DEVIL'S BATTLE

TAYLOR ANDERSON

ACE
NEW YORK

ACE
Published by Berkley
An imprint of Penguin Random House LLC
penguinrandomhouse.com

Copyright © 2023 by Taylor Anderson

ISBN: 9780593200780

The Library of Congress has cataloged the Ace hardcover edition of this book as follows:

Names: Anderson, Taylor, 1963– author.
Title: Devil's battle / Taylor Anderson.
Description: New York: Ace, [2023] | Series: The artillerymen series
Identifiers: LCCN 2022060589 (print) | LCCN 2022060590 (ebook) |
ISBN 9780593200773 (hardcover) | ISBN 9780593200797 (ebook)
Subjects: LCGFT: Novels.
Classification: LCC PS3601.N5475 D48 2023 (print) |
LCC PS3601.N5475 (ebook) | DDC 813/.6—dc23/eng/20230104
LC record available at https://lccn.loc.gov/2022060589
LC ebook record available at https://lccn.loc.gov/2022060590

Ace hardcover edition / September 2023
Ace trade paperback edition / August 2024

Printed in the United States of America
1st Printing

Book design by Daniel Brount
Interior art: Smoke background © swp23/Shutterstock.com

To Silvia

US M1841 6PDR GUN

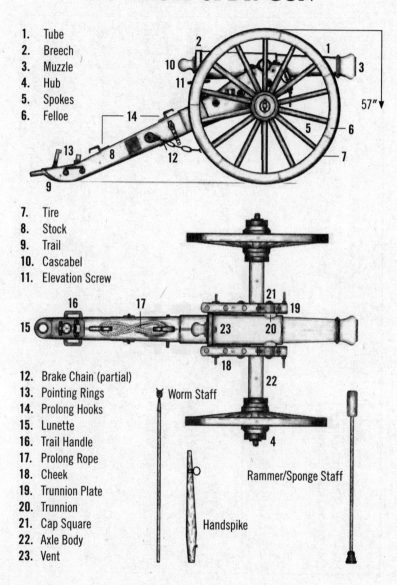

1. Tube
2. Breech
3. Muzzle
4. Hub
5. Spokes
6. Felloe

57″

7. Tire
8. Stock
9. Trail
10. Cascabel
11. Elevation Screw

Worm Staff

12. Brake Chain (partial)
13. Pointing Rings
14. Prolong Hooks
15. Lunette
16. Trail Handle
17. Prolong Rope
18. Cheek
19. Trunnion Plate
20. Trunnion
21. Cap Square
22. Axle Body
23. Vent

Rammer/Sponge Staff

Handspike

THE YUCATÁN, HOLY DOMINION, AND BEYOND

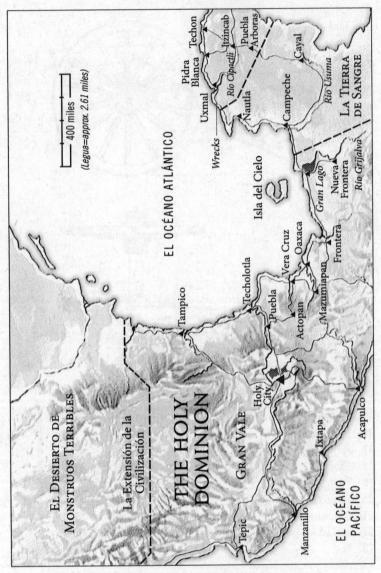

Drawn from the embroidered atlas in Uxmal. Important roads including the coastal "Camino Militar" are depicted, as far as their extent is known. Larger cities are symbolized thus: ▲

BATTLE NEAR PUEBLA

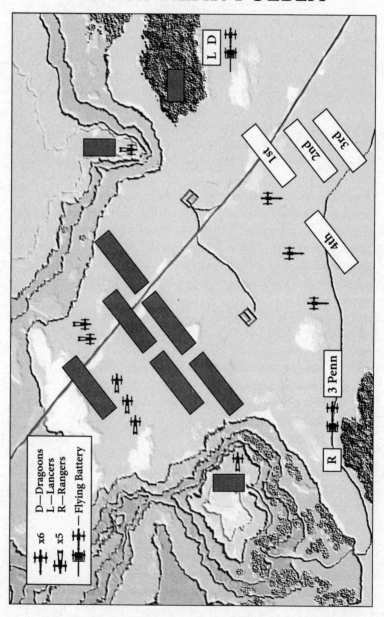

L D

1st

2nd

3rd

4th

3 Penn

R

x6 D—Dragoons
x5 L—Lancers
    R—Rangers
    —Flying Battery

Still reeling from the traumatic "passage" from their Earth to this . . . very different one, the people we first referred to as "1847 Americans" (due to the year they arrived, since we knew little more about them) were even less prepared to comprehend their circumstances than we were when the decrepit US Asiatic Fleet destroyer USS Walker *was essentially chased to this world by the marauding Japanese in 1942. Still, in surprisingly short order, Lewis Cayce (formerly of the 3rd US Artillery) consolidated all the surviving artillerymen, infantrymen, dragoons, Mounted Rifles, and a handful of Texas Rangers— even a few Mexicans who'd been unluckily nearby onshore—from three appalling shipwrecks.*

Regardless of their confusion, the terrifying lethality of this world quickly convinced Cayce that they must all work together or die. Particularly after he discovered that the savage, unimaginable beasts all around them were the least of their concerns. Humans can be far more monstrous than the strangest, most ferocious animals, and the savage Holcano Indians, their few but shockingly Grik-like allies, and of course, the vile, blood-drenched "Holy Dominion" became a constant, looming menace.

In less than a year, Lewis Cayce and his capable companions had united various city-states on the oddly shaped Yucatán Peninsula against the longfeared Dominion and its Holcano proxies, built and trained an army, and repulsed a numerically superior but arrogant to the point of incompetence "Dom" army at the "Battle of the Washboard." It was a stunning victory that convinced the locals they had a chance to live free from fear of the most significant, diabolical power known to dwell in the "Americas" of this world.

But Lewis Cayce knew that wasn't the case. The Dominion was obsessed with conquest (and blood sacrifice) and would never allow "his" new people to live in peace. Any example of successful defiance would erode Dominion tyranny over its own people and had to be exterminated. Moreover, a purely defensive stance was ultimately doomed to failure. The Dominion had to be beaten, and the only way to do that was to attack.

A bold campaign finally defeated the feared Holcanos, who, to everyone's surprise, actually joined the Allied effort. A series of small battles against Dominion Blood Priests began to illustrate just how savage this war would be, and a final titanic battle against the already disillusioned Dominion army in the region under the command of General Agon not only opened the way to the heart of the Dominion, but earned the Army of the Yucatán even more unlikely allies.

As Lewis Cayce prepared his force for an unprecedented (in American military history) advance, rumors of a mysterious place far to the south called "El Paso del Fuego" began to arise, as did nagging concerns about just how secure the Allied rear would remain . . .

Excerpt from the foreword to Courtney Bradford's
Lands and Peoples—Destiny of the Damned, Vol. I,
Library of Alex-aandra Press, 1959

CHAPTER 1

Colonel Lewis Cayce, formerly of C Company, 3rd US Artillery, and now commander of what he still referred to as his Detached Expeditionary Force as well as the entire "Army of the Allied Cities of the Yucatán," stood ramrod straight in his best (only, actually) dark blue frock coat. Carefully tailored to be stylishly tight and therefore, in his mind, unfit for combat, it could barely contain his wide, strong shoulders. A burgundy sash encircled his narrow waist beneath a freshly whitened leather sword belt, and his treasured, privately purchased and lightly embellished M1840 artillery officer's saber hung at his side. Like his belt plate and gilded shoulder boards, as well as the single row of brass eagle buttons down the front of his coat, the saber's polished steel scabbard gleamed brightly under the late-morning sun in a cloudless blue sky. Lewis's often sullen orderly, Corporal Willis, had even bestirred himself sufficiently to put a shine on the scuffed and battered black leather knee boots he wore, as well as the abbreviated brim of his 1839-pattern "wheel" hat. The latter had faded considerably, but Willis had reshaped and restuffed the saucerlike top with fresh horsehair so it stood tall and crisply round on Lewis's head like a big, blue mushroom.

Otherwise, the colonel's brown hair and full beard had been neatly trimmed by Mistress Samantha Wilde, a lovely, remarkably capable English-woman stranded on "this" Earth alongside roughly six hundred surviving

American soldiers. Despite his curmudgeonly persona, Corporal Willis was devoted to his colonel and wouldn't deliberately harm him, but his ability to manipulate tools was reckoned roughly on a par with otters', and it was preferred by all that he not bring sharp implements too close to the army commander's face. Samantha was an artist with scissors, and along with growing into the once-unimaginable authority (if not title) of assistant field quartermaster for the army, she'd become like a sister to Lewis.

His uniform for the day was completed by a new pair of sky-blue trousers—without the red artillery stripes—just arrived, along with a great many other supplies at this newly opened port by ship from the principal Allied city of Uxmal. Except for the dark blue hats, sky blue was the dominant uniform color of the entire combined army. It was mostly composed of infantry, after all, whose trousers and jackets were both that color, with white branch trim. All officers wore dark blue frock coats for dress occasions, but only mounted troopers had dark blue jackets—dragoons (yellow trim), lancers (red collars and cuffs), riflemen (white trim like the infantry), and Rangers (no trim at all). The mounted artillery had red trim, of course. That's what Lewis preferred in the field. But everyone in the army wore sky-blue trousers and for this event, in front of the whole army—that part that was present—Lewis wanted it plain he was "of" them all, not just his cannoneers. Now he gazed forward, gray eyes peering through lids narrowed against the sun, taking in the scene before him.

"Gran Lago is quite impressive for what amounts to a 'frontier' city," murmured the beefy, florid-faced Colonel Andrew Reed beside him. He was another "regular" from the "old army" originally sent to join General Winfield Scott's campaign against the Mexican dictator Antonio Lopez de Santa Anna. Most believed General Scott had surely managed without their comparatively meager participation in that other war on another world, but the good people of Uxmal and other remote cities across the Yucatán Peninsula would probably already be dead or enslaved if . . . something (Reverend Harkin still maintained it was God) hadn't brought them to this one instead. Reed was Lewis's second in command and had assumed responsibility for the infantry, largely in regard to training and organization as new regiments of "locals" were formed. That duty had fallen to others now that he directly commanded 1st Division.

"It's almost as large as Uxmal, in fact," Reed added, tone a little tight as always of late. His implication was that this relative backwater of their sworn enemy on this world was on a par with the best they had. Lewis knew that wasn't true on so many levels, but it might seem that way at a glance. Reed wasn't shy; he had plenty of courage, but the farther they advanced from their new "home" in the Yucatán toward the heart of a far more numerous enemy that inspired righteous fury and superstitious dread in equal measure, the more uncomfortable he'd become.

Lewis nodded at his words, ignoring the sentiment. "Yes. And more important, we took it largely intact."

Situated on the north coast of what should've been southeastern Mexico, Gran Lago stood on a narrow land bridge between the Gulf of Mexico and the great, brackish lake it was named for. Villas on expansive estates easily employed the slaves and lowborn freemen so it wasn't surrounded by the miles-deep slums Lewis had been told to expect around principal enemy cities. It therefore had a picturesque, almost Mediterranean quality, durably constructed of cut stone, plastered coral, and well-kept adobe. All had been freshly whitewashed after the recent calamity and in honor of this day. The buildings—particularly the high, stepped pyramid and the walls surrounding it and the gathered onlookers and formations of troops on parade in the center of the city—gleamed almost painfully bright.

One of the easternmost outposts of the "Holy Dominion," Gran Lago was well positioned to guard against the approach of monsters or invaders from "La Tierra de Sangre" beyond, and would've done so admirably if sufficiently defended. But the Dominion and the depraved Blood Priests who increasingly controlled it were arrogantly oblivious to the necessity for defense. Virtually all the troops for hundreds of miles not already called to participate in an even more distant campaign against a longer-standing enemy of the Dominion had been so intent on conquering the previously unaggressive and decidedly nonexpansionist cities of the Yucatán that Lewis was able to move his forces wide around them and force them to attack *him* here. There'd been action along the way, to be sure, but that only honed his already blooded and ever more professional army.

The great Battle of Gran Lago had broken more than the Dominion's Eastern Army of God. It broke the—apparently—long-strained and dwindling faith of its commander, General Agon, and many of his surviving troops. There'd been other contributing factors, of course, but Agon's defeat had clinched it. The Dominion was ruled by a twisted, comingled perversion of Christianity and older, darker faiths, born of a collision between

Spaniards arriving in this world aboard a Manila-Acapulco galleon at least two centuries before, and descendants of Mayan, Aztec, and perhaps even more ancient castaways. With neither group able to dominate the other, a bizarre, unholy, monolithic "compromise" faith emerged that would suffer no dissent to exist. A totalitarian theocracy arose with the formation of the "Holy Dominion," ruled by thirteen "Blood Cardinals" (one was supreme over the others), who were chosen by virtue of their blood ties to the founders. They insisted that God (in his underworld heaven) required suffering and blood sacrifice as a price for grace and salvation. Perhaps most bizarre of all, the suffering of his son, Jesus Christ, was proof—and held up as the example for all to emulate. Those who wouldn't compromise the most basic tenets of their Christian or even old pagan beliefs were hunted to extinction or hounded into exile. That was the origin of the Americans' very recognizably Christian allies in the Yucatán, in fact.

General Agon and the Eastern Army of God had suffered above and beyond what should've been required for salvation. Already beaten once and forced through multiple tortuous marches, they were abandoned by the zealous Blood Priests, a relatively new order that believed God must literally be *nourished* by the effusion of human blood, and who were not only the instigators of their misery, but had launched a coup in the Holy City of Mexico to diffuse the power of the Blood Cardinals and open that status to their own common selves. They'd complete their triumph by purging all who opposed them in a sea of blood that would, incidentally, glorify them even further in the eyes of their bloodthirsty God. It was insane, and even for the more "moderate" faithful—at least by degrees—too much. There would be civil war.

For Agon and the remainder of his army, however, the "old" faith of his enemy had proven triumphant. Again, it was obviously more complicated than that, but he'd converted to the Christian faith as espoused by the Uxmalo priest, Father Orno, and decreed that any of his troops who wished to remain and fight for the soul of the Dominion beside him must do the same. Father Orno and Reverend Harkin—a Presbyterian minister from Pennsylvania—had baptized seven thousand former Doms in the salty water of the great lake by the city. Today, in the plaza surrounding the pyramidal temple in the center of Gran Lago, General Agon would be baptized—and more—in front of his men and former enemies, in the presence of the few thousand civilians who'd remained in the city, and under the eyes of a God he was just getting to know.

"It's all very exciting . . . if true," gushed Samantha, ivory-framed fan nervously opening and closing in her hand as she voiced the qualifier present in all their minds. Samantha stood just beyond Colonel Reed in a tasteful new day dress she'd commissioned to her design, made by an elderly seamstress in the city who hadn't possessed the physical ability or inclination to flee the approaching heretics. Quite a few had been in her position, resigned to their fate, believing they'd be eaten by demons and their souls destroyed. Worse, even if the city was "liberated" by their "own," they'd be painfully "cleansed" to death. This was partially a punishment for allowing the city to fall in the first place, but more to scour the evil taint actually viewing the heretics would leave on their souls and make them acceptable in God's presence once more. After Captain Holland, commanding HMS *Tiger*, "accidentally" conquered Vera Cruz during an effort to recapture an American steamship held there, Lewis knew it was mostly so no one lived to tell that the enemies of the Dominion weren't "demons" after all. In any event, he'd encouraged his men and camp followers to be friendly with the locals, and the sutlers to do business with them if they could—all while remaining wary. Some of the locals doubtless even stayed to join them against their masters, but it was possible that many had remained to do them ill. The zealous disregard for human life—even their own—among the enemy "true believers," particularly Blood Priests, was quite astonishing.

"If true," agreed Colonel "King" Har-Kaaska, with lingering, bitter skepticism touching his voice.

If anyone fit the Doms' physical description of a "demon," it was King Har-Kaaska, along with Consul Koaar-Taak (commanding the 1st Ocelomeh Regiment) and Warmaster Varaa-Choon, currently coordinating defensive preparations at Vera Cruz. Calling themselves "Mi-Anakka," not only were they, and a mere two others of their kind known to be present on this continent, not human, they'd been in positions of authority over the pagan Ocelomeh (Jaguar Warriors) since their more conventional arrival twenty years before. They'd actually been worshipped at first, due to their furry and somewhat feline appearance—not to mention long, expressive tails—reminiscent of ancient gods sacred to the Ocelomeh. It took a while to straighten that out. The land they came from on this world (the location of which they refused to reveal to anyone) was more technologically and militarily advanced than the Indios who adopted them, however. They'd voluntarily stayed here all these years to help "their" people oppose the Dominion and other threats to civilization in the Yucatán. Meeting Varaa soon after they were wrecked on this world finally jarred Lewis Cayce into understanding that something remarkable and unprecedented had happened to the stranded soldiers he'd taken responsibility for, and he'd tried to ease them into the same realization as gently as he could. Unfortunately, they'd immediately been confronted with a traumatic battle against Holcano Indians and even stranger, far more frightening creatures than Mi-Anakka. Varaa-Choon and her Ocelomeh helped them in that fight. The strong comradery of shared combat that resulted between the marooned American troops and the Jaguar Warriors, then the Christian Uxmalos and others, probably did more to "ease" Lewis's men into an understanding of their current circumstances than anything he could've done. Even Warmaster Varaa-Choon became popular with them, and she helped clarify their situation as much as she was at liberty to. Ultimately, she and Lewis became close friends. Closer than Har-Kaaska thought wise, at first. Initially counseling restraint, he was now fully on board with the alliance. If anything, he'd even more firmly embraced the "cause" the Presbyterian Reverend Harkin and vaguely Catholic Father Orno had combined to define as their own holy mission to crush the depravity of the Doms and Blood Priests entirely.

"We've fought the Doms and their creatures so long. . . ." Har-Kaaska sighed, blinking furiously. Mi-Anakka blinking served much the same purpose as human facial expressions. It was very confusing, but Lewis had picked up enough to believe Har-Kaaska was signaling incredulity. "It will take much to convince me that a . . . ceremony of any sort can possibly transform any Dom, and Agon in particular, into . . . a person." Mi-Anakka believed all races or even species capable of thought were "people" and indistinguishable in the eyes of their "Maker of All Things." As long as they had honor. Honor was the key, the threshold upon which the divine spark separating them from animals stood. Even other Mi-Anakka without honor were no better than the lowliest insect. Worse by far, in fact. Lewis and many others, nominal Christians of various denominations themselves, had somewhat easily converted to that philosophy.

That raises the question, Lewis had to agree, gazing now at the altar and large basin Father Orno had caused to be erected at the foot of the pyramid, its steps still dark with countless years of sacrificial blood despite repeated applications of whitewash. *Can Doms really change?* he asked himself. *Can they become "people" as Har-Kaaska defines them? Agon had honor already, a sliver at least, but he fought all his life for an evil beyond anything I thought could exist. He ultimately rebelled against a greater evil, but disavowed his "own" God only when He seemed to abandon him. Can his conversion, his . . . epiphany, be trusted? Can souls as stained as his truly be redeemed? Father Orno seems to think so, and perhaps he's right.* Lewis shifted uncomfortably. "I hope so," he said aloud, answering Har-Kaaska, but reflecting on the state of his own soul as well. *None of us is pure.*

"I trust Father Orno absolutely!" Samantha said brightly, and gently rolled her eyes with a smile. "And Reverend Harkin as well. His . . . flexibility often surprises me more than any of the wonders and horrors we've seen."

"I'd have to agree with Mistress Samantha there," said Colonel Reed with a chuckle that spread to others on the impromptu "reviewing stand" nearby. Like many learned men, perhaps especially clergymen, Harkin's great hobbies had been history and the growing controversy over the subject of extinction. Recent discoveries of fossil remains around the world they came from stirred both those interests and were at odds with his religious beliefs. Harkin wouldn't accept that extinction was possible since that would imply God was imperfect. Their transportation here rekindled a resurgence of enthusiasm for his calling; who else but God could've caused it? And there was no question in his mind that they'd been delivered here to confront the evil in this land. He and Father Orno, despite lingering dogmatic disputes, were fully agreed on that. Just as important, however, in Harkin's mind at least: the extinction question had been put to rest. The improbable fossil creatures assailing his faith on the old world never died out at all; God simply moved them here.

Lewis remained unconvinced of that, but it made Harkin happy, and the good reverend was currently at Vera Cruz with Varaa-Choon, attempting to convert more allies to their cause. Lewis smiled at the thought and glanced at the officers around him: representatives of every branch of the army, still heavily leavened by a sadly dwindling but ever-hardening core of once disparate, leaderless, shipwrecked Americans turned dedicated, professional soldiers. Originally composed of only a part of the 1st US Infantry, virtually all the 3rd Regiment of Pennsylvania Volunteer Infantry, chunks of the

3rd US Artillery, 3rd Dragoons, a smattering of Riflemen and "Texas Rangers," and even a tiny cadre of Mexican lancers, those units had been reconstituted here, ranks swollen with Uxmalo, Ocelomeh, Pidra Blanca, Techono, and Itzincabo volunteers. This even before the Allied cities raised their own regiments to carry their own flags. Most of those units, three divisions' worth now, had first been commanded by American officers (often former sergeants, even experienced corporals), but only a few still were. The rest had elected their own officers as they gained proficiency and the confidence of their men. The elevation of senior officers still required the confirmation of a committee of their peers, and Lewis or Colonel Reed might still appoint or replace them (the *alcaldes* occasionally sent unsuitable toadies as rewards for political favors, knowing full well this was the case). Such men were invariably reduced in rank, even *to* the ranks, and required to work their way up. In any event, all those present had earned their positions the hard way, and Lewis gazed fondly at faces he'd grown to care a great deal about.

There was the young Major Justinian Olayne, of Irish descent, who was essentially Lewis's chief of artillery, standing with his newly promoted Sergeant Major James McNabb, a Scot by birth. (It seemed half the men who came here with Lewis had been immigrants to America first.) Olayne was knowledgeable, steady, and loyal, and no one except possibly Lewis himself knew more about what artillery was capable of and how to use it best. But where Olayne was tall and rather rangy (even the quilted padding under the front of his frock coat intended to make his chest look bigger could only do so much), McNabb was . . . "stocky" first came to mind, but there was more to it than that. In many ways, he was everything Olayne wasn't, and foremost among these things was "experienced." Olayne had seen action now, quite a bit, but McNabb was the pragmatic rock he leaned on, the distillation of leadership he needed to learn from. Lewis would've given McNabb a battlefield promotion and his own battery, but the two made such a fine pair that he wasn't sure either would flourish alone.

The Mi-Anakka Consul Koaar stood behind Colonel Reed, his new infantry uniform (all the Ocelomeh were in uniform now) almost making him look like someone had dressed a savage pet. Koaar was certainly savage in action, but he was no one's pet. He was speaking lowly to Major Marvin Beck, commanding the 1st US Infantry, and Major John Ulrich, in command of the 3rd Pennsylvania. Beck was a short version of Lewis, in a way;

broad shouldered and strongly built, but with curly black hair, side whiskers, and mustache. With his swarthy skin and the way he carried himself (Lewis had no idea what his background was and couldn't care less), Beck always personified Lewis's mental image of a Roman centurion. Ulrich was taller and the oldest officer in the army, aside from Colonel De Russy, back in Uxmal, who served the Alliance as the "Manager" of the Council of Alcaldes. He'd already retired from the regular army as a sergeant before enlisting as a sergeant in the Pennsylvania Volunteers for the war against Mexico. He was a fine leader, but still unaccustomed to his role as an "officer and gentleman." He wasn't the only one. Captain Felix Meder of the Mounted Rifles had started out as a private soldier, as had his friend Captain Elijah Hudgens, in charge of C Battery. Meder was whispering to Major James Manley, who still commanded the 1st Uxmal Infantry. Passing along, Lewis's eyes settled on the "native" Colonel Itzam, former captain of the Uxmal guard and now commander of 3rd Division. Itzam nodded respectfully, and Lewis grinned back. There were so many more.

Several who Lewis most wished were present were not. First among these was Lieutenant Leonor Anson, of course. Leonor was an utterly fascinating, lethal, and, to him, beautiful woman who'd served with her father's company of Texas Rangers practically since childhood. Marauding Mexican soldiers had murdered her mother and brothers, but settled for . . . brutalizing her, while her father, Giles Anson, had been with Houston's army during Texas's war for independence a decade before. She'd had an . . . unusual upbringing and even passed herself off as a young man when Anson's fighters joined General Zachary Taylor's army during the early battles of the war. Lewis had seen her then, from time to time, but hadn't really "noticed" her until they were stranded here. Fearless and extremely capable in a fight, she'd undoubtedly saved his life more than once, and they'd come to rely on and care for each other in ways neither ever imagined they would. It was certainly a kind of love, Lewis supposed. The reason he wasn't positive was that it seemed more like a mutually fulfilling friendship, deeper and more profound than he'd ever experienced. Like they were two parts of the same person, in a way.

He shook his head, missing Leonor's father too. Colonel Reed might be Lewis's second in command, but Major Anson was his friend and right arm. In charge of all their mounted troops, he was currently pursuing a force of

Doms, heavy with Blood Priests, led by the Blood Cardinal Don Frutos and the purely evil founder of the Blood Priest cult named "Father Tranquilo." Don Frutos was an incompetent coward, so Tranquilo was probably in charge of the three or four thousand men, fleeing not only from them but from General Agon, whom they'd betrayed. It was unknown whether they were heading straight for the Holy City in the Great Valley of Mexico over a thousand miles away, or if they meant to raise sufficient forces to expel the allies from their tentative hold on the much closer Vera Cruz—and slaughter the population there. They had to be stopped. Anson had taken his largely Ocelomeh Rangers, Coryon Burton's 3rd Dragoons, Ramon Lara's 1st Yucatán Lancers, and a section of Hudgens's battery under Lieutenant Barca to hunt them down.

A long drumroll sounded, like the one used to call the men to fall in for action, and the 1st US and 1st Uxmal, closest in front of the reviewing stand, straightened to attention. So did the former Dom troops arrayed in front of them, forming a corridor leading from the gate through the wall around the temple and up to the altar and basin Orno and some of his other priests had prepared. For now, the Doms remained unarmed, but they'd soaked their bright yellow uniform coats with black cuffs and facings in strong blue dye that turned them a somewhat unwholesome green. This not only to divorce them entirely from their former cause, but to prevent them from being killed by "friendly" fire once they joined the allies in battle as Agon hoped.

The Americans and Uxmalos couldn't be told apart from behind except by their flags—and the Americans might've tended a little taller. The 1st Uxmal was even armed with the same 1816 or 1835 muskets. All wore the same silly hats as well, but infantry had mixed feelings about them. The horsehair stuffing was meant to make troops look taller and more intimidating, but also helped cushion blows to the head (as Lewis could attest). Unfortunately, it was uncomfortably hot in this warm climate, so most of the men pulled it out. That made the hats rather floppy and shapeless, and the NCOs didn't like that at all. The men did, though, thinking it made them look rakish. Otherwise a strong proponent of the unity that uniformity in the ranks inspired, Lewis thought this tiny manifestation of individuality was good for morale. Besides, since nearly everyone did it, a kind of uniformity remained. Another thing the infantry alone liked about the hats was the straight up-and-down brim that everyone else hated. Otherwise practically useless, the brim could be shifted to the side to protect an infantryman's face from the painful and distracting vent jet of the musket fired by the man beside him in tightly packed ranks.

Father Orno stood in his black version of the American uniform (complete with horsehair-stuffed hat), brass buttons polished to a sheen indistinguishable from the golden chain around his neck supporting a humble wooden cross. Every former Dom soldier present had already gone through a similar, if abbreviated, version of what Agon was about to undergo. Those who refused had been formed into labor battalions and would spend the war as virtual slaves under guard. Lewis didn't like it, but there was no choice. Dom "true believers" were capable of anything, regardless of the consequences to themselves, and putting them to work beat killing them, which is exactly what Major Anson, Har-Kaaska, Colonel Itzam, and even General Agon himself had strongly recommended.

"Oh! Here they come!" Samantha exclaimed excitedly, gesturing down through the corridor of troops. Then her face colored. "Good heavens! He's naked!"

He practically was. General Agon, former Dominion commander of the Eastern Army of God, was short, burly, with very dark skin, nearly all of which was on display as he was led forward in nothing but a loincloth by a pair of Father Orno's healer-priests, one of whom was a woman. Lewis knew that was a strong display of Agon's new faith, as well as a test for the troops in mottled green. Women were highly esteemed among members of the Allied cities of the Yucatán, two of their cities even led by them, but Doms considered women to be property, practically livestock, less valuable than a burro. None who secretly adhered to their old faith, particularly as espoused by the Blood Priests, could bear watching Agon be led by one. Samantha must have realized this as well. "Egging it on a bit, are we?" she whispered at Lewis as her surprise faded. "What if there's trouble?"

"Having the fifers play the 'The Rogue's March' as I recommended might've been beyond the pale," Reed confessed with a quiet snort, "but if there's to be trouble, now's the time for it, while our lads're armed and Agon's aren't." The brightly polished muskets poised high on the shoulders of the American and Uxmalo troops had bayonets fixed.

"You'd never have done such a dreadful thing," Samantha scolded Reed.

Reed sighed. "No. He's behaved honorably enough since the surrender. But he killed an awful lot of our boys before then, and I'm dam . . . blasted if I'll embrace him. Not yet."

"This was all actually Agon's idea," Har-Kaaska grumbled, blinking unhappily, tail snapping back and forth behind him. "To make his conversion and submission as public and unambiguous as possible."

"You don't think that might be a ruse, to have us lower our guard?" Samantha pressed, quickly taking the opposite tack, her pretty, almost delicate features creased by a frown. "Couldn't he have warned his men what would happen? Ordered them to do nothing?"

Lewis had to force himself not to smile. A casual observer would've wondered how a woman who so enjoyed reinforcing her public persona as a flighty aristocrat not only became such a valued advisor to Alcaldesa Periz of Uxmal, helped manage their convoluted supply situation—and somehow stole the ruthless, sometimes almost dour Major Giles Anson's heart—but she truly was two people. The one she pretended to be in public was indeed a social butterfly, easily discounted and deliberately so. The one Lewis and the army's leadership—including the grizzled Ranger Anson—had come to know and admire was sharp, wily, and just as ruthless as Leonor in her way. She was also still at least as suspicious of General Agon as anyone. Lewis, Anson, Varaa-Choon, and Leonor herself might've been among the few exceptions who believed Agon was entirely sincere. They'd seen and spoken to Agon at the very end of the battle, observed his passionate denial of "his" false god and the creatures who served Him that had led to the destruction of the only thing Agon loved—his army. Lewis personally couldn't believe that passion had been counterfeit.

Major Beck spoke up behind them. "He's been incommunicado with all but Orno's priests these past five days, before it was decided to make his conversion such a spectacle. His idea again, if you'll recall. To set an example for not only his men but the people of this city." Up till now, Beck had been more interested in how the men of his regiment were behaving, watching them carefully.

"*All* of which he could have planned for in advance," Samantha maintained.

"I suppose so," Lewis had to agree. His tone hardened. "And it's difficult to just start trusting someone who was responsible for the deaths of so many of our troops in battle. I wouldn't even try if he'd been involved in any of the atrocities we witnessed on our way to intercept him—or if he'd mistreated any of our people. Some *were* taken prisoner in the Battle of Gran Lago," he reminded, "and he kept his word to Major Anson. They might not have been used as gently as I'd like, but they weren't abused."

"They didn't have them long, sir," Major Manley offered. "God knows what they'd have done to 'em if they'd won. To all of us. We know what the Blood Priests would've done." He scowled.

"True," Lewis said, then shrugged. "So I won't trust him entirely. But we're going to have to make up our minds rather soon whether to *use* him and his men." He nodded down at Agon, who'd stopped in front of Father Orno. The priests were positioning him beside the basin, brimming full of salty water from the nearby lake. It was essentially a battered wooden trough, built like a cask cut in half and about the size and shape of a large bathtub, if somewhat taller. There'd been plenty of other, far more ornate vessels cast of bronze and even gold, specifically intended for previous religious ceremonies in Gran Lago, on this very spot at the foot of the pyramidal temple. They'd been shaped to catch and fill with blood of sacrificial victims, of course. Orno, and again Agon, flatly refused to use one of them for this. In fact, one of Father Orno's and Reverend Harkin's first actions when the city was declared secure had been to collect the things and have them pounded into unrecognizable lumps of metal for transport back to Uxmal. The bronze would be used to make cannon to kill their previous users, and everyone thought that was appropriate.

Lewis watched as Father Orno advanced to the altar and raised his hands to the heavens. "Perhaps this'll help us decide," he said. In the expectant silence that resulted from Orno's pose, the diminutive priest began to speak in Spanya, the near-universally-understood mix of Mayan and Spanish, his surprisingly strong voice carrying easily to echo between the pyramid behind him, the crowded plaza, and the walls surrounding it all.

"My friends," he said simply, nodding at the stand and line of Allied troops. "Former enemies," he added to the near-naked man before him and the green-clad soldiers. "Citizens of Gran Lago," he addressed the rest, many of whom were still arriving, even climbing over the wall shutting out the rest of the city. Men were posted to make sure none who did so was armed. "Many of you here have witnessed . . . ceremonies in the shadow of temples like this." He gestured vaguely behind him. "Perhaps this very one. We understand most of these structures are very ancient, built to honor terrible false gods, many of which are thankfully long forgotten. But Gran Lago is a more recent city, and though you didn't know it, the temple behind me was made expressly for the worship and entertainment of the *devil*, masquerading as God on this world!"

There was a general murmur, mostly from the civilians, but Orno cut it off. "I have proof!" he almost shouted, holding his own heavy, leather-bound Bible up high. "My fellow priests and I bear copies of the *true* word of God brought to this world over two hundred years ago. I assure you its teachings are entirely different from the warped and perverted words you've heard in this place before, and it does *not* countenance the suffering the devil-god you've followed craves. All you have been taught is a lie, a vile abomination, a . . . justification for the tyranny of terror you've lived under and sacrificed for, all for the glorification of the devil and his evil human minions. Not God."

"He is good," Har-Kaaska grudged, eyes sweeping around the space. "At least they listen to him." Like so many other things—like where they came from—Lewis remained unsure about the beliefs of the Mi-Anakka. He understood they weren't exactly monolithic, but most believed in a single "Maker of All Things." Reverend Harkin considered them pagans, like the Ocelomeh they led, but Lewis didn't think Varaa was. She frequently referenced "the Maker," but he half suspected she'd become a Christian herself at some point over the last twenty years, and her "Maker" was simply synonymous with "God."

"He needs to be," Lewis whispered back. "And what he says needs to spread."

Har-Kaaska shook his head. "It will never happen. The closer we march to the 'Holy City' of the Dominion, the deeper we will find the roots of evil. They *like* their bloody God, *enjoy* the suffering he demands, particularly when it's heaped upon others. They'll kill anyone who speaks against him without an army at their back." He gestured around. "These people here might do the same. No"—he sighed—"as you know, I once believed you could never win against them and make this continent—this world—safe from their creeping cruelty. That's why I'm so careful about concealing the home of my people. No one can tell what they do not know. Now I believe you *can* win—after a fashion. At the very least, knock the Dominion back on its heels for a time. I wouldn't have so wholeheartedly joined you otherwise." Har-Kaaska regarded Lewis with his wide, overlarge, yellow eyes. "I still fear you don't have the necessary ruthlessness to do the job right, however."

"I might surprise you," Lewis said softly.

"Can you kill tens of thousands? Hundreds of thousands? *Millions*? All for what they believe? I think not."

"I can, for what that belief makes them do," Lewis retorted, looking back at Orno.

"I do not believe that," Har-Kaaska said. "If they were facing you in battle and refused to yield, I think you could kill every Dom there is. But what of the ragged, half-starved woman cradling the youngling and staring hatefully at you as you pass? Can you kill her? For even if they aren't really 'people' to the Doms, women will still suffer as war moves across them. Their younglings will suffer and be taught to hate."

"Well," Lewis said, clearing his throat, "let's hope it doesn't come to that." Returning his attention firmly back to the priest, he didn't see Har-Kaaska's discontented blinking.

"My priests will go among you, speak to you, pray with you, teach you that you needn't suffer for each tiny sliver of grace God gives you. You've got all you need already! You must choose not to throw it away!"

He turned to regard the imposing pyramid, its stark, angular shape rising high above. Like all such structures, smaller and much larger across the Dominion and beyond, the lines were fairly consistent. More recent "versions" such as this had thirteen distinct levels, wider at the bottom, and including the small, blocky temple at the top. All had the uninterrupted stone stairway, steeped in so much sacrificial blood that it seemed to be darkening again under the whitewash even as they watched. For all that, it was still just a place, innocent of the obscene spectacles enacted upon and around it.

"There is one more thing we must do today before the ceremony we're assembled to perform and witness can proceed," Orno called out, turning back around. "Before General Agon can publicly break with his misguided faith in the dark god of the Dominion and embrace the *one* God and His son, Jesus Christ, as his personal lord and savior, this . . . edifice we stand before can no longer be the devil's guesthouse, his palace of evil among you. As my forefathers did in Uxmal, casting out the demons in the temple there, through the power of God swelling my breast with love and forgiveness for everyone here, I now banish any evil lingering in this place and consecrate the ground of this plaza in the name of the Father, Son, and Holy Spirit, rededicating the temple in the name of Jesus Christ, through whom all can find everlasting peace and life."

Regarding General Agon with a smile, he gestured at the basin. "Step into the water now, if you please. Time for your bath."

Lewis had never seen a Catholic baptism before and just assumed that was essentially what would happen here. He didn't know if he was right or not because, in general, except for when Orno caused General Agon to kneel in the tub and proceeded to shove him underwater and hold him there interminably while he prayed loudly, Lewis didn't see or hear anything that would've clashed significantly with Reverend Harkin's technique, or probably just about anyone else's. He was struck again by the surprisingly nondenominational nature of Christianity as it was practiced in the Yucatán.

Samantha chuckled abruptly. "Remember how Harkin and Orno roared and roared at each other over baptism in general? Harkin ranted about the 'Papist washing of innocent babes' as it's practiced here, arguing the individual must consciously give himself over to God's loving care, through Jesus Christ, wholeheartedly confessing and renouncing his sins so they might be washed from his soul. Orno countered by demanding whether Harkin had ever beheld the wickedness of children!" There were amused murmurings and Samantha continued, "To which Harkin replied of course he had, in *Orno's own home*, so the submergence of infants didn't seem all that effective at eliminating sin—unless one prolonged it for a sufficiently extended period of time."

In spite of the solemnity of the occasion, Har-Kaaska *kakkked* a Mi-Anakka laugh.

"I didn't know Orno had children," Reed said in surprise.

"And a wife," Samantha assured, "with a widowed sister much taken with Reverend Harkin, by the way. In any event, Harkin is much opposed to nearly drowning his victims as well, saying since the *public* surrender to God is a symbolic act, the washing might be as well." She chuckled again. "I confess I tend to agree with him in principle, but this somehow strikes me as more appropriate here."

Sergeant Major McNabb suddenly blurted piously, "Aye. All our souls bear stains, right enough, mine likely more resistant tae removal than most—present comp'ny excepted, o' course," he added diplomatically, and Lewis almost laughed out loud. McNabb wouldn't have said that, so it could be taken either way by accident. "But I'm thinkin' the murderin' souls o' these damned Doms—'scuse me, mistress—need a harsher scrubbin' than even Father Orno's a'givin' 'em."

Finishing his prayer, Orno finally summoned Agon to arise, washed clean of his former deeds and associations, reborn in the eyes of God. To his credit, Agon managed not to *appear* as desperate for air as he must've been while the healer-priests all gathered around, wrapping General Agon in a spotless white robe. Not all priests were healers, and not all healers were priests, or even Christian. Plenty were Ocelomeh. But all healers from the Yucatán—even Holcanos—wore large silver gorgets around their necks representing the quarter moon; radiating light and holding life and knowledge. Nearly all Orno's priests with the army were healers, however, whose gorgets were suspended beneath wooden crosses. When they stepped back from Agon, the ceremony complete, all the green-clad troops spontaneously cheered. Lewis was surprised by that.

"Good heavens!" Samantha exclaimed, equally surprised. "Perhaps they really mean it?"

"Maybe so," Colonel Reed said grudgingly. "Sir?"

Lewis knew exactly what he wanted and nodded. "Three cheers. Can't let them upstage us or make us look petty, now can we?"

"No sir. Major Beck, if you please?" The former sergeant, Major Ulrich, had a fine singing voice, but no one had a parade ground voice like the commander of the 1st US.

"Three cheers for General Agon, come to God's understanding!" Beck roared.

There was the slightest hesitation before "Huzza! Huzza! Huzza!" fairly shook the plaza. The cheer might've sounded a little sullen; Agon had put a lot of these men's comrades in the ground or in the hospital. It didn't lack for enthusiasm or volume, however. No one in the Allied Army would let their former enemy overwhelm them in anything. Lewis caught Agon's eye and saw the man give an appreciative nod before he was whisked away, into the lower floor of the temple. He'd join them again when he was dressed.

Har-Kaaska clapped his hands together, a habit Varaa-Choon shared, and said, "Well, that's done. We have other things to do today."

"Very true," Lewis agreed, looking at Reed and the other officers nearby. "Dismiss the men to quarters and give them time to change out of their finery." New uniforms for everyone, along with much of the supply they'd left back at Valle Escondido on the Usuma River, had caught up with them at last. "There's still a lot of work to do strengthening the defenses here, before we move on to Vera Cruz." He chuckled. "They won't want to dirty their pretty new things."

"Have you decided exactly *how* we'll move to Vera Cruz yet?" asked Major Manley. "Shall we march by land or go by sea?"

Lewis had been leaning strongly toward the latter, if they could assemble sufficient shipping. Captain Eric Holland's little navy was growing as more and more merchant ships arrived at Vera Cruz from around the Dominion, including its possessions in the Caribbean, entirely ignorant of the fact the port had fallen to their enemies. Few had any idea the Dominion even had an enemy other than the Empire of the New Britain Isles out in the Pacific Ocean. Their ships, all of an archaic design, were easily taken, their cargoes seized. Some of the larger ones were quickly armed from the stockpile of cannon found at Vera Cruz—after alterations were made to their rig and sail pattern that would make them better sailors. Captain Holland was insistent on that. The Dominion had a very small naval presence in the Gulf of Mexico and Caribbean, but Holland had recently learned there were many more ships in the Pacific, supplying the Gran Cruzada as it lumbered up the west coast of the continent. Warships protected the transports from attack by ships of the Empire of the New Britain Isles.

No one had been much worried about that since there was no way to sail around the horn of South America on this world, the Drake Passage being reputedly choked by ice. The enemy shipbuilding industry on this coast was limited, and it had been believed that any warships would have to sail around the *world* to threaten them here. The problem was, Holland had learned of a natural, narrow passage between the Atlantic and Pacific Oceans somewhere to the south called "El Paso del Fuego." By all accounts it was an exceedingly dangerous route, likened to the Symplegades, or "Clashing Rocks" in Greek mythology, even here. Its existence had long been a carefully guarded secret, and no one knew much about it, but Lewis feared a portion of the Gran Cruzada might take ship and threaten their rear—their home—in the Yucatán and warned Alcaldesa Periz, the leader of the principal Allied city of Uxmal. She flatly refused to countenance a retreat and what would necessarily become a defensive war, probably forever. She'd insisted he win it now, while he could.

Unfortunately, the only "proper" vessels in Holland's little fleet were the recaptured steamer USS *Isidra*, now armed with several very heavy guns, and Holland's "own" HMS *Tiger*, an elderly but swift-sailing British heavy frigate that had been sold out of the navy and into the passenger service. She'd been brought to this world by the same phenomenon that transported the Americans but hadn't been wrecked. It was known that Holland intended to investigate the Pass of Fire in *Tiger*. Now that he'd been relieved of his duty protecting Vera Cruz by Varaa, he might've already left to do so.

"Even with Holland and *Tiger* gone sightseeing," Manley continued, "we seem to have been . . . gifted with enough ships to move most of the army to Vera Cruz."

"Have you been *aboard* one of those things?" Reed demanded, eyes wide. "Horrifyingly cramped, ungainly little things that make *Commissary, Xenophon*, or *Mary Riggs* seem like one of Caligula's barges, by comparison." The wrecks of those three ships (two were old whalers) that brought all of them but Samantha and her French friend Angelique Mercure (now married to Colonel De Russy) to this world, had been swiftly and efficiently broken up and stripped for anything useful. "Still," Reed continued, looking back at Lewis as NCOs shouted and the lines of troops filed out of the plaza, "we'd bypass numerous hostile cities and save a lot of time. I don't relish such a move, but it might be more expeditious. Particularly if Holland is right and there's some way the enemy might bring part of their 'Gran Cruzada' against us by sea."

The Gran Cruzada was an absolutely enormous Dom army, years in the making, dispatched to march northwest across thousands of miles of wilderness to expel a colony established by the Empire of the New Britain Isles in the far Californias. That land had been claimed by the Dominion—whether any of its subjects actually lived there or not—and the heretic invaders *would* be cast out. So great was the sheer inertia of the campaign, it had been "officially" unleashed from its already quite distant marshalling point despite the fact that some very high-placed Dom officials had already known of trouble brewing in the Yucatán. They no doubt regretted that now. But the important thing was, from the allies' perspective, the existence of the Gran Cruzada was probably the only reason they had a chance of winning this war. It had gobbled up nearly every standing force in the Dominion, and a very large percentage of fighting-age freemen had been conscripted from all over into its ranks. Agon's Eastern Army of God had been the largest regular force left within reach to oppose them. There were still millions of people in the Dominion, of course, but it would take time to raise, train, and equip more armies. And even if the Gran Cruzada was ordered to turn around and march back to the Holy City at once, it would take months for it to do so.

Lewis and his little army, currently numbering less than forty thousand effectives *including* General Agon's men, had only those months to reach and take the enemy capital, the Holy City in the Great Valley of Mexico, and install the one "friendly" Blood Cardinal in league with them as "Supreme Holiness" of the Dominion. Lewis had yet to meet the man—Don Hurac—who was currently in Vera Cruz, but he'd been reliably informed he was utterly opposed to the excesses of the Blood Priests and already close to embracing the "old faith" of Father Orno to combat them. Only he could command the Gran Cruzada to stand down when it inevitably returned, and begin the process of remaking the Dominion into a nation the people of the Yucatán could live beside in peace.

That was their own "Holy Crusade," as Reverend Harkin put it, and Lewis rubbed the bridge of his nose, a headache coming on. He was just a soldier, an artilleryman with a . . . knack for winning battles. He'd avoided politics in the "old army" with a passion, but it was enmeshed in everything here. His own army was already full of people who, without the greater cause he and Varaa, Father Orno, Reverend Harkin, and now Sira Periz and so many more had shown them, would otherwise never get along. He had Holcanos in the army now, along with other Indios from along the Usuma River, led by a war chief named Kisin. He had, of course, long been the sworn enemy of Har-Kaaska and his Ocelomeh, along with all the "city folk" on the Yucatán. Most of his people now guarded one of Lewis's primary lines of supply at Cayal, but would soon to be ordered to Campeche to do the same thing there. He had a Mexican officer commanding a fair percentage of his mounted troops—under a Ranger who'd hated Mexicans! Fortunately, they were good friends now, but he still had lingering rivalries between men who'd been "regulars" and others who'd been "volunteers," and the various branches always got on one another's nerves. That was only natural. But tensions between Irish Americans and British Americans frequently flared into fistfights, with Italian Americans and others coming down on one side or another. About the only subgroup that never gave him trouble were the German Americans. The "Southern" and "Northern" Americans were almost as bad as Irish and Brits. He sighed. And then there were the Uxmalos versus Itzincabos, or Ocelomeh versus everyone. . . . Now he'd most likely add Agon's former Doms to the mix. Sometimes he felt like he was juggling crystal goblets—badly—and they were all about to crash down around him.

The cluster of officers on the elevated stage was virtually alone now, some no doubt anxious to return to their commands, but all equally interested to hear what Lewis had to say in response to Major Manley. "Assembling sufficient transport for all of us may prove beyond even Captain Holland's surprising capacity, but ultimately, whether we march or move by sea depends largely on Major Anson," he said, with a glance at Samantha. "We've learned a lot more about the country he's chasing that murdering Don Frutos and Tranquilo's Blood Priests through, but we don't know how he'll be received by the people there. On the other hand, Tranquilo has too large a force to run around loose, and we saw all too vividly on our march down the Usuma River what Blood Priests're liable to do to civilians in 'danger' of being contaminated by us," he added grimly and frowned. "Survivors of that . . . behavior might well swell our ranks on the march, particularly General Agon's, but I'd much rather Major Anson and his 'Los Diablos' catch and kill Don Frutos and Tranquilo *before* they make their 'examples.' Better that the people between here and Vera Cruz join us of their own volition." He bowed his head to Har-Kaaska. "I know that's less likely the closer we get to the heart of their empire, so I'd like to make the most of our opportunity now."

Samantha raised an eyebrow. "You *did* turn him loose, I recall. And if anyone can stop a few thousand overzealous Dom troops and their Blood Priest overseers, Giles Anson's the man." She chuckled darkly. "He might even deliver you a number of recruits—but I wouldn't count on many prisoners."

Lewis nodded grimly. "I did 'turn him loose,' as you say. And I don't expect prisoners from the force he's gone after." He felt a sharp twinge of concern for Leonor, not really worry precisely—strange, he supposed, since few were as lethal and thoroughly aware of threats around them as she was. But likely, going into action, her father would need her by him more than Lewis did at present. Still, she'd gradually become so much a part of him that he felt oddly . . . incomplete without her. He cleared his throat. "Let's get busy, gentlemen. I'll be speaking with General Agon shortly, and it's possible I'll want to see his men perform some regiment-size maneuvers this afternoon. I'll want your input after that."

LEWIS HAD RETIRED to his command tent in the middle of the vast, fortified camp his army had erected on the east side of the city. It often struck him that, due to the nature of the world they were in, even his marching camps had come to resemble those of the long-ago Romans, protected by trenches, berms, and palisades. Not so much to defend against enemies as the voracious predators. So soon after a major battle, there were a lot more of those around than usual, it was said. That wasn't because bodies had been left for them to feed on; all the dead on both sides had been properly buried, their countless dead animals burnt, but the *smell* of death persisted. Agon's army had been forced to subsist off the land for some time, even using cannon to down larger beasts along the way. That had left a long trail of carrion, no doubt. Then again, an awful lot of livestock was required to feed so many men packed together. Predators might be tempted by that. Or it might simply be that so much blood had been spilled in the battle, the ground itself was rotting. There was no telling. In any event, this camp was practically a fort.

Lewis's soldiers were free to spend as much off-duty time in the city as they cared to, as long as they remained in squad-size groups and returned to the camp before dark. Few complained. The majority of civilians remaining in Gran Lago actually welcomed the security of the Allied Army, and many could already see the attraction of freedom from Dominion tyranny. Lewis felt like he had little control over his own civilian sutlers and camp followers, and many of them stayed in the city full-time. There'd been a number of his soldiers murdered, though—always men caught singly or in pairs, usually relieving themselves in an alley near a tavern. There was little anyone could do because there was absolutely no way to tell an honest, hopeful citizen from a rabid adherent to the Blood Priest cause, and Lewis refused to permit reprisals. It was very frustrating, and all he could do was require his men to go armed and stay sober and vigilant. That being a wildly unrealistic expectation, he had Captain Bandy "Boogerbear" Beeryman assemble strong squads of Rangers to rove randomly through the city. They'd actually caught a few troublemakers in the act or preparing to engage in mischief. None were ever brought before Lewis.

Lewis was changing out of his frock coat, his sash and sword belt tossed across his cot, when there was a loud rapping on the upright at the front of his tent, Corporal Willis striking the post hard enough to shake all the canvas. "It's that bugger Agon an' his catamite comin' for you, sir," Willis grumbled loud enough for anyone nearby to hear while pretending to speak discreetly. Lewis rolled his eyes. The scruffy, wiry, generally unwholesome Willis wasn't the best orderly Lewis could've had by any means, but he was genuinely dedicated to maintaining his position. He'd proven he wasn't a coward either, once even saving Lewis's life, but seemed mortally afraid of being returned to the ranks. That made him unflinchingly loyal and one of the few enlisted men Lewis felt comfortable talking around about anything. Leonor acted as if she cordially despised him for some reason, and Willis seemed to feel the same about her. More often than not, Lewis thought they were just putting on an act because they knew it amused him, but he wasn't always sure.

"They got *swords* too!" Willis added indignantly.

"Really, Corporal, of course they do. As you should recall, I allowed *all* the former enemy officers to keep their swords to defend themselves from their own men!"

That had been a smarter decision than he'd imagined at the time. Every one of Agon's loyal officers had been forced to defend themselves against plots to murder them in the wake of their surrender. Not all had succeeded either, but hopefully, that was over now. Pulling on his faded but well-brushed "campaign" jacket with equally faded red trim, Lewis refastened the white belt supporting his saber high around his middle, plopped his hat back on his head, and stepped out beside Willis under the overhanging fly. General Agon and his aide, Capitan Ead Arevalo, were striding quickly toward him, escorted by Father Orno, Captain Felix Meder, even Samantha Wilde, to Lewis's surprise, and a squad of Meder's riflemen with weapons slung on their shoulders. Lewis noted with interest that Agon's and Arevalo's uniforms looked much nicer than their men's, having been sewn from material that started out a nice, medium green instead of being haphazardly dyed that way. The black cuffs and facings resembled the velvet used on the collars of American frock coats, and there was even some minimal, tastefully applied gold braid around the edges. The result wasn't nearly as garish and ostentatious as what the Dom officers wore before, and Lewis strongly suspected Samantha's influence. He stepped out to meet them as more of his own officers approached.

The procession had drawn a lot of attention, men drifting over from their camps to watch. When it finally came to a stop, Felix Meder saluted. The two former Dom officers—former enemies—swept the gold-braided black tricorns from their heads and bowed without hesitation. With so many watching, Lewis knew his reaction might weigh heavily on how they and their troops were treated in general, and more specifically how they'd all move forward together. Very solemnly, he returned Meder's salute, but then shifted slightly to direct the gesture at Agon and Arevalo as well. "Welcome, gentlemen. May I say you look very fine. My compliments to your tailor."

Samantha smiled, touching her folded fan to her brow in mock salute. There was murmuring among the watchers but no rumble of outrage. Despite the bitter battle they'd fought, the rank and file on both sides had developed a grudging respect for one another. That the former Doms who remained in uniform had willingly converted away from their bloodthirsty faith when given the chance had even made some feel vaguely protective of them. The green uniforms had been a brilliant touch, since they didn't *look* like the enemy anymore. Lewis thought that had been Orno's idea and was grateful for the little priest's intuition. Arevalo straightened beside his shorter commander and glanced ruefully at his sleeve. "I have worn the yellow-and-black uniform my entire adult life and confess to being . . . disconcerted from time to time when I catch glimpses of myself and others." His expression firmed. "But this is a better, more *wholesome* color by far." He smiled. "Not to mention more practical! It certainly won't show grass stains and smut near as badly, and I'm sure skirmishers and scouts will praise the concealment it affords them!"

"If their new sentiments are sincere, I'm sure your men will be comforted by more than the color of their clothes," Father Orno proclaimed.

"Quite," agreed General Agon. "Throughout *my* military life, I have seen—and ordered—acts I deeply regretted even at the time, carried out by men whose piety was reinforced by terror. To see them now . . ." He shook his head, almost amazed it seemed. "They are prepared to fight *for* right, *against* wrong, motivated by a sense of true purpose and joy in their hearts." He held Father Orno's gaze. "As am I." Turning to look up at Lewis, who practically towered over him, he stared at him very frankly as well. "I reject the travesty of a parley and the despicable effort to murder you at our first true meeting. I had no foreknowledge of it and hope I would've had the courage to object even then. You subsequently fought us to a bloody draw—at least—and I count our meeting then as our first. I hated you," he flatly confessed, "but also deeply respected you for what you had accomplished. More than that, as a soldier, I saw you and the army you'd built as a God-given opportunity to properly engage in my chosen profession." He sighed. "To meet a true peer on the battlefield wasn't something I ever expected, and I thought my destiny had been realized."

He looked at Father Orno again. "It seems I was both right—and dreadfully wrong. It took an even more devastating defeat to open my eyes to the hideous purpose my devotion and calling had been put to, the evil my actions have supported, and the sacrilegious waste of life I've not only abetted but caused." He averted his gaze to the dusty, gravelly ground at his feet. "I might say I didn't know better, but the order I belong to, descended from the Knights of Calatrava, secretly kept legends of the True Faith and our proper purpose from fading entirely away." He glanced up at Arevalo, who stood just as tall as Lewis, and the younger man nodded encouragement.

General Agon sighed again. "For that reason, I accept an even greater measure of guilt for what I've done in the service of a vile, false god than even the wicked Blood Priests must bear."

Father Orno laid a hand upon Agon's shoulder and squeezed. "You have already confessed this to me; before us all, accepted Christ as your savior; and been washed in the purifying grace of God. God will forgive you!" Orno looked at Lewis and continued, "And I've already pronounced his penance. General Agon will lead his army beside yours in the cause we all now share: the eradication of the foul faith that spawns such as the Blood Priests."

Agon bowed his head still farther, but then looked up at Lewis again. "I know God forgives me," he said with clear conviction. "I do not deserve it, but I *feel* it in my heart. Still, I'm compelled to beg the forgiveness of another. Many others," he added lowly. "I need that forgiveness so I can earn their trust. The trust I must have to perform the penance you've set me, Father, and complete the vow I've set myself to."

Abruptly, he dropped down on both knees in front of Lewis and all his gathered officers. They exclaimed in surprise, even Capitan Arevalo, whom Agon clearly hadn't consulted about this, but Arevalo promptly joined his general without a thought.

"I have no country," Agon said. "The portion of the army that still follows me has no country either and—after God—has sworn its oath directly to me. We are far worse than outlaws in the land of our birth. Therefore, as I have begged the forgiveness of God, I beg *your* forgiveness, Colonel Cayce, and that of all your men I have wronged. If you will have it, I now swear my oath to you and the alliance you lead, to place myself and my men entirely under your command in the service of the cause and God we now share."

Lewis blinked, then looked around at the gathered faces, most as surprised as he. Only Father Orno didn't seem taken aback. "He means it, you know," Orno said.

"I believe he does," Lewis answered a little hotly, "but I'm not some kind of damned warlord! I can't have men swearing *fealty* to me!"

Orno looked confused. "What of the rest of your Americans? Is that not what they have done?"

"Of course not! They . . ." Then it hit him. His men had all sworn their oath to the Constitution of the United States—a country that didn't even exist on this world and more of an abstract ideal here and now than it ever was "back home." He and his officers were as much representatives of that increasingly ephemeral ideal as Father Orno and Reverend Harkin were for theirs, in a sense. More so. It's easier to believe in God than in mere words on a page on another world. Lewis was suddenly more determined than ever that those words should live on here—and *not* be perverted as the Doms had done the Bible. He stiffened. "Very well. I'll accept *this* oath. General Agon, repeat after me: 'I'—damn, we'll have to decide what rank you'll be, so just say your name for now—'do solemnly swear that I will support the Constitution of the United States.'"

Agon said it, apparently unconcerned that he didn't really know what it meant. Lewis continued. "Say, 'I' and your name again, then: 'do also solemnly swear to bear true allegiance to the United States of America, and I will serve them honestly and faithfully, against all their enemies or opposers whatsoever, and observe and obey the orders of the president of the United States, and the orders of the officers appointed over me according to the rules and articles for the government of the armies of the United States.'"

Agon repeated all that as well, very solemnly, but immediately asked, "Who is the president? Is that you?"

Despite the very clear seriousness of the moment and the dark, somewhat torn expression Lewis wore, there was a helpless burst of chuckles around him as Lewis shook his head, even allowing himself a hint of a smile. "No, that would be Mr. Polk. He's not here, and all you need concern yourself with at present are the officers appointed over you."

"So . . . in effect, I just swore to you."

Lewis practically groaned. "Yes, I suppose. In a way."

"Then that is good enough for me," Agon said, standing. Lewis could only imagine what it took for the man to literally kneel before him. Genuine conversion and remorse, it had to be. Arevalo rose as well. "I will ensure that every man under my command takes the very same oath," Agon said, his voice regaining some of its assurance. "I take it all *your* men have done so?"

Surprised again, Lewis nodded. "Yes, of course."

"After which they were armed?" Agon pressed, and Lewis finally laughed.

"Yes. Yes, they were. We'll reissue arms to your men, but they'll have no need of ammunition at present. You must know that if our troops are going to work well together, yours will have to learn new things—all of us must, but yours will have to make some very basic changes. I'd say you need to split your regiments in half, for example. That'll improve their mobility." He reached up and rubbed his forehead. "They'll have to learn to answer the same commands, move much more swiftly from column into line . . ." He looked meaningfully at Major Beck. "Time to reconstitute the training cadre of the First US."

"Very good, sir."

"What about the Third Pennsylvania's cadre?" Major Ulrich asked.

Lewis shook his head. "The Third's training methods work better for replacement troops, I think, plugging them right in to learn from those around them. I don't want to mix Agon's regiments with ours, and its unnecessary anyway. You'll all agree they already know how to be soldiers," he added grimly.

Justinian Olayne piped up. "I suspect the artillerymen may need the most instruction. I'm not sure we can even use their guns as they are."

"We'll have to see about that," Lewis hedged. "They might best be used in a defensive posture."

Dom artillery had good quality tubes—all 8pdrs—and there was plenty of ammunition for them since the allies had already captured and incorporated quite a few. But those had been equipped with new carriages built to the American design—stronger, lighter, and almost infinitely more maneuverable. Dom carriages were ridiculously heavy and cumbersome, and even had solid wooden wheels. They were suited only for static employment on the battlefield and were entirely unfit for the American "flying" artillery tactics that had dominated them so decisively.

Agon and Arevalo bowed again. "Very well. Clearly, we have a great deal to do. I'm at least as anxious as you to move against the enemy. I understand the controversy now is whether to do so by land or sea?"

"Not much controversy," Lewis said. "We'll move by sea as much—and as quickly—as possible. In the meantime, you're right. We train."

Agon and Arevalo started to turn away, but Lewis stopped them. "One thing, gentlemen. No one in this army—our combined army—bows or kneels to anyone but God." He performed a crisp salute. "*That's* how we show military respect to one another."

The two former Doms sharply copied the gesture, and Orno and Meder led them away, Meder dismissing the "guard." Soon, everyone had dispersed, leaving only Samantha and Corporal Willis standing by Lewis.

"That went well," Samantha said brightly. "I should return to the depot, where our supplies are heaping up. Poor Dr. Newlin will be quite overwhelmed by now."

"Most likely," Lewis replied absently, and Samantha regarded him intently. Then she nodded knowingly.

"On top of all your other concerns, you also worry about Leonor. I can certainly stay a bit longer and join you for a sip of that vile hot cocoa that disreputable cretin ruins," she declared with a magnificent sniff of disdain at Corporal Willis. "You really should replace the fool."

"An' where'd he find anybody ta care for'eem as tender as me?" Willis shrilled indignantly.

"In any hog wallow you might come cross, I'm sure," Samantha snapped.

Lewis chuckled. "You're welcome to stay as long as you like, of course, but there's no need for my sake. And we do all have a lot to do. As for Corporal Willis, he may not be the most agreeable sort, but he's responsible enough. Besides, with his attitude, I doubt he'd last a week in a line assignment." He paused. "In respect to Leonor . . . I suppose I simply miss her more than I worry. I got used to her being near. But she can take care of herself."

"How amusing," Samantha said dryly. "I'm sure I worry more about Major Anson than I miss him. I see him so rarely even when he's not chasing Doms, I've *never* grown used to his company. And he simply won't keep himself back from the action." The eyebrow rose again. "Much like you. I do worry about you, you know."

Lewis shifted uncomfortably. "No need to worry about me. I've got an entire army to stand behind now." He nodded reassuringly. "And Giles Anson can take care of himself as well."

CHAPTER 2

It was as close to pitch-black as it's possible to be, with nothing but star-light seeping down through the intermittent overcast sky and a blanket of leaves and branches overhanging a remote, ill-maintained stretch of the Camino Militar. Not the safest time to travel the coastal forest road in such a sparsely populated region full of unreasonably dangerous predators. There's a measure of safety in numbers, however, and the roughly eight-hundred-man, mixed mounted "brigade" led by Major Giles Anson pursuing the reportedly three thousand followers of the Blood Cardinal Don Frutos and the Blood Priest Father Tranquilo was composed of veteran Ocelomeh Rangers and equally experienced, largely Uxmalo lancers and dragoons under the command of Capitan Ramon Lara and Captain Coryon Burton, respectively. There was also a section of "flying" (mounted) artillery under Lieutenant Barca. The young Black man—a former slave from New Orleans—had earned the respect of the entire army on numerous occasions and quickly whipped his pair of M1841 6pdrs and their crews into everyone's first choice for duty requiring rapid movement and lethal performance.

Together, these troops and their mostly indigenous tan-and-black-striped ponies had learned to avoid or otherwise deal with the more forward animal predators, but hurried now to overtake and destroy the more vicious and far more dangerous human sort. If Don Frutos reached the fortified town of Frontera, still more than a hundred miles distant, he might significantly swell his ranks. Even if he pressed immediately on, Major Anson wasn't sure he had the men or guns to take Frontera, and bypassing it would dangerously complicate his line of supply and communication to Gran Lago.

"At least the 'rainy season' here ain't as bad or long as it is on the Yucatán," Anson murmured quietly to Coryon Burton, riding beside him. It was pointless to whisper; the horses squelching and clopping on the rocky, muddy track, and the creak and pop and jangle of the guns not far behind, iron tires exploding little stones they crushed, made plenty of noise, but their purpose and the oppressive, humid darkness seemed to require that they try not to add to it. The currently almost invisible dragoon officer nodded. He was very different from his commander. Both were tall, but where Anson was muscular without being massive, Burton was almost as thin as Major Olayne. He'd also cultivated blond side whiskers that had thickened considerably over the last year, while Anson had a dark brown mane and full, well-trimmed, gray-streaked beard. That and his sun- and weather-worn face would've easily indicated the twenty years between them in daylight. But most of the real differences would've been harder to see even then. Coryon was becoming a fine, experienced soldier, but Anson and his handful of "original" Rangers had generally been . . . harder, more ruthless fighters long before being stranded on this strange, different Earth.

They'd found all manner of terrifying monsters but could've learned to live with them over time. Other people who'd come before them had. But there was no coexisting with the *human* monsters here, and while Burton and others like him worked to build and train a relatively small but surprisingly professional modern army, the Rangers (and Ocelomeh) already knew that fighting Doms would be just as difficult for their comrades, old and new, to master as the Americans' methods were to the natives. *How* does one defeat an enemy who *revels* in bloodshed and believes God's grace—and entrance into some underworld paradise—can only be earned by misery and suffering? Anson knew, and to his relief, so did Colonel Cayce, it seemed. To beat them, they had to kill them. Undermine their faith by defeat after defeat. They'd already proven ordinary Dom soldiers were rarely as rabid and irrational as Blood Priests, and being only human, they *could* feel fear.

"Found 'em. Finally," came a familiar, husky, matter-of-fact voice in the darkness, practically in arm's reach on the other side of Anson from Burton. The young dragoon jolted upright in his local-made, Grimsley-style saddle, but if Anson was startled by his daughter's sudden appearance from the depths of the soggy gloom, he made no outward sign.

"Damn, girl," he grumbled instead, tone aggrieved. "Ain't respectful, puttin' the sneak on yer old man like that. I might have a fit, or some damn spell, an' go gallopin' off in terror."

Leonor Anson, nearly as tall as her father, but with dusky skin inherited from her Mexican mother, dark blue jacket and wheel hat, and blue-black, shoulder-length hair, she was even less visible than Burton. As nearly always, she was dressed as a man, as a soldier, and now snorted in a very unladylike fashion.

"Yeah, I'll try to remember how delicate an' skittish you are," she murmured dryly, edging her stocky native horse, Sparky, closer to her father's taller, leaner, "old-world" animal. His gelding was irreverently (and inappropriately, as it turned out, because *he* would fight) named Colonel Fannin. The two horses greeted each other companionably as they followed others in front up a twisting rise. The muted exclamations of several riders indicated others besides Burton had been disconcerted by Leonor and her small party's unexpected appearance. Everyone knew her true identity now, but like Lieutenant Barca and the Mexican lancer commander, Capitan Ramon Lara—who Anson now noted had joined them—she'd more than earned the army's acceptance. Not a few soldiers had learned to fear her more than the enemy. "I've seen you *throw* a fit from time to time," she continued thoughtfully, "but never *have* one like you described."

Anson chuckled quietly. "Only because you ain't been around me often of late," he teased, referring to her near inseparability from Lewis Cayce. There was no longer any doubt that his daughter and commander—even more wildly different than he and Captain Burton, more different than . . . any two people he could think of, in most ways—had fallen in love and come to an understanding. *They all but came out an' announced it in front of the whole damn army after the Battle of Gran Lago*, he silently, very slightly sulked, then mused, *not that anyone could tell by the way they've acted toward each other since*. In general, again for various reasons, he approved. At thirty-eight, Lewis was a little older than he'd prefer for his twenty-five-year-old daughter, but he'd somehow healed a decade-long hurt in her that no one else ever could. Even if theirs wasn't a sweeping, classical romance, it was founded on friendship and a kind of interdependence that actually seemed good for them both. That friendship, respect, and focus allowed them to maintain an entirely professional public relationship he had to admire. He was "spoken for" himself, of course, to Samantha Wilde. *The difference is, God bless her, an' I don't half deserve her, she glories in makin' a spectacle o' our attachment,* he thought ruefully.

"I've run into plenty o' things that gave me a start since we got here," believe me," he retorted cryptically.

Leonor grunted, doubting that and missing his meaning. Her father was her hero, and as far as she was concerned, the former Ranger captain—veteran of battles as far back as San Jacinto and countless bloody skirmishes against Comanches on the Texas frontier—was the most lethal fighter alive. Sal Hernandez and Bandy (Boogerbear) Beeryman, his other "original" Rangers, might be slightly quicker and better with the pairs of Paterson Colts they carried. She might be too, for that matter. But Giles Anson also had a pair of much more powerful Walker Colts, and it wasn't just the weapons that made him so deadly. It was his overall skill, judgment, timing . . . his very philosophy of fighting, now imparted to all the mounted elements he commanded in their army, that made him—and them—dangerous enough that the enemy called them all "Los Diablos."

She would've been amazed to learn that he thought *she* was the deadliest of them all. Next to Colonel Lewis Cayce, of course. Lewis wasn't the individual fighter they were. He was good with a saber, and the sheer strength of his powerful form added to his skill, but plenty of dragoons with more practice were better. His real talent lay in winning battles against more numerous opponents and inflicting disproportionate casualties. His army loved him for that. He might not be Napoleon or Wellington or even Winfield Scott, and his strategies and tactics might not work as well against better-trained, more experienced enemy commanders, but he had a natural . . . way about him, like Alexander perhaps, that bound his men to him and made them confident of victory. He could also *feel* a battle like no one Anson ever knew and adjust his tactics on the fly. When circumstances required, he could toss a carefully prepared plan entirely and quickly build another, fully formed, in an instant. Or so it seemed. What's more, most of his senior officers had learned to expect it and acquired the necessary flexibility to quickly execute his changes. Some had even developed the intuition, confidence, and initiative to do what he wanted *before* the messenger arrived. That reflected well on them, but they couldn't have done it if he hadn't taught them how. Perhaps more appropriately, if he hadn't allowed them to teach themselves. It was an interesting dynamic. Lewis had a gift for making everyone around him better than they were, which made *him* better too. Anson didn't think many armies in history had enjoyed that characteristic. The Dominion armies certainly didn't. Yet.

"How far ahead?" he finally asked, returning to the results of his daughter's scout.

"Just a little over six miles, I reckon," she replied a little uncertainly. "Sal and Boogerbear're better at judgin' distance in the dark." Boogerbear was back in Gran Lago, refitting the Rangers there, and Sal Hernandez was in Vera Cruz with Varaa-Choon, the strange catlike "Mi-Anakka" warmaster of the Ocelomeh. Anson knew his daughter deeply admired Varaa. He did too, regardless of her sharp, urbane wit, pointed ears, giant blue eyes—and long tail and tawny pelt. She was also yet another example that females could fight like the very devil.

"I wish Sal was here," Anson grumbled.

"And Varaa," Leonor agreed. "She's funny."

"Damn that Captain Holland!" Anson snorted, amused.

Only the ancient-looking but energetic Eric Holland, former captain of the wrecked *Mary Riggs* and now commanding their fledgling navy, could've "accidentally" captured the major port city of Vera Cruz. He'd taken a specially trained raiding force of Rangers, dragoons, and Uxmalo infantry, but only *meant* to recapture the paddle steamer *Isidra* and raise as much hell in the enemy rear as he could. Without much of a Dom military presence (most of the troops in Vera Cruz had long since joined General Agon or been sent to take part in the Gran Cruzada), the city just kind of fell into his lap. With the city's population subject to slaughter for allowing heretical enemies of God to conquer holy soil, Holland felt obliged to defend it. He felt responsible.

There were advantages and disadvantages inherent in holding Vera Cruz. It was the biggest, most heavily populated city on the Atlantic coast of the Dominion, accessible by sea and the tiny navy Holland had been building around his flagship, HMS *Tiger*, but it was hundreds of miles behind enemy lines and much closer to whatever concentration of Dom troops remained in the region. On the other hand, under the relatively benevolent administration of a comparatively moderate Blood Cardinal named Don Hurac, Vera Cruz had never been fertile ground for Blood Priests to flourish, and— as Anson understood it—Don Hurac was determined to protect his people from extermination, even to the extent of cooperating with heretics. Anson saw the same opportunity Lewis had and understood the evolving plan was to *get to* Vera Cruz and strike inland against the heart of the Dominion before the might of the Gran Cruzada (rumored to number over a quarter million men) could be brought to bear against them. He loved the boldness of the plan—to win the war!—but the risk was profound.

Anson's part, at present, was to hunt down and kill Don Frutos and Tranquilo before they could threaten Vera Cruz—and he was highly moti- vated for other reasons besides. They'd followed the enemy over two hun- dred miles and come across numerous small settlements, mostly farming and hunting communities, since the predators made it nearly impossible to graze livestock. Compact, heavily built homes surrounding central walled "towns" that locals could retreat to for protection in seasons when larger herds of huge herbivores passed—bringing too many (and much bigger) monsters that ate them. The walls were only wood—mere palisades, actu- ally, but built of mighty trees set deep in the earth and discouragingly sharpened about twelve feet high. They made formidable defenses, and An- son wouldn't have wanted to assault one of the settlements without artillery to smash them down. No assault was ever required, and without Dom sol- diers in residence, they would've just left the settlers alone. It turned out there weren't any there. In any of them. Not live ones.

Apparently, Don Frutos—or Tranquilo?—had learned of General Ag- on's defeat at Gran Lago because they'd instituted the same policy em- ployed among the even more remote settlements along the Usuma River: exterminating everyone they left in their wake who might aid or be influ- enced by the heretics. And Blood Priests being Blood Priests, they hadn't just killed them. They'd conscientiously done their utmost to ensure their victims suffered enough to be welcomed into paradise. Crucifixion over fire was their preference, it seemed, but some (they might've been the prettier young girls, but there was no telling now) received . . . extra attention. Most of the troopers in Anson's force had seen it before and knew their enemy, but the first such place they encountered here, inside the borders of the Do- minion itself, had shocked them. Anson himself had leaned to the side of his horse and vomited on the blood-soaked ground while Leonor somehow managed to sob without moving, the tears sheening and spilling from her eyes only magnifying the fury and hate in them.

Perhaps the saddest and most infuriating thing of all was that there'd been no sign of resistance. Why would there be? The villagers had opened their gates and welcomed their countrymen.

Their murderers.

Regardless of the warning it might give the enemy, Anson ordered the first town burnt behind them. And the next and the next. Along the road they drove carrion eaters away and buried bodies of fighting-age men who'd been taken from the settlements and couldn't be tamed. Most of these had been impaled.

Capitan Lara thought they did it to intimidate the pursuit they had to be aware of, but Leonor insisted they enjoyed it. Tranquilo and his Blood Priests, at least. They'd learned there was a difference between them and ordinary Dom soldiers, perhaps only of degrees in most cases, but General Agon had proved at least *some* had a notion of humanity and honor. He was as much an enemy of the Blood Priests as anyone. Lieutenant Barca probably had it right when he suggested they did it to frighten them, yes, but mostly to control the rest—and deny their pursuers any recruits.

It did frighten Anson's troopers. No one had any doubt what their fate would be if captured. More than that, however, it fortified their determination to make any sacrifice necessary to eradicate the evil they fought.

"Did you get a count?" Anson asked his daughter. "What were they doing?"

"About what we thought. Maybe twenty-five hundred of 'em. Restin', mostly, behind a hasty breastwork thrown up across the road. We been pushin' 'em mighty hard," she added with a note of satisfaction.

That was true enough. Despite their lengthy head start, only Don Frutos and his officers, prominent Blood Priests, and a few score more were mounted. The rest were on foot. It had been inevitable they'd catch them eventually. "Look like they'll try to make a stand?"

Leonor nodded. "Got to be down to that. With three- or four-to-one odds, they prob'ly even think they'll lick us. Might as well rest up for the fight."

"Not all of them are soldiers," Coryon reminded.

"Blood Priests fight too," Lara said and snorted. "Just not very well."

"We'll give 'em their chance," Anson ground out, then his tone turned more formal. "Get us close, Lieutenant Anson," he told his daughter. "No sense blunderin' into 'em in the dark, right up the road like they want us. We'll take a short rest ourselves, then see if we can't put the sneak on *them.*" He snorted with amusement. "Give *them* a terminal fit."

"PRETTY SOON," LEONOR told Sergeant Riss as she double-checked both her Paterson Colt revolvers in the orange-gray dawn filtering down through the trees. Unslinging the Model 1817 rifle from across her back, she flipped the frizzen forward to check the priming in the pan. Riss and his platoon of Ocelomeh Rangers were as close to being Leonor's personal command as she had. She'd started by somewhat arbitrarily choosing details to accompany her on scouts, but Riss and his squad had impressed her. All Jaguar Warriors were good in these woods, having practically memorized the virtually trackless forest of the Yucatán, but the gruff, stocky Riss seemed equally at home on the prairie or in any other wood, and his men's native horses never spooked and trod as gently and quietly as deer. Now Leonor sought them out for all her tasks, much to the ill-concealed consternation of their Uxmalo company commander. Even if only occasionally, they'd become more "her" men than his. At the moment, they were checking their own weapons: captured Dom muskets cut down to carbines or "musketoons," and quite a few captured pistols and lancer's sabers. All still carried their powerful bows as well, which launched heavy arrows with wicked, obsidian points and were actually more useful against the monstrous beasts of this land, penetrating deeper at close range than muskets. Big and heavy as they were, at their peak close-range velocity, soft lead musket balls tended to flatten on impact with the thick hide of the oversize creatures they encountered, stopping in dense muscle or against heavy bone before reaching anything vital.

"The archers are almost in position," Riss agreed. After Leonor and her companions led the way, nearly all her father's Rangers had infiltrated up and around the southern flank of the main Dom camp, beyond the flimsy barricade thrown across the road. Now hundreds of picked archers were assuming positions around the edge of a long, narrow clearing the enemy had occupied. A few lizardbirds took flight, cawing raucously, but not many more than usual. Some always flew to the seashore with the dawn to contest with their more nautical cousins for morsels washed up in the night, but most would wait until the sun dried the dew from their furry/feathery wings.

That camp's a disgrace, Leonor mused. There were apparently no latrines, and it stank bad enough to smell upwind. There was no order to it at all, and tents had been erected in a haphazard sprawl. Men without tents still slept around smoldering firepits—the damp brought a chill that night—and the only men moving about seemed focused on resurrecting the fires to cook breakfast or heat water for chocolate or the nasty-tasting bark tea. Woodsmoke hung in the air like a fog. Sentries were awake behind the barricade, gazing to the east down the Camino Militar—where Anson was *supposed* to come from—in the midst of several hundred men, sleeping in the open. If there'd been other guards, they'd all died silently as archers crept closer to their comrades. *Kind of an anticlimactic end to our long chase*, Leonor thought. *General Agon would be mortified*, she added sardonically. *Agon has a lot to learn about winning battles, thank God, but he knows how to organize and lead his army. What's left of it'll follow him too.*

"Why we use arrows first, anyway?" Riss ventured quietly. Another thing she liked about him: if he didn't understand something, he'd ask. He was good at answering questions she posed him as well.

"There's practical reasons," Leonor whispered back. "Those fellas creepin' close ain't likely to accidentally set off a musket an' spoil the surprise. Mostly, though, Doms're like Uxmalos, a lot of 'em. In their way o' thinkin, they're civilized." This with a dose of sarcasm. "Don't act it, do they? But their army don't fight with bows. Only 'savages' do that." She grinned. "An' 'savages' scare hell out o' civilized folk. Especially when they're just wakin' up."

"But . . . we will soon shoot muskets at them too."

"Yep. That'll confuse 'em on top o' the scare."

It was more complicated than that, but hopefully he'd see for himself in a moment. If her father's idea worked. He and Lewis both believed that every instant of uncertainty you flung at an enemy, no matter how subtle, was a gift. They both tried to work little touches to cause it into everything they did.

A distant bugle sounded in the thick, heavy air, and sentries at the breastworks must've seen something as well. They started rushing around, shouting at one another and kicking sleeping comrades awake. Men rose up with their weapons, groggy and staring. NCOs whipped them toward the barricade with twisted vine staffs or the flats of their swords. Slowly, the defense took shape. Leonor couldn't see far along the road, but she heard the distinctive sound of galloping horses and the rattle and grumble of rolling artillery. Bellowed orders floated toward her over the rising turmoil, and she recognized Lieutenant Barca's voice commanding his section of 6pdrs into position right on the road, probably less than two hundred yards from the enemy. Another bugle sounded, and she imagined Capitan Lara's lancers flying up the road cut to back the two cannon as they unlimbered and passed their horses and limbers to the rear. Lara's men would be mounted, pressed knee to knee, looking like three times their number with their forest of lances held high.

The camp erupted like an anthill someone kicked over, men jumping up and running in all directions. A large percentage of these wore the soiled red robes of Blood Priests or bedraggled, dingy white tunics of their initiates. They got in the soldiers' way. "Must've been a hard march for 'em," Leonor pretended to lament. Suddenly, only moments after the first alarm was raised, a monster roared on the road. It was a cannon, of course, a ton of gunmetal bronze and iron and oak formed into a Model 1841 6pdr on another world, and Leonor felt its presence even here in the form of the pressure wave it propagated through the humid air. Smoke billowed and rolled into view as a six-pound roundshot smashed through the stacked limbs and brush, as well as several men lined up behind the barricade (throwing parts of them all over or into the men around them), and struck with a geyser of damp earth just short of one of the largest, most elaborate tents. It didn't stop but carried on, its force hardly diminished, it seemed, raising shrieks in the tent as it exited, smashing a wagon to splinters and slapping into an armabuey tethered behind the vehicles.

Armabueys were basically enormous armadillos with spiky tails and other pointy deterrents to predators. Generally sedate and rather stoic creatures, if irritable on occasion, they were ubiquitously used to pull heavy burdens. Their propensity to root about made them a menace to cultivation, but they were otherwise as inoffensive as the much smaller cousins Leonor had been familiar with. This one emitted a thunderous, gurgling groan as it fell on its side, flailing mindlessly in death, shattering more wagons and knocking loose others of its kind. These had been sleeping and were spooked. They stampeded. A great swathe of tents was flattened, quite a few with men inside. Anyone who could fled from their ponderous but unstoppable rampage.

Barca's second gun roared in the cut, causing similar destruction to the first—except for the armabueys, which were doing even more at the moment. Still, armabueys were just animals, not devil-inspired heretics, and wouldn't slaughter the servants of God on purpose. Those who could had started sprinting to reinforce the barricade.

"About *now*, I expect," Leonor said aloud to herself. As if she'd personally given the order and all the Rangers heard, shrill whistles sounded and hundreds of heavy arrows arced into the massing soldiers and Blood Priests. Up close, each weapon was powerful and heavy enough to reach the vitals of very large animals. They could pass completely through a man and into another. Agonized, terrified screams erupted as more arrows quickly flew. Most of these priests and troops had grown up near the frontier, where "savages" were indeed present, and many—particularly Holcanos, whom the Dominion had allied with but betrayed—were known for *extremely* savage behavior. Barca's first gun fired again, shattering and scattering dozens with a single copper ball, even as cries of alarm from behind started distracting those on the breastworks waiting for the lancers to charge into range of their inaccurate muskets. But the screams from the rear carried on, and now arrows fell among them as well. When enough had grown more concerned by that than the terrible but understood threat to their front, Capitan Lara charged.

Lancers surged around Barca's guns and came on en masse, nine-foot razor-sharp lances of the front-rank riders coming down. Few things are more intimidating than that sight, even to veterans, and almost none of the soldiers escorting Don Frutos and his Blood Priests could claim that status. Most fired wildly without orders, in panic, without even trying to aim.

Dom muskets were as robust and foolproof (some said "crude") as it was possible to make them. The result was a weapon that reliably worked, but was clunky and inaccurate even compared to other muskets. Their bores were ridiculously oversize for the roughly .70 caliber lead balls they threw, so it wasn't particularly important they be *uniformly* oversize. Captured examples had bore diameters ranging from .72 caliber up to .76. These were reamed to .77 caliber for use with .75 caliber balls. They were kickers, but the thick paper cartridges wadded up under the ball centered it sufficiently and provided a good enough gas seal (like a sabot) that weapons thus converted were almost as accurate as the well-made .69 caliber American 1816 and 1835 models.

Just as bad as their bores, if more easily fixed, was the comparatively massive size of Dom musket locks and their shoddy geometry. They were hard on flints, and just the inertia of the cock snapping forward to strike sparks off the frizzen could wrench the weapon off target. It was found they'd even torque in the hands of an expert shot with a rock-steady rest. Conversions had their geometry tuned and a *lot* of weight filed off.

At the moment, however, the result of that ragged, panicked volley of over two hundred muskets was half a dozen wounds to men and animals, several serious, a single lancer hit squarely in the chest and a horse struck in the head. Both of the latter were killed instantly—by balls bounding up off the ground about halfway there.

The charge hadn't reached full speed and never would, so even though it slowed around the fallen, kicking horse, there wasn't a catastrophe of tumbling men and mounts. It came inexorably on in the teeth of terrified men who'd already fired their most effective shot, whose nervous fingers would never have time to reload.

"Like clockwork," Leonor exulted, practically bouncing in Sparky's saddle. The lancers, now in view, spread out as they left the cut and brought more lances down. In seconds they slammed into the disorganized defense, spearing screaming men or pounding them under their horses' hooves. Quite a few lost their lances, which either shattered or got stuck and were wrenched from their hands. They immediately employed their sabers and carbines and the clang of steel and thumping roar of firing swelled over the wails of fear and pain.

Drawing one of her Paterson Colts from a belt holster, Leonor pointed it at the growing calamity ahead. "Let's go!" she shouted, just as the whistles signaling *that* shrieked. Her pride in the professionalism of the force they'd built soared.

Mounted Rangers poured out of the woods, whooping and yelling, many pulling strings of ponies for their archer comrades to reclaim. The whipsaw of attention-grabbing horror was plain to see as heads that had turned to the fighting at the barricade spun back to them, eyes wide, mouths open. They had only heartbeats to fight or flee and most instinctively ran. Those who raised weapons were shot or hacked down, Rangers discharging handfuls of "drop shot" stuffed in their shortened muskets from yards, sometimes inches away. Patterns of small bloody holes appeared on yellow Dom army coats or dingy white undershirts. Whole heads were exploded like melons or cavernous red wounds were opened in torsos by closer discharges. Men with less traumatic wounds rolled and screeched on the ground. Leonor doubted they would if they had even a moment to think, but Blood Priests also ran. She yanked on Sparky's reins to stop him and snapped two shots at a pair, hitting both in the back of the head. They flopped forward on their faces. She wasn't as good as Sal Hernandez with her pistols from a running, pitching horse, and only had ten shots between them. She didn't mean to waste any.

"To your left, Lieutenant Anson!" cried Sergeant Riss, and she spun in the saddle to shoot a Blood Priest who'd seized a soldier's musket and was trying to stab her with the plug bayonet inserted in the muzzle. His right eye vanished in red vapor, and shards of bloody bone spewed out from his temple. He dropped the musket and clutched his face, screaming. Leonor was finished with him. Besides, another Ranger was bearing down, saber raised. In an instant, the Blood Priest's head and one of his hands were arcing away in a spray of blood. She nodded her thanks at Riss on her right. He couldn't have helped otherwise, but not only warned her, but had the presence of mind to grab her attention with the *direction* of the threat instead of just calling her name. That might've killed her.

They fought on, killing their way through men who'd awakened to absolute chaos and a chilling, ruthless aggression they'd never had aimed at them. *They're fine ones for dishin' out terror to others, the more helpless the better*, Leonor raged. *Least the damn Blood Priests are*, she reluctantly corrected. *Not much for takin' it, are they?* That was confirmed when she started hearing Rangers and lancers yelling, "*¡Tira tus amas!*" (*Throw down your weapons!*) at the soldiers, as they'd been instructed to do. Some even complied, though again it might've only been shock that made them. Dom soldiers wouldn't normally surrender any more than Blood Priests did. Any who hesitated were immediately killed, however. Blood Priests—the largest concentration of the vermin Leonor ever saw—weren't given the chance. They were summarily shot, lanced, or hacked down by sabers on sight. Naturally, a few would be wanted for questioning, and everyone was particularly looking for Tranquilo and Don Frutos. The latter should be easy to spot; a known coward and the only Blood Cardinal here, he'd likely stand out in his finery and *try* to be taken. Tranquilo had little chance. Few knew him by sight, and considering the nondescript garb of his order—white initiate tunics or apparently rarely laundered red robes for the fully ordained—"a scruffy, scrawny little bastard with eyes too close together" wasn't much of a description.

By the time Leonor shot her way through the press to the other side of the clearing and "her" boys had gathered tight around her, reloading carbines, gulping water, and quickly tending minor wounds as she reloaded her empty revolvers, Tranquilo was probably dead—along with a thousand or more Doms. Isolated clusters of the enemy, some fairly large, were starting to organize themselves, and they'd lose people finishing them off, but the massacre had gone very well so far. Pinching and pressing the last percussion caps on her second revolver, she signaled her men she was ready and they started to charge back into the fight.

"Whoa, girl, hold up," called her father, crashing Colonel Fannin through the low brush bordering the outlying cluster of trees to join her. Capitan Lara and a platoon of lancers were still with him, since he'd been with them in the charge. He'd said it was the lancers' "turn" to put up with him in a fight, but Leonor suspected he also wanted to watch over their young Mexican commander. Lara had suffered repeated serious wounds to his right arm in previous actions, and it remained almost useless at present, still healing from the last time.

To Leonor's lingering amazement, she'd grown quite fond of Lara and the few surviving members of his "lost patrol." Her mother and brothers had been murdered and she'd been raped and beaten and left for dead by straggling Mexican *soldados* a decade before. Both she and her father went a little mad after that, developing an implacable hatred for *all* Mexican soldiers. It wasn't blind hate and remained tightly focused, never extending to Mexicans in general. Leonor's mother was Mexican, after all, as had been most of their friends and neighbors. "Uncle" Sal Hernandez had been with Giles Anson at San Jacinto, and his family was also slaughtered. Only Mexican soldiers came to personify the bloody tyranny of Santa Anna in their hearts.

People elsewhere often forgot that the Texas Revolution was only part of a wider rebellion against Santa Anna and his dissolution of the Federal Republic and Constitution of 1824. Revolts flared all across Mexico, and the dictator brutally crushed them. His worst excess had been in Zacatecas, where thousands of civilians were massacred before "Texians" even took up arms against him. The *feel* of his "no prisoners" approach to war at the Alamo and Goliad—where the Ansons lost friends as well—was actually vaguely familiar to the struggle here.

After the revolution, Giles Anson and his friends formed their Ranger company as much to cope with Comanche raids as the steady hostilities on the border. Comanches were feared and hated, but respected. Fighting them was viewed as a bitter necessity. Fighting Mexicans became a form of deadly entertainment and atrocities were committed by both sides. After what she'd been through, young Leonor refused to be separated from her father and had ridden with his men ever since. Only they knew she'd been a girl, then a woman (the deadliest they'd ever known), and the arrangement continued after they joined the United States' new war with Mexico. Leonor had seen the war as a chance for wholesale revenge, and it had been for a time. It took meeting Lara after they all wound up here to open her mind and heart to the fact there was good and bad in everything. Even Mexican soldiers. Probably more than her father, maybe even more than learning to care for Lewis Cayce, Leonor suspected her friendship with Lara might've saved her soul. That left her wondering uncomfortably from time to time if there might be good in a few Doms as well . . .

"Hold here awhile, Lieutenant," Anson said more formally. His use of her rank instead of "girl" made it an order she had to obey. "Can't kill 'em all by yourself," he continued. "Besides, it's time to shut the gate on 'em an' let Coryon Burton's dragoons have their say." The clots of still-fighting Doms were trying to coalesce toward the middle of the clearing, amid their shattered camp. The Rangers and lancers were pulling back, marksmen still taking a toll on the packed mass, but their job had turned from shocking and horrifying them to keeping them corralled. Leonor knew the plan, but her blood had been up. It was good that her father reminded her that it was time to get out of the way.

A detail of lancers had remained by the shattered breastworks, now abandoned by all but the dead, to tear a gap through it. They appeared nearly finished, dragging more debris and a few more bodies to the side, when a bugle sharply heralded a company of dragoons, which flowed quickly through under their red-and-white guidon and spread out to the sides of the road. Despite the fact their uniforms hadn't yet been replaced and they reflected the hard use of a grueling campaign even before the brutal Battle of Gran Lago and the long chase since, Burton's dragoons looked magnificent. The young officer insisted on that. Their horses—mostly native stock now—were carefully groomed, and their lovingly brushed fur shone under the rising sun. Brass buttons, saber guards, and steel scabbards all flashed after painstaking polishing, and even the yellow trim on their jackets, wheel hats, and sky-blue trousers had somehow retained its color. Only the jackets and trousers themselves seemed somewhat the worse for wear, the dark blue faded to a kind of purplish-gray and the sky blue now a grayish brown.

Directly behind them came Barca's section of guns, hitched to limbers drawn by six horses apiece. Dressed like dragoons except for red trim, men rode every animal and crowded the top of the ammunition chests on the limbers. Shouted commands caused the horses to wheel about, presenting the blackened muzzles of the otherwise red-gold guns to the enemy as men bailed off horses and vehicles to deploy their prized weapons. Shouts of "Drive on!" sent the horses and limbers back toward the gap before executing another turnabout. Leonor recognized the slight form of Barca on his own horse between the guns, sitting calm and erect while his gun's crews swiftly retrieved implements and took their positions under a renewed, focused hail of Dom musket balls. Even at this distance, she clearly heard Barca roar, "Load canister!"

"Yeah," Sergeant Riss said. "Good thing we din't go back out there! Don' want any closer than we are."

Leonor nodded, anxiously looking to see how many of her people remained in the danger area—essentially the whole clearing. None she could see. Some Doms had tried chasing them as they pulled back, but fusillades of fire discouraged that. *Course, if those silly bastards out there ever faced canister before, they wouldn't stay wadded up like that for anything,* she reflected. Now, essentially out of the fight, she was surprised to feel a trace of remorse over what they were about to do. "Mighty cold-blooded today, ain't we." It wasn't a question.

Anson looked at her sharply. Surprised not by the sentiment, but the source. "You *saw* what those bastards did *to their own people* all along the trail leading here. They're vermin," he snarled. "There's still more o' them than us an' I'd kill 'em all with a wave o' my hand if it'd save a single one o' ours."

"Not really arguin'." Leonor almost sighed, then glanced at Lara before looking back at her father. "But some're just conscripts, taken from them very places we passed. Ain't *all* of 'em vermin."

"Sad but true," Lara said, possibly as surprised by what she said as her father, "but for the very reason that we value life—ours more than theirs, I'm not ashamed to say—we have no choice but to indiscriminately destroy any who assemble to oppose us. Afterward, one might hope, we may have an opportunity to pick and choose, perhaps save some of those who were victimized, as you say." His expressive eyes darkened, and he frowned. "But if we don't kill them today, we will certainly have to kill even those unfortunates later, after longer . . . association with their new masters. As you've seen on the impaling poles, Blood Priests are rather insistent on complete dedication. Even from their slaves."

"I know, I know," Leonor assured, sounding annoyed with herself. "Just a weird thought."

Anson's expression softened. He knew it was more than that. Having learned to care for Lewis Cayce, his daughter was starting to . . . feel . . . in other ways as well. He didn't know whether to rejoice or grieve for her. "Not weird at all," he said lowly. "*I* even get notions like that now an' then," he confessed. "What's 'weird' is if you never do." He nodded out at the field. "Like Blood Priests."

"Section! *By* the section!" came Barca's shouted command, rising over the growing musketry and cries of pain. "Fire!"

With a great thunderclap roar, both gleaming 6pdrs fired at once. Billowing white clouds of smoke, already with a slight yellowish tinge as always with canister and highlighted by the golden sunrays behind them, rolled out in dense, stately columns undisturbed by any wind. It would've been beautiful if not for the hell it unleashed.

Like the copper cannon balls they'd been forced to make do with (though "make do" is somewhat inappropriate; copper worked very well), they'd replaced their own expended canister with what could be made in Uxmal and Itzincab. This consisted of tinned brass cylinders (brass kept its shape in the limbers better than copper) on top of wooden sabots. Inside were ninety .69 caliber lead or copper balls packed in sawdust. Copper was lighter than lead, and gunners had to adjust accordingly. These rounds turned a cannon into a giant shotgun, and that was the effect they had on the densely packed, fearful, and demoralized Doms—like firing a pair of enormous shotguns into a pen full of rabbits.

Dom soldiers and priests closer to the guns were literally mulched into gory, steaming heaps of bloody flesh and shattered bone, hardly recognizable as anything once human. Scores behind them were swept away in instant death among many more scores of screeching wounded. Most still standing seemed stunned into immobility, but a keening wail began to rise. One of the lancers near Leonor retched. Even she was sickened, regardless of how hardened by war and death she'd become.

The guns were reloaded in seconds—both Barca's crews had once achieved six rounds fired in a minute—and with an air-shaking *Poom! Poom!* they fired again. The smoke of the previous shots had rolled over the enemy by now, mercifully concealing the results from view. "*¡Rendicion!*" called a growing number of surrounding Rangers. "Surrender, damn you all!"

Some might've tried. Even as they were slaughtered by Barca's 6pdrs, it sounded like the Doms had started fighting one another. "Damn it, call Captain Burton!" Anson shouted at Lara's bugler. The man nervously licked dry lips and blew. Almost at once, more dragoons poured through the gap and around the guns, deploying quickly in a double line, drawing sabers. Without even stopping, they charged. Almost immediately, there came a mighty crash in the smoke-choked clearing, and the dull boom of Dom muskets was replaced by the lighter popping of breechloading Hall carbines and pistols, the clash of steel, and screams. Horses squealed, men yelled and cursed, and indistinct shapes whirled and shifted in the haze. Topping it all, there was the unmistakable sound of panic, whimpering, crying, moans of terror amid running feet almost as loud as thundering hooves.

Even as carbines and pistols kept firing, the denser cloud of cannon smoke started to dissipate, and shapes were seen racing toward them. Rangers and lancers fired at them, and it sounded like there was shooting all around the clearing. Apparently, the Doms had scattered. The screaming had turned to panicked pleas for mercy as men hurled weapons away and held empty hands out before them, many dropping to their knees. Some were shot anyway. Fighting the Holcanos for so long, many of the Ocelomeh Rangers still had difficulty turning the killing off.

"Cease firing, God damn you!" Anson bellowed. "Don' kill 'em if they're surrenderin'!" To his astonishment, a few wearing red robes or white tunics tried to surrender as well. Most of these were simply shot down, but a few were secured. Increasingly, yellow-uniformed Dom soldiers were allowed to live as well, roughly knocked or shoved into groups where they could be watched by a few while their comrades kept shooting those who still approached with weapons.

"Bugler!" Anson shouted over the turmoil. "Damn it, Lara, where's that bugler?"

"Here, Major."

"Sound 'recall' to pull the dragoons back to the guns."

The tinny notes soared over the noise.

"Keep at it until they take it up," Anson insisted, and the bugler repeated his call several times before a dragoon bugle sounded in response. Very quickly, mounted men heaved their animals back around the way they came, some still shooting or slashing with sabers. Anson grimly noted a dozen or more horses with empty saddles, but these too galloped back where they came from.

The former camp was a shattered desolation of death and destruction, not a single tent standing amid the ruin. Hundreds of men were still out there, largely scattered once more, but high-pitched commands were summoning them back together, trying to create a semblance of a battle line. Quite a few Doms, particularly those closest to the woods, simply threw away their weapons and ran toward their killers, sobbing for mercy.

"¡Jesu Cristo!" Sergeant Riss exclaimed, lip curling in distaste. "I've seen the Doms beaten, thank God. Even seen 'em break. I *never* seen 'em *shattered* like this. Ruined." He looked at Anson with a kind of awe.

Anson just shook his head. "Blood Priests are one thing, but those soldiers ain't front-line troops like we fought at Gran Lago. Mostly militia, I bet. Still, wake anybody up the way we just did an' they'll fall apart."

"Even us?" Riss asked.

"Yes," Leonor answered for her father. Tone cold, she sounded more like herself again. "That's what us Rangers are mainly for: to make sure nobody *ever* gets to wake our people up like this."

Virtually all shooting had abruptly stopped, and Rangers and lancers were busy rounding up prisoners. Some were even approaching the cannon and dragoons. The dragoons had them covered and Barca's gunners stood ready, weapons loaded, lanyards stretched. It was hard to tell, but there might be four or five hundred enemies in custody. Many were wounded, and all looked terrified. Most disconcerting of all, Leonor could see more than a dozen Blood Priests here close to them. Who knew how many had rushed into the arms of others across the field? There'd be plenty to question.

Before very long, all that remained in the middle of the clearing amid the charred wreckage of the camp were bodies—and a mob of several hundred Doms. Even as they watched, more straggled, even crawled to join those gathering under a waving red banner and jagged gold cross of the Dominion. A small cluster suddenly broke away, running for the trees, but they were shot down by a ragged volley fired by their own comrades. Anson frowned at Lara as if to say, "I hope that wasn't the ones we'd like to save." It wouldn't have mattered now.

"Messenger," Anson called. One of the lancers who'd arrived with him urged his horse closer. "My compliments to Lieutenant Barca, and he's to expend as many rounds of canister as necessary to exterminate that murderous pack of vipers out there."

"Vipers, sir?" The youngster hailed from Pidra Blanca, by his accent.

"Uh, poisonous snakes," Anson expanded, then remembered the kid had likely never seen one. It struck him as ironic that on a world crawling with so many terrible, deadly monsters, there were very few snakes. Sailors who'd smuggled goods to and from Dom-held Caribbean islands said there were serpents on some of those, but no one knew them on the mainland. *Worse things probably eat 'em*, Anson thought. "Lieutenant Barca will know what I mean," he assured.

"No call to surrender?" Lara asked.

"We've already taken more prisoners than I expected, by far. Probably more casualties too," he added grimly, then waved toward the holdouts. "Shootin' those who ran, they've made it plain we won't get any more out of that bunch, an' I won't lose another life sortin' 'em out." He glanced at Leonor, who nodded agreement with a frown. "Go," he told the messenger, then looked around. "Lieutenant Anson, Capitan Lara, form details to take charge of the prisoners. Do what you can for the wounded who look like they'll make it. I'll have healers made available after our own people are seen to. Sort out the Blood Priests an' initiates. Search 'em well an' put extra guards on 'em."

"We gonna patch them up too?" Leonor asked with an expression of distaste that implied the "old" Leonor had reasserted herself.

"No," her father said brusquely, nudging Colonel Fannin forward. "They won't need it. That said, send word right away if you run across Don Frutos." He snorted. "If Tranquilo's still alive, he'll be with the holdouts, I expect."

"Where are you goin'?" Leonor asked. "Where will you be?"

"I'm off to find Burton and see what shape his dragoons're in. We'll need to get after any stragglers. Carry on."

Everyone was chilled by an almost maniacal laugh that suddenly burst out, and Anson drew back on his reins, attention pulled to one of the Blood Priests being tied in a circle around a tree. This one, lolling against the tree at its base, didn't look like he needed to be bound. There was a big hole in his upper chest, and his dingy red robe was wet with blood. More blood was flecked on bluish lips in a pale, almost whiskerless face.

"Shut your damned mouth. You think all this is funny, you heap of shit?" Anson snapped.

"Quite amusing, actually," said the man, speaking accented English instead of Spanya. That got everyone's attention. "You do not remember me? I am offended," he added.

Anson's eyes went wide. "You were one o' them bastards that had ahold o' Colonel Wicklow, when Don Frutos tried to murder us all at that 'parley' before the fight at the Washboard!"

The Blood Priest dipped his head in smiling acknowledgment. Leonor was surprised and gave him a hard stare. She'd been there too, but didn't recognize him.

"I was there!" the priest exclaimed, then winced and coughed. More droplets of blood appeared on his chin. "My goodness!" he said in a strangely happy tone, hand groping weakly for his wound, "as painful as this is, I'll soon be in paradise! I appreciate your arranging that for me."

"Don't mention it," Anson said. "What were you laughin' at?"

The man appeared thoughtful. "I suppose it won't hurt to tell you, after all you have done for me. There is nothing you can do about it in any event." He managed a slight shrug, causing even more pain. "Wonderful," he hissed through blood-reddened teeth.

Leonor rolled her eyes and drew one of her revolvers. "Speak up quick," she snorted sarcastically, "or I'll put you *out* o' your misery."

The Blood Priest held up a hand. "At once, I promise." His gaze turned to Anson. "I merely find it humorous that, after all the time you've wasted and trouble you've put yourselves to pursuing us, those you seek—Father Tranquilo and Blood Cardinal Don Frutos—will not be found here. They continued swiftly on with the bulk of our mounted contingent. . . ." He paused to reflect, each wheezing breath an effort. "Five? No, six days ago. They raced ahead while we dawdled in your path. You will never catch them now. Not only did they escape you, a messenger dragon Tranquilo appropriated at Gran Lago was sent to the Holy City with his report!"

Anson was taken aback. The Doms had a few of what he considered larger versions of lizardbirds—basically flying Grik, and probably related to them. Grik were ferocious, bipedal . . . furry/reptilian warriors about the size of a man. Once allied to the Holcanos, they aided no one now. Not even one another. Stung by their losses in battle, their contentious tribes had abandoned the coalition forged by their war leader, General Soor, and scattered once more into the wilderness. Aside from their feral young, called "garaaches," none had been seen for some time. Unlike Grik, however, messenger dragons weren't smart and couldn't communicate, but could—with great care, apparently—be trained to act like messenger pigeons. *Nothing we've done here will be secret from the enemy for long*, Anson realized, *and we've got even less time than Lewis thinks to figure out what to do next.*

The dying Blood Preist—Anson didn't know his name and didn't care to—had seemed triumphant for a moment while Anson digested his news, but finally looked disappointed. "It was hoped we might delay you longer, inflict a stiffer penalty, perhaps even destroy your smaller force. We were specifically instructed to slay *you*, if we could." He blinked. "Sadly, that did not happen, and remembering our previous meeting, I feared it would be difficult. Our soldiers were poorly trained and chose their position unwisely. Particularly since . . ." He paused, gasping, while he studied Anson keenly. "We had many sympathizers embedded in General Agon's army, true believers in the New Way and not the old regime. With the fall of that regime, the . . . removal of the reformist Don Datu from succession and installation of Don Julio DeDivino Dicha as Supreme Holiness, reactionaries like General Agon would've ultimately been dealt with by those sympathizers. The outcome of the battle at Gran Lago made that . . . less convenient, but some of our people escaped to reach us with news of the battle, as well as a description of how your Rangers—all your horsemen and great guns—had caused terrible mischief beforehand. It was believed you and they are somehow more devils than men. Is that true?"

The Blood Priest was having more difficulty now and seemed to be fading quickly. When Anson didn't reply, he resumed, but his voice was thinner, wispier. "Father Tranquilo long believed your entire force was composed of devils. How else could it arrive out of nowhere and survive—even prevail—against the efforts of God? Please"—the man coughed more blood, thick and bright—"as you can see, I can tell no one. Your secret will be safe with me."

Leonor and Lara watched as her father slowly moved his horse closer to the Blood Priest. She was mainly concerned that one of the others might attack him, with his teeth if nothing else, but they'd all been carefully secured. The thunderous cannonading in the clearing resumed, smashing the last to resist without mercy or pause, and Anson leaned over in his saddle so his low spoken words could be heard.

"That's right. Los Diablos, that's us, come to find whatever hole your sick, twisted god hides in. We're gonna bob his horns, cut off his tail, set fire to his drawers, an' *then* . . ." Anson grinned. "Well, no matter. You won't be around to see it. One thing about us devils. We got powers, see? Best of all, we got the power over those in our hands to make sure they don't go to their underworld paradise. All your sufferin's been for nothin', an' when you die here directly, you're goin' straight to hell. I reckon for you that'll mean endurin' the same sufferin' you've inflicted on others. Forever an' ever an' ever." Yanking Colonel Fannin's head around, he called back to Leonor. "I think we got all we need from him. Hang the Blood Priests. All of 'em. Initiates too. An' make sure there ain't any hidin' amongst the prisoners. The rest of 'em will know. If any act funny about pointin' 'em out, hang them too."

"You still goin' to find Burton?" Leonor asked. "Sir," she added. Barca's pair of guns fired again.

"Yeah. We gotta get this mess wrapped up an' get word back to Lewis. An' I want to get back to chasin' Tranquilo *today*." With that, he passed out of the woods, half of Lara's protective lancers following, and they galloped away along the tree line, back toward the smashed barricade.

"He's probably right," Lara told Leonor, moving his own horse up beside hers. "We have little time left to catch Tranquilo. Coronel Cayce will probably—rightly—recall us as soon as our messengers reach him. He will want us before he moves the rest of the army, and he will move it soon." He paused, looking down at the Blood Priest, whose face was constricted with horror. He might not fully believe what Anson told him, but he'd die with doubts. "Would you like to hang the Blood Priests, Lieutenant Anson?" he asked Leonor, suddenly very formal, "or shall my lancers have the honor?"

Leonor considered that. "Why don't we see if any of the other prisoners want to do it? I'm kinda curious how popular this 'new way' is. Especially 'mongst soldiers who've been right under the thumb o' those red-robed bastards."

"Interesting indeed," Lara agreed. "Shall we experiment?"

CHAPTER 3

Once a mere outpost on the easternmost edge of the Holy Dominion, Frontera (not to be confused with Nueva Frontera, four hundred miles farther east) had been aptly named when it was founded almost a century before. Now, though perhaps not a "city" even in the sense Gran Lago had become one, it was a respectable-size town with seven to ten thousand people inhabiting it and the surrounding estates. And even though it was still on a "frontier" in a manner of speaking, the region around it was somewhat less wild and the land to the northwest considerably more settled. Those living in and around Frontera were able to do so in relative safety from the monsters of the wilderness. Some still came to ravage flocks and herds of livestock, but palisades protected those farther out, and stout fences were sufficient to defend crops from smaller grazers. Almost nothing could stop the bigger ones, even in the Great Valley of the Holy City, and certain percentages of such crops were simply written off to them, "sacrificed" in a sense, but even those bigger monsters were always on the move to avoid the things that harvested them.

In any event, Frontera was a fairly prosperous place. Access to the sea allowed rapid export of produce and livestock, and the country villas and buildings within the main walls were "modern," as such things were reckoned; stuccoed and whitewashed walls roofed with clay tiles. There were the usual swarms of poor farmers in the fields and grubby laborers in town, many mere slaves, but even a large percentage of freemen made enough to dress fairly well. Hidalgos and above almost all covered themselves in fine, colorful clothing. There were no soldiers to speak of, all having been called away to join Agon or the Cruzada, yet the people couldn't imagine needing them. They were missed by their families, of course, but their purpose seemed vague and unthreatening. Most imagined their sons and husbands embarked on a grand adventure. All would return one day with fanciful tales of exotic lands. Paid hidalgos *milicia* served as police or confronted the more troublesome rampaging monsters, and the peaceful little city had been oblivious to the heretic threat from the east—until the Blood Cardinal Don Frutos and his entourage of roughly two hundred lancers and Blood Priests arrived several days before. Their coming had caused a sensation, but they hadn't themselves been in battle, and they didn't seem much more worn than anyone would after their long journey from distant Gran Lago. Only the *alcalde* and his advisors, the most influential men in Frontera, knew the real reason they came, and they'd been warned to keep the secret if they wanted to live.

"Scouts have returned, my lord," proclaimed Teniente Juaris—the highest-ranking lancer officer to remain in Don Frutos's party—as he rushed into the open-air plaza inside the *alcalde*'s palace. He wasn't speaking to the *alcalde*, who sat dejectedly on a stone bench off to the side of the larger group gathered around a flowing fountain. And despite the honorific he used, he wasn't even facing Don Frutos when he spoke. The Blood Cardinal was no longer of much use to anyone at all and sat in a place of prominence in his lightly soiled gold-embroidered red robe and white galero-like hat, its wide brim decorated with red tassels that looked like dripping blood. His pale, narrow face was drawn, his sharply trimmed whiskers rapidly going from blue-black to gray, his sunken eyes unfocused and absent. The *teniente* was clearly addressing another frail man robed in much filthier and tattered, unadorned red.

The meager, stooped figure was pacing, however, with an angry energy that belied his shriveled, wrinkled face and wispy gray hair but not the darting, ferret-like eyes. "What news?" the man demanded in a raspy, impatient voice. Regardless of his appearance and still somewhat ambiguous status even after the elevation of the new Supreme Holiness he supported, there was no doubt the Blood Priest, Father Tranquilo, had supreme authority here. If anyone dared question that, they'd be quickly and pitilessly corrected by the hulking brute shadowing his steps. Brother Escorpion might be the very last survivor of the first "reaper monks" Tranquilo had recruited himself. The order had grown considerably, but generally remained secret at present. Escorpion's knee-length tunic was the same cut as any initiate's except it was dyed red as well, and had a jagged yellow cross-stitched across the chest. His only weapon was a six-foot spear with a golden blade. He didn't really need it to perform his only function in life: to protect Father Tranquilo and do his bidding. This included destroying anyone Tranquilo told him to.

Teniente Juaris hesitated in the face of Tranquilo's growing impatience, then simply said, "The blocking force we left to delay the pursuing heretics was destroyed."

Tranquilo nodded, expecting no less. He regretted the loss of so many of his Blood Priest brethren, but there'd only been mounts for a few. He cared nothing for the soldiers. Nearly all had been conscripts gathered along the way and given the most rudimentary training. The loyalty of the handful of "professionals" left to lead them to the "New Way" of the Blood Priests had been suspect to say the least. He would've "sacrificed" all of them, regardless. This way their sacrifice served a purpose beyond merely cleansing their souls of heresy. "So, how many enemies did they slay, and how many days did they gain us?" he asked.

Teniente Juaris coughed.

"Well?" Tranquilo spat impatiently.

"It is believed they may have slain as many as a dozen of our pursuers and wounded twice that many more. A column of wagons—ours that they captured—was observed moving east under the protection of enemy lancers. Some of the wagons had wounded in them." Juaris hesitated again. "As for the time they gained for us . . . perhaps the entire day the action took."

"¡Que dios los maldiga a todos!" Tranquilo roared. "They couldn't even serve a useful purpose in death! What of my priests?"

"Any who survived the fight were . . . hanged."

Tranquilo closed his eyes and took a deep breath. He'd expected that. More and more he'd been hearing that was the treatment his priests could expect if taken. He said a silent prayer that God might accept their souls into paradise regardless of how little they suffered. "Despicable," he muttered. "We would not even send heretics we captured off so callously to meet God."

"Perhaps we should arrange for them to have as painless a death as possible so we can be sure to deny them a place in paradise!" the reaper monk growled.

"No," Tranquilo said. "Do not be that way," he scolded. "Besides, they *fear* the pain of suffering and death. We can use that to our advantage." He snorted. "Imagine their surprise when they discover the gift we have given them!" He looked back at Juaris. "What did the enemy do then? Did they finally turn about, or did they continue on after us?"

"They come, Lord. Having sent an escort for their wounded, they are fewer now, but not by much. Considering how few could fight to protect Frontera, I fear they will take it with ease. And we will have to hurry to keep ahead of them. If they reach Oaxaca or Mazupiapan . . . Those are much larger cities, but no better prepared to defend themselves. Regardless, they must be warned to prepare."

Tranquilo shook his head. "Warned to prepare against *what*?" he demanded, beady eyes sweeping the rest of those present. "Heretics? Devils from beyond the frontier who *defeated a Dominion army*? Don't you see? They cannot be allowed to know such a thing has even happened!" He glanced at the miserable *alcalde*. "Any who learn of it must be silenced, but we cannot silence everyone! Each city grows larger and more important from here to the Great Valley. We cannot continue to cleanse each one merely because they learn of their peril. We must stop the threat cold, here."

The *alcalde* of Frontera finally summoned the courage to speak. "H-how?" he asked shakily. "We have no soldiers other than the few you brought. The *milicia* will fight, but they are so few . . . I-I understand it has always been our way to destroy any of our people who allow Dominion soil to fall into the hands of invaders—settlements on the frontier overrun by savages—but Frontera! I beg of you! There are *thousands* of innocents here!"

Tranquilo rounded on the man. "Yes!" he snarled. "Thousands! Many more than the enemy! Let every man and boy who can wield a weapon go out to meet the enemy and fight to save their homes! They'll be slaughtered," he stated callously, "but they can *stop* this vile invasion if they try." He paused, considering, and the expression on his already sinister face became even harder to gaze upon. "And we will ensure that they do. We will take custody of every woman and child in and around the city. If their men will not fight for them and earn the favor of God, *their families* will pay the price. *They will earn* the grace the men of Frontera could not. Do you understand me?"

Horrified, the *alcalde* could only stare, openmouthed.

"Do you understand?" Tranquilo shrieked.

"I do," the *alcalde* whispered. "But what will we use for weapons?"

Tranquilo waved that away. "Whatever you must. Surely there are some. Bows, arrows, and spears, at least. Some of your wealthier residents must have *escopetas*. Otherwise, I don't care. Axes, cleavers, farm implements. Teeth, if need be."

"Wh-what will you and your soldiers be doing?"

Tranquilo glanced at Teniente Juaris, who looked deeply uncomfortable. *Too bad*, he thought. *He had promise.* "Some of my people will help you." His little dark eyes became black slits in his face. "The rest of us will be watching."

———

"Ohhhhh . . . !" began the hulking Daniel Hahessy in a surprisingly pleasant baritone, preparing to break into song. A former troublemaker of the very worst sort forcibly transferred out of the 1st US Infantry, he was now the Number One man on the Number Two M1841 6pdr gun in Lieutenant Barca's section. He was currently riding the foremost horse on the right side of the six-up team hitched to the limber that pulled the heavy weapon. Just three days after the action against the Doms and Blood Priests they'd been chasing, a little more than half of Anson's force had emerged from the forest into relatively open rolling hills under a bright warm sun. The Dom city of Frontera wasn't supposed to be far ahead, but it couldn't yet be seen, nestled in a valley about ten miles away at the base of rising, purple mountains. There were quite a few empty farmhouses and the occasional vacant villa, everyone apparently having learned they were coming and fled, but it was a spectacular view, and life swirled all around them.

Coveys of short-winged lizardbirds exploded from the brush alongside the Camino Militar like pheasants or giant quail, fluttering away amid high-pitched *woopwoopwoop!* sounds. It was almost comical. Great herds of massive beasts, some they'd never seen, which were so bizarre they defied description, grazed peacefully in the distance, utterly unperturbed by the passage of just over five hundred horsemen, two artillery pieces, and all their caissons and wagons. After all they'd been through, it was the kind of day that seemed made for a song, and Hahessy appeared about to oblige.

"Lord above, he's gonna sing it again! Make 'im stop, Corp'ral Hanny, can't ye?" the Scottish-born Number Two man, "Preacher Mac" MacDonald, practically beseeched his chief of the piece, Corporal Hannibal "Hanny" Cox. Hanny was riding the left-hand horse directly in front of the limber. Up ahead, the Irish Hahessy glared at the Scotsman beside him, feigning disappointment at the interruption.

"No, I can't. Won't, actually." Hanny chuckled. "I kind of like it." Hanny had come to this world as a gangly teenage recruit in the 3rd Pennsylvania Infantry, but found his true calling in the artillery. Still only eighteen, he'd shown he had wisdom and talent beyond his years and had earned the respect of everyone in the section, including Hahessy.

The 1st Section of C Battery (also known as "Hudgens's battery" for its commander, Captain Elijah Hudgens) had been on detached duty with Major Anson's wide-ranging mounted forces far more than it had been with the rest of C Battery. A few cynics might've imagined it to be exiled, partly because of the "pickup" nature of the gun's crews, but mainly due to its new section chief. Many of its artillerymen had started as infantry and some of Coryon Burton's Uxmalo dragoons had replaced heavy losses after the Battle of Gran Lago. But the section chief, Lieutenant Barca, was a young Black man from New Orleans who came to this world as the personal servant of Colonel De Russy. Yet as mixed as all the original "American" units had become as natives replaced the fallen, or men were assigned to the production of war material, hardly anyone even thought about such things anymore. Barca had certainly distinguished himself and won the loyalty of his men. If any of them, including Hahessy, heard speculation they'd been cut loose because Barca was Black, there probably would've been violence. In their estimation, their *elected* lieutenant had taken the worst section in the battery (deemed lucky to hit the planet, much less the intended target with its guns) and created the hardest-fighting, most professional and effective section in the army. If 1st Section spent a lot of time detached, it was because it was so frequently requested.

"I like the song too," said Private Apo Tuin, Hanny's closest friend and the gun's Number Six man. Apo was another Uxmalo, short and dark, with a wicked sense of humor. He also had a beautiful sister named Izel whom

Hanny was besotted with. "Besides," Apo continued, a little mystified, "you helped him with the words!"

That was true enough. Even though Preacher Mac and Hahessy cordially hated each other, it seemed they had a common interest in verse. Riding up front, side by side as they did, they'd begun inventing new words to the popular standby "Rosin the Beau" that reflected their current situation. That was nothing new. Virtually every melody known to any of the men, with a few exceptions, had new words now, or at least new verses tacked on.

"It isnae the words, it's *how* the fiend sings 'em!" Preacher Mac complained darkly. "Mockin' the lyrical speech o' me homeland—an' him a black-hearted Irishman! Nor did I want sae much aboot spirits init, did I?"

"Yer soul ta the divil, Preacher," Hahessy replied. "Did I add anythin' about spirits then? I did not. Imagine it's wine, or beer, or bloody sheep's milk if ye like. An' as for the sound of it, didn't ye birth the best words yerself? Seems only right it should have a *proper* Scotsman's sound to it."

Preacher Mac grumbled, but to everyone's surprise, First Sergeant Petty had ridden up beside them and prodded Hahessy on with a croaky "Ohhhh..." of his own. With a laugh, nearly everyone joined in, affecting their own best (or worst) Scottish brogues, even the crew of the Number One gun trundling along behind them.

> *Oh, have a drink with this wild-rovin' sodger!*
> *Raise a toast to me sorrows an' woes,*
> *But dinnae fergit tae save a wee bit,*
> *Tae splash on the graves o' me foes!*

"D'ye see?" Hahessy interjected quickly. "Sheep's milk it is. I'd never countenance wastin' good whisky so!"

> *I rambled me old world over,*
> *Faced sufferin' an' mis'ries galore,*
> *Then the Good Lord did fetch me to a whole 'nother world,*
> *Just so's I could suffer s'more!*

"Blasphemy," Preacher Mac scolded.

"Is not," called Billy Randall, the gun's Number Seven man, tightly seated on the ammunition chest atop the limber beside Apo and Kini Hau. Three men were *supposed* to fit between the handles, but usually two was the limit. Apo, Kini, and Billy were all small and thin. "How do you think we all got here?" Billy pressed.

"Not just tae suffer," Preacher Mac defended.

Nearby dragoons and Rangers had joined in, and the song swelled as they belted out the next verses, including another chorus that included "wasting" more drink—though many laughingly identified it as sheep's milk now. Neither Preacher Mac nor Hahessy had declared the song "finished," and others would add their own verses, but soon they came to the "end":

> *So have a drink with this wild-rovin' sodger!*
> *Festoon me dank grave with great stones,*
> *An' by an' by, have a drink an' come spy*
> *That the boogers ain't dug up me bones!*

"Gloomy bastards, Scots," Petty groused. "Irishmen too. Always gotta end a song in the grave."

Having expanded almost up and down the whole column, the men sang the last chorus.

> *That the boogers ain't dug up me bones, me boys, that the boogers ain't*
> *dug up me bones,*
> *Have a look see, when ye come tae see me, that the boogers ain't gnawed*
> *up me bones!*

Laughter exploded. Grinning, Hanny saw that Hahessy practically glowed—he'd never been praised for much of anything in his life—and Mac had hunkered down in his saddle, face red. The contrast was striking. *Mac doesn't need to earn the goodwill of his fellows. He already has it. Hahessy's just begun to learn what it feels like.* He suspected the big Irishman would die for any of them now, whether he liked them or not. *I did that*, Hanny suddenly realized. *Just by standing up to him and making him look at himself.* The thought made him feel very strange. Humbled was part of it, but also a little . . . afraid. "Let's have another," someone shouted, and the practically unaltered favorite "Blue Juniata" began, led by a young Uxmalo dragoon with a fine voice.

Major Anson and his daughter rode up and joined Lieutenant Barca where he was riding alongside the Number Two gun as it rattled along. Hanny and the boys behind him on the limber made to salute, but the older Ranger waved it off with a grin and held up his hand, clearly implying they shouldn't interrupt the song. It was likely that very few of the Americans knew where the Juniata River was, and none of the locals ever would, but they found the cheerful tune and simple, unpretentious lyrics as endearing as the men who brought them here. Hanny reflected that the simple song might've done more to build and bind their alliance than anything else they'd done.

When it ended, as always, there was cheering, whistles, and even a few off-color, laughter-inducing comments about the stunning number of new-born daughters named Alfarata in the alliance. Accustomed to the coarse company of soldiers, even Leonor chuckled. Shaking his head, Major Anson looked at Barca. "How are the repairs to your guns holding up to the pace we've set?" he asked. The carriages under both of Barca's 6pdrs had been shot to pieces in action at the Battle of Gran Lago.

Barca absently removed his hat and scratched the short but already curling black hair on his head. "The tubes were fine, of course, and Sergeant O'Roddy has done a fine job on the damaged or broken irons. My boys repaired the harness themselves, with good leather 'commandeered' at a villa outside Gran Lago," he added proudly. "I think your fellows made good use of some of it themselves." Anson nodded. Whoever owned the villa and its scores of slaves had also run a large nearby tannery. It was one of the biggest "industrial sites" captured so far, in fact. Anson and Lewis were beginning to wonder about that. Word was, little of strategic value—aside from the basic necessities of a modest seaport and foodstuffs, of course—was produced at Vera Cruz, and only luxuries actually came from the Holy City of Mexico. There were supposedly some foundries, more tanneries, a powder mill, and other things in smaller cities near there, but nothing like the industry required to raise a force like General Agon's had been. Certainly not the "Gran Cruzada." It was believed all heavy equipment and virtually all war production must still be centered in the oldest Dom settlements west of the Holy City along the Pacific coast. That could pose a problem.

"We're running on half the spare wheels in Captain Hudgens's whole battery—there's only one more spare along with us," Barca reminded. "But generally . . . I think we're getting along well enough. I'll be glad to replace a few of the cheeks and both the axle boxes," he conceded, referring to slabs of oak supporting the tubes by the trunnions and the heavy wooden outer axle housings for the wrought iron shaft inside. "I'd say they're still sound for now, but all the wood that was shot and splintered away has left them somewhat weaker." He smiled wryly. "Sloshing flaxseed oil—or whatever they make it from—and paint down in bullet holes won't control the rot forever."

"Speaking of rot," Leonor said lowly with a meaningful glance at Private Hahessy up ahead. The song now was "Annie Laurie," and the big Irishman was singing along with Preacher Mac, both using the original words in place of many that had changed to suit local conditions (and language).

Barca obviously knew what she meant and looked at Hanny, who'd twisted around on his horse to watch. Barca's expression seemed to ask if he'd like to answer. Hanny cleared his throat. "He's better, sirs and . . ." His face colored looking at Leonor, but he went on. "*Really* better . . . so far," he qualified, gesturing around. "He's finally got a crew—a 'tribe,' so to speak— of fellows he considers his equals, I think. Even a few he accepts as betters because they've proven they're *better men*, not just born above him." He shrugged. "I wouldn't say he has friends exactly, and we've been rather busy. Always on the move and frequently in action. He does his duty, performs his share of chores without serious complaint, and he's stopped bullying those weaker than him." He paused. "He still *provokes* men, like Mac, who'd make a closer match, but even that has more of a playful aspect to it." He stopped again to consider. "God only knows how he'll behave if he ever gets bored, but I'll vouch for him at present."

"Annie Laurie" came to an end, and Hahessy loudly blew his nose on a filthy rag he kept stuffed in his belt. Everyone looked at him as he glanced around, vigorously flapping the rag before putting it back. "Faith!" he exclaimed in a loud, mournful voice. "Sing somethin' livelier next, if ye please. Always gets me, that one does!"

"Is that a *tear* I see on yer great hackit face?" Preacher Mac asked in surprise.

Hahessy leaned back in the Grimsley-style saddle and stared down his pug nose at Mac. "An' what if it is, then?"

Taken aback, the young Scotsman merely nodded. "Then it is, I ken."

There were chuckles from those who heard. "Morale does seem to be good," Anson observed. "Men and animals are tired, and that's understandable, but I think we're doin' as well as can be expected, all alone an' three hundred miles in advance of any support. We've been fortunate acquirin' supplies, an' it's good there hasn't been more effective resistance. By the way, Mr. Barca, excellent execution the other day."

"Thank you, sir," replied Hanny's section chief, but Hanny himself turned back around, his own mood quickly darkening. *The fight in the clearing was an 'execution,' all right*, he thought. *Practically murder.* And the image of hanging Blood Priests festooning the trees around the clearing like macabre decorations still haunted him. Then again, so did the scenes they'd viewed in the dead towns and all the innocents they'd found horribly murdered along the way, not to mention the desolate, mostly starved conscripted civilians they'd managed to "save" and send back to Gran Lago. *Murder or not*, he thought, heart hardening, *I guess they had it coming.*

He would soon lose any lingering doubt.

"Captain Burton's back," Leonor noted, nodding forward. Hanny looked and saw a squad of dragoons pounding back down the line, obviously seeking Major Anson. Burton led the men who pulled up and turned huffing horses to ride alongside their commander. He saluted and Anson returned it. "See somethin', Captain?" the Ranger asked.

"Yes sir. Scouts reported a force assembling in our path a few miles ahead, but what they said didn't make sense. I felt compelled to see for myself before I brought it to your attention."

"*Never* hold back reports, Captain, no matter how strange they seem," Anson growled.

"No sir. I never would. It's just that there was no pressing threat." He gestured vaguely around, and it was true. They could see a long distance, and even the closest huge herbivores were almost a mile away. "I just thought it best to . . . clarify the report before bringing it to you."

Anson seemed to think that was reasonable. "Very well. I take it you did?"

Coryon sighed. "I believe so, sir. There *is* a large gathering of people ahead, thousands in fact. They appear to know we're coming, and I can't imagine they have any purpose other than opposing us in mind."

If Anson was alarmed, he didn't show it. "Have they thrown up any obstacles? Are they moving this way?"

"No sir. They're just . . . kind of congregated in our path, like I said. There's no discernible organization, no battle line, no flags. Most are armed with something, but their weapons aren't particularly intimidating, and I saw very few of what might be soldiers among them, though a number of those dreadful Blood Priests were seen." He glanced at Barca. "No artillery."

Anson looked at his daughter and scowled. "It's a mob of civilians, then."

"I'd say so," Coryon somberly agreed. "Townsfolk, mostly." He waved around again. "Some farmers and . . . gamekeepers from out around here, I expect." He chuckled uneasily. "Seems inappropriate to call them ranchers, with some of the strange beasts they tend, but I suppose they are."

"An' they mean to fight us?" Leonor asked.

Coryon pursed his lips. "That's the thing. That *must* be their purpose, but I can't think they want to."

"Blood Priests," Anson growled, and Coryon nodded. "I better have a look for myself. Stay here, Captain Burton. Halt the column and you're in charge until I get back. Lieutenant Anson, Lieutenant Barca." He raised his voice to call the lancer commander forward. "Capitan Lara, you an' a squad of your men with me, if you please."

Anson's party galloped forward in a swirl of dust, straight up the road. The Ranger called a halt at the crest of the rise and briefly scanned the sloping ground ahead, noting the distant walled town nestled at the bottom of the grade several miles ahead and that the "enemy's" disposition was exactly as Burton described. Kicking Colonel Fannin ahead once more, he trotted his horse still closer, causing a great deal of agitation in the mob; obvious civilians tried desperately to array themselves in something like a line, while Blood Priests shouted at them and beat them into position. Anson stopped again and raised his tarnished brass spyglass.

"Bastards," he growled as Leonor, Lara, and Barca stopped by him, Lara's eight troopers spreading out to the sides. "It's them Blood Priests whuppin' 'em at us, all right. Men—mostly older men an' boys is all they are." He looked a little longer. "Maybe twenty-five hundred, three thousand or so. All look terrified, an' less than half have a proper weapon. Farmin' tools, mostly." He spat in disgust before looking again. "Surprised they didn't send the women an' little girls to fight us too."

"You forget, Father. Doms—an' Blood Priests in particular, I guess— don't think women are much account," Leonor reminded.

Lara shook his head. "We've already seen that isn't necessarily the case out here on the edge of their empire. Women had status in Gran Lago, and don't forget Alcaldesa Consela." Consela was the mature but still very handsome head woman of a settlement on the banks of the Usuma River, all but wiped out by Blood Priests. She and Chief Kisin, the now Allied war leader of the Holcanos, who seemed quite drawn to the much older woman, had remained in Gran Lago since that's where she was originally from.

"I didn't forget," Anson retorted, "an' just because women mean more to folks here don't mean they mean more to Blood Priests—except maybe as hostages. You remember how civilians in Gran Lago reacted to our comin'?"

Leonor nodded. "Aside from a few who were anxious to meet us an' at least *hoped* we might help 'em, most just ran away—as scared of their own people as us. But they probably knew we were comin' longer, an' you didn't go right at the city, you only blocked General Agon from reachin' it." She'd been with Lewis and the main army at the time.

"Which gave 'em more time to skedaddle," Anson agreed.

"But these people haven't left," Barca observed, "so it stands to reason they didn't know we were coming—and that's how a small number of those unholy devils quickly raised so many against us. Don Frutos and Tranquilo must be in the city with the rest of their men, *making* these people buy them more time to escape!"

"Doesn't leave me inclined to give 'em their way," Anson grumbled. "How 'bout the rest of you?"

No one answered at once, clearly concerned that Anson meant to attack the civilians.

"May I ask what you have in mind, sir?" Barca hesitantly asked.

Anson handed the young artilleryman his glass. "You can just make out the sea to the right—north. Looks like a little bay. Kinda pretty. But look down at the city. I didn't see any troops, not even guards on the gate—which is standin' wide open, by the way. Nobody along the top o' the palisade, neither; course, that ain't unusual. We've seen the same at every little village we passed. The walls these people build ain't for fightin' behind, they're for keepin' big critters out. Why line the tops with fightin' platforms? Boogers'll just reach over an' snatch fellas off 'em."

"The gate *is* wide open," Barca confirmed, "and I see no one under arms but those people right in front of us."

"You think it's a trap?" Lara asked their commander.

Anson shook his head. "The 'trap' is makin' us wade in amongst them townsfolk an' slaughter 'em. Doms can say, 'Lookie how bloodthirsty them heretics are,' while we take a beatin' ourselves an' then don't feel too good about what we had to do. That bastard Tranquilo was amongst folks on the Yucatán a long while. He knows Uxmalos, Itzincabos, Techonos, even Ocelomeh. He may not know *us* very well, but he knows what it'll do to our friends."

"So what *will* we do?" Lara asked, with evident relief. No one thought Anson would enjoy killing near-helpless civilians, but no one doubted he was ruthless enough to do so if he had to.

Anson grinned at him. "Just what they expect . . . at first. I'd give my left foot for some o' Felix Meder's riflemen about now, to shoot every Blood Priest in sight."

"We have a few rifles," Leonor said, tugging the sling of her own and nodding at her father's.

"Take too long," Anson argued, "an' as soon as we shot a couple, the rest'd start hidin' behind little boys." He took the spyglass when Barca handed it back. "So weapons aside, what's the biggest difference between us an' all them poor heatherns down there?"

"We are disciplined soldiers?" Lara suggested as a question because he didn't think it was the answer Anson wanted.

"There's that, sure, but right now that don't give us as much an edge as the fact we're all mounted, even our artillerymen—an' none o' them are." He sat silent on Colonel Fannin a moment longer, gazing at the mob of townsfolk and the land all around them. "Mr. Barca, Mr. Lara, go tell Mr. Burton to bring everything up—battle formation, with lancers on the left an' dragoons an' artillery on the right. We'll advance to within two hundred paces of the, uh, 'enemy,' an' stop, understood?"

"What then?" Leonor asked.

Anson looked at his daughter. "Why, we'll charge, o' course. *Around* the defenders as fast as we can, an' make for the city gate. Lancers an' artillery'll deploy in a defensive line there, facin' out—you're in charge o' that, Mr. Lara—while the dragoons an' Rangers go in. We'll see if there's anybody left in the city to save—or catch," he added grimly.

IT WENT VERY much like that, in fact: what roughly equaled a mounted regiment of three understrength battalions—parts of Coryon Burton's 3rd

Dragoons, Lara's 1st Yucatán Lancers, and a couple of companies of Anson's mostly Ocelomeh Rangers riding into view straddling the road on the rise above the conscripted townsfolk. Barca's section of artillery moved up near the center. Flags and guidons fluttered over the veteran soldiers as they came to a halt, sabers drawn or lances held high, and other than the thunder of hooves and jangle of tack, they made no other sound. A great noise rose among those placed to oppose them, however; moans and cries of fear, even defiant shouts directed at the Blood Priests. The Blood Priests yelled louder as well, applying cudgels, even swords, as their sacrificial defenders instinctively recoiled from the terrifying sight. Anson imagined it might've been interesting to see how that eventually turned out—whether the people of Frontera would actually face a charge or murder their immediate tormentors first—but they weren't given time to decide.

Barca's guns never completely stopped rolling before they veered to the right behind the dragoons, bouncing and grumbling away from the road on the uneven, rocky ground. As soon as they passed the dragoon guidon, Burton's bugler sounded his horn and the Rangers wheeled into column to the right and their horses began to move, first at a trot, then a gallop. Barca's guns pulled in behind them, dust and debris spraying amid blurring spokes, and the dragoons brought up the rear. To the left, the bugle had signaled the lancers as well, who re-formed their column and charged in the opposite direction.

For moments, complete confusion reigned in the chaotic ranks of the townsfolk. They might've outnumbered the heretics by as much as four or five to one, but there'd been no doubt in their minds they were doomed. Suddenly, the people they'd been told were their enemies, enemies of God Himself, simply scattered before them. Some shouted with glee, others relief, but the Blood Priests understood at once and were already screaming for them to fall back on the city. This didn't make any sense . . . until all at once it did. The enemy hadn't "scattered," they'd merely split to go around them. Already the columns were bending around, aiming for Frontera.

Some of the townspeople panicked in the face of a new terrible threat to their families. Others, perhaps more levelheaded, knew the heretics could've easily destroyed them but chose not to do so. Frontera—and their families—would've been at their mercy after that. Was it possible they really didn't mean them any harm? The Blood Priests were already viewed as *an* enemy, for the way they'd coerced the townsfolk to fight, but many began to cope with the notion that they might be *the* enemy. The *only* enemy, after all. Even as hundreds of townspeople broke and began streaming back toward their homes, others started turning on their masters. Trying to keep his charges together, a Blood Priest slammed his cudgel against the back of a young man and laid him out on the ground. Whirling and bellowing for others to heed him, he was utterly surprised when a man—the youngster's father—drove a sharpened wood spear through his throat. Hundreds of stunned faces watched for an instant as the priest choked on blood and clawed at the spear, eyes bugging out in agony and surprise.

"Kill them!" the man, a burly farmer said. "Kill the Blood Priests!" he shouted louder.

"What of the heretics? They will murder our families!" a man almost wailed beside him.

"I may be wrong—I hope not—but I think the heretics avoided killing us so they might *save* our families. Only the Blood Priests have actually threatened them!"

That abruptly made a great deal of sense to a lot of desperate people, and the heretofore inviolate persons of every Blood Priest in the midst of the mob were quickly and brutally violated with every sort of sharp instrument imaginable.

"RIGHT HERE!" BARCA shouted, pointing at the ground near the gate with his saber before spurring his horse a short distance onward. "Gun Number Two, right *here*. Unlimber facing outward and load canister *but do not fire!*" The Rangers had already poured through the gate, and Burton's dragoons were streaming past between the guns as they were made ready. Not slowed by the guns, Lara's lancers had gotten there first and, already dismounted, had begun to prepare to support the artillery section with their carbines. It wouldn't be long before they knew if they had to despite the distance they'd put between themselves and the mob. Quite a few of those people were literally sprinting the nearly three miles to the gate, and whether most would make it without collapsing or not, a few would shortly arrive.

"Take implements! Load canister!" Hanny shouted, staring over the tube of his Number Two gun at the first cluster of townsfolk staggering out of the dust stirred up in front of the gate. "God, I hope we don't have to kill these people!"

"You an' me both," Apo confessed worriedly, bringing the first round up from the limber himself.

Capitan Lara urged his horse out in the space between the guns and his flanking lancers and the citizens struggling up. All were gasping, and some could barely walk.

"Stop!" he shouted in Spanya. "Please stop. We mean you no harm! We're here for the Blood Priests, not you. Even now we have people rushing inside the city, searching for your families!"

It dawned on Hanny that they might not *know* the Blood Priests were holding the women and children hostage and what Lara said might've been enough to send the townspeople berserk. They'd guessed right, apparently, because some of the men directly in front of them simply collapsed on the ground, gasping and wheezing and praying out loud.

Lara must've had the same thought as Hanny. As more people approached, he quickly repeated what he said before, adding, "We're trying to save your families from the Blood Priests! Stop here, wait. Let us help you!"

"Let us inside!" demanded a big man who looked like a farmer. A much younger man who closely resembled him was giving them a dangerous stare. "Let us find our families ourselves—and kill those who took them from us!"

Lara held up his hands. "Please," he begged. "I can't let you in. If there is fighting, you may be mistaken for the enemy. You must trust us and wait."

"*Trust* you?" someone else yelled incredulously. "Are you not heretics?"

Lara took a breath. "By our reckoning, *you* are heretics, not us, yet we came to help anyway." There was a sudden flurry of shots in the city behind him, and people started shoving and murmuring.

"Prime your guns, damn you!" Barca shouted at his gun's crews, expression hard.

"Prime," Hanny nervously told his Number Three man. The crowd had grown to hundreds now, many still too exhausted to pose a threat, but that wouldn't last. Seeing the activity around the guns, however, they began edging back.

"Don't make us hurt you," Lara pleaded. "We *are* here to help; you have my word. You hear sounds of fighting in the city? That is *our people* fighting Blood Priests *for you*, to protect your people. Wait just a while."

"Maybe it's best," someone speculated. "If they really are fighting Tranquilo's men, let them kill them so we won't be blamed."

"Fool!" shouted another. "We will *all* be blamed for letting them into our city!" This gave rise to more loud murmuring, even shouts, because everyone knew it was true.

"With respect," Lara interjected, tone now harsh, "you didn't 'let' us in, and you can't push us out. I told you: we're only here for the Blood Priests— and to save you from them if we can." He nodded toward the pair of 6pdrs, poised to fire, and the roughly two hundred kneeling lancers with carbines leveled. "You can't stop us, and all you'll accomplish is a pointless blood-bath if you try. You'd truly die fighting those who even now might be dying to save your loved ones? What kind of leaders expect that of you? You call *us* heretics, but what kind of *God* could condone it?"

The fighting in the city swelled behind them.

"JESUS!" ANSON BARKED when a musket ball clipped one of the reins just in front of his left hand. Colonel Fannin didn't really need reins, however, and the big gelding merely did what he always did when he felt his master tense a certain way, whirling around and slamming to a stop, making Anson a harder target and then presenting him with a shot at whatever caused his reaction. Anson took it, and one of his big Walker Colts boomed. Blood sprayed from the back of a townsman crouched behind a two-wheeled cart, and he sprawled on his back, a long Dom musket clattering on the hard-packed gravel-and-caliche street beside him.

"Sorry, Father, I missed that one," Leonor apologized.

"Cavortin' around Lewis too much, gettin' all girly," he pretended to scoff. "Watch for armed locals," he called out louder, urging Colonel Fannin forward again. "Ain't all Dom soldiers an' Blood Priests!"

It never was. The Blood Priests never could've won supremacy in the Dominion without a lot of support, and quite a few converts to their twisted sect lurked even here on the outskirts of the empire. Most remained hidden to those who knew them, including family and friends, awaiting the time when they could openly rise to lead—and denounce those they saw as a threat. That was the case even as far as Uxmal, and it had been impossible to root them all out. They'd already caused serious problems "behind the lines" on occasion, and no one could ever be sure they were through.

"We might've used the townsfolk outside to help with this if not for that," Leonor grimly agreed. "As it is, any fightin'-age fellas we meet are likely in cahoots with Tranquilo." It wasn't believed there could be more than two hundred Dom troops or Blood Priests, and they'd already smashed through a few barricades manned by them, hastily erected to block the narrow streets. But there'd been a sharp fight with "townsfolk" armed with obsolete but still government-owned muskets shortly after clearing the gate and they were taking increasing fire from homes and shops the farther they advanced toward the center of town. That's where the helpless people of Frontera were thought to be gathered: at the foot of a comparatively modest pyramidal temple to the strange, black-hearted version of God that all Doms seemed to worship. They were in a hurry to get there because Doms, and Blood Priests in particular, didn't leave witnesses to their failures or defeats, but it was costing them casualties.

"Damn shame," Anson agreed. "If we take any alive, we'll let the locals sort 'em out. Probably won't appreciate their neighbors defendin' the bastards threatenin' their children."

Furious firing erupted on a street paralleling the one they were on. Waving most of his Rangers forward, Anson pounded around a corner onto a cross street, followed by Leonor and her "own" little platoon of loyal scouts led by Sergeant Riss. Almost immediately, they slammed into the flank of another barricade manned by a mix of locals, Blood Priests, and Doms. A young soldier saw them first, his yellow coat stained with old blood and soot, likely from other settlements he'd helped exterminate, and his eyes and mouth opened wide in terror an instant before a .36 caliber ball from one of Leonor's Patersons opened a small red hole in his forehead and he dropped on the ground, feet drumming. Anson's big Walker added to the din of sudden carbine fire that slapped the men down, one after another in a row. "Cease firing!" Anson roared, and Coryon Burton and several more dragoons leaped the barricade on their horses, sabers flashing and slashing. A single survivor tried to flee but was cut down by a booming volley of the dragoons' Hall carbines.

"*Well* met, sir!" Burton cried happily, white teeth glaring in a face dark with blood. His hat was gone, and more blood was drying in his hair. Other dragoons were rushing up and around him as he paused.

"Knocked on the head, I see," Anson scolded. "How often do I have to tell you, evidence aside, you *need* yer damn head from time to time? This ain't even a battle, an' we can't afford to lose you."

"I beg your pardon, sir, but I might say the same to you."

Leonor snorted, and Anson shrugged. "Losses?" he asked.

Burton's grin faded. "Too many. Three dead that I know of and more wounded. It might be worse with the other companies on other roads. The enemy is determined, as usual."

There was more shooting up ahead, and now they could hear the sound of shrill screams. "Damn, we're close," Anson guessed, "an' it sounds like those sick bastards are gettin' down to business with their hostages. Silly shits who came out to fight us should've known. Should've risen up! *Damn* them," he added harshly.

"How *could* they know?" Leonor asked quietly. "*We* didn't until we saw it before."

Anson frowned and nodded. "Let's go."

BY THE TIME the Rangers and dragoons converged on the temple at the center of Frontera, they'd fought their way through many more enemies than they'd expected to meet, and there were probably still a hundred or so left. These weren't fighting them anymore, however. The Blood Priests and Doms were too busy killing women and children—slashing bellies open, most often. This was easiest for them, after all, and their victims would die in as much pain as possible, earning enough grace to be accepted into paradise.

It wasn't all going their way. There were literally thousands of women and children packed in the plaza, and many had overpowered their executioners, mobbing them under and taking their weapons, fighting back. Swords, axes, even knives stabbed, chopped, or hacked the Blood Priests, who were now almost panicky to kill as many as possible as fast as they could before they were killed in turn. To the men who'd fought their way to this point, already seeing terrible sights, this scene was straight out of hell.

The noise was incredible, so thick with screams of pain and rage and terror, the air itself seemed to have substance. Bodies were everywhere, not all of them dead. Some crawled on the blood-muddied ground, dragging their guts, wailing in agony. The women were bad enough to see, but the children were the worst. Some merely sat in shock, staring down at gashed-open abdomens, but many more tiny bodies with pain-glazed eyes lay in spreading, blackening pools. Anson and Burton immediately lost all control over their men, and with a roar of primal rage, they charged into the carnage, hacking and shooting the Blood Priests they found, or any man for that matter. The surviving women and children were terrified and confused at first, but when it became apparent they weren't the targets of the blue-clad soldiers, most tried to gather their children and draw them out of the way. Some were too maddened to care, still fighting over the corpses of their young ones, slashing—even biting—at anyone who came too close.

After what seemed an eternity but was probably only moments, it was done. A few Blood Priests, beaten insensible, had been taken alive, but all the others had been shot or literally hacked to pieces. The clamor of misery was only slightly lessened, but Captain Burton had finally managed to assemble most of his men with their horses again. (Nearly all had dismounted as they waded into the fight to avoid trampling innocents.) "Spread out in the city," he now told his troopers. "Find anyone still hiding. Some might be innocent, so don't kill them on sight," he warned. "Bring them here where the survivors can judge them."

Anson nodded approval. "Before you personally do anything, have one of the healers look at your head. For that matter, I want you to stay here and make sure all our wounded are tended to. Direct the healers to coordinate with any locals with those kinds of skills—but for God's sake, keep an armed guard an' stay alert!" Anson looked to his daughter. She was still on her horse, grimly reloading her pistols. "Take half the Rangers back the way we came an' root out any holdouts we missed. Quick but careful, understand? When you get back to Mr. Lara an' Mr. Barca, your Rangers an' Lara's lancers'll escort the men of the town back in."

Burton looked at him in surprise. "So soon?" He waved around. "To see *this*?"

"Yes, Mr. Burton," Giles Anson snapped, lip twisted in fury. "*This* above all else is why we fight, an' I want 'em to see it as we've had to!" He lowered his voice and used his hat to mop sweat on his forehead before bleakly adding, "Over and over again. God help all those fools who went to stop us an' weren't here to stop this themselves. They'll never forgive themselves that." He looked meaningfully at his daughter, and Leonor cleared her throat, saying only, "Tranquilo."

"Right." Anson sighed. "Ask who you can; see if they know where he an' Don Frutos are. Find 'em. If they slithered off again, I want 'em caught an' killed."

The reaction of the men of Frontera to the scene in the temple plaza was about what Anson expected: complete anguish and fury. Only a few were misguided enough to blame the Americans and their friends for instigating the slaughter. Survivors denied that at once, tearfully describing how the first "sacrifices" began as soon as their men and sons marched out. And those initial murders—committed when the Blood Priests thought they had plenty of time—had been even more horrific. The *alcalde* died first, in one of the more unpleasant "traditional" rituals. Held down on the altar in front of the temple, Tranquilo (oh yes, they remembered *him*) first cut out his eyes before hacking him open and tearing the beating heart from his chest, catching the last spurt of blood it ejected on his tongue. The next dozen or so townspeople died the same way, but then came word that the heretics had bypassed "Don Frutos's army" and were already in the city. Tranquilo ordered the free-for-all slaughter that ensued, and he and Don Frutos promptly vanished. It was perhaps ironically providential that the mad Blood Priest's early desire to take his time actually saved lives in the end. More than five hundred women and children were brutally slain, and quite a few more were grievously hurt, but many more would've died if the slaughter had started like it ended—and if the blue-coated soldiers hadn't come when they did.

Deemed innocent or not, it was just as well the lancers and Rangers had carefully disarmed everyone before letting them in. Quite a few might've killed themselves or others who'd talked them into cooperating with the Blood Priests and opposing the invaders in the first place. As it was, a kind of . . . searing, agonizing, even vaguely shameful numbness descended on Frontera as the bloody day advanced into evening. Leonor led a company of Rangers in pursuit of the fugitive enemy leaders but was under strict orders to return before dark. Lara's lancers patrolled outside the city while Burton's dragoons and the rest of the Rangers split their time between hunting hiding collaborators and helping locals with the grim task of caring for their wounded and burying their dead. After hearing a few surprising stories of how some of the few Dom soldiers (tasked with rounding up the citizens) had deliberately "overlooked" as many as they could, or were seen to slash throats instead of bellies when ordered to kill, Anson agreed to allow them to be buried as well. Everyone else, dead collaborators and Blood Priests alike, was carted to the bay and cast into the water for the voracious fish to strip.

Anson stayed busy in the *alcalde*'s palace, just off the plaza, where he'd set up his headquarters, speaking with haggard deputations of citizens seeking aid or reassurance. Whether they were wealthy merchants, shopkeepers, farmers, even fishermen and dockworkers who'd largely been spared the horror of the day since their homes by the bay almost constituted a separate town that the Blood Priests had ignored, his answers to all queries were virtually the same from one group to the next:

"We're at war with the Dominion an' nearly every one o' you started the day as enemy combatants. No homes or persons'll be looted, but I'll make no other distinctions between public an' private property. We'll be takin' what we need in terms o' supplies, provisions, an' livestock." He'd added "ships or large seagoin' boats" when he spoke to the people from the bay, although he didn't know how they'd move them yet. Send a few Rangers aboard, he supposed, and force their own crews to take them to Gran Lago. "No, we won't be stayin' to protect you," he had to repeat every time, and often added, "an' we damn sure won't help you round up any slaves that ran off. Take my advice an' leave 'em be. Be glad we don't decide you're all prisoners o' war an' put *you* to work for us. *You* can stay here if you want, or you can pick up an' head east to Gran Lago. That's your best bet. It's a fair-size city an' nearly empty right now. Plenty o' housin'. No, we didn't kill the people that lived there, they just left. I have no idea why none came here. Maybe they mostly headed out across the wilderness, southwest to some o' yer older cities, fearin' they'd be treated like you started to be if they came this way—or maybe the boogers got 'em all. But we're strengthenin' defenses at Gran Lago, an' no matter how we proceed with the war, we'll keep a garrison there."

The final deputation, about a dozen men dressed in working tunics, arrived shortly after dark, and Leonor herself ushered them in, accompanied by Coryon Burton. Burton had a bandage wrapped around his head, but he'd broomed some of the dust and dried blood off his blue jacket. The yellow dragoon trim was likely stained forever. Leonor looked tired and disgusted and still covered in filth from the day. "No luck," she said angrily, flouncing down into a deeply cushioned leather-covered chair beside the *alcalde*'s dark-stained wooden desk her father sat behind. "It's almost like one o' them flyin' lizards swooped down an' snatched 'em up. It gets thick with timber again in them foothills to the west, other side of the bridge. Good bridge," she reflected. "Stone, with arches. Looks old." She sighed. "Anyway, they could've left the road an' ducked into them trees at any point. Boogerbear would've stayed on the trail," she said with conviction.

"But . . ." She shrugged. "He's Boogerbear. Not even the Ocelomeh Rangers with me could find where we lost 'em."

"Too bad," Anson growled. "More lives than a god damn cat. I'd *love* to drag those two bastards up in a tree by a rope around their necks with my own two hands!"

"No more than we would!" one of the locals said strongly. He was big and well muscled, with a dark black beard. The man beside him looked like a younger, beardless version.

Anson leaned back in his chair and took a gulp from a goblet on the desk that contained some stout, very dry purple wine discovered in the palace cellar. He didn't like wine but needed something at the moment. "We might be about even," he conceded to the big man, nodding with compassion at the smaller one. "Your son?"

"Even?" cried the youngster, bristling. "Did they murder *your* mother and grandmother?" He looked at his father. "Your *wife*?" Burton caught his breath when both Anson and his daughter leaned dangerously forward, visibly forcing themselves not to stand. Sometimes they were so much alike it was scary.

"No," Anson said icily, "but men like 'em did. An' these in particular are directly or indirectly responsible for the deaths o' more o' 'my boys' than I care to count. I'm real sorry for your loss, believe me." His voice rose in challenge. "But *I* aim to do somethin' about it. Killin' 'em—an' anyone like 'em—is what I *do* now. The sad, sorry fact is, you folks *let* 'em murder your people here, so I gotta ask what *you* aim to do?"

The younger man's fury dissolved into tears, and the older one wrapped a big arm around him and pulled him close. One of those standing behind them cleared his throat. "That is Hapiki and his son, Hoziki. Like the rest of us"—he gestured at his companions—"they are farmers who live outside the walls, their families rounded up and brought inside when the Blood Priests arrived. But *they* have already fought them. Hapiki was the first to slay one of them while the rest of us panicked or still stood like fools against you."

Anson and Leonor both leaned back a little. "Is that so?" Anson reached down beside the desk and raised a big jug up from the floor, thumping it down in front of him. It looked like an ancient amphora with a flat base so it could stand on its own. "Stuff tastes like piss strained through a sock. It damn sure ain't bourbon," he lamented, then added almost dreamily, "or cool Uxmalo beer." His voice turned rough again. "But I guess it won't hurt you. Might even help. Fetch over some o' them mugs there behind you, Mr. Burton. One for everyone, includin' yourself."

The visitors were visibly surprised, but they all gathered closer around the big desk. Leonor stood and backed away, unwilling to let them so close, but at least she didn't draw a revolver. Anson stood and filled each mug himself before looking around at the men. "I'll ask again. What is it you aim to do?"

"Kill the men who killed my wife," Hapiki said simply.

Anson shook his head. "Can't. We already did it for you. An' you can't even kill Tranquilo an' Don Frutos. Not yet, anyway. Bastards've run off." He tilted his head toward Leonor. "Even Lieutenant Anson lost the trail."

"Anson . . ? Your . . . daughter?" Hapiki asked, amazed. They'd clearly known she was a woman, and that had surprised them enough, but that the leader of these soldiers had a warrior daughter was utterly beyond their experience. Without explanation, or even seeming to notice their astonishment, Anson continued, "That's right. An' if she an' the men under her command can't pick it up, it can't be done. We'll have to hang Tranquilo an' Don Frutos another day. I'm through chasin' after 'em."

Now Leonor was angry and surprised. "What for?"

"We've come too far," her father answered simply. "We're *halfway* to Vera Cruz."

"Then why not just push on through all the way?" Coryon Burton asked.

"Good question." Anson nodded at the farmers of Frontera. "Partly 'cause o' them in a way, but mostly because our communication with Colonel Cayce an' the rest o' the army is too stretched an' gets more dangerous all the time. Besides, God only knows if we even have the *power* to push all the way to Vera Cruz . . . an' what happened today makes me wonder if we got the *right*."

Leonor shook her head, confused, and Anson just said, "Think, girl. What would Lewis do? Blood Priests killed a lot o' folks here today, but there's no question they did it because we were comin'. There's a lot more towns between here an' Vera Cruz, so they'll likely do it again. An' again. As long as we chase 'em. We *ain't* got the power to leap ahead an' prevent it"—he chuckled darkly—"like Cap'n Holland 'accidentally' did at Vera Cruz. So until we do, if there ain't a good chance o' catchin' Tranquilo, we don't really have a mission anymore. We're just on a romp."

Leonor slowly nodded. "I see . . . I think." She took a gulp of her wine and grimaced. "So now we go back, rejoin the rest of the army, an' do it 'right,' is what you're sayin'?"

"Pretty much, though I figure it's even money whether we rejoin Lewis or he joins us here, first. Either way, it'll be nice to let him do the big thinkin' again. Go back to killin' who he points me at." He took his own sip and glanced at Hapiki and his son, then the others around them. "So. Knowin' that, what do *you* want to do?"

Hapiki stared in his mug, then glanced at his son. "We can't stay here. *Won't*," he emphasized. "And 'heretics' or not, it is plain you fight against the evil that descended on us here. Whether you pushed it on us or not doesn't make it less evil." He finally took a long gulp of the wine. "My son and I will join you. Join your army and join your fight against this terrible evil, wherever it is!"

Anson nodded. "Good. What about the rest of you?"

Every man present committed to do the same. Burton was tapping his chin. "How many more, do you think?" he mused, then cleared his throat. "I mean, think about it. Besides General Agon's army, this town may contain the largest number of men we've encountered who hate the Blood Priests as much as we do—and have already purged themselves of nearly all their sympathizers!" He looked expectantly at Hapiki, who rubbed his own chin through his whiskers in thought. "I'd wager every man who lost a loved one would join. Some are too old or crippled, but many would make strong warriors." His gaze fell on Hoziki. "As would their sons."

"Fine," Anson said, raising his mug. "Maybe we didn't catch Tranquilo—*yet*," he emphasized, "but at least we'll be bringin' a battalion o' new recruits to the cause." He hesitated. "I hope some of you know how to ride or the infantry'll get you all."

Red-faced, Hoziki tentatively spoke up. "What of the great guns like those we saw at the gate? Must one be a good horse rider to kill Blood Priests with those?"

Leonor actually laughed. "It helps, but no. If that's what you're set on, I'll take you to meet Lieutenant Barca myself, in the morning."

Heavy bootfalls on the stone floor drew her attention, and she peered down a hall past the interesting indoor fountain toward the entrance of the palace. "Sergeant Riss," she said, but then her eyes widened in surprise. The stocky native Ranger she'd identified was shadowed by the utterly unexpected but distinctively mountainous form of Captain Bandy "Boogerbear" Beeryman. "Where the devil did you come from?" she exclaimed, stepping quickly toward the bearded giant with a happy smile.

Boogerbear clamped her in a brief, crushing hug, then gestured vaguely over his shoulder, rumbling, "East a ways, girl. Thought I'd amble over an' see how things was goin'."

Leonor rolled her eyes and punched the big man hard in the bicep. The locals were clearly shocked by this, but wisely said nothing. Boogerbear didn't even react to the blow, focusing on Anson instead when his former Ranger captain said, "Yeah, just a short three-hundred mile jaunt. All by yourself?"

Boogerbear shook his head. "Brought two comp'nies. Thought you could use 'em. 'Specially after we met half your fellas trundlin' back to Gran Lago with wounded an' pris'ners. Course, our horses won't be fit for much for a couple o' days. We made it here from Gran Lago in five."

"They'll need more than a couple o' days," Anson grumbled. "Don't tell me you were worried about us."

Boogerbear shook his head. "Not me." He looked around and arched a brushy brow. "Looks like I was right too. Don't know if Colonel Cayce was worried, as such—he sent some sorta urgent dispatches—but Mistress Samantha surely was," he added piously.

Anson colored slightly but nodded at the reference to dispatches. "Gentlemen," he said, addressing the native farmers, "I'm very sorry for what happened to you, to some of your loved ones, but I'm glad to have you with us. Talk to your neighbors, tell 'em what we discussed. Don't hesitate to ask if you need any assistance. Far as I'm concerned, you're part o' this army now, an' we take care of our own."

Understanding they'd been politely dismissed, the big farmer, Hapiki, nodded his appreciation and herded the others out.

Anson gestured at the wine amphora, and Boogerbear leaned over and sniffed it before filling a mug one of the locals left standing on the desk. "I know you ain't much of a drinker, an' that stuff's extra nasty," Anson warned as Boogerbear raised the mug and chugged the contents.

"I don't care," the big Ranger said, filling the mug again. "It's wet. Not as like to make me squirt as the local water, neither." Thanks largely to the curious practice of boiling most of the water they drank, taught them by the Ocelomeh, that hadn't been as big a problem as the Americans would've normally expected. Hard-riding horsemen didn't always take the time for it, though, often drinking the same water their horses did.

"Dispatches," Anson reminded when Boogerbear's drinking finally slowed. "You gonna give 'em over or just tell me what they say?"

Coryon Burton hadn't said anything, only nodding a greeting when Boogerbear came in. Now he looked at Anson, shocked. "Surely you're not accusing Captain Beeryman . . ."

Leonor laughed. "He's not *accusin'* him of anything. Father *knows* he read 'em—or Lewis told him what was in 'em."

Boogerbear nodded, surprised by Burton's behavior. "Well, sure he told me. Dispatches might get lost. Can't lose what's in my head."

"You can't destroy what's in your head if you're in danger of being captured either," Burton pointed out.

"Nobody's gonna catch my head," Boogerbear said matter-of-factly.

"No." Burton reflected. "I don't suppose they would." Even he had to agree that the enemy would be about as likely to capture one of the huge, terrifying predatory reptiles it took a cannon to kill as they were to catch Boogerbear alive.

"Have we been recalled?" Leonor pressed.

Boogerbear shook his head. "Nah. Based on your reports, Colonel Cayce figured I'd catch you here, an' you were wanted to take Frontera if you hadn't already. Another reason I brought extra fellas. Captain Holland's pal Captain Razine described the bay out yonder, an' Colonel Cayce wanted it. Soon as he has the transport ships for it, you"—he shrugged—"we will get carted up the rest o' the way to Vera Cruz. That's where we'll assemble the whole army, just like Gen'ral Scott, an' strike inland against the enemy capital. Only way to support the army'll be by sea."

"How soon?" Anson asked.

Boogerbear shrugged. "No tellin', really. Couple weeks, maybe. Only so many ships, an' he has a *lot* o' fellas to move. All Agon's troops too," he added.

"Interestin'," Anson mused, then shrugged. "Well, Lewis knows what he's doin'. An' the rest makes sense. It'll save wear an' tear on animals an' equipment, give us a rest"—he grinned—"an' give us a little time to train up a few new recruits. We'll get to Vera Cruz ready to fight instead o' worn-out after a long march—an' more fightin' we maybe didn't need to do." He looked at Sergeant Riss. "Might even get another chance at catchin' Tranquilo, though I ain't optimistic. Take Captain Boogerbear out where you lost the trail in the mornin'. Maybe he can pick it up."

"Prob'ly confused it up too much ourselves," Riss confessed.

"Could be, but give it a try."

CHAPTER 4

In a city where the misery of the lower classes and idleness of the elites ensured frequent festivals to celebrate all manner of things, the Fiesta de la Cosecha de Agosto, or Festival of the August Harvest, was one of the most important and well attended, since it was one virtually everyone could appreciate. The harvest had been good and continued to be so; therefore aristocratas were flush with revenue from their estates and other holdings through virtually no effort of their own. *Patricios comerciales* on retainer to the great families organized all that tedious productivity for them, contracting hidalgos—who might aspire to become *patricios* themselves— to subcontract labor and oversee its performance, while also engaging in their own "appropriate" pursuits; everything from the manufacture of harness and farming implements, to actually transporting everything from the harvest itself to the slaves and equipment necessary to reap it with their various freight partnerships. Next to a hidalgo sailor who owned his own ship, those who thrived in the freight business generally had the shortest road to success. Being otherwise safer from the elements, however, freight companies on land tended to be more . . . violently competitive, and the weak were quickly eliminated or absorbed by the strong.

The desperate need for freight carts, armabueys, and transport of every sort was so great at this time of year, there was usually a kind of holiday from feuds of that sort. Especially *this* year, when so much local transport had been hired away indefinitely to supply the distant Gran Cruzada. Quite a few formerly bitter rivals might even make lasting alliances. The climate in the Great Valley was such that *something* was always being harvested, but slaves were usually sufficient to get the job done the rest of the year. Not this one. For once, even lowly freemen in the labor force might manage to work year-round, or at least make enough to tide them over until off-season construction projects resumed.

It was a happy time in the Great Valley of Mexico—and just as well, because it came at a time of acute unrest. The former Supreme Holiness who'd reigned for a generation had quite suddenly been called to the underworld, and the one who most assumed would rise in his place, the Blood Cardinal Don Datu el Humilde, had mysteriously vanished without explanation, leaving his own great, naked stone temple—the second most magnificent of the thirteen in the city—unattended even by a successor to perform the appropriate rites. Strangest of all, the one who should've been Don Datu's successor, Obispo de Sachihiro, had replaced the second to Don Julio DeDivino Dicha—Blood Cardinal of the Red Temple—who had himself risen to become Supreme Holiness over them all. The whole thing had been most irregular, and many were troubled by the sense of impropriety, not to mention the many changes that followed.

The once-marginalized, deemed almost extremist, Blood Priests were everywhere now. They'd long advocated a stricter, bloodier, more puritanical (they insisted) interpretation of God's purpose for his worshippers and sought the abolition of Obispos (or at least a relaxation of qualifications required to become one), thus clearing a path for one of their own to become Supreme Holiness someday. Coincidental to the irregularities that concerned so many about the succession, red-robed Blood Priests were virtually the only priests seen in the city these days. Alarmingly (from a more conservative but increasingly intimidated point of view), traditional black-robed priests were openly mocked and chastised by those in red, and some had even been assaulted. Since fewer and fewer were seen each day, it was assumed they were either joining the "reds" or actually fleeing the city.

Worst of all, yet most impossible to believe, were the madcap but persistent rumors that, even as the invincible Gran Cruzada marched farther and farther into the unimaginable wilderness of the mythical Californias to cast out invaders from the heretical Empire of the New Britain Isles based far out in the Pacific Ocean, an army of demons from the east hadn't only crushed an army of the Holy Dominion, but was even now coming here. That was impossible, of course, and no one really believed it . . . but there *was* something strange going on. All overland commerce with Vera Cruz had ceased. Officially, the terrible "Vomito Rojo" was particularly bad this year, and thousands had been gathered to paradise after earning much grace from the sickness. Unofficially . . . the devil had made a *new* Vomito Rojo that not only killed its victims but first made them raving mad. No doubt that was the source of the other dark rumors that simply wouldn't fade.

Fortunately, again, the harvest had been exceptional, people had more coin than they ever remembered, and it was generally a joyful time for all. Except for the slaves, of course. They worked just as hard as always and had no protection from the increased demand for sacrifices that came with every festival. Particularly this one, this year. One might think it ridiculously wasteful to sacrifice slaves when there was so much work to do, but waste is the very foundation of blood sacrifice, and the spectacles were wildly popular among a populace starved for entertainment. Besides, the fewer slaves, the more paid work for freemen—who were always most likely to stir up trouble.

Flames challenged the night, leaping high from mighty braziers arrayed around the base of the Great Temple of His Supreme Holiness. Though only one of thirteen such high, stepped pyramids in the city, each with thirteen levels or "floors" including the gold sheathed box, topped by the lightning bolt–like cross, this one—also naked stone—was precisely twice as tall and broad as the rest. That was only appropriate since it was dedicated to the very son of God and His Supreme Holiness dwelt inside. Even in the darkness, all the other temples of His apostles (represented by Blood Cardinals in this world) were clearly visible, equally bathed in the light of their own great braziers, and the different colors some of them bore were luridly lit. Five were a brilliant white, washed in the same slaked lime as the high wall surrounding the inner city. Most of the rest were painted in pastel colors appropriate to the "number" they represented. Don Julio's "11th" was red, the "10th"—still technically Don Hurac's—was the same yellow as the army uniform. The "9th" was decidedly silvery, and how it was kept that way remained secret. The "8th" was a gray-black, like volcanic stone, with real silver lightning bolts inlaid into its surface. The "7th" was blue, the "6th" green. It was possible that no one, including those residing in the temples or their nearby offices, knew what the colors originally meant anymore. They'd been "inherited," and the meaning was obscure at best.

At the top of the tallest pyramid, among the rising tumult of thousands of spectators and more flaring braziers that lit a cascade of bright blood flowing down the long, uninterrupted stair like a macabre liquid ruby, a small group of wildly gesticulating men stood waiting. Only the Blood Priests stationed among the crowd seemed to know what the gestures meant, and they occasionally motioned madly back, leaped about with maniacal expressions, or went into blissful trances. A few even crashed to the stone pavement and thrashed, jabbering joyful gibberish. It was disconcerting because it was something new, but it was also quite a sight and generally delighted the watchers. Some recently ordained Blood Priests seemed confused by the behavior, even disappointed that they weren't equally affected, especially when they caught pitying or condescending looks from their peers.

Each of the men high above wore bright red robes, now almost black with the blood that soaked them, and the Blood Priests among them were otherwise entirely naked. Two of the men were draped in gold chains filled with sparkling jewels of every color, with garish, flaring, furry-feather hats on their heads. All were flanked by jagged crosses like the one at the top of the golden box behind them, and in front was a long, low altar, also gold, but splashed with so much blood it was impossible to tell.

The taller, thinner of the two featured principals in the performance was once the Obispo de Sachihiro. He was a young man with predatory eyes under a heavy brow and had formerly been the successor to Don Datu. Now, with the new title of "Primer Patriarca," he was the direct successor to His Supreme Holiness, previously known to this world as Don Julio DeDivino Dicha. Any other name but "Supreme Holiness" had no meaning now. To all appearances, this shorter, rounder man stood next to his "heir" wearing a grotesque golden mask inlaid all over with more precious stones. He always went in public like that since no one but his successor was worthy to bask in the radiance of his naked countenance and live. That hadn't always been the case, but the relatively new tradition was proving convenient since the "former Don Julio" detested physical activity as strenuous as climbing to the top of his temple, absolutely hated speaking in public (which the man behind the mask must do on occasions like this), and much preferred wallowing among deaf, mute, and blind young women in a drug-induced haze.

"How many more?" hissed his impersonator, the Blood Priest Father Armonia, through the heavy, garish, blood-spattered mask on his face, gesturing wildly and nonsensically down at the crowd before leaning slightly against the altar. "*Surely* we have fed God enough this night. I'm tired and hungry, and thirsty too."

Sachihiro had to suppress a chuckle. Armonia wasn't impious—far from it—but he had an irreverent streak that appealed to the young Primer Patriarca. "You can always drink their blood," Sachihiro suggested lowly, too low for even the other nearby Blood Priests to hear. "I hear that Father Tranquilo has started doing that."

Armonia shook his head slightly. "No thank you. Tranquilo is a great man, a great priest. He's the father of all we do, after all. But he has always been perhaps a little too focused, too manic, and I think his long sojourn on the frontier has . . . unbalanced him to a degree." He snorted and lowered his voice still further. "I shudder to think what he will say about these preposterous gestures you came up with."

"He may consider them blasphemous," Sachihiro conceded. "But he understands the need for a little showmanship. Drinking blood? Really? But even his showmanship relies entirely on terror. That's not enough. We needed a touch of . . . oh, call it benign mysticism to set our rites apart from the black robes. Something besides simple terror."

"Oh, I agree entirely, and I'm sure we can make the gestures actually *mean* something, eventually. A secret code to issue instructions or elicit specific responses from the brethren, perhaps?" Armonia suggested. "It does get rather tiresome, though, all this capering about. Particularly after . . . How many souls have we already given to God tonight? The other priests did a dozen apiece. You and I together . . . twenty?"

"Nineteen."

Armonia rolled his eyes behind the mask. "Which urges me to repeat myself: how many more?"

Sachihiro smiled. "Just one." Raising a hand to one of the priests, he beckoned grandly and the thousands below roared loud in appreciation as the order was passed and a pair of Blood Priests brought a final bound and naked figure forward. "I've been saving this one," Sachihiro confided.

"I know him!" Armonia exclaimed.

"Yes, you do," Sachihiro confirmed. Turning to the next victim, he regarded a positively emaciated man. He'd once been tall and slightly overweight but now was stooped and starved, bony arms clasped tightly in the grip of his conductors. His eyes were wide with terror, but he didn't struggle, even managing to project an air of defiance.

"Good of you to join us, Obispo El Consuelo," Sachihiro said lowly, even gently. "So nice to see you again." The last time they'd met, Consuelo had accompanied his master, the Blood Cardinal Don Hurac, to consult with Don Datu—whom Sachihiro had since betrayed and killed, of course. No one had suspected Sachihiro of being in league with the Blood Priests, even more instrumental in their rise than their "patron," Don Julio himself.

"Traitor," Consuelo hissed, his mouth dry as sand, lips cracking. "Murderer!"

"How do we handle this one?" Armonia asked, tone betraying a measure of discomfort over what they were about to do to one of such high—former—standing.

Sachihiro looked at him, astonished. "Make the most of it, of course! We're about to sacrifice 'one of our own,' after all! A lofty Obispo at that! All for the glory of God and in thanks for the bountiful harvest He has nurtured with the blood we have given Him!"

Armonia nodded and stepped around the altar. Raising his arms, he began his presentation—essentially repeating what Sachihiro said, only stretching it out, embellishing it, even implying the victim had begged for this fate for the benefit of his people. Ironically, that wasn't far from the truth.

"Don Hurac is the traitor, consorting with heretics at Vera Cruz, even joining them! But you could have joined *us*," Sachihiro almost whispered at the doomed man as the Blood Priests heaved Obispo El Consuelo onto the wet, sticky altar. "It was *you* who conveyed Don Hurac's 'Madres de Hijos' and all his brats to Techolatla and hid them from me! For a time, we might have used them to force his cooperation, but now he's too firmly set against us."

"You hunted them like animals and killed them as you caught them!" El Consuelo spat up at him.

"Because I never had them all at once!" Sachihiro seethed. "One by one they were useless to me."

"You do not know the man," El Consuelo lamented. "You never understood him. His women, his children, all his people. They are the same to him."

"Rubbish," Sachihiro snorted. "And it makes no difference now in any event." He gestured vaguely around, encompassing all the temples in the city. "The rest are gone now as well. All of them. Quietly sacrificed like any other who has no value."

Father Armonia completed his sonorous, echoing address amid a flourish of meaningless gestures, and the multitudes roared their appreciation. Stepping briskly around behind the altar, he took the great two-handed sword one of the Blood Priests passed to him as another handed Sachihiro a long, wavy, green obsidian knife, its facets glittering in the light of flaring flames like an emerald spearpoint. Looking down at the strangely calm figure of El Consuelo, Father Armonia saw his lips move, but his words were lost in the expectant tumult. The surrounding Blood Priests had seen him try to speak, however, so, glancing significantly at them, he spoke loud enough for Sachihiro to hear. "I believe he has something to say."

Frowning, Sachihiro leaned over to hear the last words and a near-instant hush fell over the crowd. Whatever was said at moments like this by those who went willingly under the fire-glass knife might be monumentally portentous.

"You didn't get them all," El Consuelo croaked. "The most important person, who lends him his greatest strength, remains by Don Hurac's side." Suddenly amassing all his own strength, El Consuelo shouted out, "I serve Don Hurac El Bendito, rightful successor to His Supreme Holiness! He will come and avenge me, avenge—"

Sachihiro slashed savagely down with the knife, hard enough to snap the tip as it pierced completely through El Consuelo and slammed into the altar beneath him. Even as he savagely sawed at the man's chest and blood sprayed from his mouth and nose, the dying Obispo loudly rasped, "Avenge us all!"

Armonia didn't wait for Sachihiro to finish cutting out the heart. He'd clearly stabbed right into it in any event, a terrible breach of propriety, stealing grace in such a way. But before El Consuelo could say anything else, unlikely as that might be, Armonia brought his sword down in a powerful, practiced arc, severing the man's head with a single blow.

A shocked silence still reigned, broken only by the *thump, whop, whack, smack* of the blood-spattering head bounding down the steps, two and three at a time, picking up speed as it neared the crowd. No one wanted near it and hundreds surged back, screaming, as it landed among them.

Stunned that El Consuelo had been capable of such an outburst and still holding the knife in the quivering, decapitated corpse, Sachihiro gave Armonia a panicked look. The older man seemed to shake himself before rushing back around the altar and wildly waving his hands. "Devils!" he shrieked. "Devils in the very air around us! I *saw* one fly into poor Obispo El Consuelo's mouth, spitting its own vile words! Oh, the abject panic and pleading I saw in his eyes! Primer Patriarca Sachihiro and I *had* to strike swiftly before the devil could spout more filth, further violating Obispo El Consuelo's selfless act!" He gestured manically again and then waved at one of the attending Blood Priests. "Fetch more offerings to God, a dozen more here and at every temple in the city, to fortify Him for the fight to cleanse these terrible devils from around us!"

"At once, Your Supreme Holiness!" the priests exclaimed, shaking off their own shock. A roar of affirmation arose from the throng around the temple and one brave Blood Priest took up El Consuelo's battered head and shook it as if trying to spill the devils out of the slack-jawed mouth. With a few more emphatic gestures, Armonia turned back to Sachiriro. "He might've ruined us," he hissed. "You should have cut out his demon tongue!"

"Yes," Sachihiro said with a sigh, finally removing the green knife and examining the broken point. "But he was right, you know. Don Hurac's favorite woman—Zyan is the wicked creature's name—remained by his side when all others left him. Don Hurac couldn't wed her because she wasn't of the blood, and he was long considered . . . eccentric for the way he coddled her. But *she* is the better part of his spine, no doubt." He frowned. "She and the heretic troops that hold his city for him, of course."

"We must end that situation as quickly as we can," Armonia commented, waving reassurance at the increasingly impatient masses. "You *did* send the messenger dragon to recall the Gran Cruzada, did you not?"

Sachihiro looked vaguely defensive. "We cannot abandon the Gran Cruzada just yet. Don't forget, it was Blood Priests and their sympathizers that agitated longest for its formation. It was their chief cause for quite some time, and we could lose considerable support. There also remains the . . . unpleasant possibility that, if recalled so soon to support what some of its generals will consider usurpers—*us*—against Don Hurac, the army might splinter. Worse, part of it may even *unite* with Don Hurac against us. It will take time for our people to weed out such sympathizers in authority, so it could be for the best that General Xacolotl is already deep in the northern desert and can't simply come skipping home. I *have* sent word for him to pause his advance where it's most convenient for supply until further notice, standing ready to return quickly if called."

"And what are the views of His Supreme Holiness regarding this?" Armonia demanded.

Sachihiro's face twisted almost to a sneer. "Have a care how you speak to me. I have the utmost confidence of His Supreme Holiness, and *I* am his chosen successor. I like you, Armonia, but don't forget your place!"

Armonia reluctantly nodded. *This* certainly wasn't the "place" for such an argument. Both men took a calming breath, and the younger one continued, "In the meantime, I sent another dragon—such a pity we have so few!—to General Telu Gomez at Manzanilla with instructions to gather all remaining troops from there, Istapa, and Acapulco and bring them to us."

"Gomez is a rarity. One of us, but still a professional," Armonia conceded. "But bringing him here will leave our Pacific coast at the mercy of raids by the Imperials. What if they take one of our most ancient cities, like has happened to Vera Cruz?"

Sachihiro held up a placating hand. The crowd was ecstatic now, as another string of naked captives was being dragged up the bloody steps. Armonia was rolling his shoulders, preparing to extend the performance he'd thought was almost over. "That will *not* happen," Sachihiro assured. "Gomez won't leave those cities helpless, and he'll get here much quicker than General Xacolotl ever could. Surely the Gran Cruzada has captured the full attention of our older enemy by now, in any event. Their navy is frankly better than ours—else we could simply send the Gran Cruzada by sea—and their scouts are not blind. The Gran Cruzada is *huge*, and the Imperials will rightly be obsessed with it, worried where it is going—there can only be one place—and perhaps for a time, most interested of all in why it has stopped."

Armonia seemed to accept that, but then warned, "Divided loyalties might still be a problem among Gomez's officers. The old cities haven't embraced the New Way, and most of the Obispos come from there."

"We still have enough loyal forces in the Holy City and its environs to suppress any dissenters Gomez might bring. With their help, I'm confident the general can sort out any threat from Don Hurac as well, and destroy this . . . Coronel Cayce and his 'army of devils' that Tranquilo reports with such concern."

"The Coronel Cayce who destroyed General Agon's Eastern Army of God?" Armonia asked with thinly veiled sarcasm.

Sachihiro glanced back down at Obispo El Consuelo's headless body and suddenly heaved it off the altar to roll down the steps past the approaching "sacrifices" to come. Some of them screamed and recoiled from the sight, and Sachihiro smiled. "Yes," he agreed, ignoring Armonia's tone. "Poor El Consuelo was right about Don Hurac. He *will* try to come. So most likely will 'Colonel Cayce' and his Yucatános and mysterious 'Americanos.' I now regret not questioning Don Datu more closely about the latter before having him strangled. But what can they throw against us? Father Tranquilo rants that Colonel Cayce has built a better army than we can field, made up largely of barbarian Indios from the Yucatán!" He chuckled. "Preposterous, but even if true, they are relatively few. What can Don Hurac contribute? An 'army' of pitiful *hombres libres* and slaves, armed with garden tools and led by ignorant, wastrel hidalgos, no doubt. No educated hidalgos or *patricios* would be stupid enough to join such a mad venture. They will have fled long ago to other cities, swearing they have no knowledge of events in Vera Cruz. General Gomez will face this rabble with a *real* army, more than adequate to smash them before they ever get close to *us*. Then we can finish the work we've started: to fundamentally rebuild the Dominion into a stronger, better, certainly more *obedient* place."

He gestured grandly for the first of the next batch of sacrifices to be brought to the altar. A quivering, naked girl shrieked in terror as bloodspattered priests grasped her arms and tugged her forward. Tired as Sachihiro and Armonia were, they would have to exert themselves even more than before, drawing each sacrifice out as long and imaginatively as possible to earn enough grace for their victims and themselves—all those watching— to sweep the devils that had infested El Consuelo from the air all around them. It didn't matter that there'd been no devils. God would quickly forget Sachihiro and Armonia's little fib about that, and each offering would enter paradise with more than enough grace to make up for their brief discomfort. Sachihiro sighed. "Oh well, I didn't accept this calling out of laziness, after all. Another knife," he said absently to one of the nearly naked Blood

Priests who attended most closely as he dropped the broken one in a stone-lined chute that would allow its passage down to the very foundation of the temple. "A shorter, broader one," he added, then paused, considering his bulging-eyed victim, her mouth now a silent O of horror. "And one of the large iron hooks, I believe, but place it in the nearest brazier to heat."

CHAPTER 5

A warm, blue afternoon sky stood over what was once the principal Dominion seaport on the Atlantic side of the continent and chief distribution point of nearly all support and supply for General Agon's aborted effort to conquer the Yucatán for his former masters. From the seaward approach, Vera Cruz looked much the same as always, its distinctive landmarks unaltered. The formidable island fortress with its high lighthouse and signal tower still brooded over the anchorage, and the high, stepped pyramid at the city's center still loomed over every surrounding structure. The heights beyond the city were as distinctive as always, of course, as were the purple mountains towering to the west. But Vera Cruz was a different place entirely, ever since Captain Eric Holland's "raid" in HMS *Tiger*. Regardless of its previous role, compared to what it had become, Vera Cruz had been a sleepy, lazy, even somewhat picturesque scene of virtual inactivity, and that impression—that nothing had changed—had been carefully preserved in the bay. Numerous Dominion ships had been lured in by that, only to be captured and placed in service to their enemies. The new crews manning the mighty guns in the fort had drilled themselves to perfection, prepared to quickly demonstrate that nothing in range on the water could survive their attention. And the recaptured, repaired, and heavily armed steamer, USS *Isidra*, could maneuver to prevent any attempt to escape, regardless of the wind.

Sadly, the "piratin' business," as Holland referred to it, had slowed considerably of late. Nearly all Dominion commerce in the Gulf or Caribbean frequently visited Vera Cruz, so it wasn't known whether word finally got out from other, smaller ports, or if they'd already taken nearly every enemy ship that sailed these seas. The latter might actually be the case because, before Holland recently departed on his quest to find and inspect the "Pass of Fire" down beyond the Mosquito Kingdom, he'd used her to snap up many more merchantmen on the sea lanes between other ports. The prizes were quickly put to work, hauling freight and troops in from Uxmal and Gran Lago or patrolling far and wide. No one knew how long Holland would be gone, but he'd stop at Pidra Blanca, Uxmal, and likely Gran Lago before he returned, so it might be a while.

The landward view of Vera Cruz from the west had changed quite a lot, and no effort had been made to hide it. First, it would've been impossible to conceal the impressive defensive works that continually expanded as more troops arrived (or locals were trained) to fill them. Second, several attempts had been made by small forces from surrounding cities to "punish" the people of Vera Cruz for being conquered by heretics, and all had miserably failed. Finally, if spies did manage to penetrate the strengthening screen of Rangers, dragoons, and lancers who simply chased them down and killed them on sight, they could only report what Lewis Cayce wanted them to: the "heretic" army assembling on the coast was becoming an impressive force, its only possible purpose to advance.

"I must confess a measure of confusion," said the Blood Cardinal Don Hurac as the entire command staff of the combined army relaxed in camp chairs under a great, colorful canvas fly on the heights above the city. From there, the whole army and all its preparations were on display. Thousands of tents were geometrically arrayed, and many more troops had been put up in warehouse "barracks" throughout the city. The broad "killing zone" beyond the outermost wall (past the trenches, entanglements, and other more insidious defenses) was currently in use by Colonel Itzam's 3rd Division, moving as if on parade, its eight regiments totaling nearly seven thousand men performing large-scale battlefield maneuvers. It was quite a sight. All wore the same sky-blue uniform of the infantry and were armed with captured

Dom muskets re-bored to .77 caliber and fitted with socket bayonets. Anything metal was polished bright. Regimental flags fluttered in appropriate places, variations on those of the city-states the regiments were drawn from. Most were those of Uxmal and Pidra Blanca, though all had NAUTLA and GRAN LAGO painted on them now. The 3rd hadn't seen serious fighting, but it wasn't a virgin division anymore. One of its regiments had been left at Gran Lago, along with one from Agon's newly designated 4th Division, their job to defend the newly established forward supply depot (replacing Campeche) against possible raids from the south.

Everyone else, even a thousand of Kisin's Holcano "auxiliaries" no longer needed at Campeche, had come (oddly, now under the joint command of him and Consela, the displaced alcaldesa of the virtually exterminated frontier town of Los Arboles). Kisin was quite taken with the older but still-striking woman and seemed to respect her immensely. To everyone's further surprise (and not a little terror among the locals), Kisin brought the Grik general Soor with two hundred of his feathery, reptilian warriors. As always, Soor wanted to be on the side that would best protect his race, but he'd insisted his warriors be integrated into the Holcanos and not simply wasted on bloody, frontal assaults. Even Kisin had used them like that before, but now readily agreed. He'd apparently actually missed the savage-looking Grik with their terrible teeth and claws.

"They are good fighters," he'd enthused. "Scare hell outa the Doms!"

They scared hell out of the locals too, who'd mostly never seen their like. Needless to say, such "real" manifestations of "demons" caused a terrific stir until Father Orno publicly baptized a very penitent-looking Soor in the same way Don Hurac submitted to Reverend Harkin. Soor even piously swore he'd eat nobody but Doms, and even then only when no one was looking. This caused some friction with Kisin, whose Holcanos had been forbidden to eat anyone. That took work by both Orno and Harkin to sort out. Soor's band would always be "demons," but he'd proven even demons could be embraced by a loving God if they opened their hearts to Him. Lewis was amused by the unlikely pairing of Kisin and Soor and thought they both might be useful—if they continued to behave.

With the final arrival of Boogerbear's Rangers (including Leonor, to Lewis's relief), Barca's section of artillery, and a battalion raised at Frontera that had searched as far as Oaxaca and Mazupiapan for the elusive Tranquilo even after Anson and the rest of his force came here, the entire expeditionary element of the combined army was packed into Vera Cruz. Tranquilo hadn't been found.

Don Hurac wasn't confused about Soor, however. "I would think you wouldn't *want* the enemy to know of our dispositions," he continued, gesturing down at 3rd Division's impressive martial display, "to be fully aware we are nearly ready to march." He stood and bowed deeply to Varaa-Choon and the newly promoted Captain Sal Hernandez of the Rangers, Captain Hayne of the dragoons, and Major Ixtla of the 1st Uxmal Infantry. The last three had been there (off and on, in Sal's case) since the raid. They'd been instrumental in defending the city and starting training up the locals. The city's very own regiment, the 1st Vera Cruz, had already been assigned to Colonel Reed's 1st Division under the former hidalgo *capitan de la milicia*, now Major Don Roderigo. He seemed a solid sort and genuinely amused by the fact that his new "station" in life would've classed him as a *patricio*. The 2nd Vera Cruz would soon be ready (armed with more Dom muskets taken from armories here, but as yet unmodified) and would march with Ixtla's 3rd Division. Together with 1st Division and Agon's 4th, the combined army totaled almost twenty-nine thousand men, including four thousand horse and eight batteries of "flying" artillery. It was a formidable force, larger than anything General Taylor or General Scott ever had at their disposal, and Lewis felt a little out of his depth. He knew he was right about his strategy, though.

"Ordinarily, that would be the case," Lewis told the man, still stiff and uncomfortable in the presence of a Blood Cardinal who—regardless of his current circumstances, a reputation as a relatively benevolent specimen of his order, and the esteem he enjoyed from the people of Vera Cruz—*had* been part of the ruling system and overseen the very sort of depraved activity they were fighting against. Father Orno was convinced Don Hurac had repented with all his heart and now fought that system as well. It would be easy for Lewis to believe, just looking at the man. He now wore an unadorned gray-white robe over his short, generally oval frame, and his wide, round eyes seemed utterly sincere. A traditional, ordinary wooden cross, just like Orno's, his only ornamentation. Even the way he occasionally looked to the stunning woman named Zyan, sitting in a blue silk-like tunic with Samantha Wilde (who'd immediately, somewhat imperiously taken her under her wing), as if seeking her reassurance was touching and encouraging. *Especially in light of the news he received about the foul fate of his extended family*, Lewis mentally, grimly added. That had unmanned the former Blood Cardinal for a time, which did more to "humanize" him in Lewis's eyes than anything else. Only Zyan had been able to pull him out of it.

All the same, while Lewis found himself beginning to genuinely trust General—now Colonel—Agon (when all was said and done, the man *was* simply a soldier, after all), Don Hurac was still trying to become the "Supreme Holiness" of the Doms. Perhaps that really was the best way to help his people and get along with his neighbors, maybe the only way, but it was difficult to predict how that much power might affect anyone.

"This is a . . . unique situation, however," Lewis went on. "I was glad to hear we don't have to worry about the Gran Cruzada just yet, but according to your source, it sounds like this General Gomez will have a larger force than ours."

Don Hurac blinked incomprehension.

"I think *he* thinks you just made his point," Leonor spoke up, her husky voice amused. She'd resumed her place by his side just as soon as she returned to it, as if she'd never left. He smiled at her, vaguely torn as always, both loving and fearing how he felt about her. He'd never cared so much about anyone, and he couldn't control that care. He'd never been ruled by feelings before, except fury on occasion, but he'd learned to master that. He was helpless in the face of his attachment to this girl—this woman—and even as he luxuriated in the unfamiliar sensation, he rebelled against it as well. He suspected she felt the same and wondered how she coped.

"I would think so too, if I didn't know better." Varaa defended the little man, her long tail whipping back and forth. She cast her huge blue eyes on Don Hurac. "I do." For the benefit of others who hadn't been part of the planning sessions ever since Lewis arrived with Major Olayne and almost all their artillery (including her own "King" Har-Kaaska), she explained. "There's another more traditional Blood Cardinal in Istapa—one of the oldest Dom cities—and he also opposes the Blood Priests and the installation of Don Julio. He just wants a return to the old ways, and I doubt he'd support what we mean to achieve," she inserted dryly, "but he sent a messenger dragon to Don Hurac—the 'roost' or whatever they call it is still manned outside the city—with most of the information we have. The Primer Patriarca Sachihiro might be in day-to-day control of the Dominion in Don Julio's name, but he can't do everything he wants without at least informing the Blood Cardinals whose jurisdictions he'll bleed for troops and supplies." Her gaze had traveled but returned to Don Hurac. "You need to maintain correspondence with this man. It occurred to me that we might use the dragon ourselves, to maintain contact between the army and Vera Cruz, but our signal towers will serve just as well, and more reliably, I should think. It would be ideal if the dragon could connect us to Uxmal, but I understand the thing would have to be *taken* there first?"

Don Hurac was nodding. "The creatures have an uncanny ability to fly directly to places they have been, on command, but as you say, they must be familiar with the route." He looked uncertain. "At least I believe that is how it works."

"Perhaps we will find someone who knows, or we can experiment later," Varaa speculated. "In any event, as Colonel Cayce says, the Gran Cruzada has not yet been recalled, but a General Gomez has been commissioned to gather virtually all the remaining Dom forces in the west to deal with us. It isn't the Gran Cruzada," she emphasized, "but it will be a sizable army. Perhaps fifty or sixty thousands."

"Gomez was never a friend," Agon said, speaking for the first time. He was seated as always with the tall Arevalo beside him, also joined today by his second in command, former general, now Colonel Tun. The two looked enough alike to be brothers. "He is a professional, however. If it dawns on him to fortify the city of Mexico—I *won't* call it the 'Holy City' anymore—or even some of the other places we simply can't bypass . . ."

"We could break our army trying to take them from him," Tun finished for his friend.

Lewis nodded appreciatively. "I'm glad you see our dilemma." Looking back at Don Hurac, he continued. "Since we can't allow him to dig in somewhere and then go root him out, we need him to come after *us*, in the open where we can move. Our mobility is our greatest strength and advantage."

"The apparently universal practice—present company happily excluded, of course," Varaa-Choon inserted with a slight bow to the former Dom officers, "of . . . exterminating witnesses to acts of defiance against the Dominion may work in our favor." Varaa was blinking rapidly, tail still swishing. Even she wore the American "mounted" uniform these days, complete with black boots specially fitted to her strangely shaped feet, and the effect was striking.

"Yeah," Anson agreed. "They keep massacrin' everybody that sees us, they won't have any cities left after long. Hell, just marchin' past one might be enough to get everybody rubbed out." The pragmatic, ruthless side of the man suddenly looked thoughtful, as if actually considering that, before finally shaking his head. "I don't know him like Agon does, but I figure Gomez'll come for us. Won't have any choice. He'll have to stop us before we 'corrupt' er 'influence' too many folk."

"You are most likely correct," Agon mused. "The enemy can't sacrifice every city between here and the Great Valley. Vera Cruz will already be a knife in the side of those ruling there, increasingly difficult to explain to those with business interests here or in the Caribbean."

"It might even be *easy* to get Gomez to meet us on ground of our choosing," Colonel Reed suggested. He might never be comfortable with Lewis's relentlessly aggressive strategies, always preferring a more defensive approach, but now that they had a strong "base" again, he didn't seem as stressed as when they were wandering the wilderness.

"Probably not 'easy,'" Agon warned, raising a bitter brow, "but less difficult than it would be to lure *me* there. Now."

"I agree with Colonel Reed," said "King" Har-Kaaska, who then looked askance at Kisin. "As long as some bloodthirsty fool doesn't slip the leash and put him on his guard."

The massive Holcano warrior looked about to explode, but the tiny, almost motherly in comparison Alcaldesa Consela put a restraining hand on the man's badly scarred thigh—courtesy of a wound Anson once caused him. "My warriors, those not already absorbed into the army that saved them, of course"—Consela bowed her head graciously to Lewis—"along with a fair number from Gran Lago—where I myself was born," she reminded, "constitute a fair percentage of Kisin's, um, 'regiment.'" She looked at Har-Kaaska. "They will behave, as will Soor's warriors, but I strongly recommend we be used as scouts"—she grinned—"and in small-scale surprise attacks when some of our more . . . frightening comrades might best distress the enemy."

Anson barked a laugh. "Exactly what I was thinking. Can I get some of your people mounted with my Rangers?" He paused. "Can Soor's . . . lizard fellas even ride a horse?"

"We'd be happy to accompany you." Consela smiled. "But no, they—I believe you call them 'Grik'—do not ride. They can maintain a surprising pace on foot, however"—she pursed her lips and looked at Kisin—"as long as they keep up their strength. They eat a lot when they exert themselves."

"Well," Anson pondered aloud, "we'll just have to keep 'em fed, now won't we?"

Don Hurac finally sat, waving pleasantly about. "Military details are beyond my capacity to contextualize and will continue to confuse me, but it seems most of my concerns have been addressed. That leaves only one glaring exception. When will you march?"

Lewis frowned. Even if he knew, he wouldn't say. Certainly not "in the open" like this, as it were. He chose to deflect. "With respect, sir, that depends on a *lot* of 'military details.' In particular, we need to know what Gomez is up to, when *he* marches and what he does then. Your friend in Istapa might help with that. Otherwise, there are a lot of smaller issues to sort out. Example:"—he looked at Major Justinian Olayne—"with you on my staff, you have to replace yourself. Who should take your battery?"

"Lieutenant Barca, sir," Olayne promptly replied, somewhat to Lewis's surprise. That's who he was going to suggest.

"You're sure?"

Olayne shrugged. "He's ready." He nodded at Anson. "In point of fact, running around 'detached' so much, Barca's section has rarely been in company with the rest of Captain Hudgens's C Battery and has probably accumulated more combat experience than any other. Performed exceedingly well, I might add."

"Damn straight," Anson agreed, seconded by Captain Coryon Burton of the dragoons, and Felix Meder of the Mounted Rifles. Ramon Lara would undoubtedly agree, but he was in charge of the security detail watching over the gathering. "I'd'a suggested you give him a battery before," Anson elaborated, "but I'm selfish. I like havin' him with my mounted boys."

Lewis smiled. "Oh, he'll still be with you fairly often, I suspect. With a full battery." He looked at Olayne. "I assume you'll let him keep his current section? Transfer the lot?" That wasn't how things were normally done, but in Barca's . . . unusual case, Lewis thought it best, even now. It was sometimes hard to imagine these days, after a year and a half of acclimation to their bizarre and deadly circumstances, how utterly packed with various prejudices most of the people marooned here with him had been. Since then, most had immediately become the *minority* race by far, been immersed in wildly different cultures, even met different species of people—like Varaa—and every day was a struggle just to survive. But the Uxmalos and Ocelomeh had accepted them, followed by others, and almost every "American" ship-wrecked here had made close friends among them. Some had found sweet-hearts, and even married. And they'd found an enemy that transcended race, drawing all men of honor to oppose it together. Prejudices remained, and there'd always be rivalries between the branches. *Nothing wrong with that*, Lewis thought. But *real* prejudice, based on ethnicity, religion, and ra-cialism, Irish and English, Protestant versus Catholic, Black or white, red or brown, had amazingly all but vanished, recognized for how shallow it was compared to contending with gigantic monsters—and the Doms.

But Olayne's A Battery was long established, and old resentments might flare. Lewis wanted Barca among friends. Not to protect him, particularly; Barca could look after himself. There simply wasn't *time* for Barca to carve a new place and earn new respect if he had to. A Battery had to jump seam-lessly back into the fight, hopefully better than before.

"I hadn't even thought about separating them," Olayne said. "Oh, a few will go to leaven the new batteries. I'll have to spread men from *every* vet-eran battery around. Our artillery train has more than doubled, you know. But Barca's men are one of the reasons he's done so well. They'll even take their guns with them—you know as well as anyone how attached the lads get to them," he added significantly. "Doesn't matter if they're shot to pieces and only standing on one spoke, *that's* the gun they've served through thick and thin, and the one that's carried them through."

"Very well. I'm glad that was easily settled."

Olayne was shaking his head. "Oh, it won't be *easy*, sir. You know that as well. And the lads'll need time to make and mend and work all the batteries back up where they should be. Too many replacements and downright green recruits to train, so they'll have to learn to work with the horses as well."

"Easily settled for *me*, Mr. Olayne," Lewis said with a straight face. "*You're* the new chief of artillery." His gaze shifted to Dr. Newlin. "While we're on the subject of artillery . . ."

Dr. Francis Newlin was a slight, somewhat tousled civilian physician who'd been engaged by the officers of the 3rd Pennsylvania before the regi-ment left for Mexico. He was actually a very good doctor, but aside from a better understanding of chemistry and organizing battlefield trauma medi-cine (learned from research and history, not personal experience), there'd actually been little he could add to the knowledge of Uxmalo and Ocelomeh healers he'd met. They knew more than he about managing disease and infection, for example, particularly some of the strange local diseases he knew nothing about at all. He'd greedily absorbed as much as he could, while helping reinvent things like fulminate of mercury for percussion caps and other chemical compounds with military applications. He'd also helped organize a sensible and efficient military hospital corps. That's how he discovered that he (and even more surprisingly, Samantha Wilde) had a talent for organization and logistics in general.

Nodding and adjusting the spectacles that constantly slid down his nose, he pulled a sheaf of thick Uxmalo paper from inside a leather folder on his lap. Adjusting the spectacles again, he selected a page. "Yes," he said and cleared his throat. "There's more than sufficient eight-pounder solid shot in the city for our captured artillery." He glanced over his glasses at Agon. "Seems *someone* wasn't sending it along to you as dutifully as they should." Evidence that the former *alcalde* of Vera Cruz was corrupt was rampant, and more came as no surprise to anyone. "We already knew that to be the case, from reports sent by Captain Holland and then Warmaster Choon, so I strongly suggested that our chief logisticians, Mr. Finlay and Procurador Samarez back in Uxmal, should focus efforts on manufacturing canister of the appropriate size. They sent a good bit along. Several entire ships' cargo capacities devoted entirely to the artillery's needs, in fact. We now have a number of spare carriages of our design for previously captured cannon, for example. The trunnions are a different size from our own, you understand, so one can't simply trade them out, willy-nilly. I recommend that we preserve some of those spares *as* spares, however, and not add too many additional batteries to our mobile force until even more carriages are made," he cautioned. "On the other hand, the Dom variety are perfectly suited to static positions, and between the guns captured here and"—he looked at Agon again—"previously, we can leave the city quite well defended while continuing to put a few guns on selected ships we've taken." He waved a hand. "Those need new carriages as well—naval trucks, I believe they're called—but they're simple enough that a decent ship's carpenter can make them." Newlin looked at Lewis. "I'd be happier with *more* canister for the eight pounders right away, and you'll have it if time permits, but there's plenty of solid shot, even grapeshot."

"*Focus*, my dear doctor," Samantha urged with exaggerated patience.

"He does get so terribly diverted at times," she explained in a long-suffering tone to expanding laughter. Zyan gaped at her in apparent horror, that a woman would speak to a man like that, especially in a setting such as this.

"I am *not* distracted, and I *will* make my point," Newlin fumed, glancing back at the page and shifting his spectacles before looking up at Lewis. "Our great ambition has always been to cast our own guns or at least standardize the captured ones like we've done the muskets. Bore the eight pounders out to twelve pounders and resize the trunnions. There's certainly enough extra metal on them, and that would ease supply." He shook his head. "Sadly, though the foundry at Itzincab has managed to *cast* a few guns, and small lathes have been built to ream musket barrels as quick as you please, even make new ones, I fear that regardless of how willing, industrious, even technologically advanced our friends on the Yucatán are, they've never *needed* anything like a machine on the scale required to bore out a *cannon* tube with the necessary precision. Even with some of our lads who know how helping with the problem, it will take longer to solve. Mr. Finlay states that there's just too much 'making the tool to make the tool to make the tool' at present." He waved his hand again. "Oh, I've no doubt they could scrape something out that would shoot, even file trunnions to fit, but we can make quality ammunition for the eight pounders. Better to continue that for now."

He grinned. "On the other hand, I do have an important achievement to report. Not only have we stockpiled enough fixed solid shot and canister for our six pounders and twelve pounders to sustain a lengthy campaign, they've finally managed to make fairly reliable *exploding case shot* for both as well."

That announcement was met with pleased murmurs, but Lewis pounced at once. "What exactly does 'fairly reliable' mean to you, Dr. Newlin?"

Newlin pursed his lips. "Well, obviously I haven't seen it demonstrated, plodding along with the army, but I was involved in the design, and Mr. Finlay describes what has been accomplished in tests. The outer shells, or casings, are made of copper, of course, so they don't break into as many deadly bits as iron when the bursting charge explodes. Someone came up with the notion of putting more, smaller lead balls inside to make up for that, and I suggested fixing them in pitch to keep them from shifting about in flight. Apparently, that was just the thing needed to preserve accuracy, and there's even a modest incendiary effect. You might want to be careful about that," he added. "In any event, the overall weight is closer to that of solid shot, and the projectiles aren't as fragile, so they can be fired with full charges without fracturing in the barrel, so the range is much extended as well." Newlin gave a satisfied smile.

"But?" Lewis urged.

Newlin's smile became a disappointed frown. "But . . . Finlay says the damned, bloody *fuses* are still a problem." He shook the page in front of him. "It's the paper, you see. The paper tubes are too inconsistent. A five-second fuse burns about right, so does a ten-second fuse—plus or minus a second or two—but when someone cuts them they seem to lose all track of time and might explode the shell at the muzzle—or not at all! The only solution at present seems to be to make the damned things in one-second increments. Which means a *great* many more must be made, transported, and carried about in a limber chest. None of those things are ideal."

"What have they done about it?" Leonor piped up.

Newlin was exceedingly fond of Leonor, but gave her a sour look before continuing, "Two hundred women, children, and old men are working on nothing else, and a large number of five- and ten-second fuses—and everything else from one to seven—have been sent. I understand you don't need more than that very often, so I'd suggest using the most appropriate first . . . and then cut the others and hope for the best."

"The lads'll have to expend some in practice to get used to the new ranges," said Olayne, and Lewis nodded.

"To finish up with artillery, thank God"—Newlin sighed—"the shipments included quite a store of cut-and-seasoned carriage parts—which will please Mr. Barca, I'm sure—more primers, spare wheels, implements, irons, harness, nails, bolts, rope, canvas, even paint ingredients." He held up the pages.

"Give the list to Mr. Olayne, if you please," Lewis told him with a wicked grin at the young artilleryman.

The meeting went on like that for a while, Newlin, and then Samantha, describing the bounty now available to the whole army; tents, cartridge boxes, haversacks, knapsacks, canteens, and more uniforms for everybody but especially the infantry, due to the added regiments. Horseshoes, saddles, and tack had come for the mounted troops, who'd already been replenished to a degree, but they'd taken a lot of fresh horses in Vera Cruz, so they didn't need more shipped in. That was just as well, because they'd just about cleared them out of the Yucatán. Beyond that, they'd generally get whatever else they needed in Vera Cruz, particularly things like blankets, barrels, freight wagons to haul the supplies, shirts, socks, drawers, and more greatcoats for new troops and to replace the ones long discarded by veterans. It was hard to imagine on this warm fall day, but Don Hurac warned that it would get very cold in the mountains to the west. Vera Cruz would supply most of the provisions for the army going forward as well. That was another reason Capitan Lara was on guard, and the dragoons and Rangers patrolled so far out: to protect the workers in the fields. There'd been a good harvest in late summer, but the last harvest of the year was coming in now. There'd be plenty for everyone, including the army, since Vera Cruz wasn't supplying the mountain cities of Actopan and Puebla, or sending across the sea to Cuba anymore. Samantha had been with Don Hurac's trusted aides, compiling a list of all that was available. Supply-wise, the army was ready to march.

It was late afternoon by the time the discussion began to wind down. Everyone was tired of sitting by then, when there was so much to do. It was inconvenient getting everyone together like this, and they wanted to finalize as much as they could. Most were hungry too, but this had been a meeting of the "high command" only, and not even servants were allowed. Even— possibly especially—Don Hurac was conscious that spies might be anywhere, or hear things later if too many had news they might want. Wine, beer, and juice had been available, as had various sliced meats, cheeses, and fruits to snack on, but if anyone wanted something, they had to get it themselves, and they often got too caught up in the discussion to think of it. In spite of all that, and his own real concerns about security, it was clear Don Hurac was anxious for Lewis's views on the timetable to commence operations.

"We *can't* let Don Julio's"—he frowned—"'administration' stay in place too long," the white-robed ex Blood Cardinal said. "Aside from the danger posed by the Gran Cruzada, the longer we wait to be rid of him, the more people will suffer, and frankly," he added gloomily, "the more used to that suffering, perhaps even indifferent, they will become. Many will lose hope, but some will begin to see it as normal. The Blood Priests will be emboldened, and their fanaticism will take root and spread."

"Well, we've run around the base of every other tree in the forest, but Lewis is right. Just have to wait an' watch careful till the squirrel pokes his head out," Anson grumbled, oblivious to the fact that many of those present would be mystified by his metaphor.

"I *assume* that means we must wait on General Gomez," Varaa said, grinning.

"To an extent," Lewis hedged. "We might do a few things to stir him up if he drags his feet," he said cryptically, "but I *won't* move the whole army until Gomez is on his way. I'd rather not move it until Captain Holland returns from his scout to investigate this 'Pass of Fire' you told us about," he added with a trace of concern.

"But . . . why?" Don Hurac insisted, and Lewis sighed.

"Partly because the new regiments still need training and the rest of the army and Colonel Agon's division need to learn to move and work together. But mostly for the very reasons I stated at the beginning of this meeting: we don't want Gomez digging in. At least not in a city," he amended, tone still evasive. He suddenly stood and stretched, Leonor rising beside him. With a lift from Zyan, Don Hurac stood as well, wearing a worried expression. He didn't need Zyan's help because he was old or even grossly overweight, he was just badly out of shape. When Lewis addressed him again, his voice was rigid. "Do you dispute that I command every aspect of the military effort against the Dominion?"

"Against what it has become, of course not!"

Everyone was standing now, and Colonel Agon was regarding Don Hurac with narrowed eyes. "Quite the qualified endorsement," he said, a touch of menace in his voice.

Don Hurac waved it away. "I didn't mean it like that, General Agon. You know me!"

"It is 'colonel' now, and I *do* know you," Agon said meaningfully. "I know you never say anything without intent."

Don Hurac nodded. "Well, that may be, but I certainly didn't mean I would restore the Dominion exactly as it was. There are a great many things I would change if given the chance, but you must confess that the Dominion—even as it was—possessed a number of virtues. I would restore only those."

"Then I'm sure you understand that it will largely be up to Colonel Cayce, his allies, and his army—including my portion of it—which of those 'virtues' you will reinstate if you assume power in the *different* Dominion we will try to give you?"

Don Hurac bowed. "Of course, General—I mean Colonel—Agon! You have my sacred word!" He looked at Lewis, expression the very picture of solemn concern. "I do beg your pardon most sincerely. The last thing I want is any misunderstanding between us! That's the only reason I pressed for more information."

Lewis hesitated, then nodded. "Very well. But everyone who knows me will tell you I never discuss strategy beyond the very broadest strokes until right before, or sometimes as, I act. Especially not in front of so many people"—he waved at Olayne, Captain Hayne, even Colonel Reed—"who don't need to know its entirety just yet. Even if no enemies can hear, and no one lets something slip later, what someone doesn't know can't be forced out of them if they fall into the wrong hands. Blood Priests and their sympathizers don't all dress in filthy red robes and can look like anyone. We've painfully learned they can be anyone too, and I'm afraid that's made me a touch distrustful. I assure you that you'll be informed right before—or as—we move, just like any of my trusted officers. Is that satisfactory?"

Don Hurac managed another deep bow.

"Excellent. Everyone? I believe we're done here. Return to the duties I've had you neglecting so long."

With that, he abruptly turned and strode away, quickly joined by Leonor, Anson, and Varaa.

"That ended a little weird," Anson observed.

"Yes."

"Are you concerned about Don Hurac?" Varaa asked.

Lewis considered that. "Yes. Well, no, not really. I expect his agenda is a little murkier than ours: essentially to win the war and live our lives in peace. But he can't do anything without us—would likely already be dead, in fact—and I'm sure Agon'll be watching him like a hawk. That's one good thing. Any lingering concern I had about Agon is gone."

Leonor snorted. "We'll see." She turned her head to gaze at Lewis. She'd let her straight black hair grow down just past her shoulders now, but it still framed a pretty, almost delicate face that looked much livelier, even younger than it had when they first met. Her dark eyes were like bottomless pools, somewhat like a hawk's as well. "We *ain't* gonna just sit here an' do *nothin'* till Gomez makes his move, right?"

Anson rolled his eyes. "Course not, girl." He looked askance at Lewis. "Right?"

Varaa laughed, clapping her hands. "You silly, silly old fart!" Amazingly, she'd only recently heard that word and thought it was hilariously descriptive. Especially describing Anson, who often called her things as well. "*I know what we're going to do!*" she exclaimed. "Lewis and I always think the same, remember?"

"You know what I'm thinking, Varaa?" Leonor asked archly. Varaa looked at her and blinked.

"No."

"I do," Anson grumbled. "My daughter wants her father—an' everybody else—to vamoose. She hasn't had any time alone with Lewis since she got here with Boogerbear. Not for months. I expect she'll want to drag 'eem off for a private stroll."

"Sometimes you surprise me, Father," she said with a nod, looking at Varaa. "Much more observant than I generally give him credit for."

Anson shook his head and gestured at Samantha, who must've hurried to cut them off. "No, I ain't. Not about that. Sam—I mean Mistress Samantha, hinted at it, while makin' it plain she had similar expectations. Damn schemin' woman," he grumped. "She's just as busy as us, ain't she?"

"All the more reason, Father," Leonor scolded in a serious tone. "There's been little time, even less now, and soon there won't be any. Surely you can spare her an hour or two." She looked at Lewis, suddenly shy, hands absently stroking the grips of her Paterson Colts at her sides as if they reassured her. At moments like this she was no longer the lethal, self-assured warrior and became a very different woman in every way. "You can, can't you?"

Lewis glanced at Varaa and then Don Hurac and the other dispersing officers. "Nothing would delight me more," he said firmly. "A fine day, lovely scenery"—he paused and smiled—"a beautiful companion . . ." Leonor blushed, and Lewis chuckled. "I'm entirely at your service. Where would you like to go?"

Leonor shook her head, still blushing. "Just walk a ways with me. That's all I want. Besides, we were s'posed to stick together, you know."

"I know," Lewis agreed. "And we will from now on, I promise. Your father's just going to have to watch out for himself." His grin widened. "Especially in the company of that charming, 'scheming woman.'"

CHAPTER 6

OCTOBER 1848
HMS TIGER / THE CARIBBEAN

L and!" came the excited shout from the lookout high in HMS *Tiger's* fore masthead.

"Where away?" Captain Eric Holland roared back in his far-ranging "quarterdeck" voice. There was more than a touch of annoyance in it. A lot of his crew was made up of Uxmalo landlubbers, but even they should know to report the bearing of a sighting by now. On top of that, he was getting impatient with how many islands and shoals they were finding here, far more than he remembered from the world he used to sail. That was making it too dangerous to let *Tiger* make the speed she should with the wind they'd had, especially at night.

Holland's weathered, deeply lined face and long, braided gray hair made him look about eighty, but he had the strength and vitality of a man half that age. Personally, he doubted he was seventy yet, but hadn't kept track and didn't care one way or the other. *Just a little older than this ship*, he mused. *Tiger* started out as a fifty-gun "fourth rate," basically a very heavy frigate, laid down in the 1770s. Too slow to catch lighter frigates and too light for the line of battle, she was probably only finished in the 1790s to counter the new heavy American frigates. Once armed with twenty-two 24pdr guns, twenty-two 12pdrs, and six 6pdrs, she'd still been formidable and even fairly fast.

Weakened by a long but undistinguished career, she'd been stripped of her heavier guns and sold into the merchant service. She'd been carrying passengers (including Samantha Wilde and Angelique Mercure) from "old" Vera Cruz to Europe when she was swept to this world by the same bizarre storm that brought the Americans. With her gun deck reinforced and re-armed with ten captured 36pdrs, she was now the most powerful ship in Eric Holland's little navy—maybe in the world, if the comparatively small, slow, and poorly armed Dom warships they'd met were the best she'd encounter.

Holland loved her dearly. She wasn't as fast and agile as USS *Essex*, the American frigate he'd served aboard back in 1812–1814, during the last "British War," until she was pounded into a shattered, bleeding wreck by HMS *Phoebe* and HMS *Cherub* at Valparaiso. That left him with a smoldering hatred of the British—and short-range carronades like *Essex* had been armed with. On the other hand, old and British-built or not, *Tiger* was still a beautiful ship and a joy to sail. Especially compared to the worn-out whaler *Mary Riggs*, which Holland commanded when she and two other transports were traumatically wrecked on this world's Yucatán. *Tiger* practically sailed herself. Unfortunately, all the islands and uncharted shallows required constant attention.

"East-southeast . . . eleven mils?"

"Miles, you ignorant bugger," Holland growled. The kid at the masthead wasn't a "lubber," but a former Dom sailor, a freed "sea-slave," in other words, who came with one of the ships they'd taken. Like many of his kind, he spoke Spanya, but also reckoned distances in *leguas*. Holland would never get used to converting *leguas* to miles in his head and insisted his much younger sailors do it for him.

"We'll have to shorten sail again, I expect," came the voice of Holland's first lieutenant and second in command, William Semmes. One of the ship's original crew—and British—Holland liked him anyway.

"Aye, damn it." He waved at the suit of canvas above. "Ever' time we get her dressed just so, an' the old gal can stretch her legs, we gotta change her outfit." He simmered a moment. "Aye, get the t' gallants off her an' take a reef in her tops'ls." Shielding his eyes against the sun, even he could see the lighter-colored water ahead. "A leadsman in the chains as well, if you please. Damned shoals. Should'a slanted further out an' tacked back in, but we don't know where this bloody 'Pass o' Fire' *is*, do we?"

"Not really, sir," Semmes agreed gloomily before passing Holland's orders along. The young man was just as frustrated as his captain, just as unhappy with these treacherous waters. Still keeping himself more separate from the locals ashore than the Yankee sailor did—particularly now that he was free of *Tiger*'s former tyrannical, cowardly, and unlamented skipper—the ship was Semmes's last link to the world he came from and the only real home he had left. Holland did his best to get him "out an' about," even thrusting pretty Uxmalo girls upon him when officers were required ashore for social occasions. Semmes wouldn't have it. It was almost as if he tried to pretend nothing had changed at all, and as long as he stayed aboard *Tiger*, he could keep this strange, deadly new world at arm's length.

That was only superficially possible. They saw wonders aplenty at sea, some quite shocking and dangerous. Genuine sea serpents (or so they appeared), with relatively tiny heads on the end of long bodies (or was it only necks?), often gazed solemnly at them from a distance with huge yellow eyes as they passed. Great swimming reptiles, like smooth-skinned crocodiles with flippers, some with tall, rainbow-colored fins on their backs, were almost a daily occurrence as well. Amazing squids with spearpoint bodies (tipped with dangerously sharp, bony protrusions), ranging in size from a man's thumb to his torso, actually *jetted out of the water and flew short distances through the air* when startled. Several men had been injured by them, and the sides of the ship were festooned with what looked like broken ivory arrowheads. The most incredible sights were awesomely tremendous fish that basked on the surface like whales—only God knew how much bigger—that were capable of rapid bursts of speed and could reputedly crush *Tiger* herself in jaws they'd fortunately never seen. They steered well clear of those. Of course, the water itself almost always seethed with smaller, shockingly swift (and actually quite tasty) silvery-blue predators that combined the appearance and attributes of barracuda and tuna. Semmes's pretense couldn't be very firm or convincing.

Their search had already taken them throughout what ought to be the Bay of Honduras, confirming the quality of the charts Varaa-Choon herself made of that region twenty years before. That's what she and the other Mi-Anakka with her at the time had been doing: mapping the coastline in a topsail schooner from—wherever it was her people came from. Varaa's own speculation placed the pass in the only area that decades-ago expedition neglected, largely due to the same clutter of islands and shoals Holland was contending with off the east coast of the "Mosquito Kingdom." Varaa and her people had intended to return and do a proper job but never got the chance. That left a gap in their knowledge about three or four hundred miles wide between their current position and Panama. As he'd said, Holland had been tempted to make directly for it, but not only did he want to "test" Varaa's chart, he had to be sure.

"Signal Cap'n Razine we're shortenin' sail," he said, referring to the former Dom captain of the armed merchant ship consort *Roble Fuerte* a mile off *Tiger*'s larboard beam. "He'll see us doin' it, but I want him takin' soundings as well." He rubbed his bristly chin, looking across at *Roble Fuerte*. The ship had once looked for all the world like an old-time Spanish galleon. Unsurprising, since that's what inspired her lines. She'd had the same woeful sailing characteristics as well, however, and had been one of the first "native" ships rebuilt and rerigged to Holland's specifications. The high poop deck and forecastle were gone, leaving a long quarterdeck with a lighter rail around it. The three stubby masts had been replaced by two taller ones, a main and foremast, and a much longer bowsprit. Rigged as a brig with square *and* fore and aft sails, *Roble Fuerte* was a much better sailor. Not nearly as large and heavy, she could keep pace with *Tiger* when the former fourth rate was under plain sail.

"Hard to believe Razine's been at sea over twenty years but never been this far south," Holland complained while signal flags fluttered up a halyard and men rapidly took in a reef and adjusted the sails. The bosun and two of his mates scampered forward with a lead line. "Mostly back an' forth 'tween Vera Cruz an' Cuba, Hispaniola, an' Jamaica his whole dreary life, before we caught him haulin' freight for Gen'ral Agon. Glad we didn't kill 'im," he reflected. Razine was a true convert to the cause, had taught them a great deal about the Dominion, and Holland genuinely liked him. "Doms ain't known for sharin' or handin' out charts to where they don't want folks to go. Buggers is just as fervent about secrets as everything else! Even Don Hurac, who knew about the pass, didn't know right where it is."

The bosun's first sounding floated back, only slightly muffled by the pleasant breeze. "By the mark, twelve! Coral sand!"

"The bottom is coming up," Semmes observed.

"Aye. I figured so. Extra lookouts to the masthead to watch for rocks, coral heads, or shallows," he ordered. "Bright enough day to see 'em, at least." He turned to the man standing by the big double wheel. "Another point to starboard, if ye please." He glared meaningfully at a hard, purple line to the west, the visible coastline of the mainland. "Not as much leeway as I'd like, but we have ta hope there's a deep-water channel."

"What if there isn't?" Semmes asked.

Holland shrugged. "We'll haul back out an' around. Rather do it in daylight, if we must. Extra days sightseein'"—he sighed—"when I feel like we *should* be huntin' the caribbee or supportin' the army."

They eventually found the channel west of the islands (it turned out there were several) and slanted southwest along the Mosquito Coast for the rest of the day. The weather remained fine, and just before nightfall, they shortened sail still more. Razine wanted to anchor (Dom skippers owned their ships—they were all they had in the world—and generally anchored at night, especially in hazardous waters). Holland preferred to remain carefully, watchfully under way, both due to a sense of urgency and a strong distrust of the bottom's ability to hold an anchor. *Tiger* and *Roble Fuerte* shouldered light swells aside all night, plowing down toward where Costa Rica should be.

Eric Holland remained on deck throughout the hours of darkness, watching fretfully as the glaring stars were drowned by thickening clouds. The barometer remained steady, however, and the rising sun quickly roasted away the overcast. The coast was *much* closer, and a high, almost mountainous headland loomed in the distance. But the water was still deep—no bottom with the short lead—the weather had remained fair after all, and nothing seemed likely to change. "I'll leave you with it, then, Mr. Semmes," he told the officer who'd just come back on deck. "Take the watch if ye please." Holland released a tremendous yawn. "I'm for bed. Steer wide of that headland, soundings o' course, an' call me if you sight . . ." He blinked. "Anything unusual."

"Aye, Captain—and it's *been* my watch these last two hours, sir," Semmes gently scolded.

Holland stared at him a moment then nodded. "Aye. My apologies. No reflection on you. I couldn't've slept anyway. Now I can, I hope. Just two hours, though, mind," he stressed. "Wake me an' join me for a late breakfast. I've drawn a rough chart from memory. It's a nasty, crude scribble—I'm no cartographer, an' damn sure no artist, by God!—an' like as not it'd all be wrong *here* even if I was. But come look it over an' give me your views on how to proceed."

"Only two hours, sir?" Semmes asked doubtfully.

"All I need," Holland assured him and chuckled. "Young fellas like yerself can run fer days without a wink. You'll find it harder in yer middle years. Even more . . . *mature* gentlemen like meself either find theirselves sleepin' what's left o' their lives away—or gifted ta require little more rest than the young. I'm happy ta be amongst the latter. Two hours, Mr. Semmes."

He didn't get it. He barely got one hour before he was awakened by an excited commotion and was shortly called back on deck. "Bloody hell," Holland grumbled, buttoning a clean, blowsy white shirt and rubbing crackly eyes. It didn't take perfect vision to see what the excitement was about: several things at once, in fact. Semmes put a spyglass in his reaching hand, and he held it up, adjusting the focus. "Bloody hell," he repeated, redirecting it from one point of interest to another. "Never just one thing ta cope with at a time," he protested philosophically.

"No sir," Semmes agreed.

Just beyond the headland Holland saw before his very brief nap, they'd opened a broad, deep bay ringed with rocky, timber-covered hills and distant snowcapped mountains. Some of the more remote mountains even seemed to smolder, pushing up hazy plumes of smoke or steam. It was hard to tell which since, though the sky to the east remained sharp and clear, all the land to the west seemed to lie under a low, vaguely ominous miasma. *Deathly humid ashore*, Holland guessed. On the other hand, though the shoreline they'd previously followed had advanced more rapidly than he reckoned appropriate (he'd written that off to the generally lower sea levels they'd observed on this world), there shouldn't have been a bay here at all.

That was only one of the things that caught his immediate attention, mere background for other wonders and more pressing concerns. Most immediate was the score or more of humongous shapes, like islands unto themselves: stupendous fish that dwarfed the greatest whale Holland had ever seen or heard of. Razine called them "Peces Monstruo," yet that seemed ridiculously inadequate. At least one or two of those in view were easily twice *Tiger*'s length, and that was just the part they could see. The beasts were known to be territorial, highly aggressive, and could easily wreck a ship, but these seemed oblivious, merely basking and rolling without a care, occasionally slapping great flukes twice the size of *Tiger*'s main course, but otherwise disinterested or lethargic. Holland hoped they'd stay that way.

Deeper in the bay, six or seven miles to the west, a great gash had been torn in the earth, like a ragged wound gouged through toothy cliffs. Dramatic as it was, it took some looking to distinguish it at first from the otherwise unbroken wall of timber and a dense mist that blended the trees all together along the shore, but an unusually heavy concentration of lizardbirds swooping and fighting in a virtual cloud in its vicinity drew Holland's glass to a span of tumultuous water scouring vigorously through the gap. The rest resolved itself then. The helmsman began calling in alarm that he was having trouble with the wheel, the current even here trying to heave them off course, and Holland knew the cause at once. They'd found the fabled "Pass of Fire," and the bay was its mouth. The tidal race surging back and forth through such a narrow gap between mighty oceans would have incomprehensible power. If the passage was truly navigable, any transit would have to be timed to perfection.

That question was almost immediately answered because even as Holland stood watching, the amazing natural wonder almost seemed to *spit* a ship out into the bay, followed closely by two more, all three sweeping toward them at an astonishing rate. For an instant, Holland could only stare, transfixed by what he saw. Shaking his head, he bellowed, "Clear for action!" as he collapsed the glass and handed it back to Semmes. He was forced to stifle a bark of incredulous amusement at how quickly he recovered from his surprise at being confronted by yet *another* unexpected marvel or complication—both—in so short a time since being summoned. That seemed to be the way of this world.

"Signal Captain Razine ta clear for action as well," he told Semmes. "If those're Doms, we'll have 'em. Perhaps they can be . . . induced ta tell us what we need ta know an' we won't have ta take *our* ships through that nightmare pass!"

Semmes relayed his captain's command to the signal midshipman and then raised the glass to study the oncoming ships himself, already much closer and still moving fast. The high coast and haze beyond had made them difficult to see at first, but now they were quite clear; all sails set to catch the west-northwest wind, flags streaming hard to leeward. He grunted in surprise. "Captain, the two ships behind the first are Doms, all right. Red flags and lower sails, all with their crooked cross painted on them, define them as commissioned warships like we've seen before." They'd even taken one mostly intact at Vera Cruz, and it was being modified similarly to *Roble Fuerte*. "The leading one looks quite different," Semmes continued, tone troubled. "Dingy white sails all around and a more advanced rig. Hull form sleeker as well. My impression is the Doms are *chasing* her and she'd show them clean heels with a different wind . . ." He paused. ". . . aye, and she's lost her fore-topmast. There may be other damage." He urgently sharpened the focus again. "Bloody hell," he murmured, and Holland finally *was* surprised. Semmes wasn't given to intemperate exclamations.

"What is it?" he asked.

"Her flag, sir." He gestured up with his gaze. "Like a combination of our own." In a bizarre and uncharacteristic (for Holland) compromise, *Tiger* sailed under both the American Stars and Stripes at the mainmast head, and the British red merchant ensign with the Union Jack field at the foremast head. In spite of his antipathy for the British in general, he liked and respected the few British sailors still part of *Tiger*'s crew. And the ship *was* British. She might've become the flagship of his own little navy, but it wasn't like he'd captured her. Better to consider his relationship with her and her crew as a partnership or alliance. Semmes's portrayal of the other flag ahead didn't sufficiently describe it, though. Holland retrieved the glass.

"Damn me, I've seen that ensign, an' so have you."

"Yes. Red and white stripes like yours, but the Union Jack in a quarter field—not the current one, however. It's like an old East India Company flag before the addition of St. Patrick's red saltire."

All three ships had noticeably slowed as they left the swiftest column of water rushing through the pass, the mystery ship now just over three miles away. Under every stitch she could carry, she was still closing fast and had hoisted some incomprehensible signal. But the Doms were keeping pace and both fired bow chasers within moments of each other, sending up heavy spumes of spray just off the stranger's starboard quarter.

"Aye," Holland agreed, unconsciously rubbing his stubbly chin. "An' enemies for certain. I've a notion . . ." he added lowly before raising his voice to a roar. "Fightin' sail only, load an' run out! We'll engage the damned Doms, but don't fire on the chase without orders. Signal Cap'n Razine ta do the same an' follow us," he said aside to Semmes.

Amid the sound of thundering drums, topmen raced aloft to tightly furl the fore and main courses and adjust the topsails as *Tiger* eased to starboard, still fighting the current. Other men, called "waisters," rigged nets overhead to protect against falling debris, while the gun's crews labored to load the five monstrous 36pdrs, eleven 12pdrs, and eight 6pdrs in the ship's starboard battery and heave their muzzles out through open gunports. There was great excitement. Even in her reduced capacity, *Tiger* was faster and vastly more powerful than any Dom warship they'd encountered in the Atlantic. Her guns were far better, and their crews had been relentlessly trained and drilled. Cannon on Atlantic Dom warships were as woefully outdated as their ships' designs, extremely short-ranged, and wildly inaccurate, much like the short-barreled carronades Holland remembered with such bitterness. *Tiger* was more agile too, despite being twice as big.

Staring intently, shifting their gun's aim with handspikes to track the enemy while gunners stood poised with smoldering slow match in their linstocks, everyone expected a quick, easy victory from beyond the enemy's range. Still closing quickly while maintaining a broadside aspect as the chase held a straight course away, they were soon within a mile of the Doms— already close enough to hit—and Holland was only waiting until the stranger, now less than a quarter mile distant, was clear before he fired. There was considerable surprise and concern, therefore, when the closest Dom warship suddenly vanished behind a blooming fogbank of white smoke lanced with orange flashes and three or four heavy roundshot slammed into *Tiger*'s side. At least one blew through the thick but aged hull, and a chorus of screams arose from below.

"God damn them!" Holland snapped. "Those aren't the same guns we've seen before! Have the thirty-six pounders on the gun deck fire as they bear, Mr. Semmes."

"Aye, sir," Semmes replied, stepping to the companionway leading below. "Pass the word to Mr. Sura to commence firing as his guns bear!" While no doubt impressive, a broadside would be less accurate than independent aimed fire and harder on the old ship's bones.

"What about us, sir?" questioned the young lieutenant in charge of the upper-deck 12pdrs.

"A little closer yet," Holland said with an understanding smile. The man nodded regretfully and passed the word below. Almost at once, two 36pdrs roared nearly as one, shaking the deck under their feet. One at a time, the next three monstrous main battery weapons thundered as well. Wind quickly swept the smoke away, and the big roundshot was actually visible as dark, blurry orbs swiftly rising to the top of their trajectories. Just as rapidly, they began to fall, and the unaided eye lost them then, but Holland had the glass back up and followed each projectile to the target. The first kicked up a huge splash in the ship's wake, and the second fell short, but the last three relentlessly found their mark, one after the other.

The lenses in the spyglass had been smeared by repeated attempts to wipe away the slimy salt air film, and at roughly a thousand yards, it was difficult to tell exactly where the huge roundshot—bigger than anything *Tiger* had ever fired in action before—hit the enemy. The result was immediately obvious, however. Better armed or not, these Dom ships were still relatively small and lightly built, and shattered debris exploded from the target in a spray of large fragments that patterned the sea all around. The mainmast teetered and collapsed against the foremast, smashing the foretop down on the forecastle. Dozens of men would've just been crushed to death and scores flayed by splinters. Flapping canvas draped the side of the ship and dipped down in the water like a huge sea anchor, and the vessel nearly stalled in her tracks, beginning a helpless pirouette.

Cheers erupted on *Tiger*, *Roble Fuerte*, and even the stranger, which had turned to come in behind Razine's former merchantman as if joining their line of battle. A quick glance revealed the addition was armed with a row of light guns on her main deck, probably 6pdrs, protruding through decorative round piercings in her bulwarks. Once again, Holland had the impression of a vessel from an earlier age. The damaged Dom ship foolishly kept firing blindly through its own masking sails and tangled rigging. Inevitably, there was a flicker of flame and a rush of rising dark smoke.

"Idiots!" Holland barked harshly. "Damned if I didn't *respect* their talent, hittin' us this far away, but whatever fool officer didn't have 'em quit shootin' deserves what he's gonna get!" He watched for a moment. "That other silly bugger's still comin' on, against *three* of us now."

The second Dom ship had been sailing abreast of its consort and now pulled ahead of the floundering, smoldering wreck. As soon as it did, it opened fire as well. Holland counted sixteen flashes behind the new cloud of flowing white smoke. "Thirty-two guns. Sixteen- er eighteen-pounder main guns, I'll wager," he surmised, as *Tiger* shook from a couple more hits and holes appeared in her topsails with a loud popping sound. *Roble Fuerte* staggered from a couple of hits herself, but most of the shot kicked up splashes around them. He looked at Lieutenant Semmes, still standing stoically and attentively near. "Makes her a frigate as we reckon such things." He had to raise his voice as Razine opened fire with half his ship's own battery of twenty-four 8pdrs. "Though I don't know how they pack so many guns in somethin' that small. Let's introduce her ta the rest o' ours, shall we?"

The huge 36pdrs were still loading, but the gunners around the main deck 12pdrs, and the 6pdrs on the quarterdeck around them, were getting impatient. They roared their approval when the word was passed. Soon, they were pounding away as their guns came to bear, much faster than the heavies on the lower gun deck. *Roble Fuerte* was pouring out a spirited fire, and even the mystery ship with the strange flag was booming away, for all the good its lighter guns did. Six pounders were excellent weapons for field artillery, light enough to move with ease on land and quite powerful enough against light defenses and mere human flesh, but they weren't much use against heavily constructed ships at what was still the fairly long range (for them) of five or six hundred yards.

Ultimately, the great 36pdrs finished the fight, literally smashing the side of the enemy ship in and toppling all its masts. In moments, there were two bobbing wrecks, the first still smoldering but not fully engulfed in flames as most had expected. Its crew had stopped firing to deal with the fire. The second ship was beginning to settle.

"Bring us in within musket shot of the first one," Holland told Semmes. "No closer, in case the maniac bastards blow theirselves up." They'd discovered to their shock that, while enemy merchantmen might be captured intact, nearly all Dom naval officers seemed to be fanatical supporters of the Blood Priests who'd been working on them even longer than the army. They'd only captured that one Dom warship by a surprise boarding action at Vera Cruz. Others in danger of being taken had deliberately destroyed themselves and everyone aboard. "Heave to off her stern," Holland added. "We'll rake her ta death if she wants ta keep at it."

As they drew closer, Holland watched through his glass and saw that fighting had erupted on the enemy ship. Officers and soldiers were killing their own crew with swords and muskets, but the crew had them outnumbered and surrounded and were desperately fighting back with belaying pins and other improvised weapons. Scores were dying, and the combatants seemed entirely oblivious to *Tiger*'s approach. "Ain't that somethin'," Holland murmured. Quickly striding to the taffrail, he seized a speaking trumpet and called down to *Roble Fuerte*, close in their wake. "Cap'n Razine! They're fightin' each other up ahead. If the sailors keep their officers from blowin' up the ship er somethin', we might save a few. Wouldn't mind takin' her as a prize, if we can. The better guns alone'll be interestin' ta look at. Go over an' take station astern o' the other. Invite 'em ta surrender. They'll be guarded but well treated—*you* know how it is," he reminded.

"That one looks in danger of sinking," Razine called back, the doubt in his muffled, tinny voice still clear through his own speaking trumpet.

Holland appraised the other ship. "Aye," he responded. "Clear away your boats an' have 'em ready ta put in the water." Abruptly remembering where he was and what he'd seen earlier, he had a sudden chilling thought. The voracious smaller fish were a constant threat to men in the water and even small boats, at least in coastal shallows, but they might be the least of their concerns. What if they'd attracted the attention of the huge island-size monsters that had been so uncharacteristically placid before? Quickly scanning the sea all around, he didn't find any near. Better yet, those still in view seemed to be sullenly moving away. "Don't imagine we *scared* the big bastards," he grumbled, perplexed.

Guessing what must've concerned his captain, Semmes offered a possible explanation. "No. I don't think we *could* frighten anything as large as they are," he agreed, "but perhaps they're sensitive to loud noises, or the concussive pressure the great guns produce? I understand sound travels undiminished in water, and we *did* just raise quite a din. Do you suppose they merely chose to move away from the source of their annoyance?"

Holland looked at him thoughtfully, then grinned. "You may be right at that. Good thing ta know, if true." He turned back to Razine on his smaller ship. "Just stand by ta save anyone you can."

"What do you propose *we* do?" Semmes asked, gesturing back at the ship they approached.

"Depends, don't it? Make her a prize if we can, but board her an' have a look, at least. Just have ta see who wins the scuffle aboard."

The fighting was over by the time *Tiger* hove to, sails popping and flapping as they were adjusted to keep her as stationary as possible. The current was making that difficult, but it seemed to be ebbing now. Having killed or overpowered their officers, the Dom sailors were still clearly frightened despite having hauled down their flag and cast it into the sea, and the many shouts of encouragement from aboard the ship that ravaged them. *Odd*, Holland thought. *Though their officers appear as fanatical as any we've seen, Doms from the Pacific*—that had to be where they were from—*obviously know what strikin' their colors means.* The friendly shouts seemed to have an effect and the Doms' expressions changed from pure terror to guarded hopefulness. Holland turned away to study the ship they'd "rescued." It hadn't veered around to follow *Roble Fuerte*, but crept up alongside *Tiger* to heave to in a seamanlike fashion. The ship's longboat was already being lowered from a boom that looked like it might've been the missing fore-topmast.

"It looks like we're ta have visitors," Holland said, raising a brow. "Take a well-armed party across ta the prize, if ye please," he told Semmes. "Assess her condition an' how cooperative her crew seems ta be. Judgin' from past experience, killin' their officers an surrenderin' puts 'em pretty damn firmly on our side. No goin' back from *that*," he added dryly.

"My pleasure," said Semmes with a grin. As he started to turn and assemble his boarding party, Holland held up a finger. "Be brisk about it, especially if it looks like we'll have to take her in tow." He cast an appraising eye at the distant maw of the Pass of Fire. Amazingly, it seemed farther now than when he first saw it. They'd been sailing against its current as they closed with the enemy, but apparently hadn't even matched its terrific flow. Though the geography of this new world vaguely agreed with the old, there were countless differences, small and large, mountains where there shouldn't be, no islands where there should—and even more islands than there ought to be, on occasion. Of course, the beasts were entirely wrong. It seemed absolutely nothing alive that hadn't come here the same way they had was the same. It was all very strange and sometimes quite frightening, but for some reason that narrow, violent passage between the greatest seas of the world struck Holland as almost supernaturally wrong. Now that they'd found it, he wanted to observe it, but he'd prefer to do so from farther away. The current was helping with that for now, pushing all the ships toward the mouth of the bay, but he was sure he knew the reason. "Tides," he said darkly, nodding at the pass and then turning his attention back to Semmes.

"Sir?"

"Tides," Holland repeated. "This terrific current's the result of a *tidal surge* through that pass, as I'm sure you've guessed already. It's already begun ta slow, an' mark me, it'll ease ta nothin' in time—before it turns the other way. When that happens, this whole bay'll be like a bathtub with the stopper pulled out an' we'll all be sucked down the drain." Never a superstitious man—a rarity among sailors—Holland actually had to suppress a shudder. "We'll want ta be safely *out* o' the tub by then. Make findin' out everything ye can about the pass yer very first priority when ye cross to the prize." He looked speculatively at the now-distant leviathans, but shook his head before motioning at the boat now approaching from the other strange ship. "I'll do the same when I speak ta them."

The strangers came alongside and hooked onto larboard at the same time Semmes shoved off to starboard. Never much concerned about his own appearance, Holland felt he owed it to his ship and his cause to make a good impression on these new, unknown people, and dashed town to his cabin to change. Now he sweated in his dark blue frock coat right along with all his mostly Uxmalo officers and handful of young midshipmen. "Marines"—infantry from the detachment borrowed from Ixtla's 1st Uxmal for his "raid" on Vera Cruz—constituted the side party welcoming the strangers aboard.

The bosun twittered his pipe as five men ascended the side dressed in a variety of frock coats of different colors, open in the front with swept-back tails, revealing weskits beneath. Two wore trousers and sensible sandals firmly strapped to otherwise bare feet, but three with the finest coats and large, woven straw bicorn hats wore knee breeches, stockings, and well-made shoes. All wore curious smiles as they took in the details of the large, well-maintained ship, and particularly its mixed, almost entirely native crew. *Tiger*'s "enlisted" sailors had no uniform to speak of, except for the fact nearly all their clothes were made from sailcloth. Even their low-crowned, wide-brimmed hats, reminiscent of the practical straw hats most Yucatán natives used ashore, were sewn from canvas and heavily painted a variety of colors to stiffen them. In any event, Holland was struck by the irony that he'd atypically dressed to "look navy" so as not to stand out from his officers and petty officers, while his visitors looked anything but.

The apparent leader, a tall, portly man with a long, dark, braided beard and either as tanned as Holland or of mixed race himself, swept the large hat off his head and bowed. "I am Captain Stanley Jenks, honored to command HIMS *Nemesis*, currently commissioned by the Governor-Emperor of the Empire of the New Britain Isles as a private man-o'-war." He stood up straight, still smiling, but betraying intense curiosity. "I do hope I'm not mistaken and it's possible to address you in English. I can't speak anything else."

"Aye," Holland said, taken aback.

"Excellent! These men"—he waved behind him—"are my senior officers and advisors. I'll be pleased to name them momentarily, but first, I'm *dying* to know the identity of those who came so providentially to our aid." He gestured up at the flags. "We initially took you for countrymen, quite astounding enough in this unknown place, but then noted certain . . . dissimilarities in our flags. I can only assume you're somewhat more recent arrivals to this world, but perhaps we share certain origins or influences?"

Holland was becoming vaguely annoyed. "Like I told Lewis, goddamn Brits're everywhere," he grumbled under his breath.

"Excuse me, sir?" Jenks exclaimed, alarmed.

"Nothin'," Holland assured, forcing a smile. "Just a sort of joke with a friend." He straightened. "I'm Captain Eric Holland, United States of America." He pointed up at the Stars and Stripes. "*Former* British colony in North America, but which kicked the British out sixty-odd years ago. We weren't at war with each other when we came here last year, so I figure this British warship we helped salvage is more 'allied' than 'owned.' Only right she should fly her own flag too."

"Yes, the red ensign!" Jenks exclaimed. "We recognized it! A mercantile flag, is it not?"

"Aye. *Tiger*'s a little past her prime. She was a 'private vessel' too."

Jenks gazed around admiringly. "Nonsense. Aged or not, she's magnificent! And so powerfully armed! We noted she only used five guns of her main battery, but each side is pierced for seven more. She may be 'past her prime' where she came from, but not *here*, sir. No indeed!"

Holland nodded and gestured around. "We all feel the same, an' we're glad to have her." He wouldn't yet reveal that *Tiger* only *had* five of the massive 36pdrs to a side because nobody thought she could carry any more. He nodded at *Nemesis* instead. "Fine-lookin' ship there too. Nice lines. Recognize the flag o' the 'Honorable East India Company.' Is that what you use for the red ensign?"

Jenks shook his head. "Actually, that's the national flag of the empire. We were established by a pair of Indiamen that found themselves upon this world roughly a century ago. We adopted various of the company's forms of governance, and therefore its flag as well. There were other reasons," he began, but then smiled and shrugged, understandably unwilling to reveal everything about his country to strangers within minutes of meeting.

Holland cleared his throat. "Well, I'm equally pleased providence put us here in time ta give you a hand. Whatever else we share, historically an' situation-wise, it appears we have the same enemy. We've heard tell o' your 'empire.' Don't know much *about* it, even where it is, but we do know there's a hell of a big Dom army marchin' to throw some colony o' yours out o' California."

"Thus our occupation," Jenks said with a nod. "Though small by your standards and even those of our own navy, *Nemesis* is a purpose-built warship, a 'letter of marque' . . . "

"Privateer," Holland supplied.

"Indeed," Jenks agreed, unoffended. "She was special built to prey on cargo ships supplying that army by sea. We've known about the formation of the Dominion's 'Gran Cruzada' for a number of years, in fact. Now that it has actually set out, a general naval war has commenced." He smiled. "Along with our more . . . modest, admittedly entrepreneurial contribution. We'd even been fairly lucky of late, cruising off more remote southern settlements where Dominion merchantmen fill with grain and other agricultural cargoes. Slaves too, of course," he added offhand. "We aren't greedy, you see, going for more valuable, better-protected cargoes. It was the ships themselves we wanted"—he gestured at *Roble Fuerte*—"to convert in a very similar fashion as you seem to have done. We foresee a fine market for hulls such as that when the current unpleasantness ends."

Jenks's expression fell. "Yes, we were quite successful until suddenly, an entire squadron of enemy warships pounced upon us as if they knew our position exactly, scattering our most recent prizes. We sustained some damage to our hull in a brief exchange of fire—you may have noticed they carry heavier metal than *Nemesis*? In any event, making water rather badly and dreadfully slowed, we were forced to flee." Nothing pleasant remained in his expression. "As difficult as it is to induce Dominion ships and crews to surrender, perhaps you already know you'd be better advised to cut your own throat before surrendering to *them*? Yes. Well, we made sufficient repairs to our hull to start pumping it dry, but five of the devils had got close enough to start peppering away at us, knocking our masts and sails all ahoo."

"Five?" asked one of the young Uxmalo midshipmen, eyes wide.

"Indeed." Jenks nodded. "As soon as we repaired one thing, they bashed something else. Amazingly frustrating!"

"That's when you entered the Pass of Fire to escape?" Holland asked.

Jenks looked at him and blinked. "Good God, no!" he exclaimed in surprise, then considered. "Well, yes, I suppose. In a sense," he added. One of the men behind him chuckled nervously. "And that would be a most appropriate name," Jenks continued. "The western entrance is considerably larger than this, ringed by monstrous volcanoes, spewing fire in all directions. There's even a recent settlement near the mouth of the bay amid the ubiquitous ruins of some ancient civilization. Great, conical structures you must be familiar with."

Nearly everyone nodded now, enthralled by the account.

"Leviathans wallowing everywhere! More than I've ever seen!" Jenks gestured at the huge, distant fish. "Far more than here. *Far* more, as if they gather for some social purpose!" He shuddered and tilted his head to his ship. "We'd restored our rig to what you see now and hoped to gain an advantage, perhaps even dodging among the leviathans themselves! I don't understand why they didn't smash us. Perhaps they're less aggressive in large groups?" He waved it away. "By then, the Dommies had us, though, advancing with all their ships spread out. We'd just decided to shoot the gap between a pair of them, blasting away, when the most astonishing thing occurred: the bay began to *move*, the current so amazingly strong, we could make no headway against it. Worse, even as we tried, it only swept the enemy toward us! We had no choice but to turn away and trim the sails as best we could to maintain some control."

"Wait," Holland said. "You speak as if this all came as a surprise."

Jenks fairly goggled. "Of course it did! How could we prepare for something we didn't know *existed*? No one did. We'd sailed down beyond our charts." He looked at Holland. "Are you at all familiar with currents in the Pacific?"

"The Pacific on our old world, aye."

"I'm given to understand they're similar here," Jenks informed them. "If we do truly come from the same 'old world,'" he added cryptically before continuing. "I'm not even sure how we got as far southeast as we did unless that damnable pass had something to do with it."

"What was it like?" another midshipman asked. "Going through, I mean?" Jenks glanced at the lad, slightly impatient, as if unused to being questioned by youngsters. Holland didn't care if he was. He encouraged the "young gentlemen" to ask whatever they wanted as long as it pertained to their duties and profession. How else could they learn? Recognizing the ardent curiosity on every other face, Jenks relented, though his voice sounded haunted.

"Why, it was horrifying. Like trying to secure a loose sail with your teeth, or riding a raging river on a chip of wood. . . . I fear I'm unprepared to provide an appropriate metaphor and can't adequately describe it so soon after the fact." He looked vulnerably at his companions as if hoping one might take up the narrative; none seemed willing to do so. He sighed and looked back at Holland. "We were swept practically helplessly along between high cliffs that had shed heaps of rocks the size of houses, which strayed alarmingly into the torrent. I'm *sure* we exceeded eighteen knots, more, but there was no imaginable way to measure it even if we'd thought to try. 'Impossible,' say you, and I'd agree with all my heart if I hadn't endured it, steering constantly, myself at the wheel, hands like claws digging into the spokes. . . . I ground a decade off my teeth. The only thing that saved us was the wind blasting through the cliffs, perhaps even stirred by the rush of water itself—I've no idea—that allowed us to maintain just enough steerageway to avoid the obstacles and keep to the deepest water."

He hesitated. "There was one place where the northern wall fell away and another wide bay opened. I can even imagine the place as an anchorage in which to relax the nerves and make repairs if one was ever mad enough to deliberately take such a passage, but we saw no evidence anyone ever had. The view was phenomenal: distant mountains, a mighty forest surrounding a broad plain upon which momentous creatures grazed . . . but the sky was black with dragon gulls, and the water held a greater abundance of terrors than anyplace I've ever seen. It *seethed*, I say, and reeked of rotting death. We might've tried to linger," he reflected, "attempt to move into the bay and anchor ourselves—fight our pursuers!—but we had no warning, and I don't think we could've safely escaped the flood without preparation." He nodded at the ship Semmes had boarded and the other, which had, unnoticed till now, begun to slip beneath the waves. Debris was swirling all around in the strange, slacking current. Apparently, its own boats had been undamaged, and between those and the ones from *Roble Fuerte*, everyone who wanted to live had been saved. "There *were* still those two fellows after us."

"What happened to the other three?" Holland asked himself.

"Wrecked, I'm sure. I saw one go myself. The closest at the time. It smashed head-on into one of those monolithic rocks. Enemies or not, it was a dreadful thing to see—and contemplate as a likelihood for ourselves, I can tell you!"

"How was the passage after the, uh, bay you discovered?" asked Mr. Greg, *Tiger*'s British third lieutenant.

"Not quite as bad. I can imagine it being slightly less terrifying going from this side to that if one paused at the bay and waited for the current and wind to cooperate—not that I'll ever try it, I assure you!" he stated emphatically.

"How will you ever get back?" Greg asked.

"We'll sail right roun' the whole bloody *world* afore willin'ly sailin' back through *that* hellish crack!" exclaimed one of Jenks's men whom he still hadn't introduced.

"I believe Mr. Blakeslee has adequately summarized the sentiment of the majority of my crew," Jenks said with feeling, but then looked at Holland. "Unless you know a better way . . . I suppose not. You wouldn't be so interested in our misadventure if you'd ever been through it yourselves."

"We never have," Holland confessed.

Jenks looked confused. "Then what brought you here, if I might ask? Fortuitous for us as it was."

Holland rubbed the stubble on his chin. "Unlike you, we'd *heard* about the place, but our source had never been here. We came ta see it for ourselves. Had ta know if the Doms might venture ta send forces against us through it. Warships, even troopships."

Jenks shook his head. "I can't imagine that. You heard my tale. Two warships out of five made it through. I can't think any of their captains could've survived the attempt often enough to become accomplished. As for troops in some fat merchantman," he scoffed, "they'd have to be insane." He paused and tilted his head to the side. "Then again, I'm convinced that some of them are. Particularly this new cult of Blood Priests. They are stark raving mad. Who knows what they'll do?" He peered intently at Holland. "Or why. I don't know any more about you than you know of me. Less. You've at least heard of the empire." He paused, considering. "But the *alcalde* at one of the little villages we visited—no reason to love the Dommies *there*, I'll tell you!—mentioned some trouble for the buggers in the Yucatán." He arched a brow. "Trouble that *ate* a whole Dommie army. Had them going around conscripting even more young sons for soldiers than daughters for slaves and sacrifices. . . ."

"It's a long story," Holland said, "an' I haven't even offered you refreshments," he added apologetically, pointing at the longboat returning with

Semmes. "My first lieutenant'll want ta hear your story again, and we'll have much ta do ta deal with the prize." He paused. "Honestly, though, after what you described, my first priority'll be ta rig a hawser ta the prize an' get it—an' us—the hell out o' this bay as fast as we can."

"I'm with you there!" Jenks exclaimed, then smiled. "I look forward to furthering our acquaintance"—he gestured at his companions once more—"and I'm sure we all deeply appreciate any further assistance you might provide to a good ship and crew suddenly marooned on the wrong side of the world! We will return the favor, I assure you." He chuckled more naturally. "It might even be that the empire has already unknowingly re-paid you in some small way."

Holland looked at him curiously, and Jenks elaborated. "As I mentioned earlier, our navy is quite active at present, and that dreadful 'Pass of Fire' is likely the very last thing any Dom troopship needs to concern themselves with."

Holland nodded slowly. "Could be you're right about that, Cap'n Jenks. Hope you are." He snorted. "Don't take this wrong, an' it's nothin' ta do with you, but it sorta sets a squirrel loose in my guts ta be grateful ta Brits—o' *any* stripe—for anything. Prob'ly couldn't stand it at all if they knew they was doin' it."

CHAPTER 7

T *iger, Roble Fuerte,* and *Nemesis* stood off beyond the mouth of the bay for the next two days, measuring and timing the current and changing depths inside, even making brief forays into its embrace to explore the periphery once they were sure they could reliably predict the surge in the pass by the movements of the moon. In the meantime, Lieutenant Greg oversaw repairs to the surviving Dom warship and organized a prize crew. To no one's surprise, there was no shortage of willing volunteers among the prisoners once they realized how truly lucky they'd been to be captured. They might know very little about the people they enthusiastically swore their oaths to, but they clearly weren't the demons they'd been warned to expect to torture, kill, and eat them. A small minority refused to cooperate, out of fear or misguided piety. They remained under guard but weren't mistreated. Experience had shown Eric Holland that many would eventually come around.

Captain Jenks practically moved aboard *Tiger* during this time, and Holland found him engaging and surprisingly unpretentious and practical, quickly warming to him as they learned more about each other and their respective "nations." Convinced that Jenks had no intention of running back through the pass, Holland grew less constrained in revealing details about the Yucatán alliance and the activities of its forces. Equally sure the

Army of the Yucatán and the American Detached Expeditionary Force posed no threat to the empire, their own war against the Dominion and Blood Priests doubtless aiding the Imperial effort as well, Jenks provided Holland with the first hard information about the formerly mysterious Pacific power that so annoyed their mutual enemy.

"We brought the conflict with the Dommies on ourselves," Jenks confessed as he and Holland strolled *Tiger*'s quarterdeck, peering over the rail to leeward at the fascinating bay and frightening passage within. Still adamant he'd never go through it again, Jenks's horror of the pass had faded enough that he and Holland could objectively appreciate the wonder, even the strange beauty of the remarkable feature. "Our ancestors had *three* Indiamen at first, outbound in convoy for China from someplace I can't remember on the east coast of India when a strange storm brought them to this world." He took it for granted that Holland didn't need an explanation of that fantastic event. "Prepared to defend themselves, the ships were well armed with large crews of British, lascars, Malays, Chinese. . . ." He shrugged. "The story goes that they stopped among some very strange folk in the East Indies for repairs and learned quite a lot from them. But those folk weren't precisely *people*, if you get my meaning, and the decision was taken to move along." Holland pursed his lips, wondering about that, but nodded.

"Only two ships proceeded eastward, the third sailing back toward England with a reduced crew." Jenks blinked. "I can't believe they truly thought they'd find England as they knew it, but they were never heard from again. The others engaged in an odyssey comparable to Ulysses's before settling on a string of large, unknown islands as close to the middle of the Pacific as possible. Two critical issues immediately manifested themselves, however. They had roughly five hundred people, crew and passengers combined, at that point, and though few dangerous predators inhabited the islands and they were relatively easily secured, there were no other humans. The biblical tale of Adam and Eve is all very well . . ." He paused and regarded Holland inquiringly. Holland nodded his understanding, and Jenks continued. "Yes. Well, clearly the Lord took a hand or Cain could never have extended his line. My ancestors were in much the same unsustainable situation and no such isolated outpost could endure. I'm a sailor, not a scholar, and can't remember my lessons well, but there couldn't have been more than a score of women of all ages, um . . . 'available,' as it were.

"Needless to say, they were kept as near prisoners, both for their protection and to prevent their attachment to anyone. Can you just imagine the battles that would start? A search for more people, particularly women, had to begin at once. Early explorations eventually found some, I understand, though just as isolated and few. Rumors persist that larger populations were encountered somewhere in the Southern Ocean, but they were violently warlike and otherwise . . . undesirable for ambiguous reasons. Only when the Dominion was ultimately discovered were more people found who were *glad* to move." He arched his eyebrows. "The Dominion was younger then, not as organized, but its population already labored under blood-drenched tyranny. Our very first meeting was violent." He shrugged. "Raids were undertaken and people carried off. Considering how they flourished after their terror faded, I'm not ashamed that the empire—quite a pretentious boast at the time—made an enemy of the Dominion. I do deplore that, still desperately needing people, an uneasy peace and eventual trade was established. Mostly for women, as you might imagine."

"Why deplore trade?"

Jenks looked grim. "Because we—and the people we got—would've been better off if we simply kept raiding for them. You see, over time our industrial capacity far outstripped the Dominion, at least in terms of quality. They got things I'd rather they hadn't, and we received what's come to be considered indistinguishable from female *property* in exchange. The position of women in Imperial society is far better than under the Doms even now, though it's become rather schizophrenic. Women are either virtual slaves, working under a kind of indenture until their 'purchase price' is repaid, or they're pampered and protected and kept as cherished, fragile possessions. The latter is the most the former can hope for, in fact: to earn their 'freedom' to be married and encased in a velvet box! I can't imagine it's much of a life for most and only thank God I'm a man!"

"Female slavery," Holland mused. "There's those among us against even makin' slaves o' the *enemy*. I don't think they'll much approve o' your empire." He snorted. "An' there's a few women, one in particular, who'd prob'ly take deadly offense."

"Should I be truly concerned?"

Holland thought about it, then answered in a roundabout way. "We've done all we can here an' ain't seen nothin' else come through the pass. I'm inclined ta agree with you that nobody makes a habit of it, an' even if they'd risk a flock o' troopships to your navy, they wouldn't likely try ta send 'em through what you described. Pure madness, that. Time to shape a course back to Uxmal—kind o' the capital of our alliance. I need to get back into things. When we get there, though, your officers an' crew need ta know how ta act. I'll fill you in on the way. Suffice ta say for now, the ladies are different from what you're used to: free as birds an' more outspoken an' productive than most o' their men. Own more than half all our industry too. Only thing they *don't* do is fight in the army, an' it wouldn't surprise me if they took that up next. There's some from other tribes, like Ocelomeh, who do."

He grinned. "But your first snag's gonna be gettin' on the good side of a tough young lady about yay high." He held his hand even with his chest. "Pretty as can be—an' hard as roundshot. Her name's Sira Periz. *Alcaldesa* Sira Periz. She pays my wages, an' even Colonel Cayce won't go against her without damn good cause." He looked thoughtful. "Don't make her mad, an' she'll pay *your* wages." He nodded at the prize anchored off the headland, yards going up on the new mainmast that was swayed up and dropped in by *Tiger* the day before. "She'll pay for that too. I'll try to see you get a share." He grinned. "You *did* lead her to us, after all."

DELAYED BY THE repaired but still excruciatingly slothful Dom prize, the roughly fourteen-hundred-mile voyage up from the Pass of Fire, back across the Bay of Honduras, and up around the northeast point of the Yucatán Peninsula to Uxmal, took Holland's expanded little squadron nine dreary days. Fortunately, the wind remained cooperative and there were no storms. The sea was mild with a slight rolling swell, and no other sails were seen. Holland was impressed by *Nemesis*. With her fore-topmast restored and a new topsail bent on, the sleek ship-sloop extended their view to windward, occasionally darting back in, leaning hard, and throwing up a fine, foamy spray on the purple-blue sea. Holland was reminded of a young thoroughbred meandering around the pasture that just had to kick its heels up and run from time to time. She was a joy to watch, and vaguely old-fashioned in appearance or not, Holland had to admit that the Imperials on this world hadn't let their maritime roots go to seed. Of course, their empire was centered on islands—again—and they needed well-found ships. Colonies too. Jenks had explained the decade-old colony in the Californias was a source of desperately needed raw materials. Left vacant by the distant Dominion that claimed the region, the empire hadn't thought the Doms would dispute them for it. And they hadn't—until the advent of the Gran Cruzada.

By noon on the ninth day, they'd closed the shore enough to see the distant city of Pidra Blanca. It was quite similar to Uxmal in appearance, though not as large, and there was a much smaller anchorage. Unlike Uxmal, there was only the most rudimentary wall around the inner city as well, and nothing along the seaward side. It was an encouraging vista, however, and Holland knew they'd soon be "home." Uxmal *was* home now, Holland realized thoughtfully, and though he hadn't even been gone very long, he was glad to return, however briefly. He'd never really felt that way about a "place" before, only a ship, and he wondered what the difference was. He'd been a loyal American—still was—but even his Baltimore birthplace and numerous New England home ports through the years never stirred any loyalty or fondness in his heart. There were port cities he "liked" all over the world, but none where he felt he belonged. *Maybe that's all there is to it,* he mused. *For the first time since USS* Essex *was practically shot out from under me, "home's" a place I have a real stake in. A place doin' somethin' important an' needs me ta help.*

That evening, *Tiger* opened Uxmal bay, firing a salute that was exuberantly returned by the two little forts at its mouth, as well as the guns they'd emplaced in the wall around Uxmal itself. Slowly leading the other ships into the anchorage a short distance away from the bustling city docks, *Tiger* turned into the wind and dropped anchor as figures raced out along the yards to haul in her sails. One after another, her consorts did the same. Holland was surprised how crowded the bay felt, with more ships in it than he'd ever seen. Of course, a large number of prizes taken at Vera Cruz had been sent here for conversion, and that work was just now finishing on the last of them. *Brought 'em another,* Holland thought, smiling to himself. Few of the former were entirely ready for sea, but six rebuilt merchantmen like *Roble Fuerte* were anchored in the roads with their yards crossed as if waiting to sail with the tide.

"A lovely place, Captain Holland," Captain Jenks complimented. The Imperial sailor had returned aboard *Tiger*, crossing over from *Nemesis* as they neared their destination. He was dressed much the same as when they met, only in a finer coat with subtle, contrasting piping, and highly polished brown riding boots instead of stockings and shoes.

"It is," Holland agreed. "Oh, there's an unwholesome element such as you'll find in any port city, but smaller by far." He quirked an eyebrow. "Less . . . sophisticated too, an' not as bloodthirsty. Except for Dom spies an' operatives, o' course. As you likely know, they might be anywhere." Something seemed to occur to him. "I expect they'll take special notice o' Imperial sailors bein' here. Might even think it important enough ta risk detection ta get word out, an' we can snap 'em up," he mused. "Other than that, your lads'll want ta exercise ordinary caution. Drunk sailors alone *will* get knocked on the head an' robbed, but not likely killed. Even thieves have respect for those protectin' 'em here. One man ta watch is a . . . well, like a city councilman. Name's Tukli. Owns about a quarter o' the city's fishin' fleet an' would have it all if he could. Scrawny, sweaty, ugly little bugger, always turned out fancier than the *alcaldesa* herself. You'll know him when ye see him; dress a turd in all the lace an' brocade ye care to . . ." He chuckled and shrugged. "Still, he ain't really criminal nor evil, just greedy. He'll try an provoke ye on general principle. Always hasta be aggrieved." He rolled his eyes.

"I appreciate your candor and advice, Captain." Jenks smiled. "I shall continue to rely upon it, since I don't mean to leave your side until I'm better acquainted with the locals and their customs."

Lieutenant Semmes was nodding seriously. "A good idea, that. *I* don't even feel comfortable ashore by myself," he confessed. He looked at Holland. "You might require the lads going ashore on liberty to watch over the men from *Nemesis* until they learn their way around, as it were."

"My hope exactly," Jenks agreed.

Holland dipped his chin. "Make it so, Mr. Semmes."

Turning away, Semmes called loudly to the senior midshipman, "Lower the captain's gig and the longboat. The starboard watch liberty party will go ashore first, but every group or individual will take charge of an appropriate number of Imperial sailors from *Nemesis*. *They* will be responsible for our new friends' behavior and safety."

"Signal Captain Razine the same goes for him," Holland instructed Semmes. "I'd like all our lads ta mingle. Mr. Greg'll hold the, ah, former Doms aboard the prize at present. I don't want 'em feelin' like prisoners, but can't just turn 'em loose in the city. We'll start 'em out in smaller groups tomorrow, mixed with liberty parties that've taken the edge off their thirst, so ta speak."

"A sensible compromise, sir," Semmes said, and relayed the instructions to the signals midshipman.

"What about us?" Jenks asked.

Holland had begun scanning the dock with his spyglass. Quite a few people had gathered to watch and wave, as usual, but it wasn't exactly a crowd. Nor was there any sign of a formal reception. Just as well. Holland hated crowds, and all the times he'd been greeted by one he'd felt extremely self-conscious. He knew Lewis Cayce felt the same. Both of them were confident in their competence, and no man despises genuine praise for a difficult task well done, but neither craved exaltation for merely doing their duty. The near idolization the locals were capable of heaping on them at times made them profoundly uncomfortable—like frauds only posing as heroes. Holland finally saw a couple of coaches drawn by burros pulling up behind the dock, however, and was sure they'd been sent for him and his officers. A large boat with half its oarlocks empty was putting off from the dock even now.

"Belay launchin' the gig," he shouted, looking back at Captain Jenks. "We'll be goin' ashore directly."

Eric Holland watched Captain Stanley Jenks as the first coach carried them, Lieutenant Semmes, and Mr. Blakeslee from the dock where they landed all the way to Alcaldesa Periz's Grand Audience Hall. First they passed through the heavily reinforced north gate that was supposedly proof against the primitive Dom naval guns they'd encountered before. *I wonder how it'll stand against the 16pdrs their Pacific fleet ships have*, Holland grumped to himself. He wasn't worried much about the strengthened walls. They'd already been ridiculously thick before embrasures were opened for more of the mighty 36pdrs captured at the Battle of the Washboard, their huge muzzles now glowering menacingly out at the bay.

Jenks seemed suitably impressed. He was also apparently fascinated to see the bright-painted stone-and-mortar architecture of two-, even three-story structures lining the amazingly smooth cobbled streets in the city. Holland remembered when most of those buildings still had thatch roofs, but almost all now supported infinitely more durable and fire-resistant baked tile. Jenks appeared charmed by the tide of busy, colorfully dressed people bustling peacefully about in the inner city of Uxmal and genuinely taken aback by how confidently women strolled along alone, or commanded male employees or servants in imperious tones.

Holland himself frowned to see how many slaves were in evidence, recognizable by unadorned gray tunics, and more than when he'd last been here just a few weeks before. The cities of the Yucatán had always used slaves, mostly Holcano warriors captured by the Ocelomeh in battle, but they'd largely been employed on remote farms (more vulnerable to predators) or in various mines. Such a large number in the city was new, but then so was war to these people. Their men were in the army or working to supply it, and replacing their labor with those who made the army necessary probably made sense to them. *So long as they never get the notion the army's purpose is gatherin' slaves an' loot*, Holland thought with a touch of concern.

He didn't see that happening for a very long time, but remembered a conversation he once had with Lewis. Holland had seen every type of slavery the old world had going, and it *was* all over. Few countries were as divided about it as the United States had become, but he was so used to it, he hadn't thought much about it one way or the other. He disapproved of *racial* slavery because he'd been *around* so many races all his life. Any merchant ship's crew might've been made up of men from all over the world, and a man was a man, in his view, no matter his race. Enslaving captive warriors was something else. That sort of thing had been going on since time began, and he figured it was better to work a man than kill him.

But Holland learned early on that Lewis Cayce was as close to a radical abolitionist as the state of Tennessee was likely to produce and was also a student of history like most professional soldiers. He understood using captured enemies for labor—especially when the only alternative was to kill them—and even did it himself on his last campaign. It was senseless to use half his army to carry supplies to feed prisoners who, at first at least, would only try to kill them again if released. But Lewis was determined that the Allied cities, the fledgling "country" he was trying to give time to form, would never get used to widespread, casual slavery, and he invoked the economy of ancient Rome as his cautionary example. Rome, even during the Republic, had been almost totally dependent on slave labor to support its few "productive" citizens, and a shocking percentage of its population produced virtually nothing and sucked on the teat of a state largely financed by slaves and loot taken by conquest. Lewis believed all its people were ultimately enslaved to the corruption and whim of a state they had no stake in, no *pride* in, anymore. Holland was unusually well-read and self-educated for a "simple sailor," as he considered himself, and knew the fall of Rome was more complicated than that. Big things like that usually are. Of course, that was just it; it was more complicated than most cared to sift through, and Lewis's angle was one he hadn't considered before.

Watching Captain Jenks's reaction as they finally approached their destination, he caught himself rubbing the ever-present stubble on his chin, wishing he'd thought to shave before seeing Sira Periz. Almost oblivious to his appearance otherwise, he liked to look his best for her. The carriages came to a halt, and the drivers jumped down to open the door and help them all out. Rejoined by Capitan Razine, Lieutenant Greg, and two more of Jenks's officer/advisors Holland had finally gotten to know a little, the group was met by an escort of what looked like sharply turned-out regular infantry, but was in fact the *alcaldesa*'s personal guard.

"Never a welcome visitor," Jenks lamented dryly. "No cheering throngs, no music . . ."

"It's better this way, trust me," Holland told him, but Jenks was already viewing the high, stepped, former pagan pyramid now dedicated to "Jesu Cristo" and Father Orno's branch of Christianity, as well as the Grand Audience Hall.

"I've seen similar structures on the west coast of the Dominion, but they were places of death and misery, always radiating an aura of brooding malevolence. The difference here could not be more striking."

Holland knew what he meant. He'd seen other places like this as well, and though the great temple had certainly hosted its share of suffering in the distant past, it stood bright and clean, the stark white plaster smoothing the stone construction and gleaming gold under the setting sun. The Grand Audience Hall, a short distance across a lovely green grass plaza bounded by colorful, carefully coiffed exotic shrubs, was shaped entirely differently. It was a long rectangular structure built on an elevated mound with numerous entrances accessed by broad, evenly spaced stairways leading to a cavernous, well-lit interior. The roof seemed to be made of enormous stone slabs extending outward all around and supported by majestic columns perhaps thirty feet high. The whole thing had a strikingly classical appearance, and Holland was reminded more of the Parthenon in Athens than most other buildings he'd seen in this land.

"Good evening, gentlemen," greeted a surprisingly tall, very young Ux-malo soldier with officers' shoulder boards on his dark blue frock coat. He saluted. "I am Captain Orno, on the *alcaldesa*'s staff. You are all expected and very welcome. Will you please follow me?"

"Our pleasure, Captain," Holland said, self-consciously returning the salute and motioning the others along. Joining the young officer on the steps as they mounted them, he said, "Orno, huh? Any relation to the short, religious fellow off with the army who usually runs the joint over there?" He gestured at the temple.

"My father, sir," the young man replied with heavy irony as they stepped into the vast audience chamber itself. The floor was smooth, carefully fitted stone. Great wooden timbers supported the roof high above. The stone walls were covered with ornately carved and painted plaster, illuminated by braziers. The impressive space was empty, however, so Holland knew they were being taken to another, smaller chamber, for a more intimate reception. *More secure as well*, he thought with approval.

"I never would've guessed," he stated truthfully. "No offense, an' I consider your father a close friend, but the bugger's rather . . . shorter, an' don't look old enough ta have a grown son. An' in the army, as well."

"He is past thirty," the young Orno objected as if that explained everything. "God has blessed him. My mother and all their children survive. I'm the oldest of six brothers," the captain said. "Four sisters as well."

"Randy little goat takes bein' called 'Father' pretty literal, I guess. Your poor mother." Holland chuckled.

Leading the party to a heavy wooden door on the far left—northern and seaward—side of the building with two guards stationed outside, the captain paused before announcing them. "Father expected me to follow him into the priesthood, but I fear that my people have greater need of soldiers just now. I'm sure several of my brothers and sisters will follow in his footsteps." He grinned back at Holland. "And there may yet be more of them."

"Poor, poor woman," Holland murmured, tone still sympathetic as Captain Orno directed the guards to open the heavy door and allow them inside. Holland motioned Jenks to join him as they stepped through the wide opening into a still fairly large room dominated by a long, heavy wooden table surrounded by ordinary but well-padded chairs. Wooden benches were stacked along one wall, implying the room might sometimes be filled. There was no decorative plaster in here, and the exposed stonework and support timbers gave the place a distinctly rustic feel. Ceramic tankards and mugs were arranged on the table, and everything about the room seemed intended to foster a casual air and put visitors at ease. Holland wasn't surprised to note that Jenks's attention was immediately drawn to a huge, embroidered atlas on the far wall behind the table. Depicting the "known world," at least as it was known to Uxmalos, it represented that portion of the land from where they were in the Yucatán, almost all the way north around the Gulf of Mexico and west to the lower Californias. It was so cunningly executed that it looked more like a model, or sculpture, or God's own view looking down from the heavens.

The planned intimacy of the visit was made equally obvious by the identities, and small number, of those waiting to receive them. Other than Captain Orno, who accompanied the eight visitors inside, only eight other men and women rose to face them from behind the table. Holland immediately recognized most. There was Sira Periz, of course: the young, beautiful, almost elfin-tiny, and tragically widowed *alcaldesa* of Uxmal. Initially somewhat problematically insular, she'd grown tremendously in the last year. Leading what was undeniably the principal city in the alliance against the Doms, she'd become its beloved face to most. She and her city had given the most to support it in terms of blood and treasure, and Uxmal had more of its sons, both in sheer numbers and as a percentage of its population, in uniform than any other city. Only the Ocelomeh beat them in the latter— they were *all* in the army, in some capacity—but the marching camps the army made were closer to cities than the nomadic villages they ordinarily lived in. The only real changes Ocelomeh had to adapt to were the strict regimentation and discipline (not entirely alien after twenty years of rule by "King" Har-Kaaska) and the itchy, uncomfortable uniforms, of course.

Rising slowly beside Sira Periz and then towering over her was Colonel Ruberdeau De Russy. Wearing his immaculate dress uniform, complete with white breeches, vest, shoulder epaulets, and tails, his face was red and puffy under the enormous mustache and side whiskers he'd cultivated—more hair on his face than his head—and the brilliantly polished vest buttons seemed in considerable distress, doubtlessly secured around his widening middle under protest. Originally appointed to command the 3rd Pennsylvania Volunteer Infantry by that commonwealth's governor, he'd been unable to cope with the whipsaw events immediately after his force and the other Americans found themselves here. The terrifying battle against brutal Holcanos and feathery/furry, seemingly demonic Grik monsters they were almost immediately faced with had made that abundantly clear. He was a politician, not a soldier.

In truth, few soldiers could've kept control any better, but just enough of his junior officers held things together until Lewis Cayce (Holland and Anson too) organized another group of shipwrecked Americans, providentially joined by Warmaster Varaa-Choon and a large band of Ocelomeh, to relieve his trapped and beleaguered force. Realizing his talents lay elsewhere, De Russy put Lewis in military command and focused on diplomatic relations with their new friends. Currently, as the trusted manager of the Council of Alcaldes, he conceivably had more power than any of them, but used it only to mediate disputes and keep all the cities' representatives focused on prosecuting the war. At the moment, he wore a wide-eyed, choleric expression, but it vanished and turned almost angelic when he smiled.

De Russy's new wife, the former Angelique Mercure, stood on the other side of Sira Periz. Angelique was the French friend of Samantha Wilde, and it took her even longer to adjust to her new circumstances than De Russy. Once she had, however, she'd ensnared De Russy with her beauty and intellect and become as invaluable an advisor to Sira Periz as Samantha had been. Daughter of a moderately well-off merchant who nevertheless, like over 90 percent of the people who weren't bankers or fantastically wealthy, had been denied the right to vote by the July Monarchy in France, she'd become steeped in the snake pit of politics and yearned for a new republic. She often grew morose, wondering how her father and people fared in a France she'd never see again, but had thrown herself into helping the Allied cities become a republic. Just as Lewis Cayce wanted. Incidentally, along with Samantha, she'd practically revolutionized fashion on the peninsula as well.

Captain Holland admired the woman, but try as he might, he couldn't quite like her. She was very beautiful, and De Russy was . . . less so, to be charitable, and they made an unlikely pair. Perhaps she truly did love him, but it was hard not to suspect she'd hitched herself to him because of his position. Regardless of that, and whether he agreed with her goal or not, she'd become a little too much the predatory zealot for his taste, sometimes even agitating to unite the peninsula by force. That would never do, and the idea of potential fighting among the cities at the same time they were fighting the Doms didn't bear thinking about. Fortunately, there seemed to be little danger of De Russy and the *alcaldesa* adopting her approach.

Of the others present, Holland was acquainted with Alcalde Ortiz of Pidra Blanca, the nearest large city to Uxmal, and the long-suffering logisticians Finlay and Samarez. He knew the strange "powder monk" now in charge of Allied gunpowder production by sight, but didn't know his name. And he identified the elderly woman just beside Angelique as Concejala (councilwoman, essentially) Urita Xa, who owned a number of industrial concerns and was a staunch supporter of the cause. Unlike her *alcaldesa* and the young Frenchwoman beside her, she was dressed in the traditional long, colorful tunic belted around her waist. He didn't know why he wasn't surprised to see the ornate, long-bladed dagger on her belt.

He smiled at them all in turn, and Sira Periz swept around the table amid the noisy swishing of her very French dress and fondly embraced him as she would her father. Helplessly, he squeezed her back. Pulling away, Sira looked solemnly into his eyes and spoke in carefully enunciated English, "All of us were deeply concerned. Sailing beyond the known world to investigate this mysterious place we've been so worried about since its existence was first revealed was a dreadful risk." She smiled at Semmes, who blushed deep red, and the others she knew as well. She finally fixed Stanley Jenks with a harder, inquiring gaze.

"It seems your voyage was a success, however. You returned safe and even captured another lovely prize. I'm anxious to hear all about the dreaded Pass of Fire and the . . . unexpected acquaintance you made. I suppose this man commands the strange ship that accompanied you here under its own unknown flag?"

The Imperials snatched their hats off and bowed very deep. "Captain Stanley Jenks and Mr. Esah Blakeslee," Jenks humbly said, "subjects of His Majesty Cassius McDonald, Governor-Emperor of the Empire of the New Britain Isles. We owe Captain Holland and his squadron a debt we can never repay. He has seen fit to transfer that debt to you, and I and my officers, as well as my ship and crew, are entirely at your service."

Her smile regained all its previous warmth and she held her hand out to Jenks, who clasped it gently in both of his and gave it a chaste peck.

She hadn't been expecting that and almost jerked away with a frown. It quickly vanished, and she stepped slowly back around the table to resume her place.

"I *told* you not to do that," Holland hissed at Jenks. "They don't do that here. Besides, if somethin' crawled out o' that hedgerow growin' on your lip an' bit her, she'd prob'ly have you hanged." He'd spoken loud enough to be heard on purpose, to show he liked and trusted Jenks enough to joke with him. Everyone exploded in laughter, dissolving any tension there may have been. Sira was also amused and smiled as she introduced her companions behind the table. Holland remembered Concejala Urita Xa's name, but the powder monk's jumped in and out of his head like a frog. So did the names of Jenks's other two companions, for that matter. If it turned out he needed to remember them, he'd ask again. *One advantage o' bein' old*, he thought with an odd sense of triumph: *nobody expects you to remember everything anymore. I can focus on rememberin' things I actually give a damn about.*

"Please be seated, everyone," Sira said pleasantly. "There is boiled and cooled water, juice, some excellent *octli*, and even *pulque* if you'd prefer," she said the last with a hint of disapproval. "And please smoke if you wish." She herself took an elaborately carved, long-stemmed pipe from a wooden case on the table and put it to her lips. De Russy gallantly stood and fetched a burning taper from a socket on the wall. When Sira's pipe was drawing nicely, he lit a cigar and passed the taper to Holland and Semmes.

"I say, that smells vera' fine," Blakeslee exclaimed with wide eyes. "Our ancestors were fortunate enough tae ha' tobacco seed in their cargoes, but what we grow in the Islands is a wee bitter an' pungent in comparison."

"Ain't even *real* tobacco, I'm told," Holland said. "Might as well be. Tastes well enough, once yer used to it, an' it's just as stimulatin'—an' addictive."

"Have you no pipes at hand?" Sira Periz inquired politely.

"No, Your . . . ah . . ." Jenks looked stumped, clearly wondering how to address her.

"'*Alcaldesa*' is appropriate," Sira told him.

"Thank you, Alcaldesa. No, we follow the same practice as Captain Holland, and there's no smoking on our ship. The lads mostly chew flavored tobacco, as his do as well, though there are energizing nuts and even a variety of twig that's popular. We didn't think to fetch our pipes."

"Be good enough to send for pipes, Captain Orno." Sira looked apologetically around while the young man stood and went to the door. "You must pour refreshments for yourselves, I'm afraid." She glanced at Jenks. "No servants tonight, and very few others, as you see. Even before I knew to expect you, I anticipated discussing sensitive subjects this evening." She hesitated. "Forgive me when I say I do wish you'd not flown your flag as you arrived, however. Your empire is little more than a myth to us here, and I doubt anyone knows your flag." She nodded at Holland. "Most will likely assume it's the same as his at a glance, as I did at first. But *somehow*, a description of it will eventually reach someone who does know what it is, and they can only assume your people and ours are in contact. I don't know what effect that may have."

"Perhaps very little, Alcaldesa," Jenks said. "The passage you fear, that Captain Holland went to inspect, is . . . well, it *is* navigable, to an extent." He huffed. "*Nemesis* is surviving proof of that. On the other hand . . ." He paused to sniff curiously at one of the pitchers and poured a mug full of a syrupy, yellowish juice before taking a long gulp. "Good stuff, that," he said with a sigh, then proceeded to tell the same tale he'd related to Holland about his ship's ordeal in the pass. This audience was just as captivated as those aboard *Tiger* had been, especially when he went on to describe the Imperial navy's efforts against the Doms. More than an hour later, he finished with the assessment he'd given Holland: that even if a usefully large force escaped destruction by the Imperial navy, it couldn't survive a voyage through the Pass of Fire without obscene losses. Having seen Uxmal's defenses, he didn't think the enemy could bring sufficient strength by sea to threaten them here.

The room was thickly fogged with smoke now, and Sira sat back and sipped her own juice. "I am reassured," she said. "With Colonel Cayce's bold plan for a campaign directly at the heart of the Dominion, I confess I've had night terrors of that dreadful doorway behind us and what could happen if the enemy came in strength and fell upon us here. I know the possibility has preyed on Colonel Cayce's mind as well—one of the reasons he risks moving so quickly—but now he can be reassured as well." She stood, bowing her head first to Alcalde Ortiz, then De Russy and the others. "Thanks to many of you, I'm not only satisfied that the Allied cities are secure, but also with how the war is progressing in the northwest. I think it's high time the rest of us moved more boldly as well."

"What do you mean, my dear?" asked De Russy. He'd spoken little, mostly listening thus far, and his voice held a hint of surprised alarm. Clearly, the *alcaldesa* hadn't discussed any "bold" plan with him.

"Our main supply line to the army is too long. We need to shorten it, move the *source* of supplies forward to Vera Cruz," she replied, nodding respectfully at the powder monk and elderly Concejala Urita Xa. "War-making industries in general, but munitions manufacture in particular." She frowned. "Colonel Cayce's campaign is sure to be costly, and I want to take him more troops, while releasing many of those dedicated to support to join him in the fight. Well-meaning or not," her voice sounded dubious, "the people of Vera Cruz are not *our* people, with sons and husbands impossibly far from those they're fighting for. I want to move more civilian support forward, including as many of those loved ones as possible: dockworkers, teamsters, blacksmiths, wheelwrights, leatherworkers—healers, most important—and those who make the tools to fight with, of course. You all know better than I who should go." She paused. "And *I* must go forward as well."

"Surely not!" Alcalde Ortiz helplessly exclaimed. "We may not have established the 'union' Colonel Cayce craves, though most of the *alcaldes* are increasingly agreeable to it, but if all our cities have a single leader everyone respects and looks to, it is you."

"The notion is utterly ridiculous, my dear!" snorted De Russy, and Sira's eyes flared angrily. De Russy seemed oblivious. "Alcalde Ortiz is right. You may not yet be the president of the Yucatán, but yours is the lovely face of it!" He shook his head. "It's far too dangerous, and you cannot be spared."

"*Es-tu fou?*" Angelique scoffed, but her tone was concerned.

The anger faded from Sira Periz's face, and she smiled sadly. "It is not ridiculous, and I am *not* indispensable." She quirked an eye at Angelique. "I have no idea what you said, my friend." Turning to glare at Ortiz, she said, "And if I truly am who everyone looks to, all the more reason to go! Alcalde Truro of Itzincab accompanied Har-Kaaska and Colonel Reed down to Cayal. I can do no less. *All* our soldiers from every city must know that those who send them away to fight are near enough to see what they do for us. Our people are not used to war, yet they've fought magnificently and gone far beyond the boundaries of the world they knew." She shifted her glare to De Russy. "Not so different from *your* people, now. They fight for survival, new ideas they never imagined before, and most of all, one another! They fight for freedom from fear, not only for their families and themselves, but for their comrades. Even for strangers from other cities who share their cause, and now former enemies as well! This is *so* much bigger than it began, a mere convulsion to throw off a predator in hopes it would go away. Now our people hunt the hunter, to kill it in its lair. How can I leave them to do that alone?"

De Russy and Ortiz seemed to be looking around for support. They probably had it from Jenks and Blakeslee, but it wasn't their place to speak. Finlay seemed lost in thought, but Samarez was nodding slightly. So was the powder monk. Concejala Urita Xa's eyes were bright with satisfaction. Truth be told, regardless of how protective he felt of Sira Periz, even Holland could see the value in her presence at Vera Cruz, helping organize the support she'd described. And there was no doubt it would inspire the troops. Besides, Holland remained . . . uncomfortable about Don Hurac's motives. He firmly believed the man wanted reform in the Dominion, but wasn't quite sure to what real extent. The Blood Cardinal was obviously more open to the influence of beautiful, strong-willed women than was the norm in the Dominion. He wouldn't do hardly anything without Zyan nearby. An alliance between her and Sira Periz might at the least discover what his long-term ambitions might be.

"You'll travel in *Tiger*, no doubt?" was all Holland had to say.

"What?" De Russy exclaimed, a look of betrayal on his face. "I thought you, at least, would stand against this impetuous impulse!"

Holland shook his head. "I don't think it is one. Figure she's right, in fact."

De Russy gaped around him. "But . . ." He faltered.

Angelique stood and went to him. "It will be well, *mon cheri*. Sira knows what she does. Concejala Urita Xa can assume her executive *fonctions*, and you, *mon cheri*, will command the defense of the city, as before. *Tout ira bien*."

De Russy closed his mouth and steepled his hands before him. As his young wife said, he'd been in effective command of the troops still in Uxmal. He'd even found he rather enjoyed the administrative side of all that, and had a talent for it. He had a very low opinion of his combat command capabilities, however. He was no coward, but he'd frozen to uselessness during his very first action and recklessly overcompensated in the second. He was perfectly happy with his rear echelon role. Based on Holland's report, at least it didn't look like he'd have to find out how he'd perform in battle a third time.

"Yes. Well. I suppose we'll have to make do," he finally conceded. "Take good care of her, Captain Holland, and I charge you specifically to bring her back safely and soon, and ensure she gets no *closer* to the fighting than Vera Cruz!"

"None o' that's really up to me, Colonel, but I'll do what I can."

Captain Jenks cleared his throat. "Excuse me, please. I do have one little question." He looked around at the various faces now turned to him. "Having offered the service of my ship and crew to your cause—clearly one and the same as the empire's whether it's aware of it or not—I assume you accept that service?"

Sira Periz stood again and nodded. "Gladly, sir, and with deep appreciation."

"I'm happy to hear it. That said, please don't mistake the second part of my question as greed . . ."

Holland laughed. "He wants ta make sure we'll take care o' him an' his people," he told the room at large.

"Well . . . yes," Jenks agreed. "*Nemesis* is a private ship, after all, financed and maintained by the proceeds from her prizes. Not to put too fine a point on it, that's how her crew is paid as well: percentages of those prizes. I suppose that sums it up. To be blunt, how will I maintain my ship and pay my people?"

Sira nodded at Holland, who grinned. "That's up to you. If you want ta stay independent, carry a 'letter o' marque,' I'm sure that can be arranged. I'll warn ye, though, pickin's'll be slim on this side o' the pass." He waved vaguely in the direction of the bay. "We've already snapped up most of the ships ta be had."

"It sounds as though you'd recommend an alternative," Jenks observed.

"Aye. Take a commission like any other vessel in our little fleet. Your ship'll be maintained an' supplied at Allied ports, an' your crew'll be paid the same as a soldier in our army. Not a lot," Holland conceded, "but it's steady. An' there *will* be prize money for ships ye take."

"That may be best, under the circumstances," Jenks murmured thoughtfully, glancing at Blakeslee.

"Most likely," Holland agreed.

Jenks snorted, looking rather fondly back at the grizzled old sailor. "Judging by the expression on your ancient face—is that a grimace or a smile? Internal discomfort?—I assume there is at least one other disadvantage to that arrangement aside from financial, and surrendering our freedom of action, of course."

"Aye," Holland chuckled. "Ye'll hafta take orders from me."

CHAPTER 8

"Cold," Leonor said lowly, cupping her hands in front of her face and breathing into them as Sparky huffed and clopped up the ever-rising, rocky road winding into the mountains west of Vera Cruz. A faint fog gusted between pink fingers. Urging Arete upward and onward beside her (the big chestnut mare from another world seemed just as reluctant to move that morning as Leonor's smaller, striped, local animal), Lewis looked at the young woman in surprise. It was the first time he remembered ever hearing her complain of discomfort. Not that he blamed her. The temperature had dropped amazingly, the higher they climbed, and it was suddenly colder—especially at night—than Lewis remembered experiencing in a great long while. The first time ever on this world. That was discomforting more than the horses and Leonor's hands.

The army's time at Vera Cruz had been well spent, and aside from the heavy rains associated with the occasional storm sweeping in from the gulf, the late fall weather at Vera Cruz had been idyllic. The sky was perfectly sharp and clear without any haze to speak of, and days were pleasantly warm, generally in the midseventies. Nights had just enough nip to make a wool blanket welcome toward dawn. For the common people, mostly freemen and slaves, still working to support their protectors and strengthen defenses (without daily fear and near constant abuse from owners or masters), or training with new or established regiments in the army, life might've been described as "sublime." And those regiments and divisions were still forming and growing into disciplined, professional forces unmatched in motivation by any their instructors had seen on the world they came from. Freedom and survival, perhaps even justice for past suffering, are firm foundations for a cause.

Then, almost simultaneously, a wealth of intelligence Lewis had long-awaited practically tumbled in. *Tiger*, *Nemesis*, and *Roble Fuerte* arrived with holds full of ordnance and dedicated support personnel, news of the Pass of Fire, and an emboldened Alcaldesa Sira Periz, anxious for Lewis to commence his push toward the Great Valley of Mexico. Perhaps even more significant, a messenger dragon came flapping down right in the middle of the city, scaring hell out of everyone who'd never seen such a creature and bearing word from Don Hurac's Blood Cardinal friend in far Ixtapa. According to him, the Dom general Gomez had marched from Acapulco a fortnight before. It was time to move.

The new 5th Division had absorbed most of the city's defenders, so even if it was ready to go, the defenders had to be replaced. Even more had stepped forward in Vera Cruz to join replacements coming in from Frontera and even Oaxaca (the *alcalde* there was panicking, and his Blood Priests had escalated sacrifices to appease their vile God enough to send people fleeing to the "enemy"), and they had to be trained and equipped. Fifth Division would have to join them later. But that left Reed's 1st, Har-Kaaska's 2nd, Itzam's 3rd, and Agon's 4th Divisions ready in all respects. Concerned that spies would get ahead of them, Lewis called them all to readiness in the wee hours of the morning after everything came to a head and marched with the dawn.

That was four days before, and the going had been slow. The steep slopes up from the coast were hard on everybody, no matter how well-conditioned, but especially those who'd spent their whole lives at little more than sea level on flat terrain. And as they'd been told but probably hadn't fully grasped until now, it was *cold* in the mountains. The native troops from the Yucatán had it worst, not ever really having felt cold before. The thicker wool uniforms retained by a few of the American soldiers and the newly issued greatcoats were suddenly much appreciated. Not a single soul voluntarily dropped out, however. Some were inevitably injured by falls or sprains, or even the opportunistic wildlife at night (no large monsters had pestered the huge serpent slithering through their territory), and those caught rides in the ambulance carts until they healed, or were sent back to Vera Cruz in empty grain wagons if their injuries were more serious. There was practically no straggling whatsoever.

Looking at Leonor's cold, red hands, Lewis felt somewhat torn. Their relationship had slowly grown to the point that, had they been alone, he wouldn't have hesitated to take her hands in his to warm them—and she actually would've let him. That would've inevitably led to a tight embrace, and even gentle, tentative kisses like youngsters might've shared. The thought of that new aspect of their relationship both thrilled and frustrated Lewis because he and his very best friend—for that's what Leonor had become— were both distinctly aware of how quickly and easily those innocent kisses could escalate dramatically into something else. Both feared that would irrevocably change the friendship they treasured, especially its unusual professional characteristics. And, of course, they weren't alone.

Gazing ahead and then turning to look behind, Lewis felt an admittedly anxious pride at the sight that greeted him. It had only been full daylight a very short time, but all his divisions, plus their artillery and prodigious baggage train, were already out of camp and filling the Actopan Road four abreast for as far as he could see. From near the middle of the column at the junction of 1st and 2nd Divisions, just ahead of Don Hurac's huge, bizarre, but no doubt comfortable coach drawn by a pair of armabueys that could barely match the pace of the infantry, the ribbon of sky-blue uniforms looked like a river flowing up and down through the rocky, brush- and timber-covered slopes. "I can see about fifteen thousand men from here," Lewis said as if to himself, "and there are almost that many again beyond my view, counting Agon's division and *not* counting the Fifth." He glanced back over at Leonor. "A far cry from the seven hundred–odd fellows we started with after that terrible fight on the beach. My God, I'm beginning to think we might just pull this off."

"Of course we will!" interjected Varaa-Choon, pushing her own horse forward to join them. Colonel Reed, Colonel "King" Har-Kaaska, and most of the senior officers from 1st and 2nd Divisions were also riding with them, as was Agon's adjutant, Major Arevalo. Agon's locally augmented 4th Division, in its somewhat mottled yellow-green uniforms, had pride of place at the head of the army, for the honor and practical purposes. Lewis couldn't even see the 4th at present, but it would come back into view later as the miles-long serpent switchbacked ever upward.

The only troops even deeper in Dom territory were Major Anson's scouts and his typically fast-moving brigade of Rangers, dragoons, lancers, and riflemen—and Barca's battery of 6pdrs.

Apparently aghast that she'd "whined" in front of Lewis, Leonor abruptly lowered her hands and crossed her arms over her chest, hands now under her arms and the open greatcoat she wore. Sparky looked nothing like Arete, or her father's bay gelding, Colonel Fannin, but she and nearly all Allied cities' horses were just as controllable with knees as reins. Agon had told them only the animals privately owned and ridden by relatively wealthy Dom lancers could match them in that.

"This is my plan as much as yours," Varaa elaborated, blinking something like supreme self-confidence, "and with both our minds in accord, it cannot fail!" She grinned, tail whipping behind her emphatically.

"It *is* cold, though," Har-Kaaska groused. "I don't like it at all." He patted his strange mount, much bigger than a horse, which looked like an opium addict's dream mix of a duck, a lizard, perhaps an ostrich, and God knew what else. The creatures—or others like them—were ubiquitous, roaming on marshy plains in large herds, but were apparently wildly difficult to domesticate. "Feensa doesn't like it either," he said consolingly.

Colonel Reed looked at his counterpart and huffed, nose and ears glowing like bright beacons even against his always-reddish face. "What are you complaining about? You and Varaa, and Consul Koaar, are all covered with fur. You could run naked in greater comfort than the rest of us find in our heavy coats."

"Grow more fur," Varaa suggested, *kakking* a Mi-Anakka chuckle. "You already have some. Why not encourage it to thicken?" Her blue eyes widened with mischievous delight. "Perhaps you might nourish it! Manure works well for crops. Have you tried that?"

"If that's all it takes, I suppose you've been wallowing in it for years," Major Beck cracked. Lewis chuckled, encouraged by the banter. Beck was a fine commander of the 1st US but had always been reserved toward Varaa. She peered at him now with narrowed eyes. "It seems to have worked fairly well for you." Beck was also one of the hairiest human beings Lewis ever knew, his beard fairly exploding overnight.

Beck hesitated, face reddening, but suddenly burst out laughing. "Yes indeed! I use the produce of my own horse and smear it all over each night—after a lengthy hot bath, of course!" He turned a serious gaze on the rest of his companions. "I heartily recommend it. A strong attractant for the ladies and good for the skin as well."

Even some of the nearby troops burst into laughter, and some wag shouted out, "What sorta ladies've *you* been keepin' company, Major?" There was more laughter, and the humor spread quickly in both directions as the exchange was repeated.

"I fear you'll have a new sobriquet by the end of the day," Colonel Reed confided with a grin. Beck only shrugged. "Most of the lads already think I'm a shit . . . I beg your pardon, Lieutenant Anson," he added for Leonor's benefit.

She waved it away. "I've heard that an' worse every day of my life."

"Not from me, and I apologize," Beck persisted.

Leonor rolled her eyes.

There was a disturbance atop the massive coach behind them as four men clambered up what could only be described as a companionway onto the safety-railed roof. Leonor rolled her eyes again, at the ridiculous conveyance. Don Hurac's ten-by-eighteen-foot "headquarters" was more properly a land ship than a coach, supported by eight solid wheels with wide, iron tires, and an intricate leather spring suspension designed to ease the ride.

"Good morning to you all!" Don Hurac exclaimed with a broad smile, joining his guards and peering down from the vehicle's upper deck. Zyan was beside him, helping support him, and so—to Lewis's mixed gratitude and annoyance—were Samantha Wilde, Reverend Harkin, and Father Orno. Lewis had wanted Don Hurac along, hoping he'd persuade enemy civilians to cooperate, but he'd never dreamed such an abominable transport existed. The thing was like dragging a steam locomotive's freight car around, and without the team of huge armabueys, he imagined it would take forty horses to pull it. He wouldn't object as long as it didn't slow them, but the first time it got stuck or broke down, he fully intended to have it torched. Don Hurac could make do with a tent after that, like everyone else.

The passengers were another matter. He'd agreed to Samantha's presence—in place of Alcaldesa Periz, who'd *wanted* to come—because Don

Hurac would go nowhere without Zyan. She and the Englishwoman had established a strong acquaintance, if not friendship. But unknown to anyone until just a few days before they left, Samantha had also "gone crazy as a possum in a shithouse"—in Major Anson's still shocked, confidential, and blushing words—and "shamelessly seduced" his "helpless" self. She'd immediately insisted they be married at once and dragged Anson, Leonor, Lewis, Dr. Newlin, and Varaa in front of Reverend Harkin for a late-night wedding. Lewis had been best man for the miserable-looking groom, Leonor was maid of honor, and Dr. Newlin gave the triumphant bride away. Lewis now warily regarded the bearded clergyman, still put off by how pleased he'd seemed with himself at the time, not to mention prepared for the sudden crisis, and darkly suspected he'd actually conspired with Samantha to pull the caper off.

Leonor was certain of it, and though somewhat annoyed as well, was more understanding of Samantha's motives. The "arrangement" Samantha and her father had reached was that they'd be married after the war, but Anson made no secret of his conviction they'd all be lucky to survive that long. The odds were stacked high against them. He still seemed to almost enjoy the war, but had become increasingly fatalistic about his fate. Leonor told Lewis she thought Samantha was desperate to give her father something besides the war to live for. To care about.

Lewis could see that, but also secretly wondered if Leonor was just a little *too* understanding, and if the same scheme ever occurred to her. He rejected the notion. She had to know if she tried something like that with him, it would probably work just as well—but her days of fighting beside him would be over.

"Would anyone like some breakfast?" Don Hurac inquired brightly. "Warm food would do well to cut this abominable chill!" Even covered with at least two of his new, white robes, he theatrically suppressed a shiver.

"You *cooked* in that thing?" Major Beck asked, eyes wide.

"Not me, of course"—Don Hurac chuckled—"nor even the ladies," he added with an unconsciously condescending smile, "but my servant easily managed. The interior is quite stable. I only regret it is so crowded. The guards sleep outside, but there is still a premium on private space. There were two more such transports in the city. I honestly can't imagine why, since they were built before my time and are somewhat aged, if well-preserved. All could have been refurbished for travel in a few meager days. I do wish you'd given more warning before we marched, Colonel Cayce!"

Warning for whom? Lewis had to think. He knew Leonor and Varaa—at least—wondered the same. He shook his head. "If the enemy has managed to learn anything about our plans, they'll still think—as you did—we meant to remain on the defensive for the most part. Hopefully, they won't fortify Actopan and every village between here and there." He frowned. "Or worse, murder everyone they don't think they can defend. They won't expect us to come for them. Word'll eventually get out, ideally after we liberate Puebla. If it hasn't by then, we'll make sure it does. That should bring Gomez to us, on ground of our choosing." He arched a brow. "I don't think the usurper and other enemy leaders will want our army marching up to the gates of their 'holy city' for everyone to see a powerful force opposing their twisted rule."

Don Hurac touched a finger to his chin whiskers.

"But how will you keep word from racing ahead? That concerns me most of all."

"That part is up to Major Anson," Lewis said with a look at Leonor. "He's pretty good at that sort of thing."

"Jesus!" Anson shouted, hauling back on Colonel Fannin's reins.

"*¿Que diablos es eso?*" cried Ranger Captain Sal Hernandez, riding beside him, as both drew Paterson Colts in the face of—well, they didn't know what. Rangers and Kisin's Holcanos were generally scouting the rough flanks of the column, picking their way through the heavy brush and timber on the splayed, scree-strewn, up-and-down fingers of the slope on both sides of the road, rising high on the left and dropping off precipitously to the right. Holcanos, both human and Grik, went on foot where horses couldn't. Regular couriers brought reports. But word from Captain Hayne's dragoon scouts inspecting the road ahead was long overdue. Hayne had proposed taking a squad forward himself to make sure his men hadn't run into trouble, and Anson and Sal went with him. Within a couple of miles, it was suddenly clear there'd been trouble indeed. At least some—most, probably—of Hayne's nine-man scout troop and most of their horses lay scattered on the road. It just wasn't immediately apparent what sort of trouble they'd found.

Blue-coated corpses, now shredded and stained nearly black with blood, and equally mangled stripey horse carcasses were being noisily and savagely torn apart by twenty or more large, four-legged creatures the size of big wolves with much the same disposition. Covered in long, light-colored feathery fur that bristled at the withers, they would've even *looked* like wolves if not for their long, straight, feather-plumed tails and blood-soaked, lizard-like heads with oversize greenish eyes. Most frightening of all, their long, narrow jaws were lined with many more teeth than the most ferocious wolf ever dreamed of.

Anson's first impulse—that their Grik "allies" had turned on them—lingered only an instant. Despite a vague resemblance and similar size, Grik went on two legs and these things were plainly quadrupeds. Nor were they immature Grik "garaaches" for the same reason. Whatever they were, they became aware of Anson's party of horsemen in the same instant he stopped Colonel Fannin, and they attacked so quickly their reaction must've been instinctive. In the blink of an eye, almost every one of the pack was galloping toward the riders, long, greyhound strides propelled by wicked claws digging into the packed caliche road.

"Form line abreast an' fire at will!" Hayne shouted, voice rushed. His well-trained dragoons were already flowing forward and out to the sides, bringing up weapons. Anson and Sal fired first, quickly emptying the five-shot cylinders of their first revolvers as they were joined by Hayne's single-shot pistol and a few Hall carbines. That initial fusillade was followed by a small, ragged volley, and the air filled with smoke, yellow flashes, and high-pitched squeals and shrieks. Anson was hard-pressed to compare those shrieks to anything in his experience. The closest was probably the Grik when he fought them before: anguished screeches like a woman in agony somehow mixed with the piercing cry of a hawk. This was like that, but different. He shook his head and drew his second revolver. The things were on them now.

"Hold, damn ye!" Hayne roared at his men, who didn't even have time to make breechloaders ready again. Claws raked at nervously dancing local horses, and a panicking voice yelled out, "But sir!" The animals probably knew what the attacking creatures were, even if they'd never seen them either. They shared the same name as many other beasts in this world: "things to flee."

"Ye don't think they'll catch ye if ye run? Only start eatin' ye from yer cowardly ass forward, they will! Sabers!" Hayne bellowed, already drawing his own with a well-oiled metallic *sheenk!* and slashing down to the side. Colonel Fannin was the only horse there that was no more afraid of these foul things than he'd ever been of coyotes, even wolves. His master's revolver boomed near his head, and he reared up and kicked an attacker, midleap, pulping its head. Stomping down, he killed another, and another, all while Anson kept firing. Sal's striped horse was no bolder than the others, but the Tejano Ranger was a master trainer. At least the animal stayed tremblingly still or maneuvered as told, as Sal methodically shot beast after beast in the head. Nobody was better with a pistol than Sal.

The line had collapsed; there was no use in it now, and men needed room to swing their long blades. There were screams as two men were hauled off their horses and their companions did their best to save them. Abruptly, this became simpler. About half the murderous creatures unexpectedly broke off and fled, almost as if by command, leaving ten or more dead and wounded behind. One was still trying to drag a screaming, wounded dragoon along, the man tangling its legs and slowing it. Anson blew it down with the Walker Colt he'd just drawn. It fell without a twitch, and he circled Colonel Fannin, firing a shot into each of the things that still moved.

As quick as that, it was over. Thundering hooves came up from behind and a half company of dragoons swept past. "Touch nothin' ahead, Mr. Joffrion," Anson warned the gentlemanly, extremely formal young officer leading them. Captain Hans Joffrion seemed surprised by the order, but gravely saluted and rode on. A pair of healers, both young women in uniform, wearing the half-moon gorgets that identified them for what they were, had rushed to the sound of combat. Quickly dismounting, they checked the three wounded men (one had taken a nasty slash on the leg, but remained in the saddle) and the two who'd been pulled down but miraculously still lived. The one Anson saved was an almost boyish-looking Itzincabo, and Anson's educated eye grimly told him the kid would almost certainly lose the arm the creature had ahold of.

"Major Anson!" Joffrion called from among the carnage they'd seen in the road.

"A moment," Anson replied. "Will you be all right, Mr. Hayne?" he asked the dragoon captain, eyeing the shredded sleeve over the man's saber arm.

"Aye," Hayne said, flexing the arm and then pulling a rag from inside one of his pommel holsters to wipe furry blood off his long blade. "Form up, you silly buggers," he shouted at his men. "Quit blockin' the damned road, gawpin' at the wildlife. Ain't you never seen one o' . . . whatever the hell them things are?"

"No sir," chorused two troopers, but one nodded. Hayne peered intently at the youngster. He wasn't Ocelomeh, but had geometric tattoos extending out on his hands from under the sleeves of his jacket like one of the small village, woodland tribes. "Well, what are they, then?" Hayne demanded.

"Locals call 'em 'lobos de la muerte,' or just 'lobos,'" said Sal Hernandez. He had the barrel off of one of his revolvers and was reloading the cylinder. A difficult task on horseback, but he'd perfected it. Loose parts—like the barrel—were put in a pouch at his side so he wouldn't drop them. He shrugged. "Wolves. You probably even seen 'em yourself now an' then, skirtin' our scouts outa Vera Cruz." He looked at Anson. "I never saw 'em in the woods on the Yucatán, though, an' maybe you didn't spot any down on the plain. I figure there's too much competition from bigger, hungrier critters down outa these chilly mountains."

Anson frowned and spurred Colonel Fannin toward Joffrion and several dismounted dragoons, but still listened as Sal followed behind. "I hear these things are hard on folks travelin' this road in small groups, even mounted. An' unarmed civilians on foot by theirselves wouldn't have a prayer." Sal nodded ahead. "But ta kill those men fast enough they never got off a shot . . . we'd'a heard it. An' then ta come for us like they did? Don't make sense."

"No," Anson agreed, halting Colonel Fannin and stepping down, handing his reins to a trooper. Hayne and Sal did the same. "Who knows why they came at us? Maybe we spooked 'em"—he frowned—"or they thought we'd plunder their meal. But they didn't kill these men."

Even Sal's eyes went wide. "No?"

"No," Joffrion confirmed bitterly, handing over one of the heavy, obsidian-tipped arrows used by native hunters—including their own Holcanos and Ocelomeh. Several more were still stuck in the ground and in dead horses. Gnawed stumps protruded from some of the ravaged troopers. "They were ambushed," he elaborated, "and only six of the nine who should be here are present."

"Some got away?" Hayne speculated hopefully.

Joffrion shook his head. "I fear not," he simply said, gesturing up into the trees on the left side of the road. "There is considerable ground disturbance leading up that way, as well as a moderate blood trail. I sent a squad to investigate—but not far."

More hooves thundered up behind them, and they turned to see a half dozen Rangers led by the bearded giant, Captain Bandy "Boogerbear" Beeryman. "There was shootin'," he said matter-of-factly, gazing around at the six half-eaten men and dozen or so dead predators. "Scary-lookin' boogers," he commented, "but don't strike me likely ta take on armed, mounted men."

"They didn't, at first," Anson said.

Boogerbear had already seen the arrows and the trail. "You sent men in there?" he demanded. Joffrion nodded. "Call 'em back. Me an' my fellas'll have a look." Boogerbear meant no offense, and none was taken. Joffrion didn't even hesitate before turning to a bugler still on his horse. "Sound the recall," he ordered. Tracking was a job for the Rangers, and not only was there rarely a trail so old or disturbed that Ocelomeh Rangers couldn't stay on it, but Boogerbear was renowned even among them as having an almost supernatural understanding of it. Besides, it was virtually impossible for him to be surprised, and even if he was, there simply wasn't anyone better able to calmly, lethally sort it out.

The dragoons that Joffrion had sent up the trail emerged fairly quickly, obviously glad to be back in the open. Boogerbear always carried a finely made double-barrel shotgun across his lap in the saddle. Hoisting it up on his shoulder by the sling, he and his six companions (including Sal, who joined them without a word) dismounted, checked their weapons, and quietly disappeared in the darkness of the thick timber. Anson hauled himself back up on Colonel Fannin and turned to Hayne with a grim expression, eyes flicking from one body to the next. "See to our boys. Form a burial detail an' plant 'em careful. With all these damn wolf-lizards around . . ." He shook his head. "You know what to do. But clear the road quick. Get help if you need it. The rest of the column'll be up soon, an' we have to push on."

"What about Mr. Beeryman?" Joffrion asked.

"He'll catch up an' tell us what he found."

"What if he runs into trouble?" Joffrion persisted.

"He'll handle it," Anson replied with certainty, then waved up the steep slope. "Besides, there's other Rangers castin' about out there, not even countin' Kisin's Holcanos an' creepin' Griks. They'll have heard the shootin' too.

Some'll come. Prob'ly more likely to catch the bastards that killed the dragoons than Boogerbear. The ambush could'a happened more than an hour before we got here, an' who knows how far the sneaky shits are by now."

BOOGERBEAR AND SAL led their men swiftly up the densely wooded slope. Neither man was as naturally stealthy as the Ocelomeh Rangers accompanying them, but years of fighting Comanches had honed their skills sharp. The country they'd done it in couldn't be more different, at present, but there were advantages and disadvantages inherent in every type of terrain. They might not have as much experience moving through heavy forest as their Indio companions (though they'd caught up considerably over the last year or so), but the ground presented less of a problem. Clacky, clattery, rocky slopes were nothing new to them. Even the huge Boogerbear had learned to cross them with an almost ghostly lack of noise. And the near-complete absence of painful and entangling ground cover like cactus, nettles, and thorny brush made everything else a comparative cinch. That was important because Boogerbear was in a hurry.

He didn't care how far the column proceeded without them. They'd catch up quick enough, and the possibility of getting lost with a clear sky above the trees—day or night—never even occurred to him. But not only did he need to catch the ambushers before they reported what they knew, it was possible the three men they'd taken still lived. They wouldn't for long. Besides, whoever jumped them and mercilessly killed their comrades had to die. From Boogerbear's very cut-and-dried, black-and-white perspective, it was as simple as that.

One other thing was eating him, and that was his equally sharply defined sense of responsibility. With the exception of the flying artillery (and including even some of them, at times), Major Anson now directly or indirectly commanded all Allied mounted forces. But the Rangers (including those weird Holcanos) were basically Boogerbear's now. All riders, even Mounted Rifles and lancers, might be called on for scouting, and dragoons were better suited for scouting in force, but Boogerbear's Rangers and now Holcanos were best suited for and strictly charged with making sure the enemy never outscouted *them*. He took the ambush personally.

"More blood," Sal whispered, pointing down and around. Boogerbear gave the thicker spatter-spray a glance and nodded. There'd been blood since they'd started. Even Joffrion's dragoons hadn't obliterated that during their own brief search. It proved that someone, probably a captive, was badly injured. Given the rate of blood loss, how much time had passed since the ambush, and that they'd already hounded the trail more than a mile up and onto a kind of long shelf on the way to a higher mountain pass above, they'd probably find whoever was spilling it soon.

They did. All three captives were found, in fact, each hanging upside down from tree limbs above, facing back the way they'd been brought. Well, they weren't actually *facing* anywhere, since they'd all been decapitated and their guts torn out and draped in the low branches around them. Boogerbear's attention had been drawn by movement as they approached the place where the forest briefly parted and some of those wolf-lizard things were already snuffling around. Beyond was a tumbling, babbling stream, which might've covered quieter noises. The watchful Rangers spread out and carefully drew closer, watching how the scavengers reacted. They paid no heed. The Rangers were downwind, and their quarry wasn't to either side, at least not near enough to harm them, and the scavengers showed no concern over anything in the vicinity.

Boogerbear almost casually gestured to three of his Ocelomeh Rangers. All had bows in their hands, musketoons slung over their backs. With acknowledging nods, the ones he designated raised their bows, arrows nocked, and let their missiles fly. Two arrows tore through the chest of one creature, and it dropped, kicking, to the ground. The other gave a high-pitched squawk, thrashed across the little stream, and expired just on the other side. Boogerbear held up a hand, watching and listening a moment more, long dark beard jutting out as he almost seemed to sniff the air. Finally, he rose and gestured the others forward, and he and Sal went to examine the dead dragoons while the other Rangers remained on watch, weapons ready.

"The bunch we're after must be Blood Priests or initiates," Boogerbear grimly appraised. "Inspired by 'em, anyway. Least they cut our fellas' heads off afore they gutted 'em. Thank God fer small mercies," he added with bitter irony. "Must know we're still comin', though, or they'd'a made a proper job o' tormentin' the poor bastards." That was abundantly obvious since they'd heard no screaming, and they would have.

Sal grimly nodded and Boogerbear took a long breath. "Well, still gotta catch 'em, an' there's no time ta bury these fellas." He frowned at the closest dead scavenger. "Might hoist 'em up a little higher in the trees, I guess."

"No use," Sal sadly pointed out. "The lizardbirds'll get 'em anyway." He gravely regarded the dangling corpses. *"Lo siento, mis camaradas."*

"Yeah. Let's move," Boogerbear decided. Suddenly, he raised a hand and cocked his head to the side when they heard what could only be the dull report of a distant shot filter to them through the trees. The direction was indistinct, until there was another. Boogerbear pointed with certainty. "That way, maybe half a mile. We'll take it fast, then slow as m'lasses."

With the occasional echoing shot to guide them, they ultimately found the enemy with relative ease. Still approaching with great care in case the enemy was deliberately luring them in, they eventually saw a flash and heard a loud boom, followed by the *thwok!* of a musket ball hitting wood just a short distance ahead. Down low and creeping still closer, they finally distinguished five men ahead, barely thirty yards distant. All were facing away, clearly confronted by another threat, and strung out under the cover of a massive fallen tree. Two more were lying dead, sprawled out on the ground. At least a couple had muskets, and they were down, reloading, but all were armed with bows and dressed in knee-length brown tunics belted around their waists. Feet were encased in soft, knee-high moccasin boots much like some of Boogerbear's Ocelomeh Rangers and all the Holcanos still wore, but there was no possibility these might be allies. Different color or not, the tunics were the same cut as Blood Priest initiates'.

Then Sal got a glimpse of those pinning them down. "Holcanos," he hissed beside Boogerbear, pointing as shapes flitted swiftly and silently from behind one tree to another. "I think there's at least one o' them lizard hombres also."

"Grik?" Boogerbear asked.

"Si," Sal said, pointing in another direction.

Boogerbear grunted. "That loco bastard Kisin might be good fer somethin' after all. Let's get this sorted out." Silently signaling his Rangers to kill all the enemies below except the one in the center who seemed to be directing the others, he made no other signals or commands. Five Ocelomeh Rangers merely readied their bows, and four of them suddenly rose from the crouch they'd assumed and launched arrows at whichever man was directly across from them, all striking true. Two were literally nailed to the tree, screaming in terror and agony. One dropped, gurgling and kicking and clutching at his throat where an arrow had exited as blood sprayed out around his fingers. The fourth man staggered and shrieked, but tried to turn and raise his musket. The fifth Ranger sent one of the big, monster-killing arrows straight through his chest.

That left the center man, armed with a musket, who rolled to the side and tried to bring his weapon up. Boogerbear stood, Paterson in hand, and shot him in the crook of his right arm, blowing out the elbow. The man screamed and dropped his weapon, then dove down and tried to crawl through a small gap under the dead tree.

"No, you don't, señor," Sal called and shot him in the ass with one of his own Patersons, likely breaking the right hip joint. The man shrieked even more horribly but pulled a knife from his belt and tried to bring it up, presumably to cut his own throat. Sal had already recocked his revolver and now shot the Dom through the hand. Blood and bone fragments exploded, and the knife whirled away.

"Go drag him out. Careful, though. Might still bite," Boogerbear cautioned his Rangers, then called louder, "You fellas out there! Holcanos! Cap'n Beeryman here. C'mon in. We got the bastards."

The Rangers half carried the moaning Dom over and dropped him in front of Boogerbear and Sal. Meanwhile, a mixed squad of six Holcanos and two of General Soor's Grik warriors filtered over, still wary of their surroundings. Boogerbear was surprised to see the big, savage-looking form of Kisin himself and wondered how he managed on foot in the mountains. Anson had given him a very serious compound leg fracture when they first met, ramming Kisin's horse with Colonel Fannin and crushing Kisin's leg in between. There was still a terrible scar that the Holcano warrior seemed inordinately proud of, but at worst, he had a slight limp.

"You stole our fight!" Kisin accused darkly.

"Don't worry. I'll find you a better one soon. Guaranteed," Boogerbear retorted, then looked back down at the Dom. Now he could see that the tunic had been dyed, even with a large jagged yellow cross already sewn on. It was murky brown now too. After a moment, he remembered where he'd seen that particular size and style of cross device before.

"I'll be durned. Well, well," Boogerbear said, crouching down to look into the man's sweat-sheened face and agony-glazed eyes. "You're one o' Tranquilo's reaper monks, ain't you? Ain't seen one o' you bastards since the mornin' after a sneak attack on Uxmal an' the American camp, right after we wound up here." He looked at Sal. "You remember that big, dead turd that stirred all them Holcano slaves up an' killed a buncha civilians? Nearly killed Colonel Cayce hisself."

"I do," Sal replied, then grinned wickedly. "I also remember he was disgracefully disabled by Varaa-Choon an' Señorita Leonor—two *females*—before Colonel Cayce denied him any of the sick grace he sought through pain by hacking him apart with his saber." He shook his head in mock pity. "Such a coward too. He died squealing like a pig in a puddle of his own piss."

"That's a lie!" the Dom seethed through clenched teeth. He was right too, but he'd never know.

"Sad but true, I'm afraid," Sal assured him. "Still, I suppose that one who believes as he did—as you do—might find grace even in the suffering of ignominy, and I thought it was cruel to deprive him of the opportunity to . . . enjoy it more, as it were."

Boogerbear looked at his friend and rolled his eyes, but Sal gave a very slight but urgent shake of the head.

"Yes . . ." The wounded Dom seemed to reflect, eyes clenched in pain.

"Compared to him, however, you are bearing up quite well," Sal complimented. "Your wounds must be very painful."

"They are . . . more than I could ask for," the Dom hissed, tears streaking his face. The possible double meaning earned a snort from Kisin, and Sal sent him a scolding glance as well.

"You must be proud," Sal said, then hesitated before beginning again. "As I understand it, your order values truthfulness among its devotees above all things, not even begrudging the passage of information to enemies."

"We keep secrets, of course," the Dom gasped, "but why should we lie about things you already know about or cannot change?"

"Why indeed? A noble philosophy, certainly," Sal commended. "Let us make a bargain: if you promise to truthfully answer a few insignificant questions, I give you my word you'll go to your afterlife *festooned* with all the grace you could possibly desire."

"I'll tell you what I can," the Dom conceded, voice growing faint due to shock from his wounds, perhaps even blood loss—the arm in particular was gushing. A major artery had clearly been severed and threatened to overcome him. "It hurts a great deal. I may not need much more. . . ."

"Nonsense!" Kisin suddenly interjected with a leer. "I've known several of your Blood Priests, and they always insisted that one can never have too much grace!"

"This is a buncha shit," Boogerbear growled impatiently. "Let's just kill 'im an' get back to work."

Sal irritably held up a hand and shushed his friend. "Do we have an agreement, young man? Tell me your story," he invited, voice suddenly very gentle and understanding. "This will all be over soon, and you'll be in your paradise."

Pain and blood loss left the increasingly groggy Blood Priest amazingly susceptible to a friendly, sympathetic-sounding voice as he faded, and it didn't take long to learn quite a bit they didn't already know, after all. Finally finishing the man with his *navaja*, Sal stood and gave Boogerbear a vindicated glare as he wiped and folded the blade into the grip before dropping the long, curved object in his pocket. "*Not* a 'buncha shit,' *cabrone*," he almost gloated.

"I reckon not," Boogerbear equably agreed.

"If you were not always in such a rush to just kill everyone . . ." Sal started out hotly, but Boogerbear forestalled the impending rant by turning to Kisin. "Good work," he begrudged, "gettin' in front o' the bastards like you did. Prob'ly oughta return to your sector, now, in case somebody else tries to sneak through. I don't want any more o' that, hear?" Turning to Sal and his Rangers, Boogerbear continued, "The rest of us need ta get back to Major Anson with the news Sal sweet-talked out o' that devil there." He nudged the corpse with his boot. "I was leanin' toward just lettin' them Grik fellas eat 'im ta death, but I guess you were right this time, amigo."

CHAPTER 9

I t is warming up," newly promoted Corporal Apo Tuin commented gratefully, rubbing his hands together in front of him. The little Uxmalo was riding on the limber chest just behind Sergeant Hanny Cox, as usual, and Hanny was on the closest horse in the left-hand traces. The limber and heavy 6pdr gun hitched behind it groaned and creaked and clattered, exploding small rocks and pebbles with iron-shod wheels. The road-jostled words Apo spoke were the first from anyone in a while, and Hanny was shaken out of the saddlesore and somewhat fatigue-numbed reverie he'd been floating in for a while, raising his eyes from the brown-striped horse mane in front of him to gaze all around in a kind of confused wonder.

Apo was right. Bright, caressing rays fell across them as the morning sun crested silver-lined mountain peaks behind, further illuminating what was, somewhat oddly, Hanny thought, some of the most beautiful scenery he'd ever beheld. High mountains reared all around them, strangely green all the way to the snow line, and deep valleys cut by rivers fed by dramatic, tumbling waterfalls plunged deep into the mist alongside the rough, rocky road Major Anson's main mounted column briskly traveled. Probably the most fascinating thing to Hanny was how green everything remained despite how cold it got. Especially at night. And nothing showed signs of turning. The trees in his native Pennsylvania would be a riot of reds, yellows, and oranges by this time of year, leaves already fluttering through the air in gusty winds and heaping up in gullies.

"Feels bloody wonderful, it does," grumbled the hulking form of Daniel Hahessy on the front, right trace horse. "But the marrow in me bones is still froze. I always heard Mexico was nothin' but heat, rocks, sand, an' sarpents, not such a cold, mountainous land."

"Different Mexico," Hanny reminded, "though Captain Barca says this isn't so different from what he's read this region should be like. There may still be desert elsewhere, I suppose."

"I think it is pretty," Apo said.

"Aye," agreed "Preacher Mac" McDonough, riding up forward, to the left of Hahessy. "I'm minded o' the Highlands, in Scotland o' course," he added in a nostalgic tone, "though this is a wee bit rockier. More trees as well, I ken."

"Not much *besides* trees, though," observed Billy Randall, the Number Two gun's Number Seven man. He was crammed atop the limber chest with Apo and Kini Hau, the Uxmalo Number Five. "Hardly anybody lives along here. Seen what? Four, maybe five rock-an'-mud huts surrounded by pointy palisades all morning? No livestock to speak of either. Like they've all run off. But how would they know to—and where have they gone?"

Hanny waved around at the steep slopes. "Not many places here to build houses," he pointed out. "As for the rest?" He shrugged. Captain Barca always made a point of taking at least one of his six "gun captains"—what he called chiefs of the piece—and one of his section chief lieutenants to officer's call each morning before they resumed their trek. That morning he'd taken Hanny and Lieutenant Petty (newly promoted to section chief himself), and they'd come away with the latest information. Hanny had already passed what he heard to the other gun captains, and Lieutenant Petty had likewise informed the other section chiefs. Hanny didn't spill what he knew to his crew all at once since that was all they'd have to talk about that day.

"Word is, Rangers caught the ambushers who killed those dragoons yesterday. Took a prisoner too. Seems that Dom General Gomez marched east even earlier than anyone thought, and may have already reached the enemy capital in the Valley of Mexico."

"Well . . . that's largely what Colonel Cayce was waiting for, isn't it? What he was hoping for?" Apo asked.

Hanny nodded. "Obviously, we can't fight a battle on this mountain road, but the colonel does want his fight in the open, not in a city."

"Is there a chance of that?" Kini asked. "I mean, meeting the enemy on this scary road?"

"Them poor dragoons met 'em yesterd'y, didn't they?" Preacher Mac put in.

"That's what nobody knows: whether advance elements of Gomez's army have already pushed out as far as places like Actopan—the first real city we're supposed to come across—and fortified it." Hanny shrugged again. "There seems to be a little confusion over whether the ambushers were scouts for Gomez, or that Blood Priest Tranquilo raised more of his reaper monks on his way through an' set 'em on us. Might even be other Blood Priests are sending them out." He pursed his lips. "Either way, *somebody's* got scouts out creeping around, so the enemy could be anywhere, and we need to keep our eyes open and stay ready."

"I don't know about the rest of this new battery we're in, but *we* are ready," Apo declared.

Hahessy snorted. "We're no more prepared ta fight a battle on this goat trail than we are ta fly ta the moon."

"You know what I mean," Apo snapped back.

Hahessy sighed. "Aye, an' yer right. I think the rest o' the lads in Barca's battery are just as ready as us, fer all that. Good lads, most of 'em. Good cannoneers."

Hanny blinked with surprise to hear praise of any sort, for anyone, escape the big man's lips. Everyone else must've been just as surprised, because no one spoke for a moment. That was when Hanny heard a commotion behind them and stood in his saddle to peer back along the column. Barca's battery was spread out along the column by sections, and only Gun Number One was in view directly to the rear at the moment. Past that were more dragoons. A company of Lara's lancers was cantering up, however, its leaders slowing to edge carefully past the section's caisson, forge wagon, etc., where the road briefly widened enough to do so. Capitan Lara himself trotted up alongside the Number Two gun while he waited for his men to catch up.

"Good morning, sir," Hanny said, offering a salute.

"Good morning, Sergeant Cox." Lara returned the salute. "Gentlemen," he added, nodding at the rest.

Hanny hesitated before blurting out, "Excuse me, sir, but you've been along this way before, haven't you? On our old world, I mean. Can you give us an idea what to expect? Is the country like this all the way?"

Lara looked at him strangely for a moment before replying. "Yes, I traveled this way before. On the 'old world,' as you say." It was his turn to hesitate. "I wish I could answer your question, but this is all as new to me as it is you." He gestured around. "The road follows roughly the same path, going generally in the same direction, but it was never so narrow or frightening. And these mountains"—he sighed—"are *much* steeper, sharper, even taller than I remember. I don't know why." He pursed his lips. "It is like that, sometimes; memories of places or people do change over time, depending on one's perspective. I think it's most often the case that things—or people—revisited after extended absence are . . . smaller and less impressive than they're remembered to be. Disappointment may result," he added with a touch of sadness before recovering himself. "But that's not the case here. First, it wasn't so very long ago that I made my way through this region of the world we left, so my memory shouldn't be much distorted. Second, for some reason, things here are *much* more impressive, even severe, than I recall. Perhaps actually . . . younger, in some undefinable way." He blinked several times as if absorbing that notion himself. "Whatever makes the shorelines, people, and creatures that inhabit this world so different has clearly been at work on land as well." He shrugged somewhat vaguely. "In any event, I'm of little use as a 'tour guide,' I'm afraid, and can't even make useful suggestions to Major Anson.

"There were maps of the route in Vera Cruz, of course, and some of the locals have hauled freight along it, but most of them were more suited to employment with the supply train than with Major Anson's Rangers." Lara arched an eyebrow. "It seems they know the way—and its inherent dangers—well enough that they're unwilling to leave the road."

"Those wolf-lizards," Apo guessed.

"And other things," Lara agreed. "So it appears the only 'reliable'"—he loaded the word with sarcasm—"guides we have for the road from Vera Cruz to Actopan are the Blood Cardinal Don Hurac's guards and escorts, who remain with him back in Colonel Cayce's main column. Don Hurac himself could provide only the most rudimentary account since he always tended to sleep in his coach for as much of the journey as he could."

"What about the new commander of the First Vera Cruz Regiment? I heard he's done some traveling," Hanny said.

"Major Don Roderigo"—Lara nodded, tone implying he had a good opinion of the man—"went to Actopan many years ago, but his more recent travels were south to Mazupiapan and beyond. Even if he had more recent experience with the Actopan Road, he couldn't be spared from his regiment. I won't say the First Vera Cruz is shaky; they're every bit as devoted to the cause as the First Uxmal was at the Battle of the Washboard. Perhaps even more so in some ways. But they've seen no action as a unit, and the added sense that they're rebels persists. One never knows about rebels," he added cryptically.

"Then Colonel Agon's whole division is made up of rebels," said Captain Barca, falling back to join them, riding on the other side of the limber. "I hadn't gotten that impression from them."

Lara acknowledged his fellow officer with a nod. "Nor I," he agreed. "If anything, they seem to think of the *enemy* as rebels. Longtime rebels against God. On the other hand, despite Don Hurac's very public conversion and the fact the new troops from Vera Cruz believe him to be the legitimate ruler of the Dominion, they haven't all been as thoroughly brought to *our* God's understanding. I think some still feel like rebels against their Church. That could be dangerous." He brooded. After a long pause, he took a deep breath. "Ultimately, therefore, we must all rely equally on the dragoons to investigate the path ahead, and the Rangers to guard our flanks." He said the last with a tone of almost disbelieving irony.

"Well . . . thanks anyway, Captain," Hanny said, suddenly feeling a little awkward. Not that he'd so boldly initiated conversation with someone else's officer. Theirs wasn't that kind of army and never had been. Private soldiers were discouraged from pestering passing officers on a whim, but NCOs were more or less expected to, to learn what they could for everyone else. Some grumbled that was bad for discipline, but others—and Hanny was one of these—believed it was good for morale. Even so, it was rare for accosted officers to actually reply, usually deflecting with an off-color comment when they did. Capitan Lara's considered response had revealed a great deal about a number of things he worried about, perhaps too much.

With another polite nod at Captain Barca and the men in his battery, Lara spurred his horse forward, quickly followed by the lancers who'd been stacking up behind him.

"A very troubled fellow, I'm afraid," Barca said softly, clearly more troubled now himself.

"Think we're fer the chop, do ye?" Hahessy asked loudly.

Barca blinked and looked at the big man. "No. Nor, do I think, does Mr.

Lara." He waved around. "It's these tight confines. None of us is best suited to fight like this . . ."

"Aye," growled Preacher Mac with feeling.

". . . and if an enemy force *did* manage to slip past Mr. Beeryman's Rangers," Barca persisted, "things could go very badly for us all." He gestured irritably at Preacher Mac. "A sentiment clearly foremost in many of our minds. I do *not* expect that to happen," he continued forcefully. "Leading and screening movements of this sort, even in unfamiliar territory, is what Captain Beeryman and, indeed, Major Anson have been doing for a long, long time. I'm not saying we can't be attacked, but I don't think it can happen without warning. Certainly not by a force large enough to do us real harm."

"What about them dragoons, then? Them which got killed?" Hahessy grumbled.

"They were out front, on their own. Not in the middle of the column like us. And their killers were dealt with," Barca added. He started shaking his head, looking toward the front where Lara had gone. "No, Mr. Lara is oppressed by this narrow, nerve-racking serpent of a road. Perhaps also by the fact he *has* been along here—on another world—before. The differences will be more unsettling to him than the strange newness is to us." An ironic smile appeared on Barca's face. "Don't forget, while his lancers might perform many of the same tasks as dragoons, they don't have rapid-fire carbines and are best used all together instead of in small groups." He gestured upward. "And they're wholly unsuited for the work the Rangers are doing. On top of everything else, he may be uneasy that his security rests entirely with that branch of our army named for and led by a former mortal enemy of his. I'm confident he'll feel better when we emerge into the open once more. So will I."

Barca was right. The road wound a little farther around the flank of a mountain before coming to a broad, flat, clearing. Like a mountain meadow it was still bounded by trees, but there were streams of fresh, cold water, and they could see for miles. It was quite a stunning, picturesque sight, complete with horned quadrupedal herbivores, much like those they'd often encountered, grazing all around. Generally smaller and shaggier, these specimens were just as ill-tempered as their larger relations. Major Anson had watched with concern at first when Coryon Burton's dragoons tried to shoo the things off from their proximity to the camp and they didn't want to move. Hanny's section arrived in time to watch the effort turn somewhat comical when a platoon of Captain Felix Meder's mounted riflemen started arguing with the dragoons.

The riflemen often shot one or two large beasts for the men when the opportunity arose, and that was usually quite an adventure itself. With men racing in to fire their M1817 rifles and then galloping off to reload numerous times, the process could take a while. But it was also common practice to do it far enough from camp that the pickets wouldn't be troubled by scavengers all night. The thing here was, the riflemen thought it would be easier to butcher the edible portions off a couple of these smaller animals and then drag the stripped carcasses still encasing the offal away by the head than to haul the meat in from a distance. The dragoons disagreed—it wasn't their job either way—and preferred to do what they'd always done. Anson was watching with a frown, probably considering putting a stop to the growing dispute, but it hadn't come to blows, and the abortive efforts of the dragoons to safely shift the stubborn beasts, barely evading charging horns time and again, was providing considerable stress-relieving entertainment.

It was like some bizarre, impromptu rodeo, with men cheering the antics of the dragoons; the sarcastic, well-reasoned, often obscene cracks by riflemen; and even the belligerently agile efforts of the beasts to gore their tormenters or stomp them flat. Ultimately, both the riflemen and dragoons got their way, in a sense. Annoyed by the dragoons and egged on by hooting spectators, the riflemen finally rode up and opened fire, beginning the lengthy process of killing one of the creatures. A shot through the eye and into the brain was quickest, but next to impossible to manage on one of these things—whatever they were—with their tiny eyes and impenetrable bony skulls. Spine shots were surest, but also difficult to achieve even on these smaller animals (still larger than any bull), since the fast and accurate but relatively small balls fired by .54 caliber rifles rarely penetrated far enough through tough hair, hide, and dense meat and bone from the side to hit the spine. Shots from the front were deflected by the bony frill the creatures wore. The tactic of distracting the "dangerous end" of the animal while riders swooped in to fire directly into the spine in front of the hip had been devised. The roaring, near-helpless monster could be dispatched at leisure, then.

The fusillade of shots didn't do it, but the bone-chilling squeals of the first paralyzed animal finally stampeded the rest—with incensed, vengeful dragoons whooping after them. The second beast was only killed a great deal farther from camp than would normally be the case. Anson got the last laugh, ordering Captain Burton to provide a sufficient security detail from his dragoons (the ones most gleeful about inconveniencing the riflemen) to protect the distant party retrieving the meat.

In any event, Lara seemed almost manically cheerful, laughing at the dragoons and riflemen as his lancers and the rest of Burton's dragoons began tending their horses and building a marching camp while Barca arranged his battery by sections around it, even while the baggage train and rear guard arrived. The sun had long fallen behind the surrounding mountains, bringing the first sharp chill of the mountain night, but it still wasn't full dark before the camp was settled in, squads of men roasting fresh meat on fires. That's when Boogerbear's Ranger company came filing in at last, looking forward to the tents already erected for them. As usual, Kisin's Holcanos would sleep outside the camp. Not only did they prefer it, but their extended perimeter of smaller camps away from the main one provided another layer of warning and defense.

"Good evening, Captain Beeryman," greeted Capitan Ramon Lara as the tired Rangers turned their sore and exhausted animals over to another company, billeted with the lancers, who'd stayed with the column that day. They'd feed, water, and curry the horses, checking their feet and repairing or replacing shoes. The animals would then spend the following day ambling along with the rest of the column. Not even Boogerbear's powerful, oversize local horse, Dodger, could endure day after day of what the Rangers were putting them through, and they'd draw new ones in the morning. Lara's cheerful tone also stood in contrast to his earlier funk.

"Howdy, Ramon. Sal in yet?"

Lara nodded. "He and his company came in while we were making camp. I understand they had it particularly hard today. Downslope" was all he needed to add by way of explanation. "He and Capitan Barca are already in the command tent with Major Anson. Care to join me? I was just on my way there."

"Sure," Boogerbear replied, pulling his saddle off Dodger's back. "Check that left rear extra careful," he told the Ranger who was about to tend his horse. "Damn copper nails an' shoes," he said to Lara. "Better traction in the rocks, but the shoes bend an' nails stretch. Heads wear off 'em fast too." He shrugged. "Better'n nothin'." One thing the Allied cities of the Yucatán were woefully short of was iron. Large stocks of it had been captured in Vera Cruz, but horseshoes still had to be formed into basic shapes. Sergeant O'Roddy and others couldn't spend all their time at the forge wagon making the things from scratch. Boogerbear heaved his saddle up over the tongue of a grain cart and he and Lara, joined as they walked by Captain Meder and Captain Burton—still chuckling over the earlier display their men put on—passed the pair of guards Lara had set in front of Anson's tent.

Anson didn't like having guards, but no one else really cared how he felt about that. They wouldn't risk losing him to some crazed Dom infiltrator. Pulling the tent flap aside, the party stepped into the large wall tent and were immediately assailed by the smell of horse, sweaty wool and leather, dirty socks, and hot chocolate. Sal Hernandez was actually sitting on Anson's cot with Captain Barca and one of his Uxmalo section chiefs. Anson was in a camp chair behind a folding table, and his orderly unfolded three more of the uncomfortable chairs for the new arrivals. Big as the tent was in comparison to others, it was now quite cramped. Several candle lanterns hung from hooks dangling down from the center support, and another flickered on the table, but it was still gloomy inside.

"Have a seat, fellas," Anson told them, leaning back with a steaming tin cup in both hands, resting it on his lap. Body heat and the lanterns had warmed the inside of the tent, and Anson had removed his hat and jacket and sat in his shirtsleeves, vest buttons undone, revolver belt and braces hanging from the rearmost center tent pole. His hair was plastered to his head, and his graying beard had assumed a wedge shape. No one doubted they looked just as disheveled.

"Smoke if you like, an' there's wine," Anson said. "That sweet, sticky stuff from Vera Cruz. Can't recommend it. No pulque, o' course." Colonel Cayce had forbidden the men that stronger spirit on the march, and it was implied that if the men couldn't have any, officers shouldn't either. "Hot chocolate's good, though. Plenty sweet too."

"I'll have some chocolate," Boogerbear said, accepting one of Anson's offered cigars. No one was surprised. The big man loved the sweet stuff. He might've been willing to kill a hundred men for a single cup of coffee, but the chocolate would do. As for the cigars, Anson might've actually "invented" them on this world, and they were catching on. He didn't like pipes.

When all the men had cups of steaming chocolate and their cigars were drawing nicely, further deepening the foggy gloom in the tent but helping mask other unpleasant odors, Anson leaned forward. "Run into anything interestin' today?" he asked Boogerbear.

The big Ranger waved his cigar. "More o' the same. Dom scouts. Killed 'em with bows," he added simply. "Them the boogers didn't already get. Found some o' them too. What was left." He frowned. "Seen Kisin a couple times today, higher up above us where the horses can't go. Seems ta be doin' his job, but a messenger came down an' said some o' Kisin's injuns got jumped. Lost a couple to them brown-coated Doms. They're gettin' better," he warned, "like Dom Rangers, er somethin'. Kisin's lizardy pals bush-whacked 'em back though, an' killed half a dozen." He grunted. "Didn't eat 'em, neither." There'd been some concern that, unsupervised, their Holcano allies would resume their old habits, but nobody had ever expected—or even asked—his Grik allies to refrain from eating the men they killed. That was a surprise.

"I have to say the same," Sal agreed, examining his smoldering cigar, opinion of it unreadable. "We too saw some of Kisin's warriors. They actu-ally brought us a prisoner to question."

Anson's eyes widened in surprise.

Sal nodded at Boogerbear. "Another Blood Priest in a brown tunic. Be-fore we . . . granted his fervent desire to go to paradise, he basically con-firmed what we learned from the first one: General Gomez marched for the Great Valley long before we were aware and has sent tendrils out at least as far as Actopan. I cannot say what they know of us, but Boogerbear's right. *Some* of the enemy scouts have improved, and I don't believe we've stopped every one. We have to assume there's an enemy force of *some* size at Acto-pan, and they'll be waiting for us when we arrive."

"It's no longer necessary to 'assume,'" Burton said, tone turning sour. "My dragoons scouting down the road toward the city have seen them." Anson looked unsurprised, so clearly Burton already reported this. That was confirmed a moment later when Anson handed the young dragoon a sheet of something more like vellum than the rough paper they'd been us-ing. A map had been started on the bleached white surface, carefully trans-posed from an existing one, but now with added details. "As we expected, the enemy knows they can't defend the cities themselves without time to significantly alter the protective walls around them. Ironically, the larger the city and more impressive and durable the wall, the more difficult that is. They were built to deter large predators and lumbering herbivores, merely tall and very thick stone-and-mortar obstacles they can't smash down or climb. No thought was ever given to making them defensible against human enemies." He glanced at Barca. "Artillery in particular. They don't have embrasures for artillery of their own, or even ramparts for defenders to stand on. You all remember how long it took to essentially rebuild the wall around Uxmal? Well, it's the same thing here. They could do it, and make the cities extremely tough nuts to crack, but that would take a lot of time."

"They can't just pour a garrison in the place an' close it up either," Anson agreed. "Again, our artillery would eventually force a breach." He looked back at Burton, who nodded.

"That's about the size of it. And that means if the enemy wants to fight, to drive us off—preferably far enough from the city that civilians there never see us—they have to come out and meet us." He held up the map and pointed. "That's what they're getting ready for, here. The terrain's still pretty open at this point, but there are heights overlooking the road, which kind of squirms up through a rocky pass to the flat where the city of Actopan stands. Best my men could tell, the Doms have about three thousand regular infantry, 'yellows,' digging in on top of the heights, and have a couple of batteries going in on these two hills, here and here." He pointed. "Not a bad position actually, and they're going to have a pretty good view of the approaches."

"How far?" Barca asked quietly. "We've been moving quickly. When will we reach this place?"

"Tomorrow," Anson said. "Which leaves the question: do we hit 'em ourselves or wait for Colonel Cayce an' the rest of the army to come up? We're about even with the Doms in terms of numbers, but they don't have any horse aside from some of their scouts and couriers, and we don't have any infantry. On the other hand, our dragoons an' lancers—riflemen too," he added with a look at Meder, "can all fight as infantry. Their foot soldiers can't conjure up horses out of the blue, so we'll have the edge in mobility." He looked at Barca again. "They're emplacing *full* Dom batteries, four guns apiece, so that's eight guns to your six."

"We still have the advantage," Barca said confidently. "Our men and weapons are better, and theirs will be static. We can move around as well."

Anson nodded. "My thoughts exactly." He took a deep breath. "But my original question still stands. Take 'em down ourselves or wait?"

"The lads are itching for a fight," Meder said. That might not be literally true, especially for some of his veteran riflemen who'd been through the

Battle of Gran Lago, but even they genuinely wanted to get on with it. "And the whole reason behind our advance column is to clear the way of small obstacles for the rest of the army. Colonel Cayce's whole strategy depends on a rapid campaign, after all."

Most of those present were nodding. "Seems like the Doms got the same idea," Boogerbear rumbled evenly. "I wonder why Don Hurac's pal waited to tell him Gomez was on the move? Maybe he didn't get the word for a while—or maybe he's sittin' on the fence. Anyway, what we do boils down to whether this turns out to be one o' them 'small obstacles,' I guess. Gotta see the ground an' how the enemy's usin' it. What we can do about it."

Anson nodded his agreement. "I'm inclined to lean toward Mr. Meder's assessment. If we get bogged down by every little bump along the way, why are we even here? But it's my responsibility. My decision. I'll make up my mind when I see the ground."

CHAPTER 10

Not a bad position at all," Captain Felix Meder grumped, looking up at the Dom works across the road at the top of a rough, zig-zag slope about a mile and a half ahead. Yellow-and-black-clad infantry positions were marked in the center by garish red flags with jagged gold crosses emblazoned upon them, as were the artillery emplacements atop timbered rises on either side. Fallen trees had crashed down the incline in front of them, no doubt cut by engineers to clear fields of fire. Barca was actually sketching the scene with a piece of charcoal, legs crossed in front of him on the saddle providing support for a sheet of rough paper on a board.

"Colorful enough," Burton agreed, patting the neck of his dancing horse. "And equally obvious where they are." The midmorning sun was shattering the biting cold of the dawn and glaring brightly down on the contrasting colors Anson and his officers had advanced to view, yellows, reds, and golds standing out sharply against the various greens around and beyond the enemy. The head of their own column remained out of view, the road behind them veering around a monolithic outcropping of rock.

"Not that obvious," Anson denied. "Sure, they'll have pickets out on the flanks. Them Blood Priest reaper monks if nothin' else."

"Maybe, maybe not," Boogerbear said enigmatically. "Kisin don't think so. Says they pulled all their scouts back last night an' we ain't run across any this mornin'." Aside from Kisin, only one company of Rangers had gone scouting that day due simply to the fact that they didn't have far to look for the enemy. Some would keep watch on their flanks, of course, while others relentlessly probed forward, but the rest, under Boogerbear, stayed with Anson.

"Is that so?" Anson asked. "Where's Kisin now?"

Boogerbear pointed left, at the enemy right flank. "Where else? Pokin' around up there, best he can, tryin' to find a way around 'em. Sal rode out to do the same along the river to our right, which we been followin' all the way here. Says we're close to the head of it now an' might be able to cross." The river itself was swift and sometimes spread fairly wide across its rocky bed but rarely too deep to ford. Negotiating the steep, rocky slope down to it in the first place had been the problem all along. And there'd been no reason aside from reconnaissance to cross it until now.

A white cloud blossomed on the distant heights to the right of the road and a geyser of rocky soil erupted upward where a roundshot struck a couple of hundred yards short. It bounced again, much closer, before cracking through trees and rocks to the rear. A heavy boom echoed down the valley behind them.

"Well, they see us," Anson growled.

"A most discourteous greeting," Lara said. "Should we advance and deploy, Major Anson?"

Anson shook his head. "Not yet. Gettin' less impulsive in my old age, I guess. Less inclined ta just charge right at 'em. I want to hear what Sal—an' even Kisin, God help me—have ta say."

Lara seemed vaguely disappointed. It was no secret that he fairly yearned to assemble all seven hundred of his lancers and charge the Doms, smashing them under his men's lances and hooves. He might even get his chance at some point, but up the long, rough slope ahead, in clear view of the enemy, this probably wasn't it. Another gun thundered, the shot bounding up much closer.

"They've improved," Barca observed.

"Agon said they might," Anson responded. "The closer to their major cities we get, the more practiced and professional the local Dom troops'll get, but the less experience they'll have with combat. On the other hand, Gomez's troops *will* have some experience with frontier fightin' an' suppressin' rebels. Agon even allowed they'd probably be better than his troops were, at first. C'mon," he said, pulling Colonel Fannin's head around, "let's get back outa sight before they plunk one o' them balls in the middle of us, an' us not even knowin' what we're gonna do yet."

Back around the outcropping at the head of the column, that decision didn't take long. First, a mounted messenger came from Kisin, describing where he'd first seen defenses on the enemy right—fortified auxiliaries like they'd been hunting for days, pushed out just a couple hundred yards. Sal rode up in person to tell them he'd found a nice ford over the river, along with a rough track that curved around up another hill overlooking the one the Doms had a battery on. The word "hill" was relative, of course, these actually being the tops of mountains they'd seen from a great distance, but the peaks were now only a few hundred feet above them and the escarpment beyond. Sal said he'd seen no enemy presence at all and didn't think they cared what went on across the river. "They prob'ly don't know the land away from the roads much better than us," he reasoned, "an' can't imagine we'd explore it better'n them." He shrugged. "All our past experience supports that. Dom armies use roads ta get where they're goin'. It's scary off in the woods, an' *ever'body* sticks to the roads. Stands to reason they'll expect us to do the same."

"Can I get my guns across that ford and up the track you discovered?" Barca asked him.

Sal swept his great mustache to the sides in speculation. "Might be tough, but I don't see why not. I figured you'd want to try, an' left fellas to secure the track an' make whatever improvements they can."

Anson was nodding, a predatory smile growing on his face. "That settles it, then. I'm sure some of you noticed one of the terrain features that'd make a charge across the field straight at the Doms a pretty ugly proposition. . . ."

Lara squinted as if peering into his memory. "Yes. That ridge, or upthrust—whatever it is—just short of the enemy works. Like a wall itself, about as high as a man's waist, that extends clear across the enemy's front. It would force a terrible, costly pause and make it impossible to drive a charge home."

"That's it," Anson confirmed. "It'd make good cover, though, too, don't you think?" Watching his officers stare in confusion, Anson grinned even wider. "Here's what we're gonna do . . ."

"HEAVE, DAMN YOU!" Lieutenant Petty gasped gruffly, joining the men of the section under his command in heaving Gun Number Two up the steep, rocky grade. The effort to emplace a pair of guns on the hill across the river overlooking the Dom battery on the right had started out easy enough, bailing off the main road onto a surprisingly gentle slope down to the river. Even the river crossing itself wasn't terribly difficult for the artillerymen, though the six-up teams of horses pulling the guns and limbers had it tough, thrashing through the swift, ice-cold water across jagged, slimy rocks. It was probably a miracle that none were crippled. The men clinging to the limbers had the ride of their lives, their spines and insides painfully jolted, but the men on the horses hardly got wet. Once on the other side and up out of the riverbed was when things turned bad for everyone.

A platoon of Rangers had remained to clear and secure the trail and guide the artillerymen and platoon of riflemen supporting them to the top of the hill. It quickly became apparent, however, that a path deemed suitable for outstanding horsemen and unburdened animals was virtually impossible for teams lashed in traces pulling a heavy load. Men jumped off limbers to heave and pull, hobnailed shoes and boots skidding on flat, crumbling rocks that cascaded downhill. Rangers left guard positions to help while riflemen labored upward to leave their horses and return. Sergeant Dodd's Number One gun made it halfway up, horses straining and slipping, eyes wide in terror as the ground moved under their hooves and the weight of the gun and fully loaded limber pulled back against them. Disaster had probably been inevitable.

One of the horses collapsed in the traces with a screech, pushing a small avalanche of loose stones under the hooves of the horse behind it. Leaping in panic against the traces, that animal smashed the limber pole and thrust the jagged end deep in the flank of the horse to its right. Squealing in agony, it also went down, crushing the artilleryman on its back, blood jetting up like a fountain. Pandemonium ensued.

"Brake chain! Brake chain!" Sergeant Dodd roared as gun and limber, fallen men, and dying and terrified horses began sliding back down the slope—toward Hanny Cox's Gun Number Two. The brake chain might've even helped if someone was insane enough to jump in among so much madly shifting weight, unhook the chain from itself, and whip it around a wheel that was already picking up speed. That wasn't going to happen. Might as well leap under the feet of one of the rampaging horned monsters. Looking up in horror, the men pulling the horses hitched to Hanny's gun (he'd had everyone dismount to lead them) started to panic as well. It looked like Dodd's whole gun, crew, and team was doomed, and it was going to destroy them as well.

"Trip it! Trip that goddamn gun!" bellowed Lieutenant Petty, cupping his hands. A Ranger beside the track had been backing away in the trees, but now suddenly darted forward with an expression of determination and thrust his converted Dom carbine in the spokes of the gun, bravely holding it there for an instant until it wedged against the axle. The wood stock crunched and shattered, and the barrel pinched and bent—but the wheel juddered to a stop. In the blink of an eye, the gun and limber jackknifed, nearly turning over, but the iron tires turned sideways and scraped up a pile of scree that brought the vehicles to a groaning stop.

"Cut the horses out of the traces," Petty shouted. "Get the uninjured animals up the hill. Drag the dead and wounded ones to the side. No! Don't *shoot* that animal! What's the matter with you? We're tryin' not to alert the enemy, you idiot!"

Hanny took a long, shuddering breath before calling back behind him. "Rig the brake chain and chock the limber. Unwind the prolong rope from the hooks on the trail and pass it forward, then we'll unhitch our horses from the traces and take them up the hill as well." He took another breath. "Hopefully, we'll have enough rope and harness to pull everything up the rest of the way—with the horses already at the top!"

"Should'a done it that way tae start," grumbled Preacher Mac.

"Aye, an' it'll take a lot longer ta get it all done now, I'm thinkin'," Hahessy agreed. "We'll be late fer Major Anson's battle."

Hanny glared at the big man. "No, we won't, by God. We'll get these guns to the top of the hill—on time—if we have to pick them up and carry them on our backs! Now get to work!"

That was almost what it wound up amounting to. "*Heave*, you bunch o' baby, twig-armed maggots!" Lieutenant Petty now harshly encouraged as both gun's crews and most of the Rangers added their strength to the horses pulling both prolong ropes hooked together and attached to traces hitched to horses on the flat. All the riflemen were up there now, securing the Number One gun and preparing the ground for both weapons while keeping an eye on the still oblivious enemy and watching the rest of Anson's force deploying on the plain across the river below.

"My English is still imperfect," huffed Apo Tuin, "but maggots don't have arms, do they? And aren't they already babies?"

"I dinnae think Mr. Petty is as much concerned wi' mixin' 'is metaphors as he is endin' this bloody nightmare an' gettin' our bloody guns up an' ready before we run outa time tae do our part," Preacher Mac observed.

"Quit wasting your breath and heave," Hanny hissed.

Slowly, finally, Gun Number Two crested the slope onto the flat top of the hill, and the tired men, hands on their knees and breathing hard, took a moment to gaze at the shaping fight.

All the lancers and dragoons, as well as remaining riflemen and Rangers, had spilled out of the column into two long lines about a thousand yards from the heights, with the rest of Barca's battery unlimbering together near the center. The Dom batteries had been firing at them the whole time they formed, probably the only reason they hadn't noticed the activity of Petty's section on their flank. Heavy split-trail Dom cannon boomed on the lower hilltop just a few hundred yards away and roundshot shrieked downrange, throwing up dusty geysers of earth and shattered stone. One such eruption occurred among Lara's lancers, smashing down men and horses.

"How long are they gonna stand an' take that?" Billy Randall asked.

"Until *we* signal we're ready, damn you!" Petty snapped. "So quit yer damn malingerin' an' get your gun on line!"

Dodd's crew was quicker off the mark for a change, but a couple of his men had been helping the riflemen level the ground and clear entangling brush. Leaving their limber back behind, Hanny's crew unhitched their gun and rolled it up near Dodd's by hand, Andrew Morris and Kini Hau holding the trail up while others grasped spokes and propelled it forward. "Trail right!" Hanny huffed, racing ahead with Apo to clear stones and rotten limbs while Morris and Kini heaved the trail to the right and Preacher Mac and Hahessy kept the wheels turning, angling the gun to the left. "Center!"

Hanny said, then "Forward." A moment later, the gun was in position to the left of Dodd's weapon, that crew already unsecuring implements and preparing to load.

"Trail down and take implements!" Hanny said at last, before calling out to Lieutenant Petty, "What shall we load with, sir?"

"Solid shot, for starters," Petty replied.

"The closest enemy artillery?" Dodd questioned nervously.

"No. We could'a hit the damned artillery from where we were. All this work was to lay enfilading fire on the enemy infantry. Look at 'em down there! All stretched out in a line."

Breathing hard, Preacher Mac and Hahessy drew the worm staff and rammer out from under the trail while the new Number Three man, Naxa Actli from Pidra Blanca, unhooked the handspike from the right cheek and carried it to the trail, locking it into the irons in front of the lunette, improving his leverage when it came to his part in aiding Hanny's side-to-side aiming. Normally, he, as well as Morris and Hanny himself, would go to the limber and collect other specific implements such as thumbstall, gimlet, lanyard, vent prick and primers, and Hanny's all-important sight, but Kini brought all but the primers (stuffed in a pocket) forward inside his oversize leather haversack, along with the first fixed round of solid shot. This was most assuredly *not* "parade ground" drill, but they weren't on parade, and only tried, veteran crews could do away with so many extra steps in the "dance" without introducing dangerous confusion. By this point, no gun's crew on the field had more experience than Hanny's at instituting efficient and relatively safe shortcuts.

As soon as Naxa had locked the handspike, he'd shifted the trail roughly in line with the target before rushing up next to the breech of the gun and stabbing his vent prick down the vent. "Clear!" he shouted. Preacher Mack had already stepped in between the muzzle and the left wheel; now he reached over the iron tire and fished the fixed round of solid shot out of Kini's haversack and brought it over the wheel and up under the gun's muzzle, where he deftly shoved it in. Hahessy was already waiting, rammer head touching the muzzle, staff angled away. Now he shoved shot, wooden sabot, and powder bag down the barrel all together, pulling the staff as much as pushing it as he stepped in between the shiny bronze tube and the wheel to his right. It thunked against the breech, and he gave it a tap for luck. Hauling the rammer out of the barrel, he stepped around the wheel in unison with Preacher Mac, and the two men took their places, roughly even with the axle hubs. Naxa had been thumbing the vent, but now raced back to the handspike as Hanny placed his sight. Resting his chin between the thumb and forefinger of his left hand, now grasping the cascabel, he peered through the sight he'd already set to the elevation he'd estimated would be required. Lightly tapping the right side of the trail, he showed Naxa which way to shift it, how far being indicated by the force of the tap. Too far. Seeing him just barely caress the left side of the trail, Naxa adjusted accordingly. Briefly turning the four-prong elevation screw under the breech, Hanny stood, retrieved his sight, and clenched his fists where all could see, slightly to his sides at shoulder height. Now stepping back, he made way for Naxa and Morris to pierce the charge through the vent, prime the Hidden's Patent lock, and swiftly—gently—stretch the lanyard. The Number Two gun was ready to fire in all respects, seconds *before* Dodd's Gun Number One.

Neither was the first gun in Barca's battery to fire. That honor fell to the four 6pdrs deployed in the center of Anson's mounted force below. At an unheard command, all four simultaneously spat orange tongues of fire and rolling white balls of smoke. Even before they heard the roar of those cannon, they saw smaller gray puffs of smoke erupt in the air a little above and in front of the nearest Dom artillery. Those smaller explosions were drowned by the ones that sent them, but the screams that followed, as shrapnel and tightly packed balls scythed down from the sky, were clear.

"Bloody well works, by God," Hahessy muttered in apparent surprise.

"Course it works," Preacher Mac scolded the big man. "Didn't we test the new 'spherical case' shot fer a week ourselves?"

"Aye," Hahessy agreed. "But *nothin'* ever works in battle like in practice, does it now?"

"Well, ain't ye happy tae be wrong fer once?"

"Aye," Hahessy acknowledged. "Always a first time ta be wrong."

Even Lieutenant Petty rolled his eyes. "Gun Number One is ready, sir," Dodd reminded him. Petty nodded. "We'll hold for the moment. Signal the major," he told the mounted Ranger who'd come up beside him. A moment later, even as more case shot exploded over the enemy batteries, whose fire had at least slackened, a polished silver mirror was flashing in the sun. Shortly after, a brief response was seen through the smoke drifting across the battlefield below. "That's supposed ta start the attack on the other flank off," Petty explained. "Get 'em reactin' ta that while our mounted troops go at 'em from the front. Hmm," he added, when cut twigs and leaves started fluttering down around him, accompanied by the warbling moan of musket balls.

"Somebody down there's finally noticed us," shouted a rifleman with white corporal's stripes on his dark blue sleeve. Like most of his companions, he'd found a vaguely covered position sitting on the ground, rifle supported by crossed sticks or a fallen tree trunk.

"I guess so," Petty agreed, looking for himself. Apparently, even before the signal was made and returned, perhaps a couple of hundred Dom infantry had detached themselves from the main defensive line and come around behind the hill the enemy battery occupied. They'd have a nearly impossible task reaching the summit from that direction, but if they could get close enough for their inaccurate muskets to suppress Petty's fire, they didn't have to *take* the hill. "No point hidin' anymore," he said. "You riflemen, pick off any officers an' NCOs you see. Better marksmen can go for artillerymen if you think you can hit 'em. That's a fair stretch. Rangers, just keep poppin' at the Dom infantry. Keep their heads down, if you can."

"What about us?" Hanny asked, the *crack* of impatient rifles and *thump* of muskets already loud around them.

Petty grinned. "By all means, commence firing."

"Aye, here we go," Preacher Mac grumbled. "Startin' tae fear we'd dragged these great heavy beasties all the way up here for naught."

"When have we ever gone *anywhere* that we didn't shoot?" Hanny asked good-naturedly. "Gun Number Two . . . Ready! . . . Fire!"

CHAPTER 11

No part of Barca's battery had ever given Major Giles Anson any reason to cuss it, but he'd been growing dangerously impatient at how long it was taking Petty's section to signal it was in position. Kisin's Holcanos had been ready for half an hour and the mounted "assault force" almost as long, taking increasingly accurate fire from the artillery on the heights. Still, it had been a strange situation, probably one of the . . . quietest battlefields he'd ever attended. At least until Barca's two sections here on the line opened up. He'd been just as pleased as everyone to see the effect of the new case shot, blasting down swathes of men around the enemy guns. A few rounds exploded short, and a couple might've never gone off at all, but the percentage of on-target ammunition was at least as good as he'd expect from the government arsenal rounds they brought to this world. There was an added benefit as well. The dry, sputtering pitch that had been used to buffer the shot in each shell had deposited numerous little fires around the target, and an enemy ammunition chest suddenly exploded with a heavy *whump!* on the far left hill, launching debris high in the air amid a swirling cloud of smoke. The closest, possibly most fortunate artillerymen had been flash-roasted to death, but others shrieked in terrible pain, and smoldering men staggered and fell completely out of their position, tumbling over the hastily erected breastworks, some clearly injured, many just afraid. A couple of the cannon up there kept firing, but at a reduced rate, and their accuracy had suffered.

"Signal from Mr. Petty, sir!" cried an observer.

"About damn time!" Anson growled. "Startin' ta feel like a dance caller that lost m' damn voice with ever'body waitin'."

Small arms fire finally erupted on both flanks, echoing with a rumbling clattering sound within the surrounding mountaintop "hills." Two huge blossoms of smoke spurted down from the right where Petty's guns were, the result of twin roundshot skittering along behind the enemy infantry line instantly obvious. Dust jetted up along with a fine, red haze as men shrieked and shattered parts of weapons and bodies cartwheeled into the air. Barca had been holding his fire for a moment, repositioning his guns as the enemy found his range, and now unleashed the rest of his battery to join the fire of its absent section. Guns roared, and the shooshing case shot flew downrange in front of spitting, smoky trails. The copper shells burst over Dom infantry this time, shredding men who'd been protected from direct fire with hot patterns of metal from the sky. The distant screams grew louder.

"Bugler," Anson called to the young dragoon nearby, Corporal Hannity, he recalled. "Sound the general advance."

The harsh tones of the bugle echoed loudly and both lines of horsemen stepped forward at the trot. Everyone knew what was expected of them and exactly what to do at each signal. Things could change, of course, but these men were veterans now—at least all their officers and NCOs were. They'd know what to do if they were confronted with the unexpected. Barca's guns fired once more before pausing while comrades passed to the front. They'd resume firing as soon as the front was clear.

Keeping admirable spacing, the dragoons, riflemen, and unassigned Rangers maintained two ranks on the right, roughly a thousand men strong altogether, while Lara's block of seven hundred lancers did the same on the left, picking up speed when the bugle sounded again. It looked for the world like a grand charge was coming, building momentum as it swept up the slope. For a time there was no return fire, even as the artillery section on the right kept up its murderous cross fire and after Captain Barca resumed punishing the enemy as well. Then, when Dom cannon finally rejoined the fight, they almost invariably shot long and harmed no one. *Almost* invariably. Occasional hurried rounds struck short and bounded visibly along the

hard-packed, rocky ground, striking men and animals at moderately reduced but still lethal velocities. The entire back half of a horse exploded
when such an 8pdr shot struck just behind its rider's leg. The shrieking, cart-
wheeling, blood-spraying wreck came to an abrupt, quivering rest, the
rider as mangled as his animal. Another shot took both left legs off a horse
at the knees, and it crashed into the animal beside it. Both riders jumped
free and tumbled. One man rose shakily, holding his arm. The other rider
and both horses would never stand again.

At roughly four hundred paces, the enemy cannon started coughing
grapeshot, stands of inch-diameter copper balls spraying out like giant
shotgun blasts, and horses started falling much quicker. Men too. Anson
saw more than one riderless, blood-spattered horse galloping near. Even
musket balls started taking a toll, wounding men and animals. The range
was ridiculous for accurate aimed fire, but massed fire was increasingly effective.

"Gettin' ugly," Boogerbear shouted beside Anson. Even over the roar of
hooves, his voice was as calm and level as if he'd merely noted a distant peal
of thunder.

"Almost there," Anson yelled back, nodding forward. The depression
he'd noted earlier was close ahead, less than a hundred paces, looking more
and more like different-colored layers of rock. That's what they had to be,
and he'd seen it before, of course, but always wondered what caused it. Especially when the layers were at weird angles. "Stand by, bugler," he called
to Corporal Hannity as the step—it *looked* like a giant step on the slope—
fast approached. "Now!" he shouted. Corporal Hannity blew his bugle, and
the whole mounted force suddenly wheeled slightly to the left and came to
a stop, men dismounting as fast as they could. Only one in six riders remained on their animals, and they quickly mingled, keeping moving while
troopers tied their reins to trailing lead lines. As soon as their allotted
number of horses was secured, they turned and made for the rear as the
dismounted riders rushed into cover.

"That'll leave 'em wonderin'," Boogerbear grunted, watching as his own
horse and Anson's were pulled galloping away.

"Still has *me* wonderin'," Sal confessed, moving toward them at a crouch.
A blast of grapeshot churned the flat and suddenly vacant ground to their
front, spraying a cloud of shattered stone and dust down on them.

Anson peeked up over the crest. "What about? We're what, two hundred, maybe two hundred an' twenty yards away? Their artillery can't hurt us anymore—which won't stop 'em tryin'—all while Captain Barca keeps hammerin' 'em from the front an' side. Kisin's Holcanos are on their left, mad as hornets, an' they'll have to do somethin' about him. Only God could help 'em hit us on purpose with their muskets from here, while our riflemen can kill *them* pretty easy."

"That may be," Sal conceded, "but most of us ain't got rifles an' have to get closer to fight. Closer on *foot*," he stressed accusingly. Sal hated walking anywhere and had had enough of fighting dismounted when he was with Captain Holland's raiding force that took Vera Cruz.

"I expect we'll be close before long," Anson returned cryptically before raising his voice. "Riflemen, fire at will. Dragoons as well."

In the hands of good marksmen—and all Felix Meder's riflemen were good—M1817 rifles could certainly kill Dom infantry at this range. Because of their short barrels and leaky gas seal, the dragoons' Hall carbines were considerably less powerful even with the same powder charge and ball, but they were fairly accurate (now that the overzealous explosive force of their new Uxmal-made percussion caps had been adjusted), and at least some of Coryon Burton's dragoons were good enough to hit a man at this distance. At the very least, the dragoons could put out an impressive rate of galling fire without calling on the men armed with smoothbore musketoons to waste ammunition. Burton and Meder repeated Anson's command, and their men finally got in the fight.

Volleys of musket fire came back, but the men could hear the enemy commands. They never heard the order to "fire" before they saw the smoke of the volley, but most could still quickly duck. There was only the occasional squawk or scream when the enemy fired. Most important, now that the mounted assault was under cover, the four guns of Barca's battery still behind them had stopped suppressing the Dom infantry and retargeted the enemy artillery on the heights, pounding out exploding rounds fast enough to enshroud both positions in smoldering palls of smoke. Barca no longer even bothered to shift his guns periodically because there hadn't been any return fire against him since the "charge," and incoming cannon fire against Anson's men had abruptly ceased as well.

That didn't mean the Dom infantry had been given a break from the big guns. Fighting had intensified on the flanks as Kisin's Holcanos and the attached company of Rangers pressed in from the left, and the Doms kept shifting more and more men to try and scrape Lieutenant Petty's section of guns off the hill to the right. Those guns were firing just as fast as the rest, however, still smashing solid shot down the length of the enemy line. Anson gestured that way. "Bastards can't stand that forever. We're sittin' pretty." He glanced to the right, where the firing around Petty's hill increased even more. "Well, most of us are. An' they'll hold. Everything but what Mr. Barca asked for to support his guns behind us went to join Mr. Petty on the hill."

Sal looked slightly uncomfortable. "The more I think on the trail we scouted up there, the less confident I am they'll get their caissons up to re-supply ammunition."

Anson looked at him. "They got the guns up."

Sal nodded, but his expression still seemed a little regretful.

Anson shook his head, but his eyes focused on Ramon Lara as the lancer commander trotted up from the left. In spite of his desire to drive his charge home, his appraisal of the enemy had probably most influenced Anson's plan. "They *must* be close to breaking," he said, breathing hard.

"That's what I'm thinking," Anson agreed. Boogerbear grunted, but Sal shook his head.

"I ain't so sure," he said. "These're Doms, remember? From everything we've seen and heard, it won't even matter *which* Doms they are—whether they're already General Gomez's troops from the west, or just more different ones from around here that we ain't never fought. Agon even told us that. We *ain't* gonna make 'em run away. Not without gettin' right in their face an' pushin', at least."

"I didn't say they would do that," Lara defended.

"You said they're about to break. . . ."

Lara was nodding emphatically. "Yes. But if they won't *run* when they break. . . ."

"Here they come!" somebody roared nearby, and many others took up the warning.

Anson formed a lopsided grin as he drew one of his huge Walker Colts. "*Told* you fellas they'd get closer. Can't run, can't take it, what're they gonna do? Get back to your lancers, Mr. Lara. It's liable ta get a mite frisky."

It did, very quickly. Perhaps fifteen hundred terror-crazed but vengeful Dominion troops, pushed beyond reason, erupted from their works and sprinted at their nearest tormentors. Hall carbines and 1817 rifles tore at them at once, and the Rangers' musketoons were hacking into the mass of desperate, screaming men before Capitan Lara made it all the way back to his own. He hadn't left them unattended, of course, and his steady second in command, Teniente Espinoza, controlled the first withering volley from the lancers. It was if a great hand had swept down from the heavens and slammed the tide of enemies back, the stacking mass then smashed from the side by two swiftly loaded rounds of solid shot from the flank that literally spattered scores of men. Even to those waiting to face the mangled swarm, it was horrifying.

"Bugler, sound the final signal!" Anson shouted at Hannity. The call was "retreat," but everyone knew in this instance it only meant they were supposed to pull fifty paces back, then turn and continue firing. With a single glance at the ground and particularly the "step" in the terrain that formed so much of his battle plan, Anson had worried how he'd deal with the charge he intended to goad the enemy into. With only the riflemen armed with bayonets, his men couldn't just wait for the surge to come down on them. They had to meet their foe on the level. But not only would it be difficult and dangerous to climb the awkward, waist-high step right in the face of the enemy, they'd have it directly behind them after they did. A short withdrawal, however, leaving the enemy to spill over the drop and splash down in front of them in a torrent of confusion and disorder, should leave the survivors almost helpless. And even though Anson's force had few bayonets, almost all had wicked blades—dragoon and riflemen sabers, as well as similar, heavier lancer weapons they'd picked up on previous battlefields. Even the Rangers carried swords or sabers, increasingly the D-guard "Bowie swords" that looked like a cross between a saber and a gladius. Many were exactly that, made from foot artillery short swords. In any event, after a last furious volley left the dazed, gasping, wounded, and helplessly terrified Dom survivors now almost literally incapable of further attack or resistance, a hungry roar exploded around Anson. Without orders, almost all his lancers, dragoons, and Rangers raised pistols, blades, even musketoon butts and countercharged.

Captain Meder and Captain Burton were screaming for their dragoons and riflemen to "hold," and many of the American troops heard and obeyed, but most of the "natives," almost all the lancers and Rangers, either didn't hear Lara or Sal shouting at them or simply ignored the command. Booger-bear didn't even try to stop them. Anson started to shout at his bugler to call them back, but realized it was pointless, perhaps even dangerous. At least for a time. The Doms weren't exactly beaten yet, and those still demonstrating the will to fight had to be finished. Sadly, his own force would likely take more casualties in the next few minutes than they had in the rest of the fight up till now, but local troops had almost always engaged in a brutal, cathartic bloodletting at the end of a battle, regardless of how generally well disciplined they were. It seemed almost instinctive, even ritualistic for them, especially the Ocelomeh who'd been fighting Holcanos all their lives. And "friends" now or not, Holcano hatred of Doms went even deeper as well.

"Call the horses back," Anson told the bugler instead, yelling over the mounting roar of triumphant shouts and agonized screams. He'd emptied one of his powerful revolvers during the Dom charge and drawn the second one but wasn't shooting now. He hadn't reholstered it either, though.

"We have become just as savage as our enemy!" Capitan Lara seethed furiously, jogging up from the left, naked saber in his hand, but still bright and clean.

"Savage business, Mr. Lara," Boogerbear said with a shrug.

Lara glared at the big Ranger. So did young Meder and Burton, also stepping closer. Sal only frowned. "This may be normal for *Rangers*," Lara bitterly accused, "but I thought we were fighting against barbarism on this world!"

Anson sighed, understanding Lara's perspective, even his jab against Rangers, who'd never been renowned for merciful conduct. And Captain Meder's and Captain Burton's, who, aside from being formed by an army with rules for war, were raised in a gentler Christian tradition than even the most fervently "Christian" of their native friends here. But this was a harsher world in every respect, where the moral construct of "mercy" might be known, even strived for, but was by no means universally practiced. All cultures they'd met remained closer to base nature in various ways that Anson personally admired, yet that made it easier for him—and all his Rangers, frontier warriors from this world and the last—to avoid the delusion that mercy existed in nature. Father Orno or even Reverend Harkin might've stopped the slaughter quickly if they were here, both being recognized as moral authorities on mercy. In contrast, Anson—like Lewis Cayce—was seen as the wielder of the weapon the army they'd built had become. He'd metaphorically aimed for this very outcome—a decisive victory over an ancient and hated foe—and pulled the trigger. Now that the outcome he'd planned for had occurred—the weapon had gone off—he had to wait a moment for the smoke to clear before reasserting control. More specifically, and he wouldn't put it in so many words, he instinctively grasped how important it was to never give an order he knew wouldn't be obeyed. Especially as long as any fight remained in it, the locals *would* vent their fury on the object of their deepest fear. For a short time, at least.

"Get hold of yourselves," he told his young officers as the horse holders started arriving, joined by Captain Barca and a section of his guns. One section was still firing on the enemy at the base of the hill on the far right. It looked like the Doms had gotten under Lieutenant Petty's guns, which had ceased firing, and all they saw in response to the stubborn attackers were puffs of smoke from small arms now. "You've all seen this before. The men'll get hold of *themselves* soon enough. As soon as the Doms quit fighting them."

"Doms don't quit," Lara objected.

Anson nodded at the melee. "These ones will. From exhaustion o' body an' spirit, if nothin' else. They been through the wringer." It was his turn to shrug, as Boogerbear had. "Them that keep goin'll die. But we can push things a bit. Refocus our men." Climbing atop Colonel Fannin as the big gelding was presented to him, Anson roared, "Prisoners! I want prisoners. Don't kill all the bastards, lads—an' it's time ta get back in the fight. It ain't over."

It actually was, for all intents and purposes. The Holcanos were in the works on the ridge, whooping and shooting, and the last fighting Doms at the base of Petty's hill were turning to face them now. Anson looked significantly at Lara. "I want my lancers back in the saddle, right quick." He grinned. "If there's a Dom reserve over the crest of the pass, you can charge an' scatter 'em. Rangers an' dragoons, collect your horses an' mount up. Mr. Meder, your rifles'll be too filthy for accuracy now. Stay an' take charge of the prisoners. Use 'em to dig a ramp in that step so Mr. Barca can follow along with his guns. Messenger! Have the baggage brought up an' prepare to assemble the hospital section just past the enemy works. We'll incorporate 'em into our marchin' camp after we clear 'em out, an' that's where we'll need the healers." Wheeling Colonel Fannin around, catching the understanding, almost grateful gaze of Lara, he nodded at the young Mexican and spurred his horse off to the right where a narrow section of the step had collapsed eons ago, making an easier passage up on the flat rise beyond. Boogerbear followed, entrusting Sal to finish gathering the Rangers who, seeing their beloved commanders leaving them behind, instantly abandoned the slaughter they'd started tiring of and raced to their horses.

"First Yucatán Lancers!" Lara now shouted. "You heard Major Anson! Quit wasting time. Get mounted and follow me. Form up by fours on the flat."

As Anson had expected, even the fighting on the far right was over by the time he led his nearly entirely reconstituted force surging up and over the former Dom position. The scene behind the breastworks was ghastly, mostly due to the efforts of Petty's section and Barca's exploding case. The passing Holcanos might've left their mark, beheading a few survivors as they swept through, but at least they hadn't kept any of the heads. Regardless of the cause, the dusty, rocky earth was almost muddy with blood, and Anson had to look carefully to see an intact corpse among the scores, maybe hundreds, strung around in every conceivable shredded position. Small, brightly colored lizardbirds were already gathering to feast.

"Scouts forward, Cap'n Boogerbear," Anson said, eyes fixed on the collapsed Dom command tent and surrounding paraphernalia of a midlevel officer. He was surprised to see a blood-streaked enemy survivor wearing only breeches lashed to a pointed pole jutting from the ground in front of the ruined tent, guarded by a pair of Kisin's clearly dissatisfied Holcanos. At least a dozen red-robed Blood Priests lay scattered in the vicinity. All had been beheaded. Moving Colonel Fannin slowly forward, Anson kept giving orders. "Mr. Lara, keep half your lancers ready to respond to the scouts if they spot anything, but the other half'll join half of Mr. Burton's dragoons—an' Kisin's Holcanos when we round 'em up—in completin' the marchin' camp by enclosin' a square of appropriate size in new breastworks. The materials the enemy used to extend their line past what we'll need are ready to hand. Have to clear all this carrion away from inside it, I'm afraid. Set the Dom prisoners to that. Any who won't do it can join the dead," he added harshly. They'd soon find out whether these Doms truly surrendered or not, and how thoroughly. He simply wouldn't risk his soldiers' lives guarding the suicidally murderous. "Mr. Burton," he continued, "please take a detachment of your remaining dragoons to relieve Lieutenant Petty's little command. Lookin' at that hill from this angle, I don't know how they ever got up it, much less how they joined the fight pretty much on time. They'll be worn to a frazzle. Help 'em get their guns back down, but leave lookouts in place." He suddenly realized all the officers with him were hesitating, instead of galloping off at once to follow his orders. He looked back where he was headed and remembered why. "Sure. Might as well wait a few minutes. Won't make any difference, an' I won't have to repeat what I hear."

By now Colonel Fannin was looming over the Dom captive, and Anson sneered when he recognized the large-diameter, sharp-pointed spike the man was lashed to as an impaling pole. He'd seen far too many of those decorated with corpses on the road from Gran Lago to Frontera.

"My war leader Kisin say the Major Anson will want talk this one, so we not cut off head," the taller of the two Holcanos said. As was traditional among his people in battle, he wore his long hair stiffly spiked in imitation of the natural crests of their Grik allies, braced by some kind of sticky black goo. The once-sky-blue infantry jacket was unbuttoned over a bare chest and purposely stained a darker, mottled shade. In spite of the still-brisk late-morning temperature, he was otherwise dressed only in breechcloth, leather leggings, and moccasins. His surprisingly good effort at English instead of the virtually universal Spanya was therefore unexpected.

"He was right, an' thanks," Anson replied, dropping down from his horse, sure the guards had been left more to defend the captive from other Holcanos than to keep him from getting away. "Why don't you fellas go find Mr. Kisin an' fetch him back?"

Without a word, the two warriors hefted their weapons and loped off. Anson watched them a moment before turning his attention back to the Dom. He was fairly young and had apparently taken a blow to the head, judging by the blood matting his unusually light-colored hair. A narrow chest and arms, smooth pale skin under drying blood, and high-quality material in the stained yellow breeches meant he was no common soldier either. Certainly no laborer. "Well," Anson addressed him at last, "you must be somebody, or our friends never would'a left you alive."

The prisoner cleared his throat and thrust out a chin covered by a wispy goatee. He was trying to be brave, but his lip trembled when he spoke. "I am Capitan Don Raul de Las Lomas. At your service," he added ironically. "With the death of the vice *alcalde*, who commanded here, I presume I am the senior surviving officer. It falls to me to congratulate you on your victory—though I would prefer to do so on my feet," he bitterly injected. "Your accomplishment, if not your cause, commands my respect. It is difficult to tender appropriate esteem while I am so barbarously restrained."

Anson snorted and flicked his eyes in the direction the Holcanos went as if to imply, "What can you expect from them?"

Don Raul seemed to take his meaning. "Ah. We were told you were allied with animals, but I honestly did not believe it. How could mere debased heretics and animals truly threaten Actopan?"

Anson finally replied in the same "high Spanish" the man was using, essentially oddly accented but ordinary Spanish unmixed with Mayan. "Guess you didn't know your damned *Dominion* was allied with Holcanos before too long ago, huh? I wonder what else you don't know about all this?" He squatted down in front of the man. "My name's Giles Anson, more proper at present, *Major* Giles Anson, in the army o' the United States of America—Detached Expeditionary Force—operatin' alongside the army o' the Allied cities of the Yucatán. That's the 'debased heretics' who whipped you, an' we're all here ta wipe out *them* nasty critters"—he waved with disgust at the decapitated Blood Priests—"an' wreck your precious, perverted Dominion. We've smashed . . . call it two whole Dom armies, an' taken every city along the coast to Frontera, an' even Vera Cruz. How do you like that?"

Aside from a flicker of recognition at Anson's name, the slack-jawed surprise and horror spreading across the man's face made it obvious he hadn't known any of those other things.

"You've heard of me?" Anson pressed. The man gasped and nodded. "El Diablo Anson," he said, trembling slightly again, "and your army of *diablos terribles* who stepped out of the sea to plague the Holy Dominion! The Blood Priest . . . Patriarca Tranquilo"—he seemed to use the unfamiliar title with some slight reservation—"foretold your coming and gathered all remaining soldiers in the province to destroy you." He hesitated. "Others come as well."

Anson nodded. "So General Gomez ain't here yet? Except for maybe some scouts? Uh . . . 'exploradores'?"

The man goggled. "How did you . . ." He shut his mouth with a near-audible click.

Ramon Lara had stepped down from his horse and joined Anson, squatting in front of the prisoner. "I am Capitan Lara of the First Yucatán Lancers." He glanced aside at Anson. "I assure you *I* am no 'devil.' I would have you released to stand and be properly treated if you give your parole—your word of honor to do us no harm or try to escape—along with your estimate of how the survivors of your force will behave in defeat. It is *not* our desire to harm defeated enemies. We have treated them well in the past when we could, kept them well-fed and protected when they have allowed us to do so." He paused. "But we cannot let them harm us if they refuse to cooperate."

The young man looked lost, licking dry lips. Anson held a hand out behind him and snapped his fingers. Sal removed his canteen and lowered it by the strap. Anson uncorked it and offered it to the man, who gratefully nodded. After several gulps, Anson eased it away and said, as gently as his gruff voice allowed, "Look, we're really not even fightin' you. Well, we just did, I guess, an' that's too damn bad, but it's that bastard Tranquilo an' what he makes you do that we're tryin' to stop. The sad, sorry fact is, that slimy shit keeps puttin' poor fellas like you an' your troops in between us, is all."

"I appreciate the distinction and the assurance, and must confess a degree of . . . discomfort regarding many recent events in the Dominion. Patriarca Tranquilo and the Blood Cardinal Don Frutos behaved very strangely when they exhorted us to prepare for your coming. As if their roles were somehow reversed . . ."

Anson looked significantly up at Boogerbear, Meder, Burton, and Sal, at this confirmation those two evil men had been here.

"We made ready as best we could, enlisting as many locals as possible, training and preparing them with a tiny remining cadre," the young man continued, "expecting no more than a horde of enemies similar to those who tied me here." He looked directly at Anson. "And other bloodthirsty devils. We certainly didn't expect a professional force such as yours. My commander—the vice *alcalde*—was no soldier. *I'm* not really a soldier," the young man admitted. "My father is a *patricio* in Actopan and bought my commission in the guard after all the regulars and professionals either left to join the Gran Cruzada, or . . ." He paused, horrified. "Or General Agon."

Lara nodded. "We defeated General Agon, but he and much of his army have now joined us."

"Amazing," Don Raul breathed. "And *his* cause?"

"The same as ours in most respects," Lara hedged. "The eradication of Blood Priests, certainly."

Don Raul gazed grimly around at the red-robed corpses. "I suspect you have largely attained that goal here." He sighed. "Such a terrible business. I had never imagined war could be so dreadful."

"You ain't seen nothin' yet," Anson assured him.

"I do not wish to see more. You have my 'parole,' and I will do my best to convince the rest of my people to cause you no mischief . . . but what will happen to us now?"

Anson nodded and stood. "Prob'ly take you on to Actopan with us, then send you back to Vera Cruz when the rest of our army catches up. Your men might be put to work there, but they won't be abused. You have *my* word. Cut him loose, Mr. Lara," he said. "One question," he added after Lara used a belt knife to cut the lines binding the man to the spike and several other lancers who'd joined them helped the man to his feet.

"Yes, Major Anson?"

"What'll we find at Actopan?"

Don Raul hesitated, possibly tempted to mislead him, but he finally took a deep breath. "By tradition, I know our defeat at your hands has condemned all those who fought you today, and you promise more mercy than our own people would. I fear that the same will be the case at Actopan. Unless General Gomez has arrived there, all who would oppose you were here." He shrugged. "Actopan is helpless. I beg you to show its people the same mercy you've offered me."

"If they peacefully surrender the city, nobody'll be hurt," Anson told him.

"I would like to try to help with that," Don Raul offered. "My father will almost certainly be included among those who will decide."

"Fine," Anson agreed, swinging back up in the saddle. "Another little chore for a detachment of your riflemen, Mr. Meder. Have 'em—courteously— take charge o' the prisoner an' take him around to talk to the others. Get his scalp looked at, an' send healers with him to look at his men." His gaze landed back on Don Raul. "No funny business. I'm sendin' riflemen because they have bayonets on their weapons an' they know how to use 'em. The rest o' you fellas," he said to his other officers, "you already know what to do. Get to it."

"How far ahead do you want us? All the way to Actopan?" Boogerbear asked.

Anson considered, then nodded. "Sure, if you can. Depends on what you run into, o' course. If you make it all the way, leave some fellas ta keep an eye on it, but bring the rest back here for the night an' get a good rest in camp. We'll see what Actopan has to offer by way o' accommodations tomorrow."

"What then?" Burton asked, glancing at Don Raul. "Assuming we occupy the city as easily as the prisoner leads us to believe?" It was clear the young dragoon remained skeptical.

Anson shrugged. "It'll get a little trickier. We'll send scouts along to Puebla, but also a messenger back to Colonel Cayce. Find out if he wants us to keep pushin' or wait for the rest o' the army to come up."

CHAPTER 12

It was barely noon by the time it was all over, the camp under rapid construction and bodies being cleared. The headquarters and medical tents were the first erected, but the men all started pitching their own as their duties allowed. Though sharp, it had been a relatively short action, and many looked forward to their early halt to catch up on some rest. There'd be no rest for some, of course. The healers in particular had only just begun their grisly work, and the scouts would stay busy, but some had found reaching the new camp just as tiring and difficult as achieving their combat position had been. No one more so than Lieutenant Petty's section of Barca's battery.

The dragoons Anson sent to aid them were a help, at least getting the two guns back down the hill, but nearly half the section's horses had been killed or wounded either getting the guns in position in the first place or during the fierce fight with the Doms who tried to dislodge the section. The dragoons and their animals, already tired themselves, wore out quickly. Especially after the numerous trips they made up and down, carrying wounded to the waiting caissons and limbers by the river. These brought the wounded the rest of the way in. Barca himself led another section's teams and limbers to recover Petty's guns and crews, who wouldn't leave their weapons. Therefore it was approaching evening before Petty, riding double with Barca, and Hanny's and Dodd's exhausted crews trundled into the camp atop their borrowed horses and limbers.

Hanny slid woozily out of his saddle and dropped to the ground, clinging to the horse to keep from falling. The entire sleeve of someone's shirt—he didn't remember whose—had been wrapped around his head, blood-matted hair sticking up out of it. The sleeve was soaked with blood now as well. "You need to get your stupid head looked at," clucked the disapproving voice of Apo Tuin as the short Uxmalo hopped down from the limber and went to his friend. Hanny hadn't moved, merely standing by the horse, eyes closed tight.

"I'll be fine," he hissed through clenched teeth. "Just tired."

Apo poked the sodden bandage with a finger and Hanny squeaked. "Sure you are. Me too. But *I* didn't get shot in the head," Apo scolded.

"I didn't either. The ball hit the gun muzzle while I was aiming. Hahessy said most of it spattered him, cutting his jacket up. Probably less than half of it hit me."

Apo rolled his eyes. "So? You got shot in the head with *half* a Dom musket ball. That's worse than happened to any of our other fellas." That was true enough. Hahessy and Preacher Mac had a few cuts from those spattered lead shards (Hanny now remembered he was wearing part of Preacher Mac's shirt), and Kini Hau had been grazed by a ball on his calf. Dodd's crew hadn't been as lucky. His Number One man had been killed, and his Number Two was badly wounded. The man who'd replaced his Number One was seriously wounded as well. The dragoons, riflemen, and Rangers who'd supported them actually had it a lot worse, trading direct, close-up fire with determined Doms who'd very nearly reached the top and got among the guns. They only lost interest when Kisin's Holcanos hit them from behind. It had been a near thing. "I always thought artillery was supposed to stay back from a fight. Kill Doms from a distance. Seems they're always getting right on us. I'm going to complain to Captain Barca."

Hanny snorted and winced.

"C'mon, Hanny," came Preacher Mac's voice, and Hanny opened his eyes enough to peek at his Scottish friend. "We'll take ye tae the healers. Should'a gan earlier when the dragoons brought the other lads in."

"I won't leave my gun," Hanny insisted.

"Aye, we ken that well enough now, but it's safe in camp, the lot of us are, an' yer gun needs tendin' as much as yew. Hahessy, ye beast, take hold o' the sergeant's other arm, there. We'll carry 'im tae the healers ourselves."

"Aye," Hahessy grumbled. "He's of little enough use with all his wits, is he? None a'tall with the half of 'em soakin' yer sleeve."

"We'll take 'im, Corp'ral Apo," Preacher Mac assured. "He'll nae escape the both o' us."

"I'll go with you just as well," Apo said a little worriedly. "And Kini too. He got shot in the leg."

"I didn't get shot either!" Kini protested.

"A ball tore your flesh, so you were shot!" Apo insisted. "You know the orders. 'All injuries to be reported and treated against infection. *Especially* wounds inflicted by projectiles!'"

"That's so they can get filthy pieces of clothes out of the hole. I don't have a *hole*," Kini complained.

"An' the ball didn't pass through yer nasty breeches tae scrape ye, did it?" Preacher Mac scoffed.

"I . . . I don't like going to the hospital section," Kini finally confessed. "What if they cut my leg off?"

"They will if ye get it infected," Hahessy snapped. "C'mon along, runt," he urged, tone a strange mix of disdain and compassion. "Had a nasty infected wound me'self, I did. Long ago, in a place near as strange as this," he added enigmatically. "Got over it, aye, but saw plenty who didn't. Awful, stupid way ta die if there's no need. I'm goin ta get me own wee hurts treated, an' so's the preacher."

"Come on, Kini, that's an order." Hanny sighed.

"The rest of you, get started on the gun," Apo called behind them. A few spokes had been nicked by musket balls and would need smoothing and painting, and the tube needed cleaning and polishing, of course. They'd have to draw spare horses to rebuild the team as well. All the guns would require normal maintenance, but Dodd's Number One gun needed the most. Not only did it have just as much light damage as Hanny's, it required all new harness, even more horses, and replacement crew members too. All other guns had been spared that, at least. The last they heard was Billy Randall's voice rising, calling for the remaining men and those from the caisson to shift their gun closer to Dodd's, which had already been taken to the artillery park with the rest of the battery. Interestingly, Captain Barca had supervised the movement of the captured Dom guns into protective positions. They already knew the Doms made good tubes. Their archaic carriage design was what limited their mobility, and even accuracy. Minor aiming adjustments were very difficult to make.

The closer the five young men approached to the hospital section, Preacher Mac and Hahessy supporting Hanny, Kini limping along beside Apo, the louder were the sounds of pain. Large fires had already been built to warm the wounded against the rapidly cooling evening air, mostly Doms laid out in orderly rows waiting to be taken into lantern-lit tents. The Allied casualties had been remarkably light, fewer than thirty killed and barely fifty wounded, but Dom losses in both categories had been nearly total. Enemy artillery crews had been exterminated, smothered under a storm of case shot, and of the roughly two thousand infantry who charged the step out in the open, more than half were killed and half the survivors wounded. Perhaps five hundred remained unhurt, all told. The Holcanos and Rangers who rolled up the enemy right, rampaged through their defenses, and swept over the men attacking Petty's hill hadn't taken any prisoners at all. Some wounded were found later, close to death or pretending to be, and were "rescued," but it was estimated only a few hundred actually managed to escape. Oddly, this seemed to include a sizable force of combatants in brown tunics, reaper monks, that Kisin ran into when he first attacked. Odd because, if they truly were associated with Blood Priests, one would expect them to be least likely to flee.

"I'm not going in there," Kini protested, a long, drawn-out wail turning his deeply tanned face a decidedly unhealthy shade of gray. "They're gonna cut off my leg!"

"It's just a scratch. I seen it!" Preacher Mac declared.

"Looks more like a rope burn ta me," Hahessy agreed.

"I can walk now," Hanny told his friends—it was still strange thinking of Hahessy as a friend—"go pick him up and carry him if you have to."

Kini took a step back, shaking his head. Another screech ripped the night, macabre shadows of flailing limbs cast on the tent from lantern light as the sun slipped down past the strangely subdued peaks to the west. Kini spun and started to bolt—just as Hahessy caught him by the tall, red-trimmed collar of his jacket and hoisted him up, wriggling like a fish.

"What in blazes is the meaning of this disgraceful behavior, capering about among these injured men?" demanded a familiar but unexpected voice. Hanny turned back, woozy again, and nearly fell. Preacher Mac steadied him.

"Dr. Newlin!" Apo declared. "My apologies, sir. Private Kini Hau is an unwilling patient, and Private Hahessy is restraining him. When did you arrive? We didn't know you were with us."

Newlin was in vest and rolled-up shirtsleeves, toweling his hands and glaring over spectacles that had slid down his nose. As usual, a pipe was clamped firmly in his teeth. He harumphed. "I wasn't here till this morning. Heard the battle, of course, but I was trapped at the end of the column with a supply train, more healers, and other support that came into Vera Cruz. Alcaldesa Periz sent us to Colonel Cayce, and he passed us forward. Just in time too. For the healers, at any rate." He looked somewhat wistfully at one of the tents full of horrors. "I'm still as good a doctor as I ever was. Better, with all I've learned since we came to this world." He shook his head. "But I don't know what ever possessed me to join the Third Pennsylvania as a battlefield surgeon. I'm no match for *that*." He sighed. "I'm too slow, too used to taking my time. A dozen men would die while I tried to save one. Thank God for these youngsters and their more flexible ways!"

Apo nodded at the towel. "You're still helping."

Newlin nodded. "Yes. I may not be quick, and I won't wield a saw," he added adamantly, "but I've still got my experience and knowledge of anatomy. That's somewhat better than most. Seems autopsies are rather rare, even among Ocelomeh healers."

"It's disrespectful to cut up the dead," Apo said piously.

"Disrespectful to the *living* not to," Newlin snapped back. "In any event, I focus on some of the tougher cases I can take time with. Mostly those shot through the body." He frowned. "With these enormous missiles we all throw about at one another, few enough of those live long enough for me to see. Fewer still survive when they do. I do my best and save some of them," he finished firmly. "But what's wrong with the young trout dangling there? And I see that Sergeant Cox may be in peril of spilling his meager intellect out on the ground. Even I can't put that to rights if he does. Brains can be finicky organs, you know. Never work properly when mixed with sticks and leaves and other debris."

Hahessy shook Kini. "This one has a scratch on 'is leg an' fears they'll take it off under his chin."

"And Hanny got shot in the head," Apo said cheerfully.

"Oh my," Newlin commiserated. "Well, perhaps we might place them in the care of the healers I brought with me. They've been helping with lesser wounds until they get their bearings, so to speak, but perhaps it's time to advance them to more difficult chores, like full-body amputations and poking unused brains back into shattered skulls. What hit you, Mr. Cox? One of those eight-pounder copper roundshot? Dreadful things, roundshot, and copper is poisonous to the blood. Come along."

"You're gonna let someone who's never even *done* it cut off my leg?" Kini almost shrieked. Hahessy shook him again. "Shut up, you. There's a good lad. Die like a man, can't ye?"

The large new canvas tent Newlin led them to was brightly lit and open on both ends. Patients being tended inside were clearly those with less serious wounds, the healers all young, very pretty, and extremely female. Kini was suddenly even more horrified. "No, no, no! Don't let *them* have me! I *know* half those girls from Uxmal. They'll cut me into little pieces!"

All the young ladies wore white smocks with green collars, cuffs, and sashes around their waists. New bright brass half-moon gorgets and crosses hung around their necks. Instead of merely being gathered behind their heads in a kind of long, wild ponytail as was proper for young unmarried ladies, the ponytails were bundled into a kind of snood to keep the dark, luxuriant locks from getting in their work. Several did indeed seem to know Kini Hau, and predatory expressions flitted across faces as they contemplated having him in their power.

Newlin bowed slightly. "More victims for you, ladies. It seems some of you know the little, rather reluctant one. I expect you to filet him like the fish he resembles. For practice, of course. But do put him back like you found him. Some of you may know young Sergeant Cox. I hear he's actually a good soldier, despite his intellectual limitations. I doubt he has any brains to spare, so try to save all you can. The two larger fellows clearly have small wounds as well. Lead fragments, I shouldn't wonder. Pick them out, along with any threads you find. Mustn't let them become infected." Newlin turned to the artillerymen and nodded. "Good evening, gentlemen. All jesting aside, do as these ladies tell you and do not trifle with them in any way." He glared quite specifically at Hahessy, who nodded his understanding. Turning away, Newlin was gone.

"Just drop Kini over here," said one of the girls, grinning, holding up a large saw.

"Nooo," Kini moaned. "We are wounded heroes! How can you treat us so?" Even he now realized the girl was joking, however, and wouldn't really harm him. He might've even started to feel a little ashamed of his own behavior. He was lucky. Men were truly suffering in those other tents, friends and enemies alike.

Hanny had been remotely amused by the episode, but now felt even woozier and his head was throbbing badly. In fact, he thought he imagined it when Apo suddenly cried, "Izel?" in a tone of surprised wonder. *Why would he say that? Izel is his sister.* The girl Hanny was crazy about.

"Izel?" Apo repeated, more demanding. "What are *you* doing here?"

Hanny turned—too quick. The tent seemed to spin.

"I'm here for the same reason you are, idiot. They won't let me fight, but I can help those who can! Oh, Hanny! *¡Pobrecito!* Move him over here and lay him down. Hanny? Can you hear me? Don't you know me?"

Hanny focused his eyes. The voice was clear enough, but when he saw her reaching out to him, tears in her eyes, he knew. It *was* her! *The most beautiful girl in the world, and here I am, looking like* . . . "Izel?" he murmured, falling toward those outstretched arms as darkness swirled round him.

"Aye," he thought he heard, far away. "That's our Sergeant Hanny. Fights a bloody battle wi' a gleam in 'is eye, but confronted in the wilderness wi' the love o' his short life, the puir dafty passes oot."

ANSON'S BRIGADE (A name that seemed to settle upon any mixed force bigger than a regiment that the veteran Ranger commanded for any length of time) set out in the near-freezing darkness before dawn the next day. Steamy horse breath made a fog around the column of mounted men, brightly lit by large fires fed to warm the wounded—they and the baggage train left in the fort built from the enemy works under the protection of Felix Meder's riflemen, a company of dragoons, Kisin's Holcanos, and Petty's section of artillerymen. Essentially, all those who needed the most rest after the fight the day before. Messengers returning from the watchers Boogerbear had sent to observe the city of Actopan didn't report any new arrivals there, but did note that a couple of enemy horsemen, likely escapees from the battle, had squeezed past them in the dark, only seen when they galloped through the outer city, reached the inner gate to the city proper, and urgently requested admission. Shortly after that, there'd been quite a lot of activity. Orange light came to life inside and outside the gate, spreading across the city, flaring in windows and doorways and silhouetting people bustling about. Loud cries were heard, and eventually a growing trickle of carriages began to pull out, all heading north. Boogerbear's scouts had even seen a growing number of people on foot or riding armabuey-drawn carts begin to leave.

"Well, I guess they know we're comin'," Anson grumbled as the messengers made their way down the column to find places to sleep in the fort they were leaving behind. "No surprise. We would've had to give chase immediately with everybody we had, tired an' draggin' ass, to catch each an' every man who ran off from the fight. Still might'a missed some, an' we'd all be too beat down for whatever today brings."

Boogerbear nodded, great, hairy beard bobbing up and down. "I reckon so. You want me to take the Rangers up on around Actopan? Block the road out?"

Anson shook his head. "No, the word's out. Bound to get out, no matter what. No sense tryin' to stop people runnin' away. Send scouts ahead, though, to make sure nobody's comin' up the road from Puebla, an' warn us if they are." He paused, looking at his friend. "*Send*, don't *take*. I might need you with me today. I want the numbers in any case. We ain't a very big force, but I want to look as impressive as we can."

The day arrived, even colder at first as the sun crept up behind them, bright and sharp. They'd only managed about five miles, but the whole world around them had changed. The land was still hilly, but only sparsely forested with clumps of scrubby trees. Flat land between the hills no longer teemed with giant monsters but had given way to plowed fields under cultivation. The fields were bare at present, however, frost sparkling on the stubble of harvested grain. A few giant creatures could be seen, mostly rooting around the edges of the trees, it seemed, but like most places they'd been, even the most horrifying monsters tended to avoid civilization. And that's what they were nearing. Before, they'd seen only infrequent dwellings, modest, even humble huts perched on extreme slopes or the occasional flat. Now, as the day fully bloomed and shadows shortened, more and more picturesque villas made their appearance. Some remained relatively modest, but others were clearly the center of grand estates, supporting—more likely supported by—dozens, or even hundreds of slaves. They finally began to see some of these.

Gangs of men, marching out from the vicinity of some of those compounds to tend fields or gather the few still-standing shocks of grain onto long, fat, high-sided carts pulled by armabueys, who might've been walking in their sleep for all the awareness they showed at first, would stop and watch them now and then. Most only stood and stared, likely with no idea what they were seeing. No doubt they'd all seen soldiers before but couldn't even grasp the concept of invaders. Not here, deep in the all-powerful Dominion. A few must have done, however, suddenly fleeing in terror when the significance of blue uniforms and a distinct absence of Dominion flags finally broke through. Anson was oddly torn. Not as morally opposed to the very concept of slavery as Colonel Cayce was, he didn't exactly support it. Nor did he see slaves—of any race—as inferior beings. Most were merely unfortunate, either born as property, taken in conquest, or, as he understood it here, often laid low enough to have to sell themselves to save their own lives. But all were still victims of the Dominion, so he supposed he was fighting for them as well. Each time he saw a group of them, he was tempted to do something: round them up, send them to the rear, perhaps even set them on their owners . . . but what would he do with them then? He knew Lewis hoped to recruit them into his army, as had already happened in Vera Cruz. That would be fine—when they had time to organize, train, and equip them. No doubt most would make motivated soldiers. But first, Anson had to secure Actopan, and possibly beyond. He'd leave Lewis to decide what to do with anyone they weren't here to kill.

"Gettin' close," Boogerbear said, gesturing ahead. Anson nodded. The road they were on had dramatically improved as soon as they left camp this morning, appearing almost Roman in its construction, complete with fitted stone, a subtle crown, and even drainage ditches on either side. The *patricios* in their country villas would insist on a smoother ride than was the norm all the way back to Vera Cruz. Hills were closing in again, almost mountains, standing purple against the deep blue sky. The sun made sure they could see the city now, still seven or eight miles away, but the walls, larger buildings, ever-present pyramid, and even a couple of sharp, squarish towers were all brilliant whites and reds, gleaming in the cold, crystal air.

"Very pretty," Ramon Lara observed, riding up alongside them, quickly joined by Coryon Burton and Captain Barca. Sal had been hanging back, watching another group of retreating peasants. At least he'd thought they were peasants instead of slaves, since there hadn't been an obvious overseer. Small difference in this land, it seemed. Now Sal came clopping up to join them as well, and all the senior officers in the brigade, except Felix Meder, were arrayed in a tight line at the front of their troops. The noise of so many shod hooves on the stone road was thunderous, and the clattering guns of Barca's Third Section close behind was even louder than usual. "Most Dom cities we've seen have been kinda pretty—from a distance," Sal remarked. "Only when you get closer can you see the ugly evil."

"Riders coming," Burton said unnecessarily. They all saw the pair of Rangers galloping up on either side of the road a few hundred paces ahead, throwing grassy clods of earth behind them. The road was quite well executed, but none of their horses would be used to the relatively slick, smooth stone surface, and Anson wouldn't risk taking it at anything more than their current trot-walk, trot-walk pace. No one spoke while they waited for the horsemen to join them and report. Finally, one crossed over the road in front of them, and they both wheeled around to trot alongside, horses blowing.

"Report, Sergeant Tinez!" Sal said. Tinez had been one of the Rangers with him when they took Vera Cruz. He sketched a salute.

"Doms're pourin' out o' the city, as usual, I guess. Rich ones, poor ones . . . don't seem to matter. Most heading north toward Puebla." He snorted. "Some are just wanderin' around in panicked circles, seems to me." He looked at Anson. "But unless you want the place empty when you get there, you might need to speed it up."

Anson frowned. Empty was easier, but not best. For all his earlier ruminating, they needed to get *some* natives on their side, not only to recruit but to help move supplies—and spread the word that they *weren't* demon heretics after all. "Any sign of anyone preparing to mount a defense?" he asked.

Tinez shook his head. "No sir, though we have seen some Blood Priests.

Who knows what they'll do. Might murder everybody left, or set the place on fire." He shrugged.

Anson nodded. "Very well. Mr. Barca, continue forward on the road. Leave some dragoons to escort the artillery," he told Burton. "The rest of us'll leave the road an' continue at a canter. Horses'll be tired when we get there, but it doesn't sound like there'll be a real fight. Worst case, we might have to clear the city on foot, like we did Frontera. Damn Blood Priests!" he hissed.

Less than an hour later, they were passing through the outer town—up close, more like a slum—of Actopan. The few people they saw, mostly poor freemen or women and a surprising number of children, either fled at their approach or tried to hide. Fat, flightless, domesticated lizardbirds that everyone just called "gallinas" squawked and scattered, as did smaller things; fairly ordinary-looking rats for the most part, but also swift, ferocious little lizards that competed directly with rats for their verminous role. A few half-starved burros brayed, protesting their abandonment, and furry goats with curling horns stood around on everything, even roofs, glaring as they passed. Wide eyes in filthy faces peered from behind hovel doors or over low stone walls. There were lots of those. Short little walls laid out with a geometric precision the run-down homes, shops, and shacks couldn't match. Nearly all enclosed little gardens of some sort, a few things still growing in them. Sal sent some Rangers down side streets to guard against surprises.

Anson was out front with Lara's lancers as they neared the main south gate, standing in a high arched opening in the whitewashed stone wall surrounding the inner city. The leaves of the gate were roughly twelve feet tall and extremely thick, green copper sheathing affixed with thousands of copper nails. A handful of yellow-and-black-uniformed soldiers peered nervously down from a gatehouse on top of the wall, but nobody shot at them. The gate itself hung half-open.

That made no sense. Torn between his desire to lunge forward and secure the gate and his certainty it was a trap, Anson reluctantly held up his hand to halt the column and pulled back on Colonel Fannin's reins. The questioning look on Boogerbear's face didn't require any words. "If they close it, we can smash the damn gate down as soon as Barca gets here with his guns," Anson explained.

Lara gave the command for his lancers to spread out on either side, and Burton's dragoons and the Rangers did the same behind them. There they waited. Burton clattered up to rejoin the other officers. "How long will we sit here and stare at those fools up there in that box?" he asked.

Anson huffed. "Not very long at all."

It took less time than even he expected before the gate swung open all the way, held wide by another handful of Dom soldiers. A clatter of hooves heralded a trio of riders who emerged within the protective ring of a dozen uniformed Doms. Anson noted that even the men who'd held the gate rushed to join them, and a glance at the gatehouse revealed it to be empty. "Looks like the 'honor guard' is the last troops they have," he whispered aside to Burton and Lara, sure Boogerbear had already noticed. The three mounted men were in stark contrast with one another. The one in the center was tall and thin, richly dressed in a gold-embroidered blue tunic ending just past his knees. A gaunt face struggled mightily to maintain a dignified expression under the black-and-white whiskers that largely covered it, while large but strangely sunken eyes constantly moved back and forth across the line of blue-clad invaders and to the sides at his two companions. The man on his left was shorter, but obese enough that his horse actually seemed to strain under his weight. Though draped in a ridiculously ornate yellow-and-black uniform with silver lace swirling thickly enough to subdue the colors beneath, he couldn't have been formed less like an active soldier. The man's round red face wore a stiffly waxed black mustache and goatee, and tiny black eyes glared out beneath the bulge of his brow.

"Good lord." Coryon Burton quietly, embarrassedly chuckled. "Even General Agon never dressed so extravagantly."

"Nor did he require a sailmaker to construct his uniform," Lara whispered back.

"Quiet," Sal hissed. The enemy delegation was drawing closer, and while the "soldier" did indeed seem preposterous enough to be amusing, the presence of the third man was enough to crush all humor. He was average height, average age, average in every respect, except for the bloodred cloak with a pair of jagged gold crosses embroidered on each breast.

At first glance, Anson had hoped they'd found Tranquilo at last, but that was clearly not the case. With his hood thrown back, it was obvious this wasn't their aged, rodent-faced prey. He even wore a vaguely pleasant smile, something Tranquilo was incapable of conjuring.

"Greetings, El Diablo Anson," the Blood Priest exclaimed, still smiling. "We have heard much about you"—he glanced at the others—"at least, *some* of us have, and it is my . . . ambiguous honor to make your acquaintance at last. Allow me to introduce myself; I am Don Esteban de Felicidad Allegre, Vice Patriarca of this province."

"Gleeful happiness?" Lara almost choked, but the Blood Priest nodded benignly and gestured to his left.

"My companions here are Alcalde Fermin Xam—formerly a mere *hombre libre*, a 'freeman,' risen from poverty and obscurity, if you can imagine such a thing! The other is . . . I suppose *General* Cerdo is appropriate now, since he is the highest-ranking soldier left in the province."

"My name is *not* Cerdo, you . . ." The fat officer's face pulsed red, but he stopped himself short of offending what everyone knew was the true power in Actopan.

"You see?" Don Esteban cried. "Even though he is no *profesionale* soldier, and purchased his *grado de coronel* only recently, he is a fighter. Be warned!" he added sarcastically.

Alcalde Xam slumped somewhat in his saddle, and though still bristling, the rotund General Cerdo didn't object further. Anson actually felt rather sorry for them both, increasingly confused by the point of all this. "Pleased to meet you," he said to the two men on the right, ignoring the Blood Priest, but then turned to him. "So, if you really know me . . . us . . . you know the only reason we're not already rampagin' through the streets o' Actopan is because it's always our policy ta summon the honorable surrender of enemies, when possible, before we start killin' 'em. If you know that, you also know we treat 'em pretty good when they do." His eyes narrowed. "The only bastards we ever kill on sight, every time, is nasty, perverted, murderin' Blood Priests like you. Seems to me, you only came out here to publicly insult an' demean the only men I *should* be talkin' to right now."

Don Esteban waved a placating hand. "My apologies. I *was* somewhat harsh, I suppose. Especially to Alcalde Xam. Even I began life as a mere *hombre libre*, and the church we are reforming under Patriarca Tranquilo and His Supreme Holiness will revolutionize the Holy Dominion, creating a great empire across the world in which all men are the equals of one another under God!"

"Equally miserable under the bloody tyranny of the Blood Priests, you mean," Capitan Lara growled.

Don Esteban sneered at him. "If you prefer. And who better? Man must be governed, and God must be nourished." He looked back at Anson. "Yes, El Diablo, I know how you and your greater devil Cayce conquer: with weapons in one hand, loaves in the other, and putrid words of friendship straight from your master in hell! *That* is why I spoke as I did, to leave you no doubt who you bargain with here. Yes, your misplaced mercy toward those you subjugate is known to some. You would offer *me* terms, promising life to the 'innocent' in this city if only they will refrain from opposing you. You ask them to forsake their God and sell their souls! I *reject* your vile terms outright," he spat, "and will *tell you* what will happen instead. You will turn your pathetic little army around and flee back to that den of traitors and the despicable usurper Don Hurac at Vera Cruz. There you will await the gathering, irresistible cleansing sword of God to sweep you into the steaming sea. Enjoy the short time you have left in this world. The terrible fishes will soon pick your hell-bound bones."

Boogerbear voiced an unnerving, gravelly chuckle, and Anson smiled very strangely. "Right," he said. "Seems I've played a game like this before. Weird rules. Let's see if I get this straight. At this moment, you've got hundreds of women an' children"—he glanced at Alcalde Xam and saw the horror building on his face—"maybe even *thousands* of townsfolk gathered somewhere, waitin' to be sacrificed to your sick, slithery god. If I refuse your . . . *gracious* offer, you'll give the word an' the butchery'll start. That about it?"

"Exactly," Don Esteban sneered.

Anson scratched the whiskers on his neck, more out of habit than annoyance. The black silk cravat that Samantha had given him as a wedding present—*Where did she get the silk?* he suddenly wondered—didn't pull his whiskers like his old cotton one had. "I wonder how he's gonna do it," he said aside to Boogerbear, but his eyes were on the anxious *alcalde*. "Can't be that many Blood Priests here, not enough to cut so many folks' throats, or stick 'em all."

"Fire," guessed Lara, face filled with horror.

"That'd be my bet," Anson agreed. Alcalde Xam's eyes confirmed it. The man was clearly in agony, terrified for his people. Don Esteban's chin merely jutted slightly more in defiance. "An' even if we busted in an' swarmed to the city center—I expect that's where they'd do it. By the temple"—Xam gulped, and General Cerdo shifted his immense bulk uncomfortably—"an'

we'd be hard-pressed to get there in time to save *everybody*. Trouble is, though,"
Anson continued, glaring at Don Esteban, "it doesn't really matter if we leave
or not, does it, priest? Folks here have seen us. Even if they haven't, they
know we whipped our way all the way here. The ones who ran off last night
won't matter as much since they didn't see us—or what'll happen to Actopan whether we go in or not. They just won't be let back, is all." He shook
his head. "But anybody here, now, can't be let to live, can they?" He raised
his brows at Alcalde Xam, who finally seemed to realize his people were
doomed, regardless. "*Told* you we've played this game before."

Don Esteban caught the looks of all around, even the few soldiers who
guarded him. Sweat suddenly beaded on his forehead despite the slight chill
in the air, and he licked his lips. "A single word from me—" he began warn-
ingly.

Boogerbear shot him with his Paterson Colt, right in the nose. At this
range, the relatively small .36 caliber pistol ball still did a surprising amount
of damage; eyes bulged in their sockets, and bone, brains, hair, and blood
sprayed from the back of the head. Don Esteban spasmed, legs jerking
straight out and practically launching him from the saddle and over the back
of his horse. There he crashed down at the feet of a Dom soldier like a wet,
leaking rag.

"Guess he ain't gonna get to *say* a single 'nother word," Boogerbear
quipped, calmly recocking his pistol and pointing it at one of the soldiers.
None had even moved.

"Hold your fire," Anson snapped.

Strangely, the obese General Cerdo was first among the locals to recover,
shouting, "Stand down! Stand down!"

"The central plaza?" Anson demanded of the *alcalde*, who nodded quickly.
"I will show you!"

"Follow him in with your lancers, Mr. Lara. Straight in; stop for nothin'.
The dragoons'll follow, securin' your flanks an' rear. Rangers'll bring Mr.
Barca's guns up in case we have to blast anybody out of cover." He twisted
in the saddle and saw Barca's battery finally rushing up behind them and
sighed. "Ever since Monterrey. I *hate* this kinda shit, fightin' through a city.
Give me an open field fight any day, even two or three to one." Drawing one
of his big Walker Colts, he nodded. "Let's get on with it."

Smoke boiled up in the bright, clear sky before Lara's lancers managed to smash past a few hurriedly erected obstacles, but none had been pre-established, nor were they strongly held. Ironically, Don Esteban had apparently been confident that "Los Diablos" would be prevented from entering the city by their concern for the people there. The invaders' humanity holding them back. Anson's brigade knew better by now; only a lightning application of violence could save the most lives. And it did. Only a few of the structures around the temple plaza, packed with people and doused with oil and pitch, had been ignited by the time they got there—largely prevented by General Cerdo's few remaining conscript troops raised in that very city. A brief flurry of killing—there weren't as many Blood Priests in the far-larger Actopan as there'd been in Frontera—kept most of the buildings from being fired, and the majority of people in the ones already alight were saved by bashing down doors or even tearing down outer walls. Sturdy as the stone buildings appeared, newer ones had been built with poor-quality mortar and ropes thrown over the tops, secured by whatever would serve as a grapnel acquired close at hand, and pulled on by straining horses, collapsed them fairly easily. Sadly, the majority of townsfolk killed were actually crushed when roofs or overhead floors fell in, but there was nothing for it. Many, many more were saved from burning.

That's not to say the city didn't burn. A fair percentage did. Once the confused, terrified people were released from their burning tombs, most simply fled in all directions, as fearful of their saviors as they'd been of the flames. It took a great deal of effort to organize hardier souls to fight the fires rapidly spreading to other buildings that had been primed to burn, and then leaping to the next and the next. Lara's entire force of lancers became firefighters, pulling more and more buildings down to make firebreaks and organizing the tentatively regrowing crowd of citizens into bucket brigades, moving water from the fortunately numerous fountains around the plaza.

For Anson and Burton's Rangers and dragoons, the rest of the day was spent essentially repeating their experience in Frontera, hunting Blood Priests and their most ardent sympathizers. At first, once again, these were easy to find, happily combining to fight in the open or spring ambushes. Again, there were casualties in these encounters, but the resistance simply couldn't cope with the professionalism or firepower their adversaries brought to bear. And by the time the enemy decided to scatter, enough of the locals had coped with the situation to be willing to point out where they went. Naturally, few actual Blood Priests surrendered, and after taking more casualties storming their hiding places, Anson directed Barca to push up a section and blast them out. More and more sympathizers gave up after that, and unable to sort them out from those who'd genuinely hidden out of fear, Anson turned them over to their neighbors for justice. A few true innocents might've suffered for that, but those neighbors generally knew which ones of their own had tried to help the Blood Priests murder them. By evening, the fires were largely contained, the surviving citizenry had an entirely different opinion of their invaders, and virtually every tree in the city was festooned with dangling corpses.

Anson was standing outside the north gate, overlooking the slum of the outer city on that side, watching the activity of the people there. His eyes were red and gritty, and the cooling air on his sweat-soaked jacket was giving him a chill. He coughed in the lingering smoke from the city even as he stuck a cigar in his mouth and struck sparks onto a piece of slow match with flint and steel he kept in a vest pocket. Blowing lightly on the smoldering match, he then touched it to the end of the cigar and puffed it to life. Scraping the cherry off the match with one of the copper nail heads in the open gate behind him, he mashed the lingering sparks with his fingers and put the lighting implements back in his vest.

"I hope it isn't like this every time," came a tired voice behind him, and he saw Barca and Boogerbear stepping out through the gate to join him in the orange light of the setting sun. The high clouds above looked like pink fish flesh.

"Yeah," Anson replied. "You did well—as always—but I know what you mean. Be nice if we could just lick their armies an' let the people in the cities sort theirselves out, but this ain't been a very normal war so far." He gestured out at the slum with his cigar. "Quite a few folks still out there. I wonder if there were just as many still outside the gate we came in, just hidin' at first."

"Probably," Barca said, accepting a cigar from Boogerbear as the big Ranger stuck one in his own mouth, taking Anson's without asking to light it. Barca continued. "Unlike those with the means to flee, a horse, a carriage, even just a cart—money, food, and water, of course—common folk, some likely even slaves, would have to *walk* away with no more than they could carry. Surely there are smaller settlements, but isn't Puebla the closest large city? It's nearly two hundred miles away, through country as full of dreadful predators as any we've seen since the Usuma River, I'm told. No one would feed them or protect them from those terrible monsters in the wild on the road. And where would they go? Who would help them when they got there? Especially if they told anyone what they've seen, they either won't be believed or they'll likely mark themselves for death. We caught thirty-odd Blood Priests and hanged them—good riddance—but I can't believe none of *them* got away. Word will spread in their circles, at least, and they'll try to silence anyone else who carries it." He shook his head. "This war—this world—is absolutely insane."

Boogerbear vigorously puffed up his cigar, filling his mouth with smoke, and blew an astonishing smoke ring more like one would expect a cannon to produce. "Poor devils," he said as if he couldn't care less, in an almost obligatory tone. Barca glared at him harshly, but Anson knew the big Ranger really *did* care. He was one of the few men alive who'd seen his friend lose his famous control, and that was a shocking, terrifying thing to behold. Extremely dangerous to friend and foe alike.

"So what now, Cap'n?" Boogerbear snorted. "I mean, Major?"

"Scouts forward, o' course, an' messengers back to Colonel Cayce. See what he wants us to do. General Gomez *is* comin'. Might even be in Puebla by now. If he pushes this way, I'd love to harass the hell out of him, but we do need a few days' rest. We've pushed pretty hard, had a sharp fight"—he waved behind him at the city—"an' had to deal with a city full o' Blood Priests again. Bastards," he seethed. "Anyhow," he continued, puffing his cigar, "we picked up some good recruits at Frontera. Maybe we can do the same here. We'll let Sal take patrols out to the villas, turn the slaves loose. That's where we'll get the best recruits anyway, slave or free. Generally make better soldiers with less work than city folk. They're used to livin' outside the walls an' might even know how to ride. Might've even poked a critter before, with a spear or arrow. We can fold some of 'em right into our ranks, let 'em learn on the job. Colonel Reed might do the same with city folk, turnin' 'em into infantry, but we gotta send 'em back to him, or let him come up an' get 'em."

He paused and puffed some more, then shivered. "Damn. Temperature drops fast with the sun. Catch our deaths with all this sweatin' an' freezin'.

Shirt's like a slimy green hide, an' I expect my vest'll stand on its own when it dries. Burton secured a public bathhouse off the plaza. Hot water. Even a steam room! That's where I'm bound, an' then sleep. I ain't stayin' up all night dealin' with locals this time. Anybody need anything you fellas can't handle, I'll look at it in the mornin'."

CHAPTER 13

The self-proclaimed Patriarca Tranquilo had wandered the wilderness for many months and looked it when he came straggling into the Holy City attended and partially supported by the hulking Brother Escorpion. Escorpion was one of Tranquilo's very first reaper monks, whose order had quickly expanded. His seniority was evident by the fact he still wore a filthy, dingy red tunic instead of a brown one and carried the six-foot spear with the golden blade. No one in the Holy City would recognize that, of course. He was the last of the first of his kind, and all the others were dead. At a glance, few ordinary people could know Father Tranquilo either. Except for his particularly ragged robe, apparent frailty, and buzzard-thin legs and neck, not to mention his lack of hygiene, he looked much like so many other Blood Priests running all over the city now. The Blood Priests themselves knew him, though, or quickly knew *of* him when informed by others. That's how such disreputable-looking specimens as he and Escorpion were allowed in the inner city in the first place. No doubt he would've picked up an entourage of near-worshipful followers, in fact, if he hadn't made subtle signals. Covered by the hood of his cloak, his expression was impossible to see, yet any who knew him would've been shocked to see the blissful smile spread across his skeletal face at the sight of so many Blood

Priests—his own creation—moving purposely and unhindered in the streets of the Holy City. He'd often despaired, particularly during his long exile, that he'd ever live to see it.

Weaving through the late-morning crowd of brightly attired denizens of the open-air market, everyone fell away at his and Escorpion's approach. Many were slaves, no doubt, shopping for their masters, but everyone dressed to shop in the district closest to the Great Temple of His Supreme Holiness. None of these people had ever seen Tranquilo before, but perhaps they instinctively sensed the power he wielded over them, or Escorpion's bulk and menacing visage were enough to frighten them back. The freemen here were largely *patricios*, the elite of the Dominion; soft and pampered and incapable of even imagining the labors and suffering Tranquilo had endured on their behalf during his lengthy exile on the savage frontier. No matter. His works had preceded him, and all would soon know him when he took his rightful place beside His Supreme Holiness, his hand firmly holding the marionette's strings. He chuckled, and it sounded like a gurgling croak.

Escorpion looked at him, surprised. "It amuses you that these . . . creatures avoid us so, my lord?" He sneered. "They should be groveling before you, praying for your blessing!"

Tranquilo gurgled again. "Now, now, my son. All our work has been aimed at making these people credulous and pliable, wanting for nothing, and even increasing the numbers of the compliant upper classes. They will obey almost any command that doesn't inconvenience them directly, and few are ever called to make sacrifices. Even the lower classes will object very little when they are fat and happy and can aspire to join the upper classes in time. Only slaves and the very lowest freemen must be rigidly regulated by sacrifice and fear." He shrugged. "But there are always more slaves. Actually, I was amused by the thought that what really sent them reeling might be the power of our stench. It has been far too long since either of us bathed! Then, of course, I forget that you have never been here, never seen for yourself how it all works." He paused reflectively. "It has been many years since I was here myself."

Escorpion bowed his head. "If you say so, my lord."

Tranquilo chuckled again, gesturing to the north. "Little of how the city is arranged has changed, I assure you, and as you might imagine, that central temple, clearly visible and the tallest and grandest of all, is our destination.

In fact, we should probably hurry. Step in front of me to clear the way, if you please. I will walk behind, clutching your belt."

Escorpion looked down. "I should have saved your chair for you," he lamented. He'd carried Tranquilo in a light chair with shoulder straps, arranged like a pack basket on his back, for hundreds of miles.

"What were you to do, my son?" Tranquilo asked lightly. "When the Devil Anson attacked us in that clearing, slaughtering all our companion Blood Priests and largely destroying the rest of our force after we fled Gran Lago, you had time to save very little. Personally, I am content that you chose to carry me to safety instead of that ridiculous chair. I do perfectly well without it."

"Perhaps," Escorpion conceded, "but I swear upon my very soul that I will one day kill the Devil Anson—and all the foul Rangers he brought to this world."

"And a laudable oath it is too. I shall enjoy watching you fulfill it. First things first, however." Tranquilo gestured at the tall, naked-stone pyramid dominating all other structures in the city, even the dozen other pyramidal shapes of various colors. "Lead around to the back of the temple, opposite the bloodstained steps. The entrance we seek is there."

Despite Escorpion's efforts to move slowly, Tranquilo was practically gasping from the unusual exertion it required to walk so far. They'd arrived on horses, but since Tranquilo desired to remain inconspicuous to most, and only high officials were allowed to ride on horses or carriages within the inner city in daytime, they'd been forced to move on foot from the gate. Now approaching three heavily guarded high-arched entrances at the back of the temple, Tranquilo tugged on Escorpion's belt to signify he wanted to stop. There they stood while the gold-trimmed, red-coated temple guards approached and Tranquilo got his breathing under control.

"Move along!" the guard officer snapped. "Blood Priests or not." His lip curled, clearly showing disgust at their appearance if not his personal disdain for their order. "Look at yourselves! You mustn't linger here. They'll smell you inside!"

Tranquilo said nothing, but Escorpion cleared his throat. "We have come a great distance to call upon His Supreme Holiness."

The officer's eyes widened. "Have you, now?" he demanded incredulously. "And who the devil do you believe you are to exhibit such presumption?"

"I am Brother Escorpion. A mere reaper monk of no consequence." The giant gestured grandly at his companion. "This, however, is His Holiness the Patriarca Tranquilo, founder of God's most beloved order and singular benefactor of His Supreme Holiness!"

The officer only stared for a moment before blurting, "*¡Mierda de cabra!* Away with you both before I have you beaten."

"Teniente," a nearby NCO urgently hissed.

"What, damn you!"

"Perhaps you might look beyond our guests' appearance—and gaze upon the growing mob behind them. . . ."

Tranquilo hadn't had—or wanted—an entourage, but as word of his arrival quickly spread, he'd begun to draw a sizable crowd, following at a discreet distance. A dozen paces behind him now, upward of a hundred Blood Priests had gathered, and their numbers were only increasing. Those in front had heard what the guard officer said and seemed most displeased by the disrespect shown the virtual founder of their order.

"Hmm . . . Yes. They do seem to know him," the *teniente* said, suddenly slightly breathless. "Alferez!" he called loudly. "Go at once and see if the Primer Patriarca's secretary knows if His Supreme Holiness is disposed toward granting an audience!" He quickly turned to Tranquilo. "You do understand that no one can actually *see* His Supreme Holiness, and none but the Primer Patriarca himself may bask in the radiance of his naked countenance? If you are allowed in, there are intricate forms to follow, and ultimately, you may hear each other speak, but neither will actually see the other."

Suddenly very tired of this, Tranquilo simply sighed and urged Brother Escorpion to push the guards aside. "He will see *me*, I assure you," he cackled.

"But . . . but . . . that man has a *spear!*" the *teniente* cried, referring to the gold-bladed spear Escorpion was currently using as a walking stick. "No weapons . . ." he began again.

"That is no mere weapon. It is his badge of office. Yet he will skewer you and the rest of your guards before you can raise a hand against him if I give the word. Are you satisfied I am who I say?"

The *teniente* gave a hesitant nod.

"Very well, then, stand aside—and thank God I haven't asked for your name. Find another to take your place. I do not want to see you when my business here is concluded."

The *teniente* looked stricken. "But—with all respect—I could be crucified for leaving my post!"

"I will do worse, I assure you," Tranquilo promised. With that, he and Brother Escorpion moved to enter the central arch without another glance behind them. The entrances on either side led straight in or up to the offices and living quarters of God's true representative among the living. The center passage led downward into the holy sanctum under the earth, closest to God's underworld paradise.

Don Datu's former Obispo De Sachihiro and now the Primer Patriarca and His Supreme Holiness's designated successor sat on an ornate, elevated chair in a spacious chamber illuminated by golden braziers along the walls. Despite the heat the braziers produced, it was always somewhat damp and cool in the sanctum. He was drinking wine from a golden goblet and conferring with General Gomez, the bulk of whose Army of God in the West had arrived less than a week before and was now encamped on the narrow plain beyond the outer city between the two great lakes that lay east and west of the Camino Real. The only other person whom it might be said was fully present was Father Armonia, the Blood Priest who often stood in for His Supreme Holiness and upon whom Sachihiro relied more and more. His Supreme Holiness himself was reclined on a lounge beyond sheer golden drapes, and only his shape—and that of several sleeping women lolling around and over him—could be seen. As usual, the former Don Julio DeDivino Dicha seemed to lie sleeping or nearly so in a drug-induced stupor. He may not have heard the approaching commotion in the long stone hall, but the others did.

None of the inner guards was actually trying to stop the unlikely and disreputable-looking pair who emerged in the light of the braziers as much as they seemed to be attempting to hold them back long enough to properly announce them. Sachihiro and General Gomez stood, faces contorted with outrage over this unprecedented interruption. Armonia stood as well, but his expression betrayed only wonder.

"What is the meaning of this?" Gomez demanded. "I understood we could speak freely and uninterrupted here. Especially safe from common bedraggled vagabonds off the outer city streets!"

"State your business at once!" Sachihiro insisted, then glared at the horrified guards. "I will deal with you—and those outside—when we are finished."

Armonia cleared his throat. "Excuse me, General. Forgive me, Holy Patriarca. These men may appear to be vagabonds, and they *do* look somewhat bedraggled, but there is nothing 'common' about them." He now stood as well, bowing low in respectful greeting.

"You know them?" Sachihiro asked, astonished.

"Indeed. As do you, Your Holiness. At least by reputation. One of them at least," he added.

"I am Patriarca *Supremo* Tranquilo," the shorter, scruffier, and older of the two grandly proclaimed, stressing the lofty addition to his title that he'd only just made up. "Originator and longtime steward of the brotherhood most commonly referred to as Blood Priests." He touched his towering companion on the lower arm. "And this is Brother Escorpion, my faithful companion and protector, not to mention the sole survivor of the first generation of reaper monks I caused to be raised to defend the faith." He peered intently at Sachihiro. "Through my order, I am also your direct benefactor. Chief advisor too, if you wish to prosper." He nodded toward the still forms on the couch behind the drapes. "His as well, of course, when his intellect is present."

"My intellect is fully engaged," came a sleepy, dreamy voice. There was no telling how long the former Don Julio had been listening. "It is *good* to hear you again, Father Tranquilo," he said with genuine enthusiasm.

"Patriarca Supremo," Tranquilo corrected, and the shape of His Supreme Holiness only nodded.

"Of course, if you wish. You have earned it—as I think it is fair to say that I and young Sachihiro have lived up to our end of the bargain we made so long ago."

"Just as I always dreamed," Tranquilo agreed. "There have been setbacks," he allowed, "but all has generally gone as planned—with a few minor exceptions."

"You speak of Don Hurac?" His Supreme Holiness asked through a yawn. One of the girls beside him stirred, and he pushed her roughly off onto the rug that covered the stone floor of the sanctum.

Tranquilo hesitated, glancing suspiciously at General Gomez. Don Julio must have seen or suspected what concerned him. "The good general is one of us and an ardent supporter of yours." A chuckle. "Now that he knows who you are. Regardless of how he greeted you in ignorance, he has been one of your keenest instruments. And as for these lovely young ladies all around me, well, all have been rendered deaf, mute, and blind. Quite painlessly, for the most part. How else could I enjoy them more than once? Father Armonia impersonates me extremely well with a mask, but if these poor creatures could see me, why, I'd have to destroy them, of course. Forever replacing them just as they learn to please me. How tedious."

"Don Hurac could make himself rather tedious as well," Tranquilo said dryly, returning to the subject at hand. "Particularly now that he seems to have joined the army of heretics marching this way." The old man finally pushed the hood off his head and grimaced, blinking beady eyes and making his ancient, rodent-like countenance especially hideous. "You should have eliminated him when you had the chance."

Sachihiro coughed lightly. "Perhaps. We might have managed it while he was on his way back to Vera Cruz after a recent visit here, but Don Datu would then have been on his guard. Unfortunately, the 'chance' never presented itself again. Vera Cruz fell to the heretic armies from the Yucatán almost immediately after, and Don Hurac has been under the protection of the Diablos Americanos ever since."

"Not just their protection, but the remnant of General Agon's army as well," Tranquilo growled. Noting Gomez's expression of shock, Tranquilo inquired, "You did not know?"

"I never imagined such a thing! A few scouts, mostly some of your new reapers," he acknowledged with a reluctant nod at Tranquilo, "have reported what appeared to be local troops in greenish uniforms in league with Coronel Cayce's Los Diablos, but we all simply assumed that Agon had been destroyed. To consort with the forces of hell itself . . ."

"He has long been aligned with Don Hurac," Tranquilo said, "and the fact that the coward Don Frutos essentially abandoned his army to its fate may have driven him to break with us entirely." He held out gnarled, empty hands. "Even now I do not know if he has joined Coronel Cayce as much as he simply supports Don Hurac, but his force, along with recruits they have gathered along the way—and largely armed at our expense—has perhaps doubled the size of the heretic army." He paused and looked thoughtful. "God has been nourished by a great deal of blood over the course of its advance. I only wish more of it had been the enemy's."

Gomez puffed out his chest. "Well, I am here now with the vanguard of my army."

"I saw," Tranquilo said. "Very pretty soldiers and such an organized camp! I estimated that you have roughly forty thousand men."

"Forty-two thousand, actually, with more on the way," Gomez boasted. "I will soon lead them all out to destroy the heretics once and for all."

Tranquilo shook his head. "You must not."

"Wha . . . I beg your pardon?" Gomez said, taken aback.

"Do you have a reliable second?"

"Why . . . of course I do. General Debero is quite reliable, as a soldier, at least." Gomez paused. "Perhaps a little less so, politically. He is known to be rather conservative."

"All the better," Tranquilo said. "You must stay here with your most loyal officers and a professional cadre of troops. Let this Debero lead your army against the heretics."

Gomez bristled. "With all possible respect, Father Tranquilo, are you mad? That is *my* army out there!"

"Most of which is already dead," Tranquilo snapped. "Do not question me! I have seen what Coronel Cayce's army of heretic devils can do, and a mere forty-two thousand men who have never tasted a *real* battle before will be hard-pressed to stop him."

"Ridiculous!" Gomez huffed.

"Believe me or not, I do not care," Tranquilo countered, "but we have been far too complacent when our forces met his before, and you must prepare to provide for the defense of Texcoco, the Holy City itself, indeed the entire Great Valley until the Gran Cruzada arrives."

Sachihiro was incredulous. "Even if that became necessary, the Gran Cruzada cannot be here for months! I halted its advance, but we have not yet summoned it."

"No matter," Tranquilo said with a wave of his hand. "I already took the liberty of summoning it myself, as well as arranging for . . . other troop movements of various sorts."

Don Julio leaped up from his couch behind the drapes. "*You* summoned *my* army without consulting me?" he practically screamed with fury. "How could you even do that? Never mind, I will have you . . ."

Tranquilo made an impatient noise. "My dear 'Supreme Holiness,' it seems I must disabuse you of a terrible misunderstanding. Your elevation did not legitimize the Blood Priests. They may have been looked down upon, but they were already ingrained in society, already in control, and only a small percentage walk openly in their red robes. The same is doubly true for the Gran Cruzada. Did I not first personally conceive its creation? Don't you think that I would ensure that many of its officers were members of my order and obligated to me?" He shook his head in mock sadness. "No, you will have nothing done to me. Pray I return the favor. When all is said and done, it was I and my Blood Priests who engineered your very rise to power, and you will do as I say if you don't want something 'done' to you." He smiled at Sachihiro. "Despite the promise you have shown—the comic gestures among Blood Priests at appropriate times was inspired—it would still take no effort at all to have you replaced by one of my own." He shook his head and looked back at Don Julio's indistinct form through the drapes. "I will emphasize again, the Gran Cruzada belongs to *me*. It has always been mine. True, it remains inconveniently distant at present, but is closer than you think. Pray it arrives in time to save you. You *have* no army, beyond that of General Gomez, and he will order his troops to do as I direct if he wants to go on living."

Gomez hesitated only a moment before bowing low to Tranquilo. "What are your orders?"

The only sound from beyond the drapes was a hiss of fury.

"As I told you," Tranquilo said, "you will order your deputy to advance the portion of your army already here to meet the heretics—before they become known to the residents here. We all know the grim consequences of *that*," he added somberly. "We will fervently pray for victory, but must not expect it. To fatally weaken the enemy should be quite enough. The rest of your army will remain here as it arrives and prepare to defend the valley." He looked at Primer Patriarca Sachihiro. "You will open the city armories to Brother Escorpion so he may arm all the Blood Priests and reapers in the city if it should come to that."

Sachihiro also bowed. Tranquilo smiled at Armonia. "I understand you have military experience."

"I do, Your Holiness," Armonia replied, addressing Tranquilo as he would a Blood Cardinal.

"Excellent. You will assist Brother Escorpion in all things"—Tranquilo's gaze flicked back at the drapes—"and remain prepared to pose as His Supreme Holiness at all times . . . for whatever reason."

"Of course, Your Holiness." A curious expression suddenly swept across

Armonia's face. "I must ask. Were you not traveling in company with the Blood Cardinal Don Frutos? Where might he be?"

Tranquilo almost negligently waved that aside. "Don Frutos is perhaps the finest example of why new blood is required among the Blood Cardinals and is unfit for anything in God's creation. I could no longer abide his company and sent him on to make his way to join the Gran Cruzada as our direct representative to General Xacolotl." He smirked. "I can't imagine what possible use he will be to us there, or that he will even find the Gran Cruzada before it joins us here. Either way, he will not be missed."

"I see," Armonia said.

CHAPTER 14

The bulk of the Allied Army marched inexorably forward, winding along the narrow mountain road Anson's brigade so recently traversed like a long, blue snake sliding through the green forest "grass." *A blue racer, in fact. Narrow, seemingly endlessly long, and complete with the predominant dark blue and sky-blue coloring*, thought Lewis Cayce with a nostalgic twinge, glancing behind as he loped toward the head of the column atop his surefooted Arete. A confident and nimble horse was important here, particularly riding on the outside of the column. This stretch of road, clinging to the side of a steep, wooded mountain, was especially constricted and treacherous. Men of the 3rd Pennsylvania, which he, Varaa-Choon, Colonel Itzam, Major Olayne, and Leonor, of course—along with a small retinue of aides and messengers—were presently passing, were clearly sensible to this and obligingly compressed their ranks as much as they could as NCOs shouted forward for them to do so. Quite a few of the veteran infantrymen called greetings as the officers passed. Lewis smiled and nodded back, occasionally calling, "Sorry to enforce such intimacy upon you fellows, but you're infantry. I'm sure you're used to it."

"Grateful we are, sir!" cried a wag with his greatcoat wrapped tight. "Bloody cold it is this marnin', an' I hated leavin' me tent, where I was spoonin' with me mates!" Laughter and good-natured, off-color jibes showered him, but then moved on to artillerymen in general (with whom Lewis was still identified), spreading and rising in volume. The hilarity rolled down the line to a section of Hudgens's battery, from which the wit bounced back at high velocity. Lewis just waved and grinned. The 3rd Pennsylvania, 1st US, and 1st Uxmal remained the infantry rocks he'd always rely on most. He knew they were cold and tired, especially since their long, uncomfortable march had tended ever upward into colder and thinner air, but he couldn't be prouder of them, of his entire army, in fact. Grueling as the march had been, it hadn't sapped morale. He slowed Arete to a walk alongside the regimental color-bearers and their cased flags.

"Major Ulrich," he greeted the 3rd's commander, leading his horse at the front of his men. Lewis thoroughly approved of John Ulrich. The man was an instinctive leader, incidentally possessed of a fine singing voice. A confirmed NCO, he'd been recently retired from the regular army before joining the 3rd Pennsylvania Volunteers. His subsequent transition from "permanent" sergeant to regimental command had been awkward at first, but he'd been equal to the task. The army was full of officers raised from the ranks, but few had his experience, and his men truly loved him.

"Good morning, sir," Ulrich said, saluting.

"Good morning to you. I hope you slept well."

Ulrich looked sheepish. "Well enough," he fibbed, and Lewis chuckled. The narrow clearing the 3rd camped in the previous night was too steep for tents, and it was fortunate the weather held. Some had predicted light snow, which apparently wasn't uncommon at this time of year in this clime. Even so, quite a few men had reportedly awakened in terror, not only rolling out from under blankets, but a short distance downslope as well. No one was injured; the grade wasn't *that* steep, but it was said that Ulrich himself was one who woke up thinking he was rolling off a cliff.

Lewis raised his voice so others could hear. "We'll be stopping a little earlier tonight, and everyone can get a proper rest. I understand the road widens quite a bit, and we'll use the same ground as Major Anson's brigade the night before their action against the Doms short of Actopan." By all accounts, that "action" had been a proper battle, but no one had named it. Anson certainly hadn't. The closest town was Actopan—too far, really—and the names of the most prominent features (if they had names) were unknown. Reports had called them things like "the step," or "Petty's hill," appropriate for those parts of the fight, and men engaged there would be

commended, but the whole thing had been the first serious encounter of
the current campaign. It needed a rousing name if it was to be named at all.

"I'm sure a restful night will be most welcome for everyone," Varaa
grumped sourly, blinking her huge blue eyes and swishing her tail in annoyance. "Much of the army didn't even have a clearing and slept right
where it stopped on the road."

Lewis nodded. Discomfort aside, he hadn't liked ending the day so de-
fenseless and spread out. Despite the efforts of Anson's Rangers, they knew
they were being watched. There'd been a few encounters with wolf-lizards
or similar things, but these steep, rocky slopes were no place for larger,
more fearsome predators. "A good rest," he agreed, "and then one more
long march to Actopan." He grinned. "And hot baths!" Cheers and laughing answered this, echoing off the distant slope across the deep river gorge.
"In any event, Major Ulrich," Lewis continued in a more neutral tone, "why
don't you mount up and join us? We're going ahead to consult with Colonel
Agon and Colonel Reed." In command of 1st Division, Colonel Reed was
Ulrich's direct superior, but since Lewis had to move about so much, not
only of necessity—to consult with Don Hurac at the rear on occasion, for
example—but just to be *seen*, as many (including Varaa and Leonor) insisted,
Reed needed to stay at the front whether his division led the column or not.

Agon's 4th Division hadn't just happened to be in that position when
they entered this dangerously narrow pass. Lewis put him there on purpose, not only as the ultimate test of Agon's loyalty (if their former enemy
harbored treacherous intent, this was his perfect opportunity to stop the
army's advance in its tracks), but also—hopefully—to prove to the rest of
the army, still somewhat skeptical, that Agon *could* be trusted. He knew it
was a risk, but not only did he need to know now, for certain, that Agon
could be counted on, the rest of the army needed to know it too. The time
would come in battle when Agon's division would be beside another, and
those men had to know the only enemy they had to worry about was the
one in front of them. Obviously—just in case—Lewis had a plan to counter
Agon's treachery if he displayed any now. He couldn't be absolutely positive
Agon wouldn't suspect that too, but this was the best and most tempting
time and place he'd been able to construct to either lay the most fears to rest
or deal with a viper among them.

One way or another, the time was at hand. Going forward himself was a
risk as well, of course, but he was confident he'd quickly be able to deter-

mine if Agon's men were preparing something, and Reed would've detected anything unusual among Agon's senior officers. *Especially the one named Arevalo*, Lewis mused, glancing at Leonor. She'd once shot the man who became Agon's most trusted lieutenant, but even she now trusted Arevalo implicitly. If Reed hadn't caught any undercurrents of betrayal, Arevalo would signal them somehow.

"Of course, sir," Ulrich replied. Moving to the left side of his horse, he heaved himself into the saddle. "Carry on, Captain Cullin," he told his executive officer, who'd been striding along behind him.

Moving forward again, Lewis and his entourage passed Captain Cullin's skirmishers under Lieutenant Aiken and Sergeant Visser. Lewis joked with them as well. Beyond was the green head of the long blue snake: Agon's 4th Division. Most of their uniforms were still the old yellow and black, dyed to the odd assortment of greens they'd become, but newer additions wore finer material made in Gran Lago. All had been issued new uniforms and would wear them soon enough, Lewis supposed. Agon had told him his men were saving their finery for when they met their "deluded" countrymen in battle. Trotting alongside the former enemy infantry now, Lewis couldn't help feeling odd. And it wasn't as if the air seethed with resentment or anything like that, nor did he detect hostile glances. It was just . . . so quiet. There was no singing or joking, not even much talking. It struck him as strange.

"It's determination, Lewis," Leonor said quietly, riding just behind him. As always, it seemed she'd read his mind. "I, for one, don't feel any hostility here," she continued. "These men're movin' with a purpose, determined ta prove themselves to you, us, themselves . . . but mostly to God, I figure. The way they see it, they been tools o' the devil their whole lives, an' now they got a chance to kick him where it hurts."

"So trusting," Varaa lamented behind her. Varaa seemed to go back and forth between suspecting and trusting their new allies. Har-Kaaska was the same.

"Not *always* 'so trusting,'" Leonor snapped back at the Mi-Anakka. "Not even now." Teeth clenched, she continued, "They've been . . . abused, Varaa. All their lives. I know what that's like," she added so low that Lewis and Varaa were the only ones to hear. "But I've had my father an' friends to help me cope. Maybe not the best *way*"—she almost chuckled—"but there was support—an' a vent for my anger. My faith helped too, I guess, though that was gone for a while." Her lip twisted. "But *their souls* have been raped, an' worse. The sick faith they had in what they see now as the devil turned *them* into *his* rapists! They 'served the Creature rather than the Creator,'" she quoted, surprising Lewis as she often did with her knowledge of scripture, sometimes even correcting Reverend Harkin. "They feel hurt an' used bad, but they've turned that to 'mad.' They got as much or more cause to fight Reverend Harkin's 'holy war' as anybody in the army."

Varaa blinked thoughtfully, tail swishing. "Father Orno believes so," she agreed. "I suppose I do as well, to a degree. We'll just have to see, won't we?"

THE STOCKY FORMER Dominion general Agon, now a colonel in command of 4th Division, was perched atop his magnificent tall black horse, surely a direct descendant of the fine Spanish animals that came to this world, at the very head of his troops. Colonel Reed was with him, as was his own second in command, Colonel Tun. Arevalo was there, as always, and they'd been joined by Father Orno a day or two before. Messengers and various regimental commanders followed behind in a talkative gaggle. Agon had more of the latter than Doms were used to since he'd already split his regiments, recognizing that more, smaller ones gave him greater flexibility to maneuver. Now he'd split them again, to roughly seven hundred to one thousand men each. The same "ideal" number that Lewis tried to maintain in the rest of the army. Agon had no lancers, however, nor any mounted troops of his own. The few he'd had left from before had either been folded into Lara's lancers or become mounted messengers themselves. Detachments of Rangers and dragoons had been assigned to scout ahead.

Lewis and his companions rode up to join him, just as the road finally began to widen back out, tall, bluish, spiky grass growing on both sides. Agon smiled with what appeared to be genuine pleasure to see them. "I was wondering when you would come," he called out as they approached, exchanging salutes in the American way. "I knew you would today." He actually sounded slightly smug, if Lewis wasn't mistaken, and that surprised him. All their conversations before this had been extremely formal. Then again, now they were part of the same army, working toward a similar (if not exactly identical) cause. At least Lewis hoped they were. They needed to feel more comfortable around each other. Agon surprised him further by actually laughing at his expression.

"How did I know, you ask yourself?" Agon indicated Father Orno. "My spy informed me, of course."

"I am no spy," Orno objected strenuously. "But yes, I do often discuss your concerns with the colonel. I know the souls of these men," he added earnestly to Lewis. "They have given themselves entirely to this . . ." He paused, thoughtful. "This . . . reckoning. Although the teachings both Reverend Harkin and I adhere to generally admonish us to leave vengeance to the Lord, I can imagine no better instrument to achieve it for Him than those most grievously wronged. In that sense, we are all of us His swords in this endeavor, and whether we exact true vengeance or not, we must put a stop to those who deserve it and send them into God's presence where He can finish the job."

"Well said, Father Orno," Leonor spoke up. "Without all of Harkin's quotes distorted ta fit his meanin'."

"I don't believe I've ever heard the good reverend distort, exactly," Orno defended, "although he does occasionally paraphrase." He smiled. "It is difficult for me to say for certain. Remember, the Bibles we carry may have had the same source, but they're somewhat different translations of it. Therein lies the majority of our disagreements."

"But you came and told Agon about our test for him? How could you?" Varaa demanded, still stuck on that.

Agon held up a restraining hand. "He told me because I myself was surprised, even concerned, that you hadn't already offered opportunities for treachery, that you weren't at least a little suspicious of a former tenacious enemy. To me, that didn't speak well of your good sense, Colonel Cayce," he added in an admonishing tone. He chuckled and gestured grandly. "Now, as it is, I am satisfied." Colonel Tun grumbled but seemed to agree, and Arevalo grinned widely.

Lewis laughed out loud and slapped his thigh. "As am I," he said. "It's strange, but I suddenly feel as if a great, unidentifiable weight has been lifted from my shoulders." He sobered. "You killed an awful lot of my men," he said simply. "We killed a great many more of yours. That's . . . not easy to simply forget, and I'm sure a lot of our men never will. But regardless of that, I do believe in my heart that we're on the same side."

They all rode companionably together after that, saying little at first, but gradually opening up. Arevalo asked Major Olayne about the captured Dom artillery. Specifically why, if it was so inferior to the American guns, they'd bothered to bring it at all. Olayne countered that they'd already established three full batteries using eighteen of the good-quality Dom 8pdr tubes mounted on copies of American M1841 carriages. The tubes were more than a hundred pounds heavier, but the carriages had no difficulty accommodating the weight. What's more, an ingenious blacksmith from Ohio had devised a portable device for efficiently and precisely scraping metal off the bronze trunnions of captured guns so they could drop right into existing American carriages. The elevation screw had to be moved slightly farther back on the trail, but that was easily accomplished by boring three holes (one large one for the screw itself and two smaller ones for bolts) with an auger bit and brace. In any event, those batteries—D, E, and F—were included in planning along with the rest; had well-trained, competent (if inexperienced) crews; and were interspersed along the column just as the "original" American guns were. However, the ones Arevalo referred to were the twenty largely unmodified weapons (only the squat little limbers had been altered so they could be pulled by teams of horses instead of a single armabuey) that currently plodded along at the rear among the baggage train.

Olayne shrugged at the question. "There's nothing wrong with the tubes, you know. It's only really the carriages—too heavy and cumbersome to deploy in anything much beyond defensive or static positions. They can't race across the battlefield and add their weight of metal where it's least expected and most needed. In addition to that, not only don't they have any sights to speak of, but elevation adjustments are very crude. A 'quoin,' I believe it's called—essentially a simple wooden wedge—is shifted about beneath the breech. To top it all off, your gunpowder isn't the best. It seems to be made of quality ingredients, and it's strong enough, it just isn't sufficiently consistent for fine work. It's too mixed, you see. Grains the size of pea gravel mixed with what is practically dust, and everything in between. Even when carefully measured by weight or volume, velocities vary wildly from one shot to the next."

"Have you anything good to say about our artillery?" Arevalo asked with a tinge of annoyed sarcasm.

"Well, aside from the tubes, as I said, your artillerymen were already reasonably professional considering what they had to work with."

Arevalo frowned, and Olayne realized he might've sounded condescending. He didn't mean to. "I'm sure they can do much better with improved equipment," he hastened to add.

"But you haven't given it to them," Arevalo pointed out. "They remain with the guns at the rear."

Olayne nodded. "Yes, but they do have much to learn, not only to improve their drill—loading speed and efficiency for when they *do* have better equipment—but also how to use the new sights the tubes have already been modified to accept and actually hit specific targets they aim for. This will be accomplished with training, those sights, and better ammunition. Not only improved gunpowder, but wooden sabots strapped to the shot. The straps break on firing, but the wood is pressed up around the shot to create a superior gas seal and keep the shot centered in the bore." He smiled encouragingly. "Finally, all those guns will eventually have new carriages of their own. With your artillerymen already prepared, I'm sure they'll be just as ready and lethal as ours by then."

Olayne was suddenly uncomfortably aware that everyone had stopped talking to listen. He reddened and cleared his throat. "My apologies. I didn't mean to drone on like one of my West Point professors."

"No," Lewis said. "I think you explained it quite well." He looked at Agon. "And your infantry has already had a lot of practice maneuvering alongside ours. I wish we could've modified all your muskets, to standardize ammunition at least." He glanced behind the entourage at the marching men at the head of the column. "But I'm glad we were able to divert enough effort from the smiths in Vera Cruz to equip all your men with those interesting brackets you came up with."

There simply hadn't been time to transform all the plug bayonets of Agon's troops into the socket type that allowed men to keep shooting with bayonets affixed. Agon himself had come up with the expedient of driving two roughly forged figure eight–shaped irons onto the muzzles of his soldiers' weapons that bayonets could be inserted into alongside the bore instead of shoved into it. His troops would have to remember to affix the wicked, short swordlike weapons so the guards wouldn't obstruct the muzzles, but that shouldn't be hard. They wouldn't be able to load them if they did.

"I'm grateful for that," Agon agreed with feeling. His former enemies never had possessed any truly overwhelming material advantages over his own soldiers, except perhaps in artillery, of course, and even that was due to ingenious refinements to technology both sides possessed. Aside from that, however, he could only imagine how many of his men had died solely due to the almost ridiculously and intuitively simple—in retrospect—innovation of mounting a bayonet offset from the bore. "I look forward to introducing that modest little improvement to our mutual enemies soon," he added with a bitter, predatory tone. "It will be most effective the very first time, of course."

Lewis was nodding. "That's right. One reason I hope to arrange it so there's very little sparring with the enemy and our first major meeting has the potential to be decisive."

Agon looked at him curiously. "How do you mean to bring that about?"

Lewis sighed. "Unfortunately, it won't be as easy as the first time you and I met—and I don't mean that the way it sounds. No disrespect intended at all. Not only were you under the orders of a fool and a coward who *wasted* your men"—everyone knew he meant Don Frutos—"we had intimate knowledge of the land and terrain. You tell me that General Gomez *isn't* a fool, and we're in *your* territory now and I don't know the ground."

Agon contemplated that. "We're actually still in Don Hurac's province. Sadly, he knows little about it between the cities beyond what he has seen from the windows of his coach. I don't *have* a 'territory,' of course, and know less about this one than Don Hurac. On the other hand, General Gomez has spent his entire life in the west and won't be familiar with it either. He will have local scouts, no doubt, but few of them will be better acquainted with the land beyond the roads than Gomez is from his maps. Your Ocelomeh Rangers are far bolder scouts, more comfortable exploring new routes in dangerous lands. We may *still* be in more familiar territory than the enemy when we meet."

"I hope so," Lewis said.

"Don't forget those bands of reaper monks my fath . . . I mean, Major Anson ran into," Leonor warned.

Lewis nodded solemnly at her. "There's evidence the wildlife took a toll on them, as did our own scouts, but they didn't hesitate to strike out into the wilderness."

Colonel Reed was vigorously rubbing the bridge of his nose, looking back and forth between the speakers. "They do seem more . . . attached to

Tranquilo's Blood Priests than anyone, however," he said, then elaborated. "Colonel Agon and I were just discussing them. He's encountered them before."

"Indeed," Agon agreed. "But only in very small numbers. I perceived them as an experiment of sorts, by Tranquilo himself, to create an unquestioning elite within his order chosen from among initiates for the fervency of their faith and groomed as 'special assistants' to high-ranking Blood Priests." He blinked. "However it is that they 'rank' themselves, or achieve high status over one another. They are all officially equal, remember. These new *patriarcas* aside. And how are *they* chosen, I wonder?"

"Prob'ly depends on how many people they murder in their 'sacrifices.' They keep score," Leonor growled disgustedly.

Agon looked at her and bowed his head slightly. "You may be exactly right."

Leonor furrowed her brow. "But Blood Cardinals're all s'posed to be equal too, right? How're some o' *them* more equal than others? How come Don Hurac has a better claim as 'supreme unholiness' than whoever swiped the chair from under him?"

Father Orno laughed. "Most astute, as usual, my dear." Leonor frowned at the little priest. Reverend Harkin called her "my dear" all the time. So did De Russy. But that was just the way they were. Couldn't untrain them—any more than some of the rank-and-file Irish soldiers who called *one another* that. Orno had picked it up, along with the same slightly condescending tone that certainly hadn't come naturally to him. *Have to straighten him out later, in private,* she decided, then that thought surprised her. Even she had been changed by their circumstances. Her undisputed status as an officer and soldier, not to mention her attachment to Lewis, had made her recognize her responsibility not to cause distractions or hard feelings in situations like this. In the past, she would've just blurted out a correction, Orno would've been hurt and confused, and she wouldn't have given a damn. Let someone else smooth his ruffled feathers. She glanced at Lewis and saw his secret smile, watching her smolder. *My God,* she thought. *I'm turnin' tactful!*

"Call it 'tradition,' I suppose," Orno continued, oblivious to Leonor's annoyance. "The status of the twelve Blood Cardinals is probably based primarily on the importance of the provinces they rule. Don Hurac's, which made him 'third among equals,' is by far the most significant in the east. The previous Supreme Holiness"—he glanced at Varaa, whose "king," Har-Kaaska, had once been in that ruler's clutches—"was from a western province, though I don't know its boundaries, or even what it's called. It's certainly one of the oldest and most prestigious." He looked at the former Dom general. "You will be more conversant on these matters, surely?"

Agon frowned and nodded. "Yes, the older provinces have traditionally been the most important, though those in the center, particularly the one encompassing the Great Valley and Holy City, have increasingly competed for status. Don Julio is from the Holy City itself and was no doubt embarrassed—at least—to call General Gomez to his aid from the west." He waved that away. "But we were talking about reaper monks, were we not? Based on the number of encounters reported by Major Anson, there do seem to be more of them. Almost as if Tranquilo was inspired by Anson's Rangers to build a unit of 'devils' of his own. We will have to remain on our guard for them."

Lewis appreciated the fact that Agon had suffered more at Anson's hands than anyone, losing his entire mounted force. "That's why I haven't ordered Anson's brigade forward against Puebla yet," he told them. "Kisin's Holcanos keep close watch on it, and Gomez isn't yet there, but most of Anson's men have been waiting in Actopan until we arrive with the rest of the army. I'll send him forward then. Not only so he'll have support if Gomez *does* get there in force and he has to fall back, but so we can keep a larger number of experienced scouts out around us. We won't be as strung out once we reach more open country, but we'll still be a big target for marauders. Time for us to start moving faster, but even more carefully, if we can."

"But what will we do about Puebla?" Reed asked.

"We take it," Varaa said simply, "and keep grinding on."

Reed spared her an impatient glance. "Yes, of course, but how?"

Lewis glanced at Varaa and sighed. "A lot still depends on what others do, and ground we've never evaluated, but Varaa's basically right. As I said, we'll send Anson ahead as soon as we get to Actopan—minus Captain Hernandez, I think, and perhaps some more of Coryon Burton's dragoons." He smiled at Leonor. "I'm told Captain Beeryman is the best judge of ground in the army. That's why he'll stay with Anson. Perhaps he can describe the ground well enough for Captain Barca to draw it. I was surprised to learn he was such an artist. The sketches he sent of the recent action were very well done. In any event, together they'll take the city—or not—but we'll move up regardless. If Gomez is present by then, we'll draw him out and destroy him. If he isn't there, we either take or hold Puebla ourselves and oblige Gomez to come to us."

"So we will fight a defensive battle?" Major Ulrich asked, speaking for the first time. He didn't look happy about that. Lewis shook his head.

"No, we won't wait in the city. He may have some more of those monstrous siege guns, and that gives away all our advantages anyway. We'll move forward to meet him. Beat him in the open."

Reed let out an exasperated breath, florid face redder than usual and not just from the cold. "But *how*? I always ask, and you always reply with your grand, overall scheme, but never with details of how you intend to implement it! I know you can't say for certain until you know the conditions and the odds, but I also know you wander around every day with all sorts of plans whirring about in your head, spilling out your ears. What if you fall?" he asked pointedly. "How will any of us know what you would want if you never tell us?"

Lewis regarded his second in command. "They most certainly don't 'spill out my ears.' I'm not a secretive man by nature, but we must remember the ease with which the enemy has and can spy on us. Whatever details *any of us* 'spill' in advance should only be shared with care, with those we're directly planning *with*."

"He is right," Agon said sourly. "And though I stake my life on all my remaining men being loyal, I cannot stake my *honor* on it." He looked at Reed. "Can you? Can you swear on your honor that, even among the men who accompanied you to this world, there isn't a single one susceptible to the riches or pleasures our evil enemy might offer? I think not." He looked back at Lewis. "And besides, I doubt any of us would be in the position we are if Colonel Cayce thought we were incapable of continuing a battle largely as he would if he fell. None of us are helpless, and I believe all would seize any opportunity his initial plan presented. Is that not so?"

Lewis dipped his head. "That's how I see it. No one is indispensable. No one *can be* indispensable." He sighed. "Honestly, our army is larger than any I ever imagined commanding, but compared to what the enemy is capable of raising, it's still relatively small. Its strengths are in its training, some slightly better equipment"—he grinned at Olayne—"and a good cause, of course. Taken together, those things should overcome the enemy's numbers—but it'll cost us very dear, I'm afraid. I expect from now on, every major fight will be like the last one we engaged in with Colonel Agon, just as fierce and bloody. Many of us, perhaps all, will fall in the coming weeks and months. I won't say years, because if victory eludes us that long we'll lose. We simply can't beat a fully mobilized Dominion with *millions* of subjects devoted to continued resistance. We have to win quickly and decisively, and I'm confident everyone in a position of leadership in this army has learned how to do that by now. So"—he smiled—"that's the 'big plan,' and *all of us* will begin to piece together the little things it takes to bring it about."

Varaa grinned and clapped her hands. "See? Simple!" she said.

Fourth Division reached the broad clearing where Anson's brigade made camp before its battle much earlier than expected, just a little after noon, but scouts returned to describe the much larger and better-protected camp on the battlefield itself just a short distance ahead. Lewis, still riding at the front of the army and now joined by Samantha Wilde Anson (that would take getting used to), decided to press on. He was glad he did when he easily recognized the site from Barca's sketches, along with the step, and Petty's hill, of course, because not only had the modified Dom defenses all been left in place, a kind of small barracks had been constructed and the resulting "fort" was manned by a company of dragoons under Hans Joffrion.

With the unexpected enemy activity, mostly by reaper monks that the mounted brigade in particular had encountered along the way, the plan to establish signal towers all the way to Vera Cruz had been put on hold. They simply couldn't spare the men to garrison each one, and relays of mounted couriers remained in use. The system was still costly in terms of men and animals because couriers had to move in squads big enough to discourage or fight guerillas and roving packs of predators. And there had to be even stronger way stations where remounts could be maintained, but there needn't be near as many. Joffrion's little fort was the last such station before Actopan, and he had extra men, to defend the remounts from both the large number of frightening scavengers lingering in the vicinity of the battlefield and the reaper monks the Holcanos fought on the flank in the battle, but then simply disappeared. Knowing how determined they were, it had to be assumed they remained near.

The way station hadn't been needed for the last day or two, at least as a source for rest and remounts, but Joffrion's orders were to await Colonel Cayce and bring his command in with him. Now the large, open space that once served as a fighting position for Doms, then a camp for Anson's brigade, was quickly filling up, tents practically popping into existence like serried toadstools, cook fires already sending gray wisps of smoke to the sky as those soldiers designated to cook for their squad got an early start on supper. The sections of Hudgens's battery reunited and established an artillery park, the gun's crews rigging tents and flies and picketing their horses. The gentlemanly Hans Joffrion even provided refreshments for the officers (and ladies) who dismounted with Lewis to hear the latest news and watch the great army reassemble after its long trek.

"So, there has been skirmishing with 'reapers,' or whatever they are?" Lewis asked with a significant look at Varaa and Agon after Joffrion described an ambush on some of his men out hunting. None were killed, but two had been wounded by those big, obsidian-pointed arrows. One dead attacker had been found, dressed in a brown tunic.

"Yes sir," Joffrion said. "And worse back toward the city. Some of the villas have been pillaged and people slain in . . ." He glanced at Samantha. ". . . the most disgraceful fashion."

Samantha was actually in uniform, much like the one Leonor now wore: dark blue jacket and sky-blue trousers with no branch trim. The Englishwoman had finely tailored her outfit to compliment her lovely form, however. Leonor's even nicer shape (in Lewis's opinion) was hidden entirely under her shapeless clothing. Only her pretty face and long black hair (hanging straight and unbound, which by most of the customs of the Yucatán meant she was "spoken for") betrayed the fact she was a woman. Samantha flicked her ever-present ivory-ribbed fan at Joffrion. "You needn't sugarcoat your description on my account, Captain. I have seen dreadful things before—and I was on the beach, if you will recall." Anyone present for the Battle on the Beach shortly after they arrived on this world had witnessed horror indeed and needed no further elaboration.

"Indeed, ma'am. I hadn't forgotten."

"And don't call me 'ma'am,'" Samantha insisted with a smile. "It makes me feel positively archaic. Just because I'm married now is no reason for everyone to change how they address me!"

"Well . . ." Joffrion began, at a loss. Considering Major Anson directly commanded all mounted troops and was widely believed to be the most dangerous man alive, Joffrion visibly suspected the way he spoke to the Ranger's new wife could matter quite a lot.

"Never mind," interrupted Varaa. "You were speaking of these raiders, yes?"

Joffrion cleared his throat. "Yes. After we took Actopan, we proceeded to investigate the circumstances on some of the nearby estates and immediately discovered evidence of atrocities committed against their owners and people. Not all of them. Some of those villas are practically small fortresses. But significantly, Boogerbear—I mean Captain Beeryman—concluded that many of those that weren't molested belonged to people known to strongly support the new enemy regime. They may even be actively supporting the raiders. Feeding and sheltering them."

"What's bein' done about it?" Leonor asked.

Joffrion snorted with what might be amusement. "Beeryman continues to try to make contact with prominent people in the countryside, to induce them to support the army and people of Actopan with provisions. He offers to escort them and any stockpiled grain and livestock they might have into the city if they feel threatened. Personally," he added, "I think his excursions are primarily 'hunting trips,' with his sights set on raiders."

Leonor was nodding. "He's a Ranger. That's what we do."

Lewis smiled, raising his gaze to the long columns of troops. They'd doubled now that they had the space, essentially moving with an eight-man front, but Lewis still couldn't see the tail of the army around the rocky bend nearly two miles away. The thunderous noise of tapping drums, thousands of tramping feet and hooves, clanking canteens and tinned copper cups dangling from haversack straps, squeaking sling swivels, rumbling wagons and guns, and countless excited conversations could actually be felt through the ground, in the bones. Gray-white dust billowed downwind away from the men, looking like smoke from a massive grassfire. Colonel Itzam's 3rd Division was moving past now, up with a portion of the baggage train, and the 2nd Vera Cruz was arrayed around Don Hurac's bizarre carriage. Lewis was amazed the ship-size contraption had made it this far in one piece. His smile went away. "I don't like that," he said, pointing. Colonel Itzam, who'd just joined him again, looked himself and frowned.

"Oh my, that won't do at all. Captain Uo!" he called loudly to his Itzincabo aide. The man whipped his horse around and, finding the source of the summons, trotted over.

"Sir?" he said.

Itzam gestured. "Why is the Second Vera Cruz marching with Don Hurac's party?"

Uo looked back and shrugged. "Well . . . he complained that members of the Third Uxmal were frequently disrespectful, mocking his, ah, mode of transport. Back at the clearing where we initially planned to camp, when we brought up the rear, he requested that the Second Vera Cruz replace them in line of march so he'd have his own people responsible for his security. It made sense to me," Uo defended.

Itzam was shaking his head. "No, it doesn't. Don Hurac is essentially a foreign dignitary, accompanying this army at our sufferance, as a courtesy. If we're successful, he may well rule the Dominion someday, but he has no authority in this army. He *certainly* doesn't have his own private troops, and we can't have anyone starting to think of them like that. Least of all the Second Vera Cruz itself. That regiment is in *my* division, in Colonel Cayce's army, and Don Hurac has no place in the chain of command."

Lewis nodded approvingly at Itzam, and Captain Uo suddenly realized his error, his expression crumbling. "I'm so sorry, sir. I didn't think. I'll reassign the Second at once."

Lewis shook his head. "Not your fault, Captain. I'll speak to Don Hurac myself and politely remind him of a few things. Change the order of march tomorrow when we make our last push to Actopan."

"Sorry, sir," Itzam said as Uo saluted and galloped off. "I should've caught it myself."

"Nonsense," Lewis countered. "The army's so well integrated now, the only priority for the order of march should be the allocation of combat power. Don Hurac will bear watching, however. Can't let him start thinking of this army as his. Any of it."

"Actopan tomorrow," Leonor said, changing the subject. "It'll be good to see my father again."

"I will certainly second that," Samantha agreed with a smile. She'd folded her fan, but that didn't keep her from using it like a pointer at Lewis, to emphasize her words. "I knew we would have little time together, for however long this vexing war endures. That is why I insisted we be married; so there would at least be *some*." She touched the fan to her lips. "And he does need me, I think."

Leonor nodded slightly, glancing at Lewis. He was smiling sadly, but also nodding when he said, "I'll be glad to see him too, but won't take much of his time. Make the most of your reunion, the best way you can. I'm afraid it'll be very short."

CHAPTER 15

Ranger Captain Sal Hernandez and six Ocelomeh Rangers, Captain Thomas Hayne and four dragoons, and Captain Felix Meder and four of his riflemen were escorting Alcalde Xam himself, along with a pair of his new advisors. Like the rest left behind, these had been chosen from in and around Actopan because they were fairly well-known and generally trusted by people in the area. It only seemed right to protect high-ranking civilians on their quest to draw the countryside to their cause with respected officers in charge of a good defensive mix of troops. They were twenty in total, and that alone should've been an intimidating number since they'd seen no evidence any of the marauding bands consisting of, or led by, reaper monks moved in groups larger than half a dozen or so. They'd done a lot of damage, pillaging many nearby estates, burning villas and storehouses and murdering any *patricios* or hidalgos they even thought were teetering on the edge of accommodating the invaders. Even the free and slave workers weren't spared, though a few managed to slip away from the terrifying, bloodthirsty massacres. Their accounts, and the aftermath that Sal and Boogerbear had viewed, brought Comanche raids the Rangers had seen on another world to mind, but even the worst of those couldn't compare to the bloody-minded, terroristic depravity on display here.

Today they were going farther afield, back in the direction of the battle they'd fought, hoping to appeal to the owners of those first villas they saw. If they were still alive. And the idea now was as much to save lives as to gather supplies. The whole Allied Army would be marching through here today or tomorrow, and they'd offer everyone they contacted the chance to accompany it into Actopan.

"Where are we headed next?" Sal asked Alcalde Xam. The first large estate they'd visited, about six miles south of town, had looked undamaged from a distance, and they'd hoped to find people there. They'd been disappointed. It hadn't been a slaughter this time: they only found one body— that of the *patricio*, impaled on a stake in an otherwise lovely garden that would explode with color in the spring. The man had been a personal friend of Xam's, as had his large family. Of his wife, children, servants, and workers, there'd been no sign.

"Hmm?" Xam asked, staring straight ahead of his plodding local horse, still reliving the horror he'd seen. "Oh yes. Don Mercuto's estate. Perhaps less than a mile ahead there will be a road to the west, into those hills." He indicated what would've been viewed as distant mountaintops from the south. The land here was almost flat for a great distance all around, fields of something like winter wheat only broken by small, rounded humps here and there, with clumps of scrubby trees clustered upon them. "He isn't the best candidate to seek support from. A retired military officer himself, he is rather old-fashioned and pious." Xam conjured a snort of amusement. "Nor does he like me very much. I am just a jumped-up freeman, after all. That attitude, the unusually large number of armed hidalgos he employs—also former soldiers—not to mention the high walls around his villa, might have preserved him thus far. Being a traditionalist, however, he hates the Blood Priests even more than me, I expect, and any locals among the murdering *terroristas* will have told them. Still, he can't be as high a priority as those more likely to join us, and after what we just saw . . . what you have seen many times, I feel obliged to offer him assistance." He waved back to one of his advisors. "And he has friends among us. Perhaps they can convince him."

Two of the Rangers had been riding far out on either side of the little column, and now the one a couple hundred yards west whistled shrilly, making exaggerated motions farther away.

"Somethin' out there," said Captain Hayne, raising the brass telescope he'd borrowed from Captain Holland and never returned. "Bloody hell," he murmured. "Look yonder, if ye would." He handed the glass to Sal.

"What is it?" asked Felix Meder.

"Riders," Hayne replied. "More than us, it looks like."

"At least twice as many," Sal confirmed grimly. "All mounted an' just pacin' us at the moment. Gettin' bolder, ain't they?"

"You think they are the enemy?" Xam anxiously asked.

"Gotta be," Sal told him. "It ain't none o' us, not even Holcanos. They don't scout on horseback, an' I think they're all off toward Puebla with Boogerbear." He glanced ahead at a bare dirt road veering off from the well-surfaced one they'd been on. "Here's our turnoff."

"But . . ." Xam protested. "Surely we can't go to Don Mercuto now. That road will take us *closer* to those men!"

"Yep," said Sal. "We're out here to help folks, talk 'em in if we can, but the best way to help the most people is to kill them *hombres malos* that's raisin' the fuss in the first place. It's kinda what Rangers do."

Xam's eyes went wide. "You *want* to fight them? So many?"

Sal looked at Hayne and Meder, who nodded agreement. "Just two to one; we're in good shape. Course, I'd rather you an' your friends weren't along. It might be a touch risky." He sighed. "Guess I better leave it to you. Looks to me like them devils're gangin' up on us on purpose, temptin' us with a chance to take a chunk out of 'em. *Knowin'* we'll hate to let 'em go. They prob'ly figure we'll split, come after 'em with half our boys, an' send the other half back with you." He shook his head. "That's cuttin' things too fine. They'd like as not jump on one or the other of us then, maybe one *then* the other. Splittin' up ain't a good idea an' might get us all killed. So . . . Go home or get after 'em, all or none of us. You make the call."

Xam looked at his companions. None were soldiers, but all were armed with cutoff Dom muskets loaded with heavy charges of drop shot. Two carried swords, actually more like long-bladed machetes, and Xam had a long-handled axe indistinguishable from a tomahawk thrust in his belt. "We stay," Xam finally said. "But we don't know how to fight. We are in your hands."

Sal just nodded. "Figured you'd pick that, after what we seen earlier. Stirs a fella up, don't it?"

"Yes," Xam agreed darkly. "But what will we do?"

Sal turned on the road to Mercuto's estate. "Keep goin' as before. Ignore 'em for now." He chuckled. "Well, don't *ignore* 'em, o' course, but pretend to, see?"

"Just one thing," Meder said doubtfully. "What if those men are just bait and there are more waiting for us?"

Sal seemed to think about that for a while, then shrugged. "Then I guess we might all get killed. But if there is more, they'd'a jumped on us at some point, anyway."

They were actually heading toward the enemy now, who'd stopped on the slope of one of the little hills. After moving openly before, it seemed as if they were hoping the clump of trees would distort their outlines and hide them. It didn't work. Not only did the morning sun betray them, they'd left a path in the frost on the winter wheat that practically drew a line straight to them, even at this distance. That must've belatedly dawned on them because they moved into the trees as the *alcalde*'s party drew closer.

"How good are your riflemen, Mr. Meder?" Sal asked casually. He already knew that Meder himself, armed with his personal M1817 rifle, complete with a fly in the tumbler and a single-set trigger that the blacksmith/gunsmith/ordnance sergeant, O'Roddy, in Barca's battery had modified it with, might be the deadliest long-range marksman in the world.

"These fellows with me?" Meder asked with a smile. "They're some of my best." One was a young Uxmalo, probably about sixteen, who'd inherited his weapon from a fallen man. Another had been with Meder from the start and was probably close to sixty. The other two were bearded, in their twenties, and looked like brothers.

"Sooo," Sal drawled, "think they can hit a man at two hundred paces?"

"Easily," Meder said flatly. "As long as they can see their sights and the target," he qualified, squinting at the cluster of brush now about four hundred paces away.

"Fine," Sal said. "When we get even with 'em, we'll stop an' dismount like we're checkin' the horses' hooves, stretchin' our legs an' such. Alcalde Xam? You an' your fellas hold the riflemen's horses an' stand ready to grab the reins o' the rest an' ease back behind us, clear?"

"Yes," Xam replied nervously.

"That line of rocks up ahead looks good," Meder said. "It's about the right distance and will give us rests for our rifles. Cover too."

"I see it," Sal agreed. There was a number of long piles of rocks surrounding the grain fields, doubtless gathered by those plowing the earth over the years, probably decades. Back "home," people would've stacked them more carefully, even making low walls, but large, oblivious creatures here would only scatter them passing through.

"Everybody else ready?" Sal asked.

"Aye," Hayne replied. "I reckon ye want me dragoons ta hold fire till the bloody Doms charge closer—but what if they don't?"

"With Meder's men killin' 'em, they can't just sit an' take it. They'll charge or run away. My money's on the first choice, but if they run, we'll chase 'em."

As usual, things didn't work out exactly as planned. Sal's little column stopped (Meder was actually senior by date of commission, but there was no doubt in anyone's mind that Sal was in charge of this action), and the men dismounted beside the rock rubble to begin their charade. That's when the enemy charged them.

"Take a rest! Mark your targets and fire at will!" Meder cried, diving behind the rocks himself and steadying his weapon. Thumbing the cock back, he took careful aim at a large man in a brown tunic lunging forward atop a striped horse. He was waving a Dom lancer's saber and exhorting his marauders onward, expression almost rabid. Meder hesitated only an instant, vaguely concerned all his men might target the apparent leader, but decided they'd naturally leave the man to him. Already closer than a hundred and fifty yards, that one was coming right at him, so he didn't even have to lead him. Easy. Covering the distorted face with his front sight, Meder squeezed the trigger. *Clack-craack!* There was the slightest hesitation or "hang-fire" because of the humidity but not enough to affect a good marksman who kept aiming through the shot. A large bloody hole appeared in the center of his target's chest, insane expression turning to surprise as the man leaned to the side and tumbled off his horse. Four more shots came quickly, smoke roiling, and four more men fell dead, horses bolting on alone. Infantrymen armed with smoothbore muskets would've been just as happy to hit the horses at this range, but the riflemen were horsemen themselves and glad their more precise weapons allowed them to be more particular.

The dragoons were horsemen too, and equally picky when possible. Their Hall carbines weren't as powerful, but were nearly as accurate as the enemy thundered closer. Two more men were snatched from their saddles amid a visible pink mist, and a third was left screaming and clutching a useless, smashed arm as he veered away. The veteran riflemen reloaded their long rifles almost as fast as the dragoons made their breechloaders ready again—just in time to meet the charge sweeping upon them. Combined with Sal and the other men, armed with what were essentially shotguns, they all fired into the enemy at a distance of feet.

A roaring head exploded in a geyser of bloody bone and brains. More blood fountained from the back of a rider as a rifle ball blew it out. Most of the marauders started shooting long-barreled Dom lancer pistols, largely ineffectually, but one fired a lancer musketoon simultaneously with one of Xam's advisors, his ball smashing the man's leg near the hip even as the advisor's pattern of drop shot mulched his face. Meder swiftly, gently laid his prized rifle down and drew his own single-shot pistol and saber. Hayne had a pistol and dragoon saber too—their men all similarly armed—and Sal had a Paterson Colt in each hand. In a heartbeat, all became an intermingled riot of pistol shots, slashing blades, whirling and rearing horses, and shrieking, shouting, bellowing men.

Sal's group had just about evened the numbers before the enemy was on top of them but immediately had two men down and one still holding the horses. He was struck by the fact all their attackers, though dressed like reapers, were armed with lancer weapons—except for lances, of course. If they'd actually *been* lancers, his men would've been doomed. As it was, the advantage that being mounted should've given them was wasted. They weren't good horsemen and didn't know how to use their blades. Even dismounted, his men did. Still trying to avoid hurting horses, his men ducked around inexpert saber swings to hack thighs and bellies or stab straight into chests. Some who'd saved their pistols practically jammed their muzzles into men's sides and fired. (That made Sal wince, knowing they might damage their weapons that way.) The press was so tight, however, that even as a dragoon, Ranger, or rifleman stabbed or shot someone, that man might be doing the same to one of them on the other side of his horse—who was doing the same to another rider. A Ranger was shot in the top of the head, eyes bulging, gore splashing out, even as his killer was stabbed. A dragoon was knocked down by a spinning horse that proceeded to stomp his chest with a very emphatic crunch. The man couldn't even scream. Alcalde Xam, gamely if awkwardly doing his best, cried out when a saber raked across between his shoulder and neck. Sal shot the man who did it in the temple, and he slid off his horse and dropped to the ground.

"Mr. Hernandez—if ye'd be so kind," shouted Hayne. In a glance Sal could see that the dragoon officer had been shot or slashed in the right arm, losing his saber, and was fending off blows with his pistol, held by the muzzle in his left hand. Only the strap-encircled grip of the weapon—a pitiful buckler at best—had kept it in one piece so far. Sal snapped off a shot that took the reaper in the back of the head. Dropping his saber, he simply slumped over, and the horse walked out of the fight. "Obliged," Hayne said, dropping the wrecked pistol and scooping up the Dom's saber.

"At your service," Sal replied. He meant it. No one was a better instinctive shooter with a pistol than Sal. At least at close range. Boogerbear was close, and even Leonor was very good. Anson was better at range with his much more powerful Walker Colts. But after his first shot with his musketoon, Sal had seen his role as protector for the rest. The problem was, he'd started with a total of ten shots combined in both his revolvers, and the sad fact was they weren't very powerful and were rarely immediately deadly unless he hit his man just so. He couldn't reload under these conditions either, so when they were empty they'd be of no further use in this fight. He had to take his shots with extra care, and sometimes he just didn't have one. The few bullets he'd put in men's bellies and chests had been as much to distract as to kill. Now one pistol was empty and the other had two rounds left.

That seemed just as well since the fight was quickly ending, only three of the reapers still mounted. One was clearly dead, slumped in his saddle, and another quickly followed him as a hastily reloaded Hall blew him out of the saddle. But the third man, though slashed on both thighs, blood pouring down his legs, somehow seemed to recognize the wounded Alcalde Xam. Screaming with the pain of it, he kicked his horse into motion and raised his saber. Another quickly loaded Hall missed him, and a dazed Ranger, blood sheeting his face, was knocked aside by the horse. Sal raised his revolver and actually aimed. *Click!*

"*¡Mierda!*" he snapped. He knew he wasn't empty; he'd counted his shots . . . hadn't he? *Bad cap? Lost cap?* He had only seconds. Xam looked dazed as well, just standing there waiting, upper chest wet with blood. Cocking again, Sal quickly squeezed the trigger. The Colt fired, smoke bloomed, and blood sprayed from the man's throat, just under his jaw—but he didn't stop. Instead, he seemed to coil, launching himself off the animal at the motionless Xam, arms outstretched, saber flashing. At the last possible instant, Xam darted to the side with infinitely more agility than Sal would've expected from him, even uninjured, and the Dom reaper crashed down, face-first, right onto another small heap of rocks someone once carried from the wheat field.

It was over. Five men were down, two each from the Rangers and dragoons, and Xam's unfortunate friend, of course. He'd quickly bled out from his terrible wound. Others were hurt, including Hayne, but Sal went to check Xam first of all. The *alcalde* was staring down at the last man. Amazingly, almost white with blood loss, he still lived. "Know him?" Sal asked, rotating the cylinder in his revolver to reveal the misfired chamber. There was clearly still a ball in it, and a percussion cap was in place. "Huh," he mumbled, bringing it back around again and cocking the hammer over it.

"Yes," Alcalde Xam said sadly. "One of my sisters' sons. My own *sobrino*."

"He knew you too," Sal observed.

"Oh yes. That was clear in his eyes."

The young man, face crushed, blood gushing from his neck wound, spat a congealing gobbet on the stones. "Heretic scum!" he gurgled.

Sal pointed the Colt at a flattened nose and pulled the trigger. Click. "Bad cap," he said absently as Xam looked at him with a mix of horror and confusion. "He's done for. Minutes only. If that. I would've put him out of his misery—or not. Let me look at your shoulder."

Xam shook his head. "The cut is not deep. The blade was not sharp."

"Well . . . you're still bleedin' like a slaughtered hog."

"Um, Captain Hernandez?" said Felix Meder, stepping up with his reloaded rifle in his hands. All of his men were approaching behind him, also clearly reloaded. Only the very youngest seemed injured, displaying a bloody and swelling cheek.

"Yeah?"

"More company," Meder said, nodding in the direction they'd been heading when all this started. A bareheaded old man with long white hair, mustache, and pointed chin whiskers was riding toward them at the head of eight other horsemen. The old man was obviously the leader and wore a shiny cuirass under a warm red cloak draped over his shoulders against the still very chilly morning. Despite the absence of any uniform, the men behind him looked more like soldiers than the reapers had, and all were armed. Without being told, the Rangers and dragoons who could do so finished preparing their weapons and came to stand by Sal and Meder's riflemen.

"You better do somethin' to plug that leak, Mr. Hayne," Sal told the dragoon officer, whose sleeve was soaked with blood. "You'll soon look like the *alcalde*'s nephew there if you don't."

"Nephew, is it?" Hayne replied in astonishment, peering down. The young man was quite dead now. "A bloody terrible world, it is," he lamented.

"Yes," Xam replied. "He was a fine boy . . . once." He looked up. "I suspect you have guessed who our visitors are."

"Mercuto?" Sal asked.

Xam nodded. "We are on his land, after all. His villa is not in view—you see how the road curves around that hill? But it is not far. He will have heard the fighting."

"Ye don't reckon he wants a fight too, do ye?" Hayne asked.

"I do not really know," Xam confessed, "but I suspect he would have already attacked if he did, while we were more disorganized."

Standing ready, they waited while this new party drew near. Finally, the old man stopped his horse, gazing about at the bodies before looking down at them, expression unreadable. The men behind him fanned out to the sides but didn't raise any weapons. "Freeman Xam," the old soldier eventually said. The title was no doubt calculated to be disrespectful, but the tone was as unreadable as his face.

"Don Mercuto," Xam greeted, just as neutral.

Mercuto gestured around. "You have made a mess on my land."

"We came merely to speak to you. The mess found us. I do hope they didn't belong to you."

Mercuto snorted. "These garaaches of Blood Priests? You know better. I will have no dealings with their kind." His eyes narrowed. "Or heretics up from the coast. I know who your friends are. We watched them march past to Actopan some days ago"—he waved around—"and have been on guard against these . . . things ever since. They have murdered most of my neighbors. Not a day has passed that I haven't seen smoke rising from the direction of their holdings." His sharp old eyes bored into Sal and the other officers. "All because *you* came here."

"You blame these men for the actions of others?!" Xam exclaimed.

"If their coming was the cause."

"Their coming saved Actopan, and many others out away from the city who were wise enough to heed early warnings."

"None of which would have been needed if they did not come," Mercuto stated flatly.

"Is this how it always is, talkin' with him?" Sal growled. "Just chasin' each other around a tree?"

"Almost always," Xam conceded.

Sal looked up at the old man. "We came out here to warn you about these killers an' offer you a chance to get away from 'em. We *lost men* for you, you old bastard."

"I am . . . glad you rid me of them," Mercuto allowed, "but I did not ask it and will not join you." He held up a hand. "Nor will I hinder you or aid such servants of evil." He gestured at the reaper corpses again. "This is not my war," he ended simply.

"Gonna be everybody's war sooner or later," Sal replied. "One side or another. C'mon, Alcalde," he said to Xam. "We've wasted enough time an' blood here. Gather our dead," he said to the others. "We'll leave the rest of the 'mess' for the landowner to deal with. Maybe the boogers'll eat 'em before their friends find 'em on his place."

RIDING BACK TOWARD the main road, which they'd follow back to Actopan (they had too many wounded to continue their efforts that day), Sal was unusually grumpy. The fact they'd lost good men didn't help, but he felt almost . . . betrayed by Don Mercuto's attitude. "Nearly rather he was straight up against us than sittin' on the fence like he is," he said.

"He is pious, I told you," Xam said.

"Wrong way," Sal maintained, but caught the *alcalde* looking at him strangely. "What?"

Xam shifted in the saddle and winced. His shoulder had stopped bleeding but would need a lot of stitches. "I have never been particularly pious," he said at last. "It is usually all that mere *hombres libre* can do just to keep their freedom and their lives, and the God we are told to worship—increasingly by Blood Priests only—has little interest in helping us with either of those things. I haven't met any of your priests yet, only soldiers, so I have only the vaguest notion of this different God you follow. From what soldiers say, He does seem altogether different. But even I haven't yet decided which God is *right*, and you will find that most of my people will feel the same. It is enough for us, for now, that you saved us, and the *people* who serve your God are better than those who claim to serve ours. That may change when more people come to know your God. Perhaps things will be better," he added wistfully. "But I tell you now, the closer your war takes you to the seat of our god's power, the fewer you'll find even willing to *hear* of a different God than theirs, and the fewer who will be willing to just 'sit on the fence.'" He sighed. "I do fear your cause is doomed from the start and Actopan will yet suffer." He straightened. "But many still live who wouldn't have, and where there is life there is hope. I still live to hope that you win—no matter which god you serve."

"Cap'n Sal," called one of the Rangers riding behind them. Sal turned in his saddle. Away in the distance a great cloud was rising, and at first he thought it was another villa on fire. But the cloud didn't rise like smoke. It merely hung there close to the ground. He looked down. The stone road didn't make any dust, but the stubble-covered ground was dry enough now that the drainage ditches alongside it would. There was a massive dust cloud behind.

"Riders comin' up," Hayne's voice told him. He'd stopped his horse and turned, holding his glass with one hand. "Dragoons," he added with satisfaction.

Sal grinned back at him, but his eyes were sad. "If they'd been just a couple hours sooner . . ." He coughed and looked back at Xam. "Looks like you'll soon have a whole swarm o' priests to pester you. Two in particular—though one ain't exactly a 'priest' . . . " He shook his head and smiled. "An' a lot bigger army between you an' them Blood Priests an' reaper monks. Colonel Cayce has caught up."

Xam smiled as well. "From all I have heard of him, he sounds . . . most interesting. Many of your people do, in various ways."

"Well, you've already met Boogerbear," Felix Meder chimed in. "They don't get much more 'interesting' than him."

"Do too," Sal corrected. "He hasn't met Leonor yet."

CHAPTER 16

The biggest splash in Actopan wasn't made by Lewis Cayce or even Leonor, despite the attitude toward females that universally prevailed in the Dominion. The most attention was immediately lavished on the arrival of Colonel Agon and his 4th Division, and then utterly eclipsed by the appearance of Don Hurac el Bendito, heralded by his acting secretary as "the rightful Supreme Holiness." Agon's name had been well-known, and quite a few sons of Actopan had even been sent to his army for its mysterious, distant expeditions. To see him here, in a green-and-black uniform, leading some of those same sons as part of an invading army, was a shock to say the least. Alcalde Xam wasn't sure at first if his presence helped or hurt their cause with his people. Then Don Hurac stepped up on top of his giant coach and addressed the gathering throng, rapidly swaying most of those who wavered with an eloquent oration bordering on a sermon about the evils of the Blood Priests (which all had witnessed), who were supported by the usurper in the Holy City.

He might've even persuaded Don Mercuto if he'd been present to hear, because, by tradition, Don Hurac truly was the rightful ruler of the Dominion. He still wore the shockingly *un*traditional white robe and proper Christian cross his conversion required instead of what he called the "malevolent" red, and he'd taken to wearing an unadorned black galero on his head instead of the former bizarre contraption he'd always been seen in before, but he *was* Don Hurac, he clearly wasn't a prisoner of these strangers, and he spoke easily to the people, showering praise on Colonel Cayce and the other commanders of the army while subtly implying the whole campaign was his idea. It was a masterful performance and did their cause a lot of good with the locals. Lewis only wished he could be certain it *was* just a performance. He'd determined earlier to have words with the Blood Cardinal, but now decided to wait because it *was* part of their goal to put Don Hurac in power, after all. His public assumption of authority—he never claimed command of the army—really didn't matter. Did it?

Plummeting temperatures and a violent, windy snowstorm extended the army's reunion at Actopan longer than Lewis preferred. He'd only meant to rest his divisions for two days before pressing on, but the storm gave them four. The abruptly excellent road, which they were told only improved the deeper they went into the Dominion (even Don Hurac was clear on that), certainly wasn't a problem, even for wagons and artillery. Unfortunately, the wildly gusting wind made the cold dangerous enough that moving too soon risked a lot of casualties to exposure. Without some fresh report from their forward scouts that made haste imperative, Lewis wouldn't risk such avoidable injuries. Most of that decision was based on genuine concern for his troops, something they all sensed and appreciated, binding them to him even closer. Some was pure pragmatism, of course, since they were about to embark on the part of the campaign when every soldier counted.

All the same, it was a welcome respite, and as Lewis had suggested to Samantha, she and Major Anson made the most of it, occupying a lavish town house Alcalde Xam pointed out, the owner having fled. Hanny Cox and several members of Barca's battery enjoyed themselves as well, seeing the sights of Actopan with some of the pretty young healers they'd met. Preacher Mac had fallen for a girl as tall as he was, also just as gruff in her way, despite an angelic face. Hanny knew it was love as soon as he heard them comparing scripture. He gallantly escorted Izel, of course (suitably chaperoned by her brother Apo and an enchanting young lady he'd met). The citizens were generally welcoming and still quite appreciative, but after a pair of 1st US infantrymen were found knifed in an alley near a tavern they'd visited, where there'd been no complaints of their behavior, it became tragically clear that enemies still lurked in the city. Orders were issued that no one should wander the streets alone. During an officers' meeting in Alcalde Xam's Grand Audience Hall, Sal Hernandez and Xam himself, arm in a sling, recounted their meeting with Don Mercuto and their subsequent discussion about the difficulties they'd likely face, even from civilians, going forward. Don Hurac dismissed their concerns, Father Orno was grimly unsurprised, and Reverend Harkin looked grave.

Finally, surprising everyone, Lewis and Leonor spent more "social" time together than ever before, examining Actopan's architecture, similar to but subtly different from other cities they'd seen, perusing the wares of street venders who'd quickly resumed their business, and attending festive banquets each night. The first was hosted by Xam in the Grand Audience Hall to honor all their "liberators," and a few *patricios*, trying hard to seem devoted to restoring him to power, threw others in honor of Don Hurac. To his credit, the Blood Cardinal always appeared with his beloved Zyan at his side, stylishly dressed by Samantha. Even Leonor wore dresses to these affairs, reminding everyone how lovely she could be when her face wasn't contorted by a killing rage. No one knew that both her Paterson Colts were tucked into pockets sewn inside her gown. The few soldiers still inclined to make lewd cracks about her and Lewis's . . . unusual courtship, were quickly shut down by the vast majority who'd not only accepted it, but seemed to have concluded it was the most natural thing in the world. With the possible exception of the tragically widowed Alcaldesa Sira Periz, who quite a few Uxmalos quietly lobbied for, what other woman could ever be strong—and interesting—enough for Colonel Cayce? And who else but the colonel could ever meet the standard a mythical fury like Leonor must set for a man? The army had grown remarkably sentimental about the whole thing.

The pleasant respite was all over now. It was still cold, but the wind had faded and the collected snow was quickly sublimating under a clear blue sky and bright sun when the entire army set out for Puebla, roughly two hundred miles north. Anson's brigade lunged ahead of the swift-marching but still comparatively plodding "Army of the Yucatán," the Detached Expeditionary Force, and Agon's 4th Division, which still considered itself the "Army of God." Just a different god, of course.

"Fifth Division won't be coming up behind us after all," Lewis told Colonel "King" Har-Kaaska, who was riding along with him, Varaa, Olayne, and Leonor atop his bizarre but clearly loyal mount, which looked like a giant duck with long, powerful legs and a lizard's tail. They were all together at the front of Har-Kaaska's fat-columned 2nd Division, trailing the 1st. None of the Mi-Anakka, Consul Koaar either, had much enjoyed their stay in Actopan. After the initial reaction to their "demonic" appearance, they'd stayed away from social engagements.

"Why is that?" Har-Kaaska asked suspiciously. The 5th was largely made up of recruits from Vera Cruz, and anything about the "grand plan" that changed, especially involving "Dom units," as he still collectively considered them, set him off.

"Alcaldesa Periz seems to have assumed command of the division," Lewis informed him dryly. "Interesting, that. She's probably the first female commander of such a large force on this world." He glanced at Varaa. "Aside from yourself, and on this continent, anyway." Varaa had still never told him where her people originally came from, but had practically confirmed it wasn't the Americas. Lewis continued, "But nearly all the recent reinforcements in from the Yucatán have joined the Fifth too. It's a pretty big division now. She sent up the request, and I returned permission for her—them—to move against Techolatla, three hundred miles up the coast from Vera Cruz. There aren't many enemy troops there. Seems most of them attacked Vera Cruz when there was still just a handful to oppose them under Captain Holland and they were roughly handled. Pretty much destroyed, from what I understand."

"It's true," Varaa agreed, tail swishing. "I wasn't there yet, of course, but Captain Holland did rather well commanding troops onshore. In any event, it's a relatively safe operation to secure another large seaport and blood the new division while disarming a potential knife in our backs. The Fifth will leave a garrison there and then move up through Puebla from the east to join us." Varaa *kakked* a laugh. "Assuming we've taken Puebla by then."

"We might as well go home right now if we can't," Leonor groused. It was clear that by "home," she meant Uxmal. *Funny, so do I when I think about it now,* Lewis mused.

"Well, the strategy is sensible enough," Har-Kaaska grudgingly admitted. "Without Techolotla in our grasp, we would have to leave a sizable force behind in Puebla. And Sira Periz can be trusted," he ended with certainty. That was enough for him. Lewis marveled again at Har-Kaaska's change of attitude. Before the great Battle of the Washboard, he'd allowed "his" Ocelomeh to participate in the Allied war effort, even join its army, but never thought they could actually win. He'd believed they'd inconvenience the Dominion, possibly even delay its conquest of the Yucatán for a time, maybe even years, but defeat was inevitable. Now, though he remained a strong voice of caution in some respects, he seemed to have even stronger faith in their ultimate victory than Lewis did, late at night, when doubts crept in to plague his rest.

No one spoke for a while, each alone with their thoughts. The column had reached its stride, however, eating ground at a respectable, comfortable pace now that nearly all the snow was gone from the road. Drummers and fifers had been playing since they left, bringing still-sleepy troops up to speed, and the sight and sound of the army marching north, a dark ribbon on the snowy plain, was no doubt stirring to those still watching from Actopan. But now the marching songs began, and Lewis hoped the people behind could hear them too. The contrast between the *character* of his army and their enemies couldn't be more profound. One was serious, purposeful, but still cheerful and secure in its cause to make a safe home for freedom and crush the evil that threatened it. The other would be remembered . . . as Agon's once had been: perhaps equally determined but largely only to perform their unpleasant duty while avoiding the daily capricious punishments smiled upon by a soul-crushing God who gloried in misery. Lewis looked beside him at Leonor, then reached over and gently touched her hand. Whether they ultimately won or not, they were doing what they had to—and they were doing right.

Leonor cleared her throat and asked, "How many days to Puebla?"

"On this road, at this pace, no more than ten," Olayne opined, grinning at Lewis, who'd turned at his voice. "Thank God you held out for horses for our guns and wagons instead of settling for those ridiculous armabueys. The beasts are a marvel for pulling a ten-ton freight wagon, I'm sure, or shifting great blocks of stone"—he lowered his voice slightly—"or Don Hurac's preposterous rolling palace. But utterly unfit for rapid movement or maneuver." They finally had enough horses, either captured or purchased with gold along the way, to pull even Don Hurac's contraption. Now that they no longer had to creep up a rough, unpaved mountain road, Don Hurac either had to switch to horses (twenty of them) or be left behind.

Lewis nodded. "Let's just hope the Doms we haven't met remain ignorant of our advantage in that respect."

The weather stayed good, and the army moved swiftly over the following days, villas or large farmhouses nearly always in view, even the occasional village. Almost all were abandoned, their inhabitants alarmed by refugees fleeing Actopan. A few people remained behind, unafraid, even enthusiastic when they heard Don Hurac was with them and they saw him for themselves. Some wanted to follow, to become part of what they saw as Don Hurac's crusade. Many gave him their slaves. Lewis immediately told these people they were free, but welcome to join the army if they liked. Some did. The combination of fine weather, rare monsters to guard against, and relatively few but surprisingly supportive natives gave the march the feel of a triumphal procession. That sense came crashing down just a couple of days out of Puebla, when Anson, Boogerbear, and a small troop of Rangers returned to the column with news.

"There . . . *was* a fair-size town ahead," Anson said cryptically, expression strangely brittle, as he appreciatively accepted a steaming cup of chocolate and exchanged the tired horse he'd been riding for Colonel Fannin. The same orderly had brought them both. Mounting his favorite warhorse, he nodded at his daughter and rode alongside Lewis. "Locals called it 'Lagarto Gris'—an' there are a lot of fuzzy gray lizards scamperin' around. Imagine lizards in this weather." He shook his head, and Lewis got the distinct impression he was stalling. Finally, he continued briskly, "Anyway, the place is a corpse. Murdered civilians everywhere. Some burnt, others crucified. Most both." He paused. "Other things were done to 'em too, like we ain't seen before." Instead of elaborating, he quickly continued, "Town was pretty much intact otherwise, but with a few exceptions, an' except for the funny lizards, the only livin' things we seen were scavengers. Them wolf-lizards an' lizard-birds, for the most part."

Lewis nodded grimly. "I was afraid we'd start seeing things like that, wherever the enemy doesn't think they can make an effective defense."

"It's worse than that, Lewis," Anson continued darkly. "They didn't just murder the townsfolk, but all the refugees they could catch headin' there from Actopan. There's a goddamn *forest* o' charred crucifixes on our side o' the town. Bastards had to make sure we'd see that first, to make us feel guilty for tryin' to stop 'em!"

From the rough Ranger's tone, the enemy's tactic had worked on his heart, if not his mind. After a chug of his chocolate, he continued, "There were some survivors. Come creepin' out o' whatever hidey-hole they found. Seems there'd been catacombs under the town, like some others, but even that didn't work like it did in the Yucatán. Holcanos don't go underground. Against their dopey religion. But the God o' the Blood Priests *lives* in the underworld, an' Blood Priests got no problem with it." He took a smaller sip. "Still missed a few folks, though, an' them who weren't too scared or traumatized to speak declared that a couple thousand lancers came out of Puebla, *regular* Dom lancers, dressed in yellow an' black, with bronze cuirasses an' plumed helmets. Folks were glad to see 'em, thinkin' they'd come to defend 'em—an' the sudden swarm o' refugees runnin' from the 'diablos' comin' up from the south. That ain't what happened a'tall," he said flatly. "The lancers rounded ever'body up an' just left 'em with a small 'guard' while the rest drove all the near livestock away. Wagonfuls o' food an' loot too. Directly, a few hundred soldiers in brown tunics came to take over 'guardin'' the locals, an' the rest o' the lancers left."

Boogerbear had joined them now, also on his favorite horse, named Dodger. It was said he was named for being so good at dodging spear thrusts and arrows—little help to a lesser horseman who'd just lose his seat.

"Them new devils had to be reapers," Boogerbear said. "More o' the bastards all the time, an' gettin' better too. Better at sneakin' an' murderin', at least. An' that's what they done to every man, woman, an' child they found. They ain't soldiers a'tall." The huge, hairy man spat a mouthful of tobacco juice, suddenly more emotional than almost anyone ever saw him. "Just armed an' better-trained Blood Priests, is all. They done . . . the things Major Anson said."

"What is the situation like now, Major?" Varaa asked, tail whipping like a snake.

Anson scratched his beard. "Left Burton an' most'a his dragoons an' about half the Rangers an' lancers there with Barca's battery to protect an' take care o' the survivors." He paused. "Can't be more than three or four hundred out o' maybe . . . shit, four or five thousand. I also told 'em to help the locals—they wouldn't be stopped—drag all their dead into the city, an' burn it."

"Burn it?" Har-Kaaska demanded. "It might have been of use to us."

Anson glared at him. "You didn't hear what I said? It ain't a town anymore, it's a corpse. Can't bury it, or all the dead in it. A funeral pyre is all there was for it."

Lewis nodded and patted his friend's shoulder, showing far more emotion than usual himself. "You did right."

"Not so sure about that," Anson replied, looking at Lewis with a strange expression, kind of a mix of contrition and defiance. "'Fraid I sorta lost a little control over my brigade. Kisin showed up with some o' his Holcanos an' said he knew where the reapers were camped. Sal took a company o' Rangers an' Captain Joffrion took a company o' dragoons ta follow Kisin an' sort 'em out." He glanced at Boogerbear, who'd clearly wanted to go as well. "Didn't really ask, they just went. I thought Coryon Burton would burst a vessel." He sighed. "Then Lara said he was goin' too, to hunt down the lancers. Took about half the First Yucatán, about five hundred men."

"That's more than half," Leonor said softly.

"A little more," Anson confessed.

Lewis was actually seething now. It was apparently a day for surprises, and no one had ever seen him this angry. "And you didn't stop them?" he finally exploded with a roar clearly audible to half of two regiments. "Don't sit there on that . . . dumb animal with more sense than you and try to tell me you *couldn't* have stopped them! You're Giles Anson, bloodthirsty Ranger, killer of more men before Monterrey than half of General Taylor's army! God knows what your tally is here, where you're 'El Diablo' himself to our enemies," he bellowed sarcastically. "There's not a man among all our mounted troops—even the Ocelomeh, who revere Har-Kaaska as their *king*—who wouldn't pull a rotten tooth from one of those giant man-eating lizards with their bare hands if you asked them. Don't you *dare* tell me you couldn't have stopped two companies of Rangers and dragoons led by men who revere you from rushing off into what is, in all probability, a trap. And Lara!" Lewis's voice almost cracked with rage. Everyone knew he was very fond of the young Mexican lancer. "You let Lara chase after a force *five times his size!*"

He stopped, face red, breathing hard. Leonor had her hand on his arm, squeezing, glaring daggers of her own at her father.

"To be fair," Boogerbear interjected, voice now as level and even-tempered as always, "it ain't like they disobeyed him. Not like mutiny or nothin'."

Lewis's eyes flared even wider, but when he spoke again, his voice was back under control. Iron hard and hot as a forge fire but no longer raised. "You didn't even *try* to stop them," he stated simply, as fact.

Anson cleared his throat. "I believe I prob'ly would have, if they'd asked. I figure they knew that, so they didn't."

"Which was fine with you, wasn't it?" Lewis snarled low. "By God, if I thought Mr. Beeryman would behave any differently, I'd relieve you right now and put him in command. I may give it to Mr. Burton when we reach the ashes of this dead town, anyway."

Father Orno and Reverend Harkin had ridden up to investigate, and both looked on at the argument in horror. "Gentlemen . . ." Harkin began in a soothing voice. Anson cut him off, now angry himself.

"Do what you want, Lewis. You always do. Course, Coryon was standin' right by me with one of those fuzzy lizards in his hand when they left—an' he didn't go gallopin' after to stop anybody either. Seemed downright satis-fied *somebody* was gonna try an' catch them killers." He rubbed his face and huffed loudly. When he spoke again, his voice was different again, more tired than anything, accent largely gone, but also suffused with an air of hopelessness.

"I've seen a lot of shit. A lot of the very worst things you can imagine people doin' to each other. Caused a heap more suffering myself than I'm proud of, an' that's a fact." He waved vaguely north. "But these bastards, this enemy, beats anything I ever saw an' makes me look like a goddamn saint beside 'em." He looked at Orno and Harkin. "You'd think that would make a man like me feel a little less bad about himself, but it don't, because now I'm ashamed when it happens in *spite* of me. In spite of everything we do." He barked a laugh. "An' *we* thought Kisin and his Holcanos were sav-ages for eatin' one another. Well, they've stopped, as far as we know. Hell, they even wear clothes. We've been good to 'em when we could'a wiped 'em out, an' they've stuck to us like ticks ever since." He paused and shook his head. "Sorry. Not like ticks. Like real friends. Point is, they're still savages. *We're* still savages compared to what we'd like to be, but you want to hear somethin' funny? When Kisin saw we were in the town an' came racin' in on a horse—don't know where he got it—he came up to me to report them reapers they found an' took one look around the . . . display they left for us to see. Vomited all over my boots." He glared at Har-Kaaska. "That's why we burnt the town. So this army wouldn't have to see it when it passes. Most of these men hate the Blood Priests bad enough already. Seein' what we saw back there will just make 'em feel as helpless as me, right now. It'll kill their sleep an' scar their souls for nothin'." Still holding Har-Kaaska's gaze, he asked, "Can *you* imagine what it takes to make a Holcano puke?" He turned to the others. "Kisin was *on fire* to get off after them reapers, an' so was I. So was every man in my command." He straightened. "So no, I didn't even try to stop Sal an' Joffrion. I don't think I could've stopped everybody else, including myself, if they didn't go. It may be a trap, and they may all die. They know that. But at least the soul of the army is safe." He glanced at his daughter and saw tears streaming down her face, then looked back at Lewis. "You're right, though. I should'a stopped Lara—or sent him with the rest. His mission's different, more personal."

"Why?" Lewis asked, tone now entirely back to normal again, except for a note of sympathy.

Anson shrugged. "Because it was lancers that left the people for the reapers. That kid's got a code of honor like you wouldn't believe, teaches ethics to his men as much as tactics, holdin' lancers up as men apart like knights of old. That lancers would do what those Doms did, even Dom lancers, requires a reckonin' by other lancers, see?"

Lewis frowned. "That young man . . ." He looked up at Boogerbear. "Your horse is fresh?"

"Depends on what you mean, sir," he began with a slight smile, then smothered the joke when he saw Lewis's eyes. "An' as you mean it, he is," he said.

"Good. Speak to Mr. Meder. Take the riflemen forward to relieve Mr. Burton at the town. Then proceed with the remainder of the force already there to join Mr. Lara's hunt for the Dom lancers. If you don't catch them before Puebla is in sight, you *will* all return and meet us on the road, is that perfectly clear?"

"Yes sir."

"Good. Go."

Boogerbear wheeled his horse out of the column and pounded back to where Felix Meder's riflemen rode.

"So, I guess I'm relieved," Anson said, expression accepting. "Kind of a relief, really." He chuckled weakly at the bad pun.

Leonor rolled her eyes. "You old fool. Of course you're not relieved."

Lewis nodded. "You're strung a little tight right now, understandably so, and I can't spare you for the sake of lancer honor. Lara will have plenty of help."

"What about Sal and Joffrion?"

Lewis shook his head. "They're Rangers—and better dragoons than we ever had at home. And Kisin's Holcanos will have been keeping an eye on the reapers. It doesn't sound like the numbers are all that uneven either. Go back to the baggage train and take the rest of the day off with your wife. She's traveling with Dr. Newlin." He eyed Orno and Harkin. "I'm sure one of our esteemed clergymen can direct you straight to her."

"Of course." Harkin beamed. "Glad to."

"I should be with my men," Anson countered.

"Not today, Major. I can't spare you for revenge either. Can't spare you at all, in fact." Lewis's expression darkened. "And just after your faint description . . ." He sighed. "I've seen terrible things as well. More dreadful on this world than I ever did at home. We've seen most of the *same* things, remember. But if this was enough worse, as it would have to be to affect you so . . ." He grasped Leonor's hand, still squeezing his arm. "I wouldn't trust *myself* to remain sufficiently detached to command when those reapers are found. I'd be killed doing something foolish—or stoop to their level when it's over. You would too, and I need your soul intact, Major."

CHAPTER 17

The self-dispatched detachment of Rangers and dragoons led by Sal Hernandez and Hans Joffrion (roughly two hundred men including Kisin and his half dozen guards) pounded across a deep, tumbling stream spanned by an ancient, arched stone bridge several miles beyond the murdered town of Lagarto Gris. Lara's lancers were coming up behind, and that's where they left them, veering to the left off the maintained road onto a rough, climbing forest track.

"How far?" Sal asked Kisin, gauging the increasingly rough terrain ahead against how they were pushing the horses.

"Not far," Kisin replied. "We hurry, though. They might go."

"I doubt they'll wait if they hear us coming," Joffrion objected.

"Not *that* close," Kisin assured. "We will move more carefully soon."

"How do we know they're still there now?" Sal asked, bothersome senses starting to flutter around the back of his mind. "An' if they are . . . how come? They gotta know we'll look for 'em."

"Still there," Kisin declared. "General Soor's Griks is on this side. They come tell us if the goddamn Doms is gone." Sal was briefly distracted by amusement at the direction Kisin's improving English had taken. He wasn't learning it from the largely Spanya-speaking Ocelomeh Rangers, so it had to be coming from dragoons. He was surprised they hadn't taught him even more inappropriate or meaningless words. "I think why they stay is to raid baggage train after army is past," Kisin elaborated. That made sense of a sort. Perhaps the leader of this band of reapers was new here and hadn't learned how effective the army's scouts could be. The whole situation still nagged at Sal.

They crested a rise on a long mountain spur, the timber tightening around them. Ahead and below, the woods opened a little, revealing a stone cabin surrounded by a rotting palisade. *Probably belongs to some hermit hidalgo hunter*, Sal assumed, *or, being on a road pitiful as this is, it's the home of an employee of a larger estate*. It looked abandoned, and this was confirmed as they drew near and one of Soor's chillingly frightening "lizard" warriors stepped out of the shadows by a wrecked gate and gestured them on. Sal wondered if some terrifying beast had "gotten" whoever once lived in the place.

"We go slow, now," Kisin said. "We get closer."

"What does this enemy camp look like?" Joffrion asked. "Perhaps we should plan our approach to do something a little more imaginative than just spill out of the woods upon them."

"Not much else you can do," Kisin said, "but you look at it soon. Just ahead." He nodded forward as the washed-out dirt road rose up to the top of another long, sloping spur. "We get off, go see."

"Sergeant Buisine," Joffrion said, "hold the fellows here, if you please."

Sal looked at Sergeant Tinez just behind him and tilted his head at Joffrion as if to say, "You do the same for our boys." Tinez simply nodded back. Sal and the young dragoon officer stepped down from their horses and followed Kisin forward. Easing into the woods to the left of the road, they crept up to the top of the rise. The old-growth forest abruptly ended on the descending slope beyond, the land now covered with sparser, shorter trees, sprouting from among thousands of rotting stumps. In the middle of the valley was another tumbling stream with sparkling clear water crashing down through rounded rocks. A kind of meadow surrounded the stream on both sides, though the grass had been badly overgrazed. The obvious culprits were enormous gray shapes half a mile lower down. Sal was intrigued by their color. They looked the same as the multitudes of other horn-faced, grass-eating monsters except for their shaggy coats. He wondered—very

briefly—if their fur changed color with the seasons. He had no more inclination to ponder that because his attention was drawn at once to the camp
right alongside the stream.

There weren't any tents, just lean-tos, but there were quite a lot of them.
Certainly enough to shelter the "few hundred" Dom reapers they expected
to find, many of whom wandered from firepit to firepit, talking with their
comrades or joining them to eat. Huge gobbets of flesh were suspended
over the fires, roasting on long iron spits, but Sal decided they hadn't killed
one of the monsters grazing in the distance, they'd probably butchered some
of the livestock they'd gathered in a pen thrown together with deadfall limbs.
Sal continued to scrutinize the enemy. Every single one was dressed in the
heavy brown tunics they'd come to associate with reapers, and only a few
appeared to be armed. They'd clearly been mounted as well, judging by the
number of hobbled horses grazing at will all around. No doubt they'd gather
them at night and picket them closer for protection, but that as much as
anything betrayed how unconcerned they were by the prospect of attack.

Sal frowned. He knew Doms in general were almost insanely arrogant
and Blood Priests took that even farther. So did the reapers they'd met, but
they'd also been increasingly practical. They'd never admit that Rangers
were better at field craft than they were, but they'd begun to behave as if
they knew it, taking ordinary precautions and being more careful. This . . .
didn't make sense at all.

"Act like they haven't a care in the world," Joffrion whispered, apparently
noting the same thing himself. "Like they're just *asking* us to hit them," he
continued with a glance at Kisin.

The Holcano shrugged and made a strange hissing sound. Another pair
of Holcano warriors just suddenly seemed to appear, as if detaching themselves from the very trees. Joffrion jumped slightly, but Sal had known they
were near, whether he could see them or not. These men didn't wear a single
article of uniform, and their urine-tanned hide clothing had a very distinctive smell. "You see anything while we coming?" Kisin asked one of the scouts,
then repeated his question in Spanya. There was a fairly lengthy exchange
before Kisin reported.

"He say them arse-heads down there not do nothing since we seen 'em.
Not even send no scouts of them own. Stupid, says me, an' is. Don't know if
it true, neither, no matter what been seen. Other scouts—got twenny more

watchin'—has told o' thinkin' they seen movin' yonder." Kisin pointed at the rise on the far side of the valley. There were more stumps there, all along the stream, but the slope behind was still fairly dense with trees.

"So it *is* a trap, then," Joffrion mused, looking carefully around. "A good one too, primed with bait we can hardly refuse. Is there any way to discover what awaits us in those far trees?"

Kisin pursed his lips. "We got fellas sneakin' there now, some Griks too." He pointed left up the mountain, the clearing on either side of the stream still fairly wide for a great distance. "But them got a bloody long way to go. Take long time to see, long time come back."

"Sooo," Joffrion said, looking at Sal. "It seems the quickest way to find out what we face is to do what they expect. I propose that we kill the bait and spring the trap, then kill whatever they send down on us. They *can't* expect a force as large as ours," he reasoned. "At most, they'll be prepared for a half dozen scouts—two dozen at the very worst."

Sal was shaking his head. "I don't know about that." He nodded down at the camp. "Say there's four hundred of 'em, all told. That seems the high number based on what those poor folks in the city said, but lookin' down there, I only see a hundred, hundred an' fifty movin' around. Might be more in the lean-tos. Thing is, even if they got two, three hundred in them woods waitin' to pounce, just what we see is more than any dozen of our fellas would ever take on, no matter how mad we are. It's just nuts."

Joffrion shrugged. "So they expect us to do what we've done. Locate them, as Kisin did, and bring more Rangers and dragoons to the fight. They know how effective we've been and *must* want to cripple us badly. That's the meaning behind *all* of this, I'm sure." His expression darkened. "Perhaps even the . . . extent of the massacre at the town. All to provoke a chase and create this opportunity."

Sal scratched his lip under his huge mustache. "Sounds reasonable. An' likely to work too, whether we're expectin' it or not. Losses'll be high, regardless."

Joffrion was shaking his head. "No, because we won't do what they want. We'll form up quickly and charge down on the camp. Look for yourself." He waved. "No one is ready for us there. I doubt they even know the 'plan' themselves. No one wants to be bait, and they are quite convincing in the role. Too convincing. We kill as many as we can and trip their trap, but when they attack with their reserve, or main force—whatever—we return here to the high ground and chew them up with our rapid-firing Halls as they sweep toward us!"

"Sounds good," Sal agreed thoughtfully, scouring the plan for flaws. He was sure they existed, but couldn't find them. "Let's get at it," he said. As soon as he and Sal and Kisin exited the trees below the crest, they jogged back down to their horses. Mounting up, Joffrion summarized the situation for the NCOs, all of whom had drifted forward by now.

"As soon as we're in the open, we must go from column into line as fast as we can and commence our attack. Every moment the enemy has to prepare could cost lives. When we're among them, I want you to fight like demons, but you must respond to the recall at once. We don't know what they have to send against us, but I'm sure it will be a respectable force. A few hundred, at least." He displayed his teeth. "We'll make them wish they never saw the town of Lagarto Gris, and the few who survive by fleeing for their lives will never forget Sal Hernandez and his company of Rangers, and L Company of the Third US Dragoons!"

—————

Capitan Ramon Lara had only led his battalion-size detachment of the 1st Yucatán Lancers another four miles or so down the main road toward Puebla when one of the young Ocelomeh Ranger scouts assigned to him came thundering back. The man pulled up and saluted. "Lancers ahead, sir. Dom lancers."

"How far?" demanded Teniente Espinoza.

The Ranger looked at him. "Little more than a mile, just drawn up across the road. Waiting."

"They *knew* we would come!" the grizzled Espinoza exclaimed to Lara. "Knew we would *have* to," he seethed.

"Apparently so," Lara agreed. "Which means they not only still have spies among us, but still have contact with them. That's particularly disturbing."

"What makes you say that?" Espinoza asked.

Lara looked at him intently. "After what they did, do you suppose they predicted our actions based on what *their* honor would require of them in our place?" he asked dryly.

Espinoza nodded reluctantly. "*Ours* is liable to get us all killed," he grouched. He'd been against this expedition but was utterly devoted to Lara.

"Perhaps." Lara nodded grimly. "But today . . ." He shook his head. "'The cause'—noble as it is—has been eclipsed by the requirements of my soul. I cannot let what we saw in Lagarto Gris pass unavenged. Since the greater part of our cause is the protection of souls, and mine is nourished as much by honor as faith, I feel more than justified in seeking this reckoning."

"But aren't we also honor bound to Colonel Cayce?" Espinoza gently probed. "Have you lost faith that he will provide a suitable opportunity to avenge *all* we have seen and suffered?"

"We are, and no, I haven't," Lara declared, voice turning brittle, almost desperate. "But he wouldn't have it happen *today*. . . . I *need* it today."

Teniente Espinoza regarded his commander and friend a long moment, then finally nodded. "Very well. Let us go and wash our souls in the blood of evil men—and may God help us."

The bright sun made it feel warmer than it was, but it was drier as well, little wind blew, and the only remaining snow was in drifts under trees. The trees bordering the rolling, hilly road were all still covered in blue-green ferny leaves in spite of the season and elevation. They were also much younger and smaller here, considerably less dense, and interspersed with thousands of rotting stumps. Lara supposed that was due to the proximity of Puebla, supposedly nearly as large as Vera Cruz and the largest city the army had marched against. There were also increasing numbers of dwellings, large and small, ranging from extensive villas to simple adobe huts with thatched roofs. The latter were often in clumps, practically forming little villages, surrounded by tall, tight palisades or at least a formidable barrier of long, sharpened, outward-leaning stakes. Even though everything was abandoned, Lara found hope, as always, in the fact that people found ways to live, even thrive, in a world as dangerous as this. It was the people themselves, or at least those who ruled them, who posed the most terrible threat to their survival. He refused to speculate on the fate of those who'd fled their approach again here.

The other scouts joined them as they pressed on, all confirming what the first had related, and soon Lara saw for himself. Reaching another low rise in the road, they came upon a vast plain, cultivated for crops. Nothing was standing, everything already harvested, but it was clearly the first, best place the enemy had found for the battle they wanted. And the enemy was present in force, drawn up in a traditional lancer formation, ranks wide and several deep, straddling the road about five hundred paces distant. They looked very fine on their tall, at least vaguely white chargers, short red cloaks attached at the shoulders of gleaming bronze cuirasses. Atop the men's heads, ornate bronze helmets sprouted colorful feather plumes, and a forest of nine-foot lances stood rigidly erect over all, each bristling with gleaming sharp points and more red feathers or ribbons fluttering near the heads.

The horses clearly weren't pure, local stock. Their height and long legs were proof of that. Many still bore a hint of stripes in their coats, so like nearly all Dom lancers' or officers' horses of any color (privately purchased and bred for upper-class *patricios* or their sons), they retained the best attributes of native blood. Lara rode such a captured animal himself (dark brown, almost black, with darker streaks down its sides), as did many others. He doubted there were better horses for this sort of thing anywhere on the world he came from.

"We are outnumbered," Espinoza reminded.

"Deploy for battle," Lara said curtly. Espinoza saluted and proceeded to shout commands. Crisply, as if on parade, the five hundred or so men of the 1st Yucatán peeled away by twos to either side of the road until they formed a solid line. It was only two ranks deep and still not as long as the enemy's, but the men looked just as splendid in their own way to Lara's critical eye. Polished brass buttons flashed on dark blue uniforms. Red cuffs and collars (the only real deviation from uniforms of other branches in the army) gave them an extra sharp look. Unlike their adversaries, they wore no armor, and their horses were all different colors, mostly "pure native." But they'd known for a while the Dom armor was almost entirely decorative. It might deflect a poorly aimed lance or arrow but only began the process of expansion for a lead ball and generally made the wounds they inflicted more gruesome.

"Do you suppose they will want to talk? Agon learned to. I wonder if these Doms have?" Espinoza speculated as he returned to Lara's side.

"We have nothing to say to *them*," Lara spat, even as a baleful horn sounded and the distant horsemen started forward at a walk. "Nor do they have anything to say to *us*," he observed with satisfaction. He drew his saber and raised it high, crying out firmly and loud, "First Yucatán! Before you are arrayed wicked men in the service of abomination. They were accessories, at least, to the foul acts we witnessed the results of this morning. They *defile* the honorable title of 'lancers.' We may have trained to fight much like dragoons on occasion, riding to battle and fighting on foot as Major Anson or Colonel Cayce direct us. That is acceptable, even appropriate to the cause we are embarked upon. *Anything* for victory over the evil God and men of this land. But we remain lancers, first and foremost. *Real* lancers who can call ourselves such with pride. Those . . . *murderers* in front of us must be erased, and in the process disabused of any notion they deserve to share our proud title." He slashed his saber down. "Forward!"

Lara's battalion set out at a trot, their own lances held just as high and rigid as the enemy's. At the same instant that Lara felt a terrific thrill to finally be doing something he'd always dreamed of—bunching the muscles of his men and animals to spring forward at other men who were similarly armed, head-on—something continued to nag at him. Teniente Espinoza was right. This was not wise, Colonel Cayce wouldn't approve, and there was every possibility he would fail. He'd let pent-up frustrations and emotions, particularly the wild, disbelieving, burbling horror of the morning, rule his reason. *Just as the enemy hoped*, he suddenly realized with glaring certainty.

Too late. He was committed. There could be no turning back now, not without prior planning. And all sorts of alternate schemes exploded in his mind even now, tactics even Colonel Cayce would approve, he was sure. But his reason had waited a few seconds too long to reassert control of his passions, and it was all too late. He'd committed his command to attack a much larger force, and at the very best, this half of his regiment would be brutally mauled. More likely, it would be destroyed. Espinoza gave the command for his men to accelerate to a canter about the same time the enemy did, and as they drew closer, something else struck him. He was still clearly outnumbered, as Espinoza said, but perhaps not by quite as much as he'd expected.

The surviving witnesses at Lagarto Gris had been distraught. Anyone would be. *He* was. But they'd also been firm about how many lancers there'd been. Even now it was difficult to tell, but he didn't *think* he was charging against two thousand of them. About half that seemed closer. He didn't have time to wonder what that meant, but there was one last-minute adjustment he could make.

"Bugler!" he cried to the young Itzincabo always near him. "In a moment you will sound the charge, but first you will sound 'lances down,' then 'form wedge.' Only when the men accomplish that, if there's time, sound 'charge.' Do it now!"

Wide-eyed, the bugler sounded the first command, and all Lara's lancers lowered their weapons a little earlier than normal. The reason for that was a wedge could be tricky to shift to on the fly, with no warning. Better to have the weapons down already so the men could better maneuver to make the most of them without stabbing or knocking one another about. The bugler quickly ordered the wedge, and Lara caught Espinoza's questioning glance, but saw it turn to grim understanding. Then, just as the enemy sounded their own final notes that would bring their horsemen up to speed, Lara ordered his bugler to do the same. In an instant, the two forces were converging at a terrific rate, the thundering hooves enough to rival artillery. In those last instants before the collision, Lara's heart was suddenly free of all doubts and fears. There was no artillery, no musketry, not even archers. This was mounted combat in its purest form, little different from the time of Alexander. Pistols and musketoons would soon join the mix, but at first it would be only lances and sabers. Man and horse against man and horse. Even if he lived, he doubted he'd see anything like it again.

The enemy's faces were quite visible now, many just as torn with terror as Lara knew his own men would be. They seemed quite surprised as well, as the point of the rapidly formed wedge crashed into them near the center of their lines at a combined speed of almost sixty miles an hour. The collision was cataclysmic. Lances aside, the mere impact of horse against horse or man against man at that velocity was fatal. Lances, bones, heads, bellies— all were smashed, ripped open, crushed, and rag doll figures cartwheeled through the air. Lara had wound up about four horses back from the point of the wedge and the explosion of blood in front of him, some merely vapor, but some sloshed against him hard enough to sting, utterly blinding him and his animal. Without direction, the horse seemed to instinctively know the ground ahead would be covered with rolling, thrashing, leg-snapping obstacles and simply leaped as high and far as he could. Lara was frankly astonished when he landed, still blinded by blood, but still in the saddle, still in one piece. Furiously, he pawed at his eyes—just in time to lean back in his saddle as a lance point lunged past where his chest had been an instant before. Swinging his saber, he lopped the lance head off and brought it back up, point first, through the bottom jaw of the overextended Dom, driving his blade into the skull. The man's helmet tipped off and fell, his eyes rolled up, and he dropped off his horse.

"Capitan! This way!" came Espinoza's voice, and Lara bolted toward it, now smearing blood with his sleeve. "Here, sir." A cloth was thrust in his hand, and Lara finally wiped his face enough to see. All was chaos, with horses and men from both sides locked in what looked like hundreds of individual fights. "This way," Espinoza insisted, and Lara directed his horse to follow. From a slight distance now, he could see they had indeed smashed through the enemy center, and a growing number of his lancers were gathering around, apparently unobserved. That was understandable. A lot of shooting had erupted now, and the smoke was very thick.

"I wasn't sure that would work," Lara quietly confessed. They'd practiced the maneuver to use against infantry, but never against other riders. The result was that they'd kept the "mass" of their force largely intact—at least in close proximity—while splitting the enemy in two. Now, if they could apply enough *more* mass against the isolated sections of the enemy, they might defeat them in detail. There wasn't a good chance of that, but there was a chance.

"Right," Lara said decisively. "Keep feeding men to me as they come through, or you can extract them, Lieutenant."

"What will you do?"

"Start hitting the enemy from behind, then around the edges. Who still has lances?" he asked those around him. Not many did. "Well, never mind. Reload any firearms you have and follow me."

Lara did his best, picking at the perimeter of Doms, killing as many as he could, even charging in, his men laying about with sabers, but these Doms were at least as good at this type of fighting as his men were and their greater numbers began to tell. In less than half an hour of furious fighting, exhaustion began to take its toll. Tired men make mistakes, especially in this kind of fight, when they literally reach a point where they simply can't block a saber blow anymore. Lara had no idea where his bugler was, and even if he sounded recall or retreat, it might still be impossible for his men to break contact. He flat didn't have enough of them, and he was losing too many.

Smash!

"What the devil was that?" Lara demanded, looking back at Espinoza. The gruff old lieutenant had joined him with the last of the men he'd been able to send.

"I don't know. I think . . . look!" he suddenly shouted, pointing at the mass of the enemy they hadn't been able to do much about yet. Lara blinked, then rubbed his eyes, wondering if they were deceiving him. He had more blood in them now. "Is that? Yes! The rest of the First Yucatán Lancers! And the Third Dragoons! Come, let us drive the enemy from this side again!"

The fight didn't last much longer at all, and no one could resist the sudden, rapid firing of fresh mounted troops. Dom lancers didn't surrender, nor had they ever been known to retreat, but suddenly, as if by communal decision, they called on whatever reserves they could summon and did their best to break away. Many of the men who'd been fighting them from the start found new energy within them as well, mercilessly chasing them right alongside the new arrivals. Within minutes, the brutal melee became a running fight, and Lara, Espinoza, and half a dozen other tired, bloody lancers were sitting on equally blown horses, gasping, waiting while Boogerbear and Coryon Burton galloped up to them.

"Looks like we nearly missed a fair-size fuss," Boogerbear drawled with half a smile.

Lara cut his eyes at him and shook his head. "I made a terrible mistake. Thanks to you, however, many of my men will survive it."

Boogerbear waved that away. "Don't go on about it. We all felt the same, even Major Anson. Colonel Cayce too, eventually."

"Where is Major Anson?"

Boogerbear rubbed his nose. "The colonel made him sit this one out. Can't say he was wrong."

Burton was gazing grimly at the battlefield. "I take it this was only a rear guard. But based on the number of dead and what will likely get away, there were still around a thousand here, and you nearly destroyed them yourself. You have no reason to chastise yourself, Ramon."

Lara looked at him. "Yes. About a thousand, I think. We didn't know that at first. We saw no evidence of the rest of the force moving on and just assumed it was all here. That makes my decision to attack even more ridiculous."

"Now yer just feelin' sorry for yourself," Boogerbear gently scolded. "Better quit. If we had it all ta do over again, I 'spect Major Anson would'a had us all chasin' the bastards ta start." He paused, looking thoughtful. "Seein' as you never come up on 'em, I *do* wonder where the rest o' them Dom lancers got off to, though."

As if it came as a direct answer to his question, they heard the dull, distant thump of cannon. With only the wispiest clouds in the high, cold sky, there wasn't even the slightest possibility it was thunder.

"My God," Coryon Burton said, eyes quickly widening. "We thought Sal and Mr. Joffrion had sufficient forces to deal with a few hundred reapers, filthy, ghoulish bandits that they are. We even sent one of Barca's sections and more dragoons to support them—but that's where the other lancers went! They've set a trap for the rest of the Rangers and my dragoons!"

Boogerbear whirled his horse, calling out to Burton's bugler. "Sound recall, boy. Over an' over. Gotta pull our fellas off the chase." He looked at Lara. "Wagons're comin' up, but you'll wanna be with us, I guess. Lead your fresh lancers. Might wanna leave a few of 'em here with your worn-out boys an' wounded, though. Help 'em get back to the column. This many dead, bad boogers'll be sniffin' around. Goddamn Doms might come back too." He sighed, then continued, voice still almost irritatingly mild. "I guess we were all kinda stupid after all, scamperin' all over the place in dribs an' drabs, now gettin' yanked back an' forth. Shit."

––––––––––––

The peaceful Dom camp alongside the mountain stream exploded into pandemonium as Sal's Ocelomeh Rangers and Hans Joffrion's dragoons swept down the stump-dotted slope. If there'd been any doubt these reapers who'd slaughtered Lagarto Gris had been callously sacrificed to bait a trap, it quickly fled as fast as the utterly surprised men in the camp tried to do. Desperate orders flew, calling them to assemble, but most bolted from around their fires, out from under lean-tos, and leaped into the stream, trying to wade across the swift, freezing flow. Many were being swept away by the time they reached the knee-deep middle, screaming in panic as their boots slipped off slimy rocks and they were washed downstream, the torrent bashing them against jutting stones.

A thrill rose in Sal's chest at the boiling-up numbers, and he realized the camp must've held all the reapers after all. Just as important, no one above a few NCOs seemed to be in charge, and only a very few resisted the urge to flee and gathered in a tattered line to face them. Sal drew both his revolvers, steering his horse with his knees. Joffrion drew his dragoon saber, calling his men to do the same. It was going to be a massacre. Suddenly, less than a dozen paces from the forming Doms, the whole long line of

Rangers and dragoons seemed to slam into an invisible wall. It wasn't a wall at all, of course, but a carefully concealed trench. Horses shrieked as they tripped at speed, many snapping legs and cartwheeling through the air, landing on their screaming riders or smashing one another in a macabre kaleidoscope of horror. Experienced horsemen managed to jump clear, but many of these were crushed under rolling, squealing horses, or struck down by flying riders.

Sal had been thrown without warning before and reacted instinctively, rolling when he hit and leaping to his feet, revolvers still in his hands. He'd cracked his head a little harder than he thought, and the combination of that and his rapid tumble left him a little dazed and dizzy. Few others had recovered so well. At a glance, he determined that at least half of his and Joffrion's men had been unhorsed. Quite a few of those were badly injured or unmoving. The riders who'd managed to veer away or slide to a stop when they saw what was happening were picking their way across the trench and through the thrashing animals, but the grand charge had been smashed.

Looking at the Doms mere paces away, Sal thought they were just as stunned as he. Whoever built this trap hadn't told the bait about it. Still, despite how many enemies had already fled, the numbers looked about even.

"Get up off your asses an' get stuck into the bastards!" Sal roared, quickly choosing a large reaper waving a musketoon and shouting at his own men. Sal shot him in the temple, spraying red mist on the men beyond, dropping the Dom like a sack full of rocks. That seemed to snap everyone out of their shock, and accompanied by the sporadic booming and popping of Hall carbines, and musketoons on both sides, the bitter enemies mobbed each other with a roar.

Sal had lost his own musketoon when he rolled and the sling broke. Now he quickly emptied his first revolver into the faces of four more men before holstering it and drawing the Bowie sword from his belt. Originally remade for the Rangers Sal took to Vera Cruz from an almost ridiculous number of M1832 foot artillery swords aboard the wrecked transports that brought them to this world, Bowie swords were about the size and shape of a Roman gladius. With a D guard added to protect fingers and something like sharkskin wrapped around the brass hilt to improve the grip, they were just about the best close-quarters fighting blades Sal could imagine. They'd become standard for all Rangers, now being made—albeit more crudely—by smiths from captured iron. Sal's Bowie sword now became his primary weapon, his revolver reserved for men trying to shoot him as he waded in among the Dom reapers. The blade was best suited for stabbing, but was sharp and heavy enough to cleave as well, so he jabbed and hacked and occasionally shot his way through the growing mass of enemies, lopping off spearheads that quested for him through the press (there were a surprising number of spears), or chopping off hands that wielded them. He stabbed men aiming musketoons in exposed armpits, twisting the blade as he pulled it out to release a torrent of blood, stabbing others in the neck or belly to avoid lodging his blade in their ribs. Sal was no swordsman and had never trained as such, but he was strong and agile, knew the best places to put a hole in a man, all the best muscles and tendons to slash, and was remarkably aggressive. Against other men who weren't trained swordsmen either, he had a distinct advantage.

Shooting what looked to be an NCO in the forehead, he spun and brutally slammed his blade into another man right above the collarbone, feeling his sword tip grate on the spine deep inside. Twisting viciously, he jerked it out. The wide-eyed Dom tried to scream, but all that came out was an explosive spray of bright, foamy blood.

"Captain Hernandez!" came a cry from behind him. Ducking a clubbed musket butt, he swiped his blade down the stock, hacking off the fingers that held it. The man dropped the weapon with a bellow of pain. "Captain Hernandez, a moment, if you please."

Sal blinked and realized, for the moment, his last adversary had been the only one left close enough for him to kill. And that man was down, crying loudly and scrabbling away on his back, blood splashing from his mangled hand. Turning, he saw Hans Joffrion, hat gone, blood in his hair, left arm hanging limp by his side. The saber in his right hand was clotted with red-black blood from one end of the long blade to the other. "Well done, sir. Well done," Joffrion complimented, always polite, "but I beg your attention for a moment."

The Doms had been driven back in among their lean-tos, and many of those who'd been trying to cross the stream had returned, joining their comrades for another thrust forward. Joffrion gestured beyond them with his encrusted saber, however. "The trap has been sprung, and the jaws are about to close. It is time to recall the men to the ridge above."

That's when Sal saw what he meant. The movement they'd detected in the woods on the far slope of the valley had indicated far more than they'd imagined, and now hundreds of Dom lancers, regulars, had emerged in the open, their contrasting colors—red, brightly polished bronze, and the white horses they all rode—clearly visible even here. And there was the intimidating thicket of lances, of course. It was a wonderful, terrible sight compared to the bloody chaos on the banks of the stream.

"It all becomes clear," Joffrion said. "This action was obviously planned by whoever leads those lancers, their commander or someone higher. Who knows if he ordered the destruction of the town, but he has taken advantage. Lancers would be perfect for that. Born to the ruling elite, yet strongly influenced by Blood Priests, I'm told. At the same time, they wouldn't shy from sacrificing these lowly reapers, raised from the ranks of mere freemen, perhaps even slaves, despite their devotion to the same sect."

"That's not all the lancers Lara went after," Sal commented.

"No," Joffrion agreed. "Roughly a thousand, I should think. About half. The rest are probably lying in wait for Mr. Lara even now."

Horns blared and the lancers started to move, sweeping down the hill. It wasn't a charge—they'd have to cross the stream and trench, of course—but they'd be here in minutes. And they *could* charge once they passed the obstructions.

"There's too many of 'em," Sal said simply. "Even without the reapers that'll follow 'em when they get here."

"Indeed," Joffrion agreed. "Sergeant Buisine! Sound recall. Back to the ridge. Anyone still mounted will carry those who are not."

"Sergeant Tinez," Sal called out, seeking the man.

"He's dead, sir, smushed by a horse," came a reply.

Sal frowned. "Corporal . . ."

"Nares, sir. Just got elected to my stripes, confirmed by Cap'n Boogerbear."

"Fine," Sal said. "Pick three men an' carry some fellas up to the ridge, but then keep going. Two of you find Captain Lara. Tell him what's goin' on an' to watch for a trap. The other two head back to the city an' report to Cap'n Burton."

"Sir," Nares acknowledged with a salute, just as the bugler sounded recall and the men started pulling back from the fight. Almost immediately, the reapers pressed them. "This is gonna get tricky," Sal warned Joffrion.

"It is," the young dragoon officer agreed. "I will command the rear guard. You jump up behind Sergeant Buisine and take charge of the ridge until I join you." Sal started to protest, but Joffrion pointed at his pistol. "Those make you twice the killer I am, and you should have time to reload them if you hurry."

Sal frowned but nodded. Paterson Colts could be cantankerous. They were difficult to load quickly, and even if Joffrion could do that, the triggers were heavy enough that if a man wasn't used to them, he'd waste most of his shots. "Just hurry up," he said simply and swung up behind Buisine. "Don't be a hero; come up quick. The last men here are gonna die. If you wait too long, I'll send the sergeant back to knock you on the head an' throw you on his horse. Doubt he'll appreciate that." Joffrion nodded, smiling vaguely. "Shit," Sal murmured. "Let's go, Sergeant."

The sound of fighting resumed and grew behind them as they made their way up the slope, but the defense on the ridge was already growing by the time Sal got there; all sorts of limbs had been dragged up from the woods and laid across the road, and men were adding rocks as well. The sound of fighting swelled even louder by the time Sal looked back.

"Shit," he said again. The lancers were already crossing the stream, their horses surer-footed in the rapid water than men had been. A few were slipping and staggering, but most quickly recovered. Worse, though they weren't pressing them hard, the reapers had the last of the rear guard, probably a little more than a dozen men, including Hans Joffrion, pinned down in the trench full of dead and thrashing horses with growing musket fire. Sal couldn't imagine how they'd ever get free. It quickly became clear that they wouldn't, and he felt his guts twist. The disciplined lancers just kept coming, walking their horses forward like a glistening, white-frothing surf. Men started falling among them, but lances were taken in hand, held overhead, stabbing down as they came to the trench. In moments, all shooting had stopped, and the lancers picked their way through or over the scene of destruction. Hans Joffrion and the last of the rear guard were dead—if they were lucky.

"Bastards," hissed Sergeant Buisine.

"Yeah," Sal said. "Hafta kill 'em for that." He looked around at the roughly hundred and twenty men he still had, many walking wounded, with which to oppose a thousand or more. "Hafta kill a *lot* of 'em," he added quietly.

"We'll help, if you'll make way," shouted a voice behind that Sal never expected to hear again. He whirled and wasn't the only one amazed to see the 1st Section of Barca's battery already unlimbering their 6pdrs on the road, twenty fresh dragoons dismounting to help push the guns forward. The voice had been Sergeant Hanny Cox's, and Lieutenant Petty, scruffy, but intense looking as always, was striding up to join him. "Well, now," Petty said, getting his first look at the lancers forming back up below. Belatedly, he offered Sal a salute.

Sal waved back. "I'm glad you're here, but I'm afraid even you have your work cut out."

"Yes sir, we do," Petty replied. Men parted as Hanny's Number Two gun shoved its snout between them. The Number One gun was nosing through to the right of the road. Turning, Petty shouted behind. "Get those teams turned around, facin' away. Prolong ropes to the limbers," he said to the gun's crews taking and affixing implements, preparing their weapons to load. A couple of men nodded and started unwinding the long ropes from where they were secured on top of the trails. "Might need to pull back, but keep shootin' as we do," Petty explained to Sal, then shouted, "First range looks like seven hundred an' fifty, eight hundred yards. Load spherical case, two degrees elevation, three-second fuses." He looked back at Sal while his men rushed to load. "Boogerbear sent us with the dragoon escort. Don't think he expected this. Everything else that was left in the city went up to support Mr. Lara."

"I'm glad to hear it. We just sent word ourselves, soon as we knew what was what. Probl'y passed you."

Petty nodded. "Saw 'em. More help'll come," he assured. "Just hope we're still here when it does."

"Ready!" shouted Hanny Cox, looking intently at Petty with his hand raised in the air. A moment later, Sergeant Dodd yelled, "Ready" as well, raising a clenched fist.

Petty looked at Sal, who nodded, then he turned back to his artillerymen. "Section, by the section . . . *Fire!*"

Case shot shrieked down and exploded over the lancers, scything them down with hot shards of copper and sprays of musket balls still caked in bits of smoldering pitch. Men and horses screamed and fell, rolling, thrashing, bucking, dying. Whether they'd heard reports or not, these Doms had never experienced exploding shot and might've even panicked, but their officers were sharp enough to understand, whatever the two cannon that just appeared on the rise were throwing at them, they'd best get out from under it. Without waiting to re-form their lines, scattering more by the moment in any event, the order was given to charge. Horns blew, and the lancers bolted forward just as the second pair of shells exploded, raining metal on a few riders at the rear of the straggling but surging formation.

"Independent fire," Petty called. Now each gunner would call his own shots, cut fuses and adjust elevation as he thought best. Considering how fast the lancers were coming—already at full speed—they'd soon be switching to canister. These lancers were good, though, probably better than any they'd met, managing to re-form on the run. Their horses might be blown by the time they topped the long slope, but more would get here than if they'd come on in the more traditional way—and pitiless as it was, even canister could only do so much.

"Fire!" yelled Hanny, and the Number Two gun roared, bucking back ahead of a bright yellow jet and boiling white cloud of smoke. The shriek of the shot was barely discernible before it snapped in the air in front of the enemy, hacking out a long cone of death. Dodd's gun fired even as Preacher Mac, Hahessy, Naxa Actli, and Andrew Morris clapped onto the spokes and heaved the Number Two gun back into battery. Staring downslope, Hanny hesitated only an instant before yelling back at Apo Tuin, "Load canister!"

"Load canister!" echoed Dodd.

"Times like this, I miss Felix Meder's riflemen," Sal told Sergeant Buisine.

"Might as well open fire," Buisine replied. "Put enough metal in the air, some of it'll hit something."

Sal nodded. "Rangers, dragoons, commence firing. Rangers, throw a few balls at 'em before you go back to drop shot when they get close."

Hall carbines and musketoons started booming, the rate of fire quickly rising. Hahessy was first to slam one of the heavy cylinders full of musket balls down the barrel of a 6pdr with his rammer before standing clear. Naxa quickly pierced the charge through the vent, primed the gun, and held the hammer of the Hidden's Patent lock safely to the side while Morris stretched the lanyard. Hanny hadn't really even aimed, just guiding the gun forward with the handspike for his windage adjustment, then giving the elevation screw a turn. Careful aim was superfluous now, and one instinctively *points* a shotgun, whatever the size.

"Ready!" shouted Morris, this time.

"Fire!" bellowed Hanny, young voice cracking.

Poom! Poom!

The lancers had already closed to within three hundred paces, and the twin blasts of canister hacked the whole four-rank center out of their already laboring but admirably reconstituted formation. In its place was a churned-up heap of flesh and shattered bone. Bleeding, riderless horses made the gap wider, crashing into those around them. Amazingly, a single lancer and his horse, apparently entirely unhurt, came on all alone from the heart of the slaughter. Just as quickly as scores of Dom lancers were obliterated, those to either side closed the gap. Then a horn sounded a long, intimidating series of notes, and the bristling, ribbon-flapping forest of lances fell forward simultaneously, every razor point seemingly unerringly aimed at each of the increasingly desperate defenders.

Even over the terrible noise of battle, Sal heard a number of loud . . . bodily sounds, not all of which were just farts. And for each man who shat himself, there'd be more who wet their breeches. There was no dishonor in that, and there were no cowards here. He'd seen this before, more than once, and wouldn't have been surprised if he pissed himself now. Standing and facing hundreds of needle-point lance heads backed by nine-foot shafts, held by men in deadly earnest, accompanied by the thunder of thousands of hooves pounding under countless tons of warhorses, could have that effect on anyone. Probably everyone, if they weren't distracted by shooting.

But the shooting was starting to have an effect as well. More and more men fell from their mounts, and more horses crashed to the ground, throwing explosions of damp earth in the air. Petty's section fired once again, mulching more men and animals, but Hanny roared out, "Load double canister and hold!" clearly meaning to save his last round to break the charge when it hit. Dodd did the same, while Hanny stooped to pull the prolong rope through the lunette at the end of the trail before giving it a tug to make sure it was secure. Shouting, trying to remind Dodd to do it too, he didn't know if he was heard.

The firing all but stopped for a long instant, as if even without orders, every defender intuitively intended to do the same as Hanny, glistening Dom lances now only seconds away. Sal and Lieutenant Petty both sensed it, waiting for the perfect moment. Everyone here, even the men they'd recruited at Frontera, were veterans now, so when Sal and Petty bellowed, "Fire!" together, most were already squeezing triggers or stretching lanyards on the guns. A thunderous volley slapped out, the two cannon literally gutting the center of the lancer formation, shredding bodies with the concussion of the blasts as much as the swarm of projectiles they spat. Even the crudest small arms couldn't possibly miss, especially musketoons now loaded with handfuls of drop shot again, and the hundred and fifty or so men armed with them practically hacked the front rank of lancers to pieces. Some of those, even mortally wounded, kept their lances steady until the end—and there were many more behind them, of course. The only small advantage Sal's little force had was how narrow the front was here. The clearing in the trees to the sides of the dirt road was wider at the crest of the spur, but quickly squeezed down again for a ways. All the lancers now had to converge and narrow their front accordingly. The roar of the impact was enormous, and a depressing number of Rangers and dragoons were professionally spitted at once, the lances largely passing completely through, into the ground, and shattering with a force that sometimes unhorsed their wielders. The worst of the noise came from the lancers all crashing into one another, however. In their determination to destroy this little irritant that had cost them so much already, their otherwise excellent discipline suffered somewhat, wadding their force all together, turning them into the cork stopping the bottleneck that the defenders had been until then. There was only a moment to make the most of it.

"Drive on! Drive on!" roared Lieutenant Petty, running at the teams hitched to the limbers of his guns, waving his artillery saber. Apo shouted something, and the teams lurched into motion, taking the slack from the prolong ropes and jerking the guns out of the melee. Their crews had been trapped for a moment, fighting desperately with sabers or even implements, Hahessy crumpling a lancer's helmet with his rammer head. Andrew Morris screamed when a lance slashed his throat open and he went down, clutching his neck and blowing blood. Several lancers even swirled past the guns, and Hanny had drawn the saber he hated to inexpertly fend off their blows. He knew what was about to happen, however, and kept as much to the side as he could when the lunging guns smashed the lancers' horses down and bounced up over them, all the weapon's terrible weight focused in a few square inches at the bottom of iron tires. One of the riders had gone down with his horse, leg trapped under it, and barely had an instant to scream before the wheel practically crushed his leg off and then dropped down on his chest and head. Dead grass and leaves whiskered that part of the wheel when it turned to the top, stuck to blood and brain matter.

"Get Andrew!" Hanny shouted.

"He's dead!" yelled Preacher Mac as Hahessy bellowed curses and swiped at the enemy with his rammer staff, delaying pursuit with the remaining cluster of dismounted Rangers and dragoons. Those who had horses had already mounted and were galloping back toward the limbers. "Damn you, Hahessy, come along, you great fool. We'll be needin' tae load the gun!"

Hahessy seemed to remember his duty and, with a final bash at a horse's nose that sent it up on its hind legs and spilled its rider, he ran huffing up to join the survivors of his crew. The only family he had. "Puir Andrew's gone, then?" he asked, genuinely mournful, while he scanned the faces around. "No others?"

"Not yet," Hanny replied grimly. "Load canister—but watch those wheels! Naxa, stab the vent prick into the charge when it's in, to hold it in place until we stop!"

Loading a cannon is inherently dangerous at the best of times. Much of the proper drill involves as many motions intended to make it safer as actually loading the weapon. When following the manual, it usually takes more than one person making a mistake for anyone to be injured. There's no margin for error by anyone in combat, especially when most of those "safety procedures" have already been tossed. And there are precisely zero safe ways to load a moving cannon in combat, the limber it's essentially tied to about ten yards away, pulled by horses with men on top who can't even see behind them.

Hanny's crew managed it, though; so did Dodd's, albeit a little more nerve-rackingly. His Number Three man tripped and fell but had the sense to lay trembling but otherwise still until the axle cleared him. They still couldn't stop to shoot, however. There were too many friends still holding the Doms. Sal Hernandez had mounted a dead lancer's horse and come galloping back to the guns. His hat was gone, and a saber slash on his forehead left blood sheeting down his face, and he was sopping at it with his shirt sleeve. The jacket sleeve was torn off. "Hold there!" he shouted at Lieutenant Petty, who'd come running back from the limbers after throwing men toward the guns as replacements. Two went to Dodd's, and Hanny recognized the kid they'd picked up in Frontera—Hoziki was his name; big, strong farmer's son—moving into Andy Morris's place.

"Section, halt!" Petty yelled back where he came from, and the men on the horses stopped them. The prolong ropes went slack, and the heavy trails of the guns slapped down on the ground. Mounted men rushed up and arrayed themselves to the sides as best they could.

"I'm gonna try something. Stand by to fire right up the road," Sal said, turning his new horse and dashing back toward the fighting.

"What're you gonna do?" Petty yelled after him.

"You'll see."

"Make ready," Petty growled at his section. "Each of you, aim just right or left o' center."

"How do you know what to do?" asked Dodd.

"Damned worthless idjit!" Hahessy snapped at his former gun captain. His new "family" included the whole section, even Captain Barca's entire battery to a lesser extent, but he'd never respected Dodd. "Which Cap'n Sal just *told* us, didn't he?"

"Silence," Petty said. "But that's true," he conceded. "I know what he wants, just not how he's gonna let us do it."

Sal paused a little short of the thick clot of fighting, standing in his stirrups and cupping his hands to shout. Some of the lancers had resorted to their own musketoons and directed some shots at him, leaves and twigs snapping off trees and raining down around him.

"Anson's brigade!" Sal bellowed at the top of his voice so the likely less than twenty or thirty still standing would lend him some attention. "When I shout, 'Now,' count to ten, then run as fast as you can to the sides in the trees for another ten count." He was shouting in English, which at least some of the Rangers and dragoons knew well enough now, but none of the enemy did. "Get as deep in the woods as you can in that time, then throw yourself on the ground!" He waited a moment more, then roared, "Now!"

Spinning his horse back around, he galloped to the pair of guns and his last reserve of fighters. "Don't fire till I say," he told Petty, wiping his face free of blood again, "but as soon as you do, we'll drag these guns back up the other slope as fast as we can an' pile into that palisade around the rock cabin. You seen it? Good. We'll put the guns in the empty gates an' everybody else'll support 'em as long as we can. We'll make our last stand in the rock cabin."

Almost at once, the exhausted handful of men, still doing their best to hold back hundreds of Dom lancers (many reduced to jabbing at horses with lances themselves), suddenly sprinted away to the side of the road cut as fast as they could. A few didn't leave, probably unable, with wounds that wouldn't let them. Some may have even deliberately stayed to give the others a chance. Sal, counting to himself as soon as he saw movement, hardened his heart, hoping their sacrifice would be worth it. At the same time, the evident surprise on some of the Dom faces whose opponents had just simply . . . left, would've been comical in other circumstances. "Ready," Sal called when he reached "ten" in his mind, determined to wait as long as possible. The Doms saw them now, some charging forward at once, others stunned or struck with terror.

"Fire!" Sal said.

Both guns bucked and roared, belching the oddly yellowish canister smoke, and the effect on the tightly packed Doms in the road cut couldn't have been more horrible. The closest men and horses were absolutely shredded, and the only "good" thing, from the enemy's perspective, was that those men and animals at the front absorbed much more than their fair share of the whistling swarm of projectiles. For the nearest two score or so, however, it was as if God simply stamped on them with His mighty foot.

That's what it looked like to Sal, at least, and the enemy was thrown into panicked confusion as far back as he could see; wounded, bloody horses rolling and kicking, bounding away from the carnage and crashing down on others behind them, smashing more screaming men. Dragoons and Rangers took their chance and bolted back out of the woods, sprinting up the road toward their comrades. One was running extra fast, face twisted by a more primal terror, as the whole scene abruptly became even more horrifying and surreal. One of the great upright predators, like a twisted cross between a furry/feathery alligator and a long-legged crow, suddenly strode nonchalantly out of the woods and stopped in evident surprise to stare at the delightful smorgasbord laid out before it. It wasn't as big as some they'd seen by any means, but at roughly thirty feet from its terrible, gaping jaws to the tip of its whipping tail, it certainly wasn't an infant. Perhaps it had been roused, even drawn from its lair by the commotion? Cannon fire usually deterred the things, but the smell of so much blood might be overwhelming to such a beast.

For just an instant it glanced at the men running toward the smoking

guns, no doubt tempted to chase anything that fled, but the shrieks of terror rising to join those of pain closer by reacquired its attention. With a
bark of decision, it pounced on the closest wriggling thing, a Dom who'd
been thrown past the wreckage of horses, scrabbling away on his back. The
thing stooped and almost gently snatched the man up in its jaws. Giant
dagger teeth weren't gentle to the flesh they tore, and the man squealed horribly until the thing raised up, tilting its head back, practically swallowing
him whole. Musketoons started booming, a few balls drawing blood, but
also what seemed like indignant rage. The thing lunged, jaws snapping.

"Pull back now," Sal shouted at Lieutenant Petty. "All the way back to
the palisade. Sergeant Buisine, take the mounted Rangers an' catch as many
loose horses as you can. Mounted an' dismounted dragoons'll stay with me,
pullin' back slow, but be ready to ride double back to the guns in an instant.
That big lizard won't hold 'em for long." Sal already saw men in brown tunics, reapers from the camp who'd caught up, infiltrating around the monster through the trees on foot. They'd been given lances and seemed intent
on poking and stabbing at the beast from the sides, irritating it enough to
make it leave. Quite a few would probably die, but they'd also eventually
succeed. Like any great predator anywhere, the ones on this world would
fight for a meal, but not to the point of serious injury if they could help it.
Badly hurt predators can't catch food and starve to death.

Still attached to their limbers by prolong rope, the guns were dragged,
jouncing and rattling, sometimes veering dangerously, down and then back
up the first slope behind, the unmounted artillerymen jogging alongside
them, implements in hand. Sal and the dragoons weren't far behind, some
climbing back on horses as a few were retrieved. Finally, when the irate
roaring of the monster, no longer visible in the cut, turned to frantic squeals
and then silence, the dismounted dragoons and Rangers hopped up behind
their comrades. The first Dom lancers burst out in the open, and artillerymen who couldn't mount their own horses were pulled up behind other
riders as well. The whole remaining force, barely a quarter of what it had
been, dashed together for the meager protection of a small stone cabin and
rotten palisade. The first dribble of lancers was already on them, even as
Lieutenant Petty was positioning the guns practically hub to hub and his
men were finishing loading them again. Hall carbines and musketoons
popped and crackled, tripping a horse and emptying a pair of saddles be-

fore the rest whirled around and pounded out of sight below the crest, doubtless to report the situation to their re-forming mates.

"You should take the mounted men and go," Petty told Sal. "We'll keep the bastards busy long enough for you to get clear."

"An' leave the best section in the army, not to mention two o' the best guns, behind?" Sal snorted derisively. "I don't b'lieve so."

"They won't take these guns intact," Hanny chimed in, grimly determined. "We'll burst the barrels first. Spike them, at least."

Sal looked at the young sergeant. "It ain't the *barrels* I'm worried about, you goatwit, it's you men. Artillery's what's gonna win this war, an' you're the best cannoneers we got."

Hahessy was actually caressing the blackened muzzle of the Number Two gun. "We ain't leavin' these beauties for them heathen buggers," he announced in a threatening tone. "Damned if we will!"

"None of us are," Sal assured the big Irishman. "We *can't*," he said louder, including the rest of the men. "The dragoons' Hall carbines are a help, but they take machines the Doms don't have to make. *We* can't make more of 'em yet. Then there's the caps that shoot 'em. Felix Meder's rifles are extra useful, man for man, but won't win the war for us by themselves unless Felix gets his sights on the Dom pope, or somethin' equally unlikely. That leaves the only real advantage we have over the Doms for killin' great heaps of 'em—besides our cause an' better men, o' course—an' that's those damn gun carriages an' limbers. The way they let us use guns on the battlefield, an' get 'em right where they're needed to start. *Those're* what make our guns so much better than the enemy's, make 'em faster ta move, quicker ta aim, an' deadlier in every way. We let the Doms get hold of 'em an' start makin' their own, we lose that advantage an' prob'ly the war." He glared at Hanny. "So yeah, you'll spike 'em or blow 'em if you have to, but only if you're the last man alive. Till then, you use 'em for what they're for an' the rest of us'll keep the bastards off you."

Hanny nodded back, determined. Intellectually, he knew Captain Hernandez was right, and letting the enemy get hold of these guns might eventually have dire consequences. In his heart, however, it was more personal, more immediate. He'd come a long way since he was just another particularly clumsy infantryman in the 3rd Pennsylvania. The artillery, Captain Barca's battery, his section—and his gun in particular—had become a huge part of who he was, a significant percentage of his identity. To others, particularly Hahessy, the gun and its crew *was* his identity, his very purpose in life—to maintain it, help move it, operate it in battle. Those things were what he'd been destined to do, and his whole life had been leading him to it. Here he'd found a family at last, real brothers of every size and color devoted to the same purpose—destroying evil even worse than he had ever come close to being. It was cathartic and made him a new man. He could no more abandon this gun, the nucleus around which that family was built, than he could cut his own heart out and walk away from it.

The new man from Frontera, Hoziki, stretched the lanyard and nodded at Naxa, and it struck Hanny that Hoziki had become much the same, for reasons of his own. He'd trained in every position, yearning to be on Hanny's "first" crew, and now here he was. "Ready!" cried Naxa, just behind Dodd's Number Three man for a change. No sooner had they indicated the guns were ready to fire than the Dom lancers, now spread out a bit more, roughly ten men abreast and who knew how deep, crested the ridge at a gallop, lances already down. At two hundred paces, Sal nodded down from his captured horse.

"Gun Number Two, fire!" Hanny rasped.

Poom!

". . . umber One, fire!" shouted Dodd.

Poom!

Canister peeled away another swathe of Doms, the horses behind them leaping the rolling, squealing mass and coming on. Hahessy was already pulling the wet sponge from the hot bore, Naxa's leather-clad thumb firmly on the vent, and the sponge left the muzzle with a hollow *toomp* sound. He, Preacher Mac, Naxa, and Hoziki quickly heaved the gun back where it started, and Kini Hau was already there with his leather haversack, carrying the next charge. No command was necessary. Preacher Mac handed his own implement to Kini and pulled the charge from the haversack, jamming it directly into the muzzle without any of the "proper" precautions of movement and position. Hahessy's only concession to safety was a quick glance to ensure that Naxa's thumb was pressing hard on the vent once more before he heaved the heavy tin of canister atop the bag of powder down to the breech. Pulling his rammer, he stepped outside the right wheel.

The lancers were almost on them, bright, bristling points already seeking their targets. "Ready!" screeched Naxa over the volley of small arms, thunder of hooves, and gasping blowing breath of horses and men that joined the lingering fog of smoke standing in front of the palisade. The mounted dragoons had remained in the open, all twenty-odd of them, and, dropping their carbines to hang from white leather slings by the saddle rings, drew their sabers.

For just an instant, Hanny thought he heard the pure notes of a bugle in the near distance, shattering the chill, smoke-filled air with a familiar call. He was certain it wasn't one of the lower-pitched Dom horns, but in the desperation of the moment, the significance of that eluded him. "Fire!" he croaked.

Poom!

At roughly fifty paces, the spread of canister was perhaps fifteen or twenty paces wide, but everything in that space, as far back in the ranks as Hanny could see, either died instantly or prepared to do so slower. Men a good distance to the side of the main impact were cast down by flying pieces of weapons and men, even canister balls that exited their first victims at an angle.

Poom! echoed Dodd's gun, and the horror was just as complete a little to the right. Hanny was still hearing the wail of that bugle, however, and even as he called for his crew to load again, doubting they'd ever finish this time, he heard Lieutenant Petty's harsh shout: "Section! Cease firing! Cease firing!"

Hanny was bewildered. *Petty must be mad*, he thought. Then he saw it. A solid line of blue-clad riders was thundering down the road, widening their front as they came and spitting bursts of white smoke before them, jets of sparkly fire stabbing out. Three men were slightly ahead of the others. One was huge, bearded, riding the tallest native horse he'd ever seen as the revolver in his hand fired again and again. A younger man with red collar and cuffs rode beside him, a lance of his own couched under his arm. The other was as nattily dressed as a dragoon on campaign could be, blond side whiskers unkempt over the tall blue collar with yellow trim, just above the shoulder boards of a captain. He was leaning forward in his saddle, saber outstretched, point questing.

"Go get 'em, boys!" Sal shouted at the dragoons gathered in front of him, laughter in his voice. With a wild yell, they charged. Sal held up a moment; both Paterson Colts clearly empty, he had a Bowie sword in his hand as he grinned hugely down at the artillerymen. "I *knew* that hairy old *lunatico* would come! Mr. Burton an' Mr. Lara too. But you, *mis amigos*, kept us alive long enough to *be* alive when they did." He spurred his horse into the rapidly changing fight. "I *told* you that you'd win the war for us!" he shouted over his shoulder.

With the enemy now suddenly trying to escape the furious dragoons, Rangers, and even a large chunk of Lara's lancers, and no one attempting to kill them at the moment, the tired artillerymen almost collapsed.

"I swan," Dodd said softly, stepping over to join Hanny's crew with a couple of his men. Petty drew near as well.

"Ain't gonna win the war like this," Preacher Mac dourly predicted. "An' mark me, there'll be a peck o' trouble o'er it all as well."

"Yer gloomy Scot's humor 'as returned ta ye, I see," Hahessy grumbled at him. "We won *this* battle, now, didn't we? Sod off wi' ye."

"Battle," Preacher Mac scoffed. "Ye ken as well as I, Daniel Hahessy, this wee shindy was nae battle. Nor was it our choosin'. The Doms led us tae it wi' more cost than we ken as yet, I warrant."

Petty sighed deeply, squinted eyes still watching the fight turned to slaughter. The enemy was outnumbered now, but quite a few would escape. Mostly reapers, he suspected. "He's right, I imagine. This wasn't a battle, fellas. Not like the one we're lookin' for, but look what it cost us. Who knows what price Mr. Lara's lancers paid. He didn't have half of 'em with him. An' here we've lost the better part of a third of our Rangers and dragoons, I bet." He shrugged. "We'll gain more horses than we lost, I expect, an' pick up most of the Hall carbines as well, plus a heap more enemy musketoons. We'll eventually even make up our losses in men. But at the moment, our scouts'll be stretched, an' *some* of the enemy will have survived a fight with the terrible '*los diablos de Yucatán*.' I figure that makes this a win for *them*, an' hurtin' us at a critical time an' boostin' their own morale was what this was all about."

"Then maybe we won after all," Hanny said, voice still rough. "They hurt us, sure. Probably more than they should have. Certainly more than they could have if they hadn't split us all up. Partly our own fault, you know." He shook his head. "Poor Andrew. We need to find him. Bury him right." He glanced at Dodd. "The other fellows too." He frowned. "And Mr. Joffrion. He was a good man. A good officer." He looked at Lieutenant Petty. "But as for surviving the fight with us, sure, some will. Maybe even a few hundred." He shook his head. "But even if they let them live after running from the fight, you can't tell me those that did will be able to convince others they beat us." He took a deep breath. "So, a costly draw at worst, I think. And don't forget: those reapers are the best scouts *they* have, and we killed an awful lot of them."

Petty nodded slowly. "Makes sense." He grinned. "Maybe we oughta switch jobs, Sergeant Cox. You may not be worth a fart in a stiff breeze as an artilleryman, but you're probably smarter than me. I'd rather be back on a gun."

Hanny managed a sad grin in return. "No sir, Mr. Petty. If I agreed to that, I'd just prove I'm an idiot—unfit for your job. I'll stay where I am, and you can't shift me."

CHAPTER 18

It stormed for several days as HMS *Tiger* beat down toward Uxmal from Techolotla, leaning stiffly away from a steady, southeasterly gale that might've been powered by a hurricane sweeping shoreward far to the north. Captain Eric Holland had been told to expect somewhat different weather than he was used to in these waters, especially at this time of year, and he'd proceeded with caution. *Tiger* had become very dear to him, bigger, faster, and infinitely more weatherly despite her age than the dilapidated old *Mary Riggs* had been. She was like a gift from God to highlight an old sailor's life, and he wouldn't rashly risk harm to her, even for the sheer joy that sailing on the edge always gave him.

And she wasn't only important to him, but to the cause they'd adopted. The steamer *Isidra* might be more modern and capable of wonders Holland never would've imagined when he first went to sea—such as moving directly into the wind—but not only was she their "secret weapon" for that reason, the fuel she must carry cut deep into her cargo capacity. As it always seemed of late, *Tiger* was protecting a small convoy of captured Dom cargo ships down to Uxmal. They'd carry more newly raised troops, tools, and the people to use them back closer to the war, and *Tiger* would fill her own hold with the same sort of things. Besides, as fascinating as Holland found *Isidra* to be, aside from the greater weight of metal *Tiger* also carried (she was still their most powerful warship by far), Holland felt he was too old a dog to sufficiently learn *Isidra*'s character, and he could handle *Tiger* better than anyone.

They were barely a day out of Uxmal now, and though the wind was still brisk (veering rather bracingly around out of the northwest), the sky had turned an almost flawless blue: crisp, clean, with an illusion of near infinite visibility. The only thing keeping the lookouts from seeing halfway around the world, it seemed, was the heaving, whitecapping sea, still unsettled by the distant storm and a hard, distinctly cool breeze. Captain Holland hadn't enjoyed anything nearly as refreshing since he came to this world. *Somethin's bound ta happen ta foul it all up*, he glumly imagined. *That's just the way o' things. We'll split a sail or a yard'll carry away . . . or a seam'll open an' we'll be pumpin' for our lives*, he had to reluctantly add. He could feel the old hull working hard through his feet. As much as he loved her, *Tiger* couldn't have many useful years left. *Same as me*, he thought.

Lieutenant Semmes approached the windward rail where he stood, bearing a pair of large, steaming cups. "Cookie's just made a big batch of chocolate for the lads coming off watch. I thought you might enjoy one."

"Thanks," Holland said, taking a mug and raising it to his lips. He desperately missed coffee, but the dark, syrupy chocolate—far too sweet for him and flavored disconcertingly like the tobacco-like leaves he chewed—was still welcome. It would be even more so to the men, mostly locals addicted to the stuff, who'd been high in the rigging. Genuinely cold or not, the wind whipping all around them would've sapped the strength from their hands and left them shivering. Taking a big sip, Holland tried not to grimace. He was inordinately proud that he still had most of his teeth, and he feared the drink was sweet enough to crack them. It was an unusual feeling.

"I wonder if it gets really cold this far south," Semmes said, closely mirroring Holland's own thoughts. "It never got much cooler than this last winter," he grinned. "I suppose it *is* winter, since we're still somewhat north of the equator."

"Somewhat," Holland agreed, "an' *almost* winter," he corrected. "Captain Razine swears it gets cold occasionally, though he's only ever seen one freeze in his life. Scared hell out of him, he says. An' Varaa told me that southern winters reach almost as far northward. No tropical jungles, I suppose, like we should've found on the Yucatán. Just dense hardwood forests perhaps? Or is the whole southern continent like Patagonia?" He grinned back at Semmes. "Might be we'll find out together, someday."

"I'd like that," Semmes said, gulping his own chocolate before waving vaguely back northwest in the direction they came from. "I expect Colonel Cayce an' his soldiers have found some *real* cold up in the mountains. If they haven't, they will. I don't envy them that. I'm from Cornwall, you know, but I must have the blood of a reptile." Neither speculated aloud what the weather might be like in seas they both knew should be miserably cold in winter. The weather was strange enough here.

"Sail!" came the cry down from above. "South-southeast! Two sails . . . *three*! An' smoke!"

Nothing could be seen from deck unaided. "You, boy," Holland called to one of the youngest midshipmen. "Fetch my glass, won't you? Bring it to the fo'c'sle. There's a good lad." He glanced at Semmes. "Let's have a look." Together, they strode forward past the mainmast and longboats and directly onto the fo'c'sle deck, where the foremast stood and four of the ship's 6pdrs squatted. Unlike the quarterdeck, the fo'c'sle wasn't raised, and they didn't climb any stairs. Leaning on the stanchions over the headrails, Holland took the glass the midshipman brought and raised it to his eye. He grunted. "I see five sail slantin' north as close to the wind as they'll lie. All are gaggled together an' look just like that sorry lot we're shepherdin' down ourselves." He waved a dismissive hand over his shoulder at the mostly unconverted merchantmen laboring in *Tiger*'s wake. Only one of the four ships in the old frigate's convoy had been razed and rerigged as a brig and wasn't having too much trouble keeping up. Of course, with the wind almost directly astern, only *Tiger*'s foremast wore all its canvas. The t'gallant and reefed top'sl were all that was stretched on her mainmast. Holland adjusted the focus of his telescope. "Blast this slimy film on the lenses! All I can see . . ." He slightly relaxed. "They're all flyin' the Stars an' Stripes—or Uxmal's saltire." He shifted his gaze far beyond them, but couldn't make out much more. He thought there were a couple more sails, at least. Seeing smoke was impossible through his smudged glass. "Masthead!" he bellowed suddenly, slightly startling Semmes. "What do you make of it now?"

"Five of ours running north," a shouted voice confirmed. "Five more sail, maybe six—they are all in a line to the horizon, and I can't tell exactly how many—are closing on yet another. I *am* sure that one is *Nemesis*. She has interposed herself before the strangers and turned to present a broadside."

Holland tensed again and his eyes narrowed. "What *color* are the stranger's sails?"

"Red, Captain. All red."

Holland and Semmes simply stared at each other, both recognizing the terrible implications at once. "We were wrong," Holland said. "Damn. The god damned Doms've come through the Pass of Fire after all!"

Semmes nodded. "They must have done," he said, but quickly pointed out, "*Nemesis* is faster and far nimbler than the enemy if what we've seen of their Pacific ships holds true, but she isn't as heavily armed." Captain Jenks had refused the offer of captured 16pdrs to replace his 6pdrs. Not only was *Nemesis* too lightly built to support them, he preferred to keep her speed and agility anyway. "Making a stand, she won't last long," Semmes pressed.

"Aye," Holland growled. "We'll have to lend a hand. Fire a gun ta get Jenks's attention. He should hear it. The smoke'll get his lookout's attention at least. We may not hear his reply this far upwind, but we'll see his smoke as well. Either way, if Jenks knows we're comin', he'll haul off an' wait for us to join him." He glanced at Semmes with a half smile. "He may be a Brit—o' some species—but he didn't strike me as a idiot."

"Indeed. Whatever he is, he is no Yank, after all," Semmes bantered back, then fretted, "I just hope he sees us before he is shot to pieces."

Holland frowned at him. "Well, there's nothin' for it if he don't. With Jenks's help or no, I mean ta destroy each an' every one o' them Dom ships. Mr. . . . Aw, hell, I never remember your bloody damn name, boy. Signals midshipman! Get over here." He beckoned to the youngster. "Make to our convoy to break off an' join the one that was tailin' *Nemesis*." He looked back at Semmes. "Our ships were empty; the others might be too." He addressed the youth again. "Add that any which ain't got a cargo'll steer for Gran Lago an' wait for us there. Might be we'll need 'em," he added darkly.

"What for? Few are armed. They can't fight."

Holland scratched his stubbly chin. "Those five damned Doms ain't here by theirselves—*this* side o' Uxmal. Could be we'll hafta *evacuate* someplace," he said, tone low.

NEMESIS DID INDEED take note of their arrival, and after delivering a couple of raking broadsides that toppled the nearest enemy's foremast, she tacked around to larboard. The Doms swerved to return her greetings, and a few holes appeared in her sails, but she'd managed to cripple at least one of the enemy. She'd already done more, setting fire to another currently burning fiercely a number of miles back. Now she was making for *Tiger*, tack on tack, as Holland's bigger ship, already cleared for action with guns loaded and run out and under fighting sail alone, swept down. There was loud amusement aboard the old frigate when *Nemesis* belatedly hoisted the signal "Enemy in sight," using the code still new to her. Much faster than the enemy, especially with this wind, *Nemesis* gained a mile before wearing 'round again and heaving to, wallowing heavily in the wind-driven swells while she waited for *Tiger* to come up and heave to as well. When she did, Jenks climbed on the bulwark, clutching the mizzen shrouds with one hand, a speaking trumpet in the other. "Come to our rescue again, I see," he shouted across to Holland, who was now in the larboard mainmast shrouds with a speaking trumpet of his own.

"Glad ta do it," Holland shouted back, "but it's gettin' ta be a habit. You just can't be trusted ta run around on your own without pickin' up a string o' strays."

"I did my best to discourage them from following me home," Jenks replied ironically. "Did you know that lovely exploding case shot for the army actually fits my guns? That's how we dealt with that smoldering fellow some distance back."

"Then I take it your merchants're already loaded and the Doms pounced on you after you left Uxmal?"

Jenks shook his head exaggeratedly. "No. No cargo. The Doms were already in Uxmal Bay when we arrived. Came boiling out after us like flies, and we turned around at once. Their warships from the Pacific are faster than my merchies, you know. I didn't even dare delay to try and count those still in the bay. Since our new acquaintances were already waiting for us, I can only assume we passed them in the night." He hesitated a moment. "Ah, you thought since I had some case shot, we must have already been in port. Sadly, no. The few I had were . . . borrowed, shall we say, from an earlier shipment for experimental purposes. My master gunner has a lot to learn about fuses, I fear, and only one actually exploded in the enemy. That one was enough, it seems."

"Congratulations," Holland called back, eyeing the four remaining enemy ships still closing. They were tacking away at the moment, but would be in range when they veered back. The one *Nemesis* disabled had rolled out the rest of her masts and was now a wallowing hulk. "Let's deal with these others while we still have the weather gauge. After, I'll go on to Uxmal an' have a look how things lie."

"I would be delighted to join you!"

Holland shook his head. "No. I sent all the merchants to Gran Lago." He pointed his speaking trumpet at the enemy ships before bringing it back to his lips. "If those were already past you, others might be. Our convoys'll need protectin'."

Jenks hesitated a moment, clearly disappointed. "Very well. As you once pointed out, I must follow your orders." He gestured at the nearby enemies as well. "At least I can stay long enough to help sort *those* buggers out!"

Holland nodded back. "We'll keep our distance an' pound 'em down. Work on their riggin' an' sails with your six pounders." He grinned. "You won't be of use for anything if you get close enough ta damage their hulls— an' get your own all shot full o' holes!"

NEMESIS CAME AROUND behind *Tiger*, sails filling again as she turned, and they went in together against the four inferior but still quite formidable enemy. The Doms had been expecting it; clearly these sailors were more knowledgeable about naval warfare than their Atlantic counterparts had been, and formed their own line of battle. They couldn't sail nearly as close to the wind, however, and whatever they tried, *Tiger* and *Nemesis* frustrated their attempts to close the range within six hundred yards. Finally convinced they'd get no closer, the Doms opened fire. Dom 16pdrs could certainly do great damage at that range, but the heaving sea made actually hitting their targets more a matter of luck than skill and waterspouts erupted all around *Tiger* and *Nemesis*, but few were particularly close.

The same problem afflicted Holland and Jenks to a lesser degree. Their ships had better rigs and hull forms that let them sail stiffer and more stable.

And Holland at least, still haunted by nightmares of his long-ago experience at Valparaiso, was practically obsessed with accurate, long-range gunnery. Through daily drill and countless tweaks to his weaponry, he'd honed his gun's crews to a high degree of almost sinfully prideful professionalism. His gunners had learned to time their fire to the random pitching and rolling of the ship in virtually any weather, and Holland himself knew how to mitigate that movement more than most just by the way he handled her. Standing by the leeward rail, watching the distant flowers of smoke bloom and fade, he called out minute adjustments to the sails and tiller. Finally satisfied he'd found *Tiger*'s easiest gait, he glanced at Mr. Semmes and said, "Commence firin' as they bear. All on the trailin' ship, mind."

The first great 36pdr roared and shook the old ship almost as soon as Semmes passed the word. Its smoke swept down toward the enemy and Holland had trouble following the flight of shot. "Damned glass," he muttered again. Everyone saw the enormous splash that arose close in the target ship's wake. Another gun fired, then another, and watchers with telescopes were rewarded by the sight of flying debris before the sound of the wind-muffled crash returned. Cheers—and good-natured arguing over which gun made the strike—arose.

"Beggin' yer pardon, skipper, but cain't we shoot yet?" asked one of the men, a former field artilleryman in control of the upper-deck division of lighter guns. The gun's crews around him nodded vigorously.

Holland shook his head. "You'll hafta wait a bit, lads. Too much smoke'll spoil the aim of the bigger guns. You'll get yer chance."

Nemesis was firing briskly, but her smoke wasn't obstructing their view.

"Surely, sir, the lighter guns could fire while the heavier ones are reloading?" Semmes suggested. "Perhaps choose other targets as well. Quickly cripple them all, if possible. If we simply destroy them one at a time, I fear the survivors will flee. We can certainly catch them, but it was my impression that you wanted to make short work of them."

Holland considered, then nodded. "Good thinkin', Mr. Semmes. Doms ain't much for showin' their heels in my experience, but somebody over there might figure spreadin' the word about us'd be wise." He looked at the expectant gunners. "Very well. Let's lavish hospitality all over the buggers."

Tiger's rate of fire picked up considerably, some guns even firing when they couldn't see a thing. Holland was slightly annoyed by that. He hated waste, and most of those shots hit nothing but water. Still, many of his gunners had practiced replicating previous elevation and windage adjustments well enough to strike their enemy regardless. *Nemesis* was doing better than Holland expected as well. A break in the smoke allowed him to see a mainmast crashing down, and Jenks's crew could be heard roaring satisfaction. Over the next fifteen minutes or so, Holland called a cease-fire a couple of times to view what damage they'd done. Only two Dom warships still mirrored their course, firing furiously back. The others were wallowing helplessly, one pirouetting around a fallen foremast and bowsprit, the other—probably *Nemesis*'s victim—completely dismasted. Her falling mainmast had taken the others down with it. Both were low in the water, as was one of those still under way. It was lagging badly behind the ship in front of it.

The most satisfying thing was that the return fire from the enemy had been almost entirely ineffective. *Nemesis* had taken a couple of shrewd knocks in the hull, her pumps working hard, and her main topsail had split from a shot across its belly. Canvas flailed madly while men worked to cut it away and bend on new sail. *Tiger*, the much larger target, had only taken one hit high in the hull, and her sails had a few holes. Holland didn't know about *Nemesis*, but not a soul had been injured on *Tiger*. Apparently, the fogbank of smoke rolling down upon them had degraded the enemy's gunnery more than theirs. Holland was growing impatient, however, anxious to see how things stood at Uxmal.

"Signal Captain Jenks ta maintain station here. We're gettin' closer ta finish this. Quartermaster Neen," he called to the Uxmalo sailor at the helm, "start easin' us down a little closer, if ye please."

"We'll take more hits," Semmes warned.

Holland nodded thoughtfully, then spoke loudly so his voice would carry. "Aye, the buggers'll touch us a time er two more as we close, but not often. They'll hardly have the chance. Our lads can fire faster, an' they won't miss."

An expectant cheer spread through the ship, and the boast hadn't been an idle one. The smoke continued to favor *Tiger* as she swept down on the lead Dom ship, and her own fire smashed the thing apart fairly quickly. Turning due south, she sprinted ahead of the lagging vessel and raked her unmercifully even as she finally tried to turn away. Amazingly, none of her masts went by the board, but the shot-torn red flag with the jagged gold cross was quickly cut away.

"I'll be damned!" Semmes exclaimed. "She's struck her colors!"

"These're 'Pacific' Doms," Holland reminded, just as surprised. "More of a naval war 'tween them an' the empire out there. Jenks said such things ain't unknown. Rare as crocodile feathers," he allowed with a snort, then laughed out loud. "Which *they* ain't that rare on this world! Unusual all the same, I reckon." He gestured at the shattered lead ship, clearly already going down. Her sides showed bright wood where great splinters had been blasted away, and blood streamed from the scuppers. Terrified sailors were gathering in the stern. "Get boats in the water before the bloody damned fish eat all those devils on that one," Holland continued. "Have our lads go armed an' be awful careful!" he reminded before his eyes settled on the signal midshipmen. "Run up a signal for Mr. Jenks ta come down an' secure the prize while we go invite the derelicts ta surrender. Jenks'll stand ready ta take survivors an' prisoners aboard *Nemesis*. I want his quick, *honest* opinion of whether the prizes can be easily saved. If not, he's to send 'em all to the bottom."

Jenks swiftly reported the condition of the ships, and Holland agreed that without the threat looming over the horizon, at least two of them might've been salvaged. As it was, he feared they wouldn't have time to stop all the leaks and certainly not for *Nemesis* to tow the dismasted to safety. *Nemesis* was an excellent sailor and very fast, but despite being a little larger than these Pacific examples of Dom shipbuilding, she was considerably lighter built. Towing a heavy, wallowing hulk in these rough seas would be risky. Captain Jenks was willing to try, regardless—there was the matter of prize money, after all—but Holland decided they had to be destroyed. He wouldn't risk burning them, their smoke drawing more, and had them scuttled instead. This still created a significant hardship for *Nemesis*. Not only had Jenks decided his ship needed heavier guns after all and insisted on swaying a number of the better enemy weapons aboard, *Nemesis* had to take all the survivors as well. Practically staggering under the load, she beat away in the wake of the merchantmen that had been under her and *Tiger*'s protection. Jenks could spread the amazingly meek and appreciative Dom sailors among those ships when he caught them.

Her crew still knotting and splicing cut rigging and patching sails, *Tiger* turned to shoulder her way toward Uxmal once more.

"Shape a course that'll bring us down on the city from the east with the dawn, if ye please," Holland instructed Mr. Semmes. "If we must go amongst them devils, I'd rather take 'em by surprise.

Semmes nodded agreement. If there were as many Dom ships at Uxmal as Jenks had implied, perhaps their lookouts would be lax. And no one enjoyed staring directly into the fierce dawn sun. "Do you think there will *be* a sun?" he asked, gazing up at the mottled gray sky.

Holland nodded definitively. "Aye. Clear skies an' moderatin' seas by midnight, I'm thinkin'."

"Have you consulted the glass?"

Holland shook his head, pointing at his forehead. "Don't need to. I feel it up here. Pressure's comin' up."

Semmes just nodded again, bowing to Holland's many more decades of experience.

Sure enough, by midnight, there wasn't a cloud in the sky, and the spray of stars spread across it was bright and sharp. *Tiger* took station about fifteen miles east of Uxmal and stood off and on the rest of the night encountering nothing except great, rainbow-finned fish that had herded a pod or school of large, darting phosphorescent creatures up from the depths to feed upon. Watching the fascinating spectacle helped pass the time and kept the men's minds off what might happen when the sun came up. Two hours before dawn, Holland called for the t'gallants to be furled so his ship might be mistaken for a Dom at a glance. Enemy ships only carried topsails and courses on their fore- and mainmasts. Along with approaching out of the sun, that was all he could do, and *Tiger* steered west for Uxmal—and the vast armada Jenks had reported now infested the bay.

"Feed the lads," Holland told Semmes, "then we'll clear for action. We may have to fight both sides of the ship, so take who ye need fer that."

"The topmen will be shorthanded," Semmes warned.

"Aye," Holland conceded, "but not for long, I hope. All we need do is bash our way close enough ta exchange signals with the city an' discover their true situation. Then we'll run like the devil." He didn't need to add that if the enemy landed any lucky shots and took down a mast, they wouldn't be running anywhere. If that happened, *Tiger* would likely be swarmed under and destroyed.

Apparently thinking along those lines himself, Semmes said, "The steamer, *Isidra*, would have been perfect for this sort of thing. Especially now that she has been more heavily armed and her scantlings strengthened."

Holland was already shaking his head. "With her able ta steer wherever she wants, regardless o' the wind, she might be a wonder in a fight. For this, she's too damn slow. No doubt she could get in an' out well enough, but she couldn't get *away*. The damned Doms'd dog her all the way back where she came from, shootin' her ta pieces all the while!"

Semmes smirked. *Isidra* wasn't *that* slow, and Holland well knew it.

Dawn was flaring brilliantly behind her as *Tiger* swept down on Ux-mal Bay.

"It shames me ta insult the old ship's dignity so, but we may as well run up one o' them Dom flags we been collectin'," Holland said aside. He, Semmes, and several other officers were on the fo'c'sle gazing at the brightly lit Doms lying at anchor ahead. Perhaps a dozen were just outside the mouth of the bay, but masts stood like a forest within. Captain Jenks hadn't exaggerated.

"What's the point? Our sails aren't red," Semmes objected.

"Their merchantmen don't wear red sails either. Most of 'em, anyway," Holland reminded. "Send the damn flag up. They'll know we aren't one of theirs quick enough."

The glaring sun behind and the eye-watering glitter on the sea, perhaps even the enemy flag, brought them much closer in than they would've imagined, actually passing a pair of enemy ships—the officers on one disinterestedly waving—before anyone seemed to get wise. "Arrogant bastards," Holland grumbled. "Can't imagine an enemy runnin' right in amongst 'em so they can't see it even as it's happenin'."

Semmes pointed directly ahead. "I think whoever commands that vessel might be growing suspicious," he said a little nervously. "See? He signals us now." Holland frowned. Unfortunately, no signal books had been found on the prizes taken the day before. Witnesses among the largely enslaved crews attested that their few surviving officers had stuffed them in their coattail pockets, along with a handful of small swivel gun shot, before hurling themselves into the sea. "We'll try bendin' on a reply—any gibberish'll do—an' have the signals midshipman stop the hoist before it gets too high an' fiddle with the halyard like it's jammed in the block."

"Surely they won't fall for that old ruse," Semmes objected. Holland shrugged. "Might not be an old one, here."

Apparently, it was. The Dom warship made no effort to continue communication, but immediately started hauling around, a spring in her cable, to present her larboard broadside. Gunports flew open, and shiny bronze muzzles poked out. "Shit," Holland grunted. "To your posts!" he told the nearby officers. Gesturing up at the Dom flag above, he shouted, "Get that damned rag down at once an' run up our own flags!"

"The same as always?" Semmes quickly asked.

"Aye. Stars an' Stripes to the main masthead. Your own bloody jack on the fore!"

Grinning, Semmes turned to order it done. Striding back toward the quarterdeck, Holland roared, "Run out yer guns an' prime. Both sides!"

The Dom had her guns out first, but they weren't loaded. *Tiger*'s already were. At less than thirty yards, the old frigate heeled and turned to larboard, sails flapping as she slowed. "Starboard battery, no broadsides, if ye please. No sense shakin' the old girl apart!" Holland exhorted, still pacing aft. Peering over the side at the enemy, he continued more loudly. "Now fire as ye bear, for the waterline!"

The first great 36pdr roared almost at once, swiftly followed by the second and third. Four and five nearly did fire at the same time, but even they were muffled slightly by the sharper barking of the upper-deck 12- and 6pdrs. Clouds of jagged wooden splinters exploded from the Dom's bulwarks, launched in lethal sprays across her deck. Men shrieked and fell, or just simply dropped, shredded, to the deck, and a fog of blood seemed to hang in the air over her. That was the least of it. More robust than *Nemesis* they might be, but no Dom ship, perhaps no ship on this world, could hope to deflect a 36pdr solid shot, especially at this distance. They blasted entirely through the ship, out the other side, and kicked up splashes far into the bay. Several probably hit other ships there. Their target never had a chance, never even got to fire back. The gaping holes smashed into the hull were so immense that the reeling wreck slopped tons of water into her hold with every swaying motion and quickly began to settle. Men on the gun deck, water already pouring in through her ports, abandoned their weapons and swarmed up from below. Her crew might be slaves for the most part, almost utterly ignorant of the lands they were forced to fight for, even of the Dominion itself to a degree, but they weren't stupid. They knew quite a lot about what lurked in the sea, waiting to literally eat them alive. They flew into an uncontrollable panic as the waters reached for them.

"Jesus wept!" one of the British 12pdr gunners cried, amazed.

"Poor bastards," agreed members of the next gun's crew aft.

"Stow that womanish blubberin'," Holland snapped. "Weep over the devils later if ye must. Most of 'em likely deserve it." He pointed. "But there's a lot more of 'em. An' see? Some're makin' sail already an' cuttin' their cables ta come for us. The only thing cloudin' their vision right now is blood, not tears. Keep firin', damn you."

"At her?" a particularly short Uxmalo gunner asked incredulously, tilting his head toward the settling wreck. Holland rolled his eyes.

"That'un's no further threat ta anythin' where there's air, ye midgety idjit. She might smush a clam or two when she hits the bottom." He raised his voice so they could hear down on *Tiger*'s gun deck. "Fire as ye bear on anythin' headin' this way that's close enough ta hit us. Them 18pdrs they carry ain't spitwads, ye know!" The larboard 36s started firing, quickly followed by the lighter guns. Holland whipped his head that way.

"One of the fellows we passed by seems to have realized he made a rather ridiculous mistake and appears intent on redeeming himself," Semmes pointed out. "Likely he'll attempt a similar approach to the one we just performed."

"I expect he will at that. Only we'll rake him from one end to the other as he comes—an' if he even makes it here, we won't obligingly wait." *Tiger*'s sails had been adjusted to catch the wind again, and she'd quickly pulled past the sinking ship. "I want her disabled, Mr. Semmes. Ten dollars to the crew that gives me her foremast. That's a whole keg of beer in Vera Cruz. Each crew has three shots ta get it done before we turn back for the open water just inside the bay. Quartermaster!" he bellowed at the helmsman, pointing. "Make for the east headland. No closer than a cable, mind, or ye'll tear the guts outa her!"

"What about the fort there, sir?"

Holland hesitated. "We'll hafta pray the Doms ain't took it yet—or our lads spiked the guns when they did. Nothin' else for it! Signals!"

"Sir!" cried the signals midshipman.

"Stand by to hoist a signal to the city, to Colonel De Russy in particular. Hope the silly bugger ain't dead!"

"Someone's still active behind the walls," the bosun pronounced. "I've seen cannon fire aimed at the enemy coming from there ever since we opened fire ourselves."

"That's somethin', at least." Holland looked back at the midshipman. "Keep that signal flyin' until there's a response, then ask for whatever details they can share about their situation. Jenks'll pass the warnin', but Colonel Cayce—an' Alcaldesa Periz—need ta know what's what."

"Such a . . . casual conversation will take time," Semmes warned, tone somewhat incredulous. "Perhaps longer than we should linger in the middle of a Dom fleet that is rapidly awakening to our presence!"

Holland suppressed a smile at the understatement and nodded. "Aye. Then we'll just hafta fight all the harder before we double our efforts ta get clear." He gestured around. "Least not all these damn vessels is warships. Unarmed troopships, for the most part. I can't *believe* they were mad enough ta bring 'em through the pass." He started to simmer. "An' what of Mr. Jenks's vaunted Imperial navy?" A dark thought suddenly struck him. "I wonder. Could be they've heard more about our business than Mr. Jenks was aware an' were glad ta see Dom ships an' troops pulled off ta focus elsewhere."

Semmes had nothing to say to that, but his eyes widened at the possibility.

The larboard side guns commenced a slow, measured bombardment against the nearest approaching ship barely two hundred paces distant, and *Tiger*'s well-trained gun's crews couldn't miss. In spite of the offered "beer prize," nearly all gunners aimed for the enemy bows, and they utterly smashed it from the timbers butting up against the cutwater all the way up to the fo'c'sle deck. The bowsprit fell back and away, crashing into the water, but the ship was already slowing, rapidly flooding. A great, feral cheer rose up.

"What if we can't, sir?" the bosun pressed. "Get away, I mean."

Holland grimaced. "I place my trust in providence—an' our lovely big guns—that we will. If neither of those things suffice . . . we'll run the ship up on the coral heads yonder, set her ablaze, an' fight our way into Uxmal ourselves. But make no mistake, if that comes ta pass, destroyin' the ship'll be our chief priority."

The starboard and larboard batteries were firing nonstop now, shattering targets to either side, and Holland felt the old ship's bones creaking beneath his feet. He also felt the juddering smash of increasing numbers of heavy Dom shot crashing into her in reply. *It's gonna be close either way*, he thought.

━━━━━

Colonel Ruberdeau De Russy stood on the highest seaside rampart behind the great wall surrounding the city, hands clasped behind his back. Like nearly always, as he deemed appropriate for his position as manager of the Council of Alcaldes, he was dressed in his best dress coat with tails, epaulets, and brilliantly polished buttons; his finest white trousers; gleaming black knee boots; and feather-plumed cocked hat. Considering he was also appearing in his persona as chief military defender of Uxmal, he considered it appropriate to wear his sword belt over the burgundy sash wrapped around his proud middle that day. He usually didn't bother.

The days-long battle for the city had settled into a kind of lull while the enemy fleet in the bay moved out of easy range of their biggest guns and continued to disembark infantry and field guns to fill the disconcertingly professional circumvallation their engineers had been laboring to build. Sallies had slowed them, keeping the Pidra Blanca Road open as long as possible while refugees from there kept coming, but now that road was closed. The only roads left open for now were the one to Itzincab and the Camino Militar down to Nautla. Not that the Nautla Road had much traffic. Just as the Itzincab Road must remain open as long as possible while noncombatants fled inland to that distant, well-fortified city on the interior frontier, De Russy and his second in command, Vice Alcaldesa Concejala Urita Xa, had ordered all forces in Nautla to evacuate south to Campeche. There was no point in drawing them back to Uxmal, since the city would eventually be sealed off and isolated, especially when the Dom army that had landed at Pidra Blanca came and joined the forces here. Eventually, the circumvallation would cut the Itzincab Road as well, and no one would be getting in or out of Uxmal after that. The city would have to hold or fall on its own.

There was actually fairly good reason to expect it to hold. The walls were strong and well defended by cannon and fourteen thousand reasonably well-equipped and -trained troops and militia. Supplies were no issue either. Uxmal had long been prepared to withstand a siege. Better than the enemy was equipped to enforce one, most likely. De Russy suspected that Uxmal's greatest weakness was the man entrusted with its defense. Himself, in point of fact.

"Do you suppose Captain Holland and *Tiger* made it out?" Urita Xa anxiously asked, even as the distant roar of heavy guns out across the bay finally dwindled and towers of dark gray smoke slanted sharply away. There simply was no telling from here. The old frigate had certainly cut a swathe of destruction through the anchored ships as she exchanged signals with the city, the mast erected for that very purpose not far from where De Russy now stood still flying the flags of the final response he had directed. He sighed very deeply and turned to look at the energetic old woman standing beside him, dressed in the field uniform of an Allied officer.

"I'm sure of it, my dear," he lied. Certainly the ship had looked mostly intact if considerably battered about the last time he'd seen her through the glass now in Urita Xa's hands, but that was before she made her break for the open sea. There'd been a great deal more firing after that and he'd actually lost her in the smoke. "Not only will Mr. Holland carry specific information about our predicament to Colonel Cayce and our dear Alcaldesa Sira Periz"—he gestured at the leaning, sinking ships lying closer in the bay—"he seriously inconvenienced the enemy here." He smiled and shook his head. "I didn't know the old ship had it in her!"

Urita Xa frowned. "I hope that she did."

De Russy cleared his throat. "Yes. Well. At least Holland's reference to meeting *Nemesis* means that word will spread regardless."

"But *Nemesis* can't pass our assurance we can hold here, and the *alcaldesa* must not concern herself."

"True," De Russy hedged, unsure he agreed with that part of the signal Urita Xa insisted he send. He glanced around at their combined staff and the crew of the nearest gun to make sure no one was near enough to hear. Most were excitedly discussing the morning's entertainment, in which all they'd done was fire a few encouraging cannon. None were listening, and De Russy continued. "I . . . I have made no secret of my military shortcomings, and I must confess to you that I do not feel equal to a command of this importance. My previous efforts, on a much smaller scale, were rather less than successful."

Urita Xa put a hand on his sleeve, a small smile joining the creases on her still-handsome face. "You will do fine. *We* will do fine," she assured. "No one remains here to worry about. Your dear Angelique has already departed safely to the south with my daughters and grandchildren. Indeed, there is no one left in the city who is not here to fight. When the enemy closes the Itzincab Road, it will be no real loss. Other than that, we are surrounded by fine officers who know what to do. All we must do is look calm and confident, yes?"

De Russy regarded her fondly and chuckled. "Yes indeed, and I can do that. I was a politician, after all! No one is better at hiding their true feelings and deficiencies!"

He gazed back out over the bay. *Tiger* had caused a great deal of damage, but he was surprised to see how well and how quickly much of it was being taken in hand. Undamaged ships were clustering around those that were taking on water, and shoals of longboats that had been putting men ashore merely refocused their efforts on evacuating them first. And as if to assure them that they'd hardly suffered, a number of warships were edging in closer to the city to exchange cannon fire once again. He sighed. "You'll have some more business fairly soon, it seems," he called loudly to the closest gun's crew. "No sense in Captain Holland having all the fun today."

He saw Urita Xan smiling at him, and he shrugged. "That's all I need to do, as you say," he spoke lowly. "Other men will now direct their fire." He blew out a gust of air. "Thank God for it too. We are already rather badly outnumbered, I fear, and I am no Leonidas, or William Travis!"

"Who are they?" Urita Xan asked.

De Russy hesitated, already ashamed to have made the comparison, but he couldn't help responding, "They were other men, each far better than I, who once found themselves in a similar fix. But 'were' is the distinctive tense."

CHAPTER 19

On the first day of December, Colonel Lewis Cayce, Varaa-Choon, Reverend Harkin, and Leonor were riding with Colonel Agon at the head of his 4th Division, still first in the order of march, as the army approached the key Dom city of Puebla. They remained fairly high up, roughly seven thousand feet above sea level according to Dr. Newlin, and were moving across a vast, sparsely wooded plain surrounded by distant snowcapped peaks. It felt cold enough to snow, and the men continued to march in their greatcoats, steaming breath intermingled with pipe and cigar smoke in the ranks, but the sky remained clear and almost purple-blue. Major Anson was back riding with Boogerbear and his Rangers, casting about ahead and on the flanks, every detachment returning frequent reports. Leonor thought her father blamed himself for the losses they'd suffered in the dangerous traps laid for them. Regardless of the reason, he felt even worse for not having been with them.

Disturbingly, even as they neared the city, passing through the highest concentration of farms and villas yet encountered, they discovered that many of them had been destroyed. Everything from mud hut cabins to expansive estates with numerous outbuildings had been torched days, even weeks before, and anything resembling a grain storehouse had either been emptied or burnt. For that matter, virtually no livestock remained in evidence aside from the occasional stray armabuey rooting through the charred remains of some building, possibly drawn by the smell of a secret indoor cache, and a few of the momentous, long-necked beasts the Doms used for the heaviest of labor, nibbling almost delicately on what might've once been ornamental evergreens. Neither would be of use to a swiftly moving army. Clearly, the enemy had been sure they'd come this far for a while and determined to leave nothing in terms of provisions. The cropland itself would've likely been burnt as well if everything hadn't already been harvested and the ground weren't so damp from the recent snow.

Most foreboding of all, perhaps, was the near-total absence of people. A few bodies were seen, picked over by scavengers, their remains scattered along the road. Raucous lizardbirds lingered, raking away final morsels and screeching indignantly when disturbed from their feast, spraying revolting streams of shit when reluctantly forced to take flight. Occasional survivors, left behind by the apparently traumatic exodus, were spotted now and then, usually fleeing in terror or peeking from blackened ruins where, like the armabueys, they'd been searching for something to eat. The people caught seeking food, almost all slaves who'd hidden from their masters, were fed and cared for and finally spoke to Don Hurac when he went to them. What they described—Dom troops sweeping through and herding everyone north, destroying what couldn't be taken (including people)—made Harkin remark, "Poor devils. The events they witnessed must have been like some of those dreadful paintings of souls being cast into hell. I can't remember the artists, but suspect they were all opium addicts." He arched a brow. "Doesn't mean their depictions were wrong, of course." His voice changed slightly to his "quoting tone." "'He will wipe away every tear from their eyes, and death shall be no more, neither shall there be mourning, nor crying, nor pain anymore, for the former things have passed away.'"

"Don't think *their* God'll be wipin' any tears," Leonor said. "Unless he *licks* 'em off 'cause he likes the taste. I start to think their whole notion of the almighty comes from Romans." Harkin actually shuddered at the mental image she'd created, and several of those around looked at her questioningly. She sighed. "I don't know it by heart, but it's about rejoicin' in sufferin' because it builds endurance, character, an' hope. Not a bad passage, an' pretty true, I reckon, but they've substituted 'grace' for them other things. There ain't *nothin'* so horrible they can do to one another that it ain't a *favor*, see?"

"I can't imagine how any society could function like that," Reverend Harkin said, horrified.

"Yet it is true," Colonel Agon confirmed, "and . . ." He paused. ". . . Teniente Anson is likely more right than she knows. Dominion society still functions because the laws are, at heart, based upon the commandments God gave to Moses—and those laws are strictly enforced. Suffering inflicted on those who transgress is the path to redemption. Otherwise, the 'horrible' things the *teniente* refers to are generally reserved by the Blood Cardinals to themselves"—he frowned with a tentative glance toward the rear of the column where Don Hurac followed—"to be employed during ritualistic spectacles. You all know this. The chief difference between Don Hurac and others of his kind, even before his conversion, was that he was less zealous in his application of grace-giving suffering." His expression darkened. "And the ascendent Blood Priests and their . . . tools, such as Don Frutos and Don Julio—even more Blood Cardinals by now, I am sure—would threaten that fabric of society with an orgy of suffering."

"I agree," said Varaa-Choon, blue eyes blinking rapidly and tail whipping. "Sometimes I think that the great enemy cannot possibly survive its own excess. If we could just secure ourselves from attack long enough, this 'new' Dominion they are trying to build will collapse of its own accord." She looked at Lewis. "But that won't happen, will it?"

Lewis shook his head. "Not while we exist to defy them, on offense or defense. We'll remain the common enemy to unite them."

Leonor was nodding. "An' even if they beat us, there's those Imperials the 'Gran Cruzada' went for." She looked at Varaa. "An' after them, it'll be somebody else, I expect."

Lewis managed what looked like a genuine smile. "Well. We'll just have to beat them, won't we?"

Eventually, the tallest buildings in Puebla could be seen in the distance, an ominous haze enshrouding them. As fine and crisp as the day was, the haze could only be smoke, and they were all terribly afraid of what they'd find. If Puebla had suffered the same fate as Lagarto Gris, on a vastly greater scale, there'd be no "cleaning it up" before the army reached it. And there were the divisions that would eventually approach from Techolotla as well.

They might have seen similar things at outlying villages themselves, but they'd hoped to use Puebla as a supply depot at the crossroads. The port of Techolotla was much closer than Vera Cruz. Lewis was beginning to fear they'd have to build a fort to serve that purpose now.

"Just have to beat 'em," Leonor echoed grimly.

———

Major Giles Anson and his party of thirty Rangers, along with Major Justinian Olayne and Sergeant Major McNabb of the artillery (along to view the ground), were the first to see Puebla up close. There was only the occasional tree near the city and a couple of leafless fruit orchards. The outer city of hovels had been entirely razed, which would make a fine killing ground around the walls of the inner city—if those walls had been pierced for cannon and been provided with battlements and platforms to fight from. Anson could see men in a pair of gatehouses over the main entrance, but there was no one atop the walls. As elsewhere, they'd been built to protect against monsters, not human enemies, and he wondered anew if that was on purpose, if cities away from the center of power weren't *allowed* to have battlements. He'd have to ask if the "holy" city in the Great Valley had them. Regardless, it was pointless to attempt a stealthy approach in daylight, so he and his men stayed on the road, boldly advancing in a column of twos, Stars and Stripes and company guidon uncased in the biting early afternoon breeze.

Someone still lived in the city. The men in the gatehouses proved that, and oddly there came the occasional noise of what sounded like fighting beyond the walls. The lingering smoke was a dreadful portent after what happened at Lagerto Gris, *But maybe folks here decline to just let the Blood Priests rub 'em out?* Anson thought. That possibility left his mind entirely when something else immediately drew his attention.

"Oh my God," he hissed. Up ahead, and for the last three hundred yards or so up to the gate, a line of tall, rough-hewn crosses stood beside the road, every ten yards or so. There must've been twenty-eight or thirty. On each one a man in a dark blue jacket and nothing else had been crucified. Worse, it looked like their naked legs had been savagely whipped, and all but the very closest victim had endured the added misery of a fire at the base of the cross, not large or long enough to burn through the cross itself, but doubtless a source of unspeakable extra torment. All the fires had gone out or been extinguished, but so had the lives of those transfixed above them. A few had even been festooned with arrows as if their murderers ran out of time or patience for their sickening game. But the closest man feebly raised his head at their approach.

"Good Lord!" breathed Major Olayne, youthful face twisted with horror.

"One of 'em's still livin'!" Boogerbear exclaimed with unusual animation and spurred his horse forward.

"Jesus, yes," Anson grated. "C'mon, fellas, let's get him down!"

The whole party of Rangers surged up around the cross, quickly dismounting. "How we gonna do this?" Boogerbear suddenly asked. "They've only got him tied up around his elbows, but the bastards nailed his wrists an' ankles with spikes. Can't just pull 'em out. 'Specially way up there." He gestured at the crosspiece about twelve feet high.

Amazingly, after making a few dry, garbled sounds, the crucified man managed to speak. "Is that you, Mr. Anson?" he mumbled, but his voice grew stronger as he spoke. "I'm afraid my vision is a little blurry. Just cut it down, if you please. They raised it up and dropped it in the hole with a tripod, which"—he licked dry, blood-caked lips—"they quite naturally, if somewhat inconsiderately, carried away."

Anson jerked his gaze up. The man's face was unrecognizable through bruises, cuts, swelling, and gobbets of dried blood, but that distinctive, always polite—even now!—voice belonged to Captain Hans Joffrion. Only now did Anson see the stained shoulder boards still on the man's jacket.

"My God, Hans!" Olayne nearly shouted, seeming to shake off an appalled daze. "We thought you were dead. They couldn't find you after the fight, but . . . well, the devils've never taken prisoners before."

"Justy Olayne as well," Joffrion said, cracked lips approximating a smile. "I have *wished* I was dead, I assure you." He winced as the Rangers started chopping at the base of the cross with their Bowie swords, the vibration running up the timber.

Olayne turned to Anson, his training as an engineer asserting itself. "We must arrange tag lines so poor Hans doesn't just fall like a tree." He glanced up at his friend. "I doubt that would be very comfortable, and it might just finish him off."

Joffrion snorted. "Half an hour ago, I would have welcomed that. Now I believe I'd like to try and survive."

"You'll have quite a tale to tell the ladies," Olayne assured him.

Joffrion shook his head slowly from side to side. "No, I won't, Justy. I'll tell you fellows, and Colonel Cayce and the rest, but then I hope never to speak of it again."

Olayne nodded understanding, then spoke to the Rangers. "With your permission, Major?" Anson nodded emphatically. "Rig lines to fall in four directions," Olayne continued. "Several men will grasp each one and hold it tight while others cut almost through the timber. Then the fellows behind will pull him the rest of the way over while those in front will keep him from going too fast. Everyone else will support that . . . abominable contraption as it is lowered enough to reach. Understood?"

"Thirsty," Joffrion murmured.

"Somebody stand on your saddle an' try to get your canteen to his lips," Anson ordered.

That was accomplished, and the same man, an unusually tall Ocelomeh, also secured the lines to the ends of the crosspiece. Then the chopping recommenced. Joffrion talked, trying to keep his mind off the pain of the shaking wood. "The fight?" he asked.

Anson growled. "A goddamn disaster. My fault. Lost a lot of men"—his eyes extended to the rest of the dangling victims—"but we 'won,' I guess. If you can call it that."

"It *wasn't* your fault, Major," Joffrion denied. "None of us expected that level of imagination from the enemy. We were overconfident. As for the poor fellows behind me, most were already dead when we got here. Likely dead when they were carried off, but they nailed them up anyway. Not all, though," he added grimly. "I was lucky, in a sense; unconscious for most of the time they drove these spikes in me. Missed the worst of it, I suppose, but I came to rather abruptly as they stood me up. I . . . I heard some of the men screaming behind me for quite a while until they were killed."

Anson grimaced. "When was that, do you know?"

"Just this morning, with the dawn. I'd been in the hands of those dreadful reapers until then. Suddenly, they quickly murdered the few other survivors and quenched the fires under them. I heard the hissing of water on coals," he elaborated, then reflected, "I've no idea why they didn't roast me as well unless they had something special in mind. In any event, I knew my time was up and expected to die momentarily. But then there was a Dom officer, a regular 'Yellow,' sitting astride a horse just below me, staring up with what looked like genuine remorse. Quite unexpected. He spoke to me in Spanya, deploring what had been done, but not for any reason you might expect. It seems, in his view, without time to properly 'cleanse and convert' me, I would still die a heretic. Heretics being beyond the grace and salvation agony earns for them, I and my fellows should all have been humanely killed like the spiritual animals we are."

"Crazy bastards," Boogerbear stated.

"Quite," Joffrion agreed with a hiss as the upright cracked and swayed slightly.

"Enough cutting!" Olayne said. "Start pulling him over—gently does it!"

"One more moment, if you please," Joffrion gasped. "In case I pass out, or worse, I'd like to tell you something more."

Olayne hesitated, then nodded, struck by the irony of his friend asking to remain on a crucifix a little longer.

"Thank you. The last thing the officer did—no idea who he was since he never introduced himself—was tell me his army would not exterminate Puebla, though the Blood Priests and their 'reaper pets' might. I got the distinct impression he didn't entirely approve of them. Finally, he asked if I would pass along an invitation to Colonel Cayce, by name," he added significantly, "to meet the army of General Gomez for a battle four leagues—about fourteen miles, I believe—west of the city. At Colonel Cayce's convenience, of course. He was quite cordial."

"Not 'cordial' enough tae take ye down," Sergeant Major McNabb declared angrily.

"I'll be damned." Anson snorted. "All right, let's get him down."

"Hans, just hold on," Olayne called up, face reddening at the stupid statement. "We're bringing you down now."

As carefully as possible. The Rangers slowly lowered Joffrion to the ground. He cried out a couple of times, and the men apologized profusely, but then it was done. Joffrion was still fully awake, breathing heavily, when it came time to remove the spikes. He screamed when they started, but luckily passed out before they were done. Anson spoke to Boogerbear. "He'll never ride. Take some men and scrounge around some of those places we passed. Be quick, an' not too far," he warned. "There's still a whole city full o' Doms barely three hundred yards away. Try to find a wagon or something." He looked at the line of bodies dangling from other crosses. "Wish we could take the rest, but we've lost enough good men, and I won't go within musket shot—" He stopped and clamped his mouth shut, seeing activity in the gatehouses and watching as one of the tall leaves of the gate slowly swung outward. "What the hell? Private Okai, mount up an' get over here. We're gonna hand Captain Joffrion up over your saddle. Hold on to him."

"Wait," Boogerbear said, glaring at the gate.

A half dozen mounted men in bright civilian garb seemed almost to sneak through the gate before stirring their horses to a gallop and charging over toward them. Most of the Rangers raised weapons, but before they could fire, Anson told them to hold. Seeing what they'd nearly ridden into, the men slowed their horses and proceeded at a trot. Finally, just a few yards away, they all stopped, and two men jumped down, briskly if nervously walking in among all the large, pointing muzzles.

"No! No! Don't shoot!" one exclaimed. "We all fight Blood Priests, yes?"

"*We're* fightin' 'em, an' any Dom that stands with 'em," Anson growled warily. "What's it to you?"

"We are fighting them too! In the city. They want to kill us all!" cried the second man. The first was short and slim, the second taller, but somewhat obese. Both had pointed chin whiskers like they'd all seen on Blood Priests—or *patricios*. Sometimes hidalgos.

"Is one o' you the *alcalde* here?" Boogerbear asked.

"No, no. He was murdered. Many more also. We fight!"

It occurred to Anson that the man was speaking strangely, as if he simply assumed they'd barely understand him. He huffed. *We're just a bunch of savages to him. Dangerous savages, though.*

"We hear of your coming—secret people sneak in and tell us you fight Blood Priests, maybe even help people. You help us?"

"Oh, for God's sake," Olayne blurted. "We understand you perfectly. Stop talking like a child!"

The men looked at him in surprise. "Very well," said the heavier man. Is it true? You fight the Blood Priests and help those in the city they try to slay?"

"Could be that we've helped some. Fought *with* 'em," Anson replied. "I think we're through fightin' *for* people who don't deserve it, though. Am I right that you've been in control of that gate over there all this time? Been watchin' us take our friend down? Prob'ly watched the whole time them reapers tortured the rest to death?"

There was an uncomfortable pause. "We saw," the scrawny one conceded. "There was nothing we could do. Only this morning did the Blood Priests

unveil their evil plan for the rest of us." He hesitated. "The commander of
the Dominion soldiers in the city said he didn't have his whole army with
him and the city could not be defended in any case. He told *us* to defend it
and led his soldiers away." The man blinked. "What could we do? We are
not soldiers. Having heard you fight for the rightful Supreme Holiness,
Don Hurac, and of your generosity toward other cities, we decided to seek
terms from you instead." He sighed. "The Blood Priests discovered this—
they had a spy on our council—and several hundred of them began murdering people like crazed animals."

"What about the reapers?" Boogerbear asked.

The man blinked again and gestured vaguely. "They left shortly after the
troops." He took a deep breath. "Will you help us? We would still seek terms
from Don Hurac."

Anson's lip curled. "We like Don Hurac all right, an' we're kind of on the
same side, but we're fightin' *with* him, not *for* him. You want 'terms' from
anybody, you'll ask Colonel Cayce. He's in overall command." He pointed
at the line of crosses still standing. "But I still want to know why you didn't
help our friends." He pointed at Joffrion. "Why you didn't run out an' give
us a hand takin' him down—you were already fightin' in the city; I could
hear it. Why the hell should we help you?" he demanded, voice rising.

"We were afraid," the heavy man admitted. "The Blood Priests . . . they
say you are devils."

"We are too, by their lights," Anson snarled. "But you tell me who the
devil is now. Us or them?" He shook his head. "I've a mind to ride off an' let
you sort them nasty bastards out by yourselves. My God, you say there's
just a few hundred of 'em? You've got *thousands* packed in that city! Just kill
'em. You don't need us."

"But we do!" the skinny one almost wailed. "Some of us can fight, and
are fighting, but no one knows how to do it together. The Blood Priests are
not great fighters themselves, but they rove about in large groups, killing all
who stand against them!"

Anson hesitated, fulminating. "Shit," he finally said.

"I'll stay," Boogerbear finally said, voice strangely gentle as always. "I
wanna stay. Leave me half the fellas, an' take Mr. Joffrion back to the column. We'll keep them Blood Priests occupied, keep 'em from killin' too
many folks before you get back. We *still* need Puebla in one piece, for a depot, don't we?" he pressed.

"It would be better that way," Anson agreed, voice calmer but clearly still raging. He glared at the townspeople. "All right. You heard him. But I want a soft sprung carriage out here to carry our man by the time I count to a hundred. I'll go to Colonel Cayce and let him decide what to do." His eyes had strayed to the crosses once more. "I expect he'll send us back with more men to help, an' we'll save your damn city." He pointed at the crosses. "But if those're still standin' when I get back, I'll come in an' kill every Blood Priest that's left, then I'll kill every other man I see! Is that clear?" He looked at Boogerbear, fury still building over the men he'd lost in the ambushes, but mostly at what those who'd set them did to his Rangers and dragoons. *All* "his" men now. "By God, I don't care what Lewis says, we're back 'on the loose' again. All the mounted troops, not just Rangers. We'll show these vile bastards what Los Diablos can do."

CHAPTER 20

The army rested at a quietly stunned and subdued Puebla—surrounded by the hanging bodies of Blood Priests—for two days before turning west. Not everyone was pleased with the macabre decorations, but Lewis wouldn't have them removed. Even after the arrival of Don Hurac, Puebla remained a reluctant partner in their endeavor at best, and the dead Blood Priests not only reminded its people what the "other side" would've done to them, but also what their "saviors" were capable of. Besides, Lewis had been just as furious as Anson when Hans Joffrion was brought in, and he made no comment when Anson informed him he meant to "run wild" for a while. Samantha was unhappy, afraid for her new husband's soul, but Father Orno assured her it was safe—as long as he had an "appropriate target" for his rage. Anson hadn't lingered to be chastised in any event and apparently never rested. Instead, his mounted patrols scoured the land between the city and Gomez's proposed battlefield, scouting the ground and relentlessly hunting and destroying any enemy scouts they caught. Dom soldiers were left where they lay to molder or be scattered by scavengers. Reapers or Blood Priests were left hanging in trees all along the road, where other Dom scouts would be sure to find them. It didn't take long before the dangling corpses resembled colorful ornaments, covered with feasting lizardbirds. These served to alarm watchers left in wait for the approach of *other* scouts, and the number of decorations grew swiftly.

The whole army had been affected by the treatment of Joffrion and the others in various ways. Generally horrified, of course, but also angrier and more determined than ever. Whether their city-states had fully formed a true union or not, the unity Lewis had worked for from the start was manifest in the ranks. All were full members of the "Army of the Yucatán," but with the new additions from elsewhere, it was more often referred to as the "Army of the Americas" now. One way or another, Lewis had his American army at last. Especially after "American soldiers"—regardless of where they were from—were *crucified* by the enemy. Joffrion was out of the fight, gently transported back to Techolotla and the hospital Sira Periz was establishing there. (Her "conquest" of that city had required even less fighting than the capture of Vera Cruz, for similar reasons, and messengers had come to report her heavy division would march for Puebla as soon as Techolotla was secure.) But Joffrion's stand at the river and stoic suffering since had made him a universal (and even further unifying) hero.

When Lewis's army finally marched west, secure in its movements for the first day at least, it was with a sense of renewed purpose. Its resolve hadn't been lacking, but keenness had been somewhat subdued by the atrocities it had seen and the enormity of the task ahead. That collective . . . "unease" might be the best word, was gone, and that collective purpose burst forth again with a dedication almost unknown since those poor, half-trained units first met Agon's at the Washboard. And Agon's men were part of it now, part of this American army, marching through the slush of another light snow to the thunder of drums and joining in songs they first heard across a desperate battlefield. At the moment, as Puebla slowly receded behind them, they sang what had practically become the unofficial anthem of the army, "Blue Juniata."

"A very uplifting melody," observed Colonel Agon, riding along at the head of the army, those around him largely the same as had been there as they approached Puebla. Olayne and Sergeant Major McNabb were with them now, however, as were Coryon Burton, Felix Meder, Andrew Reed, Ramon Lara, and Boogerbear. The big Ranger had just returned, and Sal Hernandez took a rested detachment out. But there were representatives from every branch of the army.

"Perhaps a little *too* uplifting, even frivolous, considering our purpose," Reverend Harkin objected. "A hymn might be more appropriate."

"Nonsense," countered Father Orno, the diminutive priest shaking his head. "The mood of the army is ideal, I would say. There will be time for hymns later."

"I wish I could say the same for *my* mood," Samantha grumbled, tightening the earflaps she'd folded down from around her wheel hat. The wool of her new uniform, even made of the thinner, finer Uxmalo and Pidra Blanca weave, was much warmer than anything else she'd brought. She'd been abstractly aware that it got colder at the higher elevations they'd be campaigning in and ensured there'd be enough greatcoats for everyone. (Even the green uniforms of Agon's former Doms were covered by sky-blue greatcoats at present.) But she hadn't thought sufficiently ahead to provide herself with warm, stylish things and was disappointed in herself. She had an image to maintain, after all.

"You and Dr. Newlin have done a masterful job coordinating our logistic requirements," Lewis Cayce consoled.

"Perhaps," Samantha practically snapped back at him. "Well enough that things back in Vera Cruz practically run themselves. And much of the organization Dr. Newlin established will move on to Techolotla. We wouldn't be here if that weren't the case—a bit of motivation there, since we both wanted to come." She sighed, then confessed, "I fear my mood is most affected at present by the constant absence of Major Anson. I never gave it as much thought as did my female acquaintances growing up—certainly not as much as dear Angelique—but I honestly never imagined I would spend my bridal tour on a military campaign through a snowbound wilderness."

"We are not exactly 'snowbound,' nor is this precisely a 'wilderness,' my dear," Harkin gently chided her. "Nor is this any ordinary military campaign," he added with growing conviction. "We are embarked . . ."

Chuckling, Lewis cut the reverend off before he could get wound up again. "Just as there'll be time for hymns—and sermons—later," he pointedly added, "Major Anson will be released from all duties for as long as he wants when our business is finished."

Samantha glared at him. "And how likely do you think it is that he will *survive* that long, behaving as he is at present?"

"Don't worry," Leonor told her. "An' don't forget, I've seen him like this before. It may seem he's actin' reckless, but he's also more focused. You prob'ly even think he's neglectin' you—an' he is—but he's a lot safer without you, or even me, to worry about right now."

"She's right, mistress," Boogerbear chimed in. "An', bein' truthful, I don't expect he really wants you seein' him . . . the way he is right now."

Varaa-Choon sighed almost wistfully. "I wish I were with him. I am a warrior. All this plodding along, surrounded by thousands and doing almost nothing, is not the type of war I am used to." She grinned at Lewis, easing her horse closer to his. "But it will be worth it very soon! Let me look at that map you are hoarding, now that you have added Captain Beeryman's observations."

Captain Barca had drawn a fine map of the region based on several they'd found in Puebla, omitting fanciful aspects and focusing on terrain. Numerous copies had been made of his initial work, with Corporal Hannity and Major Olayne, both fine artists as well, adding details and notes of specific observations brought by returning scouts as they traveled. By the time they stopped for the evening, likely actually within sight of the enemy after a fairly leisurely march, they'd use that map, combined with what they saw with their own eyes, to finalize their battle plan. Agon was sure Gomez's maps could be little better than those Barca started from. They had to assume *some* Dom scouts had made it back and they'd know more about areas they'd personally viewed, but none of that would be compiled for the benefit of every enemy officer. Agon maintained (from experience) that wasn't the way Dom generals thought. They had their map and what scouts had told them in their heads—if they didn't forget. Their subordinates had no need to know anything beyond where their general told them to go and what to do. Initiative wasn't encouraged.

On the other hand, that very evening, every officer in Lewis's army should have a map of their very own and could add the latest details pertinent to their upcoming assignments from the "master map" in Lewis's keeping. In short, each lieutenant, probably sergeant, perhaps even private soldier in Lewis's force should have a better grasp of the ground General Gomez had chosen to contest than the general himself. Some of that ground might be difficult, however.

Varaa unrolled the painstakingly detailed drawing when Lewis pulled it out of the leather tube hanging from his saddle and handed it to her. Large blue eyes took it all in, then peered over at Boogerbear. "No change in our estimation of numbers?"

Boogerbear shrugged. "Far as we can tell. An' we been all around the enemy, even behind 'em. Still looks like about forty thousand, give or take five." He added the last like it was immaterial. "It splits down to about thirty-five thousand infantry, three thousand lancers, the rest bein' enough artillerymen for five o' their batteries—twenty-five guns—an' support, o' course. They got a helluva baggage train with lots o' goodies," he ended mildly but with a predatory gleam in his eye.

Colonel Reed frowned. Just as he had during their trek across the Yucatán, and particularly as they advanced on Gran Lago, he'd begun to grow increasingly cautious. Lewis generally welcomed his views, however, since perhaps too many of his officers might still be described as overenthusiastic, if not exactly overconfident. "Our six batteries of six guns each certainly give us an advantage in terms of artillery"—he slipped a glance at Samantha—"as long as we can keep all the guns fed."

"We are well supplied, I assure you," Olayne said, smiling reassuringly at the Englishwoman. "Never better, in fact."

"Be that as it may," Reed continued, "we started at Gran Lago with thirty-eight thousand, I believe, including Colonel Agon's Fourth Division." He bowed his head slightly at their former enemy. "We've added another division, but it isn't here. Just as significant, our advance has weakened us. We've inducted local recruits, but most have been sent back for proper training. Maintaining our own tedious supply line has cost us more troops than formal fighting, not only as escorts and garrisons, but in casualties caused by raids, monsters, and ordinary injuries and sickness." He didn't acknowledge that, largely due to the wonderfully learned native healers, they'd suffered less "ordinary" sickness than any army he ever heard of. "Then there was that recent debacle that cost us hundreds of mounted troops we could ill afford."

"Formal fightin' or not, Colonel, it's a war," Boogerbear stated flatly. "Enemy gets to change the rules, same as us. We lost men at the 'Step,' too, an' Frontera—an' to bushwhackers all along. All told, I figure this campaign's cost us about one to their ten. Still too bad, but I'll take it." He arched a brow at Reed. "Doubt . . . anybody could'a done better than Major Anson."

Reed's face was already redder than usual due to the cold, but the implied criticism turned it almost purple. To his credit, he managed to continue without his anger touching his voice. "In any event, we remain on the offensive with fewer than thirty-five thousand men. We're rather significantly outnumbered, it *is* winter, and we can only expect more avoidable casualties to exposure"—he gestured at the map Varaa held—"and according to that, the enemy is strongly placed in our path. All our past major actions against the Doms have been at least somewhat defensive in nature, though I'll concede they have been . . . surprisingly aggressive, if that isn't too contradictory. This time, we will almost assuredly be obliged to attack." He hesitated. "Perhaps we should return to Puebla and await the spring. Then, with the addition of further reinforcements and Sira Periz's division, we would be in a better position to succeed."

"Your counsel is noted and appreciated, Colonel," Lewis said, "but as you know, we can't wait. Not only would we waste"—he smiled at Orno—"the 'mood' of the army, but the enemy will surely be heavily reinforced by then. Possibly even by the Gran Cruzada." He shook his head. "Its arrival, before we secure the enemy capital and install Don Hurac in power, will be the beginning of the end for us. We simply can't cope with the numbers involved." His smile grew as he gestured at the map. "We *can* cope with General Gomez, though, 'strongly placed' or not. His plan is fairly obvious, and you'll see when you examine the map more closely. He expects us to launch a frontal assault against his admittedly commanding position—and we'll have to do it too. That's when his lancers will sweep in from the flank and tear us apart. Pretty straightforward. I'm not at all happy that we'll have to play by his bloody 'rules,' even to a point, because it'll be costly." He nodded at the map as well. "But that will be our salvation, and I mean to throw out his damn rules right in the middle of the game." He chuckled darkly without humor. "We already started changing them as soon as Mr. Barca began sketching the beginnings of a plan."

Varaa was looking at the map again, observing where Gomez's forces were placed, taking in several abandoned structures nearby, then noting some terrain features, newly added, that were apparently never properly surveyed for any previous map. She looked back up at Lewis and grinned.

"You see?" Lewis asked. "Varaa has caught it at once."

Leonor smiled as well. "Yeah. An' as she always insists, she thinks just as sneaky as you."

"It's actually rather straightforward as well, not very 'sneaky' at all," Varaa almost complained. "I only hope the enemy doesn't see it as well."

They reached "Gomez's Battlefield" in the early afternoon and got their first in-person look at the ground and how the enemy had chosen to use it. Gomez had the high ground, of course, his garish yellow infantry deployed partway up a long, gradual grade, but still across the floor of a modest mountain valley, its flanks anchored by a broad-topped, wooded bluff on the north, and steeper heights on the left that sloped gently down to the south. Beyond both stood higher, snow-washed peaks in the distance. Batteries had been placed on the nearer heights, and there was visual evidence of troops on the northern elevation, at least. The majority of Gomez's artillery was placed in the center. One thing was glaringly obvious at once, however, and Lewis motioned Colonel Agon closer.

"Clearly, Gomez has been expecting us," he stated.

Agon nodded. "Yes. His camp looks well established, as if he has been here several days, at least."

Lewis nodded. Scouts had reported as much, as well as other information he simply couldn't credit. "The defensive, blocking stance he's taken isn't dissimilar from what Anson faced at the step—but I don't see any defensive works. No trenches or breastworks. No entanglements. Not even a fortified camp. Is there some . . . trick here that I'm not seeing?"

Agon considered for a moment. "I do not believe there is any 'trick' to his disposition. What you see is merely another example of Dominion arrogance I once displayed so grievously myself. Remember, no Dominion army—before mine—was ever defeated in battle. None has ever even been attacked by a significant force. Field defenses are known to . . . my former colleagues, on an intellectual level, but not a practical one." He shrugged. "They've never practiced constructing them because they've never imagined needing them. I never did," he added a little sadly. "I'm sure General Gomez knows I and my army were defeated by you, but he won't have many details about how it happened. Particularly how decisive your own fortifications proved at Gran Lago. Remember also, he will crave the sort of classic, stand-up, open-field battle I once did and for which he is apparently prepared." Agon pointed. "And you are moving to match."

Agon's own 4th Division was peeling off to the left side of the road, each regiment uncasing its new flag—a gold field with a simple red cross and regimental number upon it. First Division, having already formed a parallel column led by the 1st US, beneath the Stars and Stripes, began deploying on the right. Four batteries of guns, twenty-four in total, wheeled in behind and passed through to unlimber to the front. This was merely a precaution. Agon had assured them there was no chance that Gomez would initiate any fighting so late in the day. He would already have his own, quite inflexible battle plan and would make no attack while the Allied Army made camp. Such an action would lead to a very disorganized and uncoordinated fight that Gomez couldn't control. Besides, he'd likely dreamed of an encounter just like this his entire life—most Dom commanders did. Gomez would want to "enjoy" the pageantry of the thing to its fullest.

Lewis's headquarters tent was already rising under Corporal Willis's braying supervision as Lewis and his staff dismounted, growing by the moment as 3rd Division's Colonel Itzam and his Itzincabo aide, Captain Uo, arrived, immediately followed by 2nd Division's Har-Kaaska and Major Wagley. The 2nd and 3rd still weren't up and wouldn't go on line when they were, but their commanders had hurried ahead. Orderlies took their horses. Details from each company already on the line scampered back to start erecting tents for themselves and their comrades, and the caissons and battery wagons supporting the unlimbered guns moved to do the same. Lewis was consistently amazed by how fast and efficiently camp was made. There was invariably a little confusion at first as engineers reoriented themselves to re-create it like they always did, but shortly they were pacing out spaces and marking company streets, tents already going up around them.

Lewis pulled his watch from the slit pocket on his jacket and gave it a glance. "Corporal Hannity will sound 'officer's call' in an hour and a half. I want every regiment and battery represented when we discuss initial assignments." He waved at the enemy, the closest large regimental blocks about a mile and a half away. "I'm actually fairly impressed by General Gomez's cunning. He has a strong position, even for the type of fight he wants, but it isn't *so* strong that we'd be justified refusing battle here."

"As if we would," Leonor murmured, and Lewis smiled at her.

"Oh, I'd love to just go around him, leaving him confused and rushing to catch up, but this road is the only route we can use to move something the size of this army," Lewis said. "Even so, I believe it's safe to say we'll largely refuse to fight like Gomez *expects*." He started looking around just as Willis hurried up with a folding table, as if he'd read his commander's mind.

"Which I was just bringin' it," the disagreeable man griped. Leonor hissed at him, and he flinched.

"You're a wonder, Corporal," Lewis said with a disapproving glance at the tall, female Ranger. "You always seem to know what I need." He unrolled the map and laid it out, Willis quickly seizing rocks off the ground and dumping them on the table to hold it down.

"He's a 'wonder,' all right," Leonor said sarcastically.

Willis gave her a put-upon glare. At that moment, adding to the mass movement, noise, and controlled chaos around them, Major Anson, Captain Meder, and Kisin, the Holcano war leader, arrived with a mixed company of Rangers and mounted riflemen almost simultaneously with Coryon Burton and a roughly equal number of dragoons. All were sweating in spite of the cold and had clearly ridden quite a distance, horses tired and huffing, steam jetting from their nostrils.

"How far did you go?" Boogerbear called out.

"A mile or so." Anson grinned. "In a straight line, anyway. Maybe ten miles, all told, with how we went squirmin' around." He got down, joined by Felix Meder. The big Holcano remained mounted. He'd never become a good horseman and was embarrassingly clumsy getting on and off. Samantha went to Anson at once, and he turned a little red when she hugged him, then picked debris from his beard.

"Oh, for God's sake," he mumbled before raising his voice. "Get blankets on them animals, an' rub 'em down good," he told his men, handing Colonel Fannin off to a corporal. "Check his shoes real careful."

"Roughly the same for us," Burton agreed, also swinging down, nodding and smiling at Meder. "Found out where the Dom lancers wound up."

Lewis pointed at a patch of heavy timber at the base of the bluff on the north side of the valley, near the enemy left.

Burton stared. "How did you know? You just got here. Did you see them?"

"No," Lewis said. "But that's where I'd put them—if we had the sort of single-purpose lancers they have. Hidden and poised to strike our flank as we advance."

"Well, that's where they are. Most of them, anyway. Quite uncomfortable too, I should think, since they appear to have been there several days, forbidden any fires so we wouldn't know they're there." He chuckled. "Poor devils."

"Lara's still out with Hernandez?" Lewis asked Anson. After briefly swelling to over seven hundred men, Lara's lancers were back to about five hundred, the rest either killed or wounded in the ambush. It wasn't a lot to face off against his enemy counterparts, but he wouldn't have to do it alone. In any event, Lara's lancers had stayed with the column when Lara himself went scouting with Sal. The Ranger nodded. "Very well," Lewis said. "If they haven't returned by the time we make assignments, I'll rely on you to pass them along. What did you see on the enemy right? No change?"

"A little," Anson said. "Double-checkin' the path around those other woods on our left, it's about four miles to the objective. They've put some infantry up there, supportin' their guns. Couldn't get close enough to count 'em, but there can't be a whole regiment. There ain't room in the space they cleared. Maybe they won't have a cold camp an' we can calculate numbers by fires. Otherwise, there's pickets for a ways at first, then nothin.' Silly boogers haven't figured out how far we can move when we want. Think if they can't do it, we can't."

"We won't always have that advantage, I fear," Colonel Reed inserted with a worried look.

"I doubt it," Lewis told him.

Agon cleared his throat. "General Gomez is considered very good. A true professional, as I was. He is from the far west, however, the older provinces, and no matter what he might have heard, he has never seen how mobile our forces are. Not only artillery, but infantry as well. Smaller regiments are *far* less ponderous than what he is used to. It took *me* long enough to appreciate that, even after I'd witnessed it. He won't expect any radical maneuvers after battle is joined, and the commanders of his very large regiments won't have the initiative to quickly react when they happen."

"That's what we're counting on," Lewis agreed.

Varaa clapped her hands. "Good. Are you at least ready to share the bones of our plan yet?"

"'Our' plan?" Har-Kaaska asked stiffly, clearly annoyed that Lewis might've sought Varaa's input without him.

"Well, of course," she replied, grinning at her king. "Whatever it is, it is the same thing I would have devised because . . ."

Leonor and half a dozen more of those present laughingly interrupted to say, "Because you think the same."

Varaa smiled and nodded. "Yes."

Reed was still frowning, now looking at the sky. Clouds were starting to gather; gray, cold, heavy-looking things. The sun still shone bright on the yellow uniforms and red flags of the enemy, but now it beamed down through a hole in the sky. "Let us hope the enemy doesn't think the same way as well," he said, voice gloomy. "All may be moot, of course. If it snows, we could wind up sitting and staring at each other for days."

Lewis shook his head. "No. We attack in the morning, regardless of the weather—barring rain that'll soak the infantry's muskets." He blew into his cupped hands to warm them, and make a point. "I don't think we have to worry about that." Looking at his watch again, he continued. "Go. Make sure your men's needs are seen to and they're getting well settled in. Pass the word to your subordinates: officer's call in an hour and a quarter."

CHAPTER 21

Thickening cloud cover made it much darker, but it was still day when Captain Barca and Lieutenant Petty returned from their meeting with the rest of the army's senior officers, the headquarters section practically overflowing. Petty was irascible as usual, seeming unfazed by what he'd heard. Captain Barca projected a strange mix of dread and excitement when he gathered every member of his battery, nearly ninety men including gun's crews and their replacements on the caissons, battery, and forge wagons, and spoke to them together. "Make an early night of it, men," he said. "You won't get long to sleep," he added cryptically. "Tomorrow might be the biggest day of our lives. Possibly the last day for some," he conceded sadly, "but commanding this battery has been my heart's delight, and even if I fall tomorrow, I will die content, among friends, my only regret that I won't be in at the finish with you."

He smiled and bright, white teeth defeated the gloom and gleamed in his dark, beardless face. "That said, I don't intend to fall, and none of you have permission to do so. It will be a hard day, however, such as are always expected of this battery—the very best in the army—and I'm sure you'll all do your duty and continue to make me proud. I hope I may share a moment with each of you before tomorrow is through, but if I don't . . . God be with you."

With that, he nodded encouragement and turned to stride away toward Captain Dukane's battery of howitzers.

"Eat, have a shit, sleep," said Lieutenant Petty as the other two section officers passed much the same advice in somewhat gentler terms. Turning, he followed Captain Barca.

"Whew!" exclaimed Preacher Mac. "Hard tae jump right off tae sleep after a speech like that!" He gave Hanny a speculative look. "Me heroic wounds're achin' a wee bit. P'raps I'll have 'em looked at by that bonnie healer lass. I dinnae ken when I'll have the chance again. Who's with me?"

"I want to see Izel," said Apo Tuin, also looking at a red-faced Hanny, who simply said, "I'll go."

Hahessy rolled his eyes. "I'll be takin' Mr. Petty's counsel fer once. The latrine, then me bedroll. Carouse all ye like, but leave it behind when ye return ta camp er I'll lay ye out quiet as a tomb, by God. Ye'll be lucky ta wake when the cap'n bestirs us fer our next adventure."

Hanny, Preacher Mac, and Apo lit the candle lantern they shared, standing between two tents, made sure their bedrolls and gear were laid out and ready, and took another lantern with them. Most of the troops in the whole huge camp must've been similarly advised by their commanders, and even with troops still arriving, things were strangely quiet in this part of camp with little moving about. Of course, it was cold, and quite a few men were gathered tightly around the hundreds of fires springing to life, cooking rations or just keeping warm. Weaving their way through the company streets, they eventually came to the headquarters section, where they observed Colonel Cayce, Varaa, Major Anson, Leonor, and Har-Kaaska, as well as Colonel Agon and Major Arevalo, and all the other infantry commanders. They'd clearly lingered after everyone else left. A muted alarm was called out, and Hanny watched many of those officers hasten toward the front, where the 1st and 4th Divisions had encamped close to where they'd deployed. Hanny looked questioningly at his friends, and they shrugged back. Without a word, they followed the moving cluster of officers.

Even as the cloud-filtered light of evening dwindled into night and hundreds of fires flared to life across the generally open ground between them and the enemy (just a few trees and a pair of likely abandoned villas were in view), a party of horsemen bearing torches could be seen making their way toward the center of the field. All were preceded by a pair of riders holding tall staffs with lightning bolt crosses atop them aloft, like standards. At least that's what Colonel Reed reported after examining them with his glass. "And believe it or not," he added, "they've even got a white flag attached to one of their foul standards!"

"Good God!" they heard Major Marvin Beck of the 1st US exclaim. "Do you suppose that's General Gomez wanting to talk? I thought that was new with you, Colonel Agon. That your people had no tradition of such things?"

"Perhaps they heard what we did?" Agon's voice speculated. It was already getting dark enough that it was difficult to tell who was who. "I doubt it, though," Agon continued. "And we never used a white flag. Remember, Gomez's army will be composed almost entirely of westerners. We have little in common with them, and they tend to consider us provincials. I suspect it's more likely they have been influenced by their contact with Imperials. The white flag would tend to confirm it. Despite the long, slow-burning war, there is trade with them. That would require actually *speaking* with them from time to time, rather than just killing them on sight."

The distant party, emissaries, whatever they were, had stopped about a thousand yards out, flaring torches now stationary. Hanny blinked when something touched his eyelash, and he noted that the far torches were starting to blur. "It's snowing," he murmured to his friends.

"Maybe they'll postpone the battle, if it snows enough," Apo whispered.

Hanny looked at him. "No way. You remember how hard we trained around Uxmal, even in the heart of the rainy season there. The Doms might expect it, though, and Colonel Cayce will see miserable weather as a gift. Not sure I don't agree with that, weighing a little misery against our lives."

"Silence!" hissed Preacher Mac, nodding at the clump of officers.

"Too bad our guns aren't ready," Olayne's voice lamented. "Still, I can *get* ready quick enough!" he added enthusiastically. "Even at this range and in the dark, with twenty-four guns already on line, I assure you we can maul them!"

Hanny heard Colonel Cayce chuckle. "How rude! All the same, even if that is General Gomez, I don't want to talk to him. Not tonight. I'm not in the mood, and it'll soon be extra cold out there. If he wants to have words in the morning, I may oblige him out of curiosity—if we're not already too busy for that."

"So much fer the evenin's entertainment," Preacher Mac groused. "Let's hurry away tae the hospital section er the lassies'll all be abed as well."

Moving that way, they found the young ladies all still up, even fairly glad to see them. Hanny sensed an . . . awkwardness at once, however, as soon as Izel took a moment to speak with him alone. He'd hoped for an embrace, perhaps even a kiss, but the girl merely looked at him with big, worried eyes.

"What's the matter, Izel?" he asked. "Aren't you glad to see me? I thought, after the time we spent together—"

She swiftly reached up and pressed her hand to his lips, tears now pooling in her eyes. "I am *very* glad to see you," she said so softly he almost didn't hear. "But why do you think we are all still up when the sensible thing to do, considering what tomorrow will bring, is try our best to sleep?"

He blinked, looking back into the brightly lit hospital tent. Izel and her class of healers did look a little busier than usual, cleaning surgical instruments, rolling bandages, threading razor-sharp bone needles with fine waxed twine, and preparing large quantities of the potions they used to clean wounds and deaden pain. Generally what they always did, he thought, just more of it. He shrugged. "I don't know. Getting caught up?"

Her tears spilled, and she became angry. "More than that," she snapped. "Tonight we prepare for battle just like you, but the biggest difference for me—and the girls who are fond of Apo and Mac . . ." She sniffed. "Even if we win tomorrow, and I'm certain God will grant us victory, you can come back and find us, tired but joyful to see you. I, on the other hand, am terrified I will see you in there"—she twitched her head toward the tent—"either *before* the battle is won . . . or much too long afterward. Worst of all, I cannot bear to see you laid out before me on a table, torn and bleeding. What if I have to watch you die . . . or help take off one of your legs?" Her voice was rising, turning almost hysterical.

Hanny thought he understood better now, but remained a little mystified. "Well . . . I sure hope not, but I guess it's possible. Chances are, though, if I'm that bad off, they'll take me to the experienced surgeons' tents." He grimaced. "Nobody ever wants to go there."

She slapped him so fast he never saw it coming. Hard too, enough to bring tears to his own eyes. "Fool!" she seethed. "Idiot boy! There will be a *big* battle tomorrow, and 'experienced' surgeons will be here, or we will be helping them elsewhere! Have you no sense? If you are brought in *any-where*, I will be told. . . ."

He stared at her in shock, saw her expression of fury transform into abject horror, then watched her flee inside the tent and crash into "Apo's girl" (he couldn't remember her name just then) and start bawling on her shoulder. He reached up and felt his stinging cheek. "What did I do?" he asked quietly, the thickening snowflakes falling around him. Shaking his head, he strode away. He hadn't gone far before Apo caught up. Hanny kept walking.

"Slow down!" Apo said. "Your legs are longer than mine."

Hanny jerked to a stop and waved back where he came from. "She's your sister, and she's crazy. I thought she liked me, and *whack*! Half knocked my brains out." He started walking again, a little slower.

"She is not crazy by herself," Apo consoled. "Rya . . . you know, Izel's friend I have been visiting," he supplied a little self-consciously, "well, she yelled at me to leave as well, after Izel became so upset. What did you do?" Apo asked, suddenly suspicious.

"Nothing!" Hanny said adamantly. "What do you . . . Damn you, Apo, what do you *think* I did?"

Apo shrugged. "I have seen her kiss you. Maybe you . . . touched her?"

"No!" Hanny seethed. "We were just talking. She was already upset, afraid we'll turn up all full of holes, and the next thing I know—*whack!* My mother never slapped me that hard for cussing."

Apo nodded seriously, and Hanny kept simmering as he stalked past the headquarters section and back into the lines of tents. "Rya was upset as soon as she saw me," Apo finally said. "She told me it was because she cared and worried. Do you think Izel felt the same?"

Hanny shrugged. "Maybe, at first. Like I said. That's what she sounded like. Then she tried to break my head."

"And you said nothing to make light of her concern?"

Hanny thought hard for a moment. "I don't *think* so."

"But you *spoke*?"

Hanny looked at his friend. "Yeah. So?"

Apo nodded. "Then you are to blame, my friend. You said you thought my sister likes you. In point of fact, she *loves* you—simpleton that you are— and I suppose that *does* make her crazy. But in her fearful condition, fearful for *you*, Izel could take any single thing you said as critical or dismissive of her concern. With nothing else at hand, she struck out at what she fears most. You! Or at least what might happen to you."

"But . . . that's crazy!"

"Already established," Apo agreed.

THAT WAS FIVE hours ago. Hanny and Apo had talked for a while by a fire (some distance from the sleeping Hahessy), and when Preacher Mac showed up, a little less disturbed by his visit but just as mystified by females, they decided to get some sleep. Tossing and turning under his blanket, replaying his and Izel's behavior over and over in his mind, then worrying about what would happen the next day, Hanny may have managed an entire hour of sleep before Lieutenant Petty woke him with an order to rouse the rest of his crew.

When he crawled out of his tent, it was a whole different world. It was sharply, bitterly cold, and a couple of inches of snow had already accumulated, with more still falling. It wasn't what he'd define as a blizzard—there seemed to be almost no wind at all—but it was hard to see very far even with the bright white snow reflecting the firelight and a quarter moon up behind the clouds. There was a little light filtering down from it. Still, it was about midnight, and they were clearly preparing to move. Barca's battery was, at least. Hanny decided conditions were good for them to see a little of where they were going, while being hard to see from a distance themselves. And the shushing snow might dampen the noise of their passage as well. He buttoned his greatcoat and pulled the shoulder-length cape up around his neck as he shook the tent frames and called lowly for his crew to crawl out and fall in.

"There's hot chocolate at Cap'n Barca's fire. Get some, but keep it quiet," Lieutenant Petty told them. "An' stay back from the fires, otherwise. We got pickets close enough to feel the heat of enemy fires, an' they might've creeped close enough to do the same. Don't want 'em to see what we're doin'."

"What *are* we doing, sir?" Hanny asked.

"Don't be an idiot, Sergeant. What do you think?"

Everyone was calling him an idiot tonight. "Uh . . . what we always do, Lieutenant?"

"What else? No great crowded gun line for Barca's battery, with lots of other guns for the Doms to shoot at. No. Least we'll have the whole battery an' not just a section this time."

"Who's in support?"

"Rangers an' Mounted Rifles an' those man-eatin' Holcanos, o' course. Like always." Petty actually grinned. "An' the entire Third Pennsylvania Regiment too."

Hanny's eyes widened. Whatever they were going to do would be sizable.

That was about three hours ago. Since then, they'd started the battery south, thudding and scrutching through the dry, loose snow, eventually coming up on the tail of the mounted troops, riflemen right in front of them. Not long after that, there was a kind of low, continuous rumble, and the 3rd Pennsylvania, a full one thousand men with the regiment kept up to strength with native replacements, fell into column behind the six guns, three caissons, and fifty-four horses pulling them all. With maybe another five hundred horses ahead (Hanny heard they had half the Rangers and all the Riflemen), they made a terrific din, and he was convinced they'd be discovered and have to fight a desperate, confusing melee in the freezing night and snow, but they continued unchallenged. Now he had absolutely no idea where they were. There wasn't a star in the sky, he could only vaguely place the moon—within about forty-five degrees, if he was lucky—and they'd twisted and turned on a winding forest road long enough to utterly confuse him. He felt like they were some distance to the southwest. They'd started out southward, anyway. That was as close as he could guess. He was pretty sure they'd begun to climb, though. The horses straining more than they would on a grade, the road under the deepening snow getting rougher, more rutted by old runoff.

"Oh, it's so coooold!" mumbled Apo, almost whining, just behind Hanny's lead horse on the limber chest. "I have never *been* this cold!"

"Shut up, you," Lieutenant Petty whispered, riding past toward the front of the guns, where Captain Barca rode. For a wonder, their section wasn't leading the battery at present.

"Nobody'll hear me over all this rumbling and clopping and crunching," Apo objected. "And I can hear all those blasted infantry jabbering behind."

"Sound like turkey hens just off the roost, Mr. Petty," supported Billy Randall, sandwiched between Apo and Kini Hau on top of the chest. He was surely the warmest of them all.

Hanny actually saw Petty frown, so the clouds must be thinner between them and the moon. It didn't seem to have slowed the frozen downpour, though.

"Well . . . just keep it down. If the infantry took to snatchin' up our horse apples an' eatin' 'em, would you do it too?"

"That depends," said Kini. "What is 'horse apples'?"

Petty snorted and kicked his horse forward.

"You ever been this cold, Hanny?" Apo asked.

Hanny nodded. "Colder. Many times. Pennsylvania can be like this for much of the winter."

"Agh, I couldn't stand it," Apo stated flatly, wrapping the blanket he'd thought to bring tighter around himself. "No wonder you are so pale. You come from a land without a sun! I never even *saw* snow before we came here. Sure never was in any, and I can't wait to get out."

"Oh, the wonders ye'll see in the army, me lads," Hahessy said up ahead on the farthest horse in the team. He had a finger in a nostril, rooting vigorously. Finally, dissatisfied, he closed the other one and snorted, firing a clotted projectile into the snow.

"Yer a rare, disgustin' creature, Hahessy," Preacher Mac pronounced.

"Aye, I'm that," Hahessy assured with satisfaction. "Rare an' wondrous, with magical powers—like a kinda *god*, I am!" Shifting slightly in his saddle and striking a pose, he detonated a thunderous fart.

There was muffled laughter that even Hanny joined, but Preacher Mac yanked off his hat and struck the big man riding beside him. "Blasphemer!" he hissed before roughly quoting: "Claimin' tae be wise, they became fools an' exchanged the glory o' the immortal God fer images resemblin' mortal man an' birds an' animals . . ." He paused before archly adding, "An' creepin' things," in a hostile tone.

"Now, Preacher," Hahessy objected, "a 'creepin' thing' I may be, but I's just funnin', is all."

"Ye shouldnae 'fun' in such ways, as ye ken full well," the offended artilleryman objected piously.

Hahessy sighed. "Aye, you've the right of it, an' we'll all be beggin' the Lard's pertection in the marnin', I shouldn't wonder," he said, uncharacteristically chastened. "Shivers me guts just ta contemplate the horror." He farted again. "D'ye see?"

The grade increased fairly dramatically after that, complete with harrowing switchbacks, even as the detachment's pace slowed to a stop-start-stop kind of progress. One of the reasons for that was eventually revealed when they saw a Dom corpse lying in the snow with one of those big, obsidian-tipped arrows right through his head, the snow around it splashed and melted by blood. There was no way to be certain in the dark if it was a Holcano or Ocelomeh Ranger arrow, though Holcanos were more likely to reuse missiles that killed a man, at least cutting off the tediously shaped points to mount on new shafts. Lurching forward once again, they moved more swiftly for a time before grinding to another halt, the side of the hill falling precipitously away on the right and allowing them their first unobstructed view of the land around since they'd set out.

The snow had stopped or at least paused for a while, and the view to the northeast was startling. Down below and barely a mile away—surprisingly close considering how long and far it felt like they'd moved—was the great sprawling camp they'd left behind. Hundreds of fires still twinkled like the invisible stars above, washing surrounding tents with orange light. Quite a few shapes moved about, tending those fires or coming and going from the brightly lit headquarters section, and it struck Hanny that if he'd been a watching enemy, he'd see just what he expected: the whole Allied Army, warm and resting, waiting for battle the next day while its leaders continued to plan. If the Doms hadn't actually *seen* their detachment head out, or others Hanny suspected had gone, nothing about the camp should give a clue now. Shifting his gaze to look for the enemy camp, he couldn't see it. The very hill or low mountain—whatever they were on—blocked his view.

Turning around, he whispered back at Apo, their sudden exposure making him extra conscious of the need for quiet. "We're doing the same job we had at Petty's Hill: sneaking up on the flank."

"You're just now figuring that out?" Apo replied, teeth chattering. "Sure we are, only on the other side, with a lot more men an' guns."

"Stands to reason we're gonna have to fight—before we get in the *big* fight," Billy Randall agreed. "We know there was Doms up here with a battery o' guns. Infantry too. We saw 'em from below when we made camp. Just don't know how many."

An unexpected chuckling voice interrupted from beside the limber. "Why, it *is* young Hanny Cox! An' look at those red stripes. A *sergeant* now, no less! I thought I heard your breakin' voice."

Hanny turned around the other way to see a familiar shape in infantry dress, three white stripes on light blue sleeves and musket slung, muzzle down, over a shoulder. The man was standing by the limber wheel. "Sergeant Visser! I haven't seen you since—"

"Since you deserted Captain Cullin's B Company of the Third Pennsylvania," Visser said with mock severity.

"I didn't desert. You *gave* me away!" Hanny gestured around. "Me and some of these other fellows."

"Just joshin', just joshin'," Visser assured. "But you boys've done well for yourselves. We've kept track, Lieutenant Aiken and I." He reached up to shake Hanny's hand. "We're proud of you, son."

Hanny gulped. His time in the infantry hadn't been stellar. Lucky, maybe, but he certainly hadn't been surrounded by friends. Most he'd made had joined him in the artillery, in fact. But Sergeant Visser had done more to make him a soldier than anyone, and he felt guilty he hadn't even visited him. Shaking the offered hand, he waved around once more. "You remember Apo Tuin, Preacher Mac, Billy Randall?"

"Sure. Good to see you boys." Visser tilted his head to the side. "There were a few others . . ."

Apo spoke up. "Gone, Sergeant."

Visser nodded sadly. "Sorry to hear that. Hell of a war. Well, I guess you can't get the reputation you have without gettin' hurt a little."

"Reputation?" Hanny asked, confused. "Only 'reputation' I remember having with you is that my musket never went off in a fight."

Visser laughed quietly. "That did seem to be a habit, though it wasn't always your fault, if I recall." Hanny couldn't see Visser's face, but his stance subtly changed. "Same old Hanny, though. Quietly competent, brave to a fault, and with no idea that anybody's noticed. Look here, son. You and your friends've been in every major action of the war, and more sharp little fights than anybody can count. You're in Mr. Barca's battery, a *Black* man—former *slave!*—who leads the hardest-fighting battery we have, and your section is the star of his battery." He snorted. "Infantry an' artillery rivalries aside, you boys are the pride of the Third Pennsylvania too! You didn't *know* that?"

Hanny was shaking his head in wonder.

"I did," Apo proclaimed, teeth still chattering.

"I didn't," Hanny said softly, still shaking his head. "Honest, Sergeant Visser, I didn't know—and don't understand it." He shrugged. "We've just been doing what we're told."

"Same old Hanny," Visser repeated. "Well," he said hurriedly as the column began to move again, "I'm glad we'll be fighting together again." His tone turned serious, determined. "And with the Third Pennsylvania by you, you'll never want for support and those heathen bastard Doms will *never* overrun a gun in your battery. You have my word on that."

"Uh . . . thanks, Sergeant," Hanny said weakly as Visser fell back to his infantrymen. "I'll be durned," he breathed.

"Face it, Sergeant Hanny, it's hee-ros we are on account o' you," Hahessy said, a little louder than was right. "An' I'm one of ye! How's that fer a laugh?"

"God," Hanny murmured.

"Don't let your head swell up and pop," Apo warned. "Maybe now you know why Izel acted so strange in her worry. Heroes aren't made where it is safe."

"I'm no hero," Hanny snapped back. "I'm scared to death all the time and just want to get through this!"

"Dae ye think it's different fer the rest o' us—aside from this great, bloated ox?" Preacher Mac demanded quietly, gesturing dismissively at Hahessy on the horse beside him. "Dae ye imagine *Captain Barca* feels different? No. We do our duty as best we can, an' God has seen fit tae protect the most o' us . . . for the now. But we *all* just want tae get through it!"

"Not all," said one of the new men, Private Hoziki. Hanny thought it was the first time the big farmer's son from Frontera had spoken since they left Puebla. "Some of us do not care if we 'get through it,'" he continued darkly, "as long as we kill enough of the enemy."

CHAPTER 22

I t wasn't quite dawn when the bugles sounded, accompanied by the long drumroll. As always, the tinny notes and low-frequency rumbling elicited miles-distant (and sometimes not so far) bugling responses from large, frightening beasts. Lewis compared it to an old-world turkey gobbling in response to a hoot owl, even a gunshot. Leonor's analogy was probably more appropriate: wolves and coyotes howling hungrily at the sound of a crying infant. Nerves on edge, most of the men in the great camp were already up, hot cups of honeyed chocolate steaming in their hands around the fires, where company-size mess sections prepared the morning meal.

The company mess had been one of Lewis's few truly unpopular innovations, particularly among the men who now had to cook for so many. Nor was it received very well by the squads that traditionally cooked for themselves in rotation. Being directly responsible to their messmates for the quality of fare, they usually did their best to make it palatable. Moreover, it quickly became apparent that appointed company cooks generally got the job as punishment or for being poor soldiers who were therefore unlikely to care what their fellows thought.

Lewis himself hadn't been sure it was a good idea, in fact, and only consented to try it at Dr. Newlin's suggestion shortly before they reached Puebla, the principal argument being based on logistics. Even Samantha disagreed with Newlin on this matter, but he'd been convinced that, not only would they eliminate literally tons of extra weight the men and wagons had to carry in terms of redundant cook pots, skillets, fire irons, etc., but there'd be less waste when it came to the quantity of provisions they had to move. He'd been wrong about the latter, at least. With a few exceptions, the men hated what the cooks did to their food and simply wouldn't eat it, so a tremendous amount went to waste at once. Uncharacteristically determined to force his point with the argument that the men *would* eat when they were hungry enough, Newlin pressed Lewis to "give it a little more time." Lewis reluctantly agreed.

That morning, however, when Lewis emerged from his tent in his best field uniform, boots and saber polished and newly whited belt over crimson sash, sky just beginning to brighten in the east, he caught the respectful but disappointed looks of many a soldier standing around fires with empty plates. As if in explanation, Corporal Willis glaringly plunked a plate of glop on his folding campaign table under the fly, retrieved a stick from behind him, and proceeded to push the plate toward him as if afraid to touch it. Lewis made a queasy face and arched a brow at him.

"Which I didn't cook for you this mornin', Colonel. Didn't think it was fair. Still, I didn't fetch *that* from the *awfulest* o' the devils tryin to poison the fellas either," Willis proclaimed triumphantly, seeing his expression. Gesturing at the plate covered with something that smelled like the inside of a boot, he went on. "Punish me if you like, buck an' gag me, whip me, *hang* me, but they done this on a *battle day*, Colonel, when the fellas need their strength more than most! Black, festerin' treason, if you ask me."

Lewis pursed his lips and nodded. "Just something hot to drink, if you please," he said, then stepped out in the open, several hundred pairs of eyes fixed upon him. "Eat your food, men," he shouted loud enough for the order to carry. "Just this once more to help you face a trying day—or fill up on tortillas and molasses, if you like, but get something in your bellies. Corporal Willis," he barked, turning.

"Sir?" Willis said, flinching back from his Colonel's suddenly angry glare.

"Find Dr. Newlin and have *him* send a messenger to Puebla, instructing the commissary agent he left in the city to dispatch the wagons with 'excess' cooking implements forward at once." He turned back to the wide-eyed, expectant faces. "My apologies, men. Clearly, sometimes new ideas aren't always better. You may be too tired to cook for yourselves tonight—more tortillas if you want—but tomorrow we'll resume the old tried-and-true system, and I won't change it again. Now spread the word as you fall in!"

The men scattered with a cheer, some contemptuously dumping their plates on the fires. Lewis looked back at Willis. "Go!"

He heard a throaty laugh and turned to see Leonor and Varaa riding over to join him, Leonor on her local horse, Sparky, and leading his own Arete, already saddled and groomed for war. No doubt Leonor had carefully cleaned, inspected, and reloaded the pistols in the pommel holsters Lewis usually forgot he had as well. Varaa was atop one of the nearly jet-black captured Dom animals. Gone was the former "battle attire" both females used to wear—silver scale armor over buckskin for Varaa, and the bedraggled, largely civilian outfit Leonor once clung to so stubbornly. Now they were dressed as smartly as Lewis, down to white belts, sashes, even officers' shoulder boards—a lieutenant's for Leonor and a colonel's on Varaa. Lewis couldn't fault that. As warmaster of all the Ocelomeh, Varaa technically outranked "King" Har-Kaaska in battle, even if she had no specific command. She still wore her long, straight-bladed, basket-hilt backsword and a strangely British-looking musket slung across her body. While Leonor's white belt supported no saber, it did keep a Bowie sword and her holstered pair of Paterson Colts close to hand. She also had one of Felix Meder's M1817 rifles, slung similarly to Varaa's weapon.

"Only you, Lewis," Leonor said with fond admiration.

"What?"

"Only you could turn a mistake that had your whole army grumblin' into a cause to fight even harder for you!"

Varaa clapped her hands and *kakked* a laugh.

"It was a stupid mistake," Lewis conceded, looking up at the sky. The clouds were turning orange, and he wondered if they'd clear. "Let's join the others—and hope I don't make any more of them today."

Together, they rode slowly through the expansive camp, joined by Major Olayne and his shorter shadow, Sergeant Major McNabb, then Marvin Beck, Colonel Reed . . . The entourage grew and grew as they moved closer to the point where the entire 1st and 4th Divisions, nearly fourteen thousand men combined, were re-forming by regiments in the impressive array they'd first assumed the afternoon before. Men of Har-Kaaska's 2nd Division, assembling as if intended as a central reserve for the 1st and 4th, cheered them as they passed. Lewis smiled and waved at them, but as always, the attention and confident hope entrusted in him made him profoundly uncomfortable. He didn't revel in such displays as General Winfield Scott— "old Fuss and Feathers"—always seemed to, *but then again, did he really?* Lewis suddenly wondered.

He'd deeply admired General Scott for a variety of reasons and frankly considered him a military genius. He'd always focused on his strategy and tactics, however, only now realizing a measure of his genius might well be reflected by the ostentatious persona he affected for his men, always appearing in a full-dress uniform. *The very picture of a commanding general, almost a caricature*, Lewis mused, *projecting absolute professional conviction at all times. Surely he did it at least as much for the confidence of his men as for himself. Perhaps, deep down, the great man felt the same uncertainty and discomfort as I do when soldiers trusted him with their lives.* He smiled and waved.

But I'm no General Scott, Lewis confessed to himself. *Not even a General Taylor, though I suppose I'm more inclined toward the latter's easiness with the men and almost . . . fraternal approach to commanding them.* Even though he was perhaps more "dressed for battle" today than he'd ever been, at least in the sense he was clean and polished and his everyday red-trimmed shell jacket had been carefully brushed, that was as far as he could bring himself to go. He commanded this army, but wasn't "over" it. He was still "of" it. *Maybe Zachary Taylor felt the same way—unless his rough dress and behavior was as much an affectation as Scott's fine dress and formality.* Lewis didn't really know. He did know it wasn't like that with him.

They were moving in behind the 1st and 4th, where Colonel Agon met them with a morning salute and grim smile when Captain Raul Uo, Colonel Itzam's Itzincabo aide, galloped up and saluted as well. Returning Agon's salute, Lewis turned to Uo. "You have a report?"

"Yes sir. Colonel Itzam's respects, an' Third Division's movement is complete." The young man blinked. "Nearly didn't make it before it was light enough to see. I didn't think we would."

"Very good," Lewis replied. "My compliments to Colonel Itzam. I don't know when we'll signal Third Division, but he knows what to do when it happens."

"Yes sir," Uo said, saluting again before dashing away to the rear.

Lewis looked around. The sky was brightening quickly over the vast expanse of white, the snow probably having reached a depth of three inches or so. At the moment, it remained pristine across the space between them and the enemy, interrupted only by newly laden trees and the empty villas standing equidistant between the combatants and on either side of a small mountain lake. A gleam of peeking sunlight seared the bright field, sparkling and flashing as it swept up the gentle slope toward the enemy, glaring on their yellow uniforms and golden guns.

"If we keep the sun coming up behind us, it will hinder the enemy's observations for a time," Agon observed.

"Hinder their artillery too," Olayne agreed.

Varaa squinted. Her eyesight was as good as a man's with a glass. "I think another party like we saw last night is beginning to assemble to advance."

"Gomez seems intent on getting to know us," Colonel Reed declared.

Lewis looked at Agon. "Can you imagine any advantage to be gained by speaking with him?"

Agon shook his head. "I see only disadvantages. He certainly won't offer to surrender, but while we talk, we'll lose the sun in their eyes—and they'll have longer to discover some of our . . . deployments."

Lewis nodded. "I agree." He took a deep breath. "I propose that we advance to meet him—with the artillery and the First and Fourth Divisions."

Olayne grinned and spurred his horse forward, passing between the divisions to where the guns had already been limbered at McNabb's orders as soon as their crews fell in. "Battalion! Prepare to advance to one thousand yards from the enemy center, action front infantry, load case, and hold. Gunners will cut their own fuses." With those batteries now present, combining 6pdrs, 12pdrs, and captured Dom 8pdrs, it was pointless for Olayne to direct fuse lengths for time of flight, but these men could be trusted to do well. Now he waited while the crews mounted their horses and limbers, all while preparatory commands echoed among the infantry, and then bellowed, "Battalion, at the trot . . . march!" He personally couldn't remember if that was the "manual" command or not. He doubted it. So many things had changed, even commands (still all in English), modified or simplified for ease of communication—they trained by the manual but then did their best from there. The artillerymen they'd formed on this world would never compete on the parade ground with Lewis Cayce's beloved "Ringgold's battery," but Olayne wouldn't have given odds to either in combat.

Blowing steam, twenty-four six-up teams—144 horses—strained forward, accelerating amid billowing snow dust and dark clods of earth, wheels spinning and throwing up sparkling, rainbow rooster tails. Justinian Olayne thought his heart would burst with pride at what they had created. *And this isn't all of it*, he reminded himself.

"We won't be duelin' the artillery first, sir?" asked McNabb, now trotting forward beside him.

"Infantry first, Sergeant Major. When the enemy guns start getting our range, we'll shift things about and detail some of ours to reply."

Lewis was watching with equal satisfaction. He remained an artilleryman at heart, of course. Olayne and McNabb had pressed onward and stopped to wait, marking the point where the guns would go into line. Varaa burst into a *kakking* fit, and Lewis looked where she was helplessly pointing.

"Well," Leonor said. "Guess General Gomez don't want to meet us that bad after all. Least not Mr. Olayne. That bunch that was gatherin' just blew up like a covey o' quail," she elaborated for those who couldn't see. Naturally, not all of them knew what quail were, but most took her meaning.

"Advance your divisions, if you please," Lewis told Agon and Reed.

Preparatory commands had already seen to the removal of cases on the colors, and the city-state flags of regiments and the Stars and Stripes of the Detached Expeditionary Force danced lazily in the meager wind. A stiffer breeze would likely rise as the day wore on, but hopefully the sun (increasingly bright and unobscured) would counteract that for the sake of the men's comfort. Few wanted to fight in a bulky greatcoat. In addition to the impediment, they'd toss it aside as soon as they started to sweat and might never get it back.

Lewis was suddenly struck by the larger number of United States flags than the forces on the field should justify, particularly among former enemies in the 4th Division. Agon caught him staring and shrugged.

"We don't have a national flag anymore and can't *impose* our new regimental standards on the Dominion. Won't, at least. Nor would we do that with your own colorful flag," he quickly assured. "But the more my people learn of what that flag stands for—unity, and the God-given rights of those it waves over most of all—the more appropriate it seems as a symbol for our struggle." He waved past the 1st US, at other examples in the 1st Division. "For all of us. There may be no true union as of yet, but we all fight for the same cause." He shrugged again. "Yours is the only flag *here* that stands for union, so we will gather under it for now." He hesitated. "I meant to ask you first, but Varaa—and Har-Kaaska—believed you would refuse."

Lewis looked at Varaa. "You did?"

She nodded. "But King Har-Kaaska quoted an old Mi-Anakka saying to the effect that it is often easier to seek pardon than approval."

"He said that?" Leonor exclaimed in surprise.

"He did."

"I'll be," Lewis murmured, then looked at Agon. "You certainly have my pardon. And the founders of the nation that flag somewhere flies over would be quite proud as well, I think. I pray it will stand for unity forever."

Twenty-four guns fired, one after the other, shattering the frozen air with thunder and shrieking projectiles. There was a long, roaring flourish of drums before the fifes struck up "The Old 1812" and 1st and 4th Divisions stepped off, muskets high on thousands of shoulders, polished bayonets gleaming. The battle for the gateway to the Great Valley of Mexico had begun.

CHAPTER 23

On the heights to the south, the booming guns sounded impossibly loud, the pressure actually shaking powdery snow from the trees. Major Giles Anson was dismounted, standing on a wooded, rocky shelf slightly above the Dom position they'd struggled all night to reach. Some of his Rangers and all of Felix Meder's riflemen were with him, under cover, waiting for Major Ulrich's signal that his infantry, also creeping closer through the confining forest below, was as ready as it could be. When the gasping, sweating (and now shivering) messenger reached them, Anson turned to Meder and said, "Let 'em have it."

"Fire!" Meder shouted, and scores of rifles cracked almost as one, slashing into the backs of Dom infantry arrayed before them but facing away, down at the battle beginning below. Stunned screams of agony and surprised terror erupted as men crashed to the ground. A hundred or more were killed or wounded in an instant, but there were plenty more.

Kisin's Holcanos and Anson's detachment of Rangers had done a fine job of first scouting, then leading those riflemen, Barca's battery, and the 3rd Pennsylvania to the top of the low mountain, unerringly true in their direction. They apparently hadn't missed killing a single Dom picket either. Kisin specifically asked for and was given the task of infiltrating closest to the enemy artillery position, and his Holcanos and scattering of Grik did just that, possibly proving at long last they were even better at such things than Ocelomeh Rangers. Unfortunately, it was now becoming clear that Holcanos couldn't count worth a damn. Instead of the thousand or so Doms Anson's plan accounted for, there appeared to be a full Dom regiment of three thousand present, and Anson had to make a new plan on the fly. He had to admit he'd learned to do that from Lewis—he hoped. At least when it came to being responsible for more than fifty or so combatants. Thank God he had John Ulrich to help. And Felix Meder too.

"Fire!" bellowed Captain Cullin, B Company, 3rd Pennsylvania, and a hundred men snapped a seething volley into the enemy from a little below and to the right of the shelf before practically sprinting out of the woods and to the side, where they went into line and started reloading. "Fire!" cried another company commander, moving up and doing the same in the lingering smoke, hacking more panicked Doms to the ground in sprays of blood before racing to form beside B Company. Given the limited space, there'd been no way to move the whole regiment up through the trees and deploy before attacking so they were in a dreadful race to get enough companies up, out in the open, and formed for battle to not only hold their own, but allow the rest of the regiment to join them. All before the Doms could recover and stop them.

The riflemen above and about fifty yards back had reloaded and fired again, independently, and at less than a hundred and fifty yards, few could have missed. Another volley of musket fire resounded as a third company of infantry emerged. The closest Dom soldiers had been savaged already, the farthest still didn't know what was happening. Only those in the middle of what was essentially a large block, or square, were aware of their danger and trying to respond. Any return fire was blocked by comrades, however, even while those same comrades were being slaughtered regardless. Anson didn't know what possessed the enemy to hold an infantry reserve in such a way. Perhaps these Doms were more inflexible than Agon's troops had been, and the need to exert strong, direct control over them even in this severely limited space around the artillery was to blame? Maybe it was the only place their officers thought they could keep them, ready to deploy against threats from below. Or maybe they were poised to attack downhill at some point, into the Allied infantry flank. Whatever the reason, Anson would make the most of it while he could.

"Carry on here, Felix," he told the rifleman. "Good luck."

"You too, sir," Meder replied, ramming another patched ball down the barrel of his rifle. Surrounded by his scattering of Rangers, Anson hurried to the rear, where their horses waited, and heaved himself up. A few large enemy musket balls were finally whizzing by, smacking against the stony bluff behind them and clipping small limbs, dumping snow. The enemy might not yet be able to fire on Ulrich's infantry on the same level as they, but more had realized they could safely engage this elevated position. Anson urged Colonel Fannin forward, leading his escort into the trees to the right. "Nothin' we can do here, boys," he called to his companions. "Time to get ready for our part." He paused and tilted his head to listen. In spite of their proximity to the fight on the bluff, the noise of it was almost drowned by the staccato pounding of artillery down below, especially now that the Doms had joined in.

Regardless of the strange, rushed plan, terrible ground, and inability to quickly mass, Ulrich and his 3rd Pennsylvania had engaged in a shockingly one-sided slaughter for much longer than they'd imagined possible. That was ending as the enemy finally managed to turn and bring unimpeded fire to bear. This was aided by the simple fact that those still in confusion or panic were almost all dead by now, piled in a moaning, heaving heap of shattered bodies actually forming a sort of grisly breastworks for the rest. Almost all the 3rd was up now, firing independently at a range of barely fifty yards, but the comparatively crude Dom muskets were just as deadly as the far superior M1816 and M1835 Springfields at that distance. The 3rd Pennsylvania began to die.

"Move! Move! Get them up!" shouted Captain Barca. All his guns had been unlimbered, their crews moving them forward by hand, aided by as many infantrymen as could find something to grab, to push or pull. Other infantry were quickly being detailed to heave the heavy ammunition chests off the limbers (each weighing about 575 pounds, fully loaded) and carry them forward as well. All while enough stray Dom musket balls slashed through the woods to this narrow path to take down the occasional man and horse.

"Trail left!" Hanny shouted, trying to direct his Number Two gun around a ragged stump, but the heaving, gasping throng around it was struggling against itself, almost smashing right into the obstruction. That probably wouldn't have damaged the gun, but men might've been badly hurt.

"*Left*, damn ye!" Preacher Ma roared at the infantrymen supporting the trail.

"That's what we were trying to do, you damned sheep-humping Scotsman," an "old" Pennsylvanian snapped back. "Sergeant Hanny said left, and we aimed the gun left!"

"He said '*trail* left,' tae steer the gun like the rudder on a boat, ye sheep-headed idjit!"

The infantryman stared. "What the hell does that mean? The gun's left or ours?"

"The gun's! Always the gun's!"

"From the front or back?"

Thunderously furious, Daniel Hahessy left his place by the right wheel, literally picking the squirming, shouting infantryman up over his head and throwing him into a depression beside the track where more snow had gathered. "Away with ye," he roared at the man, now spluttering curses and flailing to rise. "Yer too bloody stupid ta *look* at me glorious gun, much less touch it! C'mon, lads," he shouted at the others, artillerymen and infantrymen both, as they heaved on the gun again. Hanny exchanged a grin with Preacher Mac. Hahessy might still be a monster, but he was *their* monster.

The volleys roared louder as Barca's battery came out of the trees on the same track the infantry used, his crews heaving their guns down the line behind the men firing muskets—who were beginning to fall with depressing regularity, crying out and clutching limbs or rolling and screaming on the ground. Without consciously doing so, Hanny directed his own weapon a little farther along until he caught sight of Sergeant Visser. His old mentor was loading and firing his musket as fast as he could, just like everyone around him, calmly calling encouragement to those within reach of his voice. But while many of those others looked terrified, enraged, or everything in between, Visser's face wore only an expression of grim determination. "We'll push through here, if you like," Hanny shouted at him, rubbing his pink hands together to get the blood flowing back to his fingers. There was plenty of blood flowing all around on the ground, the snow now beginning to melt under the bright morning sun and turning a slushy pink. "She's already loaded with canister," Hanny added. They'd loaded the gun before they moved up, pinning the charge in place with the vent prick. It wasn't an ideal solution, was even dangerous, but the only other way to move a loaded cannon without risking the charge sliding down the barrel away from the breech was by stuffing some sort of wadding in after it. That could radically increase the pressure and change the point of impact entirely.

"By all means, Sergeant Hanny," Visser flung past his left shoulder even as he raised his musket to his right, took aim, and fired.

"Detachment, halt!" Hanny shouted. "Trail right . . . halt! Trail down. By hand to the front . . . march!"

Infantrymen flowed to the sides, still loading and firing, polished iron ramrods flashing as the 6pdr gun poked its muzzle out between them even as Hanny grasped the handspike and slightly adjusted the aim. Careful targeting was a waste of time, and he was just making sure the muzzle was pointed in the general direction of the most Dom soldiers close ahead. While he did that, Private Naxa shoved the vent prick forward before drawing it out and then tended the hammer on the Hidden's Patent lock as Private Hoziki primed the piece and stepped to the side, stretching his lanyard. Musket balls were flying around, thick as hail, snatching at clothes, creasing skin, cracking spokes, and spattering off irons. "Ready!" Naxa almost shrieked, releasing the hammer and stepping outside the wheel.

"Fire!" Hanny bellowed, young voice cracking.

Dodd's Number One gun was quicker for once, blasting out a spray of canister an instant before Hanny's, but in less than fifteen seconds, all six guns in Barca's battery had vomited hundreds of screaming musket balls, shrouded in smoke and fire, to tear into the enemy at less than fifty paces. The result was utterly horrific, mulching and heaving the closest enemy ranks back and away in a shrieking, bloody heap.

"Keep it up, let 'em have it!" Captain Barca shouted from behind, pacing from gun to gun atop his horse. "The fools are trying to turn their own guns on us. Good for the fellows down below, and of no use to the enemy. They can't engage us with all their infantry in the way!"

The 3rd Pennsylvania kept firing, at least three rounds per minute, and Dom officers and NCOs trying to dress their ranks and organize their men were dropped by Meder's riflemen above. Tension was building, terror peaking, and Hanny could feel how brittle the enemy was becoming. He glanced at Visser, who caught his gaze and seemed to understand entirely.

"Fire!" Hanny croaked, and his gun bucked back.

"Fix bayonets!" roared Sergeant Visser, Captain Cullin clearly agreeing

with his timing and repeating the order for the rest of the company. Even as
the rest of Barca's battery fired once more, Major Ulrich commanded the
entire 3rd Pennsylvania to lock their vicious triangular blades on the muzzles of their muskets. Shoving his way to the front on foot, musket in hand
(ever the infantryman, Ulrich still disdained an officer's sword), he moved
in among the color-bearers to lead his men himself. As the last 6pdr fired,
churning the steaming blood and flesh in front of it, thundering drums
signaled the charge and the 3rd Pennsylvania swept forward with a roar.
Simultaneously, amid a stutter of musketoons blasting loads of drop shot,
Anson led his mounted men into the enemy flank. They broke.

"Cease firing! Cease firing!" Barca was shouting, barging his horse forward right up alongside Hanny's gun. Their infantry was in front of them
now, companies getting all mixed up, stabbing and slashing with bayonets.
Major Anson himself could be seen, firing his powerful revolvers down at
fleeing Doms as Kisin and his Holcanos, human and Grik, made a beeline
for the enemy artillery. The Dom infantry was peeling away, spilling down
the hill behind them, slipping and tumbling down the steep snowy slope
with blue-clad infantry yipping on their tails, and in a flurry of truly horrifying killing, the Holcanos overran the Dom guns. Unfortunately, in their
destructive enthusiasm, Kisin's Holcanos also started tipping the enemy
guns over the bluff, smashing them apart as they fell among their fleeing
crews. Captain Barca charged forward through the storm of musket balls
and started slapping Holcanos with the flat of his saber, yelling at them to
stop.

"Up! Get 'em up on line, you lazy bastards!" bellowed Lieutenant Petty.
His hat was gone, and blood was sheeting down his face, eyes white as the
snow within his dark red visage. Hanny caught his meaning at once.

"Push her up alongside those last two Dom guns," he shouted at his
crew. He didn't think he'd lost anyone to the fighting yet, but a glance at
other guns in the battery revealed some of them were sorely pressed. "Sergeant Visser!" he shouted, seeing his old friend trying to re-form Cullin's
company. "Can you lend a hand on these other guns?" The sergeant nodded
and directed details to help. In moments, Barca's entire battery was on the
line on both sides of the captured Dom guns. That's when Hanny caught
his first glimpse of the vast panorama of the "main" battle below. Thousands of infantry in blue on the one side and yellow and black on the other
were arrayed across the snowy white plain, not yet close enough to shoot at

one another directly, but heavy white clouds of gun smoke drifted across them from the massed batteries of guns, ripping at the stainless earth, churning dark soil into the air, or spraying the snow red as roundshot or case snapped through the opposing forces. Barca was pointing at the artillery position behind the Dom infantry, shouting something Hanny couldn't hear, but Hanny saw more clouds of smoke billowing out from the heights across the valley. Rushing over to Lieutenant Petty, he pointed them out.

"Yeah," Petty said, observing as well. "Thought those guns were s'posed to be took care of too, but I guess it's up to us." He hesitated, squinting. "Long shot, for a fact. Start tryin' the range. I'll square it with the cap'n. You, Sergeant Visser!"

"Mr. Petty?"

"You boys in the Third're all trained on artillery, right?"

"Some . . ." Visser hedged, teeth chattering, hugging himself. Like everyone, the sweat he'd worked up in the fighting was chilling him now.

"Good enough. Fill out these crews an' put new ones together for the captured guns. Jump!" Petty sloshed away through the bloody slush around scattered Dom bodies toward Captain Barca.

CHAPTER 24

*P*oom! *Ppppoom! Poom! Poom!* went Olayne's massed guns, throwing exploding case shot at the heavy ranks of Dom infantry, sputtering fuses leaving rolling, spiraling trails of white smoke in the air as the lethal bombs shrieked away, bursting with satisfying (and still somewhat surprising) regularity above the enemy troops. Ragged gray flags of smoke marked the detonations in the air, and swathes of shattered, screaming bodies pathetically testified to the effectiveness of hot, spraying balls and shards from above. These Doms had never faced anything like it, but they stood all the same, braving the arbitrary storm of metal that slew and maimed by the score, staining the snow with slashed earth and blood. The hell wasn't equally distributed, but the Doms were dishing out a hefty dose themselves. Eight-pounder roundshot gouged the ground in front of 1st and 4th Divisions, bounding along to smash whole files of "Americans" and Agon's former Doms. They stood and took it too.

"Their execution is much improved," Varaa observed, horse quivering nervously at the unprecedented barrage, tone as neutral as she could make it.

"'Execution's' right," Leonor grimly groused, a roundshot bowling down a dozen of Agon's men in an instant before bounding up and over the rest and falling among the tents behind them. Lewis was sitting atop Arete, the veteran warhorse as still as a stone as Lewis intently surveyed the heights on the left through a spyglass. "I think Major Anson and Major Ulrich have taken the enemy battery on the left, but reserves are moving over to bolster the retreating Doms. They'll have their work cut out taking that position back." He turned to look to the right. A five-gun Dom battery on the rise to that side was still shooting down on them. "Something happened over there," he said, troubled, refocusing his glass. "We should shortly know what it was. There are messengers coming from Mr. Burton and Mr. Lara."

The messengers drew up very shortly indeed, saluting quickly, horses blowing.

"I take it Mr. Burton was unable to carry his objective?" Varaa asked.

The dragoon messenger shook his head. "Took us longer to get in position than we thought. The fight for the other battery was already under way before we were ready and the enemy was better prepared. Mr. Burton thought it best to withdraw and support Mr. Lara's action when the time came."

Lewis nodded. The very last thing he'd told Coryon Burton was to avoid high casualties at all costs, and the young dragoon officer had done the right thing. The flanking battery would be troublesome, but not nearly as much so as the large force of Dom lancers waiting to pounce. He'd wanted Burton to support Lara against them when the time came anyway.

"Very well," he said. "We'll just have to make do. We'll presently be advancing here, and I expect the enemy horse to make their move. I rely on Mr. Lara, Mr. Burton, and Mr. Dukane's battery of howitzers to disrupt their formation." He smiled wryly. "Just remind your commanders—especially Mr. Lara—to disengage before the Dom lancers drive their attack home."

The dragoon and lancer both saluted and wheeled their horses around.

"It might be close," Leonor warned.

Lewis nodded. "It will be—and we have to *let* it be, so the enemy will come at us where we want them to." He raised his voice and called to Colonel Reed. "Advance the infantry, if you please. We'll move a little closer to the right for the moment."

Reed, also mounted a short distance away, nodded tersely. He might not be as instinctively aggressive as Lewis or as comfortable with their ambitious strategies, but as always in action, his jitters were gone and he was ready. The drums thundered their preparatory warning, and then the two lead divisions stepped off into the maelstrom of battle. Lewis paused to watch the deep ranks of 1st Division with the 1st US on the left, at the point of contact, with Agon's 4th Division moving in step to the rumbling drums and stirring, cheerful music. Regimental flags streamed colorfully under the still vaguely golden sun, adding a strangely festive air to the campaign soiled light blue and dingy green ranks. For the very first time in this terrible war, Lewis's army was commencing a battle against their more numerous foes with what looked for all the world to be a conventional, traditional linear attack. *And it'll be one for a while—a costly one*, he mused with a desolate tightening in his chest. But if the surprising aspects of his battle plan were going to work like he wanted, he needed General Gomez convinced that it would all be as straightforward as he expected. Even the sneak attacks on the flanks were part of that, since Gomez would've undoubtedly heard that Lewis's tactics were unconventional, by his standards, and it might be for the best in the long run that the attack on the heights on the right had failed. Gomez would think this direct assault was the natural result of that failure and that Lewis's bag of tricks was empty. He'd be right, in a sense. All of Lewis's preplanned "tricks" were in motion, and his other surprises were largely dependent upon how Gomez reacted to the chaos Lewis hoped to create. Agon had firmly assured him that their army was infinitely better equipped to cope with confusion, even take advantage of it, than the enemy was. And considering the size of the forces engaged, most opportunities he hoped would develop must initially be seized by regiments, even companies in contact. After that, the rest of this battle would be fought in Gomez's mind as much as on the battlefield.

"They look magnificent," he said almost reverently aside to Varaa and Leonor as he watched the army, *his* army, step boldly, confidently, closer to the storm of metal the Dom infantry would soon unleash.

"I'm proud enough ta burst," Leonor agreed, "an' sad enough at the waste of it all ta cry, I reckon."

"Waste?" Varaa asked.

Leonor gestured. None of the infantry, on either side, had opened fire as yet, but they would soon enough. "All that blastin' away, shoulder to shoulder, close enough ta spit on each other. Seems so awful . . . an' so damn arbitrary. Survival's got more to do with luck than good soldierin'."

Varaa patted the buttstock of the strangely British-shaped musket slung diagonally across her back. "Just the way of things, even where I come from. As it once was for stones, then spears, then arrows, now muskets, only massed fire can break an enemy, and the Maker knows the Doms are hard to break! We must shatter their will—or enough of their bodies—so there won't be enough fit to rally and hold." She patted her musket again. "It takes lots of these—then the bayonet—for that."

Lewis had examined Varaa's weapon more than once and would've sworn it was British. It had brass furniture, the barrel was pinned, and the graceful lock was quite distinctive. The odd markings on the lock and barrel were clearly Latin numerals and letters, but the letters spelled nothing he could understand, so the numbers were equally meaningless.

"It would be different if the whole army carried rifles, like Felix Meder's men," Varaa continued. "Marvelous weapons." She waved at the ranks of men advancing on the enemy. "This whole way of war would have to end. No one could stand the casualties."

"*We* would change things, certainly," Lewis told her. "I doubt basic tactics would change among the major powers for quite a long, bloody time, however."

"You're probably right," Varaa conceded. "Even among my folk, such a change would be difficult."

They were still moving to the right, angling rearward slightly toward Har-Kaaska's 2nd Division, drawn up as if in reserve as well, when the first titanic volleys erupted from the 1st and 4th Divisions. They'd marched to within range of their own muskets—even the reworked captured weapons had an advantage over the enemy's—and now were pouring it in. Har-Kaaska urged his huge, bizarre, bipedal mount into motion and trotted over to meet them at the head of his staff officers. Lewis was surprised to see Reverend Harkin and Father Orno with the Mi-Anakka leader.

Harkin raised his hand in benediction. "When you go out to war against your enemies and see horses and chariots and an army larger than your own, you shall not be afraid of them, for the Lord your God is with you!"

Lewis bowed in the saddle. "I'm quite convinced of it, and a good morning to *you*, Reverend. And you, Father Orno." He looked at Har-Kaaska. "Any sign of movement on the right?" He obviously meant in the trees on the flank of the advancing infantry where thousands of Dom lancers were supposed to be.

"Nothing from the enemy, but quite a bit from our lads," Har-Kaaska responded sourly. "Mr. Lara got in quietly enough, as did Dukane's battery. The returning dragoons were a shambles. Didn't seem to be all that many casualties, but they raised quite a ruckus moving into position." He pointed. "You can still see them. Strung out at a right angle to the forest."

Lewis was nodding. "Just as I instructed Mr. Burton."

Har-Kaaska looked stunned. "You *wanted* the Doms to be aware of them there?"

Lewis nodded again. "There are less than a thousand of them. As far as the Doms are concerned, they just got thrown back from their attack. They won't draw much attention where they are. They can't *seem* like much of a threat, after all." He grinned. "We know better, of course, but the Doms don't. And just as important, our 'battered and beaten dragoons,' right out in the open, will keep the enemy from focusing more attention on what might remain hidden."

"I told you he was sneaky," Varaa reminded her king.

"Indeed."

Lewis was looking back to the front, where enemy volleys were tearing at his men, billowing musket smoke filling the bright, clear sky. The enemy artillery had resumed as well, but only the guns on the heights to the right would bear down on his infantry. The rest were trying to engage Olayne's massed batteries, but those guns were already shifting to new positions. Even as he watched, an exploding case shot erupted quite close to the elevated enemy battery, fired from Barca's battery on the captured heights on the left. Tiny yellow-clad shapes collapsed around the gun closest to the bursting shell.

"I want you to start moving up behind First Division," Lewis told Har-Kaaska. "Make no move to deploy in any way other than support for the First until I give the command"—he paused, considering—"or you get word from Leonor or Varaa." He smiled. "It's not impossible that I might be unable to give the word myself."

Har-Kaaska blinked unhappily, tail whipping. "Your death is not impossible, but is unacceptable. I retain considerable influence over Alcaldesa Sira Periz and will ensure that she has you severely punished if you die!"

Leonor glared at the big Mi-Anakka, but Lewis barked a laugh. "I suspect I could prevail upon her to do the same to you," he retorted, then touched Arete's flanks with the heels of his boots and allowed her to carry him forward, just behind the extreme right of 1st Division, firmly anchored by the

1st Ocelomeh Regiment under Consul Koaar-Taak and Major Ixtla. Both men were dismounted, and Ixtla hurried over. "You should not be here!" he exclaimed. "Especially up on your horses."

"You're not too closely engaged here yet, but you will be, I assure you." Lewis smiled. "If we're still with you then, we'll most likely dismount. Ah, Corporal Willis. There you are."

"Which I been tryin' t' catch up with you, anglin' whichever direction you was headed," the scrawny former artillerymen accused.

"Where's your horse?" Leonor asked sarcastically. "Could'a caught us easy on your horse."

"Deserted!" Willis exclaimed indignantly. "Miserable damned sack o' fleas deserted in the very face o' the enemy!"

Reverend Harkin, who'd followed along with Lewis when he left Har-Kaaska, arched a brow. "Did he indeed? And I suppose there is no chance I would find him where you left him if I went there to look?"

Willis ground his teeth and stomped in a circle. Now that the sun was fully up, the snow was going fast, leaving a muddy mess behind. Olayne would be having trouble moving his guns. The enemy would find it impossible to move theirs efficiently. "He could be back," Willis finally allowed. "Somebody might'a caught his traitorous ass an' put 'eem back."

"I wouldn't be at all surprised."

The sound of battle was all-consuming now, musket volleys, screams, explosions, and cannon fire making it difficult to hear drums and bugles. "You'll have to find a substitute for the present," Lewis told his orderly. "A fast horse for Corporal Willis, if you please, Major Ixtla."

"Certainly," Ixtla said, gesturing at one of his messengers to surrender his animal.

"What do I need with a fast horse . . . sir?" Willis asked Lewis suspiciously.

"You're going across to Mr. Burton. He'll be the first to see the Dom lancers begin to deploy from the trees, and I want to know it when he does."

Willis's eyes grew as wide as goose eggs. "Me? Go out there by myself—on a *horse*—where ever' damn Dom in the world can shoot at me?"

Lewis sighed. "Don't be so dramatic. Only a few thousand might possibly see you, and I doubt hardly any will actually shoot at you. Their officers are rather strict about their targets, you know."

Leonor narrowed her eyes at Willis. "Why don't I go," she suggested. "Or send just about anybody else?"

Willis silently snarled at her and, without another word, snatched the reins the messenger had offered and clumsily climbed the horse. "Soon as the lancers show, I come tell you, right?" he demanded of his commander.

Lewis nodded. "Hopefully we'll already know, but we have to be ready for this."

Willis nodded, then galloped off, swaying alarmingly in the saddle.

"I don't know why you bait him so," Lewis leaned over and whispered to Leonor, close enough that his beard brushed her ear. That's the only way she heard him over the sound of battle, but even in the midst of it all, the unexpected touch of his whiskers—she'd never known her ears were so sensitive!—stirred her. Covering her discomfiture, she raised her voice to holler back, "I don't know why you tolerate him. I can't say he's a coward. He did save your life that time, and I didn't see anybody make him. But since you won't throw him out, back to the ranks, somebody's gotta shame him up out of his hole from time to time. I reckon he hates me for it, but he's always prouder of himself later."

Lewis grunted. Leonor was an undisputed wildcat in battle, far more lethal than Willis had any desire to be, but this wasn't the first time Leonor motivated him to action by implying he wouldn't perform a task a woman was willing to do. It wasn't fair, but it worked.

An 8pdr roundshot from the heights on the right gouged the earth much too close, spattering them all with slushy mud and sending all the horses but Arete nervously capering. Lewis wiped a blob of mud from his cheek and patted his horse affectionately on the neck. "Good girl," he murmured.

"We're in clear view of the enemy," Varaa reminded. "If we don't choose to separate, perhaps we should move about a bit."

Lewis nodded. None of them were dressed significantly different from any of their troops, their shoulder boards likely invisible from a distance, but they were mounted in the midst of infantry.

"Mr. Barca seems to be getting their range," he observed as three exploding shells burst almost simultaneously, sleeting hot metal at the enemy battery. "I do take your point, however." Instead of moving, though, he simply dismounted and led Arete, walking along behind the advancing Ocelomeh infantry. It was clear he intended to stay where he was for the moment, and whoever wanted to remain by his side would have to dismount as well. He grinned at an Ocelomeh file closer (an NCO standing behind the firing line to "close the files" as men fell, keep others from running away, or help them with malfunctioning weapons), who glanced at him with relief, glad the "brass" wouldn't keep drawing disproportionate fire in his vicinity. First Division's right was about to draw plenty of fire in any event. The Doms were lengthening their line as they advanced as well. Major Ixtla's regiment was armed with the better American weapons and had been firing unanswered volleys as it advanced. The enemy would certainly respond very soon, and they'd be in the thick of the infantry fight. That's when Lewis expected the Dom lancers to move.

The snow was vanishing even quicker now, and virtually none remained in the wake of the 1st Ocelomeh, its men having churned it into a deep, thick morass of mud.

"Poor Willis," Leonor said with mock remorse. "Even if he does get shot, he'll be madder about the mess you're making of your boots."

Varaa and Reverend Harkin chuckled, but their amusement was shattered an instant later, when the 1st Ocelomeh once more ground to a halt and prepared to fire another volley. The Doms beat them to it, their massed volley slamming home at roughly seventy-five paces. Men screamed and fell, blood misting and uniform fibers exploding into the air like down. Canteens, shards of muskets, even buttons and beltplates became secondary missiles, wounding others around those who were struck directly. With so many men standing between Lewis's party and the enemy, it was a wonder anything could get through, but it did. Musket balls hissed or warbled past, snatching at uniforms or raising cries from horses. Two of Lewis's messengers fell, and the file closer he'd grinned at just moments before toppled over with his hat—and the top of his head underneath it—blown completely off.

"Damn this," Lewis growled, trying to glimpse the enemy, but being dismounted, glimpses were all he got: yellow-and-black uniforms surging through the smoke and flashing muskets.

"Fire!" someone roared, maybe Ixtla. The Ocelomeh officer wasn't with them anymore. A withering volley cracked at the Doms, as crisp and lethal as a demonstration on a parade ground. They weren't on parade today, however, a fact driven grimly home by the wounded being dragged or helped to the rear.

"Stand firm in the faith! Act like men; be strong!" roared Reverend Harkin, unslinging the M1817 rifle he always carried. Turning to Lewis, he said, "Win your battle, Colonel Cayce. I cannot help you with that. I *can* help *these* men, so I will fight my battle here."

Varaa started to object, but Lewis shook his head. "Be careful, Reverend, and be watchful. Things will quickly change here. Don't get yourself killed. I suspect your greatest battle, one *I* won't be much help with, is yet to come."

Pulling Arete around, he strode briskly toward the rear, into the space between 1st and 2nd Divisions. There, he swung back into his saddle and gazed around. Battle had been joined all across the plain, and fighting was particularly furious around the nearest abandoned villa, as if both sides were striving to gain the cover it afforded. Fighting around the more distant one suddenly fell away to nothing, however, as a large bipedal predator, its furry coat brown on top and white below, almost like a deer, suddenly leaped from behind the wall surrounding it and dashed back and forth in apparent panic, roaring threateningly in all directions. It must've taken refuge from the storm in the villa and lingered there as the armies approached as long as it could stand. Thundering volleys and pounding guns had finally driven it from its lair. Lewis was struck by how apparently unsurprised Colonel Agon's former Dom soldiers appeared to be, especially when a couple of his companies suddenly rushed the disoriented beast, yelling at the top of their lungs. With a terrified squawk, the monster turned and fled, pounding right through the enemy ranks, flattening whole files. Dozens of Doms might've been killed, smashed by the monster or crushed by comrades trying to get out of its way.

Lewis held his breath. A break like that would be tempting to charge through, and the whole 4th Division might be sucked into a premature attack. *It could even work*, he conceded to himself. That's when Agon justified all Lewis's faith in him, sounding his horns, pulling back, and re-forming his green-clad troops. Lewis exhaled in utmost relief. Yes, Agon might've passed an opportunity to win the battle, but the *plan* to minimize casualties called for breaking the enemy here, on the right.

"Neat trick," Leonor called out, now mounted beside him.

"Damn good discipline," Lewis countered. "Don't let me forget to compliment Mr. Agon."

Varaa was mounted now as well. They could see better from here, but distance and the drifting smoke made them less of a target. "Why did you leave the reverend?" she asked. "Especially if you really think his biggest fight is ahead."

Lewis looked at his Mi-Anakka friend. "Frankly, I suspect he'll be safer with Ixtla than us." He smiled at Leonor. "And Lieutenant Anson already has enough of us to look after."

A dragoon corporal galloped up, horse blowing steam and spraying mud. Stopping by Lewis, the young towheaded rider—one of relatively few "original" remaining dragoons—saluted. "Mr. Burton's respects, sir, an' the Dom lancers is spillin' outa the woods an' formin' opposite your flank."

Lewis stood in his stirrups but still couldn't see. It didn't matter. "My compliments to Mr. Burton. He and the others know what to do. The only further order I have for them is to watch out for themselves. You too, Corporal. God be with you."

"An' you, sir," the young dragoon said earnestly, saluting again. He thundered off through the drifting smoke of another volley. Almost at once, Corporal Willis came bouncing erratically up atop his own trotting horse.

"Which you never needed to send me over there a'tall," he accused, poking a finger through a hole in his left sleeve, near the cuff.

"If you'd rode faster, you'd'a got here quicker," Leonor accused. "Even pokin' along like you were, you nearly beat Coryon Burton's own messenger."

"I wasn't pokin'!" Willis flared. "Damned horse won't go no faster!"

"Certainly not, with you pulling so fiercely on his reins," Varaa agreed dryly.

"You did well," Lewis interceded. "Now go inform Har-Kaaska that the time has come to redeploy his division. If we can't see the enemy clearly, I doubt they can see us as yet. The remnants of the enemy battery on the heights might observe his maneuver, but I'm sure Mr. Barca is firmly holding their attention. Even if they do see what's happening—and recognize the significance—I doubt they have the means, and they certainly won't have the time, to warn the enemy lancers."

Willis hesitated. "You ain't just sendin' me off to get kilt?"

"Of course not," Lewis replied somberly. "Nor have I already sent word to Har-Kaaska. You do need to hurry, though."

Willis finally sketched a salute and forced his confused, borrowed horse to face the rear before urging it on.

"Quit tryin' ta pull his head in your lap, you idiot!" Leonor called after him, before turning back to Lewis. "You don't send him off to be killed. You try to protect his foolish neck. Why?"

The infantry brawl in front of them, just the sort of prolonged slugging match that mauled both sides and Lewis had hoped to avoid, made a steady, thunderous roar, both sides firing independently now. There wasn't any help for it, though, since he'd been forced to await General Gomez's next move— the charge of his lancers. That also meant, visible through the smoke or not, Lewis and his party were just as vulnerable to random musket shot as anyone.

"Move aside, move aside! Comin' through!" bellowed Sergeant Major McNabb, pushing an entire battery of captured and remounted 8pdrs up through the stream of wounded making their way to the rear. "Get those goddamn horses . . . 'Scuse me, Colonel Cayce!"

"No, you're right, of course, Sergeant Major!" Lewis called, backing Arete up. Leonor's Sparky managed that as well, though all the other horses had to be turned. Lewis didn't even ask McNabb if he remembered his instructions. The stocky, powerful Scotsman was one of the few professional artillerymen to come to this world, and he hadn't been made Justinian Olayne's sergeant major for nothing. "Send the enemy a proper greeting for me, will you?" Lewis said as the gasping gun's crew fought the mud to heave their weapons past.

"Aye, that we will!" McNabb agreed.

Lewis nodded, aware that at that moment, fully half of the rest of Olayne's guns would be moving in behind Har-Kaaska.

Leonor pressed her inquiry as if their conversation had never been interrupted. "You sent Willis to Burton just before we went close to the firin' line. Now you've sent him off to get him outa this." Men were falling even faster now, and the air around them sounded like it was full of buzzing hornets.

"You people." Varaa sighed, exasperated and blinking something that reinforced her tone. She'd been lighting her pipe from a piece of slow match in a copper tube that she'd struck alight with a device like a tiny wheel lock. "You have the strangest notions of betrothal and mating."

Lewis frowned, gesturing at Leonor. "I assure you. Our . . . understanding . . . is not typical."

Varaa laughed. "I know *that*. Perhaps I should have said you *two*. Though your father's and Samantha Wilde's circumstances were somewhat odd as well, in contrast to other customs I've observed in this hemisphere. Among the free people on the Yucatán, at any rate. And even compared to them, such things between my people are much more straightforward." Varaa vigorously puffed her pipe, visibly stopping herself from continuing in that direction. She seemed to reconsider, however. "Even among my people, however, females are generally protected. I think I've let slip that we've had many wars and only females may rebuild populations, after all. Of necessity we've learned that females should be *taught* to fight, but only allowed to do so when the whole population is threatened. When their . . . exclusive capability would make no difference in defeat, in other words."

"You fight," Leonor pointed out.

"Quite well, if I say so myself," Varaa agreed. "But at first, in this land where I'd never dream of raising a youngling, I fought 'of necessity.' Now, somewhat past my prime youngling-bearing years—though still in my prime in battle, I assure you—I fight for the same reason." She blinked her huge blue eyes at Leonor. "Will you wind up like me?" Flipping her tail, she shook her head. "In sum, Lewis protects Corporal Willis because he likes him. The man is all but useless in battle yet is devoted to Lewis's welfare. And all pretense to the contrary, I know even you find his affectations amusing. Most of all, Lewis protects him because he can—and he's helpless to protect you."

"Me?" Leonor sputtered, and Lewis shifted uncomfortably, pretending disinterest in their discussion while he observed the battle.

"You," Varaa confirmed. "You are a warrior at least as much as I, yet you love this man and could still have many younglings. Just as you have . . . guarded your father's back so long, however, you yearn to protect Lewis as well. Losses in your past have utterly invested you in their safety." Varaa frowned. "I truly fear for you if you lose either one." She sighed. "But I fear for Lewis as well. You certainly know he loves you also—probably the only thing in this world he loves besides his army and his cause—but he won't change you any more than you'd change him. You'd no longer be *who* he loved if he did. For all that, have no doubt he longs to send you to safety . . . but that would remove you from him entirely, wouldn't it? You'd return to your father, continue fighting anyway, and you and Lewis both would worry even more about each other!" Varaa glanced at Lewis, now leaning forward in the saddle, keenly staring to the right. "None of us can afford that. He must focus on his battle in that . . . interesting way he has. Even now I believe he is starting to . . . feel it. He won't worry about much else at all, for a while." Varaa grinned, showing long, sharp canines. "Which is all the more reason he *needs* us female warriors—who care so much for him— by his side!"

"Corporal Hannity!" Lewis called to his dragoon bugler. "Stand by to signal Mr. Lara and Colonel Har-Kaaska." He turned back to Varaa and Leonor, expression very different from before, his excitement more like that of a spectator at a horse race. "The enemy lancers are formed to charge, and Coryon Burton's dragoons are already nipping at them. Har-Kaaska will move to refuse our flank even as 1st Division presses forward!"

Leonor knew the plan, had even seen it drawn on the map, but she couldn't "feel" it in action as it unfolded, "see" it in motion like Lewis did now. She only knew Lewis's exhilaration meant things would soon get even more intense than they already were. She nodded grimly at Varaa, and the Mi-Anakka warmaster grinned back.

CHAPTER 25

The day was warming dramatically under the bright, clear sky, and Barca's whole battery was pounding the distant Dom artillery on the opposite heights. There was no return fire from there, and only an occasional shot screamed down at the American infantry below. Meanwhile, most of the 3rd Pennsylvania, and Anson's Rangers and Holcanos, as well as Meder's mounted riflemen were stubbornly keeping more Dom infantry from pushing up the slope to retake their position. In addition, though it couldn't reach them, plenty of Dom artillery was still churning the ranks of their comrades in 1st and 4th Divisions, from the massed Dom batteries behind the line. Olayne's guns below had started working on them, but now they were repositioning, not firing at anything, and Captain Barca had set the two Dom guns they'd managed to capture upon them. It wasn't going well.

"God in heaven!" Lieutenant Petty roared at Sergeant Visser's squad of Pennsylvanians as they did their best to load and fire the pair of Dom 8pdrs. "You look like wild *goats*, all roped together, tryin' ta pull a freight wagon up a hill! You'll be standin' on top o' the goddamn guns, eatin' paint off the carriages next."

Sergeant Visser tramped over to him as if deliberately trying to splash him with mud. "You damned jumped-up tyrant, hardly outa stripes your-self, don't you talk to *my* boys like that! They're hard-fightin' infantry who won you this nice view ta fight from in the first place!"

Petty's eyes narrowed. "You've all had artillery trainin', an' Colonel Cayce requires *everyone* to be able to serve a gun, even the damned dragoons!"

"Trained ta *serve* a gun, sure!" Visser yelled back, stomping more mud on Petty. "Not take one over entirely, shoot as fast as fellas who drill on 'em every day—an' knock a man's head off at a thousand paces!"

"But you *ain't* knockin' any heads off!" Petty bellowed, genuinely furi-ous now and actually kicking mud on Visser. "You ain't even comin' within fifty yards o' them stationary guns at barely *six* hundred paces!" He pointed vaguely at Private Hoziki on Hanny's gun right next to them and a couple other recruits from Frontera scattered around. "I've had farmers join my crews, an' Ocelomeh right outa the woods, who could do that well in a day!"

"We haven't *had* a day!" Visser ranted. "Most of my lads had a few *hours'* instruction half a year or more ago!"

"What the devil is this all about?" shouted Captain Barca, pulling up and circling his horse. Petty and Visser both pointed at each other and drew a breath, but Barca held up a hand. "Never mind, I already know. Sergeant Cox, choose half a dozen men from your gun and Dodd's and take charge of this section. You can refresh the training of Sergeant Visser's infantry-men while improving their execution. Does that meet with your approval, Sergeant Visser?"

"Why . . . yes sir, it does."

"Good." Barca glared at Petty. "The right section, on the other side of these"—he waved at the 8pdrs—"will continue suppressing the enemy fire on the opposite heights. The rest of the battery, including our new . . . acqui-sitions, will focus on the enemy guns behind the line." He pointed, but not at the guns. Suddenly, they all saw a large part of Lewis Cayce's battle plan unfolding before them. Through the smoke of the infantry brawl below, thousands of Dom lancers, pennants and flags streaming, were charging across the open ground between the forest at the base of those other heights and the army's right, intent on smashing the flank. The ridiculously out-numbered dragoons were giving ground, but still peppering at them with Hall carbines, emptying saddles with the rapid-firing breechloaders. Mostly it seemed like they were keeping the swarm of lancers from spreading out quite as much as they might've liked. That was their purpose, of course. Behind them, Lara's lancers, more dragoons, and a few hundred more Rangers—perhaps as many as fifteen hundred riders all told—were massing to hit the enemy lancers in the flank, supported by Dukane's battery of 12pdr howitzers. Even so vastly outnumbered, their effect wouldn't be insignificant, but with Har-Kaaska's entire 2nd Division double-timing up to the right of 1st Division, the enemy lancers were about to smash into a wall of lead balls and bristling bayonets. If they broke, it would throw the whole enemy left into confusion.

They'd see it all from here.

"You'll remain in command of your section," Barca continued to Petty, "but take Hanny's place as gunner on Number Two." He smiled wryly at the crusty former NCO. "Let's see *you* knock off a few heads, eh?"

Hanny picked three of Dodd's more patient men and took Preacher Mac and Private Hoziki (who'd been trading off with Naxa and knew the Number Three position as well as his own Number Four), and the transfer of personnel went quickly. Replacements for Petty's guns came up from the rear, where the caissons had finally moved up the road leading to the position. The infantrymen that Hanny's replaced were told to stand back and watch, while the rest were given shouted instructions on the fly. The gun Hanny took personal charge of was no different from other examples he'd seen: heavily built split-trail carriage (these painted red, while previous examples had been yellow) and banded with more iron than most Uxmalos had ever seen before the war. The wheels were solid, without any spokes, mounted on massive wooden axles, and rode on heavy iron tires as well. Instead of being heated and shrunk tight on the felloes like American-style wheels, however, these tires wore short lengths of iron spiked into place, leaving large knobs all around the circumference.

Hanny had to admit the carriages were tough, doubtless built to last a century, but they weighed at least twice as much as American carriages and were ridiculously bulky and awkward. The gun tubes they carried were considerably more refined, much more so than the naval guns salvaged from the first Dom warship they saw, wrecked in the mouth of Uxmal Bay. They were heavier for caliber and a redder bronze than American guns, made with more copper and less tin in the alloy, but were much more ornate with decorative, geometric shapes cast into the wedding bands and around the vent. They even seemed nearly as well bored. The only markings on Hanny's 6pdr were the registry number, weight of metal at the muzzle, identity of the foundry, and the date it was made stamped on the trunnion ends and the muzzle. A large US had been cast into the top of the tube between the trunnions. Much more important, Hanny's beloved 6pdr had a front sight screwed into the top of the bell at the muzzle and a bracket for a robust but relatively precise pendulum hausse rear sight screwed into the back of the breech. The Dom cannon had no sights at all and only a wedge of wood to adjust elevation. "How the devil am I supposed to hit anything with this?" he complained aloud as Preacher Mac loudly corrected the efforts of the infantrymen trying to load it.

"Aye," agreed Preacher Mac. He'd moved over to the Number One position to ram the powder charge, which was separate from the shot. That would take an extra step because they'd found cylindrical wads of cork or something like it to ram down on top of the shot. "An' if Sergeant Hanny, sharpest shooter in Barca's battery—meanin' all the bloody guns on this evil world— can't do it, how're these puir, ignorant footsloggers tae manage?"

"Hey," objected Visser. "You were both infantry yourselves, you know."

"An' look at this, then," Preacher Mac continued in disgust as if Visser hadn't spoken, holding up an 8pdr shot the Number Two man had started to place in the muzzle. "They should'a sent us with some o' our new ammunition fer these ridiculous things. No sabot, an' shaped like a giant egg, this is. How's that s'posed tae fly straight?"

Hanny peered at the projectile. It looked smooth and well enough made. "Kinda like a teardrop," he declared. "Maybe they expect it to stabilize itself. Clever, but it won't work. Especially without a sabot to keep it centered in the bore—and in front of all the force of the gunpowder." He had a sudden inspiration. "Use the shot itself to shove a couple of those wads down the barrel and give it a good whack. Then push another wad down on top."

"Aye, might work," Preacher Mac speculated. "Though it'll wear me out double quick."

Petty's section, with the lieutenant on Hanny's gun, had already started firing again, throwing exploding case down around the enemy gunners, hacking them down in bloody swathes. More men took their places. The mass of charging enemy lancers had been confronted by Haar-Kaaska's division, and utter chaos reigned as savage volleys wilted the horsemen like locusts flying into a grass fire. Cannon erupted from right among 1st Division's most distant regiment, sheeting canister into the Dom infantry facing it. Hanny was convinced the battle was in the balance, and here he was, doing almost nothing. "Can't be helped," he snapped in frustration, "and by the time you get tired, somebody'll have watched enough to step in for you." Raising his voice, he shouted for the crew of the other captured gun to load theirs the same way he and Preacher Mac discussed and then returned his attention to trying to aim something without sights again. Visser had been contemplating the problem as well. "You were infantry yourself," he reminded again. "I see you've gotten lazy. Your musket never had a rear sight."

"It had a *front* sight, and I never had to shoot it so far," Hanny retorted, but he was nodding. As soon as Preacher Mac heaved the heavy shot on top of two wads down the barrel to the powder charge, Hanny said, "Make a mark on top of the muzzle, as close to the center as you can. Use a knife, a rock—I don't care as long as I can see it."

Preacher Mac complied with a nod, perfectly aware of what Hanny wanted. The sun was getting high, and any scratch in the blackened muzzle would be bright. He stooped and retrieved a small stone as suggested. Standing directly in front of the loaded gun and peering back at the vent, he closed an eye, bit his lip, and laid a thumbnail on top of the muzzle. Using that for reference, he scribed a line beside it with the stone. "How's that? Might have'tae freshen it from time tae time, but the mark's there tae see."

"Good enough," Hanny said, crouching to gaze down the barrel. Everything felt wrong. The cascabel was there to rest his hand on and cradle his chin, but he could barely even reach the far side of the right-hand trail to signal Hoziki, who'd taken an oddly formed handspike and gone to the rear. "Can't do it from there," Hanny called back without moving his head. "We'll need a man on both sides. Damn stupid carriage," he added lower. The Number Four man, holding a long linstock with a smoldering match clenched in an intricately cast brass arm, thrust the base of the linstock in the mud and seized another handspike.

"Apo!" Hanny shouted, hopefully loud enough for his friend behind the limber chest for the Number Two gun to hear. "Send somebody over here to look for a gunner's quadrant among the enemy tools, or something like a dispart sight. They have to have one." The rest of the men took up the cry, whether they knew what those things were or not, and Hanny vaguely heard

Apo shout agreement. Now back to aiming, but unable to signal both men at once with his hand, Hanny had to rely on shouted directions. "Left!" he said, and Hoziki shifted the trail a little from his side, using the handspike like a lever. "Left," Hanny repeated, "left . . . left a tiny bit . . . No, damn it. Just a little right . . . there!" Hanny stood, the gun now roughly aimed at one of the enemy guns down below, the scratch on the muzzle aligned with the top of the breech as well as Hanny could eyeball it. There were probably other tools (besides Preacher Mac) for finding the top center of the tube. Like the quadrant, they had such things in their own limber chest. Hanny had never trained with them, however. What was the point? He'd adjust his fire off Preacher Mac's scratch.

"Is this it?" called Visser himself, holding a strange wooden device: a foot-long stick with a hollow triangle at one end. Something that looked like a pistol ball dangled from the top of the triangle by a string. Visser had beaten everyone else to the Dom tool chest.

"Yes!" cried Hanny. "I think," he added a little doubtfully. "Looks different from ours, but close enough. What else could it be? Give it to Mac."

Handing the device over the gun to the Scotsman, Visser stepped back beside Hanny. "What're you gonna do now? This is already way more than my boys could manage. We were just happy to load the damn thing, point it, and set it off."

"No idea about trajectory, especially with those wads, but I'm gonna try two degrees," Hanny called to Preacher Mac, who'd already inserted the quadrant in the muzzle, triangle up.

"Two degrees," Preacher Mac confirmed.

"Sorry, Sergeant Visser," Hanny apologized to the veteran. "I wasn't ignoring you, we're just kind of in a rush. Now I'm going to shift that stupid block of wood under the breech back and forth until Mac tells me to stop." Squatting down, he grasped a handle on the back of the heavy, wedge-shaped object and began easing it back, slowly lowering the breech and raising the elevation of the muzzle.

"Good God," Visser groaned. "You poor bastards have to do all this every time you shoot?" He gestured to the side where the rest of Barca's battery was still pounding away. "How do you keep your rate of fire so high?"

"Can't. Not like this. Another one of our few advantages over the Doms. Now you know why every Dom gun we capture has to have a new carriage—and sights—before we put 'em to use!"

"A wee bit more," Preacher Mac, shouted, staring at the weighted line hanging over darkened roman numerals etched in the shaft of the quadrant. Hanny stopped what he was doing and stood to press down on the breech near the vent. "That did it!" cried Preacher Mac, yanking the quadrant out of the gun and stepping back around the wheel. "At least I think it did," he added. "What else could them numbers mean but degrees? Let's see how it does!"

"Right," Hanny agreed, motioning Hoziki and the other man to finish preparing the gun to fire. This they knew how to do because they practiced to perform the same basic task, priming the vent with loose powder and igniting it with a linstock, in case they ran out of primers for their Hidden's Patent lock, or the mechanism somehow failed. Both things had happened before. Hoziki pierced the charge in the gun with his own personal vent prick, which he always carried, and then filled the vent with powder from a wooden flask somebody handed him. Pooling more powder on top of the vent, he stepped back. "Ready!" he cried.

The conscripted infantryman retrieved his linstock and blew on the slow match until it glowed brightly. Hanny looked around to make sure no one was in the path of the weapon's recoil, then nodded to himself and shouted, "Fire!"

The linstock came down, the smoldering slow match barely touching the little pile of priming powder before it flashed and whooshed, spitting an orange, smoke-shrouded jet of fire straight at the sky. An instant later, the big gun roared, rolling several feet back. Hanny sprang to the side to see around the billowing smoke cloud the gun spewed so he could watch the fall of shot. He saw it in flight, a black dot in the sky, streaking away, remarkably straight, directly toward the enemy guns. A geyser of mud erupted a few yards in front of one.

"Range is right on the money," shouted the excited infantryman serving as the Number Two.

"Aye," Preacher Mac agreed, shading his eyes with his hand. "Just gotta adjust a wee bit left. That is, if our 'wad sabot' really worked."

"It did," Hanny proclaimed with confidence. "Now let's load her up again—faster this time—and get back in the fight!" He looked at the other captured gun, its crew still watching him. "You saw what we did, damn you. Get to it!"

Sergeant Visser clapped him on the shoulder with a grin. "Always knew you'd amount to something. Give those devils hell. Me and the rest of the boys in the squad'll stay and cover you in case any of them rascals trying to retake this hill get past the fellas sent to stop 'em." His grin grew. "Pleasure to fight beside you again, young Hanny Cox!"

CHAPTER 26

Lewis Cayce was exhilarated and horrified all at once by the scene unfolding to the right of 1st Division as thousands of brave, well-disciplined, and finely turned-out Dom lancers—not to mention their beautiful horses—were churned into bloody mulch. Rapid, professional volleys continuously cracked from Har-Kaaska's division, stacked four ranks deep. The first rank reloaded by the time the fourth rank fired, the deadly volleys were almost continuous. Olayne's artillery had nosed into the line as well, coughing enough canister that the guns might've stopped the lancers unaided. And Dukane's howitzers, unlimbering within musket shot of the enemy flank with Burton's dragoons in support, were savaging the helpless lancers stacked up behind the shattered vanguard.

Lewis was appalled by the evisceration of such a fine force, so many men and animals, but—for the moment at least—more elated that his plan seemed to be coming together. If that continued, the enemy's left should soon collapse. Just as they had at the Northern Mexico Battle of Monterrey, the conflicting emotions left him somewhat sickened with himself, but his devotion to his cause and love for the army he'd built, coupled with the nature of the enemy and the war they fought here, let him suppress that feeling more than before.

"Lara's lancers are going in," Varaa observed matter-of-factly, watching

Ramon Lara's riders sweep up Burton's dragoons as they charged through Emmel Dukane's six guns, which had ceased firing as abruptly as they began and were already limbering up to move. Lewis spun Arete around to face Corporal Hannity. "Sound the signal for Second Division and Olayne's batteries on the left to cease firing." Even as Hannity raised his bugle, Lewis turned to a messenger. "My compliments to Colonel Reed. Batteries to the front, interspersed with his First Division, will open fire."

Even with the dragoons and Rangers, sabers drawn, joining Lara's lancers, he was still woefully outnumbered, but the enemy lancers had been shattered before their charge ever went home. Most of the survivors were merely milling about, blocked from advancing by the carnage in front and until moments before, savaged from their left by rapid-fire Hall carbines and canister from Dukane's guns. Now Lara's force was charging them out of the smoke and there was no way to tell how few they were. All the confused, demoralized, and increasingly terrified Doms understood was that they were receiving yet another wild, whooping, unexpected attack. A few might've stood regardless. It was their way. But too many were hurt, all were disorganized, and many were frankly too stunned by the trip-hammer blows of ferocity to try and resist yet another. Likely without even thinking, they simply surged away in the only direction from which no attack had yet come and subconsciously thought they'd be safe in their own lines.

But even those lines weren't safe. First Division was still trading volleys with the Dom infantry right in front of it. Men on both sides were screaming, falling, dying. But even the Dom infantry could sense a shift in the weight and movement on their left, whether they saw it or not. The noise alone was enough to unnerve them. They'd seen their lancers charging in, heard the calamity of sound, but the Americans in front of them that should've been recoiling from an irresistible crash on their right stood firm, firing with lethal precision and rapidity. Then, of course, they saw the gaping muzzles of Olayne's artillery nosing through the ranks of their adversaries just before the great fire-hearted blossoms of yellow-white smoke bloomed in their faces and the whirring roar of canister sheeted into them.

The balls striking bodies made the same thumping sound the men had grown used to, but they came all together, in an instant, mixed with flying clods of mud and wet snow. Worse were the secondary projectiles, long splinters and other shattered fragments of weapons, uniform buttons, even shards of bone that flew with sufficient force to wound or kill as well. The smoke roiling over the Dom lines was filled with indistinct forms cart-wheeling to the ground amid a chorus of agonized screams, and the yellow-white smoke turned orange as blood spray tinted it red. Then, before a breath could be taken, before standing men even knew if they were unhurt or dead on their feet, a call roared forth from the hell to their front that they understood perfectly, different language or not.

"Fix bayonets!"

"Keep yer alignments an' intervals as best ye can, lads," NCOs shouted. "Don't get carried away. I'll buck an' gag any man who stops to loot, by God!"

"In good order . . . charge!" came another loud voice, and the terrible drums began to roll. Even before the enemy crossed the distance between them, the fringe of fleeing lancers scraped the flank of the Dom infantry line, pulling frightened men along with them. Those still standing saw American and regimental flags of the 1st US, 1st Uxmal, 1st Ocelomeh, 1st Vera Cruz—most of the "firsts" in the army were with 1st Division—swirling toward them through the smoke atop a blue wave of figures roaring like the surf. Fragile as an egg already, in spite of tardy, panicked orders to *"¡Preparan bayonetas!"* the Dom left began to crumble.

"MESSENGERS!" LEWIS SHOUTED. "Colonel Agon will advance at once. Compliments, of course," he told one of the mounted men who urged their horses forward. Looking at another, he pointed behind them and to the left. "The same to Colonel Itzam and Third Division. He knows what I want."

Much like Har-Kaaska had deployed 2nd Division behind the 1st, Itzam's five regiments had moved to support Agon's men. Unlike Har-Kaaska, however, Itzam's only secondary role had been to keep an eye on 4th Division. As much as Lewis had come to trust Agon and his conversion to the cause, the middle of a crucial battle was not the time to discover he'd been wrong to do so, or that others of Agon's units or commanders weren't similarly dedicated. Now, with 4th Division heavily and valiantly involved in the fighting, Lewis wanted Itzam to move up obliquely to support both 4th and 1st Divisions, ready to fill any gap between them if it started to form, or just keep the pressure up if either leading division stalled. The messengers galloped away.

Lewis nudged Arete into a gallop of her own, belatedly followed by an exasperated Leonor, Varaa, and the others detailed to attend him. He drew up beside Colonel Reed, who was following behind his charging division and had seen him approach. "It goes well," Reed said guardedly, eyes straying across the mounds of dead and the steady stream of wounded moving to the rear. There were corpses everywhere, and the charging troops were literally having to climb over the heaps of Doms, lying in rows. There'd been no terrible crash as the charge went in because the enemy simply ceded the ground. In spite of everything, however, something had stiffened them after that, and they kept firing as they pulled back. A ball snatched Reed's hat right off his head, ruffling his sweat-plastered hair.

"We need to push them back faster. Get them running," Lewis said.

"I'm trying," Reed almost snapped back, waving around. "The boys are trying—and dying."

Lewis nodded. "I know."

At that moment, Captain Boogerbear Beeryman thundered up, followed more tentatively by an ashen-faced Corporal Willis. Giving Lewis and Anson's daughter a quick head bow of greeting, Boogerbear slid off his horse, Dodger, and lifted the animal's right front foreleg out of the slushy mud. "Damn," he said, prying off a shoe held only by a single nail. "I need another horse."

"You can have mine," Willis offered hopefully.

"I wouldn't think o' leavin' you afoot, Corporal," the big Ranger retorted dryly.

Reed motioned to one of his own messengers to surrender his mount and take care of Boogerbear's. The Ranger nodded his thanks and retrieved his signature, somewhat battered but extremely well-made double-barrel shotgun that was hanging from Dodger's saddle horn by a sling. There was no horn on the dragoon messenger's saddle, and he hefted the shotgun over his shoulder before mounting the borrowed horse. Looking at Lewis, he waved back behind him. "Dom lancers took off. Just broke. Prettiest thing you ever saw. Thousands of 'em, runnin' like rabbits. Infantry's a mite stubborner. They're fallin' back, but need another nudge. Mr. Lara's re-formin' his own lancers an' all the dragoons. My handful o' Rangers too. Gonna hit 'em straight in the flank." He turned his gaze to Reed. "If the Doms don't move nothin' else up in the meantime, you oughta roll them devils plumb up an' start a full-blown skedaddle." He pointed ahead where the infantry under the 1st Vera Cruz flag had slowed to fire a volley. "That's that Don Roderigo fella, ain't it? He doin' okay?"

"As well as any," Reed replied.

"Fine. Tell him to get ready to give 'em another push in a minute—then chase 'em straight to hell."

Glancing at Lewis, Boogerbear grinned through his giant beard. "We'll break this wide open for ya, Colonel."

Lewis frowned, gauging the action in front. Olayne's batteries were pushing their guns forward once more, and that should certainly wreck the enemy's firming resolve, but he had to respect how tenaciously their infantry had controlled their first break. With enough support, quickly brought to bear, they might still hold. They could certainly make things costlier than 1st Division could afford. "I believe I'll join you, Captain Beeryman, and Mr. Lara for a while."

"Colonel!" Reed began to protest.

Lewis shook his head. "Our men continue to fight splendidly, but most are still rather new to this, and it's starting to hurt. They must be *led*, sir, and see who's leading them." He raised a hand to stop Reed's objection. "You're where you should be, and I've seen far too many NCOs and junior officers lying on the ground or being carried from the fight. They've been where they were needed as well." He held his hands out to his sides. "I, on the other hand, am leading no one at present. Take command until we rejoin, but press the attack, Colonel Reed," he said intently. "We *must* break this flank before General Gomez sends significant reinforcements."

Leonor sighed and exchanged a knowing look with Varaa, and they both urged their horses to follow Lewis and Boogerbear back to the right. Passing a miserable-looking Willis, Leonor called, "Why don't you stay with Colonel Reed, Corporal? My God, you ain't even *armed*!"

Willis glared back, kicking his own borrowed mount into motion. "Then I'll by God arm myself, won't I?"

The ride around the right flank where Lara's riders were coming back together (quite a few had chased the enemy and were slow returning) was just a few hundred yards and passed very quickly, Lewis gazing past the infantry at the swirling smoke. The firing line had reestablished itself just seventy to a hundred yards beyond where it was before the charge, and Lewis felt the initial exhilaration he'd experienced over the successful unfolding of his plan beginning to fade. *Then again*, he thought, *no matter how detailed, battle plans are just outlines, and you have to remain prepared to fill in the details as you go—or throw the whole thing out and start over.* He didn't think the latter was necessary yet. He encouraged all his commanders to use initiative—within reason—and it seemed Ramon Lara was doing just that, preparing to fill in a "detail" of his own.

The lancers were already formed in a block when he arrived, those still with lances in front. Lewis saw Coryon Burton's dragoons and accompanying Rangers fastened to the block on the right, arranged in a column of fours. They'd be available to lend their weight to the charge or peel off if it became advantageous to do so. To Lewis's surprise, cheers greeted his arrival as his own little column trotted up to join Lara and Burton.

"Well done with the enemy lancers, gentlemen," Lewis said loudly as he halted Arete and returned salutes. Nearby troopers grinned and started spreading his words. "Mr. Beeryman says they're still running. And I see you're about ready to fall on the flank of the Dom infantry as well."

"It seemed the thing to do," Burton replied with a tentative smile. "Some of them ran with the horsemen, but the rest shook off the scare."

Lara nodded agreement. "Regardless of the foul cause they fight for, the enemy has never given us grounds to disdain their courage."

Lewis knew from Agon that Dom conscripts, making up the bulk of their rank-and-file infantry, were actually more motivated by terror of what their superiors—particularly Blood Priests—would do to them if they didn't fight than they were by any cause. He considered that violation of their character, their very souls, one of the greatest evils the enemy perpetrated. The fact they had to kill those men, victims themselves, in order to destroy their masters didn't sit well with him when he occasionally contemplated it.

The roar of battle, now extending virtually from one side of the miles-wide valley to the other, reached new heights, Reed's infantry likely covering the guns pushing through once more. Lara knew time was short. "With your permission, Colonel Cayce?"

Lewis held up a hand. "This is your command, your action. I'm only here to observe."

Lara nodded seriously. "Thank you, sir. Better get back to your men, Coryon," he told Burton, who was already turning.

"God be with you all," said the young dragoon from North Carolina.

"You as well," Lewis responded as he, Leonor, Varaa, and Lewis's small entourage joined Lara, trotting their horses to the head of his block of lancers.

"You comin'?" Boogerbear asked a grumbling Corporal Willis, who'd dismounted to select a Dom musketoon and cartridge box from a pile some camp followers had already begun to collect.

"Not with you an' them Rangers," Willis snarled at the giant, who could've snapped him like a twig.

"Ain't goin' over there," Boogerbear said evenly. "Sal can handle them fellas fine. Figure I'll stick with the Colonel—an' Leonor." He shook his head. "Ya' know, now an' then, they don't take as much care as they should."

"You're tellin' *me*?" Willis protested. "They need keepers. Both of 'em. Damned irresponsible, inconsiderate . . ."

Boogerbear leaned over and helped the smaller man swing back up on his borrowed horse. "Reckon so," he agreed. "Let's go get at it." Together, they hurried after the others.

From his position, mounted and with his view less obscured by the smoke on the firing line, Lewis saw that almost all of Olayne's guns were right up with the infantry now, some already firing. Dukane's battery of 12pdr howitzers was working over the shattered Dom battery on the heights to the right, blanketing it with case shot. Barca's battery, high on the left, had either silenced the Dom guns to the rear or drawn their attention. The Doms couldn't even try for Olayne's guns anymore, so close to their own infantry. Lewis also saw another reason those enemy batteries might've stopped firing: they were currently masked by fresh blocks of infantry moving forward around them. Barca's barrage was taking a toll on them as well, and some units seemed affected by the lancers still streaming past to the rear (Lewis began to suspect their continued flight had become more an effort to preserve and re-form the force than it was an actual rout), but the fact remained that he was running out of time to break the battle open. Further delay would doom them to his second-worst nightmare: a prolonged linear battle of attrition. They might still win the day, but their casualties would be horrific enough that they'd likely lose the war.

He glanced impatiently to his left. There in the distance was Justinian Olayne himself, sitting his horse beside Colonel Reed, saber raised high. With a shout impossible to hear, he swept the blade down. Three full batteries, fifteen guns—including their two heavy 12pdrs (much more powerful than Dukane's lightweight howitzers)—erupted simultaneously with a force that seemed inconceivable even compared to the massed musketry all around them. Lewis could see nothing through the rolling fogbank of smoke, but knew exactly what it hid. He'd seen it many times, and his mind's eye readily supplied dreadful images of shattered, mangled bodies and great swathes of shredded, steaming mounds, no longer recognizable as men. He looked expectantly back at Lara.

"First Yucatán Lancers!" the young Mexican cried, holding his own saber aloft with his healthy left arm while those around him, including Lewis, drew their blades as well. Leonor and Boogerbear each unholstered a Paterson Colt. A trooper behind Lara blew the preparatory command, then the order, "By the left wheel, march!" after Lara shouted it. The block of lancers and Rangers lurched forward, quickly wheeling to the left in a long, wide turn that left those on the left almost stationary but had the Rangers nearly galloping. They immediately started taking fire from Doms who'd been rushing to extend their own flank, but they came in a trickle and remained in disarray. "Charge!" Lara roared, and the bugler sounded the call. Hooves thundering and spraying mud and melting snow, they swept down on the enemy flank. Reed's division flowed forward, charging into the smoke as well, bayonets bristling, shouted "Huzzas!" mingling into a sustained, ferocious roar.

The crash when both forces met the enemy was stunning. Dom plug bayonets inserted in the muzzles of their muskets met Lara's charge like spears tearing into horses that couldn't see them. Men and horses screeched and screamed when the sharp, deadly weapons pierced them. Nine-foot lances slammed deep into Doms, most snapping before they could be hauled out of the men they struck. Lancers disarmed in such a way hauled their sabers out, slashing about them on one side or the other, hacking arms, heads, and probing muskets. Leonor and Boogerbear were snapping off shots, first emptying one revolver then another, firing directly into rage-contorted faces. Revolvers unreloadable in such an action, Leonor resorted to her M1817 rifle and Boogerbear his double-barrel shotgun, both loading and shooting as fast as they could or using the weapons as clubs. Lewis had his saber, of course, a privately purchased M1841 "artillery officer's" variant with slight embellishment and of somewhat better quality than standard-issue weapons. He'd always disdained fancy uniforms with extra braid, fine silk sashes, embroidered gauntlets, or various other fripperies some officers required, but indulged himself when it came to what he considered important, such as the best-quality saber and horse he could buy. Arete was his finest possession and the fastest, best-tempered, most stoic (but also most aggressive when necessary) warhorse he'd ever seen. He loved her dearly. His saber probably came next, then the tack Arete required—such as the expensive Ringgold saddle she wore. He also had a pair of finely tuned flintlock pistols in pommel holsters, but often forgot about them. He always preferred his saber in situations like this, stabbing, slashing, and chopping around him with great strength and passable talent while Arete kicked and stomped, accounting for at least as many enemies as he.

Leonor watched Lewis when she could, impressed by his lethality with his blade, if not necessarily his skill. She doubted he'd last long against an expert, but between the powerful strokes of his quality blade and Arete's ability to anticipate him and position him to best advantage, not to mention her own mighty kicks with iron-shod hooves, the frightened Dom infantry packed in around him didn't stand a chance. His expression was grim, but she'd learned by now that a battle wasn't fully "real" to him until he was *in* it and his odd genius for shaping it to his will only fully surfaced when he could *feel* the fight. She actually understood that to a degree because her father was much the same, if on a smaller scale. Giles Anson was never sharper, never more alive than when battle swirled around him. He was the best, most aggressive mounted leader they had. He might even be the best small unit commander, combining mounted, foot, and artillery forces. He'd clearly taken the heights on the left, after all. He couldn't do what Lewis did, however, sensing how best to combine the different branches of an entire army to force an enemy to do what he wanted.

The problem was—as she saw it—no matter how brilliantly he planned a battle, he never could finish it until he'd tasted it somehow. She wondered how much of that came from his military schooling. Almost all their officers thus educated had a dangerous tendency to lead from the front and had passed that expectation to their Allied officers as well. Then again, it might simply be part of his personality, an inability to order men into something he stayed back from. His need to be in the battle up to his neck came from something else, she believed. It was like he subconsciously made an offering to God, striking an unthinking "take me now or let me win" sort of deal. *Or is it unintentional?* she wondered.

All this came to her in an instant, but was quickly driven from her mind when her little horse Sparky suddenly screamed and reeled, a big Dom musket ball, fired from mere feet away, slapping into the animal's side right in front of her knee, blood spurting in a stream. "No!" she cried in a fury, leaning over and caving in the face of the Dom shooter with the iron butt plate of her rifle. Pulling it out of the gory hole she'd made, she watched the Dom drop to the ground. Sparky started to falter, bright orange-red blood spraying in the steam that jetted from his nostrils. "No," she said lower, chest crushing as she realized the ball had ripped Sparky's lungs. Pulling on the reins, she tried to steer him out of the tangled press. The Dom line on the right (their left) had finally shattered under the combined blows of Olayne's massed canister and Lara's and 1st Division's charges. The lingering smoke and rapid, steaming breath of so many packed together made it almost impossible to tell direction at the moment and, though most of the nearby Doms were simply trying to break contact and get away, they didn't know which direction "away" was and were running in all directions. Just as confusing, a lot were actually blocked by the depth of the mounted penetration. Few were still shooting, their muskets rendered unfireable with the short swordlike plug bayonets firmly inserted, but there were still quite enough of them desperately wielding those lethal spears.

Leonor had managed to turn her horse back the way they came, just as a pair of glistening blades were thrust into his shoulder and neck from ahead. His squeal turned into a bubbling moan, and his legs began to wobble. Even as she flailed at the closest man with her rifle, Leonor kicked free of her stirrups and stepped nimbly off when Sparky went down. With a last mournful look at her dying horse, she slung her precious rifle and stooped to seize an abandoned Dom musket with its bayonet inserted. A quick glance was all she needed to see that Lewis and the others had smashed on ahead, leaving no friends in sight. Of course, despite the fact she was generally taller than most Dom soldiers, she still had a limited view. What there was revealed countless bodies, staining every patch of unchurned snow with red-rimmed holes from hot blood spatter. There were lots of desperate Doms as well.

Thus she prepared to fight to the end in the midst of the press, surrounded by enemies. Beginning with a shout and a deadly thrust at the other Dom who'd stabbed Sparky to the ground, her long-bladed bayonet punched through his yellow coat, between ribs, to cut his heart in two. Blood sprayed from his mouth under wide, staring eyes as he dropped his own weapon and collapsed to his knees. Twisting savagely as she'd been taught before withdrawing her weapon, she was dumbfounded to see the

Dom bayonet pull out of her muzzle, locked between the enemy's ribs. It had been her experience that the damn things had to be driven out.

"Shit!" she shouted, throwing the musket at another man and reaching for the swordlike bayonet protruding from her squirming victim. It came out quite easily. Drawing her Bowie sword, she crouched with a blade in each hand. Something alerted her, and, whirling around, she dodged to the side as a bayonet quested for her, and she slammed both her blades through her assailant's throat. Blood fountained all over her as the man kept coming and almost took her to the ground as he collapsed.

A loud "Huzza!" roared to her left, and she caught a brief glimpse of sky-blue-clad forms in the drifting smoke and mentally urged them to hurry because there were still a lot of Doms between her and them. Doms who now turned toward her, possibly recognizing the only enemy between them and escape. At least she didn't fear being shot by friends. Not too much, anyway. Reed or Har-Kaaska—whoever the advancing "Americans" belonged to—would've cautioned their men to use bayonets only as long as Lara's mounted men might remain to their front. That did little to help Leonor as dozens of Doms came right at her.

"Behind you, girl!" came a shout that sounded like Boogerbear, even as she heard pounding hooves. Turning to look, she saw the big, bearded Ranger leaning low to the side in the saddle atop his horse, Dodger, mighty arm outstretched. She simply raised her own arms, and Boogerbear roughly snatched her up, swiveled at the waist, and plopped her on the horse behind him.

"Ha!" Leonor shouted gleefully, catching the breath that was nearly driven out of her. "We haven't done that in years!"

"No," Boogerbear replied evenly. "An' you're a heap bigger now. Heavier too. Figure I threw out my back."

They'd practiced that very maneuver countless times when she was younger, and she'd thought it was a kind of play, to cheer her out of her traumatized shell. It worked as much as anything had. Only later did she learn the serious purpose behind it and that her father had insisted that every Ranger who rode with him be able to retrieve his daughter if she found herself dismounted.

Boogerbear heaved Dodger around, physically pointing the horse's head away from the enemy. A scatter of Dom musket balls whizzed by. Firing was swelling elsewhere on the line but remained enough diminished here that they could hear them. "Where's Lewis?" Leonor demanded, arms tight around the big Ranger's waist.

"Right there," Boogerbear replied as Lewis, Varaa, a handful of lancers and dragoons, and even Corporal Willis streaked past and slammed into the clot of Doms. Lewis was in the lead, face beyond grim and lit by something Leonor hadn't seen before, something like furious desperation. "My God," Leonor murmured as Lewis's saber swept down and struck a Dom soldier between head and shoulder with enough force to lop the man's head completely off. He immediately swiveled in the saddle, urging Arete to stomp a soldier in front of her, then slashing down hard enough to cleave another Dom's skull down to his chin. No other enemies were willing to try him, and they parted around him, chased by the Stars and Stripes and flag of the 1st Ocelomeh, the standard-bearers in the center of a line of cheering men in sky-blue greatcoats and dark blue wheel hats, muskets held low, bayonets leveled.

"Yep," Boogerbear shouted over the roar of Olayne's cannon near the junction of 1st and 4th Divisions. "When he saw you weren't with us, he got a mite riled. Sent Lara on an' peeled off back here."

Lewis seemed to snap out of some sort of trance, sitting up perfectly erect in his saddle, then pulling Arete around and waving the bloody saber in the fleeing enemy's wake. "Don't break ranks—keep after them, boys!" he shouted at the infantry, then sent Leonor a strangely strained but extremely relieved smile. "The Doms are trying to form another line behind this one, but press these men hard enough and they'll break the rest for us!" He paused to stand in his stirrups and stare off to the left while the cheers of passing men subsided. It seemed even to Leonor that the whole Dom line, as far as she could see, was starting to buckle. "Messenger," Lewis shouted. "Find Mr. Olayne. Tell him to keep pushing half his batteries forward but limber the rest of them up and prepare to move quickly."

"Yes sir!" cried the young Uxmalo dragoon, who bolted away. The gun smoke was clearing, and Har-Kaaska's whole division was coming up now, its commander galloping over on his bizarre, bipedal mount to join Lewis while Boogerbear and the rest gathered 'round him once more. Lewis sent Leonor another relieved smile, and this time she stopped shaking (she hadn't realized she was doing that) long enough to nod and give him what she hoped was a confident smile in return.

"Colonel!" Lewis greeted Har-Kaaska when the Mi-Anakka and the strange, vaguely duck-faced . . . thing he rode (Reverend Harkin was increasingly convinced it was a relative of Iguanodon, whatever that was) came to a stop. Har-Kaaska was grinning.

"You saw that?" Har-Kaaska demanded. "My boys stopped the enemy lancers cold. Now you have shattered their infantry in front of First Division! This is a glorious day!"

Lewis understood the king of the Ocelomeh's enthusiasm. His first large-scale action against the Holcanos had been a near disaster. He'd done much better afterward, but aside from standing and presenting an impenetrable wall of musket fire and bayonets the Dom lancers—and particularly their horses—simply couldn't ride down, his division hadn't been in the meat grinder yet. Not like 1st and 4th Divisions. The artillery had performed most of the slaughter in front of him while he kept the Dom lancers at bay.

"The day is young, my king," Varaa reminded him. "There is plenty of time for glory to sour."

"She's right," Lewis said. "First Division has gone on the attack, but they've been mauled. The Doms in front of them have finally broken, and the First is pushing as hard as they can, but the enemy is forming another line farther back, and they need your support, and if possible, your relief. We *have* to keep pushing, not only to force the unsupported enemy in front of Agon to pull back as well, but to break that new line with the weight and panic of their own fleeing troops."

"It shall be done," Har-Kaaska pronounced grimly, holding up a tight fist. "We will *smash* them!"

"I'm sure of it," Lewis encouraged him. "We won't delay you further," he hinted.

Har-Kaaska nodded and turned the creature he rode. The front ranks of his division were almost on top of them. Drawing his sword, very similar to Varaa's variation on a long, straight-bladed rapier, or backsword, he waved it toward the enemy. "Second Division! Now is your time! Forward at the double time! We go to the aid of First Division and to crush the enemies of your God!" Nearly every regiment in his division had been raised in Uxmal, Pidra Blanca, Itzincab—major cities on the Yucatán where Father Orno's version of Christianity prevailed. All were members of his flock here, with priests embedded in their ranks, and this was very much a holy war to them. They roared their support as they quickened their pace. Flowing efficiently around the small mounted group, the infantry redressed their lines and pushed on. Har-Kaaska saluted Lewis with his sword and urged his mount after his men, his staff coalescing around him.

"He will do it," Varaa said with certainty.

Lewis nodded. "He'll do it or die," he agreed.

"What? We ain't goin' with 'em?" Corporal Willis asked in an acerbic tone. "We'll miss another chance ta get our fool heads shot off." He gestured at Leonor. "Like she nearly did." To Leonor's surprise, his tone had changed, and she thought she almost recognized a hint of relief in there somewhere.

"I wouldn't miss a chance at that," Lewis said, eyes focused left. "But there are other places to do it. Messenger," he called. He didn't have many of those left. One trotted his horse up close. "Do you see where Mr. Lara is re-forming the lancers and dragoons?"

"Yes sir."

"Ride over there as fast as you can. My fondest compliments to Mr. Lara and ask if he'd be so kind as to continue harrying the enemy flank. Quick strikes only, no committed charges."

"Like what Rangers are more used to," Boogerbear said. "Run in, raise hell—then get the hell out an' reload!" Lewis looked at him and frowned, eyes slipping over to Leonor's. She was still up behind the big Ranger on his horse, and both had the barrels off of their Paterson Colts, using the required tool to reload each chamber. "Yes, exactly." Lewis refocused on the messenger. "I see Mr. Dukane's battery is near him, firing into the enemy rear. Give him my compliments as well and tell him to attach his howitzers to Mr. Lara. Mr. Burton's remaining dragoons will come join us here."

"Where are we goin'?" Leonor asked.

Lewis tilted his head to the left. "I've fought against the former General Agon several times. I think it's time I fought *with* him."

"How exciting!" Varaa said, clapping her hands.

Willis grumbled something unintelligible.

"I'm gonna need another horse," Leonor said.

———————

Major Giles Anson, his Rangers, riflemen, and Holcanos, and most of the 3rd Pennsylvania had hastily fortified what amounted to another step down below Barca's guns on the slippery, now mostly muddy heights. They'd already endured a couple of costly enemy attempts to dislodge them and regain the position, and the guns above hadn't been any help. They simply couldn't depress far enough. Besides, they had other business to attend to. The pounding roar of the things had been hard on the men so close below them, however. All were somewhat stunned by the dagger-in-the-ears reports and overpressure that made them feel like their guts were being squeezed out their mouth and left men crawling and puking. Quite a few had been deafened, at least temporarily, and many with bleeding ears would probably never hear the same again. Anyone who had anything they could stuff in their ears or wrap around their heads had done so. Anson himself had pushed a pair of pistol balls into his ears. That helped. He'd worry about how to get them out later.

On the bright side, the force under Anson's and Ulrich's joint command had been in the perfect place to see the enemy left collapse, then watch 1st Division and then 2nd Division keep pushing its shattered remnants back in disarray—right into another forming enemy line. Some idiot Dom officer gave the order to fire into the fleeing men, just like Anson saw at the Battle of the Washboard. Even he'd been appalled by such barbarism (it took a lot to unsettle Anson after some of the things he'd seen in his life), particularly since that force back then had been retreating in good order and then just stood and took its insane punishment. These Doms today were infuriated by the act and attacked the secondary line themselves even as they smashed their way through it and broke it apart. Anson couldn't see anything organized left in front of Reed's and Har-Kaaska's rampaging divisions on that side of the valley.

They'd been in the middle of fighting off a Dom attack on their own position at the time, but cheered themselves hoarse regardless. Even more exciting, the chaos on the far side of the battlefield had left the "new" left flank of the Doms in front of Agon flapping in the breeze, curling back and starting to fray, while Agon's 4th Division shot and stabbed and stomped its way forward, pushing back those bleeding, desperate ranks in front of it yards at a time as well. But there were more fresh Dom reserves over here at the base of the heights than elsewhere, and they were rebuilding the line. They couldn't stretch it out back across the valley or attempt to flank Agon. Reed had been canny enough to leave enough regiments in place to prevent that. *He might not be as aggressive a campaigner as Lewis*, Anson thought, *but put him in a fight an' he fights. Does it right too.*

Unfortunately, though surrendering the bulk of his remaining army to inevitable envelopment, the Dom commander could continue his force's movement back into a vaguely rectangular semicircle right at the base of the bluff below. Anson's, Ulrich's, Meder's, and Barca's positions were increasingly precarious. It was a dream in the sense that they had a fortified lodgment with hundreds of crack infantry and eight field pieces stabbed right in the enemy's back, but also a nightmare because, despite horrific losses, there were probably at least twenty thousand Doms left down there. Anson and Ulrich might still have fifteen to eighteen hundred combined, including the artillerymen.

"Well," Ulrich said philosophically, and it quickly became clear he was thinking along the same lines when he added, "with Agon still kickin' 'em and Third Division finally comin' up—and the rest of First and Second Divisions sauntering back as they feel like it," he continued a little bitterly, "the Doms can't all come at us up here at once." He grinned at Anson. His face was bloody and blackened with powder spilled from paper cartridges he'd torn open with his teeth. "Sooo, five-to-one odds at most, I figure." A gun up above them roared, exploding a case shot among the farthest enemy troops. Ulrich shook his head and worked his jaw, trying to pop his ears. "Trouble is, climbing over us may be their only way out of that mess."

Anson scratched his beard, looking from the enemy below to the guns up above. "Only one way up here, though. The same trail the enemy used to get their own guns up. I mean, sure, the Doms can try to climb the bluffs, but we'd murder 'em. We can bring a couple of our guns down to cover that approach. Thing is, Lewis is too smart ta trap 'em like rats. They'll fight like fiends if he does that. He may do it for a while, to make 'em desperate enough to surrender, but if there ain't a way for 'em to get out an' stream up the valley, he'll open one up."

"Are you sure?" Ulrich asked.

Anson nodded. "Better he leaves a beat, disorganized enemy runnin' for their lives than he seals the bastards up an' leaves 'em with nothin' ta lose, an' nothin' left for 'em but ta take as many of us with 'em as they can. He generally has his eye set half a dozen steps ahead—I couldn't do it," he confessed. "But Lewis'll want to save as much of his army as he can for the battles ahead."

"Seems he'd want to wipe 'em out if he can so he doesn't have to fight 'em again."

Anson shook his head. "Too costly, too bloody, an' it'll be easier fightin' men who've already run. Mark my words. He'll let a good bunch of 'em go."

"Well, I wish he'd hurry," Ulrich said, gesturing down at the bottom of the bluff. Another assault, heavier than before, was preparing to come at them while 3rd and 4th Divisions had wrapped around the enemy, pressing hard, smoke swirling up from savage volleys. Much of 1st Division was forming back up on the move some distance away on a front that would converge on the enemy below as well. Interestingly, 2nd Division seemed to have split, part of it rampaging through the enemy camp, keeping the Doms running in front of them, while the other half was overrunning the guns the enemy hadn't already pulled out. Anson waved a couple of Holcano runners forward. "Do you understand me?" he asked in Spanya. Both men nodded. "One o' you devils scamper up to Captain Barca. Tell him I want one of his sections down on the track the Doms used to get up here." He pointed. "The rest of his crews'll dig holes for their guns' wheels, block up the trails, hell, put 'em on the slope an' tie the trails to trees if he has to. Barca's an imaginative kid, an' I want him to do whatever it takes to get fire down past us." He looked at the other messenger. "Get Kisin an' the rest of the Holcanos an' all the Rangers an' riflemen down there to support Barca's section on the road." He looked at Ulrich. "Might have to send some of your boys over there too."

"Just say when," Ulrich agreed. Glancing down at the building assault, just out of musket shot at present, he said, "I'll be holding here with just over five hundred men. I'll send them—if I've got them to send."

"Fair enough," Anson said, moving back out of the line of fire, where his horse and some of his Rangers waited.

CHAPTER 27

ood morning again, Colonel Agon, Major Arevalo," Lewis said
loudly but pleasantly over the constant snarl of musketry as he
rode up behind the former Dom general and his aide. Both were
calmly sitting their horses right behind the firing line, and it was impossible to miss that Agon's custom-tailored green uniform had a number of
holes in it. One on his arm near his elbow oozed blood. "Almost afternoon,"
Lewis continued with some surprise, consulting the watch he pulled from
the slash pocket on his jacket.

"Coronel Cayce!" Agon exclaimed, shouting over another thunderous
volley. "What are you doing here, so close to the action? You cannot risk
yourself so."

"He does it all the damn time, draggin' the rest of us along," Corporal
Willis grumped, gazing around at the scattered bodies. Most wore yellow
and black, but there were quite a few in mottled green. Walking wounded
were helping their more badly injured comrades back from the line. Agon
seemed taken aback by the outspoken Willis.

"I might point out that you're quite exposed yourself, Colonel Agon,"
Lewis observed.

Agon looked down. "Yes, but . . . I have a great deal more to prove
than you."

Lewis snorted. "Your loyalty? Commitment to our cause? Nonsense. I was convinced of those things long ago. Why else would I have put you on the front line of battle?"

Arevalo pursed his lips. "With Third Division directly behind us, watching us."

Lewis nodded at him. "I'm sure that reassured some in the army, but I had no doubts. Nor will anyone else after today. And Third Division is now doing what it was originally intended to."

Arevalo seemed satisfied.

Lewis nodded forward. "How is it going?"

Agon frowned. "The enemy fights very well, with tremendous determination." He took a long breath and sighed. "They are better soldiers than my 'Army of God' when we faced you before." He straightened in the saddle. "They are not as good as we are now. One supreme difference is the purity of our cause that all my men share. We also have much better training now, our muskets are more lethal—and they simply can't stand against our superior bayonets. Those—and the fortitude of our men—are the primary reasons we have achieved our current dominance."

"Dominance," Corporal Willis huffed, cringing from the passage of projectiles. Real or imagined. "Am I the only one that's wonderin' what we're all doin' still sittin' up high on horses an' makin' such pretty targets?"

"We damn sure have better bayonets," Leonor agreed fervently with Agon, ignoring Willis as usual.

Agon looked curiously at the blood-washed woman on the captured Dom horse, then gazed back at Lewis. "We have them pinned here, and much of First Division has formed back up and is marching to extend Third Division's line and trap them in place."

Lewis hesitated. "About that . . ." He pointed. "You can see the enemy is already assailing our men on the heights. They're badly outnumbered, and only the artillery has preserved them. But the guns will be low on ammunition by now. More has been sent, but there's no telling how long it'll take to arrive. I'm confident Major Anson and Major Ulrich will hold no matter the cost, but at this point in our campaign I'm not ready to pay it. I simply can't spare them and their men." He looked intently at Agon. "I can't spare you and yours either. I never intended for this to turn into a costly massacre of an intact, trapped force. I meant to break them and slaughter them as they fled. If these were the only Doms we ever had to face, I'd press it to a conclusion regardless. That's not the case today, however, and a victory that expensive would be no victory at all." He sighed. "From a practical standpoint, against a rational foe, we would've already won the day, and General Gomez—if he lives—would know he was beaten and would be anxious to save what he could and withdraw. Since we don't see any evidence of that, perhaps *now* is the time to talk to him, if we can." He gestured behind at the approach of Don Hurac's bizarre carriage. "Time to let *him* talk, as the legitimate 'Supreme Holiness.' Father Orno and you as well. It might do some good. If not, we'll open a small gate in the trap and start letting the enemy out." He held up a hand. "Don't worry. First Division will tear them apart as they run the gauntlet, and the enemy will do themselves more harm than we can inflict by fighting among themselves to get past. After that, we'll press them, harry them, *shatter* them as they flee and prevent them from re-forming to establish another strongpoint." His expression turned hard. "Those that escape—that survive our pursuit—will never be the same soldiers we fought here today."

Agon considered that, eyes drawn to the scattered corpses and continuing stream of wounded, not to mention the men in the firing line crying out and falling even as he watched. He looked back at Lewis. "This is what you planned all along," he stated. It wasn't a question.

"Yes," Varaa confirmed for Lewis. "The outcome Lewis described, that is. We are not yet there, and various steps we have taken along the way have required Colonel Cayce to choose . . . alternatives. The enemy makes his choices as well, you know. Still, it is in that skill"—Varaa shook her head, blinking—"perhaps 'knack' is a better word, that Lewis and his young officers shine most brightly."

Agon was nodding. "I tend to agree." He paused. "And it seems fitting, after all, that the enemy should be given the same final choice that I was allowed, the same one Gomez would've likely given us this morning: 'join or die.'"

"How can you say that?" Arevalo demanded, glaring at his commander. "It is not the same at all! The first option Don Frutos—who led us at the time—offered Colonel Cayce and the people of the Yucatán was '*submit* or die,' and that is *not* the same. Later, the only alternatives were to 'die well in battle or ignominiously in surrender.' You'd equate those even now that you have learned the God we served"—he pointed at the enemy—"that they *still* serve, can only be the devil?"

Agon took a long breath and shook his head. "No, Arevalo. You are right, as usual." He waved helplessly around, the roar of battle still intense, the *vip* and warble of musket balls still thick around them. "I fear that even as I yearned to crush this current enemy, memories and feelings from that other day opened a freshly healed wound." He offered Lewis a sad smile. "Like Gomez will, I am sure, I well remember that you beat me . . . and my soul is glad of it. My heart?" He shrugged. "It sometimes sees things less clearly, and there are occasional beats of regret. I hope we won't both regret not utterly smashing General Gomez."

"As do I," Lewis agreed.

"Very well," Agon said. "The enemy apparently understands the concept of parley, having tried it with us already. Perhaps now they will be ready to listen to alternatives to whatever they thought this day would bring." Agon looked around. "Major Arevalo, pass the word. We'll try a white flag as the enemy did. If they slacken fire, so shall we. If not . . ." He looked at Lewis.

"We'll bring the rest of the guns up on line and smother them with shot," Lewis said.

It wasn't long before several white flags—possibly sheets brought forward from Don Hurac's carriage—were waving in clear view of the enemy. Shouts were heard from the opposing lines and a similar flag was displayed.

"Cease firing!" shouted Colonel Tun, echoed by Arevalo as he galloped down the line. Other officers took up the shout. Soon, at least there in front of 4th Division, no one was firing anymore. Men just stood, the front ranks of their forces leaning on their muskets barely fifty yards apart, gasping steamy breaths and wiping freezing sweat from their faces. The fighting on the heights and in front of 3rd Division actually seemed to intensify, if that was possible, but it might've just been the sudden near silence here that made it seem that way.

"You want to talk, yes?" came a bellowed query in Spanya from behind the Dom infantry.

"We do," Agon shouted back.

"Why now and not before?" demanded the same voice. "You are losing, yes?"

Agon looked at Lewis as if to ask if he should continue. Lewis nodded.

"No," Agon shouted. "But our fight has reached a point where we will soon be forced to destroy you all if we continue."

"Try!" came the almost laughing response.

"I would rather not," Agon shot back after a glance behind him confirmed that Don Hurac and his entourage, including Father Orno and a ragged-looking Reverend Harkin (a bloodstained sling supporting his left arm), were hurrying forward. "More important, the rightful Supreme Holiness of the Dominion would not have it so. I'm sure your men would prefer a different fate as well," he added with a touch of sarcasm.

"You speak of the pretender, Don Hurac? He is here?"

Agon snorted loudly. "The only 'pretender' hides in a stolen temple in the Great Valley."

There was a long silence—except for a growing rumble from the enemy troops. Few if any would've been aware the throne—or whatever it was—of His Supreme Holiness was contested, but Don Hurac's name would be known by many.

"You lie!" came a clipped response, drowned by more shouting. When a voice arose to speak again, it came from a different source. "We shall meet in the space between our armies. If I do not see Don Hurac with my own eyes, our fight will resume as before."

"What of the fighting elsewhere?" Agon asked, the noise of battle still loud.

"It goes on . . . for now."

Agon looked at Lewis.

"Horseshit," Boogerbear said. He'd been uncharacteristically silent. "You didn't ask, but that's what I think," he elaborated. Leonor nodded her agreement. "The whole thing smells."

"In this case, I'm inclined to go along with the other female warrior in our midst—and the upright bear as well," Varaa said, grinning at the big Ranger. Clearly, like "badger" for her father, Leonor's description of the bearded giant had stayed in Varaa's mind.

"I b'lieve Major Anson once called you a 'self-absorbed, bug-eyed possum,'" Boogerbear retorted under his breath. "I added the 'bug-eyed' part."

Varaa blinked and clapped her delight.

Don Hurac and his companions had drawn near enough to hear the demand, however. "I accept," the Blood Cardinal said a little breathlessly. "Please inform the enemy commander that I will meet with him." Father Orno and Reverend Harkin looked equally determined to accompany him. "We must end this bloodshed now, if we can," Don Hurac added.

Agon looked at him a long moment, then nodded agreement himself.

Without even glancing at Lewis, he raised his voice again. "Very well. In the interests of humanity, Don Hurac has consented to meet with your commander between the lines. We will bring him out with a suitable escort. Your commander may do the same." He hesitated. "Surrounded as we'll all be by thousands of men with loaded weapons, I think you'll agree that it's pointless for us to expect each other to disarm. I warn you, though, if Don Hurac is harmed or there's treachery of any sort, we will kill every last one of you, soldiers, camp followers, even draft animals. Do I make myself clear?"

"You do," came the voice.

"This is an unacceptable risk and will not bear fruit," Varaa said lowly, grimly. "I wasn't sure before, but now I am. No demeaning taunts or threats in return? No protestations of invincibility? Whether there is treachery or not, whoever we're speaking to is playing for time."

"They're still trying to bash over Father—I mean Major Anson—an' Ulrich an' Barca on the heights," Leonor added. "I agree with Varaa."

"So do I," Lewis said. "But unlike yesterday . . . maybe now they've suffered enough to be tempted by what we offer." He looked at Agon. "We must do this quickly, however, or not at all."

Agon jerked a nod. "Who goes? Not you, Colonel Cayce," he quickly added.

Lewis arched his eyebrows. "Of course I'm going. From a practical command standpoint, you're the only one among us here who shouldn't. On the other hand, I think your presence might have an . . . interesting effect, particularly if you're recognized by any of the enemy officers." Stepping down from Arete at last, quickly followed by a relieved Corporal Willis, Lewis handed his reins to one of Agon's troops and nodded respectfully at Don Hurac. "What happened to you, Mr. Harkin?" he asked, indicating the sling the minister wore.

"As you may recall, I joined the fighting with First Division. The First Ocelomeh Regiment, in fact. The volume of fire was amazing, sir. Amazing. I couldn't possibly keep up with my rifle, but felt honored to be among those spirited lads." He held up his arm and lamented, "This is just a scratch, but far too many of those fine young men fell around me. Fine fellows indeed, every one."

"Are you ready to speak to the enemy?" Lewis asked.

Harkin straightened. "I am, sir."

"And you, Father Orno? How will you convince them to lay down their arms?"

The diminutive priest spread his arms at his side. "If allowed to speak, I will simply tell them the truth."

Lastly, Lewis's gaze fell on Don Hurac. "And you?"

Don Hurac cleared his throat. "I shall remind them that according to the very laws of the church they fight to defend, I am the only true and rightful successor to its leadership. The usurper and his abominable Blood Priests are the cause of this strife and all the irregularities currently in the land. I will then endeavor to explain how they have been most sinfully misled and the god they serve is false. Only I can lead them to a reconciliation with the true word, which has been so twisted."

"Fine," Lewis said, beginning to lead them all forward to the eerily quiet firing line. Tired, powder-smudged men, many of whom were lightly wounded, moved almost reverently aside as they passed. "But remember, they see you—and this army—as the 'irregularities.' That whole monologue might take too long if you want to catch their attention at once and actually get them thinking about throwing their support to you." He gestured to Agon, Varaa, Leonor, and Boogerbear. "None of us thinks this parley is sincere. They're just grabbing for time with both hands, and we can't let them have it. Get their attention quickly, Don Hurac. I know you're well-spoken. Don't waste time explaining anything. We're not supplicants here. *Command* them. That's what . . . 'Supreme Holinesses' do, is it not? You'll have all the time in the world to explain things later if you can get them to listen now. At present, we just want the fighting to end so we can save lives and continue our campaign. Give them a reason to agree to that. Pitch it to them hot and fast, and I suspect we'll know pretty quickly if there's a chance to stop this or not." He started to push through the front ranks of the firing line.

"Wait!" cried Leonor, grabbing his arm. "*You* ain't gonna just walk out there!"

"Why not?"

"What if that's what they want an' they're just waitin' to shoot whatever fool officer comes out to talk? I doubt they think *you'd* be stupid enough, but they're already expectin' Don Hurac. This is their chance to get 'eem. There might be a hundred men with orders to shoot at whoever steps out from the line."

Lewis paused for an instant and nodded with a smile, patting her hand until she removed it. "That's certainly possible. In that case I guess we'll have our answer even quicker." He looked at Boogerbear. "Hold her back a moment or two, if you please, Mr. Beeryman. You may be the only one who can manage it without serious injury." Lewis continued to smile as he pressed on into the open. Being taller than nearly all of Agon's troops, he'd already seen a gathering of enemy officers in the space between the armies. If they did intend to shoot, those men would be in the line of fire. Considering how Doms had behaved in the past, such a thing wasn't impossible, but he believed the risk was worth it. If even for a moment, the sight of just him and then Agon stepping confidently out to meet the enemy before their surprised escort and the rest of their party caught up could have a strong effect on the morale of both sides. *A good prank on Leonor too*, Lewis thought, already appraising the men before him. *She'll make me suffer for it, though*, he knew.

"Paradise awaits!" one of the taller, thinner Dom officers in a senior officer's uniform with silver lace and buttons on the yellow and black exclaimed in surprise, eyes going wide at the sight of Agon. Arevalo was breathing hard, having rushed to catch up. "We knew you had lost an army or two, and there were dark rumors you'd been taken captive, but I never thought to see you alive, much less in league with heretics!" The man waved to draw the attention of his companions, as if that were necessary. "This, gentlemen, is indeed General Agon, former commander of the Eastern Army of God. An army that no longer exists, I'm afraid. We were junior officers together—and there is no mistaking his short, round form!" The handful of Agon's guards and Lewis's dragoon escorts, including Corporal Hannity, and then Boogerbear and Varaa and a fuming Leonor, quickly surrounded Lewis and Agon. A put-upon-looking Willis brought up the rear with Don Hurac, Reverend Harkin, and Father Orno.

To the Dom officer's further surprise, Agon and Arevalo saluted him. "What's this? Don't be absurd, Agon. We may be enemies now, and it is my duty to destroy you, but we hold the same rank—and surely we are still friends!"

"In the Army of the Yucatán"—Agon glanced at Lewis—"the 'American' army we have made, I have the honor to command a division as a *coronel*." Looking back at Lewis, he continued, "Coronel Cayce, may I present General Debero de la Montaña de la Costa. Prisoners have informed us that he is second in command of the Army of God in the West, under General Gomez. Debero and I once . . . knew each other quite well."

Lewis also saluted, as did the dragoons around him. Leonor, Varaa, and Boogerbear didn't. Honoring an enemy they were trying to kill struck them as hypocritical. Still, Debero was clearly taken aback by the courtesy and tried to conceal it by quickly naming his other officers. Lewis was intrigued to see no Blood Priests present, or reaper monks in brown tunics among the enemy officers. Some of the latter were mingled with troops on the firing line, but none were brought out to meet them. Completing his introductions, Debero stared quizzically at Lewis.

"So, you are the *notorio* Coronel Cayce. I have heard a great deal about you. A most dangerous and troublesome opponent, by all accounts—though none of those have been firsthand, and I'm sure certain aspects of your reputation have been exaggerated." He stroked his chin whiskers thoughtfully. "Though perhaps the important ones have not." Measuring Lewis's height and broad shoulders with his eyes, he snorted amusement. "Actually *bigger* than I expected as well! How frequently is that the case?" His gaze drifted to Leonor and Varaa. "Nor do you disappoint in other respects. Not only are you attended by a defector, a female officer, and an inhuman demon, you've made a creditable army of barbarian rabble and . . . temporarily inconvenienced our rather larger, more civilized force. I commend you!"

Lewis smiled wryly, cocking his head to the sound of battle from the enemy's left and rear. "You're too gracious, sir, and I'm afraid I've not heard your name before." He regarded Agon and Don Hurac. "I know little enough about General Gomez except that he is 'capable.' Is he here?" Debero shook his head. "He is not. He remains in consultation with our superiors in the Holy City." He shook his head at Agon. "Nor am I truly his second. His actual deputy, a religiously zealous clerk from Don Hurac's own Yellow Temple offices, was chosen for him by Obispo de Sachihiro and a . . . disagreeable Blood Priest named Father Tranquilo. Sachihiro enjoys the new title of Primer Patriarca. Are you familiar with it? I was not. It seems he has . . . quite extraordinary influence over the recently elevated Supreme Holiness. In any event, Gomez's deputy was either struck on the head by a fragment of one of your charming exploding cannon shot or fell off his horse and landed on his head—no one is quite sure—before he could lend his martial genius to this day's proceedings. He is expected to live, at present, but of course, one never knows about head injuries."

"Then it's been your strategy we've been fighting today," Lewis surmised. "I congratulate you on how quickly you adjusted it."

"And I you, on how rapidly you countered my efforts."

Leonor rolled her eyes. "There's still fightin'. Men are still dyin'. Can we adjourn this mutual admiration society meetin' an' get on with it?"

"She's right," Lewis agreed. "We're not here to exchange pleasantries. There isn't time for that, and I personally joined this delegation to ask you to consider surrender"—he gestured to the clerics—"and present the esteemed Reverend Samuel Harkin, Father Orno, and His Eminence, the Blood Cardinal Don Hurac el Bendito, rightful Supreme Holiness in line of succession to rule the Holy Dominion. They'll tell you why you should surrender, and I hope you'll hear them out. Either way, let's keep it brief. We either have to stop further killing or get on with finishing our fight."

"Hear him, Debero," Agon urged, "and I beg you to hear Don Hurac with your souls as well as your ears. He is *no* Don Frutos, the Blood Cardinal who wallows in depravity with the Blood Priests, led my first army to its doom before fleeing to safety himself, and has no doubt been intimately involved in the treachery now guiding your actions." At least half the Dom officers gave him hostile looks, but a few seemed thoughtful.

Don Hurac cleared his throat, and to Lewis's surprise, every Dom officer faced him respectfully. Each of them knew him, or of him, and regardless who they hailed as Supreme Holiness, he was a Blood Cardinal of note and commanded their deference. *It's also just possible he'll win*, Lewis thought cynically. *Best they at least appear sympathetic.*

"My children," Don Hurac began loud enough for even many nearby troops to hear while he extended his arms as if embracing them all. "You were called to defend the Holy Dominion, and you came—as you should—but the men you fight here are not your enemy. They are merely people, like you, who wish to live in peace with their families."

"They are heretics!" someone shouted, and Lewis thought he saw movement in the enemy ranks, more brown tunics than before.

"They are not," Don Hurac said firmly, and Lewis tensed, fearing the Blood Cardinal would launch into a sermon denouncing his own people's beliefs. No one would hear him after that, and the fighting would resume at once. He didn't do it. Instead, he merely continued in the vein he'd begun.

"Nor did they start this war we now wage. Many lived so far away, on the distant Yucatán, we would never have even known each other existed in our lifetimes if the Dominion continued to expand at its historic and traditional rate." He pointed south. "For the most part, a vast wilderness still lies between us." He frowned. "But unholy men of power within the Dominion saw an opportunity to broaden and deepen their rule by advancing a dread agenda of total control through terror." He nodded. "You have all seen it; I know you have. Even far to the west where most of you came from, and its roots are not yet so deep." He waved at Agon's troops. "The Dominion attacked *them*, and when God rewarded them with victory, instead of being properly chastised and penitent, those unholy men—and I was still one of them!—could not let the humiliation of that defeat stand. Yet another army was sent, and my dear General Agon was beaten once more. He saw the light, as did I, and we both understood that God did not favor our aggression.

"But the blasphemous creatures lurking in the Great Valley and the sacred Holy City chose to forge ahead with their evil plot, murdering our beloved Blood Cardinal Don Datu, who was next in line of succession, declaring *me* an outlaw heretic enemy so I could be cast aside, and installing their own drug-addled, empty-headed puppet—Don Julio DeDivino Dicha—as Supreme Holiness. He actively aided and abetted his ascension, so he is not without blame, but he is merely the mask behind which the true usurpers"—his lips twisted in disgust—"the evil enemies of God and all the people called 'Blood Priests' plot and scheme toward total control, the enslavement of all our people, and the blood-drenched suppression of any dissent. They are the creatures we oppose today, in the name of the One True God, and who benefit from every drop of blood you spill."

Don Hurac still held his hands out at his sides, looking down in a pose of humble supplication, and there was almost utter silence for a moment, broken only by the rumble of battle all around. "This is what I and these good priests beside me came to say to you. Unlike the Blood Priests, we do not want your blood to bathe and wallow in, nor would we revel in your misery. Others of our army were even more like all of you—some of the meager few survivors of *Dominion* towns and cities the Blood Priests sought to eradicate simply for witnessing our opposition. They will kill everything that undermines their power! I ask you, knowing that, can you still fight for them? Join us, I beg, for the salvation of all our souls!"

In the silence that still prevailed, he looked into the face of General Debero, who seemed deeply moved. Others of his officers had been struck by a sudden growing anger, though it was impossible to say whether that was because of what they'd learned or simply due to what Don Hurac said. The Blood Cardinal looked at Agon, then Lewis, and shrugged as if to say, "I'm done."

General Debero cleared his throat to speak, but a loud voice behind him shouted first, "Heretics! Criminals! Enemies of God!"

"Kill them all!" roared another. Lewis didn't believe an ordinary Dom soldier would dare shout out like that from the ranks, and he was right. Quite a few more men in brown tunics were pushing their way to the front of the firing line, raising their weapons.

"General Debero," he said urgently. "I think you should . . ."

A limited, ragged, but still robust volley suddenly crashed out from the Dom line, mostly smashing into the cluster of their own officers. Almost without exception, those junior officers at the rear of the delegation (and closest to the fire) were hurled to the ground. Many others were struck as well. General Debero himself acted as if he'd been punched in the back, and a spray of blood erupted from his chest. Even as he stumbled against Don Hurac, coughing a red torrent upon the Blood Cardinal, Don Hurac was struck in the shoulder and violently spun around. Together, he and Debero crashed to the ground.

For an instant, as other men reacted to their wounds, falling, staring in incomprehension, or crying out in pain, there was otherwise a terrible silence, the majority on both sides looking on in confusion and horror. Nor were all these other victims Doms. Reverend Harkin stumbled, fresh blood spreading swiftly on his red-smudged sling as he leaned heavily against Father Orno. Two of the dragoons crumpled silently and fell on their faces. Agon himself, face pale, sat heavily in the slushy mud.

"Oh, shit," Boogerbear said calmly, drawing a revolver as Leonor shoved hard against Lewis, trying to propel him back to their lines. He shook her off, drawing his saber.

"¡Dejar de disparar!" a surviving Dom officer desperately roared, trying to stop the shooting. Even Lewis could see that only the reaper monks had done it and nearby regular soldiers were already upon them, fighting to keep them from reloading. It was a feeble, insufficient effort. A clot of perhaps sixty reapers, weapons lowered, bayonets firmly inserted, were now swarming out toward the decimated delegation, and Colonel Tun's strong voice could already be heard, bellowing for the 3rd Regiment of the 4th Division to charge.

"Protect the injured," Lewis shouted.

Boogerbear had rushed to Orno and Harkin and swept them both up to drop beside Don Hurac, who was struggling to pull himself out from under General Debero. He was covered in blood but didn't seem badly injured himself. The ball that struck him must've been mostly spent—the same one that passed through Debero first. Agon's aides were pulling their commander over to the others. He was breathing hard, but no blood ran from his mouth.

"What's the matter with you?" Leonor snapped at Lewis as she joined the pitiful, ragged line of men preparing to defend the fallen, drawing both of her revolvers. "You command our *army*. Let the Third do this." Lewis quickly hugged her to him, then gestured at their meager line with his saber. Besides themselves, Varaa, and Boogerbear, there were three dragoons, six of Agon's guards, and half a dozen Dom officers who'd come out with Debero. They were about the same distance from both lines, and the 3rd of the 4th was running, screaming with rage, but the reapers had known what was coming and were closer. Varaa gestured at them with the musket she'd unslung, its bayonet fixed, the closest enemies just steps away now. "They'll get here first" was all she had time to say before expertly deflecting an enemy bayonet and driving her own into its wielder's throat.

The dragoons' Hall carbines barked, and they quickly dropped them and drew their own sabers while Leonor and Boogerbear began shooting reapers in the face. Their Paterson Colts might be underpowered, but they were extremely accurate in their practiced hands. Most of their targets screamed and dropped dead, but a few screamed louder and longer as they tried to flee from what hurt them. Immediately lethal or not, getting shot in the face tends to refocus an attacker's priorities. Lewis killed opponent after opponent simply by dodging or deflecting their bayonet thrusts and grasping their weapons as he stepped inside their reach to slash or stab them to death with his saber. Assailants around them who might've taken advantage of his vulnerability were the primary recipients of Leonor's and Boogerbear's pistol shots.

One of Agon's guards was the first to fall screaming with a Dom bayonet in his belly. A dragoon quickly followed, victim of a similar wound. Boogerbear took a slash on his arm, but it didn't seem to affect him in the least. Even Varaa was driven back, stunned, struck in the face by a steel-shod musket butt. By then, however, after only a handful of seconds, the 3rd of the 4th was already sweeping around the beleaguered officers, shooting and bayonetting every reaper they saw. Possibly unfortunately, they didn't stop there, smashing straight on into the Dom infantry line, roaring their fury. With General Debero quite obviously dead, no one would ever know if he might've been swayed, but every member of the 4th Division had seen the delegation attacked, and most of the 3rd Regiment saw Agon go down. Even if Colonel Tun's order to charge had been specifically aimed at the reapers, which it wasn't, the men of the 3rd would've only heard "Charge." And of course, when all the other regiments saw *them* race forward to the attack, their officers would naturally assume they should do so as well.

On the Dom side, a surprisingly large number of troops was fully aware that the reapers had not only broken the truce but killed many of their own officers to do it. Furious themselves and without those officers to direct them, they were more focused on hunting the reapers among them than facing the enemy for a few fateful moments. Thus, when the frenzied charge of the 4th Division, then the 3rd, swept forward, they were taken largely by surprise.

With Father Orno's help, Don Hurac had managed to rise. Now he ranted impotently at the furious fighting in front of him. Lewis said nothing but felt much the same. The frenzied bloodletting the reapers had unleashed was precisely what he'd hoped to avoid.

"Didn't work after all," Varaa said awkwardly around a split lip, blood wetting the fur on her face.

"It might have," Lewis said darkly, glancing sadly at Debero's corpse. Agon was sitting up again, grimacing in pain, but clearly just as upset as Don Hurac. "You men," Lewis called to his and Agon's surviving guards, now heavily reinforced. "Kindly escort our wounded to the surgeons and the, uh, clergymen to the rear. The enemy officers who stood with us as well. See that they're not harmed." He looked around at the others, eyes finding Corporal Willis. The man was holding an ornate, bloody sword. "Where did you get that?" he asked.

"Offa one o' them dead Dom officers. Didn't loot him," Willis added defensively, "just took this here sword, seein' as how he didn't need it no more."

"Well . . . I'm sure it will give you great comfort," Lewis told him. "Now let's get our horses and rejoin the battle"—he frowned—"which I was beginning to think might almost be over." He paused to watch the fighting for a moment before glancing up at the heights beyond where Anson, Ulrich, and Barca were enduring a heavy push. "Which it might just be, if our friends over there can't hold."

CHAPTER 28

Trail right . . . *Right*, damn you!" Hanny Cox screamed as his half-scratch crew manhandled his Number Two gun down the steep, ragged, slush-muddy road *toward* the enemy. "Why is that always so bloody hard to understand?" They were easing the one-ton weapon down the slippery grade, muzzle forward, with two men on each wheel, one on each side of the trail, and the rest—his own extended crew and all the members of the 3rd Pennsylvania he'd picked up—sliding down behind it clinging to the prolong rope. A couple of times, one of those men on the trail had actually stood on it to help slow the gun's descent. After the long, exhausting night and morning, the misery of the snow and now-freezing mud, then hard fighting up above, this maneuver took the cake. At least it was *his* gun and not the much heavier captured weapon they'd been serving. Getting one of those down on the small flat Ulrich had chosen as the best position to stop the growing Dom assault might've been beyond them under these conditions. And pulling it out back up the hill if they had to abandon the position would've been practically impossible. So Hanny's 6pdr and Dodd's Number One gun were back together under Petty's section command—as so often seemed the case—rushing to join the rest of the 3rd Pennsylvania and all of Anson's dismounted Rangers, Holcanos, and riflemen. They were here to stop what seemed like the whole Dom army from crashing over them like a heavy wave on the beach and swarming on over the hill they'd taken and defended all day.

Major Ulrich roared and a musket volley crashed out at the teeming enemy just as Hanny saw Petty gesturing at a space to the left of where Dodd and his crew were hastily emplacing their gun. "Trail left!" Hanny shouted again, and Hoziki and Naxa heaved the trail over, and Hahessy tried to slow his right-hand wheel from turning. "Forward!" Hanny called, then "Trail right!" Preacher Mac slipped and fell, trying to brake the left wheel, but the infantryman helping him managed the task as the trail was shifted right. Preacher Mac scrabbled to get out of the way as Hanny called, "Forward," once more and the gun rolled and slipped up where Petty had been pointing—uncomfortably close to the Number One gun. "Trail down," Hanny shouted through the storm of Dom musket balls whipping past in answer to Ulrich's volley. Several men on the firing line fell, splinters sprayed from a spoke, and one of the Pennsylvania boys helping Dodd cried out and dropped, rocking on the ground and screaming. The Rangers and riflemen opened up, giving cover for the artillerymen scrambling to ready their guns. Dodd's 6pdr fired a blast of canister, the pressure so close pounding the ears and bodies of Hanny's men, already feverishly leveling the frigid mud with their boots and hands while "tamping it down" by heaving the gun back and forth across it. Other men frantically hurled rocks, tree limbs, and old deadfall trunks up over in front of the gun. Even the corpses of a few Doms who'd made it this far before Anson chose the spot to stop them were thrown on the pile.

"Load canister!" Hanny bellowed over the battle roar.

"Your limber chest ain't down yet!" Dodd shouted at him.

"So?" Petty growled. "He can feed his gun from yours till it is!"

"But I'll run short!" Dodd complained. "I'm already short!"

"Apo, Billy Randall, and a couple more infantrymen are bringing the last full chest from the caissons," Hanny assured him. "When we empty that, we won't be short, we'll be done!" He glanced at Petty, who nodded.

"That's a fact—unless they've brung more up behind us since we came down here. They were supposed to."

Shoving the load of canister in the barrel for Hahessy to ram down, Preacher Mac called, "Cap'n Barca passed by us tae check on the guns above. Said he'd be back with more ammunition!"

"That's fine," Petty growled, "but he can't miracle it up outa nothin', can he?"

"A week's pay says he does, Mr. Petty," Hanny called back.

"Sergeant er lieutenant's pay?" Hahessy asked with a grin. Each private soldier made a *reale* a day, an eighth of a *dolor* (or dollar, as most of the men called it), and that went up with rank.

"Lieutenant's," Hanny said confidently.

"Yer on," Petty replied. "An' I'll be happy ta pay up."

Hanny nodded at Private Hoziki, acting as Number Three, indicating satisfaction with how the farmer's son from Frontera had roughly pointed the gun with the handspike. With the enemy surging closer, careful aiming wasn't required. Hoziki jumped out from behind the gun, nearly tripping, and yelled, "Ready!" as soon as he was clear.

A musket ball hit the ground just a few feet in front of Hanny, spattering him from head to foot with icy mud as it bounded up and clipped a ragged gash in his trouser leg, painfully grazing his calf. Instantly aware that had the ball taken a less fortunate bounce, it would've shattered his shin and he'd have lost the leg, Hanny shuddered even as he shouted, "Fire!" Naxa smartly tugged the lanyard. With a thunderous boom and a yellow-white cloud of smoke, the giant shotgun-like load pummeled the enemy ranks even as the infantry fired another volley.

"Load canister!" Hanny cried, sending Kini Hau racing to Dodd's chest again.

"I only got this one left!" objected the Number Six man, crouching down behind the chest and dropping a round of canister in a gunner's haversack. Dodd's Number Five man would take it forward.

Hanny growled in frustration. "Kini, bring case shot if there is any. We'll cut the fuse for a muzzle burst!"

"I got one o' those," the Number Six man confirmed.

"Where the hell is Apo?" Hanny asked, voice rising in desperation. What good did it do to bring the guns down here if they couldn't feed them? It suddenly struck him that he hadn't heard the guns up above them firing for a while. Not since they were halfway down here, at least. That left him wondering where Captain Barca was as well, and he risked a glance up the slope behind them. Four men were actually pushing and dragging a heavy limber chest down the sloppy road.

"Hurry up, Apo! We're out!" Hanny shouted as loud as he could. That's when he noted a limber hitched to horses just over the top of the rise, as if waiting, apparently to dash down and pull the guns out if they had to—and if they had space to turn it around once it was here. Hanny wasn't sure they did and hoped it wouldn't come to that. Kini handed him the case shot strapped to a sabot to which the powder bag was tied, and Hanny swiftly drove the paper tube fuse he'd already cut into the wooden plug on the front of the shot before giving it back to Kini. The little Uxmalo dropped it in his leather haversack and rushed forward, presenting the haversack to Preacher Mac, who pulled the round back out and inserted it in the muzzle of the gun. Hahessy had been waiting, rammer staff poised to show he was ready, bell-shaped rammer head touching the gun by the front sight. For the last few moments the only real shooting had come from Ranger muske-toons and Meder's riflemen, the latter maintaining a steady, deadly fire, dropping an enemy with every shot. Now Hahessy hesitated just an instant, gazing through a hole in the smoke and out beyond the enemy.

"Damn me if that ain't a sight!" he exclaimed. "Lookie yonder!"

They'd all seen the enemy left fall apart, their lancers and thousands of infantry streaming away up the valley to the northwest, 2nd Division on their heels. Much of the Dom center and right had recoiled back around—straight toward Anson's force—with 4th and now 3rd Divisions pressing them hard. First Division had briefly chased the fleeing mob as well, but most of its regiments had held together, laboriously re-forming and chang-ing their front. Now it was advancing to tie up the sack the rest of the Doms were about to be caught in.

What gave Hahessy pause, however, was that the fighting in front of 4th Division seemed to have stopped. "They're havin' a parley down there or I'm a lascar."

"That may be, ye damn fool Irishman, but nobody's quit shootin' *here*! Gi' on wi' it, will ye?" Preacher Mac snapped.

"But look," Hahessy insisted. "Out past all that. Two whole batteries—one is Dukane's for sure, with his howitzers—are thunderin' out after the Doms that ran off! Pretty a sight as I've seen, it is. Ye can see the mud spray-in' from horse hooves an' wheels from here! *There's* glory for ye. *That's* flyin' artillery, by God. No draggin' their guns up an' down bloody mountains by hand in the dark for them lads! No, an' not in the freezin' snow, neither."

"Finish loadin' that goddamn gun!" Lieutenant Petty roared at him. Hahessy glared back at their officer, but then shrugged and rammed the charge down to the breech before stepping out from between the tube and right wheel.

"Frankly, I wouldn't mind riding into action for a change myself," Hanny lowly agreed with Hahessy as Hoziki shifted the handspike to point their weapon at the closest, thickest concentration of enemies. "It seems we've had to do our horses' work for them in every fight we've been in since Gran Lago."

"Aye, an' no shiftin' aboot fer us, makin' it harder fer the buggers tae hit," Preacher Mac grudgingly conceded as Hoziki pierced the charge through the vent and primed the gun. "We always get stuck on the line with the puir infantry, Doms close enough tae smell! Aye, an' the most of us were *in* the infantry once! That was all supposed tae change!"

"Ready!" shouted Hoziki and Dodd's Number Three at the same time. "Fire!"

At virtually the same instant both 6pdrs spat clouds of death at the enemy, the American and Dom infantry each also chose to fire another volley. The thunderous combination was the most deafening event the nearby participants experienced that day—and possibly also the deadliest. Dodd's final round of canister swept into the enemy and did what canister does; scores of men were chopped apart, hurled shrieking to the ground, or wounded by flying secondary projectiles formed by the shattered equipment—and even shards of bone—of their comrades. Hanny's projectile didn't slay or wound quite as many. Bursting at the muzzle, it was little more effective than it would've been at a thousand yards. There simply weren't as many balls packed into the exploding case—and the shards the case broke into were all different shapes and sizes. A few of the larger, more jagged pieces inflicted ghastlier wounds, perhaps, but that was somewhat relative. Both guns together, at such close range, were more than sufficient to stun the Dom advance.

But everything happened at once. Nearly every American musket struck somebody, .69 caliber balls punching great bloody holes in bodies, smashing limbs, or quite literally voiding skulls. Some who'd been shredded by the cannon blasts had been little more than standing corpses already, the reverse likely true as well. Unfortunately, the Doms had finally moved close enough that even they found it difficult to miss. More men of the 3rd Pennsylvania, many of whom came from another world, dropped where they stood or fell back screaming. The same with Felix Meder's riflemen, Kisin's Holcanos, and Anson's Rangers.

There were also grievous losses among the artillerymen. A disproportionate percentage of enemy fire had been directed at them, after all. Hanny's beloved Number Two gun clattered, cracked, and rang with the impacts of countless projectiles. Hahessy's and Preacher Mac's Number One and Two positions were the most exposed, and their uniforms seemed to explode with little puffs of blue wool fibers, sheared by sharp shards of lead that spattered off the gun's bronze tube and iron tires, but even though quite a few of those shards cut their skin, neither was hurt much worse than Hanny was earlier, on the calf. Luck and divine protection were the only possible explanations, because both men in the same positions on Dodd's gun spun to the ground. Hahessy's rammer staff was sheared into three splintered pieces, however, the spinning bell-shaped head fetching Hanny a stinging, dizzying blow to the right temple. Sadly for him, as he stumbled and turned, trying to keep on his feet, he saw what happened to others who'd grown closer than brothers.

Kini Hau wasn't lucky. Standing right by Hanny to watch the effect of their shot, one Dom musket ball struck him high on the left thigh, near the groin, and another—perhaps mercifully—square in the chest. Red froth blasted from his mouth and nose as he fell with a gurgling moan. Naxa dropped to a knee, screaming, "I'm shot! Oh God, I'm shot!" while blood quickly darkened his jacket on his upper left chest, under his collarbone. Even stunned as he was, Hanny recognized what was probably a mortal wound. Hoziki had apparently been spared, but he stood, wide-eyed and unmoving, staring back at him. Farther back, Hanny was glad to see Apo in one piece, he and one of the infantrymen finally dragging the heavy limber chest up beside Dodd's. The other infantryman was nowhere to be seen, and Billy Randall was sitting on the ground about twenty yards back, holding a bloody and misshapen hand.

Hanny put his hand out to grasp the cascabel of the gun where its recoil had brought it close, but he felt like he was still turning, spinning even faster, when he saw Lieutenant Petty lying on his face. A terrible rushing sound built in his ears, accompanied by a sense of hopelessness like he had never known. Like Kini Hau, Petty must've died instantly, because he fell hard enough to splash mud and he hadn't thrashed around. By some bizarre mercy, his face had found one of the few unsullied patches of snow remaining around him.

No, Hanny thought. *What will I do without Mr. Petty?* His section chief had never been the friendliest, most outgoing sort, and was certainly no "brother" like Kini and Naxa, but he'd been so . . . confident, supportive, even patient (in some ways), with his teaching. It was he who dragged Hanny and his friends into the artillery in the first place and taught them everything they knew about the big guns, as well as most of what they'd learned about leadership too, to be fair. Hanny had just been getting comfortable with being a corporal when he was made a sergeant, and he still felt like a fraud in that role. How could he remain one without Mr. Petty's guidance?

His knees became unsteady, and his vision turned dark and narrow. He felt himself starting to fall, but suddenly, Preacher Mac—even Hahessy—were there to hold him up.

"Bloody stupid bastard, gettin' 'isself killed," Hahessy growled, but there was a strange tone in his rough voice, something like genuine regret. "Why, I never would'a thought it." When the big Irishman spoke again, he was gesturing at Kini and Naxa. "Best get these lads back from the gun, don't ye think?"

Hanny's vision was slowly clearing, and the rushing in his ears gave way to the roar of battle once more. Impatiently shrugging off the hands that held him, he found he could stand on his own. Looking back to the front, he saw the enemy starting to recover as well. "Yes," he croaked, then cleared his throat. "Yes," he said more firmly, clearly. Raising his voice, he called to the infantryman with Apo. "Can you gather a few more of your fellows and help get our dead and wounded to the rear?" He gestured to the men plying their muskets to their left. An awful lot of them were suddenly lying still as well. "See if someone can help Naxa and Billy, if you please." Looking over at the Number One gun, it looked like Dodd had lost just as many men. "Are you all right, Sergeant Dodd?" he called.

"The usual, it seems," Dodd answered with a sigh.

Hanny nodded. "Apo brought ammunition and we still have enough men to fight with reduced crews. If we get word to Mr. Barca, I'm sure he'll send down some of the infantrymen we used as gun's crews earlier. It doesn't sound like they're doing anything now."

"That's not true," Apo spoke up. "Mr. Barca's been moving the other guns, leveling a place right on the slope where they can shoot down and support us. I expect he'll be down here with the rest of our own boys as soon as he can as well."

"Me an' some o' the other fellas can fill in for your losses—carry charges an' such," the infantryman offered. "Now that you've got ammunition, we'll help you kill more o' those devils than we can with our muskets!"

"That would be fine—and much appreciated," Hanny said. "What company are you?"

"Comp'ny A, Sergeant."

Hanny shook his head. "I don't know your officers. Make sure they know I haven't just poached you"—he paused, thinking—"and half a dozen of your comrades, without asking." His expression hardened. "That said, I'm *not* asking. Captain Barca will back me up and so will Colonel Cayce, in the end. I'm sure of that. I do like to keep things cordial with our friends in the Third Pennsylvania, however."

The fighting was picking back up, the air alive with the buzz of bullets. Preacher Mac and Hoziki had already pulled Kini, Naxa, and Lieutenant Petty clear and were loading canister into the gun without orders, each man performing the tasks of two until they got relief. That was fine with Hanny, who looked over to see how Dodd was managing. He'd already called the few "extra" men in the section forward and was loading much as before. Hanny frowned. *He might've shared*, he thought, but it was just as well. *My crew is better with half its men than his ever was. They'll work better with rusty infantry too.*

"Looks like the parley came tae nothin'," Preacher Mac shouted, trotting past Hanny to retrieve another charge while Hahessy rammed one home. Hanny gazed down through the smoke. It was hard to see anything but he got the feeling Mac was wrong. Whatever happened at the parley had resulted in the 4th Division *charging forward* into the Doms, cracking their line from one end to the other. The 3rd Division was charging as well, and a huge, mass melee had resulted. Unfortunately, even as the Doms gave ground, a stunning number of them were shifting *this* way. Quite a few others had seen it, and regardless of how good the position Anson had chosen was, limiting the length of the front and the number of Doms who could hit them at once, the enemy now had infinitely more depth than Anson, Ulrich, Meder, and Barca could possibly cope with.

In spite of that obvious fact and the dull resignation that stole over him, Hanny strode calmly forward and picked up the lanyard Naxa had dropped.

While Hoziki pierced the charge, primed the gun, and tended the Hidden's Patent lock, Hanny stepped outside the wheel and pulled the lanyard taut. After watching Hoziki move to the side and nod, Hanny shouted, "Ready," mostly so Hahessy would know to cover his ear, then he faced forward, toward the enemy. Just in those few moments, the transformation he witnessed now was profound. The whole Dom army, so strikingly disciplined before, seemed to have degenerated into a seething barbarian horde. All sense of organization had been lost as the regiments retreating from the American charge broke the integrity of others, intermingling and throwing them into hopeless disarray. The flank of the Dom force facing them on the heights was rolled up by their own men!

The vast majority still seemed intent on rolling right over Hanny as well, however, and escaping up over the mountain. Gritting his teeth, Hanny tensed to pull his lanyard. Just before he could, there came the pounding roar of six guns from above, one after the other, and shot shrieked down into the press. Several exploded right among the enemy, throwing smoky gobbets of bodies high in the air within towering geysers of mud. Hanny instantly knew why Captain Barca hadn't been here with them. Not only had they finally been resupplied—all their case shot for the 6pdrs was gone, and they'd never brought any for the enemy 8pdrs—but, just as important, Barca had obviously imagined how to use the fresh ammunition to best effect. Case shot that struck the ground before the fuse burnt down usually still exploded, sometimes on contact if the impact drove the fuse into the shell, but it tended to waste much of its deadly force, expending it into the earth. Fewer enemies would be killed or wounded. Groundbursts were rather spectacular, however, as Hanny had just seen, their effect on morale out of proportion to their lethality. This was especially true at the moment, the case shot exploding in mud churned by many feet, festooning soldiers already near panic with viscous goo they'd understandably misidentify. . . .

"Cap'n Barca's bloody *brilliant*!" Hahessy roared with glee, instantly coming to the same conclusion as Hanny. Infantrymen redoubled their fire, bellowing curses and insults, while swarms of heavy arrows the Holcanos and most of the Ocelomeh still used suddenly arced into the enemy, sustaining a rate of fire only Anson's, Leonor's, Boogerbear's, and Sal's revolvers could match. They couldn't do it for long, however, and that's when Hanny realized this had been prepared for. He knew it hadn't all been part of the initial battle plan (he'd seen too much go wrong to think that), but Colonel Cayce, Anson, Varaa, maybe even Captain Barca and others had, together or separately among their various elements, prepared alternate plans—who knew how many—to deal with almost any situation. The Doms couldn't do that. Their twisted society only allowed one or two brains on the whole battlefield to actually work, maybe like ants or bees, and when their various forces were deprived of the control they were accustomed to, they simply couldn't cope. Hanny whooped with excitement and pulled his lanyard, churning more Doms to the ground. It wasn't the slaughter that delighted him—far from it. It was a growing confidence he hadn't really felt since they came down here from the heights that they might somehow win the day and survive.

"Got some men for you, Sergeant!" called the infantryman he'd sent to find some. Dodd's gun roared, and the volunteers flinched.

Hanny grinned, picking two and vaguely pointing them where they were needed. "Listen to the men standing near. They'll tell you what to do. Load canister!" he shouted, taking a third young man by the arm. He thought the kid was Ocelomeh, or maybe from Itzincab, but with everyone wearing the same uniform now, only differentiated by branch, he couldn't tell things like that anymore. All were "Americans," as far as he was concerned. "You go to that short fellow sitting on the chest with the copper lid. He'll hand you a leather haversack with something heavy inside. Bring it back to me, and I'll tell you what's next." He looked at the other men. "You boys just watch for now. Watch *everybody*, not just your pals. I might put you in for anyone."

The incoming fire was still intense, if far less organized or well directed. There were no more deadly volleys. The guns on the heights were pounding as quickly as they could be loaded now, more dark earth and smoky spume rising from the explosions, mist drifting away. There seemed to be as many screams of terror as pain, and the surging mass of Doms appeared to be shifting, trying to move more past them than at them now. Hanny was shocked to see Captain Barca and Felix Meder ride up on their horses as if it were just a pleasant afternoon and there weren't still hundreds of large pieces of lead flying in the air all around them. They did at least dismount. Meder almost immediately raised his M1817 rifle and fired a shot into the surging mass of Doms.

"An officer?" Barca asked.

Meder shrugged as he lowered his rifle butt down on top of his boot and began to reload. "Plainly not a very good one, I'd say." Meder snorted. "Not any kind of one now."

Barca looked at Hanny, then gestured back at a line of corpses growing behind the infantry. Walking wounded were moving them there, as well as helping those hurt worse than they were. Hanny suddenly wondered how they'd get their wounded out. Healers were starting to come down the slope, carrying heavy packs and cases, but no wagon was going to get back up it. Hanny did a double take when he saw that some of the healers were girls. He hoped Apo's sister, Izel, wasn't one of them. Not here. "I saw Lieutenant Petty as we rode up." Barca continued, "Too many other boys too. I'm sorry I left you down here alone so long."

"I'm glad you did, now that I know why." Hanny sighed. "I'm just as glad you're here, though." He smiled faintly. "I've had enough independence for one day."

"Ready!" Hoziki cried.

"Fire!" Hanny replied without turning. The Number Two gun roared and clanked, the shishing sound of canister indistinguishable from the tires rolling back in the mud. "Load canister," he called, still looking at the two officers.

"Don't be ridiculous," Barca told him. "You had a section up on the heights, training men in action. I saw you." He pointed. "You've done the same here, essentially leading this section too, since Mr. Petty fell—unless I miss my guess."

Hanny looked at Gun Number One. "Well, I haven't really given Sergeant Dodd any orders. We've just both kind of done what we do."

"Lieutenant Hanny," Meder said with a smile, ramming a patched ball down the barrel of his rifle before returning the rammer and raising his weapon to the crook of his arm to prime.

Hanny stared at him. "I can't be an *officer*! I was just a *private* a few months ago!"

Barca and Meder both laughed. It was a very off sound under the circumstances. "You're telling *us* that?" Barca asked, incredulous. Captain Meder had also been a private when they came to this world, and Barca himself had been a recently freed slave.

"I think he really is trying to tell us that," Meder said, brow arched. "*Us.*"

To Hanny's further surprise, Major Anson and a screen of Rangers rode up next, Kisin and his Holcanos following on foot.

"Gentlemen," Anson said, waving one of his huge Walker Colts at the enemy. The arrow barrage had stopped, but the infantry and Hanny's section—*My section!* he thought with wonder—as well as the artillery above were still pounding them. Hanny didn't know how they took it. "Time to punch those bastards in the nose. The rest o' their army's streamin' past 'em, pushin' 'em up against us here, while First Division keeps squeezin' the neck o' the bottle on the whole damn bunch. Signal from Lewis says to let 'em go. Not too keen on that myself, but he's right that finishin' 'em off'll cost us too many of our own. First Division's supposed to get the word to hold back a bit an' we'll push these in front of us out of the pocket." He waved at his Rangers. "Mounted troops first. We'll charge 'em, blast 'em, then peel off. Infantry goes at 'em next. John Ulrich is down, not too bad, I think, but Cap'n Cullin'll command. I'm hopin', disorganized as the Doms are, angry infantry comin' at 'em in good order, bayonets fixed—why, they'll shatter like a cooked flint." He looked at Barca. "Can you get horses an' limbers down here to pull your guns?"

"Yes sir," Barca replied. "I have them up top, waiting to do just that."

"We gonna get ta be flyin' artillery again, if ye please?" Hahessy asked eagerly.

Anson glowered at the Irishman, but nodded at Barca before looking up above where the other guns roared. "That's right. I'd like your whole battery in support, Mr. Barca. Can you do it?"

Barca nodded. "Indeed, sir. It will take me a while to bring my other four guns down, and we'll have to leave the captures, of course." He looked at Hanny. "Once they have full limbers, though, and the rest of their crews, Lieutenant Cox's section will be available at once."

Anson arched an eyebrow at Hanny. "Lieutenant, huh? Well done." He looked at Meder. "Support Mr. Barca with your riflemen, if you please, an' be sure to send or take a strong detachment along with Mr. Cox. Support the *guns*," he stressed. "I know you got bayonets now, but I still don't think riflemen belong on the firin' line with infantry. You load too slow, an' honestly, it's a waste of superior marksmen who could be pickin' off officers, hear?" His gaze shifted to Barca again while all the guns thundered, case shot exploded, another chorus of screams arose, and the 3rd Pennsylvania's independent fire reached new heights. "Get those limbers down as fast as you can—an' load 'em down with crates of musket cartridges. At their current rate of fire, the infantry'll need plenty more before we kick off."

A Dom musket ball clipped a cloud of horsehair off Colonel Fannin's mane. The animal did a little dance to the side until Anson absently patted him on the neck, frowning at the enemy and peering hard out beyond them. He shook his head. "I can't see what First Division's up to, but pressure here oughta ease if they do what they've been told." He waved at the closest Doms, whose fire had diminished under the merciless fusillade, whole layers of the packed mob now collapsing in the slush before they could even present their own weapons. "Then, if these silly bastards still want a fight, we'll take one right to 'em. Lewis might'a told us to let 'em go—if they will—figurin' that beat Doms are less of a threat." He shrugged. "But we can still kill a heap of 'em, an' dead Doms ain't no threat at all." With that, he wheeled Colonel Fannin and led his Rangers back to the left, Kisin's Holcanos grumbling about all the running back and forth, but dutifully following.

"Mr. Meder and I are off as well," Barca told Hanny. "I'll send the limbers and the rest of your men down at once, and start the other guns moving. I'll leave the eight pounders on the heights to continue their work"—he gestured at the infantrymen Hanny had conscripted—"so you might want to keep them, regardless. Advance when the time comes, under Major Anson's or Captain Meder's orders." He glanced at the rifleman beside him. "I'm sure Mr. Meder will quickly return to lead his detachment accompanying you."

"Of course," Meder said, bowing his head. "Mr. Cox and I have fought well together before."

"Yes," Barca agreed, "and I'm confident his section will continue to shine." His expression was earnest when he addressed Hanny again. "You know it will be some time before I can join you. Getting the horses and limbers down will be difficult. The guns are another matter." He blinked. "Well, you know. All I can ask is that you continue to do your duty"—he raised his voice—"and that God will watch over you all."

"We will," Hanny assured, "and thank you. You as well."

Barca gave a clipped nod and remounted his horse. Felix Meder did the same, and together they cantered back toward the slope.

Hanny turned back to his gun's crews. They'd both paused their loading for a moment, and all faces were turned to him. He cleared his throat. "I guess we'll still have a vote, later," he said a little weakly, "but for now . . .

I'm honored to lead you. Now, let's get back to business, shall we? Fire faster, if you can. We'll be replenished when the limbers get here, so there's no reason to leave anything in that chest that Apo and the others brought down when we advance."

"*I* won't be voting for him to be lieutenant over *me*," Dodd grumbled loudly as the section resumed loading and rejoined the battle. "I've been in the army nearly as long as that jumped-up, snot-nosed kid's been alive!"

Splinters from a tree trunk in front of the gun sprayed Hahessy as he rammed a charge Preacher Mac inserted. When he stepped outside the wheel, he regarded Dodd with narrowed eyes that had nothing to do with flying debris. "What's wrong with ye, then?"

"Aye!" demanded Preacher Mac. "Ye dinnae want'a be chief yerself, an' even if Cap'n Barca was fool enough tae propose ye, an' us even greater fools tae confirm ye . . . ye ken yerself ye couldnae do it! Why raise a fuss?"

Dodd hesitated and looked at Hanny, a little defensively. "He gets too many of us killed, is why!" he finally blurted. "Another man with more experience . . ."

"Ahsh, ye blasted idjit!" Mac scowled. "It's the *Doms* that kill us, not him!"

Hoziki didn't have anything to say, but even he was glaring at Dodd.

"Aye," said Hahessy in agreement, then spoke as if revealing a great secret to the infantrymen on the crew. "It's near impossible ta imagine the now, it is, but there was a time when I was given ta malicious intemperance. P'raps even wickedness, some might say." He looked contemptuously back over at Dodd. "That 'kid,' as ye call 'im, was the only one *man* enough ta stand up ta me—which *you* never did, Sergeant Dodd!" He grinned back at Hanny, who'd been taking this in without expression. "Nay, I don't reckon our new leftenant'll *need* yer single, measly vote a'tall."

CHAPTER 29

"W hy so quiet, so glum?" Varaa shouted cheerfully at Lewis as the two of them, Leonor, Boogerbear, and Willis, and now all the remaining mounted troops who hadn't already gone chasing the enemy on the right, thundered past behind 3rd Division on their way to reach the 1st. Except for a few reserve regiments not yet committed to the fight, Agon's furious 4th Division had lost all semblance of order as whole regiments smashed into and among what they considered the wildly treacherous Doms in front of them. A frenzied melee erupted between them and a fair percentage of the enemy that was determined to hold their ground or die. Quite a few simply fled, but a surprising number actually tried to surrender—throwing down their weapons—at least until it became apparent that the green-clad troops weren't offering quarter. Most of these fled as well. Agon, Arevalo, even Father Orno went into the thick of it, screaming for the men of 4th Division to halt, re-form, stop killing, but the troop's very real, almost fanatical conversion to the "old" faith, combined with lifetimes of injustice and suffering they'd endured for the Dominion, finally had a focus. The fighting and the righteous, bloody chase left 4th Division just as disorganized and uncontrollable as the Doms had become.

If anything, it seemed that Har-Kaaska's distant 2nd Division was behaving even worse. Except for a few intact regiments coalescing around the

Mi-Anakka "King of the Ocelomeh" and Dukane's battery, the rest were ruthlessly chasing and slaughtering any of the Doms who'd broken on the right that they could catch. The only "good" thing—if it could be described as such—was that they weren't going far. A humiliated messenger from Har-Kaaska said most of them had paused to loot and burn the vast enemy camp. Dark columns of smoke were piling high into the cold afternoon sky. Still, the division had practically destroyed itself as a fighting force, and if the Doms had kept a significant organized reserve or their lancers hadn't quit the field, 2nd Division might've been completely annihilated.

Even as they passed, Lewis could see that the jubilant, predatory chaos was infecting 3rd Division too. It was pressing forward, feeding the rout, shedding companies that bashed their way into the froth of mud and blood and hate to join 4th Division's rampage. Lewis had found Colonel Itzam almost apoplectic with rage at his men—and his own inability to control them. Lewis felt the same, at a remove, and could only imagine Har-Kaaska's wrath. The army had never acted this way, and though he probably should have, Lewis never expected it. Now that it was happening, he knew it was because they'd never really fought a battle like this. In the past they'd always stood on the defense, for the most part, and even those who stood toe-to-toe against Agon at Gran Lago hadn't seen the enemy's heels. Now, after handling the enemy so roughly on his own terms, it was like Lewis's heretofore "professional" troops had gotten a little overexcited and their long-suppressed "chase instinct" kicked in when the enemy fled. That didn't make it any easier to take.

"Did you not hear me?" Varaa demanded, breathing hard, tail whipping, eyes blinking, as her horse pounded through the mud. Only a hint of snow remained in the open. "A Dominion army is *routing*," she stressed gleefully. "That has never happened! We will soon have a famous victory here!"

"He heard," Leonor said, amusement in her voice. "Sure, we're gonna win, but Lewis is sulking 'cause it wasn't the 'perfect' battle he envisioned last night. Not even close."

"I don't think . . ." Boogerbear began, but Lewis interrupted, snapping at Leonor with the first hint of genuine fury he'd ever directed at her.

"Of course it isn't 'perfect'! There's no such thing—and if you think I care a damn for that, you don't know me very well! All I care about is victory, achieved with the least cost in lives. That's why we plan for so many alternatives, and I thank God every day we have leaders who can make up their own when they have to. But *this*," he growled disgustedly, "doesn't even approximate the 'victory' I'd hoped for, and might leave us so scattered and battered it would be better if we never fought!" He pointed ahead with the bloody saber still in his hand. "Third Division was our 'reserve,' but it's in no shape to serve as such. That leaves First Division as the only island of sanity in the midst of this whole muddled brawl!"

After so tediously putting itself back together after its own charge, 1st Division, home of most of their truly veteran regiments, looked nearly as organized as it had before the battle started. Some of its regiments were a little ragged, their banners torn and cut by shot, but it alone was intact.

"It hasn't slowed its advance, however." He shot Leonor a worried glance. "It's still in the fight, still squeezing the Doms—right up against Major Anson on the heights. Colonel Reed was supposed to *halt* his advance. Keep fighting, of course, but take the pressure *off* a bit. If I know Ulrich—and your father—they'll be attacking any minute, as asked, but if the enemy, even in their panic, have no space to pull back before the assault of what is, after all, little more than a single regiment, everything we have over there, *including* your father," he stressed once again, "will likely be overwhelmed by simple numbers."

Boogerbear was nodding. "That's what I was tryin' ta tell ya, girl," he said. Varaa's enthusiasm had faded entirely.

"We have to stop Colonel Reed," Leonor said, her voice more brittle than usual.

"Exactly," Lewis agreed.

They galloped without speaking, the only distinguishable noises being the creak of leather, wet thunder of hooves, and heavy breathing of horses. The nearby clash of weapons, clatter of musketry, and continuous roar of screams and curses and bellows of rage had blended into a sound all its own. Almost no cannon were firing just then, aside from a pair on the heights. Second Division had at least overrun the enemy gun line before it fell apart, and Barca's and Dukane's batteries had silenced the Dom guns on the other heights to the northeast. The rest of Olayne's artillery had been forced into silence by fear of hitting their own men in the confusion.

The left of the 1st's battle line now became visible through the smoke beyond the right of the 3rd. Itzam's division was less jumbled here, steadied by the example of Reed's, but all were still moving forward, rumbling drums setting the pace. Lewis saw mounted officers riding behind the 1st and urged Arete into a faster gait. "Corporal Hannity," he called behind to the dragoon bugler who'd stuck to him like glue, his more distant calls ignored or unheard. "Sound 'halt' then 'rally,' if you will. Right here where the Third can hear it as well. Rejoin us when you're done. I'll need you again," Lewis reminded the bugler.

"Yes sir! Of course," Hannity replied, bringing his horse to a halt.

Lewis and the rest galloped on, Hannity's bugle already sounding by the time they reached the collection of mounted officers ahead—interrupting a heated argument when they did. It was so heated, in fact, that Major Marvin Beck, commanding the 1st US Infantry Regiment, had just flung his fine, embroidered gauntlets at the Mi-Anakka consul Koaar-Taak of the 1st Ocelomeh in an unmistakable challenge. The shouting ended at once, several officers and their aides involuntarily saluting Lewis in spite of where they were. Leonor shot them a warning glare, but Lewis's simmering irritation erupted forth, and he practically roared, "What the devil is happening here? Do you not hear the call to halt? And how can it be that I find you all bickering like children on a schoolground instead of behaving like gentlemen on a battlefield—while brave men are dying around you?"

Just as stung by his uncharacteristic anger as they were the question he asked, no one replied for a moment. Finally, Major Beck ventured, "Sir, we only now hear the signal. If we heard others, well, the infantry still chiefly relies on drum signals and it is possible they were disregarded." He cringed just a little, knowing that was a poor excuse.

"There were mounted messengers too," Varaa said, glaring at Koaar. Aside from Har-Kaaska, he was the only other member of her species on the battlefield.

"Only one has arrived, badly wounded and incapable of speech," Koaar replied. "The poor fellow's jaw was shot away," he added, blinking furiously, "and he was taken to the healers at once." Major Don Roderigo of the 1st Vera Cruz was nodding in support.

"Guess you hear the signal now, right?" Boogerbear prodded.

Major Manley of the 1st Uxmal seemed almost jolted by the statement and, with a rushed "By your leave," whirled to race along the line, shouting for the drummers to sound the halt.

"Still, I'm wonderin' what you're doin' all wadded up here anyway, fussin' with each other instead o' the enemy," Leonor said. No matter that she was officially just a lieutenant, no one questioned that she was considerably more in reality. "Shouldn't you be with your regiments?"

"Yes," Varaa agreed. "Colonel Reed commands this division, does he not? Where is he?"

Beck looked down. "He's wounded, I'm afraid." Returning his gaze to Lewis's, he touched his forehead. "A ball struck him here. It was mostly spent and didn't penetrate, but he was quite insensible when I had him carried to the healers. We don't know if it was a mild or mortal wound, at present."

"I'm sorry to hear that," Lewis said seriously, "but you're Reed's second in command. I can't imagine how his condition could result in the disgraceful display we witnessed." He looked pointedly down at one of the gauntlets on the ground.

Beck sighed nervously, glancing at Consul Koaar-Taak. "Whether I heard any signal or not, I . . . saw what happened in front of Fourth Division, including the . . . disarray that resulted. I'm also fully aware of Major Anson's position on the heights. The fighting has been quite intense just below there, and, well, it strikes me that the only way we might still lose this battle is to continue fighting it—if you know what I mean?" His eyes flicked to Consul Koaar once more. "Believing your opinion and mine are the same when it comes to gratuitous losses, I strongly suspected what your intent might be and attempted to halt the advance on my authority. . . ."

"And met resistance from myself," Koaar confessed, then hesitated, "and others." He sounded contrite at first, but his tone warmed as he spoke. "We have a great opportunity here! The bulk of the enemy's forces are trapped, panicking, and we can destroy them at last! I argued only that we should keep pressing. . . ."

"And not only refused to halt your own regiment, thus requiring the rest to stay up with it lest our line be shattered, but called Major Beck a *coward* when he disagreed," snapped Captain "Mal" Harris, face red with anger.

Drums were beating all along the lengthy line, even spreading to the left along 3rd Division's, and a semblance of order seemed to be emerging at last as the blue-clad ranks ground to a stop and attempted to dress their ranks while maintaining independent fire. Despite the lethal fusillade, Doms in front of them, pressured by their demolished flank, began shifting to the right, trying to move up the valley. They weren't shooting much either, and the improved visibility let them all see Anson's mounted troops smash into the other side of them. That communicated a surge forward that wasn't a charge, merely a recoil from Anson and the 3rd Pennsylvania, but the Doms in front of 1st Division only knew they were being pushed directly into a continuing storm of lead and muzzle flashes from behind. Possibly the only intact and organized Dom regiments on the field that day finally broke at last, their steadfast, bloodied yellow ranks producing a kind of collective moan before throwing down their weapons and disintegrating into a surging flood, desperate only to escape.

"Give me one excuse why I should not slay you here and now!" Varaa commanded loudly of Koaar, easily heard over the firing and growing surf-like roar. Her wide blue eyes regarded Koaar with an icy look, colder than any lingering patch of snow. Not waiting for an answer, she turned and said tersely, "Please accept my apologies, Lewis. In my capacity as warmaster of all the Ocelomeh, I will deal with this fool. The army need not sully itself in any way."

Koaar seemed horrified. "What did I do wrong? I only wanted to make our victory over those who have tormented us for generations more complete!"

Lewis was shaking his head. "It sounds as if you not only disobeyed an order by a superior officer in the face of the enemy, but attempted to entice others into doing the same. Ultimately, your actions subverted Major Beck's authority to the extent that the entire division he'd suddenly become responsible for had no choice but to disregard his orders as well. Worst of all, your actions, if left unchecked, would have doubtless resulted in many more losses than we must already be forced to count. What you have 'sullied' is the victory we've won, at a far greater cost than we might be able to pay. In my view, that might possibly be the worst crime you could possibly commit." He looked at Varaa. "And he can't be punished by the authority of the Ocelomeh alone since his transgression was against the army as a whole, the cause we all fight for, and the nation we strive to build."

The flood of Doms had already largely passed, and there were shouts of "Cease firing" from lieutenants and NCOs in the companies of the various regiments as green- and blue-clad soldiers began to appear among the Dom stragglers, gasping from running and fighting so hard, but perfectly willing to bayonet any lagging Doms they caught. Hannity had rejoined them, and Lewis told him to start sounding "cease firing" and, when he thought enough had done so, sound "recall."

He regarded Varaa once more. "All that said, punishing him for doing what half the army did today would only serve the purpose of setting an example, and I despise punishing one for the sins of many as much as punishing many for the sins of one." He turned to Beck. "I pray that Colonel Reed is fit to return to his duty because, even though it was thrust unexpectedly upon you, I'm deeply concerned that you don't have the force of personality to command First Division in his stead. Prove me wrong. In the meantime, you, sir, will withdraw your challenge. There will be no dueling in this army while I am in command." Looking back at Koaar, he took a long breath and spoke: "*You*, sir, are *more* guilty than most others on the field today since yours was not a crime of passion, merely chasing a fleeing foe against orders. You *argued* with your commander as you disobeyed him and abused his honor as well. *You* will be broken to the ranks to serve as a private soldier in the very regiment you commanded."

Koaar looked at Varaa and blinked pleadingly. "Warmaster . . ." he began, but Varaa snapped, "Be grateful. I would have had you beheaded . . . not least for humiliating all the Ocelomeh and your very race itself! *Earn* your way out of the hole you foolishly dug for yourself, and I may one day greet you as a friend! Do not address me again until then."

The high, clear sound of Hannity's bugle echoed in the valley between the heights, the call picked up and repeated by others farther away. The all-consuming din of battle had all but faded—except farther up the valley, where fleeing Doms must've realized they had nothing but what they carried, no food or even a blanket, and tried to salvage something from their flame-gutted camp. Far-flung members of Har-Kaaska's 2nd Division were still in the vicinity, however, and there were sporadic waves of savage fighting there. Lewis could see that Har-Kaaska's core force had grown considerably as its wayward units returned and a couple of well-managed regiments were moving to block the refugees' access to the camp and keep them flowing past it.

Nodding with approval, Lewis turned to look out across the corpse-strewn field between 1st Division and the heights. Anson's Rangers had already reassembled after their charge into the enemy over there and were now picking their way toward him, accompanied by a section of guns. The 3rd Pennsylvania was still falling in to form a column four wide and come up behind them. Leonor urged her new horse up alongside him and spoke as lowly as she could. "I know you're disappointed with how things turned out, as much because the follow-up fell apart when so many lost their heads, either mad at the attack on the parley or tastin' a win. But I'm glad you didn't take it all out on Koaar."

He looked at her in surprise. "You think I was too harsh with him?"

Leonor snorted. "Hell no. I would'a shot him on the spot, but I ain't you." She shrugged. "I prob'ly would'a regretted it later—the waste of a brave, maybe salvageable officer with aggressive instincts who got a little carried away—but that would'a been later. I can't un-kill somebody." She giggled a little, and Lewis was surprised by the sound, coming from her. "Varaa can't un-chop their heads off—an' you can't un-arrest an' un-charge 'em either. He'd'a had to hang, er be shot in the end as the 'sole example' you wanted to avoid. Crazy as it sounds, ever'body would'a known a heap more deserved it. I think they'd'a been *offended* by the unfairness of it."

Varaa had approached and heard what was said. "She is right. Even I see that, now. Koaar will be humiliated—a dreadful punishment for my people, I assure you—but he will rise again, a far more thoughtful officer. More important, this victory—and make no mistake, it will be remembered as a momentous victory that *broke* Dom troops—will not be tainted by recrimination or resentment. Your army will be exuberant and rightfully so, but all those officers who loosed the leash and prevented it from being the more complete victory you wanted will know who they were and be privately shamed. I do not think it will happen again."

Anson, Captain Cullin, Captain Barca, and Captain Meder, along with a few mounted men behind them, were cheered wildly as they rode closer to the front line of 1st Division. The Rangers, artillerymen, and even more distant infantry returned the compliment, shouts of triumph replacing the recent roar of battle. The cheering grew louder and rapidly spread as Lewis, Leonor, Varaa, Boogerbear, and all those officers from 1st Division still present rode out to meet the heroes who'd taken and held the heights.

"Well, Lewis," Anson shouted with a grin, even a sharp salute. "It was messy, but you did it."

Leonor looked scoldingly at her father, then shrugged and smiled. No armed enemy was close enough to harm them now.

Lewis returned the salute, just as formally, to Anson, Meder, Barca, and Cullin, and then those mounted on the horses and limber of the nearest gun as it drew up alongside the officers at Barca's command. Recognizing Hannibal Cox, Lewis said, "Why am I not surprised to see you here? Glad you made it, son."

"Thank you, sir."

"We all thought *Lieutenant* Cox and his crew deserved special recognition, sir," Barca said. "Though to be fair, so does everyone in my battery, the Third Pennsylvania, the Rangers and riflemen."

"What about me—and my Holcanos?" demanded Kisin, who'd ridden up behind Anson.

"You too, you bloody cannibal," Meder said, rolling his eyes.

"I do not eat people anymore," Kisin said piously.

"We all did it," Lewis said loudly, and the cheering redoubled. Much of 4th Division had started gathering around now, leaving off killing the enemy wounded on the field. They even had some prisoners among them. Lewis saw a bandaged Agon, Father Orno, even Don Hurac riding up through the press, a cordon of dragoons pushing eager soldiers back. He'd let Agon chastise his troops as he saw fit. It wouldn't take long, judging by the stormy expression on the former Dom's face. "How is Reverend Harkin?" Lewis asked, suddenly remembering the man's second wound.

Father Orno's face fell. "I fear my friend will likely lose his arm," he cried over the tumult. "The bone was shattered."

Lewis nodded sadly. He'd suspected as much from what he saw. He turned back to Anson. "And where's John Ulrich?"

"Wounded as well," Captain Cullin reported. "Shot through the body, in fact. Amazingly, the healers don't think anything vital was damaged, and he should recover." He hesitated, looking around. "Colonel Reed?"

"Also wounded," Lewis said. "We don't know how badly, yet."

"We have lost a great many good men today," Father Orno said mournfully, "to painful injuries and God's loving embrace." He straightened in his saddle. "And there will perhaps be more, if I do not misremember your plans for the aftermath of the battle?"

Anson suddenly looked skeptical. "Yeah. What are we gonna chase 'em with? Keep the scare on 'em so they can't sort themselves out?"

Lewis shook his head, consulting his watch and the sky. Clouds were moving back in, blocking the afternoon sun. A chill wind was springing up, and more snow threatened. He glanced at Anson. "With the exception of whatever mounted troops whose horses aren't blown and are able to harass the enemy retreat, I'm afraid we've done all we can today. First Division and a few regiments of Second and Third are all that might offer an organized pursuit—but they're also the only real protection we have while we put *ourselves* back together." He looked around at the growing sea of men, especially noting Agon's simmering anger once more, and raised his voice to address as many as he could.

"Most of you have only been soldiers for a very short time, and many are already veterans of ferocious fighting, stunning victories"—he glanced sympathetically back at Agon—"even honorable, if frustrating, defeat. You're *good* soldiers, as good as I could ever hope to lead. Unfortunately, though your elation at routing the enemy is understandable, the loss of discipline and organization that ensued left a large proportion of this army little better prepared to keep fighting than the enemy was." He paused to let that sink in among the suddenly near-silent men before continuing. "Sadly, a fine opportunity may have been lost as a result, a chance to beat the enemy here in one big fight and then chase them at once, in strength, to keep them running all the way to the Great Valley of Mexico. Your valor accomplished the first, but the second . . ." He allowed a trace of disappointment to touch his features. "Now we must prepare for other costly encounters before we reach our objective."

Hundreds, maybe a couple of thousand, tired, hurt, but victorious soldiers groaned in shame.

"Did you see that?" Varaa practically hissed a gasp in Leonor's ear. "They love him—and hate themselves for failing him. Did you ever see anything like it?"

"No," Leonor replied, just as low. "I've heard of gen'rals in history with that way about 'em, whose men'd jump right straight in the fires o' hell if they asked. Never thought I'd see it." She smiled. "Though now that I do, I ain't surprised. I love him too, y'know."

Varaa blinked at her, tail waving slowly above her saddle cantle.

Holding his hands out to his sides, Lewis went on in a lower, gentler tone. "Perhaps I expected too much of you," he began, and a chorus of "No! No!" started to rise, but he waved it down. "Perhaps I did," he went on louder, "but I'll never lower my expectations. This is the one and only time I will ever speak to you about that *single* aspect of what happened today that diminished its perfection"—he smiled—"though I may remind you from time to time of the truly great victory you achieved. I'll rely on all of you to make sure that . . . other thing never happens again."

The cheers were thunderous now, and Lewis nodded and smiled as he turned Arete and rode back through the ranks of the 1st US, reverently touching the Stars and Stripes held forth by the color-bearer as he passed. The cheering kept on even as the other officers followed them through and they emerged into the relative peace behind the lines.

"Damn, Lewis. I didn't know you had a speech like that in you," Anson said at once. "Should'a left you in Uxmal as our politician instead o' De Russy!"

Lewis saw Leonor looking at him strangely. "No," she said. "We need him here. Did you hear those men? He scolded 'em, an' they love him for it." She looked around. "They *know* they screwed up, but what's more, they really *won't* ever do it again."

Lewis took a long breath and let it out. "I don't hardly even remember *what* I said, but I hope you're right. We'll move First Division out beyond the enemy camp. Second Division too, as Har-Kaaska puts it back together. Support troops from all four divisions can bring their tents and such forward. Third and Fourth Divisions are such a mess we might as well let them comb the field for wounded and prisoners on their way back to this morning's camp." Lewis rubbed his eyes and scratched his beard. "Give them the night to rest and think. The long roll in the morning will probably reorganize them better than anything they do tonight."

"What if it snows?" Varaa asked, looking at the sky. "What of tomorrow, then?"

"We still push on, if we can. Depending on how deep it gets. The cold will keep being a problem until we get through the mountains and start down into the Great Valley. And I *don't* want half a dozen bloody actions between here and there. The Doms could bleed us white."

"I don't know, Lewis," Anson said, shaking his head. "I don't think so." Almost everyone looked at him expectantly. "You forget. We've never routed the Doms like this before—but they've never, *ever* been whupped as bad either. Unless they bring fresh troops up to face us—which we don't even know if they have—I doubt they'll get the same fellas we ran off today to stand very long in front of us."

"You'd *think* that . . ." Father Orno said with a contemplative expression, "but the closer we get to the dark heart of the Dominion where the Blood Priests hold sway . . ." The little priest looked at Don Hurac. So did Lewis, reflecting that he'd never seen the somewhat . . . rounded Blood Cardinal on a horse before, or really exerting himself in any way. Interestingly, he appeared more natural doing both than Lewis would've expected.

Don Hurac solemnly regarded them all. "Wise words, and true. Never underestimate the . . . persuasive powers of the Blood Priests. There is *nothing* you can do to make even those men who ran today fear you more than they do—or will—the Blood Priests. Most especially *after* today. These western troops will not have been as intimately exposed to the rising depravity of the Blood Priest order now firmly established and emanating from the capital, but with the . . . more open-minded, perhaps even moderating influence of officers such as General Debero removed, that will change. I suspect that he and others like him would have been targeted by the reapers at some point regardless of their willingness to treat with us." His expression turned wistful. "For just a moment there, while we spoke . . ." He shook his head. "Now, 'True Believers' will replace officers like him, and there will be reprisals among his surviving troops. Decimations, most likely."

"One in ten chosen at random and executed," Agon explained to those who didn't understand. "Or more likely, brutally sacrificed to their bloodthirsty God."

"They'll be the examples of what happens if you run," Lewis added grimly, looking appraisingly at Agon. "Is it possible such behavior might drive these western troops *away* from the Blood Priests? Make them more inclined to support Don Hurac?"

"*I* think so," Don Hurac replied, "if that opportunity is swiftly made known to them."

Lewis nodded thoughtfully. "All the more reason for us to get after them as quickly as we can, and give any organized blocking force they put in our path the chance to surrender and join us before we destroy it." He turned to Anson. "All mounted troops pursuing the enemy will offer quarter to individuals and small groups they encounter instead of just riding them down."

Anson looked in the direction of 2nd Division, still reassembling in the distance. "I better get at it, then. I don't see Lara's lancers over there anymore. I bet Har-Kaaska's already turned him loose. Lara won't be givin' no quarter."

Lewis nodded. "Yes, you better go. Leave Mr. Meder's riflemen and a company of Rangers, but take Mr. Burton and all his dragoons fit to ride. You might need his firepower." He glanced at Barca, but then shook his head. Barca's battery had done enough in this fight. "Send a runner to Major Olayne for a section of guns from one of his batteries that had a . . . less eventful day."

"Sounds good." Anson grinned at Barca. "I'd *always* rather have you with me, but your boys are sore an' beat."

Barca nodded acceptance. "Thank you, Major. My battery is, as always, ready and willing to join you, but a rest would be welcome."

Lewis was looking over the lines of the 1st US. NCOs were bellowing and ranting at milling troops, mostly in green uniforms, shoving them into ad hoc formations and directing them to proceed back to camp in open skirmish order to find and retrieve any wounded they could. Ambulance wagons were already arriving. Lewis saw more guns pulling in behind the section already there. "The rest of your battery has arrived, I believe, though I don't see your caissons and other vehicles."

"All the caissons are bare, sir. Any loaded chests still on them were already shifted to the limbers," Barca reported. "A section of healers joined us on the heights, and I left the caissons at their disposal to remove the wounded from there."

"Well done," Lewis said. "Yours and Dukane's batteries will go forward in support of First and Second Divisions while they establish the advanced camp. Willis? Willis, where are you?"

"Right here behind you, which I've been near all day long," came the prickly reply. "Loyal as a dog, an' he didn't even know I was here," he mumbled low.

"Well. Go now and make sure that after the wounded are taken from Captain Barca's caissons, they're reloaded with ammunition chests and sent forward along with his forge and battery wagons."

Willis sighed. "I'll get it done."

"Fine."

There should've still been a couple more hours of daylight, but the sky was darkening quickly, the air turning crisp and cold. Breath was steaming again, and cheeks and hands were reddening. Tired troops, still caught in that strange mix of victory and survival euphoria tempered by the mournful sight of so many of their own lying unmoving in the mud, adjusted the capes of their greatcoats to protect their necks and faces from the cutting breeze—and possibly the view around them. Most of the officers now had their orders, directly or indirectly, since all now knew what Lewis wanted, and it was time to get their men moving. Saluting their commander, nearly all took their leave. Soon, only Don Hurac and Father Orno, along with their guard detail, remained with Lewis, Leonor, Varaa, Boogerbear, Corporal Hannity, and several dragoons. The mob that had assembled in the center of the battlefield remained anything but organized, but it was under control. Major Beck had 1st Division formed in a column, moving in the direction of the charred enemy camp. The battered 3rd Pennsylvania had fallen in behind, paced by Barca's battery, Captain Meder's riflemen, and Kisin's dismounted Holcanos. Kisin himself had charged off with Anson and his Rangers to catch Lara's lancers. Knowing Anson, they might or might not wait for the section of guns from Olayne. A large percentage of 3rd Division had made a sloppy column and was moving the other way, sweeping 4th Division and scattered elements of the 3rd along with them.

Lewis and those around him remained still, if anything memorizing the terrible sights all around, instead of trying to avoid them. Lewis had no idea what the ultimate bill would be, but there were obviously a lot more blue-clad bodies in sight than he'd "budgeted" for this battle. An entire regiment of 3rd Division had been detailed to collect the Allied cities'—American—dead, and they were already at it. So too were the scavengers, however, lizardbirds swooping about like bats, lighting on forms that were particularly mangled, at least at first, and cawing like crows when newcomers joined them. There'd soon be other things—wolf-lizards and strange, comparatively fat and flightless versions of lizardbirds known to run in vicious packs. Oddly, these were the same creatures the locals called "gallinas" and used like chickens. Eventually, even larger and more dangerous things would appear, like the beast that was nesting within the walls of the villa when the battle began. That was why a whole regiment had the task: to discourage smaller things and, hopefully, drive off or protect against bigger ones. There'd be little time to collect and deal with their own dead in such a manner that scavengers wouldn't get them anyway. There'd be no time at all for the enemy, and the scavengers would feast. The battlefield would become just as dangerous as it had been at the height of the fighting, overnight.

Don Hurac spoke lowly, breaking the silence that had fallen upon them. He looked around at the others, something like panic on his face. "I've seen fighting around Vera Cruz, even watched while my beloved city nearly burnt to the ground. I thought those were 'battles' and believed I was prepared. . . ." He shook his head. "I was wrong. Never did I dream . . . I simply couldn't imagine such deliberate, willful, organized slaughter on such a monstrous scale as I witnessed today. I understand the why of it, even the necessity, I suppose. We have a terrible, diabolical enemy that wallows in death, luxuriates in the effusion of blood. That enemy would joyously inflict abominations such as this upon our people." He waved almost desperately around at the thousands of dead, the vast majority in yellow uniforms. "If the Blood Priests win, scenes such as this will be commonplace, but the dead will be harmless, helpless folk whose only fault is that they can't bring themselves to embrace such evil." He looked directly at Lewis. "I believe you to be an honest, temperate man. Perhaps even godly. You are certainly a man of honor. Therefore, I am left to wonder how you can calmly plan, orchestrate, and command something like this."

Leonor's face turned dark and dangerous with fury. "Are you comparin' Lewis to a *Blood Priest*, Dom?" Her hand actually strayed to one of her revolvers. "By God, if you are . . .'"

Boogerbear silently grabbed her arm and held it immobile while Varaa spoke up. "Watch what you say, Blood Cardinal," she warned. "I personally remain unconvinced of the sincerity of your conversion to Father Orno's faith"—she shrugged—"and honestly don't really care if you embrace its every teaching, but if you lied about that, what else? If we help you 'ascend,' or whatever it is you plan to do in the Holy City, and you *don't* make profound changes to the Dominion, halt its advance on the Yucatán, stop its sick, bloody rituals, and make it more tolerant of its neighbors, I will most assuredly care a great deal." She looked at Lewis. "And *he*—who *doesn't* calmly engage in things like this, certainly doesn't wallow in blood or take joy in its spilling—will be even more . . ." Varaa's huge blue eyes narrowed. ". . . unhappy than I, should he ever come to think these soldiers—quite precious to him, I assure you—spilled their blood just so you can turn things back the way they were before the Blood Priests cut you out of the succession."

"I protest . . ." Don Hurac began, an expression of horror spreading across his face.

"*I* believe his conversion was sincere," Father Orno interrupted, "his question merely rhetorical." He looked at Lewis as well. "Do not judge us harshly. I have seen myself how personally you take the loss of every life under your command, yet even I sometimes find it difficult to reconcile the man I have come to know with the one who is capable of unleashing and directing so much violence upon his fellow man."

Lewis had taken all this in with a wooden face, stung inside. Though he'd come to accept that he did enjoy the challenge of battle, the thrill perhaps, he'd finally suppressed his initial concern that he somehow enjoyed the killing. He knew that wasn't so. He'd decided the excitement, even detachment, that came over him in the heat of the fight was a coping mechanism of sorts. Something that allowed him to focus entirely on what he was doing regardless of the horror all around, so he could win the battle quicker and *save* lives.

Don Hurac's question hadn't made him doubt any of that or even really angered him. It did remind him that he hadn't "enjoyed" the battle today, was never as deeply focused as before, and the fiasco it descended into had knocked a chink in his confidence. This had been his biggest battle yet, the closest being Gran Lago, but he'd only directly commanded about two-thirds of the forces there. *Maybe this fight was just too big for me, too full of distractions.* He feared that might be the case, and if so, how could he lead his army forward against potentially even greater odds? He'd have to ponder that. Looking at Father Orno's somewhat expectant face, he realized the priest really expected an answer.

"I'm a soldier," he stated. "I've always been a soldier. My duty—my purpose—has forever been the defense of my country, its ideals, and its people. But those ideals aren't the sole property of the country I've lost. They exist in this other world too, so I embrace anyone who shares them as countrymen. It's no secret that I favor the foundation of a union here, perhaps even more perfect than the one I can no longer defend. I trust it will happen, and hope I live to see it. Beyond that, my cause is the welfare and success of this army that strives to conquer the evil threatening all the people the army represents and defends. It has been made abundantly clear by the enemy, in particular the evil that drives their forces"—he waved vaguely around—"that only great violence can possibly succeed against them." He gazed very seriously at Father Orno. "*That's* how I reconcile the contrast you see. It's really quite simple. You're part of this army yourself and supported its creation from the start. I'd assumed you felt much the same, at least about the spiritual aspect of our cause against evil, or do you find it difficult to reconcile your own feelings as well?"

Father Orno and Don Hurac both recoiled slightly, mouths opening and closing in silence. Turning, Lewis spoke to Leonor and Varaa. "I want to see Colonel Reed. I believe the healers are moving the wounded from here forward, accompanying First Division."

"May we accompany you?" Orno asked, finally finding his voice, tone apologetic and sounding unsure if he'd offended Lewis or not.

"Of course."

CHAPTER 30

It snowed all that night and through the next day, piling up a sufficient accumulation that the army couldn't move for another two days. It was probably just as well. No matter how well organized, a pursuit under those conditions would've left the men miserable and suffering. They were running low on supplies as well, particularly fodder for the horses. The same weather had distinctly slowed the arrival of grain wagons from Puebla. There would've been no shortage at all if the Doms' supply train had been captured intact. As it was, nearly the whole army had heard Har-Kaaska rage at his delinquent soldiers who'd fired the enemy camp.

Anson's mounted troops brought a few captured wagons in from farther away, along with an increasing number of wretched, hungry, frost-bitten Dom prisoners. They were harrying the retreat even now, and there'd been no real effort by the enemy to make a stand on the road through the mountains. Surprisingly, and quite sickeningly, the Doms had taken time to raze every villa, farm, and settlement they could easily reach from the road, burning the buildings and slaughtering most of the inhabitants and much of the livestock. Animals that were easy to drive were taken, to feed the broken army no doubt, and only the most prominent Dom civilians were evacuated. The rest were simply killed.

Don Hurac, now riding near the head of the army and no longer at the rear in his huge, bizarre carriage, sadly explained why it was that even before the Blood Priests rose to prominence, witnesses to other ways and cultures, certainly any strong enough to launch an invasion at the heart of the Dominion, couldn't be allowed to live. As they knew, his own Vera Cruz—the whole city—was under sentence of death. Every leader of his people had been madly xenophobic since the Dominion's founding—ironic considering the Spanish-Indio mix that started it all—but they feared external influence gaining traction and destabilizing the system they'd created above all things. Doubly ironic then that the "old way" was collapsing under assault from within.

Needless to say, none of Anson's, Lara's, or Burton's troopers who caught detachments of these murderous Doms made any effort to capture them. They were simply killed as well, occasionally in time to rescue civilians. These people knew little of value to the army and were generally confused to find themselves grateful to their "vile heretic" saviors. So great was the growing sway of the Blood Priests, however, that some of the rescued had to be restrained from harming the men who saved them. It was insane. All civilians were sent back toward Puebla on empty supply wagons.

Today was a fine day to march, however, the air a little warmer, the snow almost gone, except on the peaks of jagged, scenic mountains rearing above their forested flanks and looming all around. Lewis was no student of the geography of Mexico, beyond what he'd seen on maps, but surely this terrain was more dramatic, even extreme, than what General Winfield Scott had intended to march through. The road made it much easier, of course, and it was holding up bravely under the rumbling iron-shod guns and wagons and marching columns of men. The only unpleasantness was the melting mud alongside the road that had turned the ditches to a slippery morass, sucking at boots and pulling shoes off of horses. The army was happy, however, and music soared along the line of march, jaunty tunes by drum and fife accompanied by singing. It was hard to believe they were at war and just days had passed since their most costly fight. The only enemy detected were reaper monks that spied on their progress. Sal Hernandez particularly enjoyed hunting them.

Except for a single, brief but profound interlude, the cost had left Lewis alternating between relief and a new uncertainty sometimes bordering on despair. They'd lost nearly six thousand men in the Battle of Puebla (they hadn't thought of anything more appropriate to call it, at present), and over two thousand of those casualties had been killed. Another thousand were wounded badly enough to be sent back to Puebla, and probably on to Techolotla on the coast. The cost had been terrible (numbers for the enemy could only be estimated because so many had been eaten by the time they were counted), but the guess was somewhere around twenty thousand dead. It was a ratio Lewis would've once found acceptable. Not anymore. Still, only one major city and likely enemy concentration (Texcoco) remained before the descent into the Great Valley. After that, Lewis would march directly against the festering, evil heart of the Holy Dominion at the head of roughly twenty-nine thousand men—and another twenty thousand still coming from Techolatla under Alcaldesa Sira Periz. It was more than he'd ever expected, and it went a long way toward improving his frame of mind.

The 3rd Pennsylvania had easily earned the right to march at the head of 1st Division, immediately followed by Barca's battery. It was in the gap between them that Lewis was riding with only Leonor at his side. Not even Corporal Willis was there, and it seemed almost as if Barca's battery in front and the 1st US marching behind had deliberately left them space to themselves. And judging by the smug amusement growing on Leonor's face the longer he remained silent, taking things in, Lewis was beginning to suspect she had something to do with it.

Clearing his throat, he spoke at last. "I've, uh, very much enjoyed this quiet, peaceful, companionable time we've had together this morning, but doesn't it seem rather odd that we've had it? What I mean is, no one *ever* leaves us alone, and I simply can't believe there aren't any number of things that dozens of people want to discuss. And Varaa! Where's Varaa? If I had a tail, she'd be my shadow—as well as most of my inner thoughts, loudly expressed. Then there's your father, of course. I know he's back from patrol. Ordinarily, he would come to tell me what he discovered at once."

Leonor looked around as if noticing their relative isolation for the first time, then shrugged. "It . . . might be that I let it get around that we wanted a few private words this mornin'," she confessed. "An' other than Father's report—which he would'a made anyway if there was somethin' important— I expect you covered everything else anybody needed to know at officer's call last night—an' again this mornin'. You don't have to hold ever'body's hand every minute, ya know," she lightly scolded.

Lewis had no reply. What she said was perfectly true. He'd also been arrested by her appearance. Looking at her closely for the first time that day, he couldn't help but notice, well, how *clean* she was. Even though no one was *ever* foolish enough to try to swim in the wild, predator-rich waters of this world, troops from the Yucatán, even the Ocelomeh, were sticklers for hygiene—when possible—and had influenced Lewis's "original" Americans, who'd been far less concerned with such things. Everyone did their best with warmed-water towel baths in their tents when in camp, but even that went by the wayside on campaign, particularly in this weather. But Leonor looked like she'd taken a real bath—only possible in Don Hurac's great carriage, or (less conveniently) in the large tent her father and Samantha shared.

Samantha had insisted on a tub, but settled for a large water cask with the top sawn off that required a lengthy and laborious heating and filling process. Leonor's straight black hair, somewhat past her shoulders now, no longer swayed in oily strands but blew free and fresh in the breeze. Her face had been scrubbed slightly red and looked like tiny doses of Samantha's makeup had been artfully applied here and there. *Definitely a bath at Samantha's*, Lewis decided. Even her wool uniform had been carefully brushed, brass buttons polished.

The more time he spent with her, the more beautiful Leonor was to Lewis even when covered in mud or blood or sweat. Especially after the disappearance of the perpetual scowl she once wore. Now, even in uniform, with her perfect olive skin and readier smile, almost delicate features and big brown eyes, she took his breath away. His strong feelings, at odds with whatever plot she was hatching, had him suddenly on guard. *Probably wants me to turn her loose on a long-range scout or something*, he thought darkly. Looking away, he frowned. If any non-native female on this world could thrive in the wild on her own, it was Leonor. And aside from Varaa, she might be the only one who really didn't need any protection. Still, Lewis *wanted* to protect her even if she'd never let him.

"I still need to decide what to do about John Ulrich," he said at last. "Dr. Newlin assures me Colonel Reed will be fine once his headaches subside, and there's no reason he shouldn't resume command of First Division. I thank God for that, but at present he's almost insubordinately insistent that I'm driving the campaign too far, too fast. Nothing new from him, but he'd never so openly challenge my decisions if he was entirely himself. As always, I value his opinion, but I worry about him." He sighed. "Then there's John. He was shot through the body, for God's sake, and is far from well. The mere fact he and so many other wounded are even alive is another powerful testament to the wonders of native medicine. Dr. Newlin remains amazed. Still, John's in no shape to command the Third Pennsylvania at present, but flatly refuses to be evacuated. I understand how he feels—I wouldn't want it either—but jouncing around in an ambulance cart can't be good for him. I'm tempted to *order* him back to Puebla. . . ."

"But he's in Reed's division, an' it's really up to him, right?" Leonor finished for him.

Lewis nodded. "Opposed as Colonel Reed has always been to the deep, expeditionary nature of our campaigns, he seems to feel strongly we should all stick together—that all those who came to this world with us have a right to stay with their comrades, if possible. I can't really disagree. Sometimes it bothers me that we're already so scattered, of necessity."

"Then leave it be. Leave it up to them an' quit eatin' yourself up about it." Leonor gestured around. "Just take a breath an' enjoy the break, Lewis. Take in the sights! It's beautiful here! I'm sure things'll get hectic enough when we get closer to Texcoco."

Gazing around, Lewis had to nod. In spite of the occasional charred ruins they passed (the fields and forests had been too wet for the enemy to burn), it really was very beautiful. He had difficulty summoning anything from memory to compare it to, especially when a great flying lizard, much larger and more rarely seen than those Doms sometimes used as "messenger dragons," launched itself into the sky a great distance away. It beat its wings in the warming morning air, rising up in a spiraling circle. It was truly a majestic creature. Finally satisfied with its altitude, it extended its wings and soared effortlessly off to the south.

"Those things're . . . Damn, I don't even have the words! They give me the willies, though. If anybody was ever crazy enough ta try ta catch an' train one, I bet they could ride it!" Leonor's expression changed to one of wonder. "But wouldn't that be somethin'?"

Patting Arete on the neck, Lewis finally asked, "You really 'arranged' this time for us?" Leonor nodded definitively. "Why?" he pressed. "Not that I'm complaining," he hastened to add as her face started to color with anger.

"'Cause I wanted to."

Lewis grinned. "And the whole army naturally obliged you."

"Not the *whole* army," she allowed. "A fair chunk of it, though, I reckon. See, I've got to thinkin' about some things I want you to think about too. Sorta private things you're too thick ta think up on your own, so I gotta give you a nudge."

He raised a brow at her. "'Private,' indeed, if so much of the army knows more than I."

She ignored him and continued, "You an' me, we been 'intended' for a while now, an' I been happy with that." She looked around furtively and lowered her voice. "I never would'a done what I did after the battle if I weren't."

Lewis felt his heart jump in his throat when she mentioned that. He still didn't know how it had happened, in fact. When they returned to camp, exhausted, bloody, and sore, she'd stayed by him as he heard all the available reports, visited the hospital tents, gave his last post-battle orders, and basically put the camp to bed. She'd even joined him while they both removed their sweat- and blood-crusted jackets and rinsed their hands, arms, and faces in a basin of warm water Willis provided by the fire he'd revived in front of Lewis's tent. But somehow, after that, Leonor had simply followed him inside, and it had seemed like the most natural thing in the world—until she stood there before him and very deliberately, expression unreadable, unbuttoned and removed her damp shirt.

Lewis could still see it in his mind. Lit only by the meager yellow light of a candle lantern, goose bumps standing proud on her small shapely breasts in the cold as she *continued* undressing. He'd been struck by how vulnerable but determined she'd looked. Of course, he'd never seen anything more beautiful either—or, frankly, welcome to his soul after the day they'd endured. Even as he drank her in, however, kicking off her boots and sliding her trousers and drawers together down past her hips and onto the canvas floor of the tent, he'd still been too stunned to move. She came to him then, embracing him, and even as she pulled at his shirt, a sob wracked her body.

He knew this was the first time she'd removed all her armor and exposed herself so since being cruelly violated. He'd always admired her courage, but this was a whole different sort. His honor demanded he stop her, but his heart simply couldn't. He loved her and wanted her, but most of all, after all the death that day, she seemed to desperately need a reaffirmation of life at least as badly as he did, and something had pushed her to cross the boundary of their tender understanding. She *needed* to show her love by gifting herself to him—and feel his love in return, unfiltered by their public behavior. He suspected that, just as important, this was a test for them both, made suddenly more urgent by the events of the day. She had to discover once and for all if she could actually *do* this, and find out for sure if he really *did* want her. He felt almost positive that if he called a halt, she'd see it as a rejection, and they'd never be the same again. Even their friendship would vanish.

Finally just tearing his shirt away and pushing his braces off his shoulders, she clutched him closely, pressing her breasts against his naked chest, kissing him fiercely. His last meager defenses came tumbling down, and for the first time in longer than he could remember, he'd just . . . stopped thinking about anything, shut his mind down, and let his heart have its way.

"What *we* did," he reminded her softly.

She nodded a little shyly, then said, "When Father an' Mistress Samantha up an' got married out o' the blue before we left Vera Cruz, I honestly figured they were loco." She laughed. "Father did too. Now I'm not so sure. He's still fightin' as good as ever, an' she still might as well be the quartermaster o' the army, but they got a home to go to, to be together, even if it's just a stinky ol' tent. They're happy with that. Least Samantha'll say so, but Father is too. I can tell." She looked intently at him. "None of us might have much time left, but at least they're makin' the most of it." She straightened in the saddle and raised her chin. "I want that too, an' understandin' or not, I'm through waitin' for the war to be over. That might never happen, or we might either or both of us get killed. Not bein' gloomy, just statin' a fact." She turned and faced him again. "That . . . night after the battle, you made me happy, Lewis, like I never been before. Happy to be alive. I want *more* o' that, while I can get it, to just . . . live happy for a while." She shrugged. "An' since it ain't decent to carry on like that, I figure that means we gotta be married now."

Lewis blinked. "Now?"

"Now," Leonor insisted, then looked very angry. "Well, as soon as I shoot Corporal Willis! He *heard* us! Now the whole army knows, I bet. How am I supposed ta show my face if we ain't married?"

Vaguely amused, Lewis knew even if Willis did blab, no one would be fool enough to behave disrespectfully to Leonor. She was less impulsive

these days, but just as deadly. Even he knew better than to let his amusement show and forced a glower instead. "Willis." He snorted. "If he was
indiscreet . . . I believe he'll find he's gone a little far this time. Captain
Barca is short of experienced artillerymen. I wonder how Corporal Willis
would enjoy being assigned to the hardest-fighting battery we have?"

He looked at Leonor and smiled. "Now might be a little awkward, but I
find myself agreeing with you. I too found a . . . happiness, a lightening of
spirit, that can only be good for me. Perhaps the army as a whole," he added,
contemplating the therapeutic effects of their encounter. "I've no objection,
not even to the precedent it would set. Your father and Mistress Samantha
already did that, and even in our old army, officers' wives often joined their
husbands at surprisingly isolated outposts. I'm not even aware if they were
specifically prohibited from going on campaign, to be honest." He waved
his hand, looking at her strangely. "Of course, *you'd* insist on remaining
more than just a wife, I'm sure." It was almost a hopeful question, but she
simply nodded.

With an inward sigh, he continued, "As to any general objection that
might be raised, there are plenty of women among the camp followers who
share the same risks as everyone." He looked thoughtful. "Others might
want to marry as well, for that matter, for the same reasons you clearly
stated." The newly minted Lieutenant Hanny Cox and Izel Tuin sprang to
mind as examples. "There might be a tent and quartering issue"—he
chuckled—"but I largely blame Mistress Samantha for stirring this whole
thing up in the first place. She can sort that out as well." Leonor joined his
growing laugh, reaching over to clutch his hand. It might've only been his
imagination, but he thought he noted an air of approval emanating from
the nearest troops when that occurred.

There was the sound of a galloping horse, splattering through the mud
alongside the road. Hooves suddenly clattered on the pavement behind
them, and they turned to see Sal Hernandez. "Sorry for intrudin', but we
got trouble," he said hastily, tilting his head to the rear. "The whole gaggle o'
brass is comin' up. Figured I'd bound on ahead an' warn you, so to speak."

A large number of riders was indeed approaching, all those who gener-
ally rode with or consulted Lewis on any given day. Anson, Varaa, Meder,
Lara, and Kisin were in the lead, followed by Olayne, Agon, Tun, Don
Hurac, Father Orno, Har-Kaaska, Major Beck, and Don Roderigo. Even
Colonel Reed was among them, head still wrapped in a bandage and

accompanied by Dr. Newlin, Samantha, and Colonel Itzam. He was surprised not to see Coryon Burton and Boogerbear, but remembered the Rangers were on the flanks and following up today while Burton's dragoons scouted ahead in force. Quite a few others were present as well, of course, but they held back, slowing their horses to plod in the mud alongside the impromptu command meeting. There was only so much room on the road. Captain Barca and Major Beck up ahead took note and fell back to join the assembly.

"Good morning again, gentlemen—and lady," Lewis greeted, bowing his head slightly to Samantha. She was dressed warmly in a blue army greatcoat, but her cheeks were pink. "Captain Hernandez mentioned trouble. Do you all already know its nature?"

"No," Anson said, pushing forward with Varaa at his side. Both looked tired. They'd been out most of the night, and whether the enemy was present or not, they had to stay vigilant. Not just on guard for Doms, but to avoid the terrifying predators that roamed the night. "Just me an' Varaa for the moment." He pointed at Sal. "Well, Cap'n Hernandez too, a little. He didn't read the whole thing. A dispatch," he clarified. "Seems Alcaldesa Periz has the semaphore or telegraph towers—whichever you call em—built almost up to Puebla. Been settin' 'em up as she brings her big division this way, an' she's almost there. Anyway, my Rangers scoutin' our backtrail met a courier comin' on fast, an' we looked at the dispatch. Sorry. It was sent to the army, not just you specifically, an' with the towers up, this is the newest news we've had, if you get my meanin'. Couldn't resist lookin' at it. Besides"—he shrugged, glancing at Leonor—"I was told you'd be occupied for a spell."

"That's fine," Lewis assured, "but if you chose not to wait for a scheduled stop, I assume the message is time critical?"

"Yeah. I mean, yes sir." Anson waved around. "An' no sense sprinklin' the word out, neither. That's why I rounded up ever'body I came across on my way up to you." He nodded at a stand of trees on a rise a short distance from the road. "I'd recommend over there, sir."

Lewis was surprised. He always kept his battle plans close, but rarely withheld news of events elsewhere from the army. Then again, they'd been extraordinarily fortunate in the respect that most communications they received from Allied cities and forces generally contained good news of late. Sal's warning and Anson's demeanor reinforced his concern that wasn't the case this time.

"Very well," he agreed, noting that "his" dragoon bugler had joined them.

"Corporal Hannity, sound 'halt' and 'officer's call,' if you please. We'll have the senior officers only, at present." He looked at Anson. "I'm sure if you'd discovered any enemy activity nearby, you would've informed me at once, but we'll have extra skirmishers out regardless." He sent a small smile to Leonor and nodded toward the trees. "Shall we?"

Rumors of troubling news seemed to have swept up and down the column as quickly as Hannity's bugle was repeated, and it wasn't long before virtually every senior officer in the army had gathered around the stand of trees. Orderlies held their horses, and Corporal Willis took Lewis's and Leonor's, as well as Anson's. He recoiled with a start at the look Leonor gave him. "Damned murderous females," he grumbled as he led the animals a short distance away.

Lewis had taken the message and already read it several times before passing it on to Colonel Reed. Quickly scanning it, Reed then made sure Agon saw it next. Returning the dispatch to Lewis, who'd reached for it—it would take too long for everyone to read it—the former Dom officer quietly began explaining what he'd learned to Don Hurac, who alone remained on his horse.

"Bad news indeed," Lewis began darkly.

"The worst," Anson growled in agreement.

Lewis raised his voice so all could hear. "Most of you were aware that we had a new addition to our little fleet: a light frigate named *Nemesis* from the Empire of the New Britain Isles. She's under the command of a Captain Jenks, of that nationality. He and his people, no friends to the Doms, were essentially chased by them into our awareness from the *Pacific* Ocean"—he gestured west—"another great sea on the west side of this continent," he added for the benefit of those who might not know. "They arrived here through a dangerously narrow pass or strait that didn't exist on the world we came from, that lies somewhere south of the Mosquito Coast, in the vicinity of Costa Rica, I believe. It's called 'El Paso del Fuego' since it seems to have been created and remains influenced by considerable volcanic activity. It's also violently scoured by terrifying currents, and Jenks and his ship only barely made it through. We've learned some things from him, about the empire and enemy both, and having survived it himself, Jenks firmly believed no sane commander would willingly risk the passage." He hesitated an instant to take a breath. "Especially with troopships. Captain Holland viewed the eastern mouth and experienced the terrific currents there as well. He was of the same opinion that there was simply no way a dangerous naval force could traverse it without appalling losses," he added significantly, then waved the coarse paper the dispatch was written on.

"Unfortunately, though they might've been right about the cost—we'll likely never know—and we've had our own education regarding what the enemy considers 'acceptable losses,' it seems the Doms *did* risk it." He frowned as murmuring began and he spoke over it. "They're now loose in the Atlantic with upward of ninety ships, each more modern than any Dom vessel we've faced before and each one crammed with hundreds of troops."

Now there were outright cries of alarm, and Colonel Itzam rode over them with his demand, "Where are they bound?"

Lewis regarded him grimly. "They're already *at* Uxmal, possibly Pidra Blanca and Techon as well," he said. "If they split their forces evenly among the cities, Pidra Blanca, at least, might have fallen already."

Frightened, angry voices began to surge, but Anson snapped harshly, "Get hold of yourselves, damn you! Yer men're watchin'!" He waved at the halted column of troops less than seventy paces away. "They already know somethin's up. You want 'em to see their officers all runnin' around like . . . gallinas with their heads cut off? The whole damn army'll fall apart!"

Reed was nodding, gently pressing his hand against his forehead, but glaring furiously around. "You call yourselves officers? I've seen you stand rigid and outwardly composed in battle, but now is the true time for calm." He glanced reassuringly at Lewis. "How we react, what we do next when faced with a calamity we can do nothing about, is the true measure of a professional. Now," he continued, "will you allow the army's commander to speak so we can hear the rest?"

There was a little continued murmuring while Lewis gave Reed an appreciative nod, but when he spoke again there was attentive silence. "As I was saying, at the time the bones of this dispatch were first generated—Colonel De Russy, defending a besieged Uxmal, managed to signal Captain Holland when he approached in *Tiger*—the enemy controlled the bay and had landed enough troops to eventually encircle the city. Uxmal has formidable defenses, however. Plenty of provisions and munitions. Not only were our friends there *not* taken by surprise, most of the noncombatants had time to evacuate southeast to Itzincab. I'm sure they'll be quite safe."

"My people will help," Kisin said. "Even if the Doms take Uxmal, they won't take Itzincab. I tried once, remember? It's too strong."

"But what about Pidra Blanca and Techon?" asked one of Itzam's regimental commanders, carefully controlling his tone. He was from Pidra Blanca himself. Being farther—everyone thought—from any enemy advance, neither Pidra Blanca nor Techon were as well fortified as Uxmal.

"My apologies," Lewis said, gently waving the page again. "I simply don't know. Faced with a large-scale invasion, I'm certain Alcaldesa Yolotli of Techon and your own Alcalde Ortiz would quickly fall back on Itzincab as well. We can't know for sure the enemy even threatened those places. According to the message, the quick fall of Pidra Blanca was only feared due to its lack of a wall around the city." He took another long breath. "Speaking of the enemy, we must assume a force that large was detached from the Gran Cruzada, which we're racing against to reach the Dom capital." He paused. "Even if the entire force has been recalled to deal with us—still far from certain—an overland march to the Great Valley will take much longer than an ocean voyage. Though we must still move with haste, we can still win the race."

Colonel Itzam looked taken aback. "You mean . . . even knowing all this, of the threat to Uxmal, you still mean to press on? What are Alcadesa Periz's thoughts on this?" He pointed at the dispatch. "Surely she included them."

Lewis ran his fingers through his beard. "She . . . expressed her intention to march her division back to Techolotla and take ship for Uxmal as soon as sufficient transport was available." He paused. "Moments ago, I sent Captain Hernandez back toward Puebla with sufficient remounts to reach the *alcaldesa* before she could turn her force entirely around. My orders to her, as commander of our combined army, were to send half her division back to Techolotla and a quarter to Vera Cruz. She will remain with the rest of her troops at Puebla, for now."

"You *ordered* her?" Itzam almost barked.

"Yes!" Lewis cracked back, tone still low but with the intensity of a cannon shot. "*Alcaldesa* of Uxmal or not, just like 'King' Har-Kaaska of the Ocelomeh, she holds the rank of colonel in our army and has committed to abide by my *military* seniority and command for the duration of the war! She has no military experience, wasn't summoned to the front—came here of her own accord—and was provisionally given the locally raised division committed to our cause to command. She won't induce them to abandon that cause to go fight in the Yucatán."

"In spite of my esteem for you, Colonel Cayce, she might induce *me*," Itzam warned. "Along with more than half of the force *you* command!"

There were gasps, and Leonor started to flare with fury when all were distracted by a calming "Now, now. This is all a great shock and we must respond with logic and reason." Almost as one, everyone turned to regard Don Hurac as Colonel Agon helped him step down from his horse and move to stand among them. "If I may, Colonel Cayce?" he asked.

Lewis raised a brow and nodded. "By all means, sir."

Peering around before settling his gaze on Itzam, Don Hurac spoke: "I am fully aware that many of you here will still regard me as an enemy. That could not be further from the truth. In many ways, our respective causes align almost exactly. I am a firm convert to yours, and the . . . ancillary aspects of mine will benefit us all. That said, I must beg you to tell me how shattering this army—or encouraging your charming provincial leader to shatter it for you after all you have accomplished—can do a single thing to protect your people back home."

Itzam looked confused. "They are being attacked. We must help them!"

Don Hurac shook his head. "Think. Your city . . . Uxmal, yes? Its defenders will defeat the invader or fall long before you could possibly ever get there. Despite the rapidity of your communications from Techolotla, there is Captain Holland's sea voyage from Uxmal to consider. One way or another, the fate of Uxmal has likely already been decided, and the consequences for abandoning this campaign will be the same. If Uxmal or any of the other places that concern you *have* fallen, I have no doubt that you can take them back—your soldiers are very good—but what then? You will have spilled unnecessary blood to once more possess an empty city, and this entire campaign will have been for nothing. All the *lives* lost for nothing. *If* you ever return to complete this quest, starting at one of the coastal cities because Puebla can never be held, you will certainly face the irresistible force of the Gran Cruzada returned. Even an army such as this cannot prevail on open ground against a force that size. The war—the cause—will already be lost."

"And what if we *all* went back—only to find Uxmal has held?" Reed asked. "How much more heartbreaking and wasteful then?"

Lewis glanced at his second in command, even more surprised, wondering if the knock on the head had somehow made him more aggressive. He started to speak, but Agon beat him to it. "There remains only one way forward," the former Dom general stated. "The enemy can't beat you in the Yucatán. Much of your means of producing war material has already been reproduced or shifted to Vera Cruz or Techolotla. Your . . ." He paused. "*Our*," he stressed, "line of supply is secure. *We* can still beat the *enemy* if we conquer the seat of his unholy power, remain true to the cause we fight for"—he glanced at Don Hurac—"and install *him* in place of the Blood Priests' puppet as supreme over all the Dominion."

As usual, when it was put like that, Lewis felt a surge of unease. And it wasn't even Don Hurac himself that fanned those apprehensive embers, because it was increasingly apparent that Don Hurac's intentions were . . . well, if not exactly pure, certainly more benevolent than the current regime's. But Lewis and many others, probably his whole army, had a strong aversion to monarchies and dictatorships. Har-Kaaska's "kingship" didn't really count since he'd been popularly acclaimed by the Ocelomeh, a tribe with no territorial claim. But how benign could even Don Hurac remain once he was, essentially, an emperor?

He and Agon had clearly won their point with Colonel Itzam, however, especially after Don Hurac softly spoke up and added, "You all have my sacred word that, once I am installed as Supreme Holiness, my very first commands to the Dominion armies will be to arrest every Blood Priest they can lay hands on and cease all hostilities *everywhere* at once!"

Expression both contrite and deflated, Colonel Itzam regarded Lewis a little nervously. "Please accept my most abject apologies, sir. I fear my concern for my home city aroused . . . intemperate and ill-considered passions. I'll do my best to calm those of Alcaldesa Sira Periz as well. Another dispatch from me, reinforcing your, um, recommendations, perhaps?"

"That might be helpful," Lewis agreed. Refocusing on the unmoving column, he cleared his throat. "There's nothing more, for now. I'll certainly keep you all apprised of further developments." He paused. "And you may as well inform your men. They'll hear it eventually, and better they hear it from you, possibly phrased as Colonel Agon and Don Hurac put it, than to think we're keeping things from them. I expect, once they do, they'll be just as eager as I am to press on. Any questions?" Lewis asked, looking around at his silent officers. "Very well. Resume your places in the line of march and let's get moving."

The gathering quickly began to disperse, a few infantry officers who'd arrived on foot actually jogging back toward their regiments. As long as the snaking column was, some would probably wait until their commands caught up with them. Agon helped Don Hurac back on his horse before mounting his own. Exchanging knowing looks with Lewis, he led Don Hurac away. Colonel Reed sighed and gently touched the bandage on his forehead before speaking.

"Well, Lewis, I'm sure you're as surprised as I am by how my position has shifted regarding this campaign."

Lewis nodded. "I am. On the other hand, aside from the army, Uxmal is the closest I've ever come to calling something 'home.' When I first read that the Doms actually came through the Pass of Fire in sufficient force to threaten it, a flash of insight illuminated the thought that you might've been right all along and we should've remained on the defensive." Smiling fondly, he reached over and put his hand on Reed's shoulder. "You'll be glad to know that the fit lasted only an instant."

"Good," Reed grumbled. "I've been a fool. I'm as concerned about all the Allied cities as you are, as anyone not born there can be, but the invasion there just proves how wrongheaded I've been. We can't hide from this threat, that's clear enough now, and we can't destroy it by waiting for it to come for us. And we *have* to destroy it, root it out and kill it. I don't doubt that anymore." He managed a small smile back at Lewis. "Perhaps you should have knocked me on the head long ago."

"Many will feel the same," Har-Kaaska said. He'd stepped away to retrieve his strange mount from an Ocelomeh orderly, but returned to them sitting atop it. Taking that as a signal, Willis was advancing with Arete, Colonel Fannin, and Leonor's new unnamed animal. "I myself agree with you entirely," Har-Kaaska continued, "yet I am still torn. The Yucatán and its people have been 'home' for me so long that I have no desire to return to . . . the land of my birth." Even now he remained elusive about where that might be. "Some may still require a similar blow to the head to understand that we cannot save it by dropping everything and running back."

Varaa was nodding, tail flipping. "I believe I will ride back to Puebla and speak to Sira Periz in person. She is strong and fervently supports the cause." Varaa blinked rapidly. "But she is also quite devoted to her people and city. We all know that devotion once nearly cost us the war. She has grown considerably, and I don't think that will be the case again—once she thinks things through—but I'd like to be there to help her do that," she added wryly. Turning to Samantha, she asked, "Would you care to join me?" Sira valued Samantha's advice, and her presence might help.

"We will never catch Captain Hernandez," Samantha reminded with a meaningful look at her husband, "but perhaps another escort might be arranged?"

Anson growled but gestured agreement with a hand. It was all for show. There probably wasn't a full mile of road back to Puebla without some Allied presence on it, and Varaa was certainly capable of protecting Samantha from most things they were likely to encounter, but he simply wouldn't risk her. "Take Sal's squad of Rangers when you get to 'em."

For a while after that, no one said anything, lost in their own thoughts about the campaign and this new development. Not only were their friends, their new people in danger "back home," their rear wasn't nearly as secure as they'd counted on.

Finally, as if to lighten the moment, Leonor cleared her throat. "Soo," she began, tone unusually bright as she looked at Lewis, brow raised, lips slightly quirked, "even with so many folks as there was, I guess you figured this wasn't the best time to announce we're gettin' married pretty quick?"

"Absolutely *not* the right time," Lewis agreed with a similar expression.

"Wait! What?" Anson said sharply. "*That's* what you wanted your privacy for?"

"I believe you just announced it, my dear," Samantha said, grinning.

"Well, but . . ." Anson spluttered, glaring at his wife, before turning back to face his daughter. She and Lewis were both climbing back on their horses. "I knew you'd decided to do it someday—without even askin' *me* proper," he inserted, "but what does 'pretty quick' mean? An' why?"

Leonor turned to look down at him, cocking her head to the side as Lewis trotted Arete back toward Barca's battery. As far as he was concerned, time was wasting, and he wanted the army back on the move. "Could be we might *have* to, Father," Leonor said, tone level, deadly serious, and loud enough for Lewis to hear. He stiffened in the saddle. "Just can't take a chance on things like that," Leonor went on conversationally. "Why, just think of the shame it'd bring to the fam'ly! The whole army'd be scandalized!"

Turning again, she kicked her horse into motion and galloped up alongside Lewis—whose eyes were closed tight as he rode, teeth clenched. "Why did you do that?" he asked.

Leonor shrugged. "I felt like it. After all the years of him an' Boogerbear an' Sal pullin' pranks on me, it was fun."

"You *were* joking . . . right?" Lewis asked, tone still serious despite a nervous smile.

Leonor rolled her eyes. "Sure," she replied, but couldn't help needling him as well, "as far as I know."

Lewis snorted exasperation, then asked, "Is he pointing any weapons at me?"

Leonor turned to look. "Somethin', maybe. Not one o' those big Walker Colts, though. Prob'ly just a Paterson, like mine." She rested a hand on the grip of one of her revolvers and regarded him speculatively. "You're a big fella. Not much chance a Paterson'd kill you outright from here. Good thing too. I plan on bein' married, an' we got the rest o' this war to finish. Oh!" She laughed. "Now he's arguin' with Mistress Samantha an' Varaa. You're safe."

Lewis reached over and firmly took her hand again amid whoops and a few gleeful if indistinct "Huzzas!" in the ranks as they neared. For once, Leonor didn't glare flashing pistol muzzles at the miscreants. "We'll talk about this later, I promise," Lewis said, then added dryly, "For now, I expect I'll have even more visiting conversationalists than usual." Even under his beard, Leonor saw his jaw clench in determination. "And we all must focus on the campaign once again. Colonel Reed was right: we can't be distracted by events beyond our control. We can only pray that Don Hurac is also correct: take the Holy City and we win the war. Everything else will be sorted out. If the Gran Cruzada intervenes and we fail"—he took a long breath—"we lose."

Seeing Corporal Hannity already waiting in the gap between Barca's battery and the 1st US, Lewis called, "Sound 'forward,' if you please."

Hannity raised the bugle to his lips and blew the loud, rapid notes. Drums took up the signal in a cascading rumble that leaped from regiment to regiment, as did the shouted commands of officers and NCOs. Soon, the long blue column was moving again, toward whatever this world held in store for it.

Some few historians in the NUS are still prone to criticize Lewis Cayce for his decision to press forward with his campaign against the rotten, wicked core of the Dominion in spite of the threat looming at home. Spoiled by the luxurious wonders of radio and fast steamships in our modern world, along with the omniscient gift of hindsight, they could even be right to do so. Personally, especially given the state of communications and the time it would take to cope with the threat, I believe Cayce did the only thing he could. History may be written by the victors, the survivors at least, but it is then warped out of all recognition by their "intellectual" descendants, safe with their pipes in overstuffed chairs, intent on amassing fame for themselves at the expense of those who have earned it.

But I digress.

In general, Lewis Cayce and his scratch-built army had done very well, churning up across half a continent to the virtual gates of the Holy City. Of course there had been mistakes, aching growing pains, but those had been impossible to avoid given the necessary haste of the campaign. It's a wonder he built such a competent force given the meager time and resources he had. And there was every reason to believe that victory was in his grasp in spite of the sudden and unexpected enemy presence in the Yucatán. But when gods use men to settle disputes and all the devils do battle, calamity always seems to chase triumph. . . .

Excerpt from the foreword to Courtney Bradford's
Lands and Peoples—Destiny of the Damned, Vol. I,
Library of Alex-aandra Press, 1959

ACKNOWLEDGMENTS

Thanks—as always—to my agent, Russell Galen, and my wonderful (very patient) editor, Anne Sowards. I also want to thank the fine copy editors who have to churn their way through what might, at times, be charitably called my somewhat . . . whimsical prose, with all its own weird rules, archaic words and expressions, different pronunciations (depending on who's talking), and even occasional made-up words. I sometimes wonder whether having them work on my manuscripts is a kind of punishment, but their efforts are deeply appreciated. Especially when they catch really embarrassing continuity errors on my part!

Photo by Jim Goodrich

Taylor Anderson is the *New York Times* bestselling author of the Artillerymen series, including *Devil's Battle*, *Hell's March*, and *Purgatory's Shore*, as well as the Destroyermen series, including *Winds of Wrath*, *Pass of Fire*, and *River of Bones*. A gunmaker and forensic ballistic archaeologist, Taylor has been a technical and dialogue consultant for movies and documentaries and is an award-winning member of the United States Field Artillery Association and of the National Historical Honor Society. He has a master's degree in history and has taught that subject at Tarleton State University in Stephenville, Texas. He lives in nearby Granbury with his family.

VISIT TAYLOR ANDERSON ONLINE

TaylorAndersonAuthor.com
f TaylorAndersonAuthor